Anon

Journal of the Proceedings of the Eighty-Seventh Convention of Protestant Episcopal Church

Anonymous

Journal of the Proceedings of the Eighty-Seventh Convention of Protestant Episcopal Church

Reprint of the original, first published in 1871.

1st Edition 2022 | ISBN: 978-3-36812-508-0

Verlag (Publisher): Outlook Verlag GmbH, Zeilweg 44, 60439 Frankfurt, Deutschland
Vertretungsberechtigt (Authorized to represent): E. Roepke, Zeilweg 44, 60439 Frankfurt, Deutschland
Druck (Print): Books on Demand GmbH, In de Tarpen 42, 22848 Norderstedt, Deutschland

JOURNAL

OF THE

PROCEEDINGS

OF THE

EIGHTY-SEVENTH CONVENTION

OF THE

Protestant Episcopal Church,

IN THE

DIOCESE OF PENNSYLVANIA,

HELD IN

ST. ANDREW'S CHURCH, PHILADELPHIA,

Commencing Tuesday, May 9, and ending Thursday, May 11, 1871.

PUBLISHED BY ORDER OF THE CONVENTION.

PHILADELPHIA:
M'CALLA & STAVELY, PRINTERS, 237-'9 DOCK STREET.
1871.

COMMITTEES

TO REPORT AT THE NEXT CONVENTION.

Committee on Alterations of Canons of the Diocese.

REV. DR. WATSON,
" MR. SPACKMAN,
" DR. HARE,
. " S. E. APPLETON,

MR. G. W. HUNTER,
" ISAAC HAZLEHURST,
" JOHN BOHLEN,
" G. M. STROUD,

MR. R. R. MONTGOMERY.

Committee on Parochial History.

REV. J. A. HARRIS,
" JOHN BOLTON,
" F. J. CLERC, D.D.,
" J. W. ROBINS,
" L. W. GIBSON,

MR. JAMES S. NEWBOLD,
" C. R. KING,
" JOHN BOHLEN,
" G. W. HUNTER,
" GEO. M. CONARROE.

Committee on Parsonages.

REV. WM. RUDDER, D. D.,
" ALBRA WADLEIGH,

MR. S. K. ASHTON.

Committee on Minority Representation.

REV. DR. HARE,
" " HOWE,
" " RUDDER,

MR. G. M. CONARROE,
" ISAAC HAZLEHURST.

Committee on City Missions.

REV. DR. HARE,
" J. R. MOORE,
" DR. ROACH,

REV. DR. HOWE,
" DR. HOFFMAN,
MR. G. L. HARRISON.

Committee on Resolution with Reference to the Funds of the Diocese.

MR. ISAAC HAZLEHURST,
" AGIB RICKETTS,
" G. W. HUNTER,

MR. R. A. LAMBERTON,
" M. RUSSELL THAYER,
" THOMAS ROBINS,

MR. J. R. SYPHER.

LIST OF

Clergymen of the Diocese of Pennsylvania,

(CORRECTED TO JUNE 1st,)

AND OF THE

LAY DEPUTIES

COMPOSING THE CONVENTION OF 1871.

Those printed in *italics* were not members of the Convention.
Not present during the Convention.* Removed since. †

CLERGY.

The Rt. Rev. WILLIAM BACON STEVENS, D.D., LL.D., Bishop, 708 Walnut street, Philadelphia.

ABEL, ALFRED M., Rector of St. Luke's, Lebanon, and Hope Church, Mount Hope.

ALLEN. H. J. W., Rector of St. John's Church, Bellefonte.

Antrim Thomas M., Deacon, Assistant to the Rector of the Church of the Atonement, Philadelphia.

APPLETON, EDWARD W., Rector of St. Paul's Church, Cheltenham ; P. O., Shoemakertown.

APPLETON, SAMUEL E., Rector of the Church of the Mediator, Philadelphia.

Babcock, John H., Rector of St. Andrew's Church, Tioga.

BALDY, HURLEY, Rector of St. Paul's Church, Doylestown, and Trinity Church, Centreville.

BARKER, THOMAS B., Rector of St. John's Church, Lancaster.

*BARNARD, JAMES H., Rector of St. Luke's Church, Bustleton.

BARROWS, N., Rector of St. James' Church, Mansfield.

BARTLETT, FRANK W., Minister of Church of the Mediator, Allentown, and Missionary at Catasauqua ; P. O., Allentown.

BATTERSON, H. G., D.D., Rector of St. Clement's Church, Philadelphia.

BEASLEY, FREDERICK W., D.D., Rector of All Saints' Church, Lower Dublin, and Christ Chapel, Oak Grove ; P. O., Eddington.

Berghaus, V. Hummel, Deacon, residing at Harrisburg.

BEERS, JOHN S., Deacon, Assistant at Grace Church, Philadelphia.

BISHOP, G. LIVINGSTON, Assistant Minister of the Church of the Advent, Philadelphia.

BIRD, GUSTAVUS C.

BOLTON, JOHN, Rector of the Church of the Holy Trinity, West Chester

BOWERS, WM. V., Philadelphia.

BOYLE, A. H., Rector of Trinity Church, Shamokin.

BRINGHURST, GEORGE, Rector of the Church of the Messiah, Philadelphia.

*BROOKS, ARTHUR. Rector of Trinity Church, Williamsport.

BROWN, HENRY, Rector of St. Paul's Church, Chester.

BROWNE, PERCY, Rector of St. Philip's Church, Philadelphia.

BROWN, R. HILL, Rector of St. John's Church, Salem, and Zion Church, Sterling; P. O., Hamlinton.

BRUSH, A. P., Rector of St. James' Church, Muncy.

BUCHANAN, EDWARD Y., D.D., Rector of Trinity Church, Oxford; P. O., Oxford Church.

BURK, JESSE Y., Rector of Trinity Church, Philadelphia.

BURROWS, THOS., Rector of Grace Church, Hulmeville.

BURTON, GIDEON J., Rector of St. Matthew's Church, Sunbury.

Bush, Franklin L.

BUSHNELL, F. H., Rector of St. David's Church, Manayunk.

BUTLER, C. M., D. D., Professor in the Divinity School, Philadelphia.

CARPENTER, JOHN T., Rector of St. Paul's Church, Minersville.

CATHELL, J. EVERIST, Assistant Minister of the Church of the Epiphany, Philadelphia.

Cha e, Robert F.

CHILDS, JOHN A., D. D., Secretary of the Bishop, of the Diocesan Board of Missions, of the Managers of the Episcopal Hospital, and of the Overseers of the Divinity School, Philadelphia.

Christian, Edmund.

CLAXTON, J. W., Rector of the Church of the Advent, Philadelphia.

CLAXTON, R. BETHELL, D. D., Professor in the Divinity School, Philadelphia.

Clements, Samuel.

CLERC, FRANCIS J., D. D., Warden of the Burd Orphan Asylum, Philadelphia.

COLEMAN, LEIGHTON, Rector of St. Mark's Church, Mauch Chunk.

COLTON, RICHARD F., Professor in the Divinity School, Philadelphia, and Rector of the Church of Our Saviour, Jenkintown,

*CONNOLLY, PIERCE, Rector of the Protestant Episcopal Church, in Florence, Italy.

COOPER, CHARLES D., Rector of the Church of the Holy Apostles, Philadelphia.

Crooke, George A., D. D., Philadelphia.

Cull, Alex. H., Philadelphia.

Cummins, Alex. G.

DAVIES, THOS. F., Rector of St. Peter's Church, Philadelphia.

DAVIS, THOS. J., Rector of the Church of the Resurrection, Nicetown, Philadelphia.

†DENNISON, ROBT., E., Assistant Minister in St. Mark's Church, Philadelphia.

DIEHL, WM. N., Rector of St. John Baptist's Church, Germantown.

Douglass, Benjamin J.

*DOUGLASS, JACOB M., Philadelphia.

DRAKE. G. C., Muncy.

DRUMM, JOHN H., D.D., Rector of the Church of St. James the Greater, Bristol.

DUANE, CHAS. W., Rector of Zion Church, Philadelphia,

DU HAMEL, J. PLEASANTON, Rector of the Church of the Redemption, Philadelphia.

DUHRING, H. L., Rector of All Saints' Church, Philadelphia.

DUPUY, CHARLES M., Philadelphia.

Durant, N. Joseph.

DURBOROW, SAMUEL, Superintendent Protestant Episcopal City Missions, Philadelphia,

ECCLESTON, JAMES H., Rector of the Church of the Saviour, West Philadelphia.

EDWARDS, ROBERT A., Rector of Grace Church, Mount Airy, Philadelphia.

Edwards, Samuel.

Elwyn, Alfred, West Chester.

ELY, WM., Rector of Calvary Church, Rockdale; P. O., Lenni.

ERBEN, W. B., Rector of the Church of the Redeemer, Philadelphia.

EVANS, REES C., Rector of the Church of the Messiah, Port Richmond, Philadelphia.

FALKNER, JOHN B., Rector of St. Matthew's Church, Francisville.

FIELD, GEO. G., Rector of Trinity Church, Coatesville.

FISCHER, CHARLES L., Rector of the Church of St. John the Evangelist, Philadelphia.

FOGGO, E. A., Rector of Christ Church, Philadelphia.

*FORBES, JOHN I., Philadelphia.

FUGETT, J. P., Philadelphia.

FUREY, JOHN G., City Missionary, Philadelphia.

GIBSON, L. W., Assistant Minister of St. James' Church, Philadelphia

GOODWIN, DANL. R., D. D., LL. D., Professor in the Divinity School, Philadelphia.

*GRAFF, WM. H., Rector of St. Jude's Church, Philadelphia.

GRAHAM, RICHARDSON, Philadelphia.

GRIES, W. R., Rector of Grace Church, Allentown.

*HALL, RICHARD D., Philadelphia.

HALLOWELL, SAML. W., Rector of Christ Church, Media.

HALSEY, WM. F., Rector of St. David's Church, Radnor; P. O., Spread Eagle.

HAMMOND, J. PINKNEY, Rector of Christ Church, Reading.

*HARD, ANSON B., Chester.

HARE, CHANDLER.

HARE, G. EMLEN, D. D., Professor in the Divinity School, Philadelphia,

*HARE, WM. HOBART, Secretary and General Agent of Committee for Foreign Missions, New York.

HARRIS, J. ANDREWS, Rector of St. Paul's Church, Chestnut Hill.

HARTLEY, B., Rector of St. Luke's Church, Blossburg.

HAWKINS, WM. G., Missionary at Chambersburg.

HAZLEHURST, SAML., Philadelphia.

HAY, H. PALETHORP, Rector of the Church of the Good Shepherd, Radnor; P. O., Philadelphia.

HEATON, WM. SMITH, Rector of St. Paul's Church, Manheim, and Missionary.

HENING, E. W., in the service of the Foreign Missionary Committee, Philadelphia.

HEWITT, JOHN, Rector of St. Paul's Church, Bloomsburg.

HEYSINGER, J. L., Rector of St. Timothy's Church, Philadelphia.

Hirst, Marmaduke, Norristown.

HODGE, GEORGE W., Assistant Minister of Christ Church, Philadelphia.

HOFFMAN, EUGENE A., D. D., Rector of St. Mark's Church, Philadelphia.

HOPKINS, GEO. P., Rector of St. Paul's Church, Troy.

HOWARD, HORATIO C., Deacon, officiating in St. Paul's Church, Pleasant Mount.

HOWE, M. A. DeWOLFE, D. D., Rector of St. Luke's Church, Philadelphia.

HUTCHINSON, T. P., Rector of St. James' Church, Hestonville.

Innis, Robert F., Deacon, West Chester.

IRELAND, JOHN, Philadelphia.

Isaac, Ezra, Deacon, Philadelphia.

JAGGAR, THOS. A., Rector of the Church of the Holy Trinity, Philadelphia.

JARRETT, WM., Frankford.

Jarvis, Herbert M., Rector of the Church of Our Saviour, Montoursville.

JEROME, JOHN A., Rector of St. Mark's Church, New Milford, and Grace Church, Great Bend.

KARCHER, JEREMIAH, Minister of St. Barnabas' Church, Reading, and St. Gabriel's Church, Morlattin.

KARCHER, JOHN K., Rector of St. Paul's Church, Wellsboro.

KEELING, R. J., D. D., Rector of St. Stephen's Church, Harrisburg.

Keith, Ormes B.

†KERN, MOSES L., Rector of Trinity Church, Carbondale.

KIRKLAND, GEORGE H., Rector of St. Paul's Church, Columbia.

LANDRETH, O. W., Rector of Grace, Church, Honesdale.

LEAF, EDMUND, Rector of St. Michael's Church, Birdsboro; P. O., Pottstown.

LEVERETT, WM. C., Rector of St. John's Church, Carlisle.

LEWIS, WM. P., Rector of Trinity Church, Pottsville.

*LIGGINS, JOHN.

*LIGHTNER, EDWIN N., Danville.

LOGAN, CHARLES, Rector of St. John's Church, Northern Liberties, Philadelphia.

LOUDERBACK, ALFRED, Assistant Minister at St. Luke's, Philadelphia.

LYCETT, EDWARD L., Rector of the Church of the Redeemer, Lower Merion; P. O., Cabinet.

Mackie, Robert, Philadelphia.

MACELREY, J. H., Deacon, Minister St. John's Church, Ashley, Luzerne Co.

MAISON, CHARLES A., Rector of St. James' Church, Kingsessing, Philadelphia.

MARPLE, AUGUSTUS A., Rector of St. Luke's Church, Scranton.

Marsden, John H., York Springs.

MARTIN, ISAAC, Missionary to Seamen. Philadelphia.

MARTIN, THOMAS W., Rector of St. Mark's Church, Lewistown.

MATLACK, R. C., Gen. Sec. of the Evangelical Educational Society, Philadelphia.

McGANN, BYRON, Rector of Christ Church, Pottstown.

McILVAINE, CHARLES E., Rector of St. John's Church, Norristown.

McGLATHERY, WM., Rector of Christ Church, Towanda.

*McMURPHY, A. T., Rector of the House of Prayer, Branchtown, Philadelphia.

MEAD, CHARLES H., Rector of St. John's Church, Marietta.

Meade, Samuel H., Rector of St. Paul's Church, Phillipsburg.

MILLER, DANL. S., D. D., Rector of St. Mark's Church, Frankford.

MILLER, JACOB, Rector of the Church of the Evangelists, Philadelphia.

MILLETT, D. C , D. D., Rector of Emmanuel Church, Holmesburg.

MILLETT, JOHN H. H., Rector of the Church of the Good Shepherd, Green Ridge, Scranton.

*MOMBERT, I. ISADOR, D. D., Rector of St. John's Church, Dresden, Germany.

MONTGOMERY, WM. WHITE, of W. N. Y., Downingtown.

Morgan, J. J. A., Rector of St. Luke's Church, Altoona.

MOORE, JOS. R., Rector of St. George's Church, Kenderton, Philadelphia.

MOORE, WM., Rector of St. Mark's Church, Northumberland.

MORRISON, A. M., West Philadelphia.

*MORSELL, WM. F. C., Assistant to Rev. Dr. Beasley; P. O., Torresdale.

*MORTON, HENRY J., D. D., Rector of St. James' Church, Philadelphia.

MORTON, ALGERNON, Deacon.

MUNROE, WM. H., Rector of Emmanuel Church, Kensington, Philadelphia.

MURPHY, JOHN K., Rector of St. Michael's Church, Germantown.

MURPHY, JOS. W., Rector of the Church of Faith, Mahanoy City.

MURRAY, CHAS. E., Rector of the Church of the Covenant, Philadelphia.

Neilson, W. H., Minister of Trinity Chapel, Philadelphia.

NEVIN, ROBERT J., Rector of Grace Church, Rome, Italy.

NEWLIN, JOS. D., Rector of the Church of the Incarnation, Philadelphia.

NEWMAN, LOUIS C., Missionary to the Jews, Philadelphia.

NEWTON, RICHARD, D. D., Rector of the Church of the Epiphany, Philadelphia.

NEWTON, WM., Rector of the Church of the Nativity, Philadelphia.

Noakes, Benj. T.

Nock, Joseph A., Philadelphia.

ORRICK, WM. P., Rector of St. John's Church, York.

*PADDOCK, WM. HEMANS, Philadelphia.

PADDOCK, WILBUR F., D. D., Rector of St. Andrew's Church, Philadelphia.

PARET, WM., D. D., Rector of Christ Church, Williamsport.

*PEARCE, J. STURGIS, Rector of St. Martin's Church, Marcus Hook.

PECK, JOHN M., Rector of Christ Church, Danville,

*PERINCHIEF, OCTAVIUS, Rector of Christ Church, (Swedes) Bridgeport, Montgomery County.

*PERKINS, W. S., Bristol.

PERRY, JAMES DE WOLF, Rector of Calvary Church, Germantown.

PRATT, JAMES, D. D., Philadelphia.

PRIOR, A., Pottsville.

QUICK, CHAS. W., Rector of the Church of Our Saviour, Philadelphia.

REED, J. SANDERS, Rector of Trinity Church, Easton.

REESE, PHILIP P., Rector of Holy Trinity Church, Centralia.

RICKERT, A. A., Deacon, Assistant at the Church of the Good Shepherd, Philadelphia.

Ridgely, G. W., Philadelphia.

RITCHIE, ROBERT, Rector of the Church of St. James the Less, Philadelphia.

ROACH, ROBERT T., D. D., Rector of St. Paul's Church, Philadelphia.

ROBINS, JAMES W., Head Master of the Protestant Episcopal Academy, Philadelphia.

RODNEY, JOHN, Rector Emeritus of St. Luke's Church, Germantown.

*ROWLAND, HENRY J., Philadelphia.

RUDDEROW, JOEL, Rector of St. Paul's Memorial Church, Lower Providence ; P. O., Oaks, Montgomery Co.

RUDDER, WM., D. D., Rector of St. Stephen's Church, Philadelphia.

RUMNEY, THEO. S., D. D., Rector of Christ Church, Germantown.

RUSSELL, PETER, Rector of St. James' Church, Perkiomen.

SAUL, JAS., Rector of St. Bartholomew's Church, Philadelphia.

SHIRAS, ALEX., D. D., Philadelphia.

SIMES, SNYDER B., Rector of Gloria Dei Church, Philadelphia.

SIMPSON, E. OWEN, in charge of Bishop's Church, Philadelphia.

SMITH, HENRY R., Minister of St. John's Church, Pequea; P. O., Cain's.

SMITH, SAMUEL E., Rector of St. Andrew's Church, West Philadelphia.

SPACKMAN, HENRY S., Chaplain of the Episcopal Hospital, Philadelphia.

Steck, Chas. S , Hughesville.

STEWART, W. H. N., LL.D., Assistant Minister of St. Clement's Church. Philadelphia.

STOCKTON, WM. R., Rector of St. Peter's Church, Phœnixville.

STRYKER, P. W., Rector of St. Thomas' Church, White Marsh.

SUDDARDS, W., D. D., Rector of Grace Church, Philadelphia.

SUPPLEE, ENOCH H., Assistant to the Rector of St. Philip's Church, and Principal of an Institute for Young Ladies, Philadelphia.

Teller Geo. S., Rector of St. Paul's Church, Lock Haven.

Tetlow, John, Deacon, Philadelphia.

THOMAS, RICHARD N., Rector of St. Matthias' Church, Philadelphia.

*THOMSON, C. W., York.

*TORTAT, A. E., Rector of St. Paul's Church, West Whiteland, and St. Peter's Church, Great Valley; P. O., Newtown Square.

TROWBRIDGE, ISAAC L., Deacon, Philadelphia.

TWEEDALE, SAMUEL, Assistant Minister of St. Mark's Church, Frankford.

VAN DYNE, C. H., Rector of St. Peter's Church, Hazleton.

*VAN PELT, PETER, D. D., Philadelphia.

WADLEIGH, ALBRA, Rector of St. Luke's Church, Germantown.

WALKER, JAMES, Rector of St. James' Church, Eckley.

*WARD, HENRY DANA, Philadelphia.

WARRINER, E. A., Rector of St. Paul's Church, Montrose.

WASHBURN, D., Rector of St. John's Church, Ashland.

WATSON, BENJ., D. D., Rector of the Church of the Atonement, Philadelphia.

WATSON, EDWARD SHIPPEN, Rector of St. James' Church, Lancaster.

*WELLS, H. T., LL.D, President of Andalusia College, Andalusia.

*WHITE, WM. A., Rector of St. Timothy's Church, Roxborough; P. O., Leverington.

WHITEHEAD, CORTLANDT, Rector of the Church of the Nativity, Bethlehem.
Wilson, Peter Quick, Deacon.

WIDDEMER, EPHRAIM S., Church of the Merciful Saviour.

WILLIAMSON, ROBT. H., Rector of St. Stephen's Church, Wilkesbarre.

YARNALL, THOS. C., D. D., Rector of St. Mary's Church, West Philadelphia.

LAY DEPUTIES.

ADAMS COUNTY.
Huntington, Christ Ch.—No Deputies.

BEDFORD COUNTY.
BEDFORD, *St. James.*—No Deputies.

BERKS COUNTY.
MORLATTIN, *St. Gabriel.*—*Isaac Yocom, *David Lord, *Levi Yocom.
READING, *Christ Ch.*—Isaac Eckert, *Geo. W. Morgan, Henry M. Keim.
READING, *St. Barnabas.*—Peter Jones, *Thomas Addison, *Nicholas Jones.
MORGANTOWN, *St. Thomas.*—*David Plank, *L. Heber Smith, *John Plank.
BIRDSBORO, *St. Michael.*—George Brooke.

BLAIR COUNTY.
ALTOONA, *St. Luke.*—James Kearney, *Robert Scott, *G. W. Stewart.

BRADFORD COUNTY.
PIKE, *St. Matthew.*—No Deputies.
TOWANDA, *Christ Ch.*—E. T. Fox, *S. W. Alvord, E. W. Hale.
TROY, *St. Paul.*—No Deputies.
ATHENS, *Trinity.*—No Deputies.

BUCKS COUNTY.
BRISTOL, *St. James.*—*Henry L. Gaw, *Burnett Landreth. John Ward.
NEWTOWN, *St. Luke*—*Alex. Chambers, Geo. A. Jenks.
YARDLEYVILLE, *St. Andrew*—Thomas Heed, James Paff.
HULMEVILLE, *Grace.*—Edmund G. Harrison, Joseph K. Vanzandt, John P. Thompson.
CENTREVILLE, *Trinity.*—George G. Maris, William Stavely, *William J. Biles.
DOYLESTOWN, *St. Paul.*—Nathan C. James, *W. H. H. Davis, *James Gilkyson.

CARBON COUNTY.
MAUCH CHUNK, *St. Mark.*—*Asa Packer, James I. Blakslee, George Ruddle.
SUMMIT HILL, *St. Philip.*—*Matthew E. Sinyard, *Wm. D. Zehner, Wm. S. Hobart

CENTRE COUNTY.
PHILIPSBURG, *St. Paul.*—*David W. Holt, Hobart Allport,
BELLEFONTE, *St. John.*—W. F. Reynolds, *Edward Graham, *E. W. Hale.

CHESTER COUNTY.
GREAT VALLEY, *St. Peter.*—John L. Philips, Amariah Strickland.
NEW LONDON, *St. John.*—Thos. M. Charlton, John C. McDonald, *Benj. F. McDonald.
WARWICK. *St. Mary.*—Thos. K. Bull.
PEQUA, *St. John.*—S. Baxter Black, John Cox, Henry W. Worrest.
W. WHITELAND, *St. Paul.*—*John W. Stone, *Wm. E. Lockwood, *Geo. W. Jacobs.
W. VINCENT, *St. Andrew.*—*Jno. Strickland, *Nathan G. Grimm.
HONEYBROOK, *St. Mark.*—No Deputies.

WEST CHESTER, *Holy Trinity.*—James H. Bull, Henry Buckwalter, *Addison May.
PHŒNIXVILLE, *St. Peter.*—*John Griffin, Carroll S. Tyson.
DOWNINGTOWN, *St. James.*—Joseph B. Baker, Charles L. Wells, William Edge.
W. MARLBORO, *St. James.*—No Deputies.
COATESVILLE, *Church of the Trinity.*—Horace A. Beale, *John Stone, *Jones Happersett.

CLINTON COUNTY.

LOCK HAVEN, *St. Paul.*—*H. T. Beardsley, P. S. Merrell.

COLUMBIA COUNTY.

BLOOMSBURG, *St. Paul.*—J. J. Brower, Elias Mendenhall.
DERRY (EXCHANGE), *St. James.*—No Deputies.
CENTRALIA, *Holy Trinity.*—*Joseph M. Freck, *Robert Gorrell, *J. J. Hoagland.

CUMBERLAND COUNTY.

CARLISLE, *St. John.*—Frederic Watts, E. M. Biddle, *Wm. M. Henderson.

DAUPHIN COUNTY.

HARRISBURG, *St. Stephen.*—Jno. B. Cox, *Daniel D. Boas, William Buehler.
————, *St. Paul.*—Robert A. Lamberton, *Thomas Fitzsimmons, John A. Middleton.

DELAWARE COUNTY.

CHESTER, *St. Paul.*—*John Larkin, *J. B. McKeever, Robert Hall.
Chester, St. Luke.
MARCUS HOOK, *St. Martin.*—William Trainer, David Trainer, *Abner Vernon.
RADNOR, *St. David.*—John Mather, Mark Brooke, John B. Thayer.
————. *Church of the Good Shepherd.*—*Gorham P. Sargent, Charles W. Cushman, Samuel Greasly.*
CONCORD, *St. John.*—*John G. Standbridge. Joseph H. Cloud.
ROCKDALE, *Calvary.*—R. S. Smith, Samuel K. Crozier, W. D. Brown.
MEDIA, *Christ Ch.*—E. P. Borden, James S. McCalla, *Edward A. Price.

FRANKLIN COUNTY.

CHAMBERSBURG, *Trinity Ch.*—George W. Brewer, *Allen C. McGrath, *Joseph T. Wright.

HUNTINGDON COUNTY.

HUNTINGDON, *St. John.*—No Deputies.

LANCASTER COUNTY.

LANCASTER, *St. James.*—John L. Atlee. Newton Lightner, Thos. E. Franklin.
————, *St. John.*—*Geo. J. Diller, Isaac Diller, J. M. W. Geist.
CHURCHTOWN, *Bangor.*—No Deputies.
LEACOCK, *Christ Ch.*—*Wm. Hamilton, *Joseph Slack.
PARADISE, *All Saints.*—E. W. Eshleman, *A. L. Witmer. *A. P. Wilmer.
COLUMBIA, *St. Paul.*—*D. J. Bruner. *B. F. Steiger, George H. Richards.
MARIETTA, *St. John.*—S. F. Eagle, *H. S. Watts, E. Haldeman.
MOUNT HOPE, *Hope.*—No Deputies.
GAP MINES, *Grace.*—No Deputies.
MANHEIM, *St. Paul.*—*John M. Dunlap. H. S. Stauffer, *J. B. White.

LEBANON COUNTY.

LEBANON, *St. Luke.*—James R. Jones, George Drake.

LEHIGH COUNTY.

ALLENTOWN, *Grace.*—*Jas. W. Wilson, Dewees J. Martin, *Wm. H. Ainey.

LUZERNE COUNTY.

WILKESBARRE, *St. Stephen.*—Agib Ricketts, Samuel R. Marshall, V. L. Maxwell.

SOUTH WILKESBARRE, *St. Clement.*—E. W. Sturdevant, *Andrew Lee, John W. Horton.

CARBONDALE, *Trinity.*—*J. M. Poor, *Chas. Burr, *A. O. Hanford.

PITTSTON, *St. James.*—No Deputies.

SCRANTON, *St. Luke.*—H. B. Rockwell, C. P. Matthews.

ECKLEY, *St. James.*—*Richard Sharpe, *Francis Weiss, Hiram Belford.

WHITE HAVEN, *St. Paul.*—John R. Crellin, Robert J. Westover, Albert A. Lewis.

HAZLETON, *St. Peter.*—*James C. Haydon, *William Glover, *Frederick Lauderburne.

Green Ridge, The Church of the Good Shepherd.—J. Gardner Sanderson, *J. Atticus Robertson, *Charles Du Pont Breck.

LYCOMING COUNTY.

MUNCY, *St. James.*—*G. L. J. Painter, Henry Johnson, Joseph Gudykunst.

WILLIAMSPORT, *Christ Ch.*—*George Webb, *James Smeaton, James H. Perkins.

————————, *Trinity.*—J. W. Maynard, H. F. Snyder, *G. Bedell Moore.

MONTOURSVILLE, *The Church of our Saviour.*—*Robert H. Archer, *James Rawle.

MIFFLIN COUNTY.

LEWISTOWN, *St. Mark's.*—James H. Mann, *Richard H. Lee, *Henry Frysinger.

MONTGOMERY COUNTY.

WHITE MARSH, *St. Thomas.*—Jesse Shay, W. H. Drayton.

PERKIOMEN, *St. James.*—Charles P. Shannon, *William Fronefield, *D. M. Casselberry.

NORRISTOWN, *St. John.*—*Wm. Wills, *Francis Bacon, Jno. McKay.

POTTSTOWN, *Christ Ch.*—*Samuel Wells, *Wm. J. Rutter, Charles Rutter.

LOWER MERION, *Redeemer.*—George F. Curwin, James C. Booth, Francis C. Yarnall.

JENKINTOWN, *Our Saviour.*—No Deputies.

CONSHOHOCKEN, *Calvary.*—Walter Cresson, *Theodore Trewendt, *Charles Lukens.

CHELTENHAM, *St. Paul.*—John W. Thomas, Robert Shoemaker, Thomas T. Lea.

LOWER MERION, *St. John.*—Isaac Hazlehurst, David Morgan. Joseph B. Townsend.

UPPER PROVIDENCE, *St. Paul's Memorial Ch.*—*C. W. Gumbes, *Chas. Davis, *Caleb Cresson.

GWYNEDD, *Messiah.*—No Deputies.

MONTOUR COUNTY.

DANVILLE, *Christ Ch.*—P. Baldy, Jr., Daniel D. Long, *Henry Earp.

NORTHAMPTON COUNTY.

EASTON, *Trinity.*—*T. R. Sitgreaves, John O. Wagner, *W. H. Davis.

BETHLEHEM, *Nativity*—*Wm. H. Sayre, Henry Coppeé, H. S. Goodwin.

NORTHUMBERLAND COUNTY.

SUNBURY, *St. Matthew.*—Wm. J. Greenough, N. Ferree Lightner, *Eben G. Scott.

NORTHUMBERLAND, *St. Mark.*—John McFarland, John H. Jenkins.

SHAMOKIN, *Trinity,*—Chas. P. Helfenstein, *John H. Dewees, Richard B. Douty.

PHILADELPHIA COUNTY.

PHILADELPHIA, *Christ.*—Samuel Wagner, Edward L. Clark, Joseph K. Wheeler.

St. Peter.—James S. Newbold, Chas. Willing, Geo. C. Morris.

St. Paul.—Eleazer Fenton, *Thomas Latimer, William Cummings.

St. James.—Geo. W. Hunter, William F. Griffitts, Frederick Fraley.

St. Stephen.—Thomas Neilson, Ludovic C. Cleeman, *Lewis Rodman.

St. Andrew.—Thomas Robins, Arthur G. Coffin, *Frederick Brown.

Grace.—M. J. Mitcheson, Isaac S. Williams, Andrew H. Miller.

Epiphany.—*Lewis R. Ashhurst, Robert B. Sterling, Charles E. Lex.

Ascension.—Thos. R. Maris, Chas. Pesauque, Alfred Zantzinger.

St. Luke.—George L. Harrison, Andrew Wheeler, Wm. W. Frazier, Jr.

Atonement.—Samuel F. Ashton, Lafayette Baker, William C. Houston.

St. Mark.—Richard R. Montgomery, Edward S. Buckley *David Pepper.

Mediator.—John Ashhurst, Jr., *Horace Everett, Francis Hoskins.

St. Clement.—P. Pemberton Morris, George N. Allen, John Lambert.

Holy Trinity.—John Bohlen, *Lemuel Coffin, W. P. Cresson.

Covenant.—John P. Rhoads, James A. Kirkpatrick, James C. Allen.

St. Thomas.—*U. P. Vidal, Morris Brown, Sr., *Alfred S. Cassey.

OXFORD, *Trinity.*—Wm. Overington, Harry Ingersoll, John Cooke.

LOWER DUBLIN, *All Saints.*—Charles R. King, Alex. Brown, *S Wilmer Cannell.

N. LIBERTIES, *St. John.*—William P. Fodell, Charles Beamish, Henry Walker.

Advent.—*Abel Reed, George Remsen, *Edward Evans.

Calvary.—George B. Bonnell, Geo. M. Coates, Alfred Hopper.

SOUTHWARK, *Trinity.*—Wm. S. Price, Charles M. Peterson, Henry Green.

Evangelists.—Edwin Kelley, Henry Nichol, *George Lendrum.

Gloria Dei.—Geo. M. Sandgran, Richard Sharp, Robert B. Salter.

St. John the Evangelist.—Wm. H. Myers, George G. Roberts, A. J. Baton.

Church of the Messiah.—Henry M. Watts, M. Mesier Reese, Wm. Jordan.

FAIRMOUNT, *Redemption.*—Wm. H. Eastwood, *Adam Bustard, *Robert Taylor.

SPRING GARDEN, *St. Philip.*—John Agnew, Mifflin Wister, Joseph R. Rhoads,

Nativity.—Wm. Hobart Brown, *Joseph Allen, Lewis Thompson.

St. Jude.—Jacob S. Miller, Wm. M. Abbey, *B. L. Middleton.

Intercessor.—No deputies.

St. Matthias.—Wm. H. Rhawn, Henry S. Godshall, Joseph M. Cardeza.

Incarnation—Geo. Williams, C. M. Husband, W. J. Philips.

Holy Apostles.—Lewis H. Redner, Geo. C. Thomas, Wm. D. Thomas.

FRANCISVILLE, *St. Matthew.*—George M. Stroud, Thomas Cain, Henry L. Hoff.

Church of the Good Shepherd.—Joseph M. Christian, William Tardif, Jr., Horace J. Subers.

W. PHILADELPHIA, *St. Mary.*—C. P. B. Jeffreys, *Wm. Yarnall, Henry C. Townsend.

St. Andrew.—Wm. H. Wilson, J. R. Sypher, H. W. Siddall.

Church of the Saviour.—John D. Taylor, *A. J. Drexel, Henry P. Rutter.

Kensington, *Emmanuel.*—John Scanlan, Douglass McFadden, Chas. S. Howe.

Moyamensing, *All Saints.*—Wm. Ridings, Wm. Sterling, James Kidd.

Crucifixion.—Samuel T. Demar, Peter C. Williams, Dennis Green.

Our Saviour.—James Moore.

Germantown, *St. Luke.*—James M. Aertsen, R. P. McCullagh,*Thos. H. Montgomery.

Christ Ch.—H. H. Houston, A. Miskey, Charles Spencer.

St John the Baptist.—Wm. A. James, *John J. Crout.

Calvary.—*L. P. Thompson, Saml. K. Ashton, J. Robbins.

St. Michael.—Arthur Wells, S. Harvey Thomas, Galloway C. Morris.

Holmesburg, *Emmanuel.*—Lewis Thompson, Andreas Hartel, P. Blakiston.

Kingsessing, *St. James.*—D. Henry Flickwir, Thomas Sparks, *Isaac T. Jones.

Frankford, *St. Mark.*—Wm. Welsh, Benj. Rowland, Jr., John Clayton.

Port Richmond, *Messiah.*—Henry Christian, *Wm. J. Bell, John W. Bain.

South Penn, *Zion.*—Dell Noblit, Jr., Thomas R. Alexander, Henry N. Rittenhouse.

Manayunk, *St. David.*—Wm. B. Stephens, Orlando Crease, Edward Holt.

Rising Sun, *Resurrection.*—George Blight, *David Thomson, *Wm. Brooks.

Maylandville, *Trinity.*—No Deputies.

Chestnut Hill, *St. Paul.*—M. Russell Thayer, Wm. C. Mackie. *Franklin H. Bowen.

Roxborough, *St. Timothy.*—J. Vaughan Merrick, T. F. Cauffman, Wm. H. Merrick.

St. Alban.—*Jacob Casselberry, James L. Rahn.

Bustleton, *St. Luke.*—*Amos A. Gregg, John Willian, Jr.

Branchtown, *House of Prayer.*—Bennett Medary, Jr., *Wm. Muns, *Charles S. Shaw.

Mount Airy. *Grace.*—C. B. Dunn, *George W. Maulsby, C. M. Bayard.

Frankford Road, *St. John.*—*Wm. Ellis, *Robert Whitechurch, Cornelius Stephens.

Hestonville *St. James.*—N. P. Shortridge, James M. Cadmus, A. H. Franciscus.

Tacony, *Holy Innocents.*—*S. A. J. Salter, *George F. Keene, *Samuel S. Wenzell.

Falls of Schuylkill, *St. James the Less.*—Ellis Yarnall, Benjamin J. Ritter, George M. Conarroe.

Clay Mission.—J. Rush Ritter, *Benezet Irons, *Wm. Winters.

Bridesburg, *St. Stephen.*—William Matlack, *Charles Blackiston, *Jacob Cook.

St. George.—Wm. N. Marcus, Hugh Whiteley, John Slater.

Kenderton, *St. George.*—Thomas Maddock, *Elijah Wyatt, Percy Lauderdale.

St. Paul, Aramingo.

SCHUYLKILL COUNTY.

Pottsville, *Trinity.*—Ed. Owen Parry, *Charles Baber, *Charles M. Hill.

Ashland, *St. John's Memorial.*—*D. J. McKibbin, *William Reifsnyder, *Lewis A. Reily.

Minersville, *St. Paul.*—No Deputies.

St. Clair, *Holy Apostles.*—*George Rogers, *R. H. Coryell.

Schuylkill Haven, *St. James.*—No Deputies.

Tamaqua, *Calvary.*—*G. L. Boyd, *Preston Robinson.

Mahanoy, *Faith.*—Wesley Hammer, *Henry Jackson, *E. F. Washburn.

Tuscarora, Zion.

SUSQUEHANNA COUNTY.

NEW MILFORD, *St, Mark.*—No Deputies.
MONTROSE. *St. Paul.*—*Charles L. Brown, *William H. Cooper, *James E. Carmalt.
GREAT BEND. *Grace.*—*L. E. Colsten, *Charles G. Estabrook. *Oliver Trowbridge.
SPRINGVILLE, *St. Andrew.*—No Deputies.

TIOGA COUNTY.

WELLSBORO, *St. Paul.*—*John L. Robinson, *William Bache, *M. B. Prince.
BLOSSBURG, *St. Luke.*—*James Withington, *William D. Knight.
MANSFIELD, *St James.*—*F. A. Allen, *William Holland.
FALL BROOK, *St. Thomas.*—No Deputies.
TIOGA, *St. Andrew.*—John W. Guernsey, Thomas D. Baldwin.

WAYNE COUNTY.

HONESDALE. *Grace.*—Z. H. Russell, E. Stanton, E. W. Hamlin.
PLEASANT MOUNT, *St. Paul.*—*Henry W. Nicholls, *William W. Brown.
SALEM, *St. John.*—No Deputies.
STIRLING, *Zion.*—No Deputies.

WYOMING COUNTY.

Tunkhannock, St. Peter.

YORK COUNTY.

YORK, *St. John.*—Robert J. Fisher, *Michael Schall, *William C. Chapman.

JOURNAL.

PHILADELPHIA, ST. ANDREW'S CHURCH,

TUESDAY, May 9th, 1871, 5 O'CLOCK, P. M.

This being the day appointed for the meeting of the Convention of the Protestant Episcopal Church in the Diocese of Pennsylvania, a number of Clergymen and Lay Deputies attended at St. Andrew's Church, Philadelphia.

Before the organization of the Convention, Evening Prayer was read by the Rev. Charles E. McIlvaine, and the Rev. E. A. Hoffman, D.D.

The Secretary then announced the necessary absence of the Right Rev. the Bishop of the Diocese, by reason of sickness, and proceeded to call the names of the Clergy entitled to seats, from a list prepared by the Bishop, when 119 answered to their names.

The Secretary proceeded to call the names of the Lay Deputies, as recorded by him, from the certificates presented in the form prescribed by the Canon, when 196 answered and took their seats.

Mr. Wm. Welsh nominated the Rev. Dr. Howe as President of the Convention during its sessions, in the absence of the Bishop, and he was thereupon elected *viva voce.*

The Rev. Dr. Howe having taken the Chair, the Convention proceeded to the election of a Secretary and Assistant Secretary.

The Rev. Dr. Childs was nominated for the office of Secretary: there being no other nomination, the balloting was dispensed with, and he was thereupon duly elected *viva voce*.

Mr. James C. Booth a Lay Delegate from the Church of the Redeemer, Lower Merion, Montgomery County, was then nominated for the office of Assistant Secretary, and there being no other nomination, he was, in like manner duly elected Assistant Secretary.

The Secretary reported the following business as unfinished at the last Convention, and referred to appropriate Committees:

On Alterations of Canons of the Diocese.
On Parsonages.
On Education of Sons of the Clergy.
On Minority Representation.

The President appointed the following Standing Committees:

COMMITTEE ON CHARTERS:

Rev. E. Y. Buchanan, D.D.,	Rev. Wm. P. Lewis, D.D.,	Rev. E. A. Warriner,
Mr. Thomas R. Franklin,	Mr. Frederick Fraley,	Mr. H. Coppeé.

COMMITTEE ON CLAIMS OF CLERGYMEN TO SEATS:

Rev. G. E. Hare, D. D.,	Rev. T. F. Davies.	Rev. A. A. Marple.

COMMITTEE ON CLAIMS TO SEATS AS LAY DEPUTIES:

Mr. G. W. Hunter,	Mr. C. R. King,	Mr. A. Ricketts.

The Rev. Mr. Falkner nominated the following for Standing Committee of the Diocese:

Rev. H. J. Morton, D.D.,	Rev. Benj. Watson, D.D.,	Mr. John Clayton,
" D. R. Goodwin, D.D.,	Mr. Thomas Robins,	" Wm. F. Griffitts,
" G. E. Hare, D.D.,	" John Bohlen,	" Richard S. Smith.
" M. A. DeW. Howe, D.D.		

The Rev. E. S. Watson nominated the following for Standing Committee of the Diocese:

Rev. H. J. Morton, D.D.,	Rev. J. K. Murphy,	Mr. R. R. Montgomery.
" E. A. Foggo,	Mr. R. S. Smith,	" T. Neilson,
" T. F. Davies,	" W. F. Griffitts,	" W. S. Price.
" J. D. Newlin,		

The Rev. Dr. Watson nominated the following as Deputies to the General Convention:

Rev. M.A.DeW. Howe,D.D.	Rev. A. A. Marple,	Mr. Lemuel Coffin,
" D. R. Goodwin,D.D.,	Mr. Wm. Welsh,	" T. E. Franklin.
" G. E. Hare, D.D.,	" George L. Harrison,	

The Rev. E. S. Watson nominated the following as Deputies to the General Convention:

Rev. Wm. Rudder, D.D.,	Rev. Albra Wadleigh,	Mr. E. S. Buckley,
" E. A. Hoffman, D.D.,	Mr. M. R. Thayer,	" P. Baldy, Jr.
" Wm. Paret, D.D.,	" G. W. Hunter,	

Mr. Aertsen nominated the following for Trustees of the Christmas Fund:

Mr. Thomas Robins,	Mr. John S. Newbold,
" Edward L. Clark,	" Thomas H. Montgomery.

Mr. Thomas Robins nominated Mr. B. G. Godfrey as Treasurer of the Convention Fund.

Mr. Thomas Robins nominated Mr. R. P. McCullagh as Treasurer of the Christmas Fund.

Mr. G. W. Hunter nominated the Rev. J. W. Robins as Registrar of the Diocese.

On motion of the Rev. J. W. Claxton, it was

Resolved That the Secretary of the Convention prepare and distribute ballots containing the names of each nominee for the several offices to be voted for by this Convention.

On motion of the Rev. S. E. Appleton, the Revised Regulations were suspended for the purpose of introducing the following, which was adopted:

Resolved That the operation of the fifth of the Revised Regulations (which concerns the order of business of the Convention) be, and the same is hereby, so far suspended as to admit the Report of the Board of Missions, and the discussion incident thereto, as the order of the day for Thursday next, at 10 o'clock, A. M., provided that the elections shall have been then concluded.

The Rev. Dr. Childs announced that it was the desire of the Bishop that the services on the succeeding day should be, Morning Prayer at 9 o'clock, Holy Communion at half past 10 o'clock.

Thereupon, on motion of the Rev. Mr. Baldy, it was

Ordered, That this House hold two sessions every day, to wit: from 9 A. M. to 2 P.M. and from 5 P.M. to 8 P.M., provided that on Wednesday the Convention shall assemble at 9 A.M. for Morning Prayer, and at 10½ A.M. for the Communion.

On motion of the Rev. Dr. Hoffman, it was

Resolved, That Clergymen of the Protestant Episcopal Church belonging to this Diocese, not entitled to seats in this Convention, Clergymen of other Dioceses, Clergymen of the Churches of England and of Ireland, and of the Church of England in the Colonies of Great Britain; also candidates for Orders in the Protestant Episcopal Church in the United States, be admitted to the sittings of this Convention.

The Standing Committee presented the following report:

The Standing Committee herewith present a form of Charter of the Church of Saint Timothy, Philadelphia, but decline to recommend its approval, as it is not authenticated by any signatures.

The Committee have approved of the Charter of the Church of the Good Shepherd, Green Ridge.

JOHN CLAYTON,

MAY 9, 1871.   *Secretary.*

The Secretary read an invitation from the President of the Pennsylvania Horticultural Society, to visit the Floral Exhibition this evening at the Society's Hall, and stated that he had received tickets of admission for distribution among the Deputies.

On motion of the Secretary, Charters of Churches, approved by the Bishop and by the Standing Committee, were referred to the Committee on Charters.

On motion, adjourned.

JOHN A. CHILDS,
Secretary.

PHILADELPHIA, ST ANDREW'S CHURCH,

WEDNESDAY, MAY 10, 1871, 9 O'CLOCK, A. M.

The Convention met pursuant to order.

Morning Prayer was read by the Rev. N. Barrows, and Rev. Wm. Paret, D. D.

At 10½ A. M., the Communion Service was conducted by the Rev. Dr. Buchanan, Rev. E. A. Foggo, Rev. J. T. Carpenter, and Rev. Jos. W. Murphy.

At the conclusion of Divine Service, the President called the Convention to order.

The President read a communication from the Bishop of the Diocese, stating his inability to be present at this day's session, and requesting that the reading of his Charge be made the order of the day for Thursday at 12 M.

On motion, the calling of the roll was dispensed with, except the names of those who did not answer yesterday. The Secretary then called such names, when 38 of the Clergy and 75 of the Lay Deputies appeared and took their seats.

The minutes of yesterday's proceedings were read and approved.

The Bishop's Address was read by the Rev. Leighton Coleman, as follows:

BELOVED BRETHREN,, CLERICAL AND LAY:

I bid you welcome to another of our Annual gatherings. How rapidly they succeed each other! How swiftly the intervening time passes away! Yet each Convention, as it comes and goes, leaves its distinct legislative impress on the Church, and each year of active work tells with marked effect on its strength and growth. To detail the incidents that show the work and increase of our Church, so far as they come under the Bishop's supervision, is one of the principal designs of this Annual Address, while another purpose of it is, to furnish suggestions and state views on the various ecclesiastical and benevolent and educational movements which are going on around us. The following are my official acts during the past Conventional year:

On the Sunday after the adjournment of the last Convention, being the 22d of May, I visited the Church of the Redemption, Fairmount; preached, confirmed 12 persons, and addressed them.

In the evening, in St. Thomas' African Church, confirmed 18 persons, and made an address.

Tuesday, 24th, Evening, in the Church of Our Saviour, Jenkintown, I preached, confirmed 7 and made an address.

Wednesday, 25th. A M., in St. Stephen's, Bridesburg, after preaching, I confirmed a class of 15, and addressed them, then admitted the Rev. Wm. Jarrett and Rev. Geo. W. Hodge to the Priesthood. and administered the Holy Communion.

Sunday, 29th. A. M., in St. John's, New London, I preached and confirmed one person.

In the P. M., I preached in the Methodist Church, in Oxford, and confirmed two persons. In the evening I went to the Lincoln University, and in the Chapel preached to the students.

Tuesday, 31st. P. M., in St. Gabriel's, Morlattin, Douglassville, I preached, confirmed 8, and addressed them.

Saturday, June 4th. 5 P. M., laid the corner-stone of St. George's Church, Cardington, and made an address.

Sunday, 5th. A. M., in All Saint's Church, Lower Dublin, I preached, confirmed 11, and addressed them and administered the Holy Communion. P. M., in Emmanuel Church, Holmesburg, I preached, confirmed 14, and made an address.

Wednesday, 8th. Evening in the Church of the Atonement, I confirmed 23 and addressed the class.

Sunday. 12th. Trinity Sunday. A. M., in Calvary Church, Rockdale, I visited and addressed the Sunday School; preached, confirmed 10, and addressed them. P. M., in Christ Church, Media, I preached, confirmed 11 and made an address.

Sunday, 19th. A. M., in Trinity Church, Oxford, I preached, confirmed 17, and addressed them. Evening, Gloria Dei, Philadelphia, I preached, confirmed 7, and made an address.

Wednesday, 22d. Attended examinations of the Philadelphia Divinity School, and the meeting of the Joint Boards of its Trustees and Overseers.

Thursday, 23d. At Bethlehem. At the meeting of the Trustees of Lehigh University, and also presided at the Commencement exercises of the University, and conferred the Degrees.

Friday, 24th. In St. Luke's Church, Philadelphia, after a Sermon by the Rev. R. B. Duane, D.D., I admitted James Caird, Algernon Morton, G. Livingston Bishop, Aaron Bernstein, Philip M. Reese, and Wm. F. Floyd to the Diaconate, and advanced the Rev. Geo. H. Kirkland to the Priesthood.

Sunday, 26th. A. M., in St. James' Church, Kingsessing, I preached, confirmed 11, and addressed them.

Wednesday, 29th. A. M., in St. John's Church, Carlisle, preached, confirmed 11, and addressed them. P. M., confirmed a sick person in private. Evening, on occasion of the commencement of the Mary Institute, I delivered an address on the Christian Education of Women, in St. John's Church.

Friday, July 1st. At 1 o'clock, P. M., the committee on the Endowment of the Episcopate of the proposed new Diocese met at my house. Mr. Thos. E. Franklin was chosen Chairman and Mr. P. Baldy, Jr., Secretary.

Sunday, 3d. At St. James' Church, Pittston, I preached, confirmed 16, and addressed them.

Wednesday, 6th. Visited Northumberland, and at 4 o'clock P. M., I preached in St. Mark's Church. Evening in St. Matthew's Church, Sunbury, I preached, confirmed 12 and made an address.

Thursday, 7th. P. M., in St. James' Church, Muncy, I preached and confirmed 3 persons.

Friday, 8th. In St. Paul's Church, Lock Haven, I preached, confirmed 5 and addressed them.

Sunday, 10th. At Williamsport. In the morning I preached in Trinity Church, and introduced to the Parish their new minister, the Rev. Arthur Brooks. Evening, in Christ Church, I preached, confirmed 47, and made an address.

Monday, 11th. Evening, in the Church of Our Saviour, Montoursville, I preached and confirmed 2 persons.

Tuesday, 12th. Evening, in Trinity Church, Shamokin, I preached, and confirmed 7 persons, and addressed them.

Sunday, 24th. Evening, preached in St. Stephen's Church, Wilkes-Barre.

Wednesday, August 3d. Buried in Wilkes-Barre the child of Mr. Pryor Williamson.

Sunday, 7th. A. M., St. Stephen's Church, Wilkes-Barre, I administered the Holy Communion and preached.

Saturday, 13th. Laid corner-stone of St. John's Church, Ashley, and made an address.

Sunday, 14th. A. M., preached in St. Stephen's Church, Wilkes-Barre. Evening, read the service and preached in the same place.

Sunday 21st. Officiated all day in St. Stephen's Church, Wilkes-Barre.

Sunday, 28th. A. M., I preached in the School House in Woodside; in the afternoon I preached in the School House, Drifton. Evening, I preached in St. James', Eckley, and confirmed 5, and made an address.

Sunday, Sept. 4th. A. M., I consecrated the Church of the Holy Trinity, Centralia, preached, confirmed 7, and made an address. P. M., in St. John's, Ashland, I preached, confirmed 14, and made an address. Evening, I again preached in the Church of the Holy Trinity, Centralia.

Tuesday, 6. Met with the Endowment Committee of the proposed new Diocese in Wilkes-Barre.

Thursday, 8th. A.M., I instituted the Rev. John Milton Peck into the Rectorship of Christ Church, Danville; I preached the sermon and confirmed 3 persons.

Sunday, 11th. A.M., in St. Paul's Church, Montrose, I preached, confirmed 27, and addressed them. P.M., in St. Mark's Church, New Milford, I preached. Evening, in Grace Church, Great Bend, I preached, confirmed 3, and made an address.

Friday, 16th. Evening, in Trinity Church, Carbondale, I preached, confirmed 13, and addressed them.

Sunday, 18th. A.M., in St. Paul's Church, Pleasant Mount, I preached, confirmed 6, and addressed them. Evening, in Grace Church, Honesdale, I preached, confirmed 4, and made an address.

Sunday, 25th. A.M., in the Church of the Redeemer, Lower Merion, I preached, confirmed 6, and made an address. Evening, in the Bishop's Church, I preached.

Saturday, October 1st. P.M., in Christ Church, Leacock, I preached, confirmed 10, and addressed them.

Sunday, 2d. A.M., in St. John's Church, Pequea, I preached, confirmed 4, and made an address. P.M., I preached in the Methodist Church, Waynesburg. Evening, in Bangor Church, Churchtown, I preached, confirmed 12, and addressed them.

Monday, 3d. A.M., I officiated in St. Thomas' Church, Morgantown, and preached.

Wednesday, 5th. Evening, in St. James' Church, Hestonville, I preached, confirmed 11, and addressed them.

Thursday, 6th. A.M., in the Church of the Epiphany, Washington, D. C., I took part in the consecration of the Rev. Dr. Pinkney as Assistant Bishop of Maryland.

Sunday, 9th. A.M., in the Church of the Messiah, Port Richmond, Philadelphia, I preached, confirmed 13 (two being for Calvary Church), and addressed them.

Tuesday, 11th. Went to Williamsport.

Wednesday, 12th. A.M., in Christ Church I ordained J. Everist Cathell to the Diaconate, and the Rev. Arthur Brooks and Rev. James Caird to the Priesthood. The Rev. Phillips Brooks preached the sermon.

Thursday, 13th. A.M., in Montoursville, I consecrated the Church of our Saviour, and preached the sermon.

Sunday, 16th. A.M., in St. James' Church, Lancaster, I preached, confirmed 40, and made an address. Evening, in St. John's Church, Lancaster, I preached, confirmed 38, and addressed them.

Friday, 21st. In Grace Church, Newton, Massachusetts, I ordained to the Priesthood the Rev. Henry Christian Mayer, the Rector of the Parish. The Rev. Phillips Brooks preached the sermon, and the Rev. Dr. Stone, of Cambridge, presented the candidate.

Monday 24th. to Wednesday, 26th. I was in New York, in attendance on the meetings of the Board of Missions of the Protestant Episcopal Church.

Saturday, 29th. At 3 P.M. I laid the corner-stone of the new building of the Church Home for Children, near Angora Station on the West Chester Railroad.

Sunday, 30th. A.M., in the Church of St. John the Baptist, Germantown, I preached, confirmed 8, and addressed them. Evening, in the Church of the Holy Trinity, I presided at the Second Annual Meeting of the Indian's Hope Association, and made an address. Bishop Clarkson was present and also made an address.

Tuesday, November 1st. Deposed from the ministry the Rev. Faber Byllesby, in the presence of the Rev. Dr. Childs and the Rev. Joel Rudderow.

Wednesday, 2d. At 4 P.M., I laid the corner-stone of the Chapel of the Church of the Messiah, northeast corner of Broad and Federal streets, and made an address.

Thursday, 3d. Attended Meeting of the Joint Board of Trustees and Overseers of the Philadelphia Divinity School.

Sunday, 6th. A.M., in Christ Church, Reading, I preached, confirmed 26, and made an address, and also administered the Holy Communion. P.M., I confirmed a sick lady in private for Christ Church. Evening, in St. Barnabas' Church, Reading, I preached, confirmed 6, and addressed them.

Monday, 7th. Evening, in St. Paul's Church, Cheltenham, I met the clergy of the South Eastern Convocation, and preached the opening sermon.

Tuesday, 8th. P.M., confirmed a sick lady in West Philadelphia, for St. Andrew's Church, Mantua.

Sunday, 13th, A.M., in St. Mary's Church, West Philadelphia, I preached, confirmed 21. and addressed them. P.M., in the Church of St. James the Less, I confirmed 6, and addressed them. Evening, in St. Luke's Church, at a General Meeting called in behalf of City Missions, I made an address.

Sunday, 20th. A.M., consecrated the Chapel of Trinity Church, Oxford, at Crescentville; preached the sermon and administered the Holy Communion. Evening, made an address at the Fourth Anniversary of the Missionary Society of the Church of the Mediator.

Wednesday, 23d. At noon, visited the Academy of the Protestant Episcopal Church, it being Commendation Day, and made an address to the School.

Thursday, 24th. Thanksgiving Day. I went to Conshohocken and officiated, and preached in Calvary Church.

Sunday, 27, A. M. In Oak Grove Chapel, Bucks County, I preached, confirmed 3 and addressed them. P. M., preached in the Chapel. Evening went to Hulmeville and preached, confirmed 15 and addressed them in Grace Church.

Wednesday, 30, A. M. Visited the Philadelphia Divinity School, presided at the Matriculation Exercises and made an address. Evening I preached in a hall in Radnor Township, to the congregation of the Church of the Good Shepherd.

Friday, December 2d. Evening, I preached in the School House at Gwynedd, and confirmed 7 persons, and made an address.

Sunday, 4, A. M. In St. Michael's, Birdsboro, I preached and confirmed 3. Evening, in Christ Church, Pottstown, I preached, confirmed 10 and addressed them.

Sunday, 11 A. M. In the House of Prayer, Branchtown, I preached, confirmed 6 and addressed them. Evening, in the Church of the Good Shepherd I preached, confirmed 16 and addressed them.

Monday, 12. Evening in the Baptist Church, Chestnut St., I made an address in behalf of an effort to provide Lodging Houses for young women from the country and sales-women, &c.

Wednesday, 14. A. M. In St. Matthew's Church, Philadelphia, I ordained Isaac Lewis Trowbridge, M. D., Deacon, and Rev. Enoch H. Supplee, Priest. The Rev. William Newton preached the sermon. Evening, in St. Andrew's, Mantua, I preached, confirmed a class of 14 and addressed them.

Thursday, 15. Evening, I made an address before the Philadelphia Bible Society in the Methodist Church, corner Broad and Arch streets.

Friday, 16. Evening, I preached one of a course of sermons in connection with the opening of the New Church of the Holy Apostles, Philada.

Sunday, 18, A. M., Allentown. In Grace Church I preached, confirmed 15 and addressed them. In the School House in Catasauqua, I preached and confirmed 2. In the Evening, in the Church of the Mediator, Allentown Furnace, I preached, and confirmed 10.

Monday, 19, Bethlehem. Evening, in the Church of the Nativity, I preached, confirmed 8, and addressed them.

Friday, 23. This being the 100th Anniversary of the Ordination of Bishop White to the Diaconate and also the day appointed for the interring of his remains beneath the chancel of Christ Church, I preached in Christ Church a commemorative discourse suitable to the occasion.

Christmas Sunday, A. M. The new Church of the Incarnation was occupied for the first time, and I preached the opening sermon, and administered the Holy Communion. Evening, in the Bishop's Church I preached.

Monday, 26. Evening. presided at the Board of Missions.

Tuesday, 27, A. M. In All Saints, Lower Dublin, I admitted to the Priesthood the Rev. W.F. M. Morsell, and the Rev. H. W. Graff. I preached the sermon. Evening, in Grace Church, Hulmeville, I preached, confirmed 7 (2d confirmation) and addressed them.

Wednesday, 28. P. M. In the First Presbyterian Church, in this city, I made an address at the Funeral Services of the Rev. Albert Barnes.

January, 1871. Sunday 1, A. M. I visited Christ Church, preached, confirmed 12, an l addressed them, and administered the Holy Communion. P. M. I went to St. George's, Cardington, and preached the opening sermon in the new Church. Evening, in Trinity Church, Southwark, I preached, confirmed 15, and addressed them.

Sunday, 8. At Mauch Chunk, A. M. In St. Mark's Church, I preached, confirmed 27, and addressed the class. P. M. Attended the service of the Children's Church and made an address. Evening, in St. John's, East Mauch Chunk, I preached, confirmed 14, and addressed them.

Monday, 9. A. M. Visited St. Mark's Parish School, and addressed the children. Evening, in St. Philip's Church, Summit Hill, I preached, confirmed 10, and addressed them.

Tuesday, 10. Evening, in St. Peter's, Hazleton, preached, confirmed 4, and addressed them.

Wednesday, 11. Evening, in the Church of Faith, Mahanoy City, I preached, confirmed 4 and addressed them.

Thursday, 12. Evening, in St. Luke's, Scranton, I preached, confirmed 17, and made an address.

Friday, 13. Evening, in the Church of the Good Shepherd, Green Ridge, I preached, confirmed 6, and addressed them.

4

Sunday, 15. At Wilkesbarre. A.M., I preached in St. Stephen's Church. P. M., I baptized Alice, infant daughter of Charles M. and Helen H. Conyngham. Evening, I confirmed 16 in St. Stephen's Church, and addressed the class.

Thursday, 19th. Evening, in Spencer Hall, Divinity School, I delivered a Missionary Address before the James May Missionary Society.

Sunday, 22d, A.M., in the Church of the Redemption, Fairmount, I preached, confirmed 8, and addressed them. Evening, in the Clay Mission Chapel, I preached, and confirmed 3.

Monday, 23d. Presided at the Annual Meeting of the Society for Promoting Christianity among the Jews, in St. Luke's Church.

Sunday, 29th. A.M., at Zion Church, I preached, confirmed 17, and addressed them. Evening, at the Church of the Evangelists, I preached, and confirmed 20 persons.

Friday, February 3d. Presided at a meeting at Episcopal Rooms in behalf of the Home Colored Mission.

Sunday, 5th. Evening, I preached in the Chapel of the Epiphany Mission.

Saturday, 11th. A.M., consecrated the Chapel at Forrestville, and preached the sermon, and administered the Holy Communion.

Sunday, 12th. A.M., in St. Paul's Church, Minersville, I preached, confirmed 3, and addressed them. Evening, in Trinity Church, Pottsville, I preached, confirmed 27, and addressed them.

Monday, 13th. In Pottsville in the morning, in two different houses I confirmed respectively a crippled man and a sick woman for Trinity Church. Evening, in St. Clair, in the Church of the Holy Apostles, I preached. Before service I baptized the two infant children of Dr. Coryell, Emma Johns and Virginia Johns.

Sunday, 19th. A.M., in St. Paul's Memorial Church, Perkiomen, I preached, and confirmed 5. P.M., in St. Peter's Church, Phœnixville, I preached, confirmed 21, and addressed them.

Sunday, 26th. A.M., in the Church of the Mediator, I preached, confirmed 18, and made an address. Evening, in the Church of the Covenant, I preached, confirmed 9, and addressed them.

Monday, 27th. Went to Wilkes Barre to attend the funeral of Judge Conyngham.

Sunday, March 5th. A.M., in St. John's Church, N. Liberties, I preached, confirmed 4, and administered the Holy Communion. P.M., in St. Luke's Church, I preached, confirmed 20, and addressed them.

Wednesday, 8th. Buried at Laurel Hill Dr. Charles M. Wetherill, Professor in Lehigh University, Bethlehem. Evening, in St. John's Church, Norristown, I preached, confirmed 13, and made an address.

Thursday, 9th. Evening, in St. Matthew's Church, I confirmed a class of 30, and addressed them.

Friday, 10th, P.M., in St. Clement's Church, I confirmed 35 persons, and made an address.

Sunday 12, A.M., in St. Luke's Church, Germantown, I confirmed 14 persons. P.M., in Calvary Church. Germantown, I confirmed 4 persons. In both cases I was too unwell to preach or to make an address.

From this time I was sick and unable to go out until

Wednesday, 29th. When in the Church of the Holy Trinity, I confirmed 24, and made a short address.

Sunday, April 2d. A.M., in St. Peter's Church, I confirmed 58. and Bishop Armitage made an address to the class. P. M., in the Church of the Epiphany, I confirmed 42. Dr. Newton preached.

Tuesday, 4th. Evening, in the Church of the Incarnation, I confirmed 49, and addressed them.

Wednesday, 5th. Evening, in Emmanuel Church, Kensington, I confirmed 46, and made an address.

Thursday, 6th. Evening, in St. James' Church, Bristol, I preached, confirmed 10 and addressed them.

Good Friday, 7th. A. M., in St. James', Philadelphia, I confirmed 17, and addressed them. Evening, in Grace Church I preached, confirmed 17, and made an address.

Saturday, 8th. Easter Evening, 5 P. M., in St Mark's, I confirmed 43, and addressed them.

Easter, 9th. A. M., in St. Michael's, Germantown, I confirmed 10, addressed them and administered the Holy Communion. Evening, in St. Matthias' Church, I confirmed 30, and addressed them.

Monday, 10th. P. M., presided at meeting of the Committee of the Board of Missions on the African Mission.

Tuesday, 11th. Evening, at the Chapel of the Holy Comforter, I confirmed 5, and addressed them.

Wednesday, 12th. Evening, at Calvary, (Monumental Church) I confirmed 24, and addressed them; before service held two private confirmations of a sick man and a sick woman (in their respective houses).

Friday, 14th. A. M., in the Lincoln Institute I confirmed a sick boy in private. Evening, in St. Jude's Church, I confirmed 16, and addressed them. Also confirmed a sick man in private.

Saturday, 15th. Evening, St. Stephen's, Bridesburg, I confirmed 7, and made an address

Sunday, 16th. A. M., in St. Philip's Church, I preached, confirmed 31, and made an address. Evening, in St. Mark's, Frankford, I preached, confirmed 44, and addressed them.

Tuesday, 18th. Evening, in Christ Church, Germantown, I preached and confirmed 30 persons.

Wednesday, 19th. Evening, in All Saints Church, I confirmed 23, and made an address.

Thursday, 20. Went to Wilkes-Barre, and in the evening at the request of the Vestry of St. Stephen's Church, I delivered in that Church a Memorial discourse on the life and character of the late Judge Conyngham.

Friday, 21st. A. M., I consecrated St. John's Church, Ashley, Luzerne County, and preached the sermon.

Saturday, 22d. Went to Blossburg, Tioga County.

Sunday, 23d. A. M., I preached in St. Luke's Church. Evening, in same Church I preached, confirmed 11, and addressed them.

Monday, 24th. A. M., consecrated St. James' Church, Mansfield, preached and administered the Holy Communion. P. M., in the same Church, confirmed 20, and addressed them.

Tuesday, 25th. Went to Tioga. P. M., confirmed a sick person in private. Evening in Presbyterian Church, I preached, confirmed 5, and addressed them.

It was a sore disappointment that, owing to the burning down of the new and pretty Church, the consecration of it was defeated; though it was gratifying to see that the energetic spirit which had sustained the earnest Church people here was undaunted, and that at once erecting a temporary structure, they had resolved as soon as possible to build a new, and it is to be hoped, a Stone Church.

Wednesday, 26th. Went to Wellsborough. In the afternoon, I preached, confirmed 17, and addressed them. Afterward confirmed a sick person.

Thursday, 27th. Went to Troy, Bradford County. Evening, I preached in St. Paul's Church.

Friday, 28th. At Williamsport. In the evening, in Trinity Church, I preached, confirmed 16, and addressed them.

Saturday. 29th. Returned to Philadelphia.

Sunday, 30th. A. M., in St. Paul's, Cheltenham, I preached, confirmed 12, and addressed them. Evening, in the Hall used by the congregation of St. George's, Kenderton, I preached, confirmed 9, and made an address.

Monday, May 1. Presided at Meeting of Board of Missions.

Tuesday, 2d. Evening, in Holy Trinity Chapel, I confirmed 28, and addressed them.

Wednesday, 3d. Evening, in the Church of the Holy Apostles, I confirmed 21, and addressed the class.

Thursday, 4th. Evening, in Christ Church, Media, I preached, and confirmed two persons.

Friday, 5th. A. M., in the Church of the Holy Trinity, Westchester, after a sermon by the Rev. Dr. Watson, I admitted to Deacon's Orders Robt. F. Innis, and to Priest's Orders the Rev. William H. Jarvis. In the afternoon, in the same Church, after an address to the congregation, I confirmed 16 persons. In the evening, in the Presbyterian Church, I delivered an address before the Ladies' Bible Society.

Sunday, 7. A. M., in the Church of the Advent, Philadelphia, preached, confirmed 19, and administered the Holy Communion. In the afternoon in St. David's Church, Manayunk, made an address, at 36th Anniversary of the Sunday Schools of that Parish. In the Evening. In the same Church, confirmed 28 and made an address.

The summary of work outside of Office duties, is as follows :

Officiated times, 204; No. of Confirmation services, 127; Persons confirmed, 1738; Sermons preached, 129; Addresses delivered, 121; Corner-stones laid, 4; Churches consecrated, 6; Persons Ordained Deacons, 10; Persons Ordained Priests, 11; Marriages, 5; Burials, 3; Baptisms, 3; Instituted 1.

It is with feelings of sincere gratitude that I here record my obligations to the Right Reverend, the Bishop of Delaware, for the very prompt and serviceable aid which he rendered during my late sickness. By this means my list of visitations was kept intact, with one exception—and the Churches suffered no detriment. His report is to be found appended to my address. I also here tender my acknowledgments to the Right Reverend, the Bishop of Wisconsin, for his kind aid in confirming a class at St. Paul's, Chestnut Hill.

Clerical changes within the Diocese during the last Conventional year :

The Rev. F. E. Arnold has resigned the Rectorship of St. John's, Lower Merion ; Rev. H. J. W. Allen has become the Rector of St. John's Church, Bellefonte ; Rev. John H. Babcock has become the Rector of St. Andrew's Church, Tioga ; Rev. G. C. Bird has resigned Grace Church, Honesdale ; Rev. Frederick M. Bird has resigned the rectorship of Trinity Church, Shamokin, and removed to New Jersey ; Rev. G. Livingston Bishop has become Assistant Minister in the Church of the Advent, Philadelphia ; Rev. John A. Bowman has resigned St. Paul's Church, Wellsboro ; Rev. Arthur Brooks has become Rector of Trinity Church, Williamsport ; Rev. A. Bernstein has been transferred to the Mission work among the Jews in Europe ; Rev. A. H. Boyle has become Rector of Trinity Church, Shamokin; Rev. Faber Byllesby has been deposed from the Ministry; Rev. Robert F. Chase has resigned the Rectorship of the Church of St. Matthias, Philadelphia; Rev. Edmund Christian has resigned the Rectorship of the Church of the Holy Apostles, St. Clair; Rev. Samuel Clements has resigned his position as Principal of the Mission House; Rev. J. Everist Cathell has become Assistant to the Rector of the Epiphany, Philada.; Rev. Thomas H. Cullen has resigned the Rectorship of St. Paul's Church, Bloomsburg; Rev. Joseph N. Durant has gone to Barbadoes; Rev. Edward L. Drown has resigned the Rectorship of the Church of the Saviour, West Philadelphia; Rev. J. H. Eccleston has become Rector of the Church of the Saviour. West Philada.; Rev. John Irving Forbes has resigned the Rectorship of the Church of the Nativity, Bethlehem; Rev.Wm. Floyd is laboring in North Carolina; Rev. J. P. Fugett has resigned the Rectorship of St. John's Free Church, Frankford Road; Rev. Lewis W. Gibson has resigned Montoursville, and become Assistant Minister of St. James', Philada.; Rev. Richardson Graham has resigned St. John's Church, Concord; Rev. William H. Graff has become the Rector of St. Jude's Church, Philadelphia; Rev. Charles R. Hale has resigned the Chaplaincy in the U. S. Navy, and removed to the Diocese of Western New York; Rev. Chandler Hare has resigned St. James' Church, Pittston; Rev. Wm. Hobart Hare has resigned the Rectorship of the Church of the Ascension, Philadelphia, and accepted the appointment of Secretary and General Agent of Foreign Committee of Missions; Rev.W. S. Heaton has become Rector of St. Paul's. Manheim; Rev. John Hewitt has become the Rector of St. Paul's Church, Bloomsburg: Rev.John Ireland is officiating in St.Alban's, Roxborough; Rev. Wm. Jarrett has resigned St. Stephen's, Bridesburg; Rev. H. M. Jarvis has become the Rector of the Church of the Saviour, Montoursville; Rev. John K. Karcher has become the Rector of St. Paul's Church, Wellsboro; Rev. Charles T. Kellogg has resigned the Rectorship of St. Jude's Church, Philadelphia, and removed to New Jersey; Rev. O. W. Landreth has left Altoona, and become Rector of Grace Church, Honesdale; Rev. John Long has resigned his Missions and gone to Cleveland, Ohio; Rev. J. H. McElrey is in charge of St. John's, Ashley; Rev. J. H. H. Millett has left Whitehaven, and become Rector of the Church of the Good Shepherd, Green Ridge; Rev. Joseph R. Moore has become Rector of St. George's, Kenderton; Rev. William Moore has become the Rector of St. Mark's Church, Northumberland; Rev. J. J. A. Morgan has become the Rector of St. Luke's Church, Altoona; Rev. W. H. Neilson has become the Assistant Minister of the Church of the Holy Trinity, in charge of Trinity Chapel; Rev. William Newton has become the Rector of the Church of the Nativity, Philadelphia; Rev. J. M. Peck has become the Rector of Christ Church, Danville; Rev. Octavius Perincheif has become the Rector of Swede's Church, Upper Merion; Rev. J. B. Pedelupe has resigned the Church of St. James, Bedford: Rev. Philip P. Reese is officiating in Centralia; Rev. H. J. Rowland has resigned the Assistantship of St. James, Philadelphia; Rev. George W. Shinn has resigned the Rectorship of St. Paul's Church, Lock Haven; Rev. Joseph A. Stone has resigned the charge of the Chapel of the Holy Comforter. and removed to the Diocese of Delaware; Rev. Richard N. Thomas has become Rector of St. Matthias' Church, Philadelphia; Rev. Isaac S. Trowbridge, M. D., is officiating as Assistant in St. Matthew's, Philadelphia; Rev C. H. Van Dyne has become the Rector of St. Peter's Church, Hazleton; Rev. Courtlandt Whitehead has become the Rector of the Church of the Nativity, Bethlehem.

Candidates for Orders in the Diocese of Pennsylvania.

A. D.
1863 July 2, W. G. P. Brinckloe.
" December 3, Joseph Berry Hill.
1865, October 4, George T. Kaye.
1867, March 7, Stephen Maguire.
" May 2, Joseph L. Miller.
" June 6, Isaac N. Christman.

A. D.

1868, November 5, Henry C. Pastorius.
"   "   5, John W. Kaye.
"   "   5, Thomas W. Davidson.
1869, January 7, William H. Josephus.
"   February 4, John Coleman, Jr.
"   "   4, William S. Cochran.
"   March 4, John H. Burton.
"   "   4, Robert James Bowen.
"   May 6, William B. Burk.
"   June 3, William H. Platt.
"   " 3, John T. Wright.
"   " 3, Thomas R. List.
"   " 3, John G. Bawn.
"   July 1, Samuel G. Lines.
"   " 1, Mortimer T. Jefferies.
"   " 1, F. H. Strecker.
"   " 1, Charles D. Barber.
"   November 4, William F. Garrett.
"   "   4, G. F. Rosenmiller.
1870, January 6, J. M. Williams.
"   "   6, Charles E. Benedict.
"   "   6, Pierre E. Jones.
"   "   6, Rush S. Eastman.
"   "   6, Albert C. Abrams.
"   March 3,   Charles E. Milnor.
"   April 7,   George P. Allen.
"   "   George Coutts Athole.
"   "   George Alexander Keller.
"   "   H. P. Chapman.
"   "   R. Julius Adler.
"   July 7,   James Creigh.
"   "   George W. Hinkle.
"   October 6,   Edward E. Hoffman.
"   "   N. Frazier Robinson.
"   "   George Fox Martin.
"   Sept. 30,   Zina Doty.
"   Nov. 3,   William Levi Bull.
"   "   H. C. Cunningham.
"   "   George M. Christian.
"   December 1, Langdon C. Stewardson.
1871. January 5, S. M. Burton.
"   March 4,   Titus R. Godber.
"   "   Chas. E. Fessenden.

The following clergymen have been received on letters Dimissory from other Dioceses:

January 10th, 1870, Wm. McGlathery, New Jersey.
March 8th,   "   H. Palethorpe Hay, D.D., Tennessee.
"   19th,   "   Joseph W. Murphy, North Carolina.
"   25th,   "   Edmund Christian, Demerara.
April 8th,   "   Samuel Clements, Ohio.
"   11th,   "   J. B. Pedelupe, Missouri.

May 7th,	"	Robert Ritchie, Massachusetts.
" 9th,	"	J. Blake Falkner, Connecticut.
" 26th,	"	Theo. S. Rumney, D.D., New York.
June 4th,	"	Robert Mackie, Melbourne.
" 17th,	"	Frank R. Girard, Wisconsin.
July 9th,	"	E. Owen Simpson, Ohio.
" "	"	O. H. Van Dyne, Long Island.
" 25th,	"	Octavus Perinchief, Maryland.
September. 8th,	"	William Moore, New York.
" 24th,	"	Arthur Brooks, Massachusetts.
October 10th,	"	Thomas A. Jaggar, New York.
" "	"	Ephraim S. Widdemer, Albany.
" 4th,	"	Ezra Isaac, Iowa.
August,	"	John M. Peck, Vermont.
October 27th,	"	H. J. W. Allen, Pittsburgh.
" "	"	Joseph A. Nock, Virginia.
November 1st,	"	Wm. H. Graff, Delaware.
" 10th,	"	Wm. Newton. Ohio.
" 14th,	"	Cortlandt Whitehead, Colorado.
" 21st,	"	J. Sturgis Pearce, Connecticut.
December 28th,	"	John Hewitt. Massachusetts.
January 4th,	1871,	Herbert M. Jarvis, Connecticut.
" 16th,	"	John K. Karcher. Pittsburgh.
February 9th,	"	Peter Quick Wilson, Albany.
" 15th,	"	J. J. A. Morgan, Long Island.
" 21st,	"	W. H. Neilson, Jr., Long Island.
April 13th,	"	Thomas Mason, Antrim, Delaware.
May 3d,	"	G. W. Ridgely Easton.

The following named Clergymen have been transferred by letters dimissory to other Dioceses :

May 24, 1870,		W. W. Newton, Massachusetts.
" "		Thomas S. Yocum. Ohio.
July "		Joseph S. Colton, Maryland.
" "		Frank R. Girard, Minnesota.
Sept. 23,		Joseph A. Stone, Delaware.
" 24,		Henry K. Brouse. Rhode Island.
" 29,		James W. Bonham, Illinois.
Oct. 22,		Henry C. Mayer, Massachusetts.
" 27,		James Caird, Albany.
" "		Chandler Hare, Central New York.
Nov. 1,		Charles T. Kellogg, New Jersey.
" 12,		Fred. M. Bird, "
" 17,		Edmund Roberts, Pittsburgh.
" 18,		Samuel H. Mead, New Jersey.
" 21,		John A. Bowman, Central New York.
Dec. 6,		Edward L. Drown, Massachusetts.
" 14,		George W. Shinn, Albany.
" 17,		Thomas H. Cullen, "
Feb. 21, 1871.		J B. Pedelupe, Maryland.
Mar. 31,		Aaron Bernstein, England.
May 1,		J. Newton Spear, New Jersey.

Thus it will be seen that with the exception of about five

weeks, a large portion of which I was laid aside by sickness, I have been constantly at work the whole year. The office work this year has been unusually large and was of a nature peculiarly difficult and wearing to mind and heart. In the discharge of these duties I have ever sought the aid of the Holy Ghost, and have ever aimed to act and speak under the full consciousness of my responsibility to my Diocese, and to the great Shepherd and Bishop of souls. I do not expect that my views or opinions will always meet with the approbation of all classes of Church people in the Diocese. No man can hold such a public position, and have to deal with so many perplexing questions, and such diverse sentiments, and give satisfaction to all parties. It were hopeless to attempt such a thing, and if attempted would only result in the sacrifice of right and truth and duty. It should be borne in mind that, as the Overseer of this Diocese, the Bishop bears a paternal relation to the Clergy and Laity, similar in kind to those of a Pastor to his flock. It is his duty, therefore, as the head of this ecclesiastical family to give his counsel and advice on many matters pertaining to the welfare of the Church outside of those cases of discipline, whether punitive or advisory, which come under the several provisions of the Canon law.

In thus giving advice and counsel in the various matters laid before him, the Bishop is surely warranted in looking for that regard to his judgment which his high office demands, and also for those gentlemanly courtesies which prevail in refined society and among Christian gentlemen.

As a Diocese we have been, this year, singularly exempt from death. Only one of our Clergy has been called home, the Rev. Harrison Lambdin. This young man was known only to a few of you, as he was only recently admitted to Deacon's Orders, and had never officiated, except in two or three instances, in the Diocese. Of an ardent and sensitive nature, and full of religious earnestness and zeal, he had passed through the term of his candidateship and looked forward with much hope to the full exercise of his ministry. Just after his ordination he was called to accompany a sick brother to Europe, but while travelling there disease, which it now seems had lain dormant in his system, began to develop itself, and the brothers hastened home, each tenderly solicitous of the other, and each fearing for the other.

Shortly after Mr. Lambdin's return, he was suddenly taken away; for when at the morning light the brother went to his room to call him he found him asleep in Jesus. Thus was he early transferred from the sanctuary here, to minister in the temple not made with hands, and though the hopes of loving parents and friends were blighted by this unlooked-for death, yet have those hopes, we believe, found a fuller and nobler fruition in the happiness and rest, which his sainted spirit now enjoys in the Paradise of God.

During the past conventional year, however, we have lost a noble layman, and I feel sure that you would blame me, did any motives of personal delicacy keep me from mentioning his melancholy death. You all anticipate my reference to Judge Conyngham. For fifty years, lacking but five weeks, he had been a vestryman and warden of St. Stephen's, Wilkes-Barre. Forty-five years have passed since he first took a seat in the Diocesan Convention. Twenty-one years have elapsed since he was first elected a deputy to the General Convention. In all these offices, and in all these years, he has been faithful to his trust. You all remember his commanding figure; his noble face; his warm greetings; his earnest speeches; his punctual and diligent attention to the business of the Convention; his constant presence at all the religious services of this body. But "he is not, for God took him," took him almost as He took his early friend and fellow-lawyer at the Luzerne Bar—the late Bishop Bowman—by a sudden way-side death, away from home, and under circumstances peculiarly distressing. While on a mission of paternal love, going to bring back a sick son in the far off South—among perfect strangers, the accident befell him which in two hours resulted in death, and he passed away, repeating, as his last words, the comforting assurance of the Patriarch Job, " I know that my Redeemer liveth." Of his character, I need say nothing here, as I have already, at the request of the vestry of his parish, delivered a memorial discourse on his life and services; yet I am sure that you miss him to day and mourn with me the loss which this Diocese, and the whole Church, has sustained in the sudden removal by death of this eminent citizen, jurist, and Christian.

The Missionaries in the employ of the Board of the Diocesan Missions have been laboring with zeal and fidelity during the past year. New points of interest are every now and then being opened to us, and eight Churches have been built the past year in as many of our Mission Stations—while the number of persons confirmed averages twenty-five per cent. of the number of the communicants reported. Had the same rate been maintained throughout the Diocese the number of persons confirmed would have been 5,000 instead of 1,738. This result is exceedingly gratifying, and speaks well for the energy with which our Missionaries discharge their duties. On the other hand, we have the sad fact, that the receipts of the Board this year are much less than last, and that there is a lamentable apathy in the several Churches in reference to this work, and in reference to their duty to supply the Lord's treasury with means to carry on the Lord's work.

It should be remembered that it has been by the aid of Mission funds that nearly every Church in the proposed new Diocese has been planted and sustained, and it is by continuing this Missionary aid that the Church is to be perpetuated and enlarged. The larger number of Missionaries and Mission Stations being located within the boundaries of the proposed " New " Diocese, and it being all important to the welfare of the Church that these should be sustained, I beg leave to suggest to the Convention, the propriety of authorizing the Board of Missions to guarantee to the Missionaries now in their employ their Missionary stipend, as now paid, for a full year from the time when the new Diocese shall be organized, viz: a year from November next. This measure seems necessary from the fact that while nearly all the receipts from the Board are expended on Missions in the territory about to be set off, only about one-seventh of this money comes from the parishes within that district. It seems to me, therefore, to be both graceful and proper to extend to the New Diocese this helping hand, until they shall have had a year, at least, to perfect their own missionary plans.

There has been one subject which has engaged my special attention the past year, and upon which I desire to say a few words. I refer to City Missions.

During the year 1869, several meetings were held by the clergy of our Church, for the purpose of settling upon some plan of action, whereby we could all unite in the duty of City Evangelization. Various reports were made and schemes proposed, but it was found impracticable to adopt any one with sufficient unanimity to secure the confidence and co-operation of all, and hence the effort at last came to nought.

The result of these several meetings, while it gave me pain, gave me also a determination that by God's grace, I would on my own responsibility begin and carry on so important a work. Hence on the 1st of May last, I organized the PHILADELPHIA PROTESTANT EPISCOPAL CITY MISSION, for the extension of the knowledge of the Gospel of Jesus Christ among all classes of the community, and especially among those who are under no parochial oversight.

As the Superintendent of the Mission, I appointed the Rev. Samuel Durborow, and under him several Clerical and Lay Assistants.

A Central House was secured and services were arranged for in different parts of the city. Sunday and Night Schools were established, district visitations were commenced, tracts and circulars were distributed, the poor and afflicted were relieved and the Gospel was preached, not only in the Central Mission House, but in hired halls and in the several public Charitable Institutions which have been opened to us.

We began the work without money and in simple faith in God. We felt that something ought to be done, and we dared neglect it no longer; and in my position as Bishop I saw only one way, and that was, in humble reliance on God's blessing, to take up the duty and go on with it in hope and trust, believing that it was of God and that He would aid my efforts. That Blessing which we expected has been granted. The work has increased beyond all expectation, and the funds for carrying it on have been almost mysteriously furnished, so that while we have never had any excess of means, we have had almost always enough to sustain our plans.

Having conducted the Mission a year on my own responsibility, I now propose that the work shall be put under the care of a Board of Clergymen and Laymen. This I do in order to secure their counsel and co-operation in the work—in order to call out a greater interest in the Churches, thus represented —in order to afford a guarantee that the Mission is on a broad and equable basis, and in order to give it greater permanence and strength. The gentlemen whom I have selected are tried and well-known, and their presence and co-operation will give to the Mission increased scope and efficiency.

We meet to-day, Brethren, under most peculiar circumstances. Six years ago, we cut this once great Diocese into two parts, erecting that portion west of the Alleghanies into the Diocese of Pittsburgh. The growth of that Diocese since then has shown the wisdom of our action. What remained to us after that division, has, through the blessing of God, so increased, that another division has been called for and made, and in a few months, the larger territorial portion of the present Diocese of Pennsylvania, will be organized and officered as a new Diocese. The separation takes place with our hearty concurrence, and our earnest wishes for the full realization of the hopes which its advocates have so largely cherished. I have no hesitation in saying that should God bestow upon that portion of His vineyard, a wise and godly Bishop, it will soon show the blessed effects of this much needed measure, and that its growth and expansion will soon be apparent to all. Yet while we recognize the necessity of this separation, we cannot realize that this is the last time that the various Churches of this Diocese will meet together, as Clergy and Deputies in Convention, without a feeling of sincere sadness and regret. The ecclesiastical life of each Parish has thus far been lived in connection with the fostering care of this Convention, and most of these Parishes have been the nurslings of our Missionary boards. You are now to leave this, your mother Diocese, and establish your own Church Home, to become in turn, perhaps, the mother of other Dioceses, that shall in time, go out from under your sheltering arms, and set up for themselves, new, but kindred organizations. The many and pleasing friendships, which I have formed in every congregation—the sweet memories of personal kindness and domestic hospitality, which cluster around nearly every Parish, and the sacred associations of various services which link me with the several Churches and Chapels of the proposed new Diocese, make it hard for me to separate from you or to take my formal and official leave.

I beg to assure you all, that from the depths of a grateful heart, I thank you for the courtesy and esteem, and attention which you have all so generously bestowed upon me. Your deeds and words of kindness are well remembered and safely treasured, and will often as years go by furnish delightful reminiscences upon which my memory will feast with delight as I call up one and another, and another of the Clergy, or the Parishes, and go over anew the interesting events of the past.

No Bishop in any Diocese has been more respectfully or cordially received and cared for than I have been. You have ever esteemed me as one set over you in the Lord, and personally and officially, therefore, do I thank each and all for the courtesy, the attention and the respect which has been accorded to me in all Parishes, and by nearly all the Clergy of that portion of the Diocese which will never meet with us again in our annual Convention.

We are to work together side by side, and let us, by God's grace, stand up shoulder to shoulder in the battle which the Church of the living God is waging with error of every kind, and let our only strife be who shall work the hardest for Christ, and who shall do most in building up our Holy, Catholic, and Apostolic Church.

The following Report of Episcopal Acts, on behalf of the Bishop of the Diocese, was made by Bishop Lee:

WILMINGTON, DEL., *May* 2, 1871.

RT. REV. W. B. STEVENS, D. D.

MY DEAR BISHOP:

I herewith send you a statement of Episcopal Acts performed at your request in the Diocese of Pennsylvania. Confirmations have been held as follows:

March 15, 1871, In St. Paul's Church, Chester				36
"	17,	"	Church of Atonement, Philadelphia	15
"	19,	"	St. Andrew's, Philadelphia	22
"	19.	"	St. John Evangelist, Philadelphia	19
"	22,	"	Centreville	3
"	22,	"	Doylestown	4
"	24,	"	Gloria Dei, Philadelphia	21
"	26,	"	St. Stephen's, "	20
"	26.	"	St. Paul's, "	13
		Total		153

The Committee on Claims of Clergy to seats, having had nothing submitted to them, had no Report to make.

The Rev. Dr. Claxton offered the following Resolutions, which, having been seconded by Mr. Isaac Hazlehurst, were unanimously adopted:

Resolved, That the members of this Convention respond with affectionate sympathy to the sentiments of the Bishop's address, in regard to the character and worth of the late Judge Conyngham, who was for so many years an honored and influential member of this body.

Resolved, That while deeply mourning the loss sustained by the Church in the removal of Judge Conyngham, we would humbly record our gratitude to Almighty God for the eminently good example of this, His servant, now departed, and for all the valuable services rendered by him in the Parish of which, for almost forty years, he was one of the chief pillars, and in the Conventions of our Church, Diocesan and General.

Resolved, That so much of the Bishop's Address as refers to the late Hon. John N. Conyngham be suitably transcribed, under the direction of the Secretary, and, with a copy of these Resolutions, it be transmitted to his family; to whom we offer the assurance that we feel their affliction to be, in its measure, our own, and that of the whole Church of the Lord Jesus.

Resolved, That a copy of the above be sent to the Rector, Church Wardens, and Vestrymen of St. Stephen's Church, Wilkes-Barre.

On motion of the Rev. J. R. Moore, it was

Resolved, That so much of the Bishop's address as relates to City Missions, be referred to a special Committee of three to report before the close of this Convention.

On motion of the Rev. E. A. Foggo, it was

Resolved, That the portion of the Bishop's address which refers to the support of the Missionaries of the new Diocese for one year from November next, be referred to a special Committee of five to report to this Convention.

The President apppointed Rev. E. A. Foggo, Rev. J. A. Harris, Rev. R. C. Matlack, Mr. Charles R. King, Mr. Wm. Welsh.

Mr. Thomas Robins read the following Preamble and Resolutions :

WHEREAS, The Right Rev., the Bishop of Delaware, did, during the recent illness of our Diocesan render important services in the fulfilment of appointments and in performing Episcopal duties in this Diocese, greatly to the relief of our Bishop and to the satisfaction of the parishes which he visited. Therefore

Resolved, That the thanks of this Convention be presented to Bishop Lee, for his kindness in fulfilling appointments and performing Episcopal services in this Diocese, during the illness of Bishop Stevens.

Resolved, That the Treasurer of the Convention, be and he is hereby directed to pay to the Right Rev. Bishop Lee the sum of Two Hundred dollars, and charge the amount to the account of the Episcopal Fund.

Resolved, That a copy of these resolutions be transmitted by the Secretary to Bishop Lee.

On motion of Mr. Thomas Robins, the Resolutions were adopted.

The Secretary announced that the minutes, and the Report of the Standing Committee, and the Report of the Treasurer of the Episcopal Fund, were severally laid upon the table.

The Report of the Standing Committee was read as follows :

The Standing Committee report that they organized on the

24th of May, 1870, by electing Rev. Dr. Morton, President, and Charles E. Lex, Secretary, pro tem.

On the 5th of January, 1871, Mr. Lex resigned as a member of the Standing Committee, and on the 2d of February, 1871, John Clayton was elected by the Committee to fill the vacancy occasioned by the resignation of Mr. Lex, and on the 2d of March, 1871, Mr. Clayton was elected Secretary of the Committee.

June 15th, 1870, consent was given to the consecration of Rev. Wm. Pinkney, D. D., as Assistant Bishop of the Diocese of Maryland.

October 5, 1870, consent was given to the election of the Rt. Rev. Robert H. Clarkson, D. D., Missionary Bishop, as Bishop of Nebraska.

During the official year they have recommended for ordination to Priests' Orders,

Rev. William Jarrett,
" George H. Kirkland,
" Enoch H. Supplee,
" James Caird.
" Arthur Brooks,
" William Moore,

Rev. Henry C. Mayer,
" W. F. C. Morsell,
" Henry R. Smith
" W. H. Graff,
" Herbert M. Jarvis.

They have recommended as Candidates for Priests' Orders,

Rev. George H. Kirkland,
" J. Everist Cathell,
" Ezra Isaac.
Mr. G. Livingston Bishop,
" Robert F. Innis,

Rev. George M. Christian,
" William Levi Bull,
" William H. Platt,
Mr. Peter E. Jones,
" I. Newton Christman.

They have recommended for ordination to the Holy Order of Deacons,

William F. Floyd,
James Caird,
Aaron Bernstein,
Philip P. Reese,

G. Livingston Bishop,
Algernon Morton,
J. Everist Cathell,
J. L. Trowbridge,

Robert F. Innis.

They have recommended as Candidates for the Holy Order of Deacons,

George W. Hinkle,
James Creigh,
Coupland R. Page,
George M. Christian,
William Levi Bull,
Henry C. Cunningham,

E. E. Hoffman,
N. Frazier Robinson,
George F. Martin,
Langdon Cheves Stewardson,
Selden Mercer Burton,
Titus R. Godber,

Zina Doty.

October 5th, 1870, an application from All Saints' Church, Paradise, Lancaster County, for consent to sale of the parsonage, was granted.

November 3d, 1870, the application of Trinity Church, Easton, for permission to mortgage their Church property, was granted; also, the application of the Church of the Crucifixion, Philadelphia, for permission to convey certain real estate, known as "The Home for the Homeless," to a Board of Trustees, for the purpose of greater efficiency in carrying into effect the objects for which it was purchased. At the same meeting, permission was given to St. Clement's Church, Philadelphia, to create a mortgage of $2000 (two thousand dollars), on their property, south side of Cherry street, west of Twentieth street, in addition to those heretofore sanctioned.

The following disbursements have been made by the joint direction of the Bishop and Standing Committee, by drafts on the Treasurer of the Convention and Episcopal Funds.

John Short, services..	$15 00
King & Baird, printing..	2 50
W. S. Perry, 1st vol. Historical Collections of the American Colonial Church, for the use of the Diocese......................................	10 50
John Short, repairing furniture..	3 50

The following Churches for three years, have made no Parochial Report to the Convention, nor have Missionary Reports been made in their behalf, nor have they employed a clergyman, or requested of the Bishop the services of a missionary.

St. Peter's Church, Plymouth, Luzerne County; Church of the Holy Communion, Philadelphia; St. John's Church, Allentown Furnace, Lehigh County.

The design of a Seal for the Diocese, has been approved and engraved, as directed by the last Convention.

In the matter of the proposed establishment of a new congregation in West Philadelphia, to be called "St. Stephen's Chapel," the following resolution was adopted:

Resolved, "That the Standing Committee does not advise or consent to the establishment of a new congregation within five squares of any existing Church in West Philadelphia."

6

On the 6th of May, 1871, a memorial was received from certain persons, asking permission to form a congregation, to be known as "Saint Timothy's Church," to be located at the Church edifice, on the south side of Reed street below Eighth, Philadelphia, and to be recognized as a Parish of the Diocese. This application involved the question, whether a congregation can form a new organization, and take possession of a Church, heretofore occupied by another congregation, which latter congregation had been ejected from the premises by the civil law. There being no protest or remonstrance against the establishment of the proposed congregation, the consent of the Committee to the organizing of the same was given; although the Committee declined to recommend for approval the form of Charter submitted, as the same was not authenticated by any signatures.

The Committee herewith present the account of the Treasurer of the Convention and Episcopal Funds, which has been examined and is correct.

JOHN CLAYTON,
Secretary.

Philadelphia, May 10, 1871.

On motion of the Rev. Mr. Abel, the Bishop's Charge was made the order of the day for Thursday, at 12 M.

The President having stated that the hour of 2 P. M. had arrived, on motion adjourned.

JOHN A. CHILDS,
Secretary.

PHILADELPHIA, ST ANDREW'S CHURCH,

WEDNESDAY, 5 o'clock, P. M.

The Convention assembled pursuant to order, the Rev. Dr. Howe presiding.

The President stated that the order of the day was the election of the Standing Committee, and appointed the Rev. S. E. Appleton and Rev. H. Baldy tellers of the Clerical vote, and Messrs. J. L. Atlee and J. W. Thomas tellers of the Lay vote.

The House proceeded to ballot for members of the Standing Committee.

Pending the counting of the votes by the tellers, the Standing Committee presented the following report:

The Standing Committee herewith present the Charters of the Church of the Good Shepherd, Radnor, Delaware Co., and of Grace Church, Parkesburg, Chester Co., with the information that they approve of the same. The form of charter of the "Church of St. Timothy," Philadelphia, has been duly authenticated by the addition of signatures, and is also approved.

JOHN CLAYTON,
Secretary.

On motion of Mr. Wm. Welsh, the Report was referred to the Committee on Charters.

On motion of the Rev. Dr. Hare, it was

Resolved, That the Committee on City Missions be increased by the addition of two members, so as to consist of three clergymen and two laymen.

The President appointed the Rev. Dr. Hare, Rev. J. R. Moore. Rev. Dr. Roach, Mr. G. L. Harrison, Mr. G. W. Hunter.

Rev. Dr. Hare read the Report of the Committee on Alteration of Canons of the Diocese (See Appendix B).

On motion of the Rev. Mr. Saul, the Secretary was directed to have the Report printed with the Journal, and that its consideration be referred to the next Convention.

Mr. Thomas E. Franklin, on behalf of the Committee appointed by the Bishop to secure an endowment for the Episcopate of the proposed new Diocese, presented the following paper, and asked that it be read by the Secretary, which was granted :

To the Right Rev. Wm. Bacon Stevens, Bishop of the Diocese of Pennsylvania, and to the Convention of the said Diocese now assembled :

The Committee appointed by the Right Rev. the Bishop of the Diocese, to secure an endowment for the Episcopate of the proposed new Diocese in Pennsylvania, authorized by the Convention of 1870, beg leave to make the following statement:

That immediately upon their appointment they entered upon the discharge of the duty thus assigned them, and to the present time have been able to secure subscriptions for the said endowment, from individuals and parishes within the limits of the proposed new Diocese, to the amount of $38,000.

That they have labored under constant embarrassment in obtaining subscriptions and pledges, from what may with propriety be termed the general response of the Church within those limits that the proposed division of the Diocese without an equitable division of the several Diocesan Funds now belonging to the Diocese of Pennsylvania, would be an act of injustice, and that having hitherto contributed to the funds now in the custody and control of the present Diocese of Pennsylvania, they consider themselves entitled to a just proportion of said funds, to be appropriated in aid of the endowment of the new Diocese. The Committee, participating in the sentiment thus expressed by the constituency they represent, unanimously offer the following resolution, and earnestly urge its passage by this Convention:

Resolved. That all the Diocesan Funds now belonging to the present Diocese of Pennsylvania be equitably divided.

Resolved, That all of the Funds now belonging to the present Diocese of Pennsylvania, which are not restricted from alienation from the Diocese to be composed of the five counties, be given to the proposed new Diocese, provided the same do not exceed one-half the entire amount of such Funds.

Pending the consideration of the Resolution, the tellers of the vote of the Laity for the Standing Committee, presented the following Report:

Whole number of votes cast...114
Necessary to a choice... 58

CLERICAL MEMBERS.

Rev. Dr. Morton received...105
    "   Howe   " 81
    "   Hare   " 79
    "   Goodwin " 73
    "   Watson " 73
Rev. T. F. Davies " 40
  " J. D. Newlin " 38
  " E. A. Foggo " 36
  " J. K. Murphy " 35
Scattering... 10

LAY MEMBERS.

Mr. R. S. Smith received...
  " W. F. Griffitts " 102
  " T. Robins " 81
  " J. Bohlen " 79
  " J. Clayton " 78
  " R. R. Montgomery 38
  " W. S. Price " 36
  " T. Neilson " 33
Scattering... 15

The Convention having resumed the consideration of the Resolutions, Mr. J. R. Sypher offered the following:

Resolved, That the whole subject, relating to a division of the Episcopate Fund for the support of the new Diocese proposed to be set off, be referred to a committee of seven, to report at this Convention.

The tellers of the Clerical vote presented the following report:

Whole number of votes cast...144
Necessary to a choice... 73

CLERICAL MEMBERS.

Rev. Dr. Morton received...130
    "   Howe   " 94
    "   Hare   " 91
    "   Goodwin " 88
    "   Watson " 84
Rev. T. F. Davies " 59
  " E. A. Foggo " 53
  " J. D. Newlin " 50
  " J. K. Murphy " 47
Scattering... 17

LAY MEMBERS.

Mr. R. S. Smith received...137
" W. F. Griffitts " 133
" T. Robins " 97
" J. Bohlen " 89
" J. Clayton " 87
" R. R. Montgomery 59
" T. Neilson " 52
" W. S. Price " 52
Scattering.. 7

The President announced that the Rev. Dr. Morton, Rev. Dr. Howe, Rev. Dr. Hare, Rev. Dr. Goodwin, Rev. Dr. Watson, and Mr. Richard S. Smith, Mr. Wm. F. Griffitts, Mr. Thos. Robins, Mr. John Bohlen, Mr. John Clayton, having received a majority of the votes of both orders, were duly elected the Standing Committee.

On a motion to adjourn, a division was called for, when it appeared that there were 118 ayes and 110 noes. The President declared the Convention adjourned.

JNO. A. CHILDS,
Secretary.

Philadelphia, St. Andrew's Church,

Thursday, May 11, 1871, 9 o'clock, a. m.

The Convention met pursuant to order. Morning Prayer was read by the Rev. W. P. Orrick, and Rev. J. Bolton.

The President having taken the Chair, the Secretary called the names of those who had not hitherto answered, when one of the Clergy, and eight of the Lay Deputies answered, and took their seats.

The minutes of yesterday's proceedings were read and approved.

The President stated that he was authorized by the proper authorities of the Deaf and Dumb Institution, and of the House of Refuge, to invite the members of this Convention to visit those Institutions.

On motion of the Rev. Dr. Clerc, the invitations were accepted, and the Secretary instructed to transmit the thanks of the Convention to those Institutions.

On motion, it was

Resolved, That as the Standing Committee report that St. Peter's Church, Plymouth, St. John's Church, Allentown Furnace, and the Church of the Holy Communion, Philadelphia, have failed for three (3) years to make Parochial Reports to the Convention, and that no Missionary Reports have been made on their behalf; and during the same period they have neither of them employed a Clergyman, nor requested of the Bishop the services of a Missionary, the said Churches have no longer a right to send Deputies to this Convention.

On motion of the Rev. Mr. Bronson, it was

Resolved, That the Secretary of this Convention be directed to have a printed notice placed conspicuously in the vestibule of the Church, enjoining silence there during the progress of Divine service.

The President stated that the order of the day was the election of Deputies to the General Convention, and appointed the Rev. J. Bolton, Rev. A. M. Abel, and Rev. C. W. Fischer, tellers of the Clerical vote, and Mr. R. R. Montgomery, Mr. W. Buehler, and Mr. W. W. Frazier tellers of the vote of the Laity.

The House proceeded to ballot for Deputies to the General Convention.

On motion of the Rev. Dr. Hare, the Committee on City Missions was allowed to sit during the sessions of this Convention.

On motion of the Rev. Dr. Lewis, the Committee on Charters was allowed to sit forthwith.

Mr. G. W. Hunter offered the following as a substitute for the resolution of Mr. Franklin, in yesterday's proceedings, on a Division of the Diocesan Funds:

Resolved, That the Rev. Dr. Hare, the Rev. Dr. Paret, Mr. Thomas Robins, Mr. Wm. Welsh, Mr. T. E. Franklin and Mr. H. S. Goodwin, together with the Secretary and Treasurer of this Convention, be a Committee to consider the claims of the proposed new Diocese to a portion of the Episcopal Fund, with power to make an equitable division of such part of the said fund, the income of which is not restricted to the Diocese having Philadelphia within its limits. The said Committee to report its action to the next Convention.

The tellers of the Lay vote for Deputies to the General Convention, presented the following report:

Whole number of votes cast...................................... 113
Necessary to a choice.. 57

CLERICAL DEPUTIES:

Rev. Dr. Hare received 85
"   Howe   " 80
"   Goodwin " 74
Rev. A. A. Marple " 74
" Dr. Rudder " 39
" Dr. Hoffman " 36
" A. Wadleigh " 33
" Dr. Paret   " 29
Scattering... 1

LAY DEPUTIES:

Mr. G. L. Harrison received...................................... 78
"   Wm. Welsh   " 72
"   L. Coffin   " 72
"   T. E. Franklin " 65
"   M. R. Thayer   " 37
"   P. Baldy, Jr. " 37
"   G. W. Hunter   " 35
"   E. S. Buckley " 31
Scattering... 24

Mr. Wm. Welsh offered the following as an amendment to the substitute of Mr. Hunter:

Resolved, That in the event of the organization of a new Diocese, authorized by the last Convention, one-half of so much of the existing Episcopal Fund as is not inalienable from the old Diocese by the act of the donors, be and the same is hereby appropriated towards an Episcopal Fund for the new Diocese, when it is fully organized.

Resolved, That a Committee of five be appointed with authority to carry the foregoing resolution into effect.

At this time the Bishop entered and took the Chair.

The tellers of the Clerical vote presented the following report:⁻

Whole number of votes cast.. 136
Necessary to a choice 69

CLERICAL DEPUTIES:

Rev. Dr. Howe received..	96
" Hare "	92
" Goodwin "	86
Rev. A. A. Marple "	77
" Dr. Rudder "	46
" Dr. Hoffman "	43
" Dr. Paret "	44
" A. Wadleigh "	41
Scattering..	11

LAY DEPUTIES:

Mr. W. Welsh received..	71
" G. L. Harrison "	90
" L. Coffin "	78
" T. E. Franklin "	78
" M. R. Thayer "	45
" G. W. Hunter "	51
" E. S. Buckley "	40
" P. Baldy, Jr., "	44
" C. Gibbons "	21
Scattering..	13

The Rev. Dr. Howe, on behalf of the Bishop, announced that the Rev. M. A. DeW. Howe, D.D., Rev. D. R. Goodwin, D.D., Rev. G. Emlen Hare, D.D., and Rev. A. A. Marple, Mr. George L. Harrison, Mr. Lemuel Coffin, Mr. William Welsh, and Mr. Thomas E. Franklin, having received a majority of the votes of both orders, were elected Deputies to the General Convention.

The hour of 12 M. having arrived, the Bishop proceeded to read his Charge (See Appendix A).

On motion, adjourned.

JOHN A. CHILDS,
Secretary.

7

The Convention assembled, and was called to order by the President.

The President stated that the subject before the Convention was the amendment of Mr. Wm. Welsh to Mr. Hunter's substitute. The question being called for, it appeared, on a division, that there were 62 ayes and 73 noes, whereupon the President declared that the amendment was lost.

The question then recurred to the substitute of Mr. Hunter, which was not adopted.

The question then being on Mr. Sypher's Resolution, it was, on motion of Judge Thayer, amended by inserting the words " or the next " before the last word " Convention."

On motion, the Resolution, as amended, was adopted, and the following persons were appointed :

Isaac Hazlehurst,	A. Ricketts,	Thomas Robins,
Geo. W. Hunter,	R. A. Lamberton,	J. R. Sypher.
M. Russell Thayer,		

The Secretary stated that the Reports of the Trustees and of the Treasurer of the Christmas Fund had been laid on the table (See Appendix F).

The President having stated that the order of the day was the completion of Elections, Mr. Welsh offered the following, which was adopted :

Resolved, That balloting for other nominees be dispensed with, there being only one nominee for each office, and that the vote be taken *viva voce*.

On motion of Mr. Welsh, the Trustees and the Treasurer of the Christmas Fund, and the Treasurer of the Convention Fund, nominated on Tuesday's session of this Convention, were severally and duly elected.

The Report of the Board of Missions of the Diocese was then read by the Rev. S. E. Appleton (See Appendix C).

The Rev. J. Bolton read the following Preamble and Resolutions, which were adopted.

WHEREAS this Convention recognizes the various convocations of the Diocese as peculiarly adapted for missionary work, and as they are in fact missionary organizations, to whom the Church looks for important results in spreading the Gospel and planting Churches —

Resolved, That the Convention hereby expresses its approval of the missionary work they have accomplished in the past, and invokes God's blessing upon their labors in the future.

Resolved, That to obtain a full and exact statement of all that is done for Diocesan Missions in this Diocese, the several convocations be requested to furnish each a report of their missionary work to this body, to be appended to the ordinary annual report of the Board of Missions of the Diocese of Pennsylvania, and that they furnish said reports to the Board at its meeting in April.

The Rev. J. A. Harris read the following Preamble and Resolution of the Committee appointed at the second day's session to Report on so much of Bishop's address, as relates to the support of Missionaries after the separation of the new Diocese.

WHEREAS, The committee have learned that the Board of Missions have resolved to give one year's salary, from the date of final separation of the proposed new diocese, to all missionaries of their appointment who may continue to serve throughout the year.

Resolved, That the Convention approve of said action of the Board.

(Signed)   E. A. FOGGO,
                                          Chairman.
                    By order of the Committee.

The Resolution was adopted.

Mr. Geo. W. Hunter read the following report of the Committee on City Missions, appointed at the second day's session of this Convention:

The committee to whom was submitted so much of the

Bishop's Address as refers to City Missions, respectfully report:

The great and growing need of some such missionary work as that inaugurated by the Bishop in our vast city, where, in spite of all religious instrumentalities now employed, more remains to do than is yet attempted to be done, justifies the zealous and holy effort of the Bishop to meet this need ; and your committee think that the earnest thanks of this Convention are due to him for this effort.

But on considering carefully the whole matter, your committee are met with grave difficulties, which appear to be in the way of legally carrying on the design as it seems to have taken shape in the mind of the Bishop.

I. There is, first—though this is the least of these difficulties—the contrariety of the scheme to the resolution passed by the Convention in 1858, constituting the present Board of Missions for the whole Diocese. This could be met by excepting Philadelphia from the field of that Board.

II. Again, umbrage might be given to settled ministers, having feeble congregations, by establishing a missionary station within a short distance of their Churches, and really or apparently interfering with the success of their labors.

III. Or thirdly: and this your committee cannot help considering the chief impediment—the Canon law of the General Convention may be contravened.

Under Title I, Canon 12, section vi., Philadelphia is made the cure of all its settled ministers, and no missionary can officiate therein without the consent of a majority of such settled ministers.

But while this law must not be contravened, yet obedience to it will much hamper the greatly needed missionary operations, as it would be extremely difficult to get, as it is required from time to time, the assent of the necessary number.

The only escape from this difficulty is, as it seems to your committee, to avail ourselves of Title III., Canon 5, § II (1), and let the Convention divide the city of Philadelphia into four parochial cures, bounded by Market and Broad Streets, or which is perhaps better, into seven thus: Parochial cures to be bounded by the Delaware and Broad Street.

1. The first bounded by Vine street on the north, and Pine street on the south.

2. All above or to the north of Vine street.

3. All below or to the south of Pine street.

Parochial cures bounded by Broad street and the Schuylkill.

4. All above or to the north of Vine street.

5. All below or to the south of Vine street.

Parochial cures west of the Schuylkill:

6. All above or to the north of Market street.

7. All below or to the south of Market street.

But this matter is too important, and demands more mature consideration than can be given to it during the session of this Convention.

Your committee propose, therefore, the following resolutions:

I. *Resolved*, That a committee on the subject of city missions, which shall take into consideration and report upon some plan of dividing the city into different cures, so that the assent of a majority of the settled ministers may be more readily obtained when needed, since there will be fewer in number, be appointed to sit during the recess.

II. *Resolved*, That the resolutions passed in 1858 establishing the Board of Missions be suspended so far as to remove the city of Philadelphia from the field of its labor.

III. *Resolved*, That this Convention respectfully invoke the attention of the Bishop to the facts set forth in the above report of the committee.

IV. *Resolved*, That the earnest thanks of this Convention are hereby conveyed to the Bishop for his zeal and perseverance in endeavoring to reach that large class among us who neglect almost entirely the opportunities of hearing the Gospel preached, though living all their lives within its sound.

V. *Resolved*, That the committee be discharged.

All of which is respectfully submitted.

G EMLEN HARE,
GEO. L. HARRISON,
JOS. R. MOORE,
ROBERT T. ROACH,
GEO. W. HUNTER.

PHILADELPHIA, May 11th, 1871.

The resolutions were severally adopted.

An amendment to the preamble of the Constitution of the Church in this Diocese was offered by Mr. Geo. W. Hunter, so that it shall read " Diocese" instead of "State" of Pennsylvania, and was referred to the Committee on Canons.

Notice was read by the Secretary of the proposed alteration of the Constitution of the P. E. Church in the United States by the General Convention, in respect to the formation of new dioceses.

The Rev. J. Andrews Harris read the following:

REPORT OF THE COMMITTEE ON PAROCHIAL HISTORY.

To the Convention of the Diocese of Pennsylvania, meeting May 9, 1871:

The Committee on Parochial History respectfully report that during the past year their work has been rather that of the arrangement than the accumulation of material.

A vast number of pamphlets, &c., amounting to several thousands, and relating to a great variety of subject matter, had been gathered in past years; and these documents were, for the most part, piled on the shelves or on the floor of the Committee's room, without any classification or arrangement. To effect an orderly disposition of them, under the varying heads of their subject matter, has been almost all that it has been possible to accomplish since the last report; and even this would have been impossible but for the means placed by the last Convention at the Committee's disposal to secure the paid services of a trustworthy person to do this work; and the Committee take pleasure in testifying to the zeal and efficiency of Mr. John Short, the Janitor at the Episcopal Academy, to whom the labor was entrusted.

The following sketch of Parochial History has been sent in during the year, viz.: from The Church of the Nativity, Bethlehem.

The Committee respectfully urge upon Rectors or Vestries who have not yet sent sketches of the histories of their respective parishes, to do so at an early day ; as the main purpose for which the Committee was appointed is to secure materials for a *complete* history of the Church in Pennsylvania.

A few Convention Journals have been received from other Dioceses; and other pamphlets and books have been presented by various individuals.

A set of bound volumes of Journals of the Conventions of this Diocese has been completed ; and the first volume of Dr. Perry's "Historical Collections of the Church" has been added by purchase to the archives of the Committee.

A vacancy has been created by the removal of the Rev. Charles R. Hale from the Diocese.

The Committee feel called upon to renew the expression of their regret that no fire-proof depository is under diocesan control, for the preservation of the documents entrusted to their keeping.

They offer the following :

1. *Resolved*, That the vacancy created by the removal of the Rev. C. R. Hale, be filled by the appointment of the Rev. L. W. Gibson.

2. *Resolved*, That, in addition to any amount still remaining to their credit, the sum of fifty (50) dollars be appropriated to the use of the Committee for the current year.

All of which is respectfully submitted.

J. ANDREWS HARRIS, *Chairman.*
JOHN BOLTON,
JAMES W. ROBINS,
GEO. W. HUNTER,
GEO. M. CONARROE,
JOHN BOHLEN,
FRANCIS J. CLERC.

On motion of the Rev. Mr. Harris, the resolutions appended to the report were adopted.

Mr. Charles R. King read the following report of the Committee on the Education of the Sons of the Clergy ·

The undersigned, a committee appointed by the Bishop of

the Diocese at the last annual Convention, under the following resolution:

Resolved, That the subject of providing for the education of sons of the Clergy, be referred to a committee of three, to be appointed by the Bishop, and report to the next Convention,—

Present the following report:

The propriety and duty of some action to accomplish the objects of this resolution are too evident in a body composed of those who are to be the recipients of its benefits, and of those who are in constant familiarity with the struggles of our ill-paid clergy, to require any appeal, especially when the matter has been so earnestly presented and urged by our Bishop.

In 1848, Bishop Potter, in his address to the Convention, called attention to the importance of providing for the education of the children of the clergy whose means are straitened, who live remote from schools of a superior character, "and whose children must soon enter on life with no resources but their talents and their worth." The result of this appeal was the establishment of a fund for the education of the Clergy's daughters, which was placed in the hands of trustees, who in 1849 obtained an act of incorporation, and have been the recipients of moneys which have been partly invested, and partly distributed under the direction of the Bishop, to aid in the education of the daughters of Clergymen. In subsequent reports Bishop Potter several times suggested to the Convention, and to the benevolent of our communion, the propriety and advisability of creating free and permanent scholarships with the same end in view, and the trustees in their annual reports have constantly repeated the suggestion.

While provision has thus been made for the education of the Clergy's daughters, there is only partial provision as yet made at the Episcopal Academy in this city, and to a certain extent through the generosity of some private Episcopal Schools in the Diocese, for the sons of the Clergy.

Bishop Stevens, in his address to the Convention in 1869, calls attention to the "fact that there is no organized provision in the Diocese for the education of the sons of the Clergy," and earnestly appeals for the establishment of some means by which the hard burdens of many of the Clergy might thus be lightened. He says, and all who know the self-denying toils and worrying cares of these poorly paid ministers will agree with him, "There ought to be in and for this Diocese, under the same general provisions as those laid down in the Clergy's Daughters' Fund, a fund for the education of the sons of our ministers, so that through the simple agency of our Bishop, these brethren can secure help towards giving their sons such an education as will fit them to honor their parents and their Church, and make them capable of eventually aiding both. I cannot speak too strongly of our need in this respect. Few greater blessings could be given to our hard working ministers, than such provision for their sons." Your Committee would therefore recommend the following action :

Resolved, That Trustees be appointed by the Convention to receive any moneys which may be given either for a permanent fund or for immediate distribution for the education of the sons of the Clergy of this Diocese, the distribution to be made under the direction of the Bishop, who shall have the designation of the incumbents of all scholarships which may be created, except in the case of annual contributors to the fund of not less than $200, who shall have the right to nominate the incumbents to the scholarships created by them during the continuance of their contributions.

All of which is respectfully submitted.

CHAS. R. KING,
H. H. HOUSTON.

PHILADELPHIA, May 10th, 1871.

The resolution appended to the report was, on motion, adopted.

Mr. G. M. Conarroe read the following :

REPORT OF THE COMMITTEE ON MINORITY REPRESENTATION.

The committee appointed at the last Convention to take into consideration the feasibility and propriety of securing minority representation (by means of cumulative voting or otherwise) in elections by the Convention of this Diocese, respectfully report:

8

That the subject of minority representation is one which has recently been receiving more than common attention, both in England and in the United States; and the justness of the principle which allows the minority a proportionate share in the representative or governing body is becoming generally recognized. Such representation has been in some cases secured by restricting the voters to two out of three candidates (or to some proportion less than the whole number), thus giving one representative to the minority. On this principle our school directors are elected. At the recent election for Judges of the Court of Appeals of the State of New York, six judges were to be elected. Only four were allowed to be voted for on one ticket. The four majority candidates and the two highest of the minority candidates were therefore elected.

The plan of cumulative voting, however, is considered more fair in principle than the designation of an arbitrary proportion in the representation. The plan is simply this: Each voter is entitled to as many votes as there are persons to be voted for, and he may cast them all for one person, or distribute them among the candidates as he may think best. Under cumulative voting, the minority should be entitled to secure their proportion of the governing body. Thus a minority of one-fifth may elect two members in a board or committee composed of ten persons.

The application of the plan of cumulative voting to political elections was first suggested, in England, by Mr. James Garth Marshall. It has been since endorsed by Mr. Mill, Mr. Hare, Earl Grey, Mr. Thomas Hughes, and other leading men in English public life. It has been applied to parliamentary elections wherever more than two members are to be elected, and was applied to the elections held under the recent Education Act. The beneficial results attained by it have been almost universally acknowledged. Says the London *Times*: "It has been everywhere confessed that the adoption in one form or another of the principle of cumulative voting was essential to maintain the character of our institutions, and that through it, and through it alone, could the redistribution of electoral power (which all prescient statesmen regard as inevitable) be reconciled with the preservation of our representative government."

In this country the principle has been warmly endorsed by many of our most eminent and thoughtful public men. In Pennsylvania, Mr. Buckalew has had it applied to the elections in his district. At the last election for Overseers of the Alumni of Harvard College, it was most satisfactorily tested. It has been incorporated into the recently amended constitution of the State of Illinois. A committee of the United States Senate has recommended its adoption as a part of the Federal Constitution.

If this principle in representation is becoming so rapidly recognized by statesmen as just and proper in political elections, certainly the Church should not be backward in conceding to those in her councils an equal meed of justice. The Diocese of New Jersey has nobly set an example. A canon was adopted in the Convention of that Diocese last year, which is in the following words:

OF ELECTIONS BY BALLOT.

"SECTION 1. In all elections by ballot, each voter shall be entitled to as many votes as there are persons to be elected; which votes he may cast all for one name; or he may divide them among any number, not exceeding the whole number to be voted for; and any ticket having such excess shall be rejected.

"SECTION 2. There shall be a nomination to the Convention at least three hours previous to any election by ballot, of all persons for whom it is proposed to vote, and no vote shall be counted for any name not so nominated."

It has been said in England, and the sentiment is equally applicable here, that a plan "by which a fair share of the representation is secured for the minority is not only just to them, not only useful to the community at large, by securing a hearing for both sides of the question (and every question has two sides at the least), but is beneficial to the majority themselves, for it secures them a truer representation.

When it is not adopted, the candidates put forward are very frequently, if not most frequently, not those whom the majority of the majority would prefer, but those whom the minority of the majority insist upon being nominated, by threat of dividing the party."

It has been objected that if cumulative voting were allowed in a convention, the minority might be likely to secure more than their share of representation, and thus perhaps override the majority. But this is founded on the fallacious supposition that the majority will possess no intelligence, and will not be able to protect themselves—a thing which it is impossible to believe. The majority can have no difficulty in protecting themselves. The majority in the convention will be the majority in the committee. Taking the only reasonable view of the case, viz.: that the majority and minority are equally intelligent, the result of cumulative voting must be that the representation of each in a committee will be proportionate to their respective numbers, which is simple and exact justice.

It has been well said that "the power of decision can never be endangered by the proportionate representation of minorities, *but the deliberate formation of opinion is exposed to great hazard if the moderating influence of dissenting minorities be excluded.*"

If the objections against the cumulative votes are fairly sifted, it will be found either that they proceed upon the fallacy that a majority of a convention are the whole of the convention, or that the complaint really is that a tenth of the voters ought not to have a tenth of the electoral power.

Your committee recommend the adoption of the plan of cumulative voting in elections for the Standing Committee of this Diocese, and to that end they submit the following resolution:

Resolved, That in Canon 7, section 1, between the word "order" and the word "vacancies" the following be inserted:

Every voter shall be entitled to as many votes as there are persons to be elected: and he may cast all such votes for one person, or he may distribute them among any number of candidates not exceeding the whole number to be voted for. Any ticket having an excess of votes over the whole number of persons to be voted for shall be rejected.

A nomination of all persons for whom it is proposed to vote, shall be made to the Convention at least three hours previous to the election; and no vote for any person not thus previously nominated shall be counted, and no candidate shall be considered as elected who shall not have received a number of votes equal to a majority of all the persons (of each order) voting at such election.

M. A. DeW. HOWE,
WM. RUDDER,
GEO. M. CONARROE,
ISAAC HAZLEHURST.

I concur in recommending the passage of the resolution proposed.

G. EMLEN HARE.

On motion of the Rev. Dr. Goodwin, the subject was postponed to the next Convention.

On motion of the Rev. Dr. Goodwin, it was

Resolved, That the subject of minority representation be submitted to the General Convention for consideration.

The Rev. Dr. Drumm offered the following:

Resolved, That it is the right of the Rector or Minister in charge of a Parish, to preside at all parochial and vestry meetings, where the Charter does not contain anything which forbids it. But if there be no Rector or Minister in charge, or if he be unavoidably absent, or if he waive his right, one of the Church Wardens or Vestrymen shall preside.

On motion of the Rev. J. W. Claxton, the resolution was laid on the table.

The President appointed Charles R. King, H. H. Houston, and Edward L. Clark, Trustees of the Fund for the Education of the Sons of the Clergy; and the Committee on City Missions, Rev. Dr. Hare, Rev. Dr. Roach, Rev. J. R. Moore, Messrs. Geo. L. Harrison and Geo. W. Hunter, to which were added, on motion of the Rev. J. R. Moore, the Rev. Dr. Howe and Rev. Dr. Hoffman.

The Rev. Dr. Buchanan read the following report:

The Committee on Charters respectfully report that they have examined all the Charters referred to them by the Convention, viz.: Church of the Good Shepherd, Green Ridge, Luzerne

County; Church of the Good Shepherd, Radnor, Delaware County; Grace Church, Parkesburg, Chester County; The Church of St. Timothy, Philadelphia; and find them all to be in accordance with the requisitions of the Canons, and with the form of Charter recommended by the Convention.

They therefore beg to submit the following resolution:

Resolved, That Church of the Good Shepherd, Green Ridge, Luzerne County; Church of the Good Shepherd, Radnor, Delaware County; Grace Church, Parkesburg. Chester County; and the Church of St. Timothy, Philadelphia, be and they hereby are admitted to union with the Protestant Episcopal Church in the Diocese of Pennsylvania.

EDWARD Y. BUCHANAN, *Chairman.*

On motion, the resolution accompanying the report was adopted.

On motion of the Secretary, it was

Resolved, That the next Annual Convention be held in St. Andrew's Church, Philadelphia, on the second Tuesday in May, 1872.

On motion of the Secretary, it was ordered that 1,500 copies of the Journal be printed.

On motion of Mr. George W. Hunter, it was ordered that the charge be bound with the Journal, and 1,000 copies extra be printed.

The Rev. Leighton Coleman offered the following preamble and resolution, which was adopted:

Whereas, In view of the contemplated division of the Diocese of Pennsylvania during the current year, this body is probably the last Convention of the clergy and lay delegates of this Diocese as now bounded ; therefore be it

Resolved, That we are unwilling, after having been so long and so closely associated together, to part without recalling the kindly memories of the past, and expressing our earnest hope and prayer that these pleasant recollections will be warmly cherished in the years to come, and that the heartiest friendship, cordiality, and Christian brotherhood will ever characterize the relations of the several dioceses represented in the Conventions which are to succeed the one now about finally to adjourn.

The Rev. Jas. Saul offered the following resolution, which, on motion, was referred to the Committee on Canons:

Resolved, That Canon VII be amended so as to provide for the election of the Standing Committee biennally, instead of annually, by inserting the word *other* after the word " every " in the first line of said Canon.

On motion, the thanks of the Convention were tendered to the Rev. Dr. Howe, for the kindness and impartiality with which he discharged the duties of the Chair.

On motion, the thanks of the Convention were tendered to the Rector, Wardens, and Vestrymen of St. Andrew's Church, and also to the Institutions that had extended their several courteous invitations to the members of this Convention.

The Secretary read the following report:

The Committee, to which were referred the annexed resolutions of the Diocesan Convention of the year 1869 on the subject of making provision by insurance for the relief of families of deceased clergymen, respectfully report that they have conferred with the management of the Corporation for the Relief of the Widows and Children of Clergymen, as directed by said resolution; and, after maturely considering the subject referred to them, they made the following proposition to said Corporation:

First. That the Rector of each Church Corporation that might desire to have a policy of insurance on the life of any incumbent, should be assumed as of *thirty* years of age, and in an insurable condition of health; that any Church Corporation paying the annual or commuted premiums for any sum represented by a policy, should have the said sum payable to it for the benefit of the widow and children of any Rector that might die in the service. This proposition was declined by said corporation as being in conflict with the ordinary rules of life insurance, and embarrassed by so many conditions dependent upon the state of health and ages of incumbents, as to be too riskful.

Second. The Committee proposed that each Church Corporation should deposit either annually, or in some gross sum, such amount as it might deem proper by accumulation for a provision for the widow and children of any Rector dying in its service. That the Corporation for the Relief, &c., should accumulate such deposits at the rate of six per cent. per annum, and upon the death of any Rector in the service of the Corporation, such deposits with bonuses, varying for the length of time the deposit had remained on interest, should be paid to the depositor for the benefit of the widow and children of any Rector dying in the service of the corporation making such deposit.

This proposition was also declined on the ground that the Corporation for the Relief, &c., did not feel authorized to entertain it.

In further discharge of their duties the committee have conferred with the officers of some of the other Life Insurance Companies, with a view to the adoption of propositions similar to those above stated, and find them equally objectionable to such Companies.

The committee believe that the arrangements of the Corporation for the Relief, &c., both for insurances on lives, and the accumulation of money deposited with them, are of the most favorable character, and they would earnestly recommend to every Church Corporation in the Diocese to make some reasonable provision for the family of every Rector that it may at any time have, by contracting with the said Corporation for a policy on the life of such Rector, or by making a deposit to be accumulated for the benefit of the family of any rector that may happen to die in its service.

And the Committee respectfully ask to be discharged from the further consideration of the subject.

F. FRALEY,
THOS. H. KIRTLEY,
ROBERT B. STERLING.

PHILADELPHIA, May 9th, 1871.

The report was accepted, and the Committee discharged.

On motion, after reading the rough minutes of this day's session, and religious exercises, the Convention adjourned *sine die.*

JOHN A. CHILDS,
Secretary.

APPENDIX A.

A CHARGE.

BELOVED BRETHREN:

In selecting a topic for my primary Charge in 1864, I brought before you "The Undeveloped Powers of the Church," and endeavored to show how much latent and undeveloped power resided in our ecclesiastical body, which only needed to be drawn out and applied to make it many fold more influential and effective in its practical workings and result. To-day I shall speak upon a subject of equal interest, and which the aspect of the times, and the nature of our office, render it necessary that it should be clearly brought out and defined. That subject is, "The Clergy and the Laity, their respective rights and duties in the Protestant Episcopal Church in the United States of America."

NOTE.—Owing to the length of this Charge, several portions were omitted in the reading of it, and several other parts, having been read from my first rough notes (which my sickness at the time prevented me from filling out), are now elaborated according to the original design.

Many interesting points which might well claim attention have been necessarily omitted, in order to bring the charge within a reasonable size, and none of the topics introduced are discussed in an exhaustive way.

I have given my views freely, fully aware that they do not accord with others of equal authority in the Church of God, yet I have put them forth because I honestly believe them to be in accordance with the Word of God and with the Standards of our Church.

9

To treat this subject fully, would require a volume, rather than an hour's charge: yet I deem it all important that the relations of the Clergy and Laity should be well ascertained and broadly marked, so that there shall be no clerical encroachment on the rights of the Laity, and no refusal on the part of the Laity to recognize the position and office of the Clergy.

Only those who sit in the Bishop's seat, and have laid upon them the " care of all the Churches " in a large Diocese, can know how vital it is to the peace and welfare of the Church, to have these points defined and authoritatively settled.

Nearly all the troubles in Parishes arise from clerical infringement on the one side, or lay infringement on the other.

Grievous breaches of Christian charity, and pastoral relations, have arisen from questions of clerical and lay rights; and a very little difference of opinion, as to *where* authority really lies, has been the sharp end of a wedge, which, driven home more and more by the blows of contending parties, has cloven asunder many a Church, and riven apart many a pastoral connection.

Within the past year I have been appealed to more than in any previous year of my Episcopate, to settle canonical or constitutional questions—to adjust differences, and to give opinions, in points where both parties professed a willingness to submit to the decisions of the ecclesiastical authority. I have thus been compelled to give to this subject a great deal of thought and research, and the result of my investigations, imperfect as I feel them to be, I now proceed to lay before you.

The first topic to which I call your attention, is the

rights of the Clergy growing out of their office, and regulated by canon and rubric.

That the Christian ministry is a Divine institution, can be "proved by sure warranty of Scripture."

That to this ministry the Lord Jesus promised his special and perpetual presence and blessing, can be equally established.

That the ministry of our Church is derived by due course of canonical succession, "from the Apostles' times," in its three-fold order of Bishops, Priests and Deacons, is the teaching of our Ordinal, and the best authenticated statements of ecclesiastical history.

To this duly constituted ministry has been entrusted three great gifts or rights, each involving great privileges and duties, viz.: the right to preach the Word, the right to minister the Sacraments, and the right to govern the flock—those homiletical, sacramental and governmental rights which constitute the Minister, a Preacher, a Priest, and a Pastor.

Let us look, first, at the Homiletical rights and duties, or the Minister as a PREACHER.

When our Lord, at the beginning of his ministry, selected his Apostles, St. Mark (iii. 14,) says, " He ordained twelve, that they should be with him, and that he might send them forth to preach."

The first passage which He expounded in the Synagogue of Nazareth, was one from the prophet Isaiah, which declared that the Lord had anointed him "to preach the Gospel to the poor," and his constant practice was to "preach the kingdom of God."

His last commission to his disciples, just before his ascension from the Mount of Olives, was, "Go ye into all the world, and preach the Gospel to every creature."

The Apostles, as far as we know, carried out these injunctions, and " went everywhere preaching the word." St. Paul distinctly says, " Christ sent me not to baptize, but to preach the gospel," and instructing Timothy as to his duties, he urges him with special fervor to "preach the word." These, with numerous other quotations, prove that the foremost duty of a Christian minister is to " preach Christ and Him crucified."

Throughout the New Testament we find that preaching, or the making known of the truths of the Gospel by the living voice, was the condition precedent to believing, as believing was the condition precedent to baptism.

The place assigned by our Lord and his Apostles to Preaching, verbally; by their recorded directions, and practically, by their own usage, is the place it should occupy now.

If we say that the condition of things is now altered, and that ministers of the present day preach mostly to those baptized in infancy, and who are already in a state of regeneration, and that what we need therefore is not preaching to awaken and instruct, but frequent communion to nourish and perpetuate the new birth effected in the infant by baptism, then we fall into two errors;— first, of making infant baptism supplant the institution of Preaching; and secondly, of making the Sacrament of infant Baptism take the place of faith. On the contrary, the very fact that so large a proportion of the audiences of the day are persons baptized in infancy, who yet have not " with their own mouth and consent openly, before the Church, ratified and confirmed " their baptismal vows, thus increasing their guilt and danger; is a strong argument for giving increased prominence to Preaching, as a means of arousing them to a sense of their perilous condition, and of explaining to them their duty, and of exhorting them to embrace the terms of gospel salvation. We need preaching all the more now, because the tendency of the sacramental system is to lull men into a state of false security, and to make them satisfied with Sacraments and ceremonies, rather than seek, by prayer and through faith in the Lord Jesus, " the inward spiritual grace," without which " the outward and visible signs" are of no avail to the salvation of the soul.

Much use is made by those who disparage preaching of the words of Scripture found in the Old Testament, and quoted by our Lord, " My house shall be called an House of Prayer." It would be well to remember that this declaration was made in reference to the Temple at Jerusalem, a place not ordained for preaching, but for offering sacrifices, and in which there was no preaching as an appointed part of the service. When our Lord quoted the saying, he still applied it to the Temple, and quoted it against the Jews, who, while professing to hold the edifice in honor as God's House of Prayer, had yet, by filling its courts with shambles and money changers, made it a place of trade and trick, and hence " a den of thieves." It had nothing to do with the Christian Church, and is an argument based on the sound of the words, rather than on their sense. The ministry which Christ has commissioned in his Church is specially distinguished from the ministry which God commissioned under the Levitical Ritual, by the striking fact, that while the Jewish Priests were selected by a tribal choice, and entered upon their priestly duties by inheritance, and were required to minister in one place, and could do nothing but offer sacrifices with their accompanying rites, the Christian ministry is selected out of various tribes and nations, by an inward and spiritual call, and enter upon their duties by a distinct setting apart to their work and office, by those in authority in the Church, and are required to go into "all the world and preach the gospel to every creature."

The minister, therefore, who undervalues preaching, shows that he undervalues God's Word, and Christ's Commission, and his Ordination vow, and sets up his private judgment against the command of our Lord and the injunctions of the Church.

Here, then, is one of the paramount duties of the minister. It is a duty which he shares with no one, for the responsibility of teaching the flock rests on him alone. Nor can he avoid that responsibility by allowing others to occupy his pulpit, and preach error therein, and then shelter himself behind the fact that it was another, not himself, who spoke the words of error or deceit. The minister *is responsible* for the utterances of his pulpit, whether present or absent; and when error is proclaimed from his pulpit, and he fails to " banish or drive it away " by a counter statement of the truth, or, by silence gives a tacit approval of the same, he is, in the judgment of all right-thinking men, liable for the damage done to his flock, by the " wolves in sheep's clothing" who have ravened upon them, under his cognizance, and without any let or hindrance from him.

Would that I could impress upon you the fearfully

solemn duty which lies upon you as Preachers of the
Word. Did you feel it more, your. sermons would be
more filled with Christ, and glow with his love, and your
hearts would be all alive to the salvation of souls. You
would preach, now the threatenings of the Lord, and now
the wooings of the Gospel. You would speak now as
standing amidst the thunderings of Sinai; now as if bow-
ing beside the Cross of Calvary—keeping back nothing
that is profitable, but declaring " the whole counsel of
God, whether men will hear, or whether they will for-
bear."

In the strong words of the Dean of Canterbury,
" surely a more solemn position cannot be conceived than
that of him who stands and preaches to a congregation.
From each of those upturned faces there looks out a soul
for which Christ died. In that post of vantage stands
Christ's ambassador, pleading, constraining, admonish-
ing. To each of them, he speaks as none else can speak.
They are come expressly to be dealt with in God's
name. The words which he uses, the motives which he
urges, will never be charged with being too serious for
the occasion. He can assume, and they will grant,
truths which elsewhere would not pass unchallenged.
In private and in society, pride, rivalry, antagonism,
come in to withstand the truth. The man is on his
defence mounting guard over the fair front of his building. But here the heart is in its inner chamber, listening for the whispers of truth. Behind these faces work
conviction, sympathy, longing desire. " I am the man ";
" God be merciful to me a sinner "; " Let me spend and
be spent "; " O that I were gentle, and holy, and pure !"
" These are the thoughts that the Preacher is able to

waken; these the springs of life that he can touch.
Let us reflect that every Sunday at noon there are in
our land many thousands thus employed in speaking,
many hundreds of thousands in thus listening, and we
shall have some idea of the vastness of the agency of
which we treat.   *   *   *   *   Let us not depre-
cate them, but strive to multiply them ten fold." *

The 2d point to be considered is, the rights and duties
of the Minister in the administration of the Sacraments,
and in conducting the public worship of the congregation,
or what may be termed his Priestly work.

At his ordination, the Bishop lays upon him the
charge " be thou a faithful dispenser of the word of God
and *of His holy Sacraments*." These are as stated in the
XXVTH. of the XXXIX. Article, " Baptism and the Supper
of the Lord." In this same article the Church declares,
that " those five commonly called Sacraments, that is to
say, Confirmation, Penance, Orders, Matrimony and
Extreme Unction, are not to be counted for Sacraments
of the Gospel."

It inheres, therefore, in the very office of the Ministry
to dispense these holy Sacraments. They are fountains
of blessing placed under the care of Christ's ordained
servants for the benefit of the people committed to their
charge.

The Clergy at their Ordination promise to minister
these under two limitations or restrictions, viz.: first,
" As the Lord hath commanded," and second, " As this
Church hath received the same according to the commandments of God."

---

* Essays and Addresses by Henry Alford, D. D., Dean of Canterbury. Strahan &
Co., London, 1869 p.,4L.

The first restriction or limitation, requires that the Sacraments shall be ministered according to the terms and conditions of their original institution by Christ himself, as declared to us in the New Testament. These terms and conditions are incorporated almost *verbatim* in the formularies for Baptism, and the Lord's Supper, and are so clearly marked as to need no special indication now. The essential form of baptism resides in the use of water with the accompanying words of our Lord, requiring its application to the person of the believer, in the name of the Father, and of the Son, and of the Holy Ghost. The essential form of consecration of the elements of bread and wine, so that they become sacramentally, to all who eat and drink worthily, the body and blood of Christ, lies in the use (by a lawfully Ordained Priest) of our Lord's own words as detailed to us by St. Paul, at the time of the Institution of the Holy Supper " on the night on which he was betrayed." All the rest of these Sacramental services is of mere human ordering and invention; and hence have changed with the changing phases of the Church; and the simplicity of rite which marked Apostolic baptisms, and Apostolic celebrations of the Supper of the Lord, has given place to the elaborate and carefully guarded formularies of our Prayer Book.

These formularies are the growth of centuries of Christian thought and wisdom; and the Church hath thus gathered around these central forms of Christ's own institution, the carefully filtered sacramental teaching of the Bible and of the primitive Church, and so has made her offices instructive, as well as directory; and surrounded the sacraments with all that befitting ceremony

10

and teaching, vow and promise, prayer and praise, exhortation and confession, which make these the most hallowed of our services, because they bring us most nearly into the presence chamber of the Great King.

Our Church, by her forms, "The Ministration of Private Baptism of children in houses," and "The Communion of the sick;" shows that the validity of neither of these Sacraments depends *on the full use* of her public formularies. That the essential elements of each are preserved in the words of their original institution, "as our Lord hath commanded" though the surrounding drapery of words be altered by the various revisions which the Church has sanctioned from the Apostles' times.

It is not enough, however, for a Minister to say, I will administer these Sacraments "as our Lord hath commanded," and thus strip the service of all that the Church has added to our Lord's words; for, in addition to this he has promised to minister them "as this Church hath received the same according to the Commandment of God." So that the Minister is bound to use these forms, and these only, in ministering the Holy Sacraments.

In reference to both these Sacraments, however, the Church has imposed certain limitation and conditions.

These are in reference to Baptism, 1st, imposing the obligation of God-fathers and God-mothers, though "Parents shall be admitted as sponsors if it be desired."

2d. That the Baptism shall be administered according to the form prescribed by the General Convention. Where frequent baptisms occur, the rubric permits the omission of certain didactic parts of the service, though it also requires that "the intermediate parts shall be used once at least in every month (if there be a baptism,) for the better instructing of the people in the grounds of Infant Baptism."

In connection with this subject, the rubrics for "the ministration of Private Baptism of children in houses," enjoin two duties upon the minister:

1st. That he "shall often admonish the people, that they defer not the Baptism of their children longer than the first or second Sunday next after their birth, or other Holy Day fallen between, unless upon a great and reasonable cause." This rubric is based upon a declaration put forth in 1536, by the authority of Henry VIII. entitled "Articles to establish Christian quietness, &c.," stating "that infants * * * * by the sacrament of baptism do also obtain remission of their sins, and be made thereby the very sons and children of God. Inasmuch as infants, dying in their infancy, shall undoubtedly be saved thereby, else not."

The words "else not," which negatively asserted the damnation of unbaptized infants, were omitted in the rubric before the confirmation service in the first and second Books of Edward VI, and also in the revision in 1661. At that time, this portion of the rubric was transferred to the Baptismal office, and was so changed as to read "It is certain by God's word, that children which are baptized, dying before they commit actual sin, are undoubtedly saved." Without, therefore, declaring any opinion concerning the future state of infants dying unbaptized, the Church, by this first rubric in the office of Private Baptism, evinces her anxiety that infants should be brought as early as possible into Baptismal Covenant with God, and makes it the duty of the minister to warn the people against any needless delay. This rubric, by general desuetude has become practically inoperative. The social usages of the day, as well as the universal desire of the parents to be present at the baptism of their children, and the unwillingness of Rectors to have so many baptisms after the second lesson (perhaps each Sunday in large congregations), have conspired to render nugatory or almost so, this direction. Yet there it stands, and though the clergy in many places may not be able to comply literally with its directions, they can at least use it as a warning to their parishioners, against the delay too often manifested to bring children to baptism, and as a rebuke to the frivolous excuses so frequently given for putting off this sacrament; for it is the wilful neglect of a precious privilege, and a wanton disregard of those covenant relations, by which God is pleased to bring our children into union with himself.

The 2d duty enjoined is, that the minister "shall warn them that without like great cause and necessity, they procure not their children to be baptized at home in their houses," The reasonableness and propriety of this rubric, is evident to all, and the Clergy should discourage as much as possible, private baptism in houses, except in the special cases for which the private office was complied.

In reference to the Sacrament of the Lord's Supper, the limitations and conditions imposed by the Church on the clergy are, their duty to advertise open and notorious evil livers, and those who have done any wrong to their neighbours, that they presume not to come to the Lord's table—also, "the same order shall the minister use with those betwixt whom he perceiveth malice and hatred to reign, not suffering them to be partakers of the Lord's table, until he know them to be reconciled." While it is the duty of the minister to repel these classes, the Church also makes it his duty to admit to the Lord's table, all who have been "confirmed, or are ready and desirous of being confirmed," not being barred by these previously noted disabilities; and also all those, who can honestly and heartily respond in the affirmative to the exhortation, beginning—"Ye who do truly and earnestly repent you of your sins," who "are in love and charity with their neighbors," who "intend to lead a new life, following the commandments of God, and walking from henceforth in his holy ways," and who can "draw near in faith."

The Church also requires that this Sacrament shall be celebrated according to " The order for the administration of the Lord's Supper or Holy Communion," as set forth in our Prayer Book and established in General Convention. In the use of both of these Sacraments there are certain discretionary parts which are indicated, either by the rubrics of the offices, or by supplementary offices, such as that for " The Ministration of Private Baptism of children in houses," and that entitled " The Communion of the Sick."

Outside of these allowed rubrical discretions, and supplementary offices, no variation can be made by any Minister on his individual authority. He must, unless he violates his ordination vow, " Minister the *doctrine* and *Sacraments,* and the *discipline* of Christ as the Lord hath commanded, and as *this Church* hath received the same," for he has distinctly and publicly declared before

God and in His Church "I will so do, by the help of the Lord."

The Clergy have the right to refuse the Sacraments to those who do not come under the provisions of their original institution; or of the rubrics and invitations pertaining to the offices themselves. This right is recog-, nized by § II., Canon 12, Title II. of the Digest. Thus, for example, he has the right, as has been already stated, of repelling from the Holy Communion the three classes of persons designated in the prefatory rubric, viz.:

1st. "Open and notorious evil livers." The class which comes under this head, is thus described by Canon 109 of the English Constiutions and Canons, "If any offend their Brethren by adultery, whoredom, incest or drunkenness, or by swearing, ribaldry, usury, or any other uncleanness, or wickedness of life, such notorious offenders shall not be admitted to the Holy Communion till they be reformed." This Canon, while it does not cover all the cases of those who may be termed "open and notorious evil livers," sufficiently indicates the animus of the Church, while yet it leaves a large margin to the discretion of the Clergy.

2d. "Those who have done any wrong to their neighbors by word or deed, so that the congregation is thereby offended," i. e., it must be such a gross wrong as shall create public scandal, and bring by its continuance our holy religion into disgrace.

3d. "Those betwixt whom he perceiveth malice and hatred to reign." This need not be of such a public and notorious character as the previously specified cases; but the words refer rather to these personal, family, and social quarrels, which are so often bitter and resentful, and which cannot dwell in a soul filled with the love of God.

"The power of the keys" placed in the Minister's hands by this rubric, should be exercised by him with prayer, prudence, and patience. I have known Churches in this Diocese almost rent asunder by the hasty action, under this rubric, of young and inexperienced Clergymen. It is no light thing to cut a person off from the Holy Communion of the Body and Blood of Christ. It severs him from the highest Christian privilege, affixes to his character the deepest moral stigma, and hence never should be resorted to until after due advertisement to the offender, after affectionate and faithful warning, after all proper means have been resorted to, to convince of sin and lead to reformation. The Clergy should never forget that in all these cases there lies, by virtue both of rubric and Canon, an appeal to "The Ordinary," a right justly conceded to the Laity to protect them against the improper exercise of Ministerial authority under the provisions of this rubric.

While the Clergy, therefore, have the right to refuse these Sacraments upon certain rubrical grounds, the Laity also, when entitled to these Sacraments, have a right to the full use of all the forms and offices by which they are to be administered in this Church, without any additions or alterations. For example, the officiating Minister has no right of his own will, to omit the sign of the cross in Baptism. The discretion of using it or not, does not lie with him, but with those who bring the child; for the rubric says it may be omitted "*if those who present the infant shall desire it.*" Hence the Minister is bound to sign the child with the sign of the cross unless the parent or sponsors desire otherwise. So also in the use of the words immediately after signing the child; the Minister has no right to omit or alter a single word of the declaration which the Church requires him to say, beginning with words, "Seeing how, Dearly Beloved Brethren, that this child is regenerate," etc. The Laity can demand of the Minister the fulfilment of his duty, so to use the office as this Church hath received the same; neither omitting aught that this Church requires, nor adding anything which this Church has not authorized; for changes of our forms of administering the Sacraments by addition, as well as by subtraction, are equally reprehensible, and are equal violations of Clerical vows and promises. We do not want these forms overlaid with the borrowed rites and ceremonies of other rituals, how beautiful or effective soever these may be; nor do we wish to have them stripped of any of their befitting words and time-hallowed forms, thus despoiling the order and the beauty of those noblest of all offices, which are found in our Book of Common Prayer.

In conducting the public worship of the congregation, the Minister is the recognized leader and director of the services.

This right inheres in him by virtue of his " Orders " and " Mission." The law which is to guide him in the conduct of public worship, is found in the Prayer Book, and in the Constitutions and Canons of the Protestant Episcopal Church.

To this law he has promised obedience and conformity. In promising this obedience and conformity, he recognizes the right of the Church to ordain and establish its own rites and ceremonies. In voluntarily

seeking to enter the Ministry of this Church, he voluntarily and deliberately accepted and approved the formularies and the canons which the Church established;
and upon the faith of his vows and promises at his
ordinations,—vows and promises publicly demanded of
him by the Bishop, "in the name of God and of His
Church," and by him plainly pledged in the presence of
the " congregation of Christ;"—he was solemnly invested
with " authority to execute the office of a Priest in the
Church of God."

It would occupy too much of your time to go into any
detail as to the efficacy and bearing of the various rubrics
and canons which are designed to regulate the conduct
of the Minister in Divine worship, and I shall confine
myself to one point which has given rise to no little
trouble and discomfort, both to Minister and people, I
mean the question who shall control the music of the
Church?

In the rubric before the Psalms in metre it is expressly declared that it is " the duty of every Minister,
either by standing directions or from time to time to
appoint the portions of Psalms which are to be sung,"
with such assistance as he can obtain from persons
skilled in music, " to give order concerning the tunes to
be sung at any time in his Church," and " to suppress
all light and unseemly music, and all indecency and irrev-
erence in the performance." It is to be noted here,
that the metrical Psalms and Hymns constitute no part
of, and find no place in, the Morning or Evening Prayer.
They may be sung *before* or *after ;* but not in, or during,
Morning or Evening Prayer. It is further to be observed, that the whole question whether they shall be

11

used or not, is left "at the discretion of the Minister," and as they are only "allowed" and not enjoined, he may or may not use them at his pleasure. But if he uses any, he must confine himself to these, or to those which by a resolution of the General Convention in 1868, have been specially licensed by the "Ordinary" in the several Dioceses. The design doubtless of restricting the use of metrical Psalms and Hymns, not only to certain portions in Divine worship, but to those only which have been "set forth or allowed" by the General Convention, was to do away with the evil which exists in the Church of England, where, by usage, multitudinous hymn books of all grades and shades of Churchmanship and theology have been introduced; so that not only different Dioceses, but even different Parishes, have their various hymnals. There was no metrical version of the Psalms in the Church of England until 1562, when the version by Thomas Sternhold, John Hopkins and others was published by John Day, and was "set forth and allowed to be sung in Churches," though this version was not regularly annexed to the Book of Common Prayer until 1576, "after which," says Lord Stowell, " those Psalms became the great favorites of the common people." Since then other versions published by royal privilege, and a multiplicity of Hymnals without any authority, have been introduced, so that there is no uniformity in the Psalmody or Hymnody of the Mother Church of England, and each Rector selects that book which seemeth to him best.

Our American Church has not only restricted this indiscriminate use of metrical Psalms and Hymns, but, by the words of the rubric before the Psalms in metre, places the control of the music of the service in the hands of the Clergy. With this right no Vestry or Music Committee can interfere. The Minister alone is responsible for this part of the worship, and he can share it with no other.

Furthermore, I consider that this rubric gives the Minister control over the *instrumental* as well as *vocal* music: and that he is to repress all "light or unseemly music," whether by organ, or other instruments. This touches a delicate question, but I know, and so do you, Brethren, how much of this "light or unseemly music" is introduced into the Church; how often secular and operatic pieces are made to resound in the House of God; and how often the seriousness induced by the services, and the sermon, is dissipated by the gay performance of some irreverent organist.

The House of Bishops in their Pastoral Letter of 1856, thus expressed itself on this point, speaking of "the share which the organist and the choir are called upon to take in the public duty of devotion"—the Pastoral Letter says: "In the ancient Church there was a far higher solemnity attached to the office of the Chorister than we behold in our day. He was consecrated to his task by a sort of inferior ordination, and if he was found to act unworthily, he was openly degraded in a certain form of words, because 'what he sung with his lips, he did not believe in his heart.' Assuredly there was good reason in the principle of this, although the form has long ceased to be found in any Church of Europe. For, the singers in the public congregation should praise God in their hearts, or they cannot escape the sin of taking His name in vain. Their work is professedly a part of the worship prescribed, and it must needs be a mockery, if it be not an act of religion. We cannot, therefore, regard it as any thing short of a most grievous and dangerous inconsistency, when the house of prayer is desecrated by a choice of music and a style of performance which are rather suited to the opera than the Church—when the organist and the choir seem to be intent only on exciting the admiration of the audience by the display of their artistic skill; and the entertainment of the concert-room is taken as a substitute for the solemn praises of that Almighty Being 'who searcheth the hearts and trieth the children of men.'

" Yet this very serious and prevalent abuse was designed to be prevented by the positive rule laid down in the Prayer-Book, immediately before the authorized collection of the Psalms and Hymns. For, there it is expressly made the duty of the minister to forbid all unseemly music, and to give order for such as he may approve in the worship of the Sanctuary. This salutary rule, however, is too apt to be forgotten."

We need and ought to have a grand, expressive, reverential body of music, which shall make the Song-part of our worship as solemn and sublime as the Prayer-part is; a music that shall, by its special type of melody, lift up the soul in lofty emotions of praise, just as the martial type of music stirs the blood of the soldier, or the dramatic type excites the passions with the scenes with which the strains of song are associated.

We are gradually working our way up to such high compositions, but we are still behind both our privilege and our duty, in the worship of praise in the great congregation, nor can we compass what we want, until the great majority of "Tune Books" now in use are cast out of our Churches, and until our choirs shall be regarded as only the leaders of the congregation, guiding, but not engrossing the service of song. With such ample scope for music as our Liturgy furnishes, with such grand words as the Church puts into our mouths, with such noble occasions, joyous and penitential, Sunday and Holy Day, to evoke sublime and heart-stirring melody, our Church ought to cultivate such music as best befits its services, and such as shall make the house of God to resound with the tuneful voices of a united congregation, as they "worship the Lord in the Beauty of Holiness."

The 3d subject to consider under the general head of the rights and duties of the Clergy, are those rights and duties which pertain to him as a PASTOR.

By these I mean all those duties and rights which lie outside the pulpit and the chancel, and which inhere in or pertain to his office, as a shepherd or ruler of the flock.

The first class of rights and duties under this head are those which cluster around his duty towards the young of his flock.

These may be grouped under two heads—

1st. Those pertaining, and growing out of his duty and right to catechize children.

2d. Those pertaining to and growing out of his duty to prepare persons for confirmation.

By Canons and Rubrics, as well as by virtue of office, the public religious instruction of the children of the Parish, is placed in the Rector's hands. The first rubric after the catechism says, " The Minister of every parish shall diligently, upon Sundays and Holy Days, or on some other convenient occasions, openly in the Church, instruct or examine so many children of his Parish sent unto him, as he shall think convenient, in some part of this Catechism."

The next rubric directs " all Fathers, Mothers, Masters and Ministers, shall cause their children, servants and apprentices, who have not learned their catechism, to come to the Church at the time appointed, and obediently, to hear and to be ordered by the Minister, until such time as they have learned all that is here appointed for them to learn."

It is very evident that these rubrics cannot be fully carried out in our American Church; yet standing as they do, they are a perpetual reminder of the duties of Priest, Parent and Master, and a continual protest of the Church against allowing the young of the flock, to grow up without a knowledge of the cardinal facts and doctrines of our holy faith.

While we find catechetical instruction in the primitive Church, though differing somewhat from that now in use, yet it had gradually been discontinued, except so far as to teach the children the Creed and the Lord's Prayer, and sometimes the Ten Commandments. At the time of the English Reformation, there was but a small amount of theological knowledge among the people, and it was to remedy this defect that this catechism was published in 1549, in Edward the VIth's first Prayer Book, where it stood as part of the Confirmation office, so that those who came forward to receive that rite, should have an intelligent understanding of the truth. The catechism remained a part of the Confirmation service until 1661, when it became separated, and took its present form among our offices.

Three hundred years ago, how little did the laity
know of the truth as it is in Jesus! and in that age of
few books, little learning, and great ignorance, how invaluable was such a compendium, which, with its simple
words, lays open to much real gospel knowledge, without burdening the mind or wearying the memory. At
that time there was little, if any, home instruction in
the Bible. There were no Sunday Schools in the modern
sense of the word. There was but little preaching that
the children could comprehend; hence, if they were not
thus brought to the Church and catechized by the curate,
they would have almost necessarily remained in spiritual
darkness.

In addition to this, we must remember that three centuries ago, when these rubrics were framed, the domestic
and social life of England was quite different from what
it now is with us. The good old family regimen, which,
in those days, rigidly kept up parental authority, and
which made the household in all its grades—child, servant, apprentice—a domestic unit; scarcely exist in this
land, where children so early throw off parental control,
where apprentices have no common bond or sympathy
with the master or mistress, and where servants are regarded as mere hirelings, for whose moral care we feel
but little if any responsibility. We must remember,
also, that then there was but one recognized Church in
all England, and not the numerous sects of dissenters
which now exist; that then, there was but one Parish
Church to which all the inhabitants of that Parish were
legally attached; that then, there were no parochial or
Sunday School buildings into which the children could
be gathered and taught, and hence the Church was the

only place where they could be conveniently assembled.

Living as we do under an entirely different state of social and Church life, surrounded by numerous denominations of Christians, having ourselves no prescriptive or civil privileges or rights over others, with various kinds of Sunday School instrumentalities all around us, we may not be able to carry out the *letter* of this rubric; for, as Bishop Mant well says, "it appears to be the opinion of some of our best ritualists that this is one of the Rubrics which require to be understood with limitations, or at least will fairly admit of them."*

We must, therefore, interpret this rubric in the light of these facts, and adjust it as far as possible to our present condition, so as to bring out at least its true intent and purpose. The purport of the rubric is, that children shall be taught the Catechism; that parents, mothers, and mistresses shall see that their children, servants, and apprentices resort to the Minister for such instruction; that the Minister *himself*, and not by proxy, shall instruct or examine such as come; that this examination shall be openly in the Church; and that it shall take place "upon Sundays and Holy Days, or on some other convenient occasions." As this rubric does not direct that this examination shall take place on *all* Sundays, etc., it has been ruled by high authority (Bp. Mant), "that a Clergyman is not obliged to catechise the children every Sunday or Holy Day, but only as often as the occasion of his Parish may be fairly deemed to require."

It is to be observed here that while the Rubric in the English Prayer Book restricts the catechising by the

---

* ("The Clergyman's Obligations considered," etc. Oxford, 1830, p. 73.)

Curate to "Sunday and Holy Days," the rubric in the American service adds, "or on some other convenient occasions," leaving it for the Minister to judge what these "convenient occasions" are and how often they shall occur. On this point, therefore, the Sunday School more than covers the public catechising as required in our Prayer Book, for the Sunday School is held every Lord's day while this catechetical instruction may not be given on any Sunday or Holy Day, but on "some other convenient occasion," as the Minister shall think fit.

The spirit of these directions at the end of the Catechism I hold to be complied with—

1st. When the Minister *himself* catechises such young of his flock as are "sent unto him."

2d. When he does it *publicly*, i. e., either in the Church, the Chapel, the Sunday School-room, where his teaching may be heard by others than those whom he is required "to instruct and examine."

3d. When he does this at regular or stated times, not less than once each month. According to the rubric at the end of the Catechism, in the first Book of King Edward VI. (1549) the curate was to catechize the children "once in six weeks at the least," and was to devote "half an hour before evensong" for this purpose.

To carry out the spirit of these rubrics, two canons, one of the General Convention and one of the Diocesan Convention, are binding upon us.

The 19th canon of Title 1, directs that "the Ministers of this Church who have charge of parishes or cures, shall not only be diligent in instructing the children in the catechism, but shall also by stated catechetical lectures and instruction, be diligent in informing the youth and others *in the Doctrine, Constitution and Liturgy of the Church.*"

Canon IX. of the Diocese of Pennsylvania, requires that " Every Minister of a parish shall encourage the formation of Sunday Schools, and *the efficient prosecution of instruction in them, in conformity with the principles of the Protestant Episcopal Church.*"

These canons, taken with the rubrics after the Catechism, show conclusively, that the Church holds her Ministers accountable for the religious instruction of the young ; that the children are to be gathered in the Church or in the Sunday School, that the subject-matter of instruction must be the Catechism, and whatever will give sound information concerning the Doctrine, Constitution and Liturgy of our Church.

Thus, it is the minister's duty, by canon, by rubric and by office, to feed the lambs of Christ, as well as the sheep ; nor has any lay-agency by whatever name called, any right to step in between the pastor and people, and take out of his care the young of his flock.

There is danger that the modern Sunday School shall usurp the catechetical part of the minister's duty. This the Rector should carefully guard against, for though the Sunday School is an invaluable auxilliary, as subsidizing and organizing so much lay agency in the work of Bible instruction, yet nothing can discharge the Minister of his responsibility to supervise this instruction, and guide this agency in the right direction. He must, as a Minister of this Church, himself, publicly catechize the children, he must encourage the formation of Sunday Schools, he must instruct the young of his flock in the " Doctrine, Constitution and Liturgy of the Church."

The next point to be considered is his duty in preparing children for Confirmation.

In analyzing the rubrics bearing on this subject, we find—

1st. That the persons to be presented shall be of competent age, having come to years of discretion.

2d. That the minimum of religious knowledge which can be satisfactory, is their ability to say the Creed, the Lord's Prayer, the Ten Commandments, and the Catechism.

3d. That the Minister of the Parish is the sole judge " of all such persons within his parish as he shall think fit " for that rite.

4th. That he shall hand to the Bishop a list of such persons, with his hand subscribed thereto, before Confirmation.

Thus the selection and preparation of the class for Confirmation, is vested solely in the Rector. The Bishop has no such revisory power as is given to him by the English rubric, which says: " If the Bishop approve of them;" and can neither confirm any one not so presented, nor reject any one thus " placed before him." The Bishop acts here as a mere functionary, without any personal or official responsibility in the case. Yet a careful consideration of these rubrics, and the service itself, shows that the Minister is surrounded by wholesome restraints, and that his discretion is limited by certain conditions. Thus, though " children " are to be presented for Confirmation, yet these children must be " of competent age," must have " come to years of discretion," must have learned and " be able to say the Creed, the Lord's Prayer, the Ten Commandments, and the Catechism," and must be such as intelligently understand the Baptismal promise and vow, which they, in the presence of God and of the congregation "ratify and confirm."

While, therefore, neither the Church of England, nor our own, has formally designated what is a "competent age," or what may be regarded as "years of discretion," yet the use of these words fixes to a certain extent the proper period.

The "competent age," implies an age competent to the discharge of the duty required, *i. e.*, to understand the nature of the Baptismal vows, and the meaning of the Creed, the Lord's Prayer, the Ten Commandments, and the Catechism, as the bodies of faith and practice.

The "years of discretion" mean years wherein one is able to act with prudence, discernment, judging critically of what is correct or proper, united with caution. No child can be regarded as come to years of discretion, until he have that discernment and discrimination, by which he can choose intelligently the service of God, and resolves understandingly, to follow His holy will. Bishop Hobart, in his sermon " The Candidate for Confirmation instructed," says: " By this order, (referring to the preface) the Church evidently designs more than that they shall be merely able to say the *words* of the Catechism. They must have a full knowledge of its meaning, and as it embraces a comprehensive view of the plan of redemption, of Christian doctrine and duty, and of the privileges of Christians; these must be understood and realized before children can be qualified for receiving that holy rite, in which they pledge themselves to the belief of Christian doctrine, and to the practice of Christian duty, and in which their Christian privilege are assured to them."

Bishop White says: "The precise age is wisely left undetermined, because of the difference in the capacities. In England, the age of fourteen is generally recommended." "It has been my desire," he goes on to say, "to follow that example from an opinion that the generality of young people may be made to comprehend at the time of life specified, the grounds of their duties to God, and to their neighbors, and to have distinct ideas of the several articles of the creed, for it would be a mistake to confine the preparation to an ability to repeat the catechism. The form here referred to, supposes them to have learned what their sponsors promised for them, which cannot be without their knowledge of the sense, as well as of the letter, of the Creed, the Lord's Prayer and the Ten Commandments."

With these views of these eminent Bishops I fully agree, and except in extraordinary instances, no children should be presented to the Bishop for Confirmation before they have attained fourteen years. Some English Bishops have fixed the age of fifteen, but by the general consent and usage of the Bishops of our Church fourteen is the recognized period for presenting children to be confirmed.

In following the example of all my predecessors in the Episcopate of Pennsylvania, and fixing the age of fourteen as the normal period at which children, if properly prepared, should be brought to the Bishop to be Confirmed, I not only shall relieve the Rectors of much painful embarrasment when children are pressed upon them to be presented before they are fully qualified or have come to years of discretion; but I also, by this announcement, bring to the minds of parents and sponsors a definite period to which they should direct their minds, as the time, when, by previous prayer and instruction, their children and god-children shall assume their baptismal vows, and begin, by God's grace and in God's strength, a godly and a Christian life.

Far be it from me to limit the work of the Holy Ghost to any fixed period of life. I believe in child-piety. But I want it to consist, not in a parrot-like repeating of words without an intellectual or moral appreciation of their sense, but in a competent knowledge of God's word, an understanding of the simple plan of salvation through faith in the Lord Jesus, and a putting forth of that faith in Jesus. I long to see the time when, as a necessary resultant of the prayer and faithful teaching of parents and sponsors, our chancels at Confirmation seasons shall be filled by "children of competent age," intelligently prepared, and voluntarily ready, to consecrate themselves in life's morning to the service, and to the imitation, of the Holy Child Jesus.

I want to see the Church more than ever draw the young to her bosom by her loving acts, and enlist them in her work by her guiding words; but I want the love, and the work, to be of the heart, and from the heart, not a mere lip service or body worship; not of the letter that killeth, but of the spirit that giveth life. I never forget that our Saviour says of children, "Of such is the Kingdom of Heaven."

The second class of rights and duties of the Clergy and which come under the general head of *Pastoral*, are the performance of those offices of the Church for which provision is made in the Prayer Book.

1st. The right to perform the Marriage service. Marriage being a Divine Institution, it is but proper that the Minister of God should have a right to unite proper parties in marriage. Hence, in our land, such a service performed by a regularly ordained minister is valid in law, provided it be done in consonance with the Legislative statutes of the several states where the form is used. Upon these legal points (*e. g.*, whether the Bans are to be published or not; the age at which the law allows of such contracts; the necessity of having a license from the civil courts, etc.), the Clergy ought to be well informed, as ignorance of some of these points, has, in several instances, involved legal prosecution and fine. Usage has given to each Rector the right to marry those connected with his Parish; and as the woman by courtesy has the choice of the Minister, hence the Rector of the Parish in which the woman resides has the right to perform the service. As, however, personal relationship, or parochial attachments to a previous Rector, sometimes induce a Bride-elect to choose some Clergyman other than her Pastor, then it is the duty of the Minister thus asked to officiate to refuse to do so, unless there is given the express consent of the Rector of the Parish. This is an act of courtesy due to the Rector, and is one of those clerical amenities which ought scrupulously to be observed. I have known several cases where the Rector has peremptorily refused to allow another Minister to officiate on such occasions. While there may be extreme cases in which such a refusal would be justifiable, yet generally it is not wise to deny such a request, and a refusal often breeds dissatisfaction and heart-burnings which ought ever to be avoided.

This undue stickling for the right is generally regarded as an undue seeking after marriage fees, and works to the discredit of the Minister so refusing.

The civil law upon the subject of marriage is, in this country, so lax, and the facilities by which marriage can be obtained so easy, as to make it the more imperative on the Clergy to be very cautious and particular, and to use all possible guards as to the parties seeking to be married by them; and every suspicion of an improper or clandestine union, ought to meet their firm refusal to be a party to such transactions.

"The Order for the Visitation of the Sick" is one of those offices which require to be used with great discretion, as it contains forms and directions easily abused by men devoid of prudence and judgment. No one can read it over without being touched with its earnestness, directness, and warm evangelical tone; and when rightly used, it cannot fail of being a source of great comfort and grace to the sick and the dying. It is evident from its construction that it is to be used but once over the sick person; being, as it were, the formal recognition by the sick of the pastoral relation of the officiating Priest. One use of it during the period of illness, being sufficient to meet all its rubrical demands. Usage has almost rendered this office a dead form. Yet it was never designed to be such, and there is much that can be pleaded in its behalf as a salutary and useful office, the revival of which would be attended with undoubted blessing.

It need not be used at the first or second visit to the sick: but during the early period of sickness, if the strength of the patient permits, a time might be appointed when it could be said in the presence of the sick and the well, to both of whom its warnings and exhortations and promises address themselves with divine force.

Whether this visitation office be used or not, our Church hath declared her mind as to what is the duty of the Minister visiting the sick, and in the rubrics in the middle of the service has pointed them out with great distinctness and minuteness. He is to " examine the sick person whether he repent him truly of his sins, and be in charity with all the world." He is to exhort him to forgiviness of injuries done to him, and to make amends for injuries or wrongs done by him. He is to " be admonished to make his will and to declare his debts," and he " shall not omit earnestly to move such sick persons as are of ability to be liberal to the poor." It is quite evident that this rubric cannot be obeyed in all its requisitions, and is one of those where a large discretionary power is left with the Minister. At the time when the earlier Canons and rubrics upon which the present rubrics are based, were set forth, there was a peculiar necessity for some of these directions, especially those relating to the devising of property and making provisions for the poor. " Formerly," says Archdeacon Sharp,[*] " by the Canon law every one was bound to bequeath a part of his estate to religious uses, and in some such proportion, too, as he left his children ; so that if he had three children, for instance, Christ was to be reputed a fourth, or be made an equal share with the other three in the inheritance ; if he had but one son, Christ was to be esteemed as a second son, and so on (Decret. par. ii. Cans. 13, Qu. 2). And what was so bequeathed to the Church

---

[*] "The Rubric in the Book of Common Prayer," etc., by Thomas Sharp, D.D., page 59.

was usually deposited in the Bishop's hands, and went partially to the support of the fabric of the Church, and partially to the support of the Minister thereof." As we learn from the injunction of King Edward VI., that this old Canon law was grossly abused, and that much of the money thus bequeathed was devoted to superstitious uses, such as "Pardons, pilgrimages, trentalles, decking of images, offering of candles, giving to friars, and other like blind devotions," so by these same injunctions were these bequests forbidden and "the poor man's box," or Alms Chest, "was directed to be set up for the reception of what people were wont to bestow to the superstitious uses above mentioned; and the Curates were required to make their exhortations to sick people in favor of this new institution."

"Since the publication of these directions," says Archdeacon Sharp (p. 70), "the things they treat of are by time and some circumstances altered from what they then were. There is a better provision now made by law for the disposition of intestates' estates; there is not the necessity there formerly was to admonish the people on this head. There are also provisions made by law for the better maintenance of the poor, which may render the use of the poor man's box of less importance than it formerly was; insomuch that those public chests for alms are now rarely to be met with, or if they remain standing yet in some of the Churches, they remain rather as monuments of a former institution for the maintenance of the poor, than stand as instruments of their present supply. These things being considered, will make an alteration likewise on the stress to be laid both on the Canon and rubric, which latter is likewise softened or relaxed in the expression; and is not, as now worded, so properly a command which may not be dispensed with, as it is a monition to the Clergy who attend the sick, especially when they make their wills, to remind them of the poor, and of the acceptableness of of alms-deeds in the sight of God."

I need scarcely add that while these rubrics give the right and enjoin the duty upon the Clergy to move the sick to make his will and be liberal to the poor, yet they are to discharge this duty in the most delicate manner, and only when the circumstances of the case make it judicious and proper. The civil law in this country, and especially in Pennsylvania, is exceedingly jealous of all ministerial influence in connection with bequests and wills, obtained from sick or dying persons; and the General Assembly in 1855 passed a law rendering null and void all bequests, or conveyances of estates, real or personal, to religious or charitable uses, "except the same be done by deed or will attested by two creditable and at the same time disinterested witnesses, at least one calendar month before the decease of the testator or aliener," (Purdon's Digest, Stroud and Brightly 1119). The purpose of this act was to prevent any alienation of property by persons supposed to be sick unto death, under influences which might at such times of fear, or weakness, or infirmity, warp their judgments, and cause them to make such disposition of property in the hour of mortal peril as they would not make if in sound health, and uninfluenced by such ecclesiastic or mortuary surroundings.

No little stir has lately been made as to the right of the clergy to refuse, at any time, to use the Burial Office of our Church at the interment of the dead.

The rubric at the beginning of the Office is very clear. It distinctly states, that "the office ensuing is not to be used for (1) any unbaptized adult—(2) any who die excommunicate, or (3) who have laid violent hands upon themselves." The propriety of these three exceptions will appear upon a moment's consideration. "The Order for the Burial of the Dead," is a Christian office, prepared by a Christian Church, to be used by a Christian Minister, and designed for Christian people. Its whole structure contemplates its use over those who have been "received into the congregation of Christ's flock;" hence, any person coming to years of discretion, and wilfully neglecting the Sacrament of Baptism, whereby they become engrafted into the body of Christ's Church, do, by this very neglect, exclude themselves from all right to Christian burial. But our Church in her mercy for babes, does not, as the Church of England does, deny to an unbaptized infant this office; but, by adding to the first rubric after the word "unbaptized," the word "adult," permits it to be said over unbaptized children; as not willing to visit the sins of parents and guardians in neglecting to bring them to that holy sacrament, upon the helpless infant.

A person who dies " excommunicate," has surely no right to the service of a Church, from which, by his own open and notorious evil living, he has been cut off in accordance with the rubric and laws of the Church, and the injunctions of its Divine Head. Having eaten the Bread of the Church, he has "lifted up his heels against her," and by his own act, has excluded himself from all right and title to her sacred offices.

In the case of Suicides; the Bible distinctly says, "No murderer shall inherit the kingdom of God." Yet, where the act of self-murder is the result of mental derangement or temporary hallucination, so as to take away from the victim all moral accountablility, then I hold, that the Minister may lawfully use this office, but the case should be so clear, as to leave no doubt in the public mind, otherwise, great harm might be done to the Church. But while the Minister is not to use this office in the case of those three classes, he is at liberty to officiate at such funerals, provided he do not use this office, for it is to be observed, that the rubric does not say that the Minister shall not officiate at all at the funerals of these classes of persons, but only that "*this office ensuing*" shall not be used in such cases, leaving the Minister to act at his discretion, both as to attendance and form of service to be used in such cases. Here let me call attention to the fact, that the rubrics of this Burial office contemplate but two places where it is to be used, viz: the Church and the Graveyard. No provision is made for funerals from private residences, and the structure of the "Order," never contemplated such a use of it. It is thus a tacit discouragement of funeral services at the house, and a perpetual invitation to the surviving friends to bring their dead into the Church, that as a loving mother, she, who received them to newness of life at the font, may give them her last blessing, as they are borne in the silence of death to the grave.

For the purpose of dispensing the word and sacrament and conducting the public worship and officiating in these occasional offices, the Minister has the right to use the

Church edifice, and its ecclesiastical or educational appendages, for all Priestly and Parochial work. His election as Rector by the vestry, and acceptance of the same, virtually puts him in possession of the Parish buildings for Parish purposes, and in law, he is by this election, made the legal head of the corporation. This right is distinctly set forth in "The Institution Office," by the presenting to the newly instituted Rector, by the Wardens of the Parish, the keys of the Church, the delivery of which, invests him with the full right to use the building for all purposes of divine worship, and the presentation of which, is the official recognition by the vestry, of the Minister as the head of the Parish.

The civil courts (*e. g.*, The Supreme Court of New Jersey, vide Lynd *vs.* Menzies, 4 Vrooms, Rep., 162), have decided, that the clergy have the right to use the Church on all occasions of divine service, and that an action lies against the Wardens and Vestry, should they attempt to debar him his rectorial right.

The last right which time permits me to mention here, is the right of the Minister "to claim and enjoy all the accustomed temporalities appertaining to his cure." The Bible clearly establishes the principle that those who are called of God, to the ministry in the Church, who give themselves "wholly to this one thing, and draw all their cares and study this way," are entitled to a competent temporal support in the same.

This is strongly brought out and established by St. Paul, in the 9th chapter of the 1st Epistle to the Corinthians. In verse 7th, he shows, by allusion to the soldier, the husbandman, and the shepherd, that each is to be recompensed by, and from, the service in which each is employed. In verse 9th, by analogy of God's care for oxen, he argues his higher care for his ministering servants. In verse 13th, he alludes to the fact, that the Priests and Levites derived their support under the Mosaic economy, from the tithes, first fruits, shew-bread, and other gifts, so that they lived "of the things of the temple," and were "partakers with the altar," and then he adds, "even so hath the Lord ordained, that they which preach the gospel, should live of the gospel."

This then is the ordinance of Christ for, says St. Paul, "THE LORD hath ordained" it. It is not, therefore, simply an inference or an analogical argument, or an apostolical direction, *but a deliberate "ordinance" or law of Christ*, binding on the Clergy, so far as it requires them not to seek their support from secular occupations, but to "live of the Gospel;" and binding upon the laity in that it lays upon them the obligation to give of their "carnal things" to the full maintenance of the Ministry set over them in the Lord, so that they who are "taught in the word" shall "communicate unto him that teacheth in all good things."

The force of these last words, quoted from the 6th verse of the 6th chapter of St. Paul's Epistle to the Galations, is intensified by the consideration that the original intransitive verb here translated, "communicate," means literally to "go shares with," *i. e.*, so to share the temporal necessities of those who preach "the word of life" as to make the relief of their needs a bounden and conscientious duty; and the injunction is still further enforced by the warnings of the next verse, "Be not deceived, God is not mocked." As if he had said, deceive not yourselves with the idea that you are doing your full duty in this particular when you give grudgingly or slenderly; and do not mock God by "turning up your nose," (for that is the literal meaning of the word rendered mock,) at his ordinance to "communicate with him that teacheth" in the things of this life, and so neglecting or only half-doing your bounden duty; for the undeviating law of nature and of grace is, that the reaping shall, both in quantity and quality, correspond to the sowing. By withholding due support to the teachers of the word, you minister to your carnal appetites, and thus sow to the flesh and "shall of the flesh reap corruption," while on the other hand a ready willingness to share the burdens of the Clergy, is a doing of God's will, and so is a sowing to the spirit, and such "shall of the spirit reap life everlasting." These are solemn words, and should be well weighed by the Laity as the scriptural basis of the right of the Clergy to a decent and competent support. What the people give should not be regarded as so much given to the Rev. Mr. A, or the Rev. Mr. B, but so much for the support of the Minister of Christ set over them by the Holy Ghost; and the honour of God's House, and the dignity of God's worship, and the respect due to God's ministers, are so many factors which should control the salary and support of the Clergy of the Church. Believing also that the settlement of a Minister over a Parish at a definite stipend is a contract express or implied, binding upon both parties, I hold that neither party can be released from this contract without the consent of the other; or in case of a difference without an appeal to, and concurrence of, the Ecclesiastical authority of the

Diocese. As the Minister would be justly blamed who should strike for higher wages and refuse to officiate until his demand was acceded to by the Vestry; so the Vestry are to be blamed when they wrongfully withhold from their Rector his stipulated salary, or when, without his consent, or even perhaps notification of the purpose to do so, they cut down his salary in order to express their disapprobation of his course, or with the view, by thus crippling his resources, of forcing him to resign. This is a mean and unchristian course, violates an implied sacred contract, and is dishonest in the sight of God. Yet, alas! how often is it the case that business men, sitting as a Vestry, will act towards their Minister as they would not dare to act towards a fellow Vestryman.

The call to a parish is usually accompanied by a statement of the stipend to be paid, and if the Minister faithfully renders the services, to which, in accepting the call, he virtually pledges himself, then the vestry are bound to fulfil their part of the contract, and pay all that they promised. When for causes other than those over which the Minister and Vestry have control, the revenues of the Parish fall off, and the amount promised cannot be made up, then, by mutual conference, some new arragement should be entered into, by the Rector and the Vestry, whereby the salary should be adjusted to the reduced finances, or by mutual consent, the relationship may be dissolved. When the reduction of the income of the Church is evidently owing to the incumbent, then it is the duty of the Vestry to make a proper representation of the facts, proving this to the Rector, and respectfully to ask him, either to change the

14

course which is the occasion of his being obnoxious, or to resign the Parish, or to consent to such a reduction of salary, as shall be made necessary by the lessened revenue. This should always be done in a quiet, orderly and Christian manner, because it is a dealing between Christian men in matters affecting the honour of Christ's Church. Should differences arise, then the appeal, according to the words of the Institution Office, and the Canons of the General Convention, lies to the Bishop or Standing Committee, should there be no Bishop, and he or they, are to be the final arbitrators and judges of the case.

Having thus considered some of the leading points concerning the rights and duties of a Rector, under the several heads of Preacher, Priest and Pastor, I now proceed to the other branch of my subject, and hope to show the rights of the Laity in the Church of God, as secured to them by the New Testament, the Prayer Book, and the Constitution and Canons of the Church,

To trace out the history of Lay-rights and the changes in reference thereto, in different ages of Christendom, would be an interesting chapter of ecclesiastical history, and would furnish lessons of experience well worthy the study of thoughtful minds.

Several of these rights or privileges were gradually withdrawn from the Laity either by positive synodal action or by the growing assumptions of the hierarchy, until the doctrine generally taught was, either that the Church was in the Bishop, or that the Clergy constituted the Church, with sole right to rule its affairs. Thus the Laity as having anything to do with the government of the Church were ignored, and though attempts were occasionally made to recover their rights, yet they generally miscarried.

The Church of England presents a most singular condition of things in reference to this subject. The head of the Church is a Lay person. The law which imposes the Prayer Book as the Liturgy of the Church of England, is made by a lay Parliament. The Bishops are nominated by the Prime Minister, who is a layman, and the last Court of appeal on all questions of theology and ritual, is the Judicial Committee of the Privy Council of the Queen, composed mostly of laymen.

The Wardens and Vestries of the Churches in England have no power to elect their Rectors. The laity have no voice in Diocesan affairs, or in either of the Convocations. The Clergy and Laity of a Diocese are both debarred any free choice in the election of a Bishop, which is always done by the Cathedral Chapter on the *congé d' élire* of the Sovereign.

In the strong words of the Rev. Dr. Vaughan, the Vicar of Doncaster, " The Church of England has practically lost its machinery for self-modification. To deal conclusively with questions of doctrine or even of ritual, Convocation has no power, and Parliament little fitness. The one represents but a part of the Church—but a part even of the Clergy—even of the Clergy of one Province ; the other includes many who are not in the Church at all." *

This anomalous condition necessarily results from the union of Church and State, and the evils consequent on this union are being each year made more glaring and apparent.

---

* " Liturgy and Worship of the Church of England, by C. J. Vaughan, D. D." London, 1867, p. 365.

So morticed in is the Church with the present civil constitution, so intertwined with long established usages which have the force of laws, so rooted in the deepest traditions of English History and linked with the proudest monuments of its intellectual and moral greatness, that it would be a sad sight to see the ties which bind the two together ruthlessly torn apart, for in so doing there would be an uprooting, a prostrating, and desolating force at work which would imperil every thing upon which the true glory of England is based. Yet the signs of the times plainly indicate that the disestablishment of the Church of England is in the not far distant future.

Gradually and by various political, educational and ecclesiastical movements, there is a loosening of the old ties, and a preparing for a new state of things.

The action of Parliament in the disestablishment of the Irish Church, was the warning note to the Church of England. It has shown the way, by which it can be done, and having demonstrated the feasibility of such disunion, the lesson will not be lost, and the experience of the past will guide more surely the operations of the future. The thoughtful minds, both of the clergy and laity, are looking wistfully into the omens of the future. They are carefully watching what may be termed the storm-signals, that herald the approach of the feared devastation, and are wisely planning and forecasting, so that when the time of trial shall come, they may be found waiting and ready.

Turning now to our own communion, I remark with pleasure, that the rights of the Laity in this Church are greater than in any other particular or national Church.

These rights are based on, and sanctioned by, God's word, the Book of Common Prayer, and the Constitution and Canons of the General and Diocesan Conventions.

In reference to these rights as based on God's word, suffice it to be said here, that the first council at Jerusalem, was an assembly of Apostles, Elders and Brethren, (cf Acts xv. vs. 22, 23 with 25), that the laity choose the first seven deacons, whom the Apostles ordained; that the laity were permitted to preach the word, and that, in the language of the present Bishop of Salisbury, "it cannot be denied, that they had a real share first in the selection of persons who were to receive ordination, whether as Bishops or Priests." *

I have already briefly indicated the line of argument on this head, as it lies in the New Testament, and need not, therefore, enlarge on it here.

In reference to the Prayer Book, there are numerous points, where it distinctly and clearly recognizes and provides for the rights and privileges of the laity.

In the very title page of our Prayer Book, I find three most important words, which bear directly and forcibly upon this subject. The first is found in the word " *Common*," " The Book of *Common* Prayer."

By 'Common Prayer,' we mean a service of public worship of Almighty God, participated in orally, by minister and people alike, a service, where the people are not silent listeners, but wherein they vocally participate, both in the prayers and praises, of a common worship.

The clergyman is generally the mouth-piece of the people, and in most of the prayers at least, the people

---

* Moberly's Bampton Lectures, 1868, Lect. vii.

simply respond ' *Amen*:' but there are large and important parts of the service which are peculiarly the heritage of the people, and to which the laity have an inalienable right. The General Confession, the Lord's Prayer, the following Versicles, the Chants and Anthems, the Psalter, the Creed, the responses, to the Commandments, and sundry other portions, belong of right, to the lay-part of divine worship. No clergyman, therefore, can consistently so arrange the service, as to deprive the lay people of the privilege of the full use of their portion of the Liturgy, and when such portions are given to the choir, to the virtual exclusion of the great congregation, there is, to that extent, an infringement of the rights of the lay worshippers.

The beauty of such musical responses, when well rendered, and their attractiveness to certain cultivated tastes, are not to be considered alongside of the wrong done, often times to a large part of the congregation, who, are thus forced to remain silent, because not able to respond as they have been accustomed to do, and have a right to do, in those parts of divine service specially assigned to them. So far as this effect is produced, to that extent the service ceases to be *Common Prayer.* Take, for example, the practice of chanting the responses to the Commandments in the Communion office; here I think, is a case where it is particularly desirable that each one in the congregation should personally and vocally "ask God's mercy for their transgressions for the time past, and grace to keep the law for the time to come." The response, "Lord have mercy upon us, and incline our hearts to keep this law," is a prayer, to be said on our knees, and being purely precatory, and not like the "Tersanctus," a grand triumphal hymn, which seems by its very nature, to demand an outburst of music: ought not to be taken out of the mouths of the people, and committed, as it too often is, to a choir. All the congregation can say it, but all cannot 'sing' it, and none should be deprived of the privilege of the use of the words, in order to gratify the musical tastes of a Rector or choir. It is one of those recent innovations in our American usage, which, like the sudden bursting in of the organ and choir at the 'Amen,' at the end of the prayers, often grates harshly upon the devotional feelings of the people, as it wrests from them an ancient and established privilege, and defeats, to a great extent, the very purpose for which the responses were introduced. The more I see of these encroachments of the choir upon the responsive parts of the service, the more solicitous do I feel that the laity should hold firmly to their indefeasible right to this, their special portion. While I desire to see higher musical taste cultivated in the Church, and a more general practice of congregational singing, yet I do not want to see portions undeniably set apart for the laity, circumscribed or taken away from them, by the organ and choir.

In reference to the Choral service with which this subject is associated, I wish distinctly to say that I have no objection to singing all that is appointed to be " said or sung" under certain conditions, viz.: that such a service should be desired by *all* the congregation, and that the musical, should, in all respects, be subordinated to the devotional element. In a large city, where there may be found many persons who would enjoy such a service of song, and where, drawn together by the principles of elective affinities, these persons form a congregation for that purpose, there can certainly be no objection to their doing so, and I should bid them God-speed. But when there are only one or two Churches in a town, and the Rector of either of them, because he may be a cultivated musician, or may have well drilled choiristers, delivers over to them, those responsive parts of the service, in which all the people have a common right, and so excludes from their privilege those who do not sing, then, I conceive, that such minister is doing wrong to a large portion of his congregation, by hindering to that extent, their public devotions, and by defeating one of the very ends for which the service was framed, viz., "*Common Prayer.*"

The next special right of the Laity found in the title page of our Prayer Book, is their right to "the administration of the Sacraments and other rites and ceremonies of the Church according to the " USE " of the Protestant Episcopal Church in the United States of America."

The word "*use*" here, is an ecclesiastical term to signify the ritual of a Church.

Before the 11th century the Bishops of the several Diocese were accustomed, within certain limits, to ordain for the use of their several dioceses, the rites and ceremonies to be used therein; these, while they generally conformed to the Roman ritual, diverged one from the other, until there grew up many different forms of liturgic worship within the English Church called the "*uses*," or customs of Sarum, York, Hereford, Bangor, Exeter, Lincoln, and even different Cathedrals and Monasteries had their different " uses."

The term then, as employed on the title page, is synonymous with precept, form, or ritual of the Protestant Episcopal Church. As our Church is confessedly a " Particular or national Church," and as according to the 34th Article " every particular or national Church hath authority to ordain, change, and abolish ceremonies or rites of the Church ordained only by man's authority, so that all things be done to edifying;" so the Protestant Episcopal Church, having by its supreme authority established a use, or ritual, that, and that only, can be used, or is binding on her Ministers. Every candidate for Holy Orders, before his ordination as Deacon, subscribes to a declaration, saying: " I do solemnly engage to conform to the doctrines and worship of the Protestant Episcopal Church in the United States of America."

Every Deacon, before he is ordained to the Priesthood, declares before the Bishop, and in the presence of the whole congregation, that he will, by the help of God, " give faithful diligence always so to minister the doctrine and sacraments and discipline of Christ, as the Lord hath commanded, *and as the Church hath received the same.*"

It follows that the Laity, have the right, full and indefeasible, to the service just as set forth by the General Convention of 1789; and no Minister can abridge it, or expand it, can take from it, or add to it, without, to that extent, infringing on a right which is guaranteed to all the members of the Church.

When, therefore, the Clergy introduce new rites and ceremonies not recognized in our Prayer Book, or when they refuse to use the offices of our Church as set forth in the Prayer Book, then they are trenching on the rights of the Lay people, as well as breaking their most solemn vows. Nor does it avail to tell the people that these new rites and ceremonies are found in the older service books of the English Church, or in the Liturgies of primitive times. The compilers of our Prayer Book had all these before them when they prepared our forms ; and by deliberately and formally setting forth one form of worship, they virtually excluded all others. When the Continental Congress selected what should be the terms, forms, and conditions of its government, and established by law an AMERICAN Republic, it, by that act, not only made it binding upon every citizen to adhere to and obey that Republic, but excluded all other forms of Republican Government. Nor would it have saved a man from the penalty of the law, if he pleaded in defence of a transgression of that law, that he followed the custom of the Helvetic Confederacy, or of the Dutch Republic, however valuable the constitutions, the laws, and the governments of these several Republics.

The Protestant Episcopal Church in the United States is a perfectly organized and a perfectly self-governing body. She does not by a national organization cut herself off from the Church Catholic, for her union with that, is not through Canons and rubrics and ritual, but through an Apostolic ministry and ancient creeds, conserving and perpetuating " the faith once delivered to the Saints." We claim to be part of the " One Holy Catholic and Apostolic Church," but the claim is based not on a similarity of rites and ceremonies with any one or more branches of the Church, but that we have preserved in our Ministry, and in our sacraments, and in our formularies of faith, the Apostles' doctrine and fellowship. We are Catholic because we hold by faith to Christ the living, the universal Head, and derive thence, through ministerial and sacramental institutions of his own ordaining and continuance, our corporate life and power. "Particular forms of Divine worship and the rites and ceremonies appointed to be used therein," are, as the Preface both to the English and American Prayer Books says " things in their own nature indifferent and alterable and so acknowledged," and to this agrees our 20th article, which says, " the Church hath power to decree rites and ceremonies," etc. And as the Protestant Episcopal Church in these United States has by its highest legislative assembly, as well as by each of its Diocesan Conventions, adopted and accepted the Book of 1789 as its national use or ritual, so is the Minister bound to conform his performance of Divine service in accordance with that use, and so have the Laity the right to claim at the hands of their Minister that he shall conduct the worship according to the forms and rubrics of that Book.

The 34th of the 39 Articles bears directly on this point, and says, " Whosoever through his private judgment, willingly and purposely doth openly break the traditions and ceremonies of the Church, which be not repugnant to the word of God, and be ordained and approved by Common authority, ought to be rebuked openly (that others may fear to do the like), as he that offendeth against the common order of the Church, and hurteth the authority of the magistrate, and woundeth the consciences of the weak brethren."

For it must be borne in mind, that laity as well as clergy, were in the General Convention that framed that

Book, and that laity as well as clergy joined in setting it forth with due authority.

It has been declared, however, again and again, that neither the vestry as such, nor individual laymen, have anything to do with the manner in which the Rector conducts Divine Service. So long as the Rector conforms to the rites and ceremonies and administration of the Sacraments, as laid down in the Prayer Book, neither the vestry nor individuals can interfere. But as the conduct of public worship is a series of acts done jointly by minister and people, the people, on their part, as well as the minister on his, are perfectly competent to say whether those several acts which make up the forms of worship, are, or are not, in accordance with the rubrics and forms. It is not a question of opinion but of fact; not a matter of theology, but of accordance with or divergence from a well-known and authoritatively enjoined standard. When the layman, using his eyes and his ears and his common sense, beholds any discrepancy between the things done and the things required, he has the right to point them out and remonstrate, because the service is made for him, and not he for the service—because the Church, by its highest legislation, has guaranteed him these rights, and no clergyman can deprive him of them, or mutilate them without due process of law. I do not refer to that petty fault-finding which the Rector of nearly every parish meets with in some narrow, illiberal, or splenetic layman, but to that calm, decided, intelligent remonstrance and appeal, which no clergyman should set aside, and which, if he cannot satisfy, should be submitted to the judgment and decision of the Ecclesiastical authority.

The question here arises, what can the laity do when the clergy preach and teach, by sermons or symbolism, erroneous and strange doctrine or introduce rites and ceremonies, contrary to, or not recognized by, the American Liturgy? Have they no redress? I answer distinctly they have. Canon 2, §1. Title ii, of the Digest: "Of offences for which ministers may be tried and punished," says, "Every Minister of this Church shall be liable to presentment and trial for the following offences," and then the section goes on grouping the offences under five specifications. The second of these is as follows: "Holding and teaching publicly or privately and advisedly, any doctrine contrary to that held by the Protestant Episcopal Church, in the United States of America."

By Canon 1, section 1, of the Canons of this Diocese, "The trial of a clergyman not being a Bishop, shall be on a presentment in writing, specifying with clearness and certainty, as to time, place and circumstance, the crime or misdemeanor, &c.; the said presentment to be made to the Bishop, either by the Convention or by the Vestry of the Parish to which the accused belongs, or by any three presbyters of this Diocese, &c."

Here then are two bodies, one of which is composed partly of laymen and partly of clergymen, and the other wholly of laymen, who are competent to present a clergyman for holding and teaching erroneous doctrine. This implies their right to judge of the character of that doctrine, at least in its *prima facie* aspect, and though they are not the ultimate judges, as to the truth or error of the doctrine, yet they can take initial action and put a clergyman on his trial for alleged error. Were it not so, and had not the laity some rights in reference to maintaining the doctrine, discipline and worship of the Protestant Episcopal Church, it would contravene the whole spirit of the 8th article of our Constitution, which recognizes the right of the laity in connection with the clergy, to frame even articles of faith and forms of worship, and would be a monstrous grievance to which they ought not to submit.

Upon this point Dr. Seabury says, in a discourse on "The relations of the clergy and laity," "So far from discouraging the laity, I would earnestly call on them in the name of God, to examine the Church's standard, to compare with it the teaching and conduct of her clergy, to sustain and encourage, as by their prayers and labors, while we preach agreeably to our standard, and to oppose us, as a Christian may, when we depart from our standard and invalidate its authority. The clergy do indeed, demand in the name of Christ, submission to their judgment, but they demand it no farther than as they speak with the Church, in the words of the Church, and he who will not obey the Church, 'let him be unto thee as a heathen man and a publican.' I say, therefore, freely, I have no sympathy with those who represent a Bishop's words or a Priest's words as the rule of a Christian's conduct. I repel such an imputation on the catholic principles which I advocate, as false, and as when applied to the ministers of Christ over our own Church, the result either of ignorance or prejudice." "St. Athanasius," he goes on to say, "was but a Deacon in the Church of God, when he withstood many of the Bishops, and in later times, we have the shining examples of Lawrence, Nelson and Stevens, and other pious intelligent laymen, who have borne their

testimony to catholic truth and duty, when a majority
of the Bishops and Arch-Bishops of the State-tramelled
Church of England, were ashamed of the faith of Christ,
and prepared to undermine and betray it. These were laymen who upheld the standard of catholic faith and duty,
in opposition to the time-serving Bishops of a degener-
ate and heretical age." p. 19-21.

This language of Dr. Seabury is not too strong. History teaches us that no Church is safe from Priestcraft,
in its worst forms, where the laity have no right to judge
of doctrine and ritual, but must uncomplainingly
receive and humbly believe whatever the Priest shall
teach. Upon this point St. Cyprian says, "The lay
people who obey the Lord's precepts and fear the Lord,
ought to separate themselves from a sinner, who is set
over them, and not mingle in the sacrifices of a sacrile-
gious Priest, inasmuch as they chiefly have the power
of choosing those who are worthy or refusing those who
are unworthy, which very thing we see descends from
divine authority, namely, that the Priest be chosen in
the presence of the laity, under the eye of all, and be approved as fit by the public judgment and testimony."

A higher authority than the Bishop of Carthage, even
St. John the Apostle, exhorts the laity to whom he addressed his first epistle, "Beloved, believe not every
spirit, but try the spirits whether they be of God, because many false prophets are gone out into the world."

Here, then, we find the limitations within which it is
the duty of the laity to heed the teachings of the clergy.
Outside of the Bible as "the rule of his conduct in dispensing the divine word," the Book of Common Prayer
as his rule "in leading the devotions of the people," and

the books of Canons of the General and State Conventions, as his rule "in exercising the discipline of the Church" (points distinctly brought out in the Institution office), the minister has no commission to speak or act, and the people are under no obligation to listen or obey. I call upon the laity to watch with zealous care, the introduction, one by one, and little by little, of usages and doctrines contrary to the plain directions of the Prayer Book, and the teachings of our Creed, Catechism and Articles of Faith.

These encroachments will, if persisted in, gradually destroy the good old way of worship, and have already, in some places, set aside the simple and beautiful services of the Church, for the more ornate and sensuous, and Rome-like ceremonies of the ritualistic school. *Obsta Principiis* should be the motto of the laity in these days when the Church has within her pale, men who openly denounce Protestantism as a failure—the Reformers who gave their bodies to be burned, as cowardly traitors—the English Reformation as a hideous blunder, and who, by gaudy vestments, by unwonted and symbolical postures —by a Romish bedecking of the chancel and altar—by the additions and interpolations of the usual mode of worship—by the reproduction of names, terms and usages, distinctly papal, seek to innoculate the Church with Romanism, and thus pervert and destroy the heritage of our fathers. It is the duty of every sound Churchman, to lift up his voice against such innovation or any innovations, and to see to it, that the American Liturgy in its integrity, shall be the only use and ritual in the American Church.

The third point brought out in the title page of our

Prayer Book is, that the laity have a right to "The forms of prayer and administration of the Sacraments and other rites and ceremonies of the Church, according to the use of the *Protestant* Episcopal Church in the United States of America."

Let me ask your attention briefly to this point.

1st. Our Church is by name and constitution a Pro-tfstant Church.

There is much that goes under the name of Protestant and Protestantism now-a-days, which we, as a Church, must and do condemn. Protestantism is not the un-shackling of the mind from rightful authority, and giving it over to unbridled license. It is not an uprooting of the apostolic and primitive foundations of the Church, and substituting therefor, whatever man may choose to build up on the shifting sand of modern thought.

It is not a breaking down, or a breaking away from every thing that was for centuries used in the adorn-ment of Churches, and the proper rendering of divine service, because the same may have been used and abused, by a corrupt Church.

It is not a mere system of indefinite negations, a pro-test against, and denial of, certain dogmas; but itself asserting and advocating no primitive and fundamental truth.

It is not, a following of Luther, or Calvin, or Knox, or Cranmer, in all the opinions and plans of those re-formers in Germany, France, Scotland or England.

The specific Protestantism of the Church of England, and of our American Church, is the natural outgrowth of the Anglican Reformation; conducted at that day (in contra-distinction to the Lutheran), by the constituted authorities of the Church, within the Church, and on strictly Church principles. It was a protest against papal assumptions of power—papal perversions of the the truth—papal usages and ceremonies, onerous, superfluous and derogatory to spiritual worship on the one hand; and a re-asserting of the primitive faith, and a reestablishing, as far as the times would permit, of primitive discipline and purity of worship on the other.

The necessity for the continuance of the Protestant feature of our Church, will exist as long as the causes exists which gave birth to Protestantism. So long as the Bishop of Rome usurps the jurisdiction which he now claims—so long as the creed of Pope Pius the IV,—the decrees of the Council of Trent, and the dogmas recently promulgated by the so-called Œcumenical Council, are enforced as the true articles of faith, the belief in which is necessary to salvation: and so long as that Church, by its excessive, superstituous and puerile ritual, has destroyed almost the simplicity and spirituality of divine worship; so long, must we, as a Protestant Church stand firmly by our Protestantism; for never were these errors more rife, these claims more arrogant, these ceremonies more deceitful and soul destroying.

It was not, therefore, without specific design that the word "PROTESTANT," was first introduced into the title of our Church, in "A declaration of certain fundamental rights and liberties of the Protestant Episcopal Church of Maryland," by the framer of that declaration, Dr. Wm. Smith, the first Bishop-elect of Maryland.

As we read over that "Declaration," drawn up and issued by the clergy in Maryland, in August, 1783; and "The fundamental rules adopted by the clergy and laity of Pennsylvania in May, 1784; and the Act of Association of the Protestant Episcopal Church in the State of Pennsylvania in May, 1785; and other similar documents pertaining to the formation of the several Dioceses, and of the General Convention: we observe how distinctively are brought out the points which I have already mentioned, as marking the rightful and true meaning of the word *Protestant*, as a distinguishing term of our American branch of the Holy Catholic Church.

To this sound Protestantism our whole Church is fully committed by *name*, by *Constitution*, by *Doctrine*, by *Discipline*, by *Liturgy*; and every person, who by baptism becomes a member of our Church, is entitled to that distinctive teaching and ritual, which the word Protestant indicates and enjoins.

Hence everything, be it a rite, ceremony, or doctrine, which would take the Church back to the errors which the Anglican reformers removed and protested against, is to be reprobated and resisted by the laity.

Everything, which would make us as a Church conform to the "Uses" which have been deliberately laid aside by the Mother Church, and which have never been adopted by our own, is also to be guarded against as innovating upon the right of the laity to a Protestant service. They can claim at the hands of the clergy whatever that word 'Protestant,' when rightfully interpreted in accordance with our Constitution, Canons and Liturgy requires; and every attempt to bring back into the Church ceremonies or rites which were deliberately cast aside by the framers of our Liturgy, is, to that extent an Un-Protestantizing of our Church, which the laity should carefully watch and firmly resist.

The attempt made in certain quarters to decry Protestantism as a "failure," and to ignore it as a name of our Church, is based on a false view of Protestantism, and is as illogical in its reasoning as it is untrue in its conclusions. The Protestantism recognized in our Church by her standards and formularies is, as I have stated, essential to its growth and purity. Take away from our Church the Protest against excessive, needless, and puerile services which it makes by its reformed and simple ritual, and we are remanded back to the old Church books before the Reformation, which are described in the Statute of 1549, which abolished them as "Antiphones Missals, Grayles Processionals, Manuals, Legends, Pies Portuasses, Primers," etc. Take away from our Church that Protest which it makes against the errors of the Church of Rome, as specified in several of the 39 Articles, and as indicated in many of our rubrics, and we open the door to the elevating of the Apocrypha to the level of Canonical Scripture; to the denial of the sufficiency of the Holy Scriptures for salvation; to the placing along side of the Nicene and Apostles' Creeds, the Creed of Pius IV.; to the denial of the justification of man before God only for the merit of our Lord and Saviour Jesus Christ; and to a recanting of the declaration made in no less than twenty of the 39 Articles against the errors and deceits of the Church of Rome. Take away from our Sacraments, as set forth in our offices of administration that Protest, which our Church, in these offices, makes against the Canon of the Mass as performed in the Roman Church, and we shall be required to believe the doctrine of transubstantiation, with all those resulting dogmas which our 31st Article truly calls "blasphemous fables and dangerous deceits."

Take away from our Church the Protest which she makes in her 22d Article, in which she declares that "the Romish doctrine concerning purgatory, pardons, worshipping and adoration as well of images as of relics, and also invocation of saints, is a fond thing vainly invented, grounded upon no warranty of Scripture and repugnant to the word of God," and you open the door to the admission of all these insidious and soul-destroying errors which circle around these denounced dogmas.

Are we prepared for this, and much more that must necessarily follow, if we dissect out of Articles, and Liturgy, their distinctive Protestant character and teaching? Yet this is what the decriers of Protestantism would fain do, and what some are even seeking to do, by steathily filching away one principle of the Reformation after another, and by abjuring the so-termed "hated name," as one of the terms by which our Church is known.

We cannot be too much on our guard against the acts and the teachings of men who, while they have solemnly promised conformity to the doctrine, discipline, and worship of the *Protestant* Episcopal Church, yet covertly seek to destroy her Protestantism, and substitute therefor, a bastard Catholicity, which is neither Scriptural, unchangeable, or universal.

Thus we find in the very fore-front of our Prayer Book the recognition of these three great rights of the Laity, viz.: their right to a *Common* Prayer; their right to an *American* "*Use;*" and their right to a *Protestant* Church.

Turning now from the Book of Common Prayer to the Legislative history of the Church, we find in the Constitution and Canons of the General and of Diocesan

Conventions, the existence of many important rights and duties belonging to the Laity. The first suggestion of introducing the lay element into the Councils of the American Church was by Dr. Wm. White, in a pamphlet, "The Case of the Episcopal Church in the United States considered," 1782. In 1784 Dr. White suggested to the Rev. Dr. Magaw, Rector of St. Paul's Church, Philadelphia, the carrying out of these views into actual practice, and the conversation resulted in a meeting of the Clergy of the Parishes of Christ Church, St. Peter's and St. Paul's, with two laymen appointed from each of these Parishes at the house of Dr. White, on the 29th of March, 1784.

The object of this meeting was to take into consideration the necessity of speedily adopting measures for the forming of a plan of ecclesiastical government for the Episcopal Church."

This was followed by a large meeting at the same place on the evening of March 31st, at which it was resolved " as preparatory to a general consultation," to " request the Church Wardens and Vestrymen of each Episcopal congregation in the State to delegate one or more of their body to assist at a meeting to be held in this City on Monday, the 24th day of May next; and such Clergymen as have parochial cure in the said congregation to attend the meeting," etc.

At this meeting there were present 4 Clergymen and 21 Laymen, representing 16 different Churches. Two most important principles were established by the action of this body. One, stated in the 5th of the fundamental principles, " that Canons and laws be made only by the authority of a representative body of the Clergy and

Laity conjointly;" and the other, stated in the 6th Resolution, "that no powers be delegated to a general ecclesiastical government, except such as cannot conveniently be exercised by the Clergy and Vestries in their respective congregations." This, says Bishop White (Memoirs of the Church 86), was the first ecclesiastical assembly in any of the States consisting partly of Lay members. He then devotes several pages of his " Memoirs of the Church " to the reasons which caused him to propose such a measure as Lay representation in the Pamphlet already alluded to, and ably defends a measure which has been productive of such blessing to our American Church.

This meeting was followed by others, culminating, so far as Pennsylvania was concerned, in " An act of association of the Clergy and congregations of the Protestant Episcopal Church in the State of Pennsylvania, signed in Christ Church, Philadelphia, on the 24th of May, 1785, in which it was determined " that the Clergy and Lay deputies in convention shall deliberate in one body, but shall vote as two distinct orders, and that the concurrence of both orders shall be necessary to give validity to every measure."

Similar meetings, endorsing generally the principles already referred to, were held in New York, New Jersey, Massachusetts, Rhode Island, Virginia, Maryland, and in South Carolina. In the latter State, at the first meeting in May, 1785, a Layman, Hugh Rutledge, Esq., a deputy from St. Philip's, Charleston, was elected chairman.

The way was thus gradually prepared for a more comprehensive organization. Accordingly "on the 27th of September, 1785, there assembled agreeably to appointment in Philadelphia, a convention of clerical and lay deputies from 7 of the 13 "States," (White's Memoir, 22), viz. New York, New Jersey, Pennsylvania, Delaware, Maryland, Virginia, and South Carolina. This Convention on the 4th of October, adopted a "Constitution," drafted by Doctor White, which embodied the grand principle of co-ordinate lay representation, both in Diocesan and General Conventions. This Convention also, in the most marked manner, showed how it regarded the lay element as having equal rights with the clerical, in determining the faith and worship of the Church, by adopting a resolution "that a committee be appointed consisting of one clerical and one lay deputy, from the Church in each State, to consider of and report such alterations in the Liturgy, as shall render it consistent with the American Revolution and the Constitutions of the respective States, and such further alterations in the Liturgy as it may be advisable for this Convention to recommend to the consideration of the Church here represented." Several changes were made in this Constitution, until it reached its present form in 1789, but none affecting the rights of the laity, which were strictly secured and guarded, both in Diocesan and General Conventions. Indeed, so complete is the power of the laity, that according to the true and original words of the 2d Article of the Constitution of 1789,* *one* layman, if he chance to be the sole representative of a Diocese, can call for a vote by orders, which vote gives to the laity the power of

---

*Note.—vide Hawkes and Perry's Reprint, 99. Dr. F. Vinton's Manual, 190.

controlling the action of the House of Clerical and Lay Deputies, and thus the right of the clergy and laity respectively are placed by this article of the Constitution in their own keeping and protection.

Thus the laity have the *legislative* right, in connection with the clergy, to make the Constitution and the Canons of the General and Diocesan Conventions.

They have the *liturgical* right, in connection with the the clergy, to establish the forms of divine worship, and the rites and ceremonies appointed to be used therein.

They have the *elective* right, in connection with the clergy, to choose the Bishop, and Standing Committees of the respective Dioceses, and the Domestic and Foreign Missionary Bishops.

They have the *administrative* right, in connection with the clergy, to select the fields of labour and the men to work them, in the Domestic and Foreign missions of the Church, both as it respects the Board of Missions of the General Church, and the two Executive Committees by which the plans of the General Board are carried into effective operations.

They have the *educational* right, in connection with the clergy, to direct in the management of the General Theological Seminary, and also, in all Diocesan Divinity Schools for the training of young men for the ministry. Yet Dr. Pusey,* speaks of this action of the American Church, as an "unhappy precedent made in very evil times," as "radically wrong," and says that by so doing, "she has abandoned a bulwark of the faith, a function of the office inherited by the Bishops," though he kindly declares, that she has not thereby forfeited her claim to

---

* Councils of the Church, p. 24 *et seq.*

be a part of the Church,—and that she has not abandoned "the faith itself, nor the Apostolic Succession."

In this same work (p. 27) Dr. Pusey says, "The admission of laymen to a co-ordinate voice in councils, on the faith, is not an heretical act, yet it is an innovation upon that rule which the inspired Apostles left with the Church. To depart from this rule, must need be the commencement of a perilous course, the issue of which God alone knoweth, and from which may He preserve us."

These statements of Dr. Pusey have been most completely refuted by the learned Bishop of Maryland,[*] and he has shown conclusively, that not only did we not adopt any new principle unknown to the Church of England,—not only did we not adopt any new principle in itself considered, but that "all which was undertaken or done, was to provide under the new circumstances in which we were placed, for the carrying out a principle inherited from the Mother Church."

Before I leave this point there is one other remark which I desire to make. Dr. Pusey, in the same volume from which I have been quoting, says, "It is true that laymen were present at the council of Jerusalem," but he adds, "it is also true that the council of Jerusalem was infallible, to which infallibility these laymen could not add anything, and so could not in truth add anything to the council itself." p. 29. "The people were present at the council of Jerusalem but to hear and obey the words of God delivered through the Apostles' mouth to them, and the whole Church of God." p. 30.

This assertion, it seems to me, only gives greater force

---

*Art. 1, Jan. 1858, Church Review.

to the claims of the laity, for if in the first council ever held—if in a council consisting in part of the Apostles of our Lord, men specially commissioned by Christ, and filled with the Holy Ghost—if in a council which legislated for all the then Christian Churches, laymen were admitted, and the decrees of said council were issued in the name of the *Brethren*, as well as "Apostles and Elders," how much more may they claim the right to sit in councils, which are not infallible, as that was, and where the chosen Apostles of Jesus are not present. An element which James, Peter, John, Paul and Barnabas, recognized and honoured by associating it with their own power and authority, in sending forth the first conciliar decrees, ought not to be set aside or depressed, or be spoken of as "an innovation upon that rule which the inspired Apostles left with the Church," for no such '*rule*' can be shown, and in the words of Hooker,* "till it be proved that some special law of Christ hath forever annexed unto the clergy alone, the power to make ecclesiastical laws, we are to hold it a thing most consonant with equity and reason, that no ecclesiastical laws be made in a Christian Commonwealth, without consent as well of the laity as of the clergy."

In connection with this subject of Lay-rights comes up the question, can the Vestry dismiss a regularly Instituted or settled minister? The present legislation of the Church upon this subject, in cases where no charges are preferred, and which do not come therefore under the Canon (2 Title II.) entitled, "Of Offences for which a Minister may be Tried and Punished," is found

*Eccl. Polity, Book viii, 508.

in The Institution Office and in Canon 4, Title II. of the Digest.

The letter or address of Institution given by the Bishop says, *inter alia*, " We authorize you to claim and enjoy all the accustomed temporalities appertaining to your cure, until some urgent reason or reasons occasion a wish in you or in the congregation committed to your charge, to bring about a separation and dissolution of all sacerdotal relation between you and them ; of all which you will give us due notice: and in case of any difference between you and your congregation as to a separation and dissolution of all sacerdotal connection between you and them, we, your Bishop, with the advice of our Presbyters, are to be the ultimate arbiter and judge." This is plain and explicit.

The Bishop alone has not the full power of arbitrating and judging, as Presbyters must be associated with him. It does not say how many Presbyters, nor how they shall be selected ; but as §II. Canon 2, Title III., declares that " In every Diocese, where there is a Bishop, the Standing Committee shall be a Council of advice to the Bishop," and as in every Diocese one-half of this Standing Committee (and in one Diocese, all,) is composed of Presbyters, so the provision of the Institution Office will be duly complied with when the Bishop calls in the aid of the Presbyters of his official council of advice.

While the office, in its legal force, is only binding on those clergy and parishes where the Minister has been Instituted by it, it yet annunciates two principles, which are of special value :

1st. That for a certain " reason or reasons " this relation may be dissolved ; and these reasons may be found either in the Minister or in the congregation, implying that the congregation have an equal right with the Rector to seek a separation of parochial ties; and it also implies that either party may take the initiative in effecting such separation, due notice of the same being given to the Bishop, but no formal action being required of the Bishop.

2d. In "case of any difference" between the Rector and congregation as to separation, then the whole matter is to be referred to the Bishop, and he, with the advice of his Presbyters, is to be the sole arbiter and judge. The interposition of the Bishop and Presbyters is conditioned on the difference between the Rector and the Parish.

From the words of this letter of Institution, then, I gather the following points:

1. That the Rector, upon some urgent reason or reasons, may, with the consent of his congregation and "due notice" to the Bishop, dissolve his connection with the Parish.

2. That the Parish, upon some urgent reason or reasons, may, with the consent of the Rector and after "due notice" to the Bishop, dissolve their relation with their Rector.

3. But when differences arise on either part, then the whole matter is to be laid before the Bishop, who, with the advice of his Presbyters, is to be the sole arbiter and judge in the case; this decision is to be imperative and binding on both Clergy and Laity.

Such is the law in reference to Instituted Ministers. This Institution Office, however, is not an obligatory one. It can be used, not at the instance or wish of the

Clergy alone, but only "at the instance of the Vestry' (par. 3, § 1, Can. 12, Title I); thus the Laity of the Church must be the first to ask for it; and furthermore, the conditional words, "if that Office be used in that Diocese" (*ibid*), implies the right of a Diocese to decline its use, and the existence of Dioceses where it is not used. Furthermore, there must be not only a Parish but a "house of worship" (*ibid*), otherwise this Office cannot be used. Further still, a Deacon cannot be Instituted, the Office can be used only for those who "have received Priests' Orders," yet according to par. 1, § II, Canon 6, Title I, a Deacon who "shall have satisfactorily passed the three examinations required for Priests' Orders," can "be settled over a Parish or congregation."

So much for the law as it regards the Institution Office.

The only other law upon this subject is found in Canon 4, Title II, of the Digest, entitled, "Of the Dissolution of a Pastoral Connection."

Prior to 1859, there was another Canon on this subject (XXXIV. of 1832, XXXII. of 1808, IV. of 1804), entitled, "Of differences between Ministers and their congregations," which had special reference to cases of controversy between Ministers and the Vestry or congregations, which controversies were of such a nature as could not be settled by themselves.

The Canon then pointed out how the parties were to proceed, how they were to bring the case before the Bishop and Presbyters, and the penalties attached to a refusal to accept their decision or comply with their recommendation.

This Canon, made in 1804 to meet a special case, continued on our Statute Book fifty-five years, when it was repealed by the action of the House of Clerical and Lay Deputies, and said repeal was concurred in by the House of Bishops, in October, 1859. This repeal left in our Digest only one Canon on this point, the one entitled "Of the Dissolution of a Pastoral Connection."

The very title of the Canon shows that the Pastoral connection may be dissolved, and the subject matter of the Canon states what shall be the penalty to both parties, in case the relation is dissolved, other than in the canonical way. "In case a Minister, who has been regularly instituted or settled in a parish or Church, be dismissed by such Parish or Church, without the concurrence of the Ecclesiastical authority of the Diocese, the vestry or congregation of such parish or Church, shall have no right to a representation in the Convention of the Diocese, until they have made such satisfaction as the Convention may require."

Here it is directly implied that the parish or Church can dismiss a Minister *with* the concurrence of the ecclesiastical authority, and incur thereby no penalty.

The question here arises, what is meant by the term "The Ecclesiastical authority of the Diocese." The answer to this question is found in § iii. Canon 2, Title III, of the Digest, which says, "when there is no Bishop the Standing Committee is the Ecclesiastical Authority for all purposes declared in these Canons," from which it follows, that where there is a Bishop, *he* is the ecclesiastical authority for all purposes declared in these Canons, unless specially excepted.

Another question may arise, viz., Is the dismissal of

a Minister by a vestry the same as being dismissed by
"a parish or Church?"

Ordinarily, the 'vestry' represent in all things, the
corporation, Parish, Church, congregation. The vestry elect the Minister, fix his salary, and are responsible
for his support. The vestry elect deputies to the Diocesan Convention. Through the vestry only, when there
is no Rector, does the ecclesiastical authority communicate with the several churches or parishes, and the law
knows of and recognizes Episcopal Churches or parishes,
or congregtions, only through the vestries of the same,
upon which body it would serve its processes, and by the
acts of which body its corporate action would be valid
and legal. Thus, for every purpose of parochial action,
having reference to ecclesiastical or civil law, the vestry
is the acknowledged exponent, and its acts are esteemed
and counted as the acts of the parish or Church. So
far as I remember, there is no provision in any form
of charter used in this Diocese, or act of incorporation
granted by our Courts, for calling together the communicants or the parishioners, to take action on any
question of a parochial character, other than that which
provides for the assembling for the Easter elections. I
do not say that it is not lawful to convene the congregation or parish for any parochial purpose when the
Rector or vestry may deem it to be proper, but that
there is no express provision in the charter for so doing, and therefore, as by the charter, the right of electing a Minister is vested in the vestry, and as by the
charter, the vestry are custodians of all the interests
which affects the temporality of the Church, and as in
several instances, in different dioceses, this right of the

vestry, acting in conjunction with the ecclesiastical authority, to sever this parochial connection, has been fully recognized; hence I believe that the act of the vestry is legally and properly the act of the parish or church, and when they act under this Canon, it is the "parish or Church" which acts, through that selected and accredited body, through and by which, it has its corporate and legal title and existence.

This Canon, as it will be seen, contemplates no charges against a minister and no trial for offences, and "applies" as Dr. Hawks' (Constitution and Canons, 307) says, "to nothing but the single case of a desire for separation, which may exist without any other disagreement between the parties."

This Canon, while it guards the right of the clergy against the wrong action of a vestry, by referring the matter to the ecclesiastical authority, at the same time protects the right of the laity to have over them in the Lord, a Rector in whose character and ministry they can have confidence and peace. This right of the laity is further protected by the fact, that the minister cannot resign his parish against the wishes of his people, and without the concurrence of the ecclesiastical authority, without incurring severe penalties.

Thus, the Canon works equally for both parties. Protecting the Rector from the hasty dismissal of the vestry, and the vestry from the hasty resignation of the Rector, and both parties have an ultimate appeal. In reference to this whole matter, it should ever be borne in mind that the Church was not made for the clergy, but the clergy for the Church, and both for Christ's glory; and that there are cases, where the purity and

18

honor and prosperity of the Church would be best sub-
served by the severance of pastoral ties, and where it is
the bounden duty of the vestry to take such canonical
action as shall secure such severance.

Thus we see that in all departments of Church law
and Church work, from the charter which incorporates
a Parish to the framing or abolishing of rubrics in the
Prayer Book by the General Convention, there ever exists between the Clergy and the Laity a joint legislative
and administrative power. There is, however, such a
system of checks and counter-checks, that neither can
carry out any plan to the exclusion of the other, and
only by united action can any measure be established.

"Let us never forget," says the present Archbishop of
Canterbury, "that there is some truth in the common
saying, that there is a clergyman's and there is a layman's mode of looking at almost every one of the great
questions of the day. The Clergy and the Laity will
each be likely to gain a clear view of truth and duty
by taking into account the feelings and reasonings which
prevail in the class to which they themselves do not belong. Laity and Clergy alike, we are all engaged in
one common work, and though we may view it in different aspects, we require each other's help in doing it,
and we shall not, I trust, fail to have each other's prayers."[*]

The wisdom of these words has been daily illustrated
in the practical working of the American Church. The
reflex influence of our Church Constitution which incorporates and vivifies these rights of the Laity, and sur-
rounds them with the guards and counter-poises of

_____
*Charge as Bishop of London.

clerical co-partnership, is already beginning to influence the Church in the Old World.

The Mother Church of England and the Sister Church of Scotland, are seeking in various ways to introduce the Lay element into their convocations and councils. The Sister Church of Ireland, disestablished on the 1st of January last, by act of Parliament, has adopted the leading features of the Constitution of the American Church, especially in those parts which give a certain co-ordinate authority and power to the lay portion of the Church. Not long since I received from the Secretary of "The Church of Ireland Representative Body," the Constitution of the Church of Ireland, being the statutes passed at the first General Convention of that body; and the very first statute is in these words: " The General Synod of the Church of Ireland shall consist of three orders, viz: the Bishops, the Clergy and the Laity." Here we see the principle which Bishop White was the first to introduce into the Constitution of the American Church, adopted by the First Convention of the Church in Ireland. Not only so, but we find all through the declarations and statutes of this body, the leading ideas which are embodied in the fundamental laws of our Church; such as the division of the legislative body into two houses, the right of vote by Orders, the election by the respective Dioceses of their Bishops, the annual session of the Diocesan Synods, and the election by the parochial or other constituencies of the members composing the Synod.

The Church of England in her colonies has in many instances copied these main features of our Constitution, and the Anglican Communion throughout the world is yearning for, and gradually working up its way to, the incorporating of the lay element with the clerical in those points where they can be lawfully helpful in the legislation and administration of the Church of Christ. We believe that such principles are in accordance with the teachings of the New Testament; that they best secure the rights of the individual conscience, and the rights of private judgment; that they furnish a just balance and check to sacerdotal ambition, and that false dogma which would make the Church to be in the clergy a dogma which is the basis of the Papal hierarchy.

These principles furnish a guarantee for a broad and healthy legislation for all portions of the Church, and devolve upon the laity a responsibility and a duty, which require of them thought and wisdom, and prudence, and prayer, that they may discharge aright the burdens thus laid upon them, as co-workers with the clergy in the Lord's vineyard.

Finally, these principles tend to bring out into strong relief, that idea of the "Personal Priesthood of the Believer," by which all lay people become in one sense, Priests unto God, a holy Priesthood, the depositaries of a spiritual power, which enables each one to say with the Apostle, "I can do all things through Christ strengthening me."[*]

What a power then is lodged in the lay element of the Church! And what need there is that it should be an enlightened, a wise, and a calmly administered power! To this end the Church owes it to herself that all who legislate for her, be it in a Vestry, a Standing Committee, a Diocesan or General Convention, should be com-

---

*Moberly's Bampton Lectures, 1868, viii. Lect.

municants of good standing. This is a point that all Parishes should look to, in choosing Vestrymen, that all Vestries should look to, in choosing Deputies to the Diocesan Convention, and all Diocesan Councils should look to, in electing Delegates to the Triennial General Convention.

For, as the civil law allows no man to hold an office in the State, unless he is a citizen of the same, so the Church should allow no man to sit in her lesser or greater legislative assemblies, who has not "openly before the Church" made a public profession of his faith in Christ, and sealed that profession with the Holy Communion.

The Laity themselves, in view of their great responsibility, should carefully prepare themselves to discharge these duties, not only by cultivating the graces which make up Christian character, but also by acquiring such an amount of theological, ecclesiastical, and canonical knowledge, as will enable them to act understandingly, and legislate wisely, on the important questions which now, and will hereafter, agitate the Church. The effect of our system has already been to train up many admirable and astute canonists and legislators, and to call into the service of our General Convention the ablest minds of the Laity. It may safely be said, that in no religious body is there, in proportion to its communicants, such a number of well-read men in biblical and canonical matters, as there are in the Protestant Episcopal Church. The very Constitution of our Church, and the details of its workings, through all its ramifications, call out lay talent and lay effort. They are thus educated up to this active agency, and beginning in the humble sphere of the Vestry, and going up thence to the annual Convention, and thence on to the Standing Committee, thence on to the Board of Missions, and thence, by a selection which takes but four choice men out of each Diocese, up to the Triennial Council of the General Church, they are taught and trained in the various successive duties, of the several stages through which they pass.

In addition to this, our Church has become a teacher to her sister and her mother churches. Looking at first upon our plan with distrust, if not with positive condemnation, the whole Anglican Church from Canterbury to Montreal, in the North; and Australia in the South; has been intently watching our experiment. As the English Bishops, and Clergy and Statesmen have seen their fears and prognostications give way before recognized facts, they have changed their views, and are seeking, with certain modifications, and so far as their peculiar institutions will permit, to conform their legislative and synodical action to our own. It is not, perhaps, too bold a speech to say, that there are those here before me who will live to see the Church of England, the Church of Scotland, the Church in India, the Church as synodically organized in the colonies of Great Britain, all detached from State alliance, all organized on the principle of complete self-government, all exercising full and unfettered ecclesiastical power, all having received back the right to choose their Bishops, and all incorporating the lay element in the judicial and legislative and administrative work of the Church of Christ.

I have thus, dear brethren, set before you, though with

conscious imperfection, the important subject of the reciprocal and inherent rights of the Clergy and Laity in the Protestant Episcopal Church.

God hath joined the Clergy and the Laity together in the mystical body of his dear Son. God hath made them joint heirs of the grace that is in Christ Jesus and of the kingdom of heaven. God, who has wisely appointed divers orders in the Church, hath set them together in their several vocations and ministries in Vestries, Conventions and Councils, and let not man put asunder this divinely united power.

What is necessary in order that the Church may derive the highest benefit of these co-ordinate powers is, there should be a full recognition of each of the rights of the other—a strict guard against infringing the one or the other, a concentration of the efforts of both upon the one great end of advancing Christ s kingdom, and that mutual charity, moderation and forbearance, by which misunderstandings will be prevented, unity be preserved, and the highest effectiveness be secured. God grant that the time may never come when the two shall be arrayed, the one against the other.

Let us remember that we all, Clergy and Laity, are engaged in one and the same work—the building of the spiritual House of God. That the walls of this building being laid on the corner-stone Christ Jesus, and on the foundation of Apostles and Prophets, have been gradually framed and fashioned, age after age, by what Lord Bacon well calls " the holy wisdom and spiritual discretion of the master builders and inferior builders in Christ's Church."* That in the erection of this spir-

* Works, ii., 512.

ritual temple, the Laity have their appointed work as well as the Clergy; and that if the Clergy, by reason of their Divine commission, may be called " the wise master-builders;" the Laity may also be termed " builders"—inferior, indeed, in a proportionate manner, as to the time and talents given to the work, but still "builders," still " co-workers," still helping on the building as it " groweth into an holy temple of the Lord."

And when the top-stone of this spiritual edifice shall be brought forth at its completion, then shall the Divine Architect, who has subsidized all this various talent and agency, give to Clergy and Laity alike their due reward. Then shall we see, in the light of eternity, how that both were used for the upbuilding of His kingdom, which is an everlasting kingdom, and His dominion which shall never end, and in which heavenly kingdom the redeemed Clergy and Laity shall reign alike as Kings and Priests unto God forever.

APPENDIX B.

The Committee on Alterations of Canons, met within a fortnight after the adjournment of the Convention of 1870, and have since that meeting, met repeatedly. They respectfully report as follows:

Among the matters referred to this Committee, were two Resolutions, one proposing to strike from Canon XIII, so much as allows a Church to be admitted into union with the Convention, on the basis of "Articles of Association," and another, determining for Parishes the question who is to preside in Vestry and Parochial meetings. Your Committee unite in the opinion that neither of these restrictive measures is expedient.

Five other matters were referred to the Committee, viz., to suggest amendments to the Canon-law of the Diocese, where it conflicts with the Canon-law of the General Convention; to report with regard to the expediency of dispensing with the ballot, when there is but one ticket nominated; to consider the propriety of requiring an election of deputies to the General Convention to be made at only such Conventions of the Diocese as immediately precede the holding of a General Convention; to consider and report with respect to the mode of altering Canons; to review the Revised Regulations and such Resolutions as are to be found on the Journals, and report what modification or change seems to be required.

Your Committee, besides submitting a document exhibiting the result of their deliberations, at length, in the form they would propose, respectfully recommend the passage of the following resolutions:

1. That in Section 1 of Canon VI, the passage beginning "And to entitle him to such testimonial," and ending "to the Standing Committee thereof," be stricken out, as conflicting with Title 1, Canon XII, Section 7 of the Digest.

2. That Canon VII, Section 1, be amended to read as follows: "At every Stated Convention a Standing Committee, to consist of five of the clergy and five of the laity, shall be chosen by ballot, by the concurrent vote of the members of each order, provided, that the balloting may be dispensed with in cases where only five clergymen and five laymen are nominated. And vacancies occurring by death or otherwise, in said Committee, shall be supplied by the concurrent vote of the remaining clerical members and lay members of the Committee."

3. That in Canon XIV, the title be amended so as to read "Of Vacant Parishes," and that the first section be omitted.

4. That Canon XV, Section 1, be amended to read as follows: "At every Stated Convention of this Diocese, there *may*, and at the Stated Convention immediately preceding the stated General Convention, there *shall* be chosen by the concurrent ballot of the clerical and lay votes, Deputies to the General Convention, whose appointment shall continue until the next stated Convention, and until others are chosen in their places, provided that the balloting may be dispensed with, in cases where only four clergymen and four laymen are nominated.

5. That the following be added to the Canons of the Diocese, under the heading "Of Alterations in the Canon-Law."

1. On the first day of every Convention, a Committee, to consist of three clergymen and three laymen, and to be called the Committee on Canons, shall be appointed.

2. All proposals to alter, or add to the Constitution or the Canons of the Diocese, shall be referred to this Committee.

3. No existing Canon shall be changed, and no new Canon shall be enacted on the day on which the change or enactment may be proposed.

6. That Canon XVI (respecting the repeal of former Canons) be omitted.

7. That Resolutions of a permanent nature, which have been passed by former Conventions, viz.: the Resolutions concerning the establishment of the Diocesan Board of Missions; concerning the Convention, the Episcopal, and the Christmas Funds; concerning draughts on these funds by the Bishop and the Standing Committee; be incorporated with the Canons, after striking out therefrom, so much as requires the election of the Treasurer of the Convention, to be made by ballot, and making such merely verbal changes as may be necessary.

8. That Revised Regulations I, 1, be amended so that it shall read simply, "The Convention shall meet at five o'clock P. M., on the day appointed.

I, 2, so that the section shall be without the words "it shall proceed in the despatch of business."

I, 4, 4, omit "without advancing."

I, 4, 13, omit the whole.

Invert the order of I, 4, and I, 5.

Change I, 5, 3, so as to read "appointment of Committees, viz.: Committee on Charters, Committee on claims of Clergymen to Seats, Committee on claims of Deputies to Seats, Committee on Canons, Committee on Parochial History."

Add to I, 5, the following:

"3. The above Order of Business and Rules of Order may

be suspended by a vote of two thirds of the members present, but not otherwise."

Omit Revised Regulations, IV.

Make Revised Regulations V. a foot note to Canon XIII.

Omit Revised Regulations VI. 1, 2, 3, also VII.

9. That in the Form of Charter, in the third paragraph, the phrase "State of Pennsylvania" be exchanged for the phrase "Diocese of Pennsylvania."

10. That the Revised Regulations, amended as above, shall be incorporated with the Canons.

11. That the order of the Canons be so changed that such incongruities as the precedence now given to penal matters may be avoided.

12. That there be prefixed to the Act of Association, Constitution, and Canons, a Table of Contents.

13. That one thousand copies of the Act of Association, the Constitution, and the Canons (the last as by the above Resolutions amended), be printed under the direction of this Committee.

And whereas, the Resolution of the Convention providing for the annual appointment of a Registrar (Journal of 1867, p. 61), seems to conflict with the Constitution, which gives the custody of records to the Secretary of the Convention, the Committee recommend the passage of an additional Resolution, to lie over, if approved, to the next Convention, viz.:

14. That the following words in the Sixth Article of the Constitution of the Protestant Episcopal Church in the Diocese of Pennsylvania, viz.: "to preserve their journals and records," be stricken out, provided the next Convention of the Diocese shall so decide.

On behalf of the Committee,

May 10, 1871.   G. EMLEN HARE.

CONSTITUTION AND CANONS OF THE PROTESTANT EPISCOPAL CHURCH IN THE DIOCESE OF PENNSYLVANIA.

Published by Order of the Convention.

*An Act *of Association of the Clergy and Congregations of the Protestant Episcopal Church in the State of Pennsylvania.*

Whereas, By the late Revolution, the Protestant Episcopal Church in the United States of *America* is become independent of the ecclesiastical jurisdiction in *England ;* in consequence whereof, it is necessary for the clergy and congregations of the said Church to associate themselves for maintaining uniformity in divine worship, for procuring the power of Ordination, and for establishing and maintaining a system of ecclesiastical government ;

And whereas, At a meeting of sundry Clergymen and Lay Deputies from sundry congregations of the Protest-

---

* *Resolved,* That the President, the Rev. Dr. Magaw, the Rev. Mr. Campbell, Mr. Shippen and Mr. Hand, be a committee to prepare an Act of Association of the Clergy and Congregations of the Protestant Episcopal Church in the State of Pennsylvania, who shall meet in Convention.

The Committee was instructed to regard the following points as fundamentals for their proceedings, they having been unanimously agreed to by the Convention :

First. That the Clergy and Lay Deputies vote as two distinct orders.

Second. That a Clergyman cannot vote as the representative of his particular church ; but that a Lay Deputy or Deputies be sent to represent each congregation.

Third. That each congregation be entitled to a vote ; and that where two congregations are united, each congregation shall be entitled to a vote, and shall send a Deputy or Deputies.

Fourth. That the Convention meet annually, on such day as shall be declared in a law or rule, to be made by the next Convention for that purpose ; and that the next meeting shall be held in Christ Church, Philadelphia, on Monday, the 22d day of May, 1786, at 11 o'clock, A. M.

Fifth. That such of the members of the Convention as are met on the day of the annual meeting, shall be a quorum ; in which quorum the votes of the majority shall be decisive.— Journal of 1785, p. 11.

ant Episcopal Church in this State, held in the city of *Philadelphia*, on the 25th day of *May*, in the year of our Lord 1784, there was appointed a Committee to confer and correspond with representatives from the Church in the other States, for the purpose of constituting an ecclesiastical government, agreeably to certain instructions or fundamental principles; [*]

And whereas, The said Committee being assembled in the city of *New York*, on the 6th and 7th days of *October*, in the same year, did concur with Clergymen and Lay Deputies from sundry States, in proposing a Convention from all the States, to be held in the city of *Philadelphia*, on the *Tuesday* before the feast of *St. Michael* next ensuing, in order to unite in an ecclesiastical constitution, agreeably to certain fundamental principles expressed in the said proposal; [†]

And whereas, The body which assembled as aforesaid in *New York* did recommend to the Church in the several States, that previously to the said intended meeting, they should organize or associate themselves, agreeably to such rules as they shall think proper:

---

[*] Which are as follows:

First. That the Episcopal Church in these United States is, and ought to be, independent of all foreign authority, ecclesiastical or civil.

Second. That it hath, and ought to have, in common with all other religious societies, full and exclusive power to regulate the concerns of its own communion.

Third. That the doctrines of the gospel be maintained as now professed by the Church of *England*; and uniformity of worship be continued, as near as may be, to the Liturgy of the said Church.

Fourth. That the succession of the ministry be agreeable to the usage which requireth the three orders of Bishops, Priests and Deacons; that the rights and powers of the same respectively be ascertained; and that they be exercised according to reasonable laws to be duly made.

Fifth. That to make canons or laws, there be no other authority than that of a representative body of the Clergy and Laity conjointly.

Sixth. That no powers be delegated to a general ecclesiastical government, except such as cannot conveniently be exercised by the Clergy and Laity in their respective congregations.

[†] Which are as follows:

First. That there be a General Convention of the Episcopal Church in the United States of *America*.

It is therefore hereby determined and declared by the Clergy who do now or who hereafter shall sign this act, and by the congregations who do now or who hereafter shall consent to this act, either by its being ratified by their respective vestries, or by its being signed by their Deputies duly authorized, that the said Clergy and congregations shall be called and known by the name of *The Protestant Episcopal Church in the State of Pennsylvania.*

And it is hereby further determined and declared by the said Clergy and congregations, That there shall be a Convention of the said Church; which Convention shall consist of all the Clergy of the same, and of Lay Deputies; and that all the acts and proceedings of said Convention shall be considered as the acts and proceedings of the Protestant Episcopal Church in this State; *Provided always*, That the same shall be consistent with

---

Second. That the Episcopal Church in each State send Deputies to the Convention, consisting of Clergy and Laity.

Third. That associated congregations, in two or more States, may send Deputies jointly.

Fourth. That the said Church shall maintain the doctrines of the gospel as now held by the Church of *England*, and shall adhere to the Liturgy of the said Church, as far as shall be consistent with the *American* Revolution, and the Constitution of the respective States.

Fifth. That in every State where there shall be a Bishop duly consecrated and settled, he shall be considered as a member of the Convention *ex officio.*

Sixth. That the Clergy and Laity, assembled in Convention, shall deliberate in one body, but shall vote separately, and the concurrence of both shall be necessary to give validity to every measure.

Seventh. That the first meeting of the Convention shall be at *Philadelphia*, the *Tuesday* before the feast of *St. Michael* next; to which it is hoped and earnestly desired, that the Episcopal Churches in the respective States will send their Clerical and Lay Deputies, duly instructed and authorized to proceed on the necessary business herein proposed for their deliberation.

In compliance with the last article, the following persons are appointed, viz.: *Clerical Deputies*—The Rev. Drs. White and Magaw, and the Rev. Messrs Blackwell, Hutchins and Campbell. *Lay Deputies*—Messrs. Richard Peters, Gerardus Clarkson, Samuel Powell, William Atlee, Jasper Yates, Stephen Chambers, Edward Hand, Thomas Heartly, John Clarke, Archibald McGrew, Plunket Fleeson, Edward Shippen, Joseph Swift, Andrew Doz, John Wood, Nicholas Jones and Edward Duffield.

the fundamental principles agreed on at the two afore-said meetings in *Philadelphia* and *New York*.

And it is hereby further determined and declared by the said Clergy and congregations, That each congregation may send to the Convention a Deputy or Deputies; and where two or more congregations are united, they may send a Deputy or Deputies for each congregation; and no congregation may send a Clergyman as their Deputy; and each congregation represented in Convention shall have one vote.

And it is hereby further determined and declared by the said Clergy and congregations, That the Clergy and Lay Deputies in Convention shall deliberate in one body, but shall vote as two distinct orders, and that the concurrence of both orders shall be necessary to give validity to every measure; and such Clergymen and Lay Deputies as shall at any time be duly assembled in Convention, shall be a quorum; and on every * question, the votes of the majority of those present of the two orders respectively, shall decide.

And it is hereby further determined and declared by the said Clergy and congregations, That all such Clergymen as shall hereafter be settled as the ministers of the congregations† ratifying this act, shall have the same privileges, and be subject to the same regulations, as the Clergy now subscribing the same.

And it is hereby further determined and declared by the said Clergy and congregations, That the Convention shall meet on *Monday*, the 22d day of *May*, in the year of our Lord 1786, and forever after on such annual day,

---

* Compare Constitution VI., VII. and IX.

† Compare Journal of 1786, p. 14, and Journal of 1790, pp. 24, 25.

and at such other times, and at such places, as shall be fixed by future rules of the Convention.

And it is hereby further determined and declared by the said Clergy and congregations, That if the Clergy and congregations of any adjoining State or States shall desire to unite with the Church in this State, agreeably to the fundamental principles established at the aforesaid meeting in *New York*, then the Convention shall have power to admit the said Clergy and Deputies from the congregations of such adjoining State or States, to have the same privileges, and to be subject to the same regulations as the Clergy and congregations in this State.

Done in Christ Church, in the city of Philadelphia, this 24th day of May, in the year of our Lord, 1785. Witness our hands, in ratification of the premises.*

WILLIAM WHITE, D. D., Rector of Christ Church and St. Peter's, in Philadelphia.

SAMUEL MAGAW, D. D., Rector of St. Paul's Church, Philadelphia.

ROBERT BLACKWELL, Assistant Minister of Christ Church and St. Peter's, Philadelphia.

JOSEPH HUTCHINS, Rector of St. James', Lancaster.

JOHN CAMPBELL, Rector of the Episcopal Churches of York and Huntingdon.

JOSEPH SWIFT, Deputy for Christ Church.

SAMUEL POWELL, GERARDUS CLARKSON, Deputies for St. Peter's Church.

PLUNKET FLEESON, JOHN WOOD, ANDREW DOZ, Deputies for St. Paul's Church.

---

*The signing of those Deputies who were sent to the Convention without written power, was deferred until such powers can be procured.

Edward Hand, Deputy for the congregation of St. James', Lancaster.

Nicholas Jones, Deputy for St. Gabriel's, Morlattin, Berks.

John Campbell, Deputy for the congregation of York and Huntingdon.

John Crosby, Jr., John Shaw, Deputies for St. Paul's Church, Chester.

SUPPLEMENT TO THE ACT OF ASSOCIATION.

Whereas, Doubts have arisen whether, under the Act of Association, any alterations can be made in the Book of Common Prayer and the Administration of the Sacraments, and other Rites and Ceremonies of the Church, except such as became necessary in consequence of the late Revolution:

It is, therefore, hereby determined and declared, That further alterations may be made by the Convention, constituted by the said Act, provided only that " the main body and essentials " be preserved, and alterations made in such forms only as the Church of *England* hath herself acknowledged to be indifferent and alterable.

And it is hereby further determined and declared, That the power given by this supplement to the Convention of the Protestant Episcopal Church in this State, may, by the said Convention, be conveyed to a Convention of the said Church in the United States, or in such States as are willing to unite in a constitution of ecclesiastical government, if the same shall be judged most conducive to charity and uniformity of worship.

Done in *Christ Church*, in the city of *Philadelphia*, this 27th day of *May*, in the year of our Lord 1786. Witness our hands in ratification of the premises.

CONSTITUTION.

ADOPTED IN 1814, AND SINCE AMENDED.

WHEREAS, By an Act of Association, agreed to and adopted in Convention, on the 24th day of May, 1785, sundry of the Protestant Episcopal Churches within this Commonwealth were united under the name of " The Protestant Episcopal Church in the State of Pennsylvania "—which Association now embraces all those Clergy and congregations who did at that time assent to, or have since assented to the same.

And whereas, Since that time, by General Conventions of the Protestant Episcopal Churches within the United States, a Constitution and Canons have been formed for the government and discipline of the same, which recognize each State as constituting a District or Diocese, with the right to the Churches within the same to exercise a local government over themselves, which has been accordingly exercised by the Protestant Episcopal Churches within the State of Pennsylvania, associated as aforesaid, and it being now deemed expedient more expressly to set forth the system of local government to be exercised within this Diocese, the following, with the Act of Association, is declared to be the Constitution of the Protestant Episcopal Church in the State of Pennsylvania:

I. This Church, as a constituent part of the Protestant Episcopal Church of the United States of America, accedes to, recognizes, and adopts the general Constitution of that Church, and acknowledges its authority accordingly.

II. There shall be a stated Convention of the Church in this State, at Philadelphia, on the first Tuesday in

May, in every year, unless a different time and place be fixed on by a preceding Convention.

III. The Bishop shall have power to call a special Convention when he may judge it conducive to the good of the Church, or when applied to for that purpose by the Standing Committee; and in case of a vacancy in the Episcopal chair, the Standing Committee shall have power to call a special Convention.

*IV. The Convention shall be composed of Clergymen and Laymen. The Bishop and Assistant Bishop, if there be one, shall have a seat and vote in the Convention. Every Clergyman of the Church, of whatever order, being a settled Minister of some Parish within this State, or being a president, professor, tutor, or instructor in some college, academy, or seminary of learning, incorporated by law, or being a missionary under the direction of the ecclesiastical authority of this Diocese, or a chaplain in the navy or army of the United States, or otherwise employed in the work of the ministry, according to the order of the Protestant Episcopal Church, and with the sanction of the ecclesiastical authority, shall be entitled to a seat and vote in Convention, if he has been actually and personally, as well as canonically, resident within this State for the space of six calendar months next before the meeting of the Convention, and has for the same period been employed in performing the duties of his station: *Provided*, That any temporary absence from the State by reason of sickness, and any such absence, not exceeding in the whole two calendar months in any one year, and any such absence with the written permission of the Bishop of this Diocese, or of the Standing Committee in

* This Article was amended in 1824, 1829, 1838, 1854 and 1855.

case of a vacancy in the Episcopal chair, shall be taken into account in computing the said residence: *And provided also*, That no Clergyman of advanced years or infirm health,* who has been once entitled to a seat in Convention, shall lose his right to a seat therein by reason of his having ceased to have charge of a Parish, or to be in the service of a seminary of learning, or to be a missionary as aforesaid.

No church shall be admitted a member of this Convention, which does not, by its charter or articles of association, expressly accede to the Constitution, Canons, doctrines, discipline, and worship of the Protestant Episcopal Church in the United States, and to the Constitution and Canons of the Protestant Episcopal Church in this Diocese.

Each regularly established Protestant Episcopal Church in this State, now a member, or which shall hereafter be admitted a member of the Convention, may send to the Convention a Lay Deputy or Deputies, not exceeding three in number, to be elected by the vestry of said Church: *Provided*, That no person shall be competent to serve as Deputy, unless he has been a worshipper in the church he represents six calendar months next before his election.†

When two or more churches are united under one vestry, Deputies may be sent from each church, subject to the proviso aforesaid.

The deputation from each church shall be entitled to one vote and no more.

---

* " *Resolved*. That no Clergyman shall be entitled to a seat in any Convention on the ground of inability to discharge the duties of a Parish on account of impaired health, unless such Clergyman shall, previously to each Convention, have satisfied the ecclesiastical authority of the fact, and the nature and probable continuance of the disease."—*Journal of* 1850. pp. 71–72.

† " *Resolved*, That the Churches of the Diocese be affectionately and earnestly requested to select their Deputies to the Convention from such of their people as ' come to the Holy Communion.'"—*Journal of* 1863, p. 84.

No deputation from any church shall be entitled to a vote at the same Convention at which the church shall be admitted as a member.

When any·church which has been admitted a member of the Convention of this Diocese shall, for three years, have made no parochial report to the same, no missionary report being made in its behalf, and, during the same period, shall neither have employed·a Clergyman as its parish minister, nor requested of the Bishop to have the services of a missionary, the said church shall no longer have a right to send a Deputy or Deputies to the Convention; and it shall be the duty of the Convention to declare the same. But any such church shall again acquire that right, if, on its application, accompanied with a report of its condition satisfactory on the points herein mentioned, the Convention shall agree thereto; and this right shall take effect from and after the rising of the Convention so agreeing.

V. The Bishop shall preside in the Convention; but in case of a vacancy or necessary absence, the members shall elect a president from among the Clergy.

*VI. A Secretary shall be chosen upon the assembling of the Annual Convention, from among the members thereof, who shall remain in office until the meeting of the next Convention. His duties shall be to take minutes of their proceedings, to preserve their journals and records, to attest the public acts of the body, and faithfully to deliver into the hands of his successor all books and papers relative to the concerns of the Convention, which may be in his possession. Such other officers also shall be appointed as the Con-

---

*Amended in 1829 and 1849.

vention may find occasion for, to remain in office for
such time as they may direct.

All officers and committees appointed by ballot must,
in order to their election, receive a majority of the
whole number of votes cast at such election by each
order: *Provided,* That there shall be no election, except
of Secretary and Assistant Secretary, unless there are
present at the time a majority of the clerical members,
and a majority of the lay representations, who shall
have appeared during the session, and been admitted to
seats; and such election, except that of the Secretary
and Assistant Secretary of the Convention, shall be held
at five o'clock in the afternoon of the second day of the
sesssion: *And provided also,* That if no such majority
of the clerical members and of the lay representations
be present at that time, or if said elections be not completed, such elections shall be postponed until ten
o'clock of the morning of the next day, when the same
shall be procceded in without regard to the number
then present.   And in all cases of a failure or omission
to elect any officer or annual committee, the persons
then in office, or belonging to the committee, shall continue in their station until others shall be chosen.

VII. The Clergy and Lay Deputies in Convention
shall deliberate in one body, and shall vote as such, except when it is required otherwise by five members.
In such a case, the Convention shall vote as two distinct
orders, and the concurrence of both orders shall be necessary to give validity to a measure; and such Clergymen
and Lay Deputies as shall at any time be duly assembled
in Convention shall be a quorum; and on every question
the votes of a majority of those present, or, if required

by five, the votes of a majority of those present of the two orders respectively, shall decide.

VIII. The Standing Committee and Council of Advice shall consist of ten members, five Clerical and five Lay members. At their first meeting, they shall elect one of their Clerical members to be President, and another of their members to be Secretary. They shall keep regular minutes of their proceedings, subject to the inspection of the Convention. Any three of the members (the whole having been summoned) shall be a quorum, except for such purposes as, agreeably to their own rules, may require a larger number. They may make rules of meeting and business, and alter or repeal them from time to time.

IX. The election of a Bishop of this Diocese shall be made in Convention, in the following manner: The order of the Clergy shall nominate and appoint by ballot some fit and qualified Clergyman for that office, and if this appointment be approved of by the Lay order, he shall be declared duly elected. In the above mentioned nomination and appointment, a majority of each order shall determine a choice: *Provided*, That two-thirds of all the Clergy entitled to votes be present, and two-thirds of all the congregations entitled to votes be represented, otherwise two-thirds of the votes of each order shall be necessary to determine a choice.

X. The mode of altering this Constitution shall be as follows: A proposition for amendment shall be introduced in writing, and considered in the Convention, and, if approved of, shall lie over to the next Convention; and if again approved of in the next ensuing Convention, by a majority of the two orders voting thereon separately, the change shall take place, and the Constitution so altered shall be valid and obligatory.

CANONS

OF THE

PROTESTANT EPISCOPAL CHURCH

IN THE

DIOCESE OF PENNSYLVANIA,

ADOPTED IN 1829 AND SINCE AMENDED.

CANON I.

Of the Evidence of the Residence of Clergymen removing into this Diocese, necessary to entitle them to seats in the Convention.

SEC. I. To qualify a Clergyman coming from another 1
State, District or Diocese, for a seat in the Convention, 2
it shall be necessary first to obtain from the Bishop a 3
written testimonial of his having been received as a 4
Clergyman of this Diocese. And the Bishop shall be 5
satisfied that such Clergyman has been called to settle 6
in some Parish in this Diocese, or is to be otherwise 7
employed in the work of the ministry, according to 8
the order of the Protestant Episcopal Church, and 9
with the sanction of the Ecclesiastical authority, and 10
that he has come hither with that purpose and expec- 11
tation ; or that he is engaged as a professor, tutor, or 12
instructor of youth in some college, academy, or other 13
incorporated seminary of learning, or as a missionary, 14
under the Ecclesiastical authority of this Diocese; or 15

21

16 that he has been stationed within this Diocese as a
17 Chaplain in the army or navy of the United States, and
18 in such cases the Bishop shall give the testimonial re-
19 quired: *Provided always,* That whenever the Bishop
20 shall deem it expedient, he may further inquire of the
21 Bishop, or if there be no Bishop, of the Standing Com-
22 mittee of any Diocese in which the said Clergyman has
23 previously resided, concerning his orderly compliance
24 with the institutions and government of the Protestant
25 Episcopal Church; and if the answer to the said in-
26 quiry shall specify acts contrary thereto, done by said
27 Clergyman, the Bishop may withhold the said testimo-
28 nial until he is satisfied of the good intentions in the
29 premises, of the said Clergyman for the future.

1 SEC. II. This testimonial shall be the evidence of the
2 commencement of the canonical residence and right to
3 a seat in the Convention, required by the Constitution,
4 as regards Clergymen hereafter coming into this Dio-
5 cese.

CANON II.

Of the Evidence of Appointment of the Lay Deputies to the Convention.

1 The appointment of Lay Deputies to the Convention
2 of this Diocese shall be certified in writing by a warden,
3 or two vestrymen, of the proper Church; and the cer-
4 tificate shall state that the deputy, or each deputy
5 named in it, if the certificate be for more than one, is,
6 and has also been for not less than six months before the
7 time of his election, a worshipper in the Church or Par-
8 ish he is deputed to represent.* And no other certifi-

---

1 *Resolved,* That the Churches of this Diocese be affectionately and earnestly request-
2 ed to select their Deputies to the Convention from among such of their people as "come
3 to the Holy Communion."—*Resolution of May 29, 1863.*

cate or evidence of the appointment of any Lay Deputy   9
or Deputies to the Convention of this Diocese shall be   10
allowed or received.   The certificate shall be in dupli- 11
cate, and one copy forwarded to the Secretary of the   12
Convention, the other given to the Lay Deputies.   A   13
copy of this Canon shall be annually sent, by the Secre- 14
tary of the Convention, to every Church in this Diocese, 15
with the notice of the meeting of the Convention.   16

CANON III.*

A List to be made of the Ministers in this Diocese.

Sec. I. Within one week before the meeting of every   1
Convention of this Diocese, the Bishop shall prepare, or   2
cause to be prepared, a list of all the ministers of the   3
Protestant Episcopal Church, canonically resident in   4
this Diocese, annexing the names of their respec-   5
tive cures or parishes, or of their stations as mis-   6
sionaries, or of the colleges, academies, or other semi- 7
naries of learning, incorporated, in which they are en- 8
gaged, or in regard to those who are not engaged in   9
parishes, missions, or institutions of learning, as above, 10
their places of residence only.   And such list, corrected 11
as hereinafter mentioned, shall be laid before the Con- 12
vention on the first day of meeting, and be appended   13
to the Journal, and shall be transmitted to the Secretary 14
of every General Convention.   15

Sec. II. The list of the clergy of this Diocese so pre-   1
pared by the Bishop, and by him amended, according   2
to the changes that may occur, whether by death, or-   3
dination, discipline, or canonical removals from, or ad-   4

---

* Compare Constitution, IV., and Revised Regulations, II. 2.

5 missions into this Diocese, shall be evidence of a cler-
6 gyman's having a cure, or mission, or engagement in
7 some seminary of general learning.* And no clergy-
8 man, while suspended from the ministry, shall have a
9 place on said list.

1   Sec. III. The right of any clergyman of this Diocese
2 to a seat in the Convention shall, if disputed, be de-
3 termined, according to the provisions of the Constitution
4 and Canons, by the Convention itself; whether his name
5 be inserted in the list aforesaid or omitted.

1   Sec. IV. The Bishop shall take such measures for
2 notifying the admission of ministers into this Diocese
3 as may prevent unwary and ignorant people from being
4 imposed on by persons pretending to be authorized min-
5 isters of this Church. And his certificate shall be the
6 evidence of such admission.

1   Sec. V. It shall be the duty of the clergy to attend
2 regularly at the meeting of every Convention. At the
3 opening of the Convention their names shall be called
4 over, and absentees noted.

CANON IV.

*Of the Admission of a Church or Congregation into union
with the Protestant Episcopal Church in this Diocese.*†

1   Sec. I. To entitle a Church or congregation to ad-
2 mission into union with the Protestant Episcopal Church

---

* Compare Canon I, Section I.

1 † 1. It is recommended that all the Churches in this Diocese should be incorporated
2 according to law, and that in all cases where charters have not been obtained, appli-
3 cations be made to the Judges of the Supreme Court.
4   2. In order that such charters may conform to the essential principles of the Church,
5 as regards doctrine, discipline and worship, it is further recommended that they shall,
6 before application to the Judges, be laid before the Bishop and Standing Committee
7 for their examination and approbation; and in order to obtain as much uniformity in
8 this behalf as local circumstances will admit, the form of charter to be found in the
9 appendix, is recommended.

in this Diocese, it shall be required that the vestry sub- 3
mit to the Convention the original articles of association; 4
or, if incorporated, their original charter, or a copy 5
thereof, duly authenticated according to law: and that 6
it shall appear therein, that such Church or congregation 7
accedes to the Constitution, Canons, doctrines, discipline 8
and worship of the Protestant Episcopal Church in the 9
United States, and to the Constitution and Canons of 10
this Diocese; and it shall appear further, that the said 11
act of association or charter has been submitted to the 12
Bishop and Standing Committee, and by them respec- 13
tively approved; or, if the approbation of either the 14
Bishop or Standing Committee, or both, is withheld, he 15
or they shall report to the Convention, with the articles 16
of association or charter, the reasons of his or their dis- 17
approbation. 18

SEC. II. The Convention shall refer the whole matter 1
and documents of cases of this kind, to a committee of 2
three clerical, and three lay members of the same, to be 3
appointed as soon after the organization of the Conven- 4
tion as conveniently may be, who shall make report 5
thereon to the Convention for its final determination. 6

CANON V.

Of the opening of the Convention, &c.

A. The Convention shall meet at 5 o'clock, P. M., on 1
the day appointed. 2

B. On the following day there shall be divine service, 1
the administration of the Holy Communion, and a sermon 2
by one of the presbyters, to be appointed to this office 3
by the Bishop, which shall give place when the Bishop 4
delivers a sermon or charge. 5

1   C. A sermon preached at the opening of the Conven-
2 tion shall be at its entire disposal, to be published by
3 its order, but not otherwise. Episcopal charges delivered
4 before the Convention, shall be published by the same,
5 without any motion in relation thereto.

CANON VI.

Of the Order of Business, &c.

I. Order of the business of the Convention.

FIRST DAY (Tuesday).

1   A. Election of Secretary and Assistant Secretary.

1   B. Report of Unfinished Business by the Secretary of
2 the last Convention. Journal 1854, p. 72.

1   C. Appointment of Committees, viz.: Committee on
2 Charters, Committee on Claims of Clergymen to Seats,
3 Committee on Claims of Deputies to Seats, Committee
4 on Canons, Committee on Parochial History.

1   D. Reference of Charters, and Claims to Seats, to the
2 appropriate Committees.

1   E. Nomination to offices to be filled by the Convention.
2 Journal 1849, p. 58.

1   F. Resolutions fixing the hours for meeting and ad-
2 journment. The House, however, not to be considered
3 as adjourned at any hour fixed by such resolutions,
4 without a motion to this effect put and carried.

1   G. Resolutions respecting persons to be admitted to
2 the sittings of the Convention.

SECOND DAY (Wednesday).

1   A. Divine Service.

1   B. Bishop's Address.

C. Report of the Committee on Claims of Clergymen 1
to Seats. 2

D. Report of the Committee on Claims of Deputies to 1
Seats. 2

E. Elections, agreeably to the Constitution, at 5 1
o'clock, P. M., any pending business to be at this time 2
suspended by the presiding officer for this purpose. No 3
business at this time to be proceeded with, except such 4
as appertain to said elections. 5

F. Report of the Standing Committee of the Diocese. 1

G. Reports of the Treasurers of the Convention Fund, 1
and the Episcopal Fund. Also, other Reports conveying 2
information merely, or not likely to give rise to debate. 3

H. Report of the Board of Missions, and the consider- 1
ation of the Missionary work of the Diocese, at 8 o'clock, 2
P. M., all other pending business to be suspended. 3

THIRD DAY, &c. (THURSDAY, &c).

A. Elections not previously completed. Time, 10 1
o'clock, A. M. 2

B. Proposed alteration of the Constitution, Canons, or 1
Revised Regulations. 2

C. Report of the Committee on Charters. 1

D. Reports of Committees not named above. 1

E. Unfinished business of the previous Convention. 1

F. Miscellaneous business. 1

II. Rules of Order.

A. The business of every day shall be introduced with 1
a form of prayer prescribed by the Bishop. 2

B. When the President takes the chair, no member 1

2 shall continue standing, or shall afterwards stand up,
3 unless to address the Chair.

1   C. No member shall absent himself from the service
2 of the house, unless he have leave, or be unable to attend.

1   D. When any member is about to speak in debate, or
2 deliver any matter to the house, he shall rise from his
3 seat, and shall, with due respect, address himself to the
4 President, confining himself strictly to the point in
5 debate.

1   E. No member shall speak more than twice in the
2 same debate, without leave of the house.

1   F. A question being once determined, shall stand as
2 the judgment of the house, and shall not again be drawn
3 into debate, during the same session, unless with the con-
4 sent of two-thirds of the house.

1   G. While the President is putting any question, no
2 one shall hold private discourse, stand up, walk into, out
3 of, or across the house, or read any book.

1   H. Every member who shall be in the house when
2 any question is put, shall, on a division, be counted, un-
3 less he be particularly interested in the decision.

1   I. No motion shall be considered as before the house,
2 unless it be seconded, and reduced to writing when
3 required.

1   K. When any question is before the house, it shall
2 be determined on before anything new is introduced,
3 except the question for adjournment.

1   L. The question on a motion for adjournment shall
2 be taken before any other, and without debate.

1   M. When the house is to rise, every member shall
2 keep his seat until the President leave the chair.

III. The above Order of business and Rules of Order 1
may be suspended by a vote of two-thirds of the mem- 2
bers present; but not otherwise. 3

CANON VII.*

Of the Secretary of the Convention.

A. A Secretary shall be chosen at every Annual Con- 1
vention, by ballot, after *viva voce* nominations. If but 2
one person is nominated the balloting shall be dispensed 3
with. The Secretary shall continue in office until the 4
meeting of the next Convention, and until his successor 5
is chosen. He shall attend at the time and place ap- 6
pointed for the meeting of the Convention, shall receive 7
the testimonials of those who shall there attend as Lay 8
Deputies, and shall record the names of those who 9
present testimonials in the form prescribed by the Canon. 10
The insertion by the Secretary, in the list so made by 11
him, of the name of any person who has presented a 12
testimonial of his appointment as a deputy, shall be 13
prima facie evidence of the right of such a person to a 14
seat; but as soon as the house is duly organized, a com- 15
mittee on elections shall be appointed, to whom the 16
testimonials of Lay Deputies shall be referred. 17
There shall also be appointed by the Convention, in 18
the same manner, an Assistant Secretary. If during the 19
recess of the Convention a vacancy should occur in the 20
office of Secretary, the duties thereof shall devolve upon 21
the Assistant Secretary, if there be one; if not, or if 22
the Assistant Secretary should die or resign, a Secretary 23
shall be appointed by the Standing Committee. 24

B. He shall give not less than one month's written 1

---

* Amended in 1844—Journal, pp. 33 and 34.

2 notice of the time (the day and hour) appointed for the
3 meeting of the Convention, to every clergyman within
4 the Diocese, according to a list, to be furnished by the
5 Bishop; and, as far as is practicable, he shall give a
6 similar notice to the church-wardens and vestrymen of
7 every congregation. And such notice shall be accom-
8 panied with the form of the certificate of the appointment
9 of lay deputies.

1   C. On the printing of any Pastoral Letter of the
2 House of Bishops, he shall transmit the same to the
3 clergy and to vacant churches, to be read to the congre-
4 gation on some occasion of public worship, and also for
5 general perusal by the members of the Church, under
6 such reasonable regulations as expediency may require.

1   D. He shall transmit annually to each of the Bishops,
2 and to the Secretary of every Diocesan Convention, a
3 copy of the Journal.

1   E. He shall also transmit to every General Conven-
2 tion a certificate, to be signed by himself, or by the
3 President of the Convention of this Diocese, containing
4 a list of the clergymen in this Diocese, and the amount
5 of funds paid, or secured to be paid (distinguishing
6 them), to the General Theological Seminary, together
7 with the nomination of trustees of that seminary; and
8 also, a like certificate of the appointment of Clerical
9 and Lay Deputies.

1   F. Besides the duties before specified, he shall per-
2 form all others usually appertaining to the office of
3 Secretary, or enjoined on him by the Convention."*

---

1   *Resolved, That previous to the adjournment of the Convention, sine die, the rough
2 minutes shall always be read and passed upon.—Journal, May 1841, p. 34.

CANON VIII.*

Of the Standing Committee.

SEC. I. At every stated Convention, a Standing Com- 1
mittee, to consist of five of the Clergy and five of the 2
Laity, shall be chosen by ballot, by the concurrent vote 3
of the members of each order. And vacancies occuring 4
by death or otherwise, in said Committee, shall be 5
supplied by the concurrent vote of the remaining Cleri- 6
cal members and Lay members of the Committee. 7

SEC. II. This Committee shall have in special charge 1
the care and investment of the Convention Fund, and 2
also of the Fund for the support of the Episcopate, wheth- 3
er arising from the legacy of the late Andrew Doz, Esq., 4
or otherwise given in charge or trust to the Convention. 5

SEC. III. In case of a vacancy in the Episcopate, the 1
powers and duties to be performed by the Bishop, as re- 2
gards discipline, except the pronouncing sentence of de- 3
position or degradation from the ministry, shall belong 4
to and be performed by the Standing Committee. In 5
case of such vacancy, the Standing Committee shall also 6
have power to act in the granting of testimonials to 7
clergymen removing into this Diocese agreeably to the 8
Canons. 9

SEC. IV. In the case of the absence of the Bishop of 1
this Diocese in foreign parts, expected to continue for 2
six months or more, the Bishop, before his departure, 3
shall, with the consent of the Standing Committee, 4
request the Bishop of some neighboring Diocese, or 5
some other Bishop or Bishops, to perform the Episcopal 6
acts and duties pertaining to this Diocese, during his 7

*Altered in 1853. Journal, p. 54.

8 absence; or, if the Bishop neglect or refuse to do so,
9 the Standing Committee may do the same, at any time
10 after his departure from the United States. All other
11 acts and duties of the Bishop being such as may be
12 performed by the Standing Committee in case of a va-
13 cancy in the Episcopate, shall be equally performed by
14 them during any absence of the Bishop, as aforesaid.
15 And the Convention during said absence of the Bishop,
16 shall, at each meeting thereof, elect its President.

1 SEC. V. The record of all the proceedings on a pre-
2 sentment of a clergyman or layman shall be preserved
3 by the Standing Committee; and for that purpose, shall,
4 after a final decision, be delivered to their Secretary.

1 SEC. VI. The Standing Committee shall, before the
2 meeting of each Annual Convention, prepare a report
3 to be submitted thereto, of every Church, a member of
4 this Convention, which for three years has made no pa-
5 rochial report to the same, no missionary report being
6 made in its behalf and which, during the same period,
7 has neither employed a clergyman, as its parish minister,
8 nor requested of the Bishop to have the services of a
9 missionary.*

CANON IX.

Of the Board of Missions.†

1 A. The Missionary work of the Diocese shall be con-
2 fided to a Board of Missions, to consist of twelve clergy-
3 men and twelve laymen, of which Board the Bishop,
4 and in his absence the Assistant Bishop (if there be one),
5 shall be ex-officio, the head.

---

1 *Standing Committee may, under limitations, draw on certain Funds. Canon X, 4.
†Journal of 1859, pp. 65, 76.

B. The Board of Missions shall be appointed by the 1
Standing Committee, with the concurrence of the Bish- 2
op, or in his absence, of the Assistant Bishop; one third 3
of the number to serve for one year, one-third for two 4
years, and one-third for three years; and annually, after 5
the expiration of the first year, one-third of the number 6
shall be appointed as aforesaid. 7

C. The said Board is authorized to make their own 1
by-laws, subject to the approval of the Bishop and 2
Standing Committee, and to elect such officers as they 3
shall deem necessary. 4

D. The Board shall annually report their proceedings 1
to the Convention. 2

CANON X.
Of Funds of the Convention.

A. Episcopal Fund.

Each Church in union with this Convention shall pay 1
to the Treasurer of the Convention, on or before the 2
thirty-first day of December in every year, towards the 3
maintenance of the Episcopate in this Diocese, a sum to 4
be fixed by a Committee; which Committee shall con- 5
sist of the President of the Standing Committee of the 6
Diocese, of the Secretary of the Convention, and of the 7
Treasurer of the Episcopal Fund; the sum not to ex- 8
ceed six per cent on the salary of the Minister or Min- 9
isters, or $37\frac{1}{2}$ cents on each reported communicant, as 10
the above mentioned Committee of three shall decide.* 11
The income of the Episcopal Fund shall be exclu- 12
sively appropriated for the use of the Bishop who shall 13
have the city of Philadelphia within his Diocese.† 14

* Journal of 1858, pp. 52, 54.
†Revised Regulations, vi. 4.

B. Convention Fund.

1 The Treasurer and the Secretary of the Convention,
2 shall assess on the several parishes in the Diocese (on the
3 same basis as is above adopted for the Episcopal Fund),
4 sums sufficient in the aggregate to pay all the contingent
5 expenses of the Convention, including the mileage of
6 clergymen attending the same. On or before the first
7 day of December in every year, they shall make an
8 estimate of the expenses aforesaid, and after assessing on
9 each parish its proportion, shall advise the proper officers
10 thereof, accordingly. Whereupon it shall be the duty
11 of the officers of said churches to transmit the amount
12 assessed to the Treasurer of the Convention without delay.*

C. Christmas Fund for Disabled Clergymen.

1 All appropriations from this fund shall be made by a
2 Committee of five laymen, appointed annually by the
3 Convention, of whom the Treasurer shall be one; and
4 the said Committee shall make an annual report of their
5 proceedings to the Convention.
6 No appropriation of more than 250 dollars per annum,
7 shall be made to any individual, and no appropriation
8 shall be made, except upon evidence satisfactory to the
9 Committee, that the individual is entitled to a seat in the
10 Convention of the Diocese, and is at the time disabled,
11 by age or physical infirmity, from being employed in per-
12 forming the duties of his station.
13 If any surplus of the Christmas Fund shall remain af-
14 ter the expenditures of the year, the same shall be in-
15 vested in some productive fund, under the direction of

* Journal of 1865, p. 68.

the Standing Committee of the Diocese, to be converted 16
into money, in case of need, under the same direction.* 17

D. At every Stated Convention there shall be chosen 1
a Treasurer of the Convention, who shall remain in office 2
until his successor is appointed. His accounts shall be 3
closed on the first of May, examined by the Standing 4
Committee, and reported to the Convention. The 5
Standing Committee are authorized to fill any vacancy 6
in this office, or that of the Secretary of the Convention. 7
The Treasurer of the Convention shall be the Treasurer 8
of the Episcopal Fund.† 9
At every Stated Convention, there shall be elected a 10
Treasurer for the Christmas Fund.‡ 11

E. Draughts on the Convention and Episcopal Fund.
The Bishop and Standing Committee, or in the ab- 1
sence of the Bishop, the Standing Committee alone, shall 2
have authority to draw on the Treasurer of the Conven- 3
tion and on the Treasurer of the Episcopal Fund, or on 4
either of them, for all necessary and reasonable expenses 5
incurred in the administration of the Diocese, in all 6
cases not provided for by the Convention ; reporting all 7
such disbursements to the next Convention.§ 8

CANON XI.

Of Vacant Parishes.

When a parish becomes vacant, it shall be the duty 1
of the vestry to give notice thereof to the Bishop, or, if 2
there is no Bishop, to the President of the Standing 3
Committee, forthwith. 4

---

*Journal of 1841, p. 25.
†Revised Regulations, IV.   Journal of 1867, p. 33.   Journal of 1841, p. 25.
‡Journal of 1870, p. 20.
§Journal 1866, p. 60.

CANON XII.

Of the Celebration of Marriage.

1 No member of this Church shall celebrate any marriage,
2 without being satisfied that it is not forbidden by the law
3 of God, or of the Commonwealth of Pennsylvania, or by
4 the Canons of the Church. And if both or either of the
5 parties be minors, it shall be necessary that the consent
6 of the parents, guardians, master, or mistress (as the case
7 may require), be first obtained, unless they live out of
8 the United States, and that fact be known or proved to
9 the minister; and that such consent be certified to him
10 by some credible person or persons acquainted with them
11 and the minor, or be otherwise sufficiently proved or
12 known to him. Whereupon the minister, not knowing
13 or having reason to believe that there is any lawful im-
14 pediment, may, and if either of the parties be of his con-
15 gregation, it shall be his duty to join them in marriage.
16 The certificate aforesaid shall be in writing, if he re-
17 quires it.

CANON XIII.

Of Parochial Instruction.

1 Every minister of a parish shall encourage the formation
2 of Sunday Schools, and the efficient prosecution of instruc-
3 tion in them, in conformity with the principles of the
4 Protestant Episcopal Church. And he shall report the
5 number of scholars and teachers in his annual parochial
6 report.

CANON XIV.

Of Registers of Baptisms, Marriages and Deaths, and of Parochial Reports.

1 SEC. I. Each clergyman shall keep an account of all the

baptisms, marriages and funerals solemnized by him in 2
he discharge of his ministry, specifying the name and 3
late of the birth of the child baptized, with the names of 4
the parents and sponsors, the name of the adult baptized, 5
the names of the parties married, and the name of the 6
person buried; and also, the time when each rite was 7
performed. 8

SEC. II. These entries shall, by the minister, or, if so 1
ordered, by the vestry, by the clerk or sexton of the 2
Church, be recorded in a suitable book to be provided by 3
the vestry, which shall be the Church register, and shall 4
belong to, and remain with the vestry, as a part of the 5
Church records. And the minister of each parish shall 6
also keep a list of all the communicants within his cure, 7
as nearly as they can be ascertained; and also, a list of 8
the persons confirmed from time to time by the Bishop. 9

*SEC. III. Every minister of a parish or parishes in 1
this Diocese, shall present or forward, at every Annual 2
Convention, to the Bishop, or, if there be no Bishop, to 3
the President of the Convention, a statement of the 4
number of baptisms, marriages, funerals, and persons 5
confirmed in his parish or parishes, severally, since the 6
last like report; and, also, of the number of the com- 7
municants, distinguishing the additions, removals, and 8
deaths since the last report; also, he shall add a state- 9
ment of all other matters of fact, that may throw light 10
on the state of his parish or parishes. 11

---

* Minister to report, also, the property of the parish, and its indebtedness, his salary
and arrears. Journal of 1849, p. 51. See. also, Digest of General Canons, Title 1.
Canon XV., Sec. I.

CANON XV.

Of Deputies to the General Convention.

1 SEC. I. At every Stated Convention of this Diocese there
2 may, and at the Stated Convention immediately pre-
3 ceeding the Stated General Convention there shall be,
4 chosen by the concurrent ballot of the clerical and lay
5 votes, Deputies to the General Convention, whose ap-
6 pointment shall continue until the next Stated Conven-
7 tion, and until others are chosen in their places. Pro-
8 vided that the balloting may be dispensed with, in cases
9 where only four clergymen and four laymen are nominated.

1 SEC. II. Should a vacancy occur by death, or other-
2 wise, in the deputation to the General Convention, it
3 shall be supplied by the concurrent vote of the remain-
4 ing clerical and lay deputies.

1 SEC. III. Deputies to the General Convention may
2 present an account of their expenses in their travel and
3 attendance to the Standing Committee, who shall make
4 a reasonable allowance for the same, to be paid out of
5 the Convention Fund.

CANON XVI.

*Of a Tabular Report.**

1 SEC. I. The Bishop and Standing Committee, or if
2 there be no Bishop, the Standing Committee only, shall
3 prepare a condensed report and tabular view of the state
4 of the Church in this Diocese, previously to the meeting
5 of every General Convention, for the purpose of aiding
6 the Committee on the State of the Church, appointed

---

* Journal of 1855, p. 55. Compare Digest of General Canons, Title 1., Canon XV.,
Sec. 5.

by the House of Clerical and Lay Deputies, in drafting 8
their report. 9

SEC. II. The tabular view aforesaid shall be appended 1
to the Journal of the Annual Diocesan Convention, next 2
previous to the General Convention, for the use of which 3
it shall have been made. 4

CANON XVII.

Of the Trial of a Clergyman not being a Bishop.

SEC. I. The trial of a Clergyman, not being a Bishop, 1
shall be on a presentment in writing, specifying with 2
clearness and certainty, as to time, place and circum- 3
stance, the crime or misdemeanor, by violation of the 4
Canons, or otherwise charged: the said presentment to 5
be made to the Bishop, either by the Convention, or by 6
the vestry of the Parish to which the accused belongs, 7
or by any three Presbyters of this Diocese entitled to a 8
seat in the Convention: the said vestry or Presbyters 9
pledging themselves to make good the accusation. If 10
the presentment be made by the Convention, they shall 11
by ballot appoint a committee to sign and prosecute the 12
same. 13

SEC. II. Such presentment being made to the Bishop, 1
and being accompanied by a further statement in writing 2
of the names of the witnesses, and of the purport of 3
their evidence, and by such documentary evidence as is 4
relied on, the Bishop shall cause a copy of such present- 5
ment to be served upon the accused by a summoner ap- 6
pointed by the Bishop, and shall call upon him by written 7
summons, to show cause, at a day and place therein 8
named, why a commissary should not be appointed as 9

10 hereinafter set forth; and upon the return of the sum-
11 moner that he has served the same, and no sufficient
12 cause to the contrary being shown, the Bishop shall ap-
13 point a suitable person to be a commissary, who shall
14 repair to the city or county where the crime or misde-
15 meanor is alleged to have been committed; and having
16 either then or previously appointed a convenient time and
17 place, and given not less than fifteen days' notice there-
18 of by a summoner appointed by the Bishop to the party
19 accused, and also to the chairman or a committee appoint-
20 ed by the Convention, or to either church-warden of the
21 vestry, or to any one of the three Presbyters presenting,
22 the commissary shall then and there proceed to examine
23 the witnesses, on both sides, carefully taking down their
24 examinations in writing, which being approved by the
25 witnesses, shall be signed by them respectively; and, if
26 it be required by either party, some person qualified by
27 law to administer an oath or affirmation shall be request-
28 ed to do so in his behalf: and the examination so taken,
29 with any documentary evidence certified by the commis-
30 sary and inclosed under his seal, shall by him be deliv-
31 ered or transmitted to the Bishop without delay; where-
32 upon further proceedings shall be taken, unless, upon
33 satisfactory evidence of error or mal-practice, the Bishop
34 shall deem it necessary to justice to order a further ex-
35 amination; in which case the same or another commis-
36 sary, as the Bishop shall determine, shall be appointed
37 as before, and with similar powers and duties: *Provided*,
38 *nevertheless*, That before the trial the commissary shall
39 issue a citation, with reasonable notice, to the respective
40 witnesses, to attend at the time and place of trial; and
41 in case of their personal attendance, their testimony may,

at the request of the party presenting, or party accused, 42
or by order of the commissary and assessors, be taken anew 43
orally and reduced to writing again ; but the non-attend- 44
ance of the respective witnesses, shall not in any case be 45
a ground for refusing to read such depositions as have 46
been duly taken: *And provided also*, That if the party 47
accused desire it, the examination of witnesses and trial 48
shall be in public, and that said party shall be entitled 49
to a copy of the evidence if he require it. 50

SEC. III. Either before the appointment of a commis- 1
sary, or after a report made by him, the Bishop shall 2
have power to dismiss the presentment, and declare the 3
accused party discharged, if the accusation contained in 4
it appears to him an insufficient cause of presentment 5
in itself, or to be clearly unsupported by the evidence. 6

SEC. IV. Upon the report of the commissary being 1
made to the Bishop, and no further examination being 2
ordered, nor the presentment dismissed by him as afore- 3
said, the Standing Committee shall nominate twelve 4
Presbyters of this Diocese having a seat in the Conven- 5
tion, of whom the accused may choose four, or in case 6·
of his refusal or neglect so to do, the Standing Commit- 7
tee shall select four ; and the Presbyters so chosen shall 8
be the assessors. And the commissary and assessors 9
having agreed upon some convenient time and place, and 10
having caused not less than thirty days' written or print- 11
ed notice thereof to be given to the party accused, and 12
also to the chairman or a member of the committee ap- 13
pointed by the Convention, or to either church-warden 14
of the vestry, or to any one of the three Presbyters pre- 15
senting, the said notice to be given by a summoner ap- 16

17 pointed by the Bishop, shall then and there proceed to
18 the trial, upon the evidence and report of the commis-
19 sary, and upon such other evidence as may be produced;
20 which new evidence shall be reduced to writing, and ap-
21 proved and signed by the witnesses respectively, as be-
22 fore. The commissary and assessors having deliberately
23 considered the evidence, shall, within ten days after clos-
24 ing the same, declare in a written judgment signed by
25 them, or by a majority of them, that the accused is guilty,
26 or that he is not guilty of the charges laid in the pre-
27 sentment, in the order therein set forth; which judg-
28 ment, with all the evidence received, shall be delivered
29 forthwith to the Bishop: *Provided always*, That the ac-
30 cused shall be allowed to be present at all the examina-
31 tions of witnesses and other proceedings, whether held
32 by the commissary, or by the commissary and asses-
33 sors, and to offer explanations, or a defence of the acts
34 with which he is charged: *And provided also*, That the
35 matter of such explanations or defence shall be reduced
36 to writing by the accused, and be presented with the
37 evidence to the Bishop.

1 SEC. V. If the accused shall neglect or refuse to ap-
2 pear before the commissary, when summoned according to
3 Sec. II. of this Canon, the examination shall proceed as
4 if he were present. And if the accused shall neglect or
5 refuse to appear before the commissary and assessors (ex-
6 cept for some reasonable cause, to be judged of by them),
7 when summoned according to Sec. IV. of this Canon,
8 and no defence be there made under his authority, they
9 shall declare him to be in contumacy, and report the
10 same to the Bishop, and sentence of suspension from the
11 ministry shall pass against him for contumacy; but the

said sentence may be reversed by the Bishop, if within 12
three calendar months the accused shall tender himself 13
ready, and accordingly appear to take his trial on the 14
presentment: but if he shall not so tender himself before 15
the expiration of the said three months, the sentence of 16
degradation from the ministry for contumacy shall forth- 17
with be pronounced by the Bishop, and shall be publicly 18
read in the churches.   19

SEC. VI. The accused, on his first appearance, whether   1
before the Bishop at the return of the summoner previ-   2
ous to the appointment of a commissary, or before the   3
commissary, or before the commissary and assessors, shall 4
be called on to say whether he is guilty or not guilty of 5
the offence or offences charged against him.   On his   6
neglect or refusal to answer, the plea of *not guilty* shall
be entered for him.   And if he be found, or confess him- 8
self, guilty of the matters charged in the presentment, or 9
any of them, the Bishop shall pronounce the sentence 10
according to the Canons; but in case of a vacancy in the 11
Episcopate, the Standing Committee shall report the 12
proceedings to the Bishop of some other Diocese, as near 13
as may be to this, by whom the sentence according to 14
the Canons, may be pronounced: *Provided always*, That 15
the Bishop, upon satisfactory proof of error or mal-prac- 16
tice in the proceedings of the commissary and assessors, 17
or on account of error in their judgment, either in law or 18
fact, may, if he deems it necessary to justice, grant a new 19
trial to the accused; in which case new assessors shall 20
be appointed, and the other proceedings be conducted as 21
directed by Sec. 4 of this Canon.   22

SEC. VII. The proceedings in the case being complete,   1

2 according to the requisitions of the Canon, the sentence
3 or penalty pronounced by the Bishop according to the
4 Canon, shall be final.

1 SEC. VIII. Whenever any clergyman of the Protestant
2 Episcopal Church, resident in this Diocese, shall be ac-
3 cused by public rumor of any misdemeanor or offence
4 known to the Canon Law of the Church, or recognized
5 by the law of the land, he shall have the right to present
6 a petition to the Bishop, or, in case of his absence, or in-
7 ability to act, to the Standing Committee of the Diocese,
8 demanding an inquiry into the truth of the alleged mis-
9 demeanor or offence. Upon receipt of the said petition,
10 which shall be signed by the Clergyman, the Bishop, or
11 Standing Committee, as the case may be, shall forthwith
12 appoint a Court of Inquiry, consisting of three Clergymen
13 and two Laymen of the Diocese, none of whom shall be
14 of kin to the petitioner, nor be at all connected with
15 the subject-mater of inquiry. The said Court shall have
16 power to hear the statements and proofs to be submitted
17 by the petitioner ; and shall also have power in their dis-
18 cretion, fully to investigate the truth of the public rumor.
19 After having fully satisfied their consciences in the
20 matter, the said Court, or a majority of its members, if
21 they find the said public rumor unfounded, shall have
22 power so to declare by their judgment in writing ; but
23 if, on the contrary, they find that there is reasonable
24 ground to presume that the said public rumor is well
25 founded, they shall so declare by their judgment in wri-
26 ting. In either case, the return by the Court, accompa-
27 nied by all the testimony taken before them, and the
28 other papers in the case, shall be made to the Bishop or
29 the Standing Committee, as the case may be. And in

the case of a finding that the public rumor is well found- 30
ed, the said Clergyman shall be forthwith proceeded 31
against, and put upon his trial for the misdemeanor or of- 32
fence, in accordance with the Canon Law of the Church. 33

CANON XVIII.

Of the Proceedings in the Trial of a Layman, after repulsion by the Minister from the Holy Communion.

SEC. I. If any person repelled from the Holy Com- 1
munion, according to the rubric, shall allege to the 2
Bishop that injustice has been done, or if, notwithstand- 3
ing he shall have professed himself willing in truth and 4
sincerity to comply with the requisitions expressed in 5
the rubric, in order to be restored to the Holy Com- 6
munion, his repulsion shall be continued, he may present 7
his complaint in writing to the Bishop, setting forth the 8
grounds thereof, and desiring that he may be restored to 9
the Communion. 10

SEC. II. Unless the Bishop shall in a summary manner 1
direct him to be restored, an inquiry and examination 2
shall be made in manner following. The notice given 3
to the Bishop by the Minister repelling, shall stand in 4
the place of a presentment of the party repelled; and 5
the proceedings thereon shall be the same as are before 6
provided in the case of a presentment made against a 7
Clergyman, not being a Bishop, after the report of the 8
commissary, except that besides the Clerical assessors, 9
the Bishop shall nominate twelve laymen of this Diocese, 10
of whom the accused may choose four, or in case of his 11
neglect or refusal, the Standing Committee shall appoint 12
four, and the four persons so chosen or appointed, with 13

24

14 the four Clerical assessors, to be chosen or appointed as
15 aforesaid, having added one layman to their number,
16 shall be the assessors, and proceed to the trial in like
17 manner as is provided in the case of a Clergyman, not
18 being a Bishop.

1   SEC. III. They, or a majority of them, having heard
2 and deliberately considered the allegations and testimony
3 on either side, shall declare in writing their judgment,
4 whether the party presented has been rightfully repelled,
5 according to the rubric, or not; and whether his repul-
6 sion ought or ought not to be continued; and shall
7 forthwith report their judgment to the Bishop; and
8 unless the Bishop shall see cause to order a re-hearing of
9 the case by the assessors, or, if desired by the party re-
10 pelled, by other assessors to be nominated and chosen,
11 or appointed in manner aforesaid, he shall communicate
12 the judgment to the minister repelling, and to the party
13 repelled, which shall be final and conclusive: *Provided*,
14 That if the judgment shall direct a further continuance
15 of the repulsion, it shall nevertheless be subject to all
16 the conditions and provisions of the rubric.

CANON XIX.

Of taking the Depositions of Witnesses.

1   If, in any case, either of a Clergyman not being a
2 Bishop, or of a Layman, the testimony of witnesses shall
3 be requisite, whose attendance before the commissary or
4 at the trial, cannot, in the opinion of the Bishop, be
5 procured, their depositions shall be taken and reduced
6 to writing, upon such notice to the party presenting or
7 party accused, and under such other regulations as the

Bishop shall prescribe, and shall, when taken in con- 8
formity, be read in evidence, with the same effect as if 9
taken by the commissary, or at the trial. 10

CANON ·XX·.

Of Persons against whom Presentments are made, not to
be found, or removed ; and of the service of Notices or
Citations.

Sec. I. If a presentment be duly made against a 1
Clergyman, not a Bishop, and after reasonable diligence 2
he cannot be found in this Diocese, or has removed from 3
it, and notice of the presentment cannot on that account 4
be served on him, and return be made accordingly by 5
the summoner, in such case, the Bishop, with the advice 6
of the Standing Committee, having considered the char- 7
acter of the accusation, and the probability of its truth, 8
may suspend the accused from the exercise of all his 9
ministerial functions. But such suspension shall be re- 10
moved, if within three months the accused shall appear 11
and accept service of a citation, returnable within thirty 12
days. If the accused shall not so appear within twelve 13
months, the Bishop, with the consent of the Standing 14
Committee, may pronounce sentence of degradation 15
against him. 16

Sec. II. Every notice or citation to either party, re- 1
quired in consequence of a presentment, shall be directed 2
to the summoner appointed for the occasion, according 3
to the Canons respectively; and return thereof shall be 6
made thereon in writing; and the leaving a copy at the 5
last place of abode of the person to be cited, or deliver- 6
ing it to him in person, shall be deemed good service ˙7
thereof. 8

CANON XXI.

Of Penalties.

1   Sec. I. If any Clergyman of this Church, not a Bishop,
2 shall be guilty of crime or of misdemeanor, by violation
3 of the Canons, or otherwise, and shall thereof be duly
4 convicted, or shall confess himself guilty, he shall be ad-
5 monished by the Bishop, or suspended from the ministry,
6 or degraded therefrom according to the character and
7 circumstances of his offence.

1   Sec. II. After an accused Clergyman, not a Bishop,
2 has been convicted by the commissary and assessors, the
3 said commissary and assessors shall forthwith proceed to
4 consider and declare, in writing, and under their signa-
5 tures, what in their opinion is the due punishment of the
6 offence, of which the accused has been found guilty,
7 having respect to the character and circumstances of the
8 offence, whether admonition by the Bishop, suspension,
9 and for what period, or under what conditions; or
10 degradation; and they, or a majority of them, being
11 assembled for this purpose, shall not separate or adjourn,
12 until they have so declared their opinion of the punish-
13 ment due; and their said declaration shall be forthwith
14 delivered or transmitted to the Bishop, together with
15 their judgment of conviction, and the evidence in the
16 cause.

1   Sec. III. If the Bishop approve of the punishment so
2 declared, he shall in writing give sentence accordingly;

but if he do not approve of it, he shall, in like manner, 3
impose such other less punishment hereby authorized, as 4
he shall think justly due. 5

SEC. IV. If a Layman repelled by his Minister shall, 1
after trial, be found guilty, his repulsion shall continue, 2
subject to the conditions of the rubric. 3

SEC. V. If a Clergyman, not a Bishop, shall confess 1
himself guilty on any presentment duly made, the Bishop 2
shall determine on his punishment, whether admonition, 3
suspension, and for what term, and on what conditions, 4
or degradation from the ministry. If a lay person, after 5
appealing to the Bishop, from the sentence of repulsion 6
from the Holy Communion, shall, at any period before 7
or during investigation or trial, confess himself guilty of 8
the offence or offences for which he was repelled, the 9
Bishop shall determine the duration of his repulsion, or 10
the conditions on which it shall be removed: *Provided* 11
always, and in all cases of repulsion from the Holy Com- 12
munion, that if the person repelled be visited with ex- 13
treme or mortal sickness, the Minister of the Parish, if 14
satisfied that he is truly penitent, but not otherwise, may 15
administer the Holy Comunion or authorize it to be ad- 16
ministered to him before his death, though the term of 17
repulsion be not expired. 18

SEC. VI. In every case of degradation from the ministry, 1
the Bishop who pronounces sentence shall, in addition to 3
the provision of the general Canons, without delay, cause 4
the sentence of degradation to be published from every 5
pulpit in this Diocese, where there may be an officiating 5
Minister. 6

CANON XXII.

Of Alterations in the Canon-law.

1   A. On the first day of every Convention, a Committee
2 to consist of three clergymen and three laymen, and to
3 be called the Committee on Canons, shall be appointed.

1   B. All proposals to alter or add to the Constitution or
2 the Canons of the Diocese shall be referred to this Com-
3 mittee.

1   C. No existing Canon shall be changed, and no new
2 Canon shall be enacted on the day on which the change
3 or enactment may be proposed.

FORM OF CHARTER OF INCORPORATION.

WHEREAS, The following named persons, citizens of this Commonwealth, viz:

have, together with other citizens, associated for the purpose of worshipping Almighty God, according to the faith and discipline of the Protestant Episcopal Church of the United States of America; and have for that purpose formed a congregation at
in   and are now desirous to be incorporated agreeably to the provisions of the Act of the General Assembly of Pennsylvania, entitled "An Act to confer on certain associations of the citizens of this Commonwealth, the powers and immunities of corporations or bodies politic in law, and the supplements thereto." They therefore declare the following to be the objects, articles, and conditions of their said Association, agreeably to which they desire to be incorporated, viz:

First, That the name of the Corporation shall be, "The Rector, Church Wardens and Vestrymen of

Second, This Church acknowledges itself to be a member of, and to belong to, the Protestant Episcopal Church in the Diocese of Pennsylvania, and the Protestant Episcopal Church in the United States of America. As such, it accedes to, recognizes and adopts the Constitution, Canons, doctrine, discipline, and worship of the Protestant Episcopal Church in the Diocese of Pennsylvania, and of the Protestant Episcopal Church in the United States, and acknowledges their authority accordingly.

Any member of this Church, or Corporation, who shall disclaim or refuse conformity to the said authority, shall cease to be a member of this Corporation, and shall not be elected, or vote in the election of Vestrymen, or exercise any office or function in, concerning, or connected with, the said Church or Corporation,

Third, The rents and revenues of this Corporation shall be, from time to time, applied for the maintenance and support of the Rector, ministers, and officers of said Church, and in the erection and necessary repairs of the church, church-yard, parsonage house, and other houses which now do or hereafter shall belong to the said Corporation, and to no other use or purpose whatsoever.

Provided, That all the property of the said Corporation shall be taken, held, and enure, subject to the control and disposition of the vestry of the same; *and provided* that the clear annual value or income of the real and personal estate held by the said Corporation, shall not at any time exceed five thousand dollars.

Fourth, The Rector of this Church shall be elected by the church-wardens and vestrymen in such manner as the statutes and by-laws shall ordain. The vestry of said Church shall consist of   *persons, lay members of the said Church, and citizens of Pennsylvania, who shall continue in office for one year, and until others be chosen, and the election of whom shall be made every year, on Easter Monday, by a majority of such members of the said Church *as shall appear by the vestry books to have paid two successive years immediately preceding the time of such election for a pew or sitting in said Church, or (in case of a free church), who shall be recognized by the Rector and Wardens thereof, as usual attendants upon the services of the same, and contributors to the said Church for one year.*

---

*Not less than six.

Provided, That until the next Easter Monday after the expiration of five years from the date of this charter, members of said Church who shall in any way have contributed to the erection of the Church, or to the support of the Rector or ministers thereof, shall be entitled to vote at the election of vestrymen; and provided, that in case of the failure to elect vestrymen on that day, the corporation shall not on that account be dissolved; but the election shall be holden on some other day, in such manner as the by-laws may prescribe; and any vacancy occurring in the vestry shall be supplied by the remaining members thereof. At the meeting of the vestry, the Rector, if present, may preside, and in all matters except such as concern the property of the Corporation, shall be entitled, in common with the several members of the vestry, to one vote.

Fifth, No person shall be Rector or Assistant Minister of this Church, unless he shall have had Episcopal Ordination, and unless he be in full standing with the Protestant Episcopal Church in the State of Pennsylvania, and in the United States, and recognized as such by the Bishop of this Diocese, or in case of a vacancy in the Episcopate, by the Standing Committee of the Diocese.

Sixth, The said vestry shall have full power to choose their own officers; and they shall annually at the first meeting after their election, choose one of their own number to be one church-warden, and the Rector for the time being shall elect another of the said vestrymen to be the other church-warden of the said Church. In case of a vacancy in the office of Rector at the time of the election, the other church-warden shall also be chosen by the vestry, to remain until the election of a

25

Rector, or a new election of the vestry, and during such vacancy, all the powers of the Corporation shall be exercised by the vestry, as fully and entirely as if no such vacancy had occurred: *Provided always*, That it shall be the duty of the said church-wardens and vestrymen to elect another Rector to supply the vacancy as soon as conveniently may be.

Seventh, This charter may be amended in the following manner, that is to say: Any proposed amendment shall be submitted to a stated or special meeting of the vestry, and if the same shall be approved by a majority of the whole of the members thereof, the same shall be submitted to a meeting of the members of the congregation, who are entitled to vote for vestrymen, and if approved by a majority of the persons present at such meeting, the same shall be submitted to the next Convention, and if it be approved, shall be, and form part of the charter, upon the subsequent confirmation thereof, by the court which granted the original charter, or other competent authority.

Eighth, In case of the dissolution of the said Corporation, all the property of the same shall vest in trustees, in trust, to hold and convey the same to, and for, any future congregation of members of the Protestant Episcopal Church, which may be formed in the same neighborhood, and to and for no other purpose; and the said trustees shall consist of such persons as may be appointed by the proper court on the application of an interested party.

Ninth, The following named persons shall be the church-wardens and vestrymen, to continue in office until the election on Easter Monday next, and until others be chosen, viz:

FORM OF THE CERTIFICATE FOR LAY DEPUTIES TO CONVENTION.

It is hereby certified that at a meeting of the Vestry of
Church,,   , in the County of
held on the   day of   18 , Mr.
was duly elected a lay deputy to the Convention of the Protestant Episcopal Church in the Diocese of Pennsylvania, to
be held in   .., on the   ·   day of   next ;
and that the said deputy is now, and has also been for not less
than the six calendar months next before his election, a worshipper in the said   Church.

Dated this   ·   of   , 18

} WARDENS.

} VESTRYMEN.

N. B.—If more than one deputy be chosen, a certificate in
the above form may be given to each, or, which is better, the
names of all may be included in one certificate, varying the
language accordingly.

N. B.—According to Canon XI, "No other certificate or
evidence of the appointment of any lay deputy or deputies to
the Convention of this Diocese shall be allowed or received."

N.B.—*Resolved*, That the Churches of the Diocese be affectionately and earnestly requested to select their deputies to
the Convention from such of their people as "come to the
Holy Communion."—*Resolution of May* 29, 1863.

Form of Parochial Report.

——— ——— ——— ——— ———County.
——— ———Church,   Admitted——— ———
The Rev.   Rector.   Rev.   Assistant,
and   Wardens.
   Baptisms—Adults,   ; Infants,   ; total,   .
   Confirmed,   .
   Communicants—Added, new   , by removal   , died or removed
present number   .
   Marriages
   Burials
   Public Services—On Sundays   , on other days   , total
Average attendance on Sundays   .
   Children Catechized—Times,
   Sunday Schools—Officers and Teachers   , Scholars
   Bible Classes—Teachers   , Members   .
   Parish Schools—Teachers   , Scholars   , other Parish agencies
   Church—Sittings   ; Chapels (the statistics of which are included in
this Report), Sittings   : School Buildings   ; Parsonage   ; Ceme-
tery   ; Salary of Rector $ per annum; Arrears of salary   ;
Number of free sittings   , Extra Sunday services, free to all   .

MONEY RECEIPTS FROM ALL SOURCES.

   Pew Rents, $; Offertory at Holy Communion, $; Collections in Church, $; Subscriptions, $; Donations, $;
Investments, $; Other sources, $; Total, $.

EXPENDITURES AND APPROPRIATIONS.

   Current Expenses (including Salary of Rector) $; Repairs and
Improvements, $; Payment of Debts, $; Episcopal and Con-
vention Fund, $; Support of Sunday Schools, $; of Parish
Schools, $; Parish Library, $; Parochial Missions, $;
For the Poor, $; To Missions, Foreign, $; Domestic, $;
Home Mission, for Colored People, $; Diocesan, $; City
Missions, $; For the Jews, $: Episcopal Hospital, $;
Church Building, $; Bibles, Prayer Books and Tracts, $;
Book Societies, $; Christian or Theological Education, $;
Disabled Clergymen, $; Miscellaneous, $; Total, $.

APPENDIX C.

TWELFTH ANNUAL REPORT OF THE BOARD OF MISSIONS OF THE DIOCESE OF PENNSYLVANIA.

The Board of Missions of the Diocese of Pennsylvania herewith presents its Twelfth Annual Report.

MEMBERS OF THE BOARD.

The members of the Board whose terms expired in June last were re-appointed, Mr. James S. Whitney taking the place of Dr. Coppeé. The Rev. W. H. Hare and the Rev. G. W. Shinn have removed from the Diocese, and their places on the Board have been supplied by the appointment by the Standing Committee with the Bishop's approval of the Rev. Percy Browne and the Rev. E. A. Warriner.

The Board is now constituted as follows:

The RT. REV. WM. BACON STEVENS, D.D., LL.D., (*ex-officio*) President.

TERM OF SERVICE EXPIRING JUNE, 1871.

The Rev. M. A. De Wolfe Howe, D.D.,   The Rev. E. A. Warriner,
"   "   S. E. Appleton,   Mr. John Welsh,
"   "   T. F. Davies,   "   J. S. McCalla,
"   "   W. P. Orrick,   "   Edw. L. Clark,
"   "   Percy Browne,   "   Frederick Fraley.

TERM OF SERVICE EXPIRING JUNE, 1872.

The Rev. B. Watson, D.D.,   The Rev. R. C. Matlack,
"   "   D. Washburn,   Mr. B. S. Godfrey,
"   "   John Bolton,   "   Jas. S. Biddle,
"   "   J. K. Murphy,   "   Lemuel Coffin,
"   "   J. W. Claxton,   "   Edw. S. Buckley.

MISSIONARIES AND STATIONS.

The following Missionaries were newly appointed :

The Rev. J. B. Pedelupé, Bedford,
" " Jos. W. Murphy, Mahanoy City,
" " C. H. Van Dyne, Hazleton,
" " J. H. H. Millett, Green Ridge,
" " J. Sturges Pearce, Village Green,
" " Wm. Moore, Northumberland,
" " W. S. Heaton, Manheim.

The following have resigned during the year :

The Rev. W. S. Heaton The Rev. J. H. H. Millett,
" " John Long, " " F. Byllesby,
" " J. B. Pedelupé, " " Wm. Ely,
" " J. K. Browse, " " Edm. Christian.

The Missionaries and Stations are now as follows :

		Counties.
Rev. W. S. Heaton,	Manheim,	Lancaster.
" J. L. Heysinger,	New London, Oxford,	Chester.
" Geo. P. Hopkins,	Troy,	Bradford.
" J. A. Jerome,	New Milford and Great Bend,	Susquehanna.
" Thos. Burrows,	Hulmeville and Attleboro',	Bucks.
" R. H. Brown,	Salem and Sterling,	Wayne.
" W. G. Hawkins,	Chambersburg and Shippensburg,	Franklin.
" J. W. Carpenter,	Minersville,	Schuylkill.
" N. Barrows,	Mansfield,	Tioga.
" Geo. G. Field,	Coatesville,	Chester.
" J. H. H. Millett,	Green Ridge,	Luzerne.
" F. W. Bartlett,	Allentown Furnace and Catasauqua,	Lehigh.
" Benjamin Hartley,	Blossburg,	Tioga.
" H. C. Howard,	Pleasant Mount,	Wayne.
" H. Baldy,	Doylestown,	Bucks.
" Joseph W. Murphy,	Mahanoy City,	Schuylkill.
" C. H. Van Dyne,	Hazleton,	Luzerne.
" Wm. Moore,	Northumberland,	Northumberland.
J. H. McElré.	Ashley,	Luzerne.

TREASURER'S ACCOUNT.

During the year ending May 1st, 1871—

39 Churches out of Philada. contributed	$ 829 60
26 " in " "	5,025 30
Collection at Convention	59 21
Contributed by individuals	821 50
Total contributions	$6,735 61
Interest on U. S. Bonds	134 62
Total Receipts	$6,870 23

Of which were—

For general purposes	$5,013 33	
Special for Missions of the Board	839 98	
do do do and City Missions	600 00	
do not of the Board	416 92	
		$6 8 70 23
Balance in hand May 1st, 1870		2,675 66
Total		$9,545 89

The expenses have been—

For Missionaries and Mission Stations, and Secretary of the Board	$7,557 35
Missions and objects not of the Board	566 92
Rent	150 00
Printing and advertising	80 80
Insurance on Bonds	2 00
Total Payments	$8,357 07
Leaving a balance on hand May 1st, 1871	$1 188 82 •

The following tables exhibit the financial condition of the Board for the last eleven years :

The total receipts for the year ending

May 1st, 1861	$5,740 69
" 1862	7 779 55
" 1863	5,336 18
" 1864	6,789 85
" 1865 including $200 reported to the Board,	8,026 44
" 1866	5,461 60
" 1867	8,206 07
" 1868 including $87 50 reported to the Board,	8,542 69
" 1869 " $90.00 " " "	8,821 04
" 1870	7 928 91
" 1871 including $121 97 reported to the Board,	6,870 23

NOTE.—Beside the amounts reported to the Board which have been entered in the Treasurer's Account, the Board has been informed that "the Parish Appropriations and Individual gifts from St. John's Church, Carlisle, for Chambersburg, since May last, amount to upwards of $300."

The receipts from Churches were as follows:

Year ending	Churches out of Philada.	Churches in Philada.
May 1st, 1861	56— $ 946 92	27—$4,443 25
" 1862	83— 1,003 64	39— 5,525 83
" 1863	66— 1,208 71	33— 3,730 50
" 1864	55— 2 070 14	25— 4,339 70
" 1865	68— 2,087 11	37— 5,698 17
" 1866	40— 1,084 16	28— 4,233 58
" 1867	53— 1.292 34	37— 5,871 38
" 1868	43— 1,086 84	37— 6,499 39
" 1869	32— 1,047 17	29— 6,169 81
" 1870	33— 758 47	29— 5,703 93
" 1871	39— 829 60	26— 5,025 30

WORK OF THE BOARD.

The work in which the Board is engaged has been a work of faith, and love and patience. Its design is to spread the knowledge of the truth as it is in Jesus to the waste and neglected places of our Diocese. In many counties of our State but meagre provision is made for needy and famishing souls, and it is our desire to furnish them with the Gospel of our Lord and Master. During the past year the Board has not been without tokens of the Divine favor and blessing.

The following extracts from the Reports of several of our missionaries will show that, so far as their work is concerned, we have reason to thank God and take courage:

Extract from the report of our Missionary at Oxford and New London, November 2d, 1870:

"During the last three months I have continued uninterruptedly in the discharge of my duties. Our services have been resumed in the Hall at Oxford, and with considerable encouragement. You will perceive the importance of holding this point, when I mention that I have thus far succeeded in finding twenty-nine persons here, or in the vicinity, who have been confirmed in our Church. I must also remind you that at the University for colored young men, three and a half miles distant, there are from six to nine communicants, and others who prefer our services. Among these young men are several of good promise, and four (I think) who design to enter the ministry."

Extract from the Report of the Missionary at Pleasant Mount, Wayne county:

"I think some importance may be attached to the mission started five miles north of this village, where the services of our Church have never been heard before, and where there had been services of no kind for twelve months. I have held six Sunday afternoon services, with an average attendance of sixty-nine. At the last one held, one hundred and ten persons were present, showing an increased interest."

The Missionary at Mahanoy City reports starting an encouraging mission at Shenandoah, a growing mining town, five miles from Mahanoy City.

Extract from a report of the Missionary at Green Ridge :

"Since my last report, there have been the regular Sunday services here, both morning and evening, with a gratifying and encouraging increase from Sunday to Sunday in attendance. The Sunday school also appears to be in a healthy condition, and promising well for the future of the Church."

The Missionary at Hamlinton, Wayne county, is most abundant in labors, sustaining services at seven stations, holding three services every Sunday and traveling from 16 to 22 miles.

Extract from report of Missionary at Doylestown, March 18th, 1871 :

"Since my last report the Church improvements at Doylestown have been completed at a cost of about $8,000, over two-thirds of which have been paid. The parish is gradually growing, both in numerical strength and pecuniary ability, and I trust the day is not far remote when it will be able to stand alone."

Extract from report of the Missionary at Mansfield :

"Our new Church building was finished and opened for Divine worship on the 21st of December last. It is a neat gothic, wood edifice, costing over $4,000, seating about two hundred and forty persons. Since it was opened there has been a very gratifying attendance. The erection of this beautiful little Church has been a work of long waiting, toil and patience."

This Church was consecrated by the Bishop in April, at which time he confirmed a class of twenty candidates, among whom were some of the leading and influential citizens of the place.

The Church and parsonage at Tioga were destroyed by fire, but with an energy worthy of commendation, the people have built a new Church.

The Missionary at Coatesville has erected a chapel and is doing a good work.

At Chambersburg a Church is nearly ready for consecration, and the young parish is in a healthy and prosperous condition.

Especial attention is called to the encouraging condition of affairs at Ashley, Luzerne county, where a new Church has been built, and a good work is being done by the Missionary.

26

The Missionary at Hulmeville reports :

"Services are held every Sunday morning in Grace Church in this place, and every afternoon at one or other of the three mission stations. We have an adult or congregational Bible class every Sunday evening with an average attendance of about forty-five. During November and December we had a peculiarly interesting time, and twenty-two joined our Church."

From these extracts of Missionary Reports, it will be seen that in the field which we occupy, there is abundant encouragement to incite us to our duty. The Board has in its employment men of faith and zeal, willing to spend and be spent for the cause of Christ and His Gospel. Their fidelity and self-denial have commended them to our approval. We cannot doubt that their labors have redounded to the glory of God, and the salvation of men. Their reports tell of new missions started and Sunday schools formed. They tell of the sustaining of our Church's services to the comfort of many of her scattered children. They tell of the instruction of the young in the fear and admonition of the Lord. They tell of the building of new Churches. What are we doing to support and multiply the number of the laborers in this our vineyard ? Alas, here is where the Board feels discouraged as its Annual Report is presented. We are compelled to announce the mortifying fact, that instead of receiving an increase of funds to carry on our work, there has been a decrease. By the Treasurer's Report it will be seen that this year we received about $1,000 less than we received last year. Let the simple, unvarnished story of missionary toil, and fidelity and suffering undergone in this Diocese be told in the ears of Christians, and surely their hearts will be stirred with sympathy and aroused to a generous liberality.

One of our clergy looking upon a needy field in which to plant a new station, and then upon the small encouragement offered to engage in the effort writes, " Alas ! how unprovided with means our poor Church is for this kind of work. I ask and receive not—I go in person and am told to stay at my post. I stay and work on, and am unable to pay my debts without humiliating begging—but this is my cross perhaps. His will be done whose kingdom come, is our most frequent prayer."

The Board earnestly prays that there may be an enlarged spirit of liberality in the behalf of its work for the coming year.

TREASURER'S ACCOUNT.

BOARD OF MISSIONS

OF THE

DIOCESE OF PENNSYLVANIA.

Dr.　　　　*Board of Missions of the Diocese of Pennsylvania,*

1871.			
May 1	Paid Rev. Benjamin Hartley	$441	66
"	" John L. Heysinger	467	11
"	" do (Reported to the Board)	26	97
"	" George P. Hopkins	300	00
"	" Wm. S. Heaton	382	50
"	" John A. Jerome	200	00
"	" R. Hill Brown	260	00
"	" Faber Byllesby	104	17
"	" J. T. Carpenter	483	40
"	" Wm. Ely	62	50
"	" George G. Field	250	00
"	" Samuel H. Meade	50	00
"	" J. H. H. Millett	250	00
"	" Henry K. Brouse	41	67
"	" F. Weston Bartlett	350	00
"	" Thomas Burrows	350	00
"	" Edmund Christian	166	34
"	" W. George Hawkins	375	00
"	" N. Barrows	250	00
"	" Horatio C. Howard	250	00
"	" J. P. Pedelupé	262	00
"	" Joseph W. Murphy	212	50
"	" Hurley Baldy	150	00
"	" Charles H. Van Dyke	225	00
"	" Wm. R. Stockton	62	50
"	" John Long	87	50
"	" Wm. Moore	183	33
	do (Reported to the Board)	45	00
"	" J. S. Pearce	50	00
"	" Daniel Washburn	100	00
"	" Aaron Bernstein	116	65
"	" Isaac Martin	50	00
"	" John G. Furey	75	00
"	" Joseph H. McElrey	62	50
"	Missionary services at Milford	100	00
	" " Newtown and Yardleyville	100	00
	" " St. Clair	50	00
"	St. George's Church, Philadelphia	100	00
"	Church of the Crucifixion, Philadelphia	56	92
"	Church of the Good Shepherd, Radnor	200	00
"	Rt. Rev. Bishop Stevens, general Missionary expenses	438	55
"	Rev. John A. Childs, D.D., Secretary	300	00
"	Treasurer Lehigh and Schuylkill Convocation	85	00
"	" Susquehanna Convocation, (Reported to the Board)	50	00
"	Rent	150	00
"	Advertising	16	20
	Amount carried forward	$8290	47

By the following contributions from Parishes from May 1st, 1870, to May 1st, 1871 :

BERKS COUNTY.
St. Gabriel's Church, Douglasville.......... $14 00

BLAIR COUNTY.
Grace Church, Altoona.................... 17 00

BRADFORD COUNTY.
St. Paul's Church, Troy.............. ...... 5 00

BUCKS COUNTY.
St. James' Church, Bristol..... .... $42 00
St. Paul's Church, Doylestown............. 13 51
Christ Chapel, Oak Grove................. 7 50
63 01

CARBON COUNTY.
St. Mark's Church, Mauch Chunk.......... 36 83
do   do   special.... 35 00
71 83

CENTRE COUNTY.
St. Paul's Church, Philipsburg............. 10 00

CHESTER COUNTY.
Church of Holy Trinity, West Chester, (special) 117 11
do.   do.   Reported to the Board. 26 97
144 08

COLUMBIA COUNTY.
Church of Our Saviour, Montoursville, (Reported to the Board)..................... 10 00

DELAWARE COUNTY.
St. David's Church, Radnor................. 10 00
Calvary Church, Rockdale.................. 40 00
Christ Church, Media...................... 5 61
55 61

LANCASTER COUNTY.
Hope Chapel, Mt. Hope................... 1 42
St. Paul's Church, Manheim, S. School...... 25 94
27 36

LEBANON COUNTY.
St. Luke's Church, Lebanon............... 22 00
Colebrooke Station....................... 1 00
23 00

LEHIGH COUNTY.
Grace Church, Allentown.................. 10 00

Amount carried forward................ $450 89

DR. *Board of Missions of the Diocese of Pennsylvania,*

1871.		
May 1	Amount brought forward......................	$8290 47
	Paid M'Calla & Stavely, printing....................	64 60
	" Fidelity Trust Company......................	2 00
	Total payments.........................	$8357 07
	Amount carried forward........................	$8357 07

in account with James S. Biddle, Treasurer. CR.

Amount brought forward..............		$450 89
LUZERNE COUNTY.		
Trinity Church, Carbondale................	25 00	
St. James' Church, Pittston..............	16 00	
St. James' Church, Eckley.................	10 00	
St. Paul's Church, White Haven............	3 90	
St. Philip's Church, Summit Hill.........	2 34	
St. Peter's Church, Hazleton..............	5 00	
Drifton Mission...........................	10 00	
Church of the Good Shepherd, Green Ridge..	6 80	
		79 04
LYCOMING COUNTY.		
Christ Church, Williamsport, (Reported to the Board)...............................	50 00	
St. John's Church, Muncy, (Reported to the Board)...............................	20 00	
		70 00
MONTGOMERY COUNTY.		
St. James' Church, Perkiomen.............	5 25	
St. Thomas' Church, Whitemarsh..........	5 00	
St. John's Church, Norristown.............	25 02	
Church of Redeemer, Lower Merion, special.	100 00	
St. Paul's Church, Upper Providence.......	7 48	
do. do. special.	6 92	
		149 67
NORTHUMBERLAND COUNTY.		
St. Mark's Church, Northumberland, (Reported to the Board).....................		15 00
PHILADELPHIA COUNTY.		
Christ Church.............................	50 00	
St. Peter's Church........................	725 00	
St. James' Church.........................	176 55	
St. Stephen's Church......................	215 39	
St. Andrew's Church	186 35	
do. do. special................	100 00	
Grace Church.............................	100 00	
Church of the Ascension..................	61 42	
St. Luke's Church........................	500 00	
Church of the Atonement..................	100 00	
St. Mark's Church........................	463 50	
do. do. special..................	100 00	
Church of the Mediator...................	50 00	
do. do. S. School, special....	133 40	
Church of the Advent.....................	126 18	
Zion Church..............................	34 10	
do. S. School....................	25 00	
Trinity Church, Southwark................	20 00	
All Saints' Church, Lower Dublin..	53 50	
do. do. do. special....	100 00	
St. Mark's Church, Frankford.......	120 00	
do. do. do. special.........	200 00	
Amount carried forward.................		$3606 89

DR.   *Board of Missions of the Diocese of Pennsylvania,*

Amount brought forward........................	$8357 07
Balance, Cash in hand...............................	1188 82
	$9545 89

We have examined the foregoing account, compared it with the vouchers, and find it correct : the balance $1188 82 being to the credit of the Treasurer in the Philadelphia National Bank. The Treasurer also exhibited a certificate of deposit of the Fidelity Insurance and Trust Co., for $2000, of U. S. 5–20 Bonds.

LEMUEL COFFIN,   ⎫
BENJ. G. GODFREY, ⎬ *Auditing Committee.*
                ⎭

PHILADELPHIA, May 19, 1871.

in account with James S. Biddle, Treasurer.   CR.

Amount brought forward...............		$3606 89
PHILADELPHIA,—Continued.		
St. James' Church, Kingsessing.............	45 00	
St. Andrew's Church, West Philadelphia....	20 00	
St. Paul's Church, Chestnut Hill..........	119 25	
Church of the Redeemer, Seamen's Mission..	15 39	
Church of the Holy Trinity.................	520 00	
Church of the Incarnation.................	55 00	
Calvary Church, Germantown..............	146 58	
St. Mary's Church, West Philadelphia......	31 92	
St. Luke's Church, Germantown.............	100 00	
Trinity Church, Oxford....................	381 77	
		5025 30
SCHUYLKILL COUNTY.		
Church of Faith, Mahanoy City.............	5 20	
Mission at Shenandoah....................	3 80	
		9 00
SUSQUEHANNA COUNTY.		
St. Paul's Church, Montrose,............	20 00	
do. do. special...........	30 00	
St. Mark's Church, New Milford...........	3 00	
Grace Church, Great Bend.................	3 00	
		56 00
Collection at Convention..................		59 21
Mrs. Edward Coleman, for Blossburg........	100 00	
Miss Greene, Phila., for Rev. W. S. Heaton..	112 50	
Mrs. and Miss Buckley....................	8 00	
"Z," for Missionaries of the Board and City		
Missions...............................	600 00	
Lewis R. Dunlevy's birthday offering.......	1 00	
		821 50
Interest on U. S. Bonds...................		134 62
Total Receipts................................		$6870 23
Add balance in hand May 1st, 1870...........		2675 66
		$9545 89

1871.			
May 2	By balance in Philadelphia Bank..........		$1188 82

The above receipts were :

For general purposes..					$5013 33
Special for Missions of the Board.................				839 98	
do. do. do. and City Missions				600 00	
do. for other objects.........................				416 92	
					$1856 90
Total..					$6870 23

JAMES S. BIDDLE, Treasurer,

1714 *Locust Street.*

APPENDIX D.

PAROCHIAL REPORTS.

Those in italics not in Union.
Those marked thus * not entitled to send deputies.

ADAMS COUNTY.
Christ Church, Huntington.
No Report.

BEDFORD COUNTY.
St. James' Church, Bedford. Admitted 1866.
No Report.

BERKS COUNTY.
St. Gabriel's Church, Morlattin (Douglassville). Admitted 1785. Rev. Jeremiah
Karcher, Rector. David Lord and Henry Yocom, Wardens.

Baptisms—adult 1, infants 3, total 4; confirmed 8; communicants, added, new 8, present number 90 (about); public services, on Sundays 26, on other days 10, total 36; Sunday Schools, officers and teachers 19, scholars 88; Bible class, teacher 1, members 6; Church 1, sittings, all free, 250; parsonage 1; salary of Rector $400 per annum; arrears of salary, none.

Money receipts from all sources—Offertory at Holy Communion $21.68, Collections in Church $31.17, Subscriptions $309.20, Rent of parsonage $200; Total $562.05.

Expenditures and appropriations—Current Expenses (including salary of Rector) $445, Episcopal and Convention fund $10, Support of Sunday School $89.15, Diocesan Missions $24 (including $10 for Convocation); Total $568.15.

This decrease, however, is mainly but seeming. For several years past a Sunday School, identified with our Chapel, had been maintained in a Public School House but a few squares from our Church. The number of scholars attending this school was reported from year to year in addition to that of those attending the schools held at the Church. But I found that, as the sessions of the two schools were at different hours, both were generally attended by the same set of children; and hence, in the main, it was only having two sessions of the same school. This being the case, the separate Mission School has been discontinued, as it greatly increased the expenses of the school without any practical results.

St. Michael's Church, Birdsboro. Admitted 1853. Rev. Edmund Leaf, Rector. Reese Evans and Joseph R. Kurst, Wardens.

Baptisms, infants 12; confirmed 3; communicants, new 3; present number 27; Marriages 6; burials 5, public services, on Sundays 50, other days 7, total 57; children catechized in the Sunday School; Sunday School, male teachers 4, female 7, total 11; pupils 85; salary $600.

Collections—Parochial—Alms $24 76, for Sunday School $176 19, current expenses $20, Subscriptions for Salary $523; Total $743 95.

Extra-Parochial—Diocesan Missions $15, Domestic $130, Convention and Episcopal Fund $5, Church Hospital $6, Total $156. Total parochial and extra, $899 95.

During the past year occasional services have been held at the Cemetery Chapel, where also we have a Sunday School numbering 6 teachers and 40 pupils, not included in the above report.

BLAIR COUNTY.

St. Luke's Church, Altoona. Admitted 1859. Rev. J. J. A. Morgan, Rector-elect. S. M. Woodcock and James Kearney, Wardens.

Baptisms, infants 11; marriage 1, burial 1, public services, on 14 Sundays 34, on other days 13, total 47; children catechized, times 1; Sunday Schools, officers and teachers 21;

scholars 113; Bible classes, teachers 2, members 16; Church 1; school building 1, parsonage 1; number of free sittings all.

Money receipts from all sources—Pew rents, pews free; collections in Church $117.93, subscriptions $734.50, Total, $852.43.

Expenditures and Appropriations.—Current expenses (including salary of Rector), $1030, repairs and improvements $30, payments of debts no debt, Episcopal and Convention Fund $12.50, support of Sunday Schools $106.21; Domestic Missions $20.19.

The undersigned has had the St. Luke's Memorial Church parish in charge since the 18th of January last. Being in Deacon's orders, the Bishop has appointed the 23d inst. for my ordination and institution into the rectorship of the Church. There is every encouragement to believe the parish has entered upon a new career of Church life and Church work. The people are making generous provision for my support and comfort.* All congregational and temporal matters give token of prosperity. A class of 28 is in course of preparation for confirmation on the occasion of the Bishop's visit so soon to transpire.

The large demands upon the parish for its own needs, have caused some delinquency for the present, in collections for general purposes, which we hope to avoid in the future. The seats in this Church are *all free*, and it is sustained by the voluntary offerings of the members of the parish.

BRADFORD COUNTY.

St. Matthew's Church, Pike. Admitted 1814.

No report.

Christ Church, Towanda. Admitted 1844. Rev. Wm. McGlathery, Rector.

No report.

----

*My salary has been raised within the past 10 days from $1000 to $1200 per annum, unasked and without a word or hint from me. The most they gave before was $720 per annum.

St. Paul's Church, Troy. Admitted 1845. Rector, Rev. George P. Hopkins. .

Baptisms, adult 1, infant 1; communicants, died 1, removed 2, present number 33; burials 4; public Sunday services at Troy 47, for the most part in the morning; do. at missionary points 31; services on other days 55; Church accommodations, edifice 1, sittings 250; salary furnished by voluntary subscriptions, amount not rendered, but far below the necessities of the minister, since the commencement of his labors here. Suscriptions for Church lamps, $40; expenses for lighting, heating and attending Church $60, Sunday School $3, Sunday School books $4, Convention fund $6.50, Foreign Missions $3, Domestic Missions $3, Diocesan Missions $5.

Sunday School small, from the fact of there being few children in our Church.

At two Musical Festivals gotten up by persons belonging to our congregation, the first given in the fall, the last during the winter, $180 were cleared. This money is reserved in bank for improving Church building.

Eight years lacking a few months have transpired from the commencement of my missionary labors in these parts. Number of communicants at that time 12, present number 33. Number of persons confirmed within the above period 36; baptized, adults 19, including by immersion 2. Most of those who have connected themselves with our communion have been educated in non-Episcopal societies.

Trinity Church, Athens. Admitted 1864

No report.

BUCKS COUNTY.

St. James' (the Greater) Church, Bristol. Rev. John H. Drumm, D. D., Rector. A. Murray McIlvaine and Henry L. Gaw, Wardens.

Baptisms, adults 5, infants 13, total 18; confirmed 10; communicants, present number 120; marriages 12, burials 11; public services, on Sundays 114, on other days about 50; Children catechized at least once a month; Sunday Schools 2, officers and teachers 17 in the parish Sunday School, and 2 in that at Bensalem; scholars 153; Bible Classes, teachers 2, members about 20. Church 1, sittings about 400; Sunday School building 1, parsonage 1, Cemetery around the Church. Salary of Rector $1200, arrears of salary none, number of free sittings none, set apart as free none, but several are really so, and especially at the evening service there is full accommodation (and a welcome) for all who may come.

Money receipts from all sources.—Pew Rents $1500, Offertory at Holy Communion $98.03, Collections in Church $175, besides those given below; subscriptions about $225 for Sunday School, &c.; other sources $500, Total $2498.

Expenditures and Appropriations.—Current Expenses (including salary of Rector), $1600, repairs and improvements $275, Episcopal and Convention fund $40, support of Sunday Schools about $150, Parochial Missions $20, for the Poor $98.03, to Missions, Foreign mite boxes $25.62, Domestic $33.50, and in mite boxes $19, Oregon Mission $87, Diocesan $30.87, for the Jews $15.17, Episcopal Hospital $51, Church Home for Children $26.65, Disabled Clergymen $22; Total about $2500.

Financial condition—Encumbrances—Mortgages on Church edifice none, on parsonage $1000, Ground Rent on buildings or lands none, other indebtedness none.

The Rector being strongly impressed with the necessity of doing something to relieve the spiritual destitution of the country around Bristol, has established regular missionary services at Tullytown and Emilie. As he is not able to procure assistance, he has thus to hold three services every Sunday, and to travel about eight miles. He reports with thankfulness, that the parish is in good condition, but he is confident that it would be greatly increased in strength and usefulness if it had an additional minister and a parish school.

St. Luke's Church, Newtown. Admitted 1835. Mr. Cochran lay-reading. Alex. Chambers and John Barnsley, Wardens.

Baptisms, infants 4, total 4; communicants, present number 11; marriage 1; public services, on Sundays 50, on other days 2, total 52; average attendance on Sundays 50; Sunday School, officers and teachers 10, scholars 73; Church 1, sittings 175; School building 1; Parsonage 1; Cemetery 1; Salary of Rector $300 per annum; number of free sittings 20.

Money receipts from all sources.—Pew rents $250, collections in Church $50.25, donations $5, other sources $25, Total $330.25.

Expenditures and Appropriations.—Current Expenses (including salary of Rector), $300, repairs and improvements $24.66, Episcopal and Covention fund $5, Episcopal Hospital $5.50, Disabled Clergymen $2.40, Total $337.56.

Financial condition.—Aggregate value of property of the Parish, real and personal $6.000, indebtedness $300.

We have, during the year, purchased a parsonage for $2000, on which we have collected and paid $1700, leaving yet unpaid $300.

St. Andrew's Church, Yardleyville. Admitted 1835.

No report.

Grace Church, Hulmeville. Admitted 1837. Rev. Thomas Burrows, Rector. Edmund G. Harrison and Samuel H. Harrison, Wardens.

Baptisms, adults 11, infants 3, total 14; confirmed 22; communicants, added, new 22, by removal 5, died or removed 6, present number 58; marriages none; burials 6; public services, on Sundays 80, on other days 8, total 88; average attendance on Sundays 100; Sunday Schools, officers and teachers 10, scholars 116; Bible class teacher 1, members 50; Church 1, sittings 200, Parsonage 1, cemetery 1; salary of Rector $800 per annum; arrears of salary none.

Money receipts from all sources.—Pew Rents $400, offertory at Holy Communion $12, collections in Church $22.28, subscriptions $200, Donations $40, other sources $557.06, Board of Missions $200; Total $1431.34.

Expenditures and Appropriations.—Current Expenses (including Salary of Rector) $821.78, Repairs and Improvements $40, Payment of Debts $280, Episcopal and Convention Fund $5, Support of Sunday Schools $33, for the Jews $2.50, Disabled Clergymen $2; Total $1184.28.

Financial condition.—Aggregate value of property of the Parish, real and personal, $6300, Ground Rent on buildings or lands $1000.

During the year an adult Bible class has been held on Sunday evenings. The lessons have been a week in advance of the Sunday School, thus affording teachers an opportunity of studying for their class duties. This Bible class has been attended with very encouraging results. The attendance has averaged about fifty. We use the Protestant Episcopal Berean series of Sunday School Lessons.

During the past winter we have had a rich outpouring of the Holy Spirit, and have enjoyed times of refreshing from the presence of the Lord.

I have kept up missionary services at Attleboro, 2 miles distant, twice each month. The attendance is good.

Oxford Valley, 3 miles, and Fallsington, 5 miles distant, have been taken up as Missionary points. I preach in each place once a month. The attendance is very good, and the prospect is encouraging.

Through the liberality of friends in Philadelphia I have been furnished with a horse and wagon, the people of my several charges generously agreeing to bear the expenses of keeping my horse. I am thus enabled to visit more, and reach my appointments with comfort.

A review of the past year presents evidence of the blessing of the Lord. To his name be the praise and glory.

————

Trinity Church, Centreville. Admitted 1840. Rev. H. Baldy, Rector. William Stavely and William Biles, Wardens.

Baptisms, adults 2; confirmed 3; communicants, added, new 3, died or removed 1, present number 28; public services, on Sundays 42; average attendance on Sundays 50; Sunday Schools, officers and teachers 17, scholars 90; Bible class teacher 1, members 11; Church 1, sittings 125; salary of Rector $282 per annum.

Money receipts from all sources.—Pew Rents $94, Offertory at Holy Communion $14.27, Collections in Church $46.92, Donations $141.08, other sources $146.36; Total $442.63.

Expenditures and Appropriations.—Current Expenses (including Salary of Rector) $282, Payment of Debts $18.60, Episcopal and Convention fund $5, Support of Sunday Schools $75, Parish Library $50, to Missions, Domestic $4.71, Episcopal Hospital $3 32, Book Societies $4, Disabled Clergymen $4.20; Total $442.63.

St. Paul's Church, Doylestown. Admitted 1847. Rev. H. Baldy, Rector. John Brock and Lewis Worthington, Wardens.

Baptisms, adults 5, infants 11, total 16; confirmed 4; communicants, added, new 4, by removal 4, died or removed 5, present number 44; marriages 2; burials 2; public services, on Sundays 70, on other days 45, total 115; average attendance on Sundays 90; children catechized frequently; Sunday Schools, officers and teachers 10, scholars 70; Church 1; sittings 230; parsonage 1; salary of Rector $532 per annum.

Money receipts from all sources.—Pew Rents $560, Offertory at Holy Communion $95.18, Collections in Church $135, Subscriptions $3453.50, Donations $100; Total $4343.68.

Expenditures and Appropriations.—Current Expenses (including salary of Rector) $692.43, Repairs and Improvements $3117.50, Payment of Debts $336, Episcopal and Convention Fund $15, Support of Sunday Schools $70, to Missions, Foreign $22.75, Domestic $31, Home Mission, for Colored People $10, Diocesan $13.51, Episcopal Hospital $12.75, Bibles, Prayer Books and Tracts, $9.21, Disabled Clergymen $13.53; Total $4343.68.

CARBON COUNTY.

St. Mark's Church, Mauch Chunk. Admitted 1836. Rev. Leighton Coleman, Rector. Hon. Asa Packer and Francis R. Sayre, Wardens.

Baptisms, adults 6, infants 46, total 52; confirmed 42; communicants, added, new 39, by removal 6, died or removed

6, present number 189; marriages 5; burials 6; public services, on Sundays 120, on other days 240, total 360; children catechized, times 12; Sunday Schools, officers and teachers 28, scholars 270; Bible classes, teachers 3, members 35; Parish schools, teachers 2, average attendance 52; Church 1, sittings 450, Chapel (the statistics of which are included in this Report) 1, school building 1; salary of Rector $2000 per annum, arrears of salary, none; number of free sittings, *all free.*

Money receipts from all sources.—Offertory at Holy Communion $100.40.

Expenditures and Appropriations.—Current Expenses (including salary of Rector) $2641.28, payment of debts $2200, Episcopal and Convention Fund $50, Support of Sunday Schools $213.15, of Parish Schools, extra, $60, to Missions, Foreign $85 (including $25 from the Sunday School) Domestic (including mite chest receipts and Sunday School contributions) $421.63, Home Mission for Colored People $20, Diocesan (including Sunday School contributions) $261.83, for the Jews $10.28, Episcopal Hospital $45.82, Church building elsewhere $130, Book Societies $50, Christian or Theological Education $65.79, Disabled Clergymen $59.04, Miscellaneous $410, towards a Bell and Cabinet Organ for St. John's Chapel, $128.43, Receipts of the Mite Society $63.44, towards the Endowment of Bishop Thorpe School $1000; Total $8011.09.

In the various items mentioned above, are included the contributions of the Sunday Schools, which amount altogether to the really handsome sum of $1502.17. They are invaluable helpers in every good work, and especially by their self-denying and systematic offerings.

I am most thankful in being privileged, to record another year of harmony and prosperity, as well in things spiritual as in things temporal. The number of persons baptized and confirmed is largely in excess of any former year, while I trust our religious life is correspondingly advancing. I cannot be too grateful for the affection and confidence of my dear people, and the hearty and liberal manner in which they have coöperated with me in all parochial and missionary enterprises.

On Easter Day, by a generous offering from adults and children, provision was made for the extinguishment of the debt upon St. John's Chapel, East Mauch Chunk, and it is hoped that during the current twelvemonth the building may be finished and ready for consecration.

During the year, in addition to services at Summit Hill and White Haven (reported elsewhere) I have officiated occasionally at Heckelbirnie, Penn Haven, and Weatherly. The statistics of St. John's Chapel are included in the foregoing report.

St. Philip's Church, Summit Hill. Admitted 1850. Rev. Leighton Coleman, Rector. Wm. S. Hobart and Matthew E. Sinyard, Wardens.

Baptisms, infants 5; confirmed 9; communicants, added, new 8, died or removed 2, present number 38; burials 2; public services, on Sundays 40, on other days 10, total 50; Sunday Schools, officers and teachers 22, scholars 175; Church 1, sitting 200; number of free sittings, all free.

Expenditures and Appropriations.—Current Expenses (including salary of Rector) $115.10, Episcopal and Convention Fund $5, to Missions, Foreign $7.88, Diocesan $4.49, for the Jews $1.28, Episcopal Hospital $3.63, Disabled Clergymen $5.32, Miscellaneous $20, Contributions of Sunday Schools to Domestic Missions, through the Domestic Missionary Army $33, through the Mite Chest $44.40, to other objects $88.83, total for the Sunday Schools $166.23; grand total $328.93.

During the year I have been enabled, in connection with my duties elsewhere, to maintain regular services in this parish on every Sunday, except the second of each month, and occasionally during the week. The congregations continue very good, and their interest unabated. A valuable addition was made to our numbers in the class confirmed at the last visitation by the Bishop. The contributions of the children of the two Sunday Schools (the second being at Bloomingdale) have been remarkably liberal (especially so to Missionary objects), notwithstanding the several suspensions of business which have occurred in the past twelvmonth. I regret to have to record the removal to another field of the late Superintendent of both schools, Mr. Chas. E. West, who has laid the parish under great obligations by his exemplary devotion to this important branch of our work.

CENTRE COUNTY.

St. Paul's Church, Phillipsburg. Admitted 1827. Rev. Samuel H. Meade, Rector.
Robert Loyd and David W. Holt, Wardens.

Baptisms, adults 5, infants 3, total 8; confirmed, class awaiting; communicants, added, new 4, died or removed 6, present number 69; marriages 3; burials 9; public services, on Sundays 60, on other days 1, total 61; average attendance on Sundays 100; children catechized, times 60; Sunday Schools, officers and teachers 18, scholars 105; Bible classes, teacher 1, members 10; Church 1, sittings 200; parsonage 1; salary of Rector $1000 per annum; arrears of salary none; number of free sittings, all; extra Sunday services, free to all, all services.

Money receipts from all sources.—Seats free, Offertory at Holy Communion $50.98, Collections in Church $25.08, Subscriptions $1931.13; Total $2007.06.

Expenditures and Appropriations.—Current Expenses (including salary of Rector) $1022.24, for time that I served, Repairs and Improvements $151, payment of debts, none to pay, Episcopal and Convention Fund $12, support of Sunday Schools $89.65, to Missions, Foreign $12.84, Diocesan $5, Miscellaneous $714.33; Total $2007.06.

Financial condition.—Encumbrances, Mortgage on Church Edifice none, on other buildings none, Ground Rent on buildings or lands none, other indebtedness none.

On the 14th of November, 1870, I retired from this parish.

After an absence of five months, accepting the unanimous call of the Vestry and Church to return, I resumed the charge on the 16th of April, 1871—the first Sunday after Easter. Prior to my retirement, the Church had become entirely self-supporting, and opened its doors on Easter Monday, 1870, as a *Free Episcopal Church*, with feelings of deep gratitude for the timely assistance rendered by the Board of Diocesan Missions.

St. John's Church, Bellefonte. Admitted 1839. Rev. Henry J. W. Allen, Rector.
James Armor and W. Montgomery, Wardens.

Baptisms, infant 1; commmunicants, added, by removal 1, present number 50; marriage 1; burials 5; public services, on Sundays 56, on other days 28, total 84; children catechized, times 6; Sunday Schools, officers and teachers 9, scholars 70; Bible classes, teacher 1, members 5; Church sittings 300; salary of Rector $1200 per annum; arrears of salary, none.

Money receipts from all sources.—Pew Rents $700, Offertory at Holy Communion $200.38, Collections in Church $50, Subscriptions and Donations $1200, other sources $570; Total $2620.38.

Expenditures and Appropriations.—Current Expenses (including salary of Rector) $11, Episcopal and Convention Fund $26.10, to Missions, Foreign $15.36, Domestic $16.17, Diocesan $20.34, for the Jews $6, Episcopal Hospital $15.10, Disabled Clergymen $15.97, Miscellaneous, French Relief Fund, $23.68.

This report covers the time during which I have had charge of the Parish, viz.: from the 8th of October, 1870. The new Church has been finished, and was occupied on Easter Sunday for the first time. It is considered to be one of the finest Church edifices in this part of the State. It is completely furnished with carpets, cushions, a new and beautiful font of Caen stone, and chancel furniture of an appropriate ecclesiastical pattern—the last being the gift of Samuel Reynolds, Esq. of Lancaster. The old organ has been repaired, and adorned with a new front. Two memorial windows, of the best class

of workmanship, add greatly to the beauty of the Church.
They are respectively to the memory of two deceased parishioners, viz.: Judge James T. Hale and Judge James Burn-
side. The debt on the Church is small, and will soon be
cancelled.

CHESTER COUNTY.

St. Peter's Church, Great Valley. Admitted 1785. Rev. A. E. Tortat, Rector. John
L. Philips and Benjamin Stewart, Wardens.

Communicants, died or removal 4; present number 23;
burials 3; public services on Sundays 42; average attendance
52; Sunday School teachers 4, pupils 35; Church accommodation, edifice, 1; sittings, 150; parsonage sold; cemetery 1;
salary of Rector $500; number of free sittings 75. Our Sun-
day services are free to all.

Money Receipts.—Pew Rents, $40, Offertory at Holy
Communion, $21, collection in Church, $33.82, investments,
$465; Total, $559.82.

Expenditures.—Current expenses, including salary of Rector,
$550, Repairs and Improvements $120, Episcopal and Convention Fund, $10, support of Sunday Schools, $14, Missions,
Foreign, $5, Domestic, $5, Diocesan, $20, Episcopal Hospi-
tal, $6, Prayer Books $2, Disabled Clergy, $5, Total $737.

St. John's Church, New London. Admitted 1793. Rev. J. L. Heysinger, Rector. Thos.
M. Charlton and Joseph Hodgson, Wardens.

Confirmed 3; communicants, added, new 1, by removal 1,
present number 28; marriage 1; public services, on Sundays
52, on other days 1, total 53; children catechized, times several; Sunday Schools 3, officers and teachers 30, scholars 220;
Church 1, sittings 150; cemetery 1; salary of Rector $200
per annum; arrears of salary $92.50; number of free sittings
150.

Money receipts from all sources.—Collections in Church
$11.15, Subscriptions $150, Donations $46; Total $207.15.

Expenditures and Appropriations.—Current Expenses (including salary of Rector) $115, Repairs and Improvements

$6, Episcopal and Convention Fund $5, Disabled Clergymen $5, Miscellaneous $1.15; Total $132.15.

Financial condition.—Aggregate value of property of the Parish, real and personal, $2000.

OXFORD.

The Missionary work begun at Oxford last year, in connection with St. John's, has been carried on with a good degree of success the present year. Public service has been held on Sunday 40 times, and on other days 6 times.

In June last a Festival and Fair was held by the ladies, to raise funds for the Mission It resulted in a net gain of $306, which has been safely invested to aid in the erection of a Church edifice. In addition, a gentleman of the town not connected with the Church, has offered us a valuable lot of ground, or the means to purchase one, as may be preferred by us, as a site for a Church. An effort is now making to have this properly secured. A very good Cabinet Organ has also been purchased during the year, and paid for. The total amount of money appropriated within the year for current expenses and other objects, exclusive of the Church lot, is $611.84. None of this was used by the Missionary for his own support.

KENNETT SQUARE.

In addition to my labors as Rector at St. John's, and Missionary at Oxford, I also have charge of Kennett Square, under the special supervision of the S. E. Convocation. The following summary exhibits the present condition of this difficult but not unimportant field of labor:

Baptisms, adult 1, infant 1, total 2; confirmations, no visitation; communicants, added, new 2, by removal 4, died or removed 4, present number 14; marriages none; burials 2; public services, on Sundays 84, other days 5, total 89; children catechized, times 12; Sunday Schools, officers and teachers 6, scholars 25, Bible class 1, teacher 1, members 12;

Church services are held in a school-house, fitted up for the purpose; sittings about 75, all free.

Collected for current expenses during the year $125.

Owing to providential hindrances, the Bishop was not able to make a visitation. A small class now awaits confirmation

---

St. Mary' Church, Warwick. Admitted 1808. Daniel B. Mauger, Warden.

Communicants, present number 30; burials 9; Sunday School 1, teachers 9, pupils 70; property other than Church building and lot $900.

St. John's Church, Pequea. Admitted 1810. Rev. Henry R. Smith, Rector. Joseph Hamilton and Henry W. Worrest, Wardens.

Baptisms, adults 2, infants 14, total 16; confirmed 4; communicants, added, new 7, died or removed 9, present number 33; marriages 4; burials 10; public services, on Sundays 47, on other days 12, total 59; average attendance on Sundays 71; Sunday Schools, officers and teachers 7, scholars 36; Church 1, sittings 260, parsonage 1, cemetery 1; salary of Rector, $800; arrears of salary, none; number of free sittings 100.

Money receipts from all sources—Pew Rents $444.47, Collections in Church $148.07. Subscriptions $371.90, Investments $426; Total $1390.44.

Expenditures and Appropriations.—Current Expenses (including salary of Rector) $909.34, Repairs and Improvements $371.90, Episcopal and Convention fund $17, support of Sunday Schools $36.46, to Missions, Foreign $15.50, Domestic $12.02, Episcopal Hospital $13.50, Disabled Clergymen $14.72; Total $1390.44.

Financial condition.—Aggregate value of property of the Parish, real and personal, $12,000; Encumbrances, none; other indebtedness, none.

During the past year I have travelled, in the actual work of my ministry, 3748 miles, mostly in the saddle or on foot; preached 140 times, delivered 35 addresses, baptized 9 adults and 24 infants, solemnized 6 weddings, officiated at 19 funerals, made 203 pastoral visits, and presented 26 persons for confirmation. During the greater portion of the year I travelled about 30 miles each Sunday, and held service and preached at three stations—every alternate Sunday holding service in 3 different counties. Although this labor has made serious inroads upon a vigorous constitution, I have no complaints to utter, inasmuch as among its fruits may be found increased congregations and contributions at the outlying stations, and the largest average attendance in St. John's that we have ever had, notwithstanding the transfer of four families, numbering seven communicants, to Grace Church, Parkesburg.

St. Paul's Church, West Whiteland.   Admitted 1828.   Rev. A. E. Tortat, Rector, Azariah Thomas and Wm. B. Davis, Wardens,

Baptism.—Infants, 2; communicants, died or removed 5, present number 39; burials, 1; public service on Sundays, 41, on other days, 1, total, 42; average attendance on Sundays, 120; children catechized, times 6; Sunday Schools, officers and teachers 6, scholars 46; Bible class, teacher 1, members 7; Church 1; sittings 350; cemetery 1; salary of Rector $500, arrears of salary, $100; number of free sittings 100; our Sunday services are free to all.

Money receipts from all sources—Pew Rents $374, offertory at Holy Communion $37, collections in Church $76, Subscriptions $300, Donations $15, Investments $60; Total $861.

Expenditures and appropriations—Current Expenses including salary of Rector $540, Repairs and Improvements $500, Episcopal and Convention Fund $7; support of Sunday Schools $15, Foreign Missions $10, Domestic $10, Diocesan $20, Episcopal Hospital $4, Bibles, Prayer Books and Tracts $3.92: Christian or Theological Education $5, Disabled Clergymen $5; Total $1,11.92

A parsonage for the united Churches of St. Paul's and St. Peter's is very much needed, for the success of the parishes and the comfort of the Rector. Who will help us in our necessity?

St. Andrew's Church, West Vincent, Admitted 1834.

No report.

———

Grace Church, Parkesburg. Admitted 1871. Rev. Henry R. Smith, Minister. Wm. P. Banks and George W. Worrest, Wardens.

Baptisms, infants 2; communicants 13; public services, on Sundays 71, on other days 2, total 73; average attendance at evening service 70; Sunday School, officers and teachers 6, scholars 51.

Money receipts from all sources $100, devoted entirely to parochial needs. I am much indebted to Messrs. C. E. Fessenden, of the Divinity School, and T. R. Godber, a candidate for Orders, for valuable services at this station.

———

St. Mark's Church, Honeybrook.

No report.

———

Holy Trinity Church, West Chester. Admitted 1838. Rev. John Bolton, Rector.

Baptisms, adults 10, infants 20, total 30; confirmed 17; communicants, added 10, new 5, by removal 2; died or removed 1, present number 225; marriages 15; burials 9; public services, on Sundays 3, on other days 2, total 5; average attendance on Sundays 500; children catechized, times 12; Sunday School, officers and teachers 25, scholars 250, Bible class, teacher 1, members 38. Church 1, sittings 600; school building 1, parsonage 1; salary of Rector $1800 per annum; arrears of salary, none; number of free sittings 100.

Money receipts from all sources—Pew Rents $3210, Offertory at Holy Communion $301.31, Collections in Church $559.78, Donations $660, investments none; Total $4731.09.

Expenditures and Appropriations—Current Expenses (including salary of Rector) $3036.55, Repairs and Improvements $900, Payment of Debts $100, Episcopal and Convention Fund $50, Support of Sunday Schools $75, Parish Library $100, Parochial Missions $281.45, for the Poor $321.31, to Missions, Foreign $124, Domestic $94.08, Home Mission for Colored People $23.10, Diocesan $94.08, for the

St. James' Church, West Marlboro, Admitted, 1849.

No report.

The Church of the Trinity Admitted 1869. Rev. George G. Field, Rector. Horace
A. Beale and John Stone, Wardens.

Baptisms, adults 2, infants 2, total 4; confirmed, no visitations; communicants, added, new 4, by removal 6, died or removed 2, present number 35; burial 1; public services, on
Sundays 106, on other days 27, total 133; children catechized,
times monthly; Sunday School, officers and teachers 4, scholars
40; Bible classes, teacher 1, members 8. Church 1, sittings
180; salary of Rector $800 per annum, arrears of salary
considerable; number of free sittings, all.

Money receipts from all sources—Offertory at Holy Communion $124.83, collections in Church $178.72, Subscriptions
$879, Donations $500; Total $1,677.55.

Expenditures and Appropriations—Current Expenses (including salary of Rector) $893.73, Repairs and Improvements
$500, Episcopal and Convention Fund $10, Disabled Clergymen $20.83, Oregon and Washington $40.

Financial condition.—Aggregate value of property of the
Parish, real and personal $5800, mortgage on Church lot
$5000.

The Chapel was finished last July, and is nearly clear of
debt: a modest, inexpensive and convenient building, it has
added much to the convenience and stability of the congregation.

CLINTON COUNTY.

St. Paul's Church, Lock Haven. Admitted, 1857.

No Report.

COLUMBIA COUNTY.

Paul's Church, Bloomsburg. Admitted, 1793. Rev. John Hewitt, Rector. E. R.
Drinker and B. F. Hartman, Wardens.

Baptisms, adults 2, infants 27, total 29; confirmed, no
communicants, present number 142; marriage 1;
public services, on Sundays 2; children catechized

twice a month; Sunday Schools, officers and teachers 16, scholars 105; Bible class, teacher 1, members 36; Church 1, sittings 390, Parsonage 1, Cemetery 1; salary of Rector $1200 per annum, arrears of salary, none; number of free sittings 20.

Money receipts from all sources—Pew rents $1095.33, Collections in Church $1208.36, Investments $1200; Total $4704.09.

Expenditures and Appropriations—Current Expenses (including salary of Rector) $1575, payment of debts $1237.20, for the Jews $5.33 Sunday School offerings $527.66; Total $3345.19.

The present Rector took charge of the Parish on Christmas Day, 1870. Indebtedness incurred by the building of a new and beautiful gothic stone Church, has compelled the congregation, for the present, to limit their offerings for objects outside the Parish.

Since the first Sunday in March the Rector of St. Paul's has been holding services on alternate Sundays at Catawissa, where he has organized a Sunday School which already numbers eighty-seven scholars. A petition will be presented at this meeting of the Convention for a charter of a new parish at this place.

Financial condition.—Aggregate value of property of the Parish, real and personal, $32,000, Encumbrances, $4,000, other indebtedness $5,000.

Holy Trinity Church, Centralia. Admitted, 1868. Rev. Daniel Washburn, Rector. Rev. Philip P. Reese, Deacon, in charge. Robert Gorrell and Thomas R. Stockett, Wardens.

Baptisms, adults none, infant 1, total 1; confirmed none; communicants, added, new 7, died or removed 1, present number 18; marriage 1; burial 1; public services, on Sundays 47, on other days 12, total 59; average attendance on Sundays 70; children catechized, every Sunday; Sunday Schools, officers and teachers 10, scholars 120; Bible class, teacher 1, members 11; other Parish agencies, Mite Society; Church 1, Sittings 250; Salary $1000 per annum.

Jews $7.77, Episcopal Hospital $70.17, Church Building $400, Disabled Clergymen $18; Total $5695,51.

Financial condition.—Aggregate value of property of the Parish, real and personal, $50,000, Mortgage on buildings $6,000.

St. Peter's Church, Phœnixville. Admitted 1840. Rev. W. R. Stockton, Rector. John Griffin and Ellis Reeves, Wardens.

Baptisms, adults 6, infants 17, total 23; confirmed 21, awaiting confirmation 12; communicants, added, new 21, by removal 8, died or removed 7, present number 120; marriages 6, burials 9; public services on Sundays 3 (morning, afternoon and evening), the third service is for the study and explanation of the Scriptures, on other days 12, total 168; Sunday School, officers and teachers 22, scholars 170; Bibleclasses 2, members 20; Church 1, sittings 250, parsonage 1, finished Nov. 1870.

Money receipts from all sources—Pew Rents, about $550, Offertory at Holy Communion $65, Collections in Church $218 09, for coal $54, Donations to Rector from Mr. David Reeves $300, from Mr. Samuel J. Reeves $240, proceeds from Church fair for Rectory $144 32, for musical instrument for Sunday School $40, Rectory fund $5,445.06, Collections for Sunday School $35; Total $7,091.47.

Expenditures and Appropriations—Current Expenses (including Rector's salary), $1,362, Episcopal Hospital $6.50, Episcopal and Convention Fund $20, for the Poor $18.06, Sunday School $75, Diocesan Missions (through S. E. Convocation) $10, Disabled Clergymen $10.53, paid on account of Rectory and Church improvements $5,589.38. Mr. David Reeves and Mr. Samuel J. Reeves have greatly improved the Church grounds, &c., at their own expense, cost not included in the above; Total $7,091.47.

Financial condition.—Aggregate value of the Parish: viz. Church lot worth $5,000, Rectory lot worth (50x160) $2,000, Church building worth about $12,000, Rectory worth $7,000, total $26,000.

Encumbrances on Church edifice none; on Rectory none. The Vestry have, however, authorized the making of one for a thousand dollars, to pay for pavement on Church street and other improvements, and to settle the balance of $692.15 still due on the Rectory, over and above what was provided for or anticipated.

Remarks.—The Church and Rector have met with a severe loss in the death of Mr. David Reeves, as he was a very liberal contributor to the Church and the Rector.

St. James' Church, Downingtown.   Admitted 1844.   William Edge and Charles L. Wells, Wardens.

Baptisms, infants 3; communicants added, by removal 3, died or removed 8, present number 60; marriages 3, burials 6; public services on Sundays 103, on other days 41, total 144; average attendance on Sundays 40; children catechized frequently; Sunday Schools, officers and teachers 9, scholars, 40, Bible classes, teachers 9, members 40. Church 1, sittings, 250, parsonage 1, cemetery 1, salary of Rector $1000 per annum, arrears of salary, none; number of free sittings 20.

Money receipts from all sources—Pew rents £923 50, Offertory at Holy Communion $49.39, Collections in Church $63.91, Donations $50, other sources $102.50; Total $1,194.30.

Expenditures and Appropriations—Current Expenses (including salary of Rector) $1,186.60, Repairs and Improvements $106, Payment of Debts $60, Episcopal and Convention Fund $20, Support of Sunday Schools $15, Parish Library $25, Parochial Missions $27.41, S. E. Convocation, this Diocese; For the Poor $49.39, to Rev. Mr. Cook, Indian Mission, $10, Episcopal Hospital $25.50, Disabled Clergymen $7; Total $1,531.90.

Financial condition.—Aggregate value of property of the Parish, real and personal $15,000, encumbrances, mortgages on Church edifice $1000, Ground rent none. The Rev. W. White Montgomery took charge of this Parish April 1st, 1870, and officiated until April 1st, 1871.

No report.

The Church of the Trinity   Admitted 1869.   Rev. George G. Field, Rector.   Horace A. Beale and John Stone, Wardens.

Baptisms, adults 2, infants 2, total 4 ; confirmed, no visitations; communicants, added, new 4, by removal 6, died or removed 2, present number 35 ; burial 1; public services, on Sundays 106, on other days 27, total 133 ; children catechized, times monthly; Sunday School, officers and teachers 4, scholars 40 ; Bible classes, teacher 1, members 8.   Church 1, sittings 180 ; salary of Rector $800 per annum, arrears of salary considerable; number of free sittings, all.

Money receipts from all sources—Offertory at Holy Communion $124.83, collections in Church $173.72, Subscriptions $879, Donations $500 ; Total $1,677.55.

Expenditures and Appropriations—Current Expenses (including salary of Rector) $893.73, Repairs and Improvements $500, Episcopal and Convention Fund $10, Disabled Clergymen $20.83, Oregon and Washington $40.

Financial condition.—Aggregate value of property of the Parish, real and personal $5800, mortgage on Church lot $2200.

The Chapel was finished last July, and is nearly clear of debt: a modest, inexpensive and convenient building, it has added much to the convenience and stability of the congregation.

CLINTON COUNTY.

St. Paul's Church, Lock Haven.   Admitted, 1857.

No Report.

COLUMBIA COUNTY.

St. Paul's Church, Bloomsburg.   Admitted, 1795.   Rev. John Hewitt, Rector.   E. R. Drinker and B. F. Hartman, Wardens.

Baptisms, adults 2, infants 27, total 29 ; confirmed, no visitation; communicants, present number 142 ; marriage 1 ; burials 9 ; public services, on Sundays 2 ; children catechized twice a month; Sunday Schools, officers and teachers 16, scholars 105; Bible class, teacher 1, members 36; Church 1, sittings 390, Parsonage 1, Cemetery 1; salary of Rector $1200 per annum, arrears of salary, none; number of free sittings 20.

Money receipts from all sources—Pew rents $1095.33, Collections in Church $1208.36, Investments $1200; Total $4704.09.

Expenditures and Appropriations—Current Expenses (including salary of Rector) $1575, payment of debts $1237.20, for the Jews $5.33 Sunday School offerings $527.66; Total $3345.19.

The present Rector took charge of the Parish on Christmas Day, 1870. Indebtedness incurred by the building of a new and beautiful gothic stone Church, has compelled the congregation, for the present, to limit their offerings for objects outside the Parish.

Since the first Sunday in March the Rector of St. Paul's has been holding services on alternate Sundays at Catawissa, where he has organized a Sunday School which already numbers eighty-seven scholars. A petition will be presented at this meeting of the Convention for a charter of a new parish at this place.

Financial condition.—Aggregate value of property of the Parish, real and personal, $32,000, Encumbrances, $4,000, other indebtedness $5,000.

Holy Trinity Church, Centralia. Admitted, 1868. Rev. Daniel Washburn, Rector. Rev. Philip P. Reese, Deacon, in charge. Robert Gorrell and Thomas R. Stockett, Wardens.

Baptisms, adults none, infant 1, total 1; confirmed none; communicants, added, new 7, died or removed 1, present number 18; marriage 1; burial 1; public services, on Sundays 47, on other days 12, total 59; average attendance on Sundays 70; children catechized, every Sunday; Sunday Schools, officers and teachers 10, scholars 120; Bible class, teacher 1, members 11; other Parish agencies, Mite Society; Church 1, Sittings 250; Salary $1000 per annum.

Money receipts from all sources—Pews free, Offertory at Holy Communion $3.50, Collections in Church $33.66, Subscriptions $223.66, other sources $1095.86; Total $1356.68.

Expenditures and Appropriations—Current Expenses (including salary of Rector,) $254.97, Repairs and Improvements $100.46, Payment of debts $856.99, Episcopal and Convention Fund $5, Support of Sunday Schools $85, Missions, Domestic $2.50, for the Jews $3.67, Convocation Fund $1.75; Total $1310.34.

Aggregate value of property of the Parish, real and personal, $4000.

By permission of the Bishop and upon the invitation of the Vestry, I took charge of this Parish on the second Sunday in December, 1870. Having been in charge of the Parish only a few months, I am not able to make a very full report.

CUMBERLAND COUNTY.

St. John's Church, Carlisle. Admitted, 1821. Rev. Wm. C. Leverett, Rector. Frederick Watts and Wm. M. Henderson, Wardens.

Baptisms, infants 7, total 7; confirmed 12; communicants, added, new 11, by removal 8, died or removed 6, present number 123; marriages 7; burials 6; public services, on Sundays 88, on other days 86, total 174; children catechized, times 10; Sunday Schools, officers and teachers 20, scholars 105; Bible classes, teacher 1, members 10; Church 1, sittings 330, parsonage 1.

Money receipts from all sources—Pew rents $1432, Offertory at Holy Communion $100.88, Collections in Church $569.98, Donations $774.96, other sources $85.50.

Expenditures and Appropriations—Current expenses (including salary of Rector) $1552.32, Payment of debts $774.96, Episcopal and Convention Fund $40, Support of Sunday Schools $129.82, Parish Library $19.53, for the Poor $102.67, Missions, Foreign, $25.81, Domestic $49.76, Home Mission, for Colored People $16, Diocesan $77, Midnight Missions $10, for the Jews $14,66, Episcopal Hospital $15.11, Bibles

Prayer Books and Tracts $13, Christian or Theological Education, $15, Disabled Clergymen $25.86, Miscellaneous $81.82.

Beside the appropriations mentioned in the parochial return, special gifts from members of the parish have been made during the past year, for the new Church Building at Chambersburg, amounting, in the aggregate, to upwards of $300.

The debt of the parish has been reduced by the payment of several hundred dollars, since the last Convention, and a spirit of earnestness and efficiency prevails in the congregation.

Increased accommodations, of the most desirable kind, have been made in the new building for "The Mary Institute;" and this School under its accomplished Lady Principal, with competent instructors in the several departments, offers to both Boarding and Day pupils advantages of the highest order.

Much has been done in the past year, as previously, to cheer the heart of the Rector in his work.

DAUPHIN COUNTY.

St. Stephen's Church, Harrisburg. Admitted 1825. Rev. R. J. Keeling, Rector. William Buehler and D. D. Boas, Wardens.

Baptisms, adult 1, infants 10, total 11; confirmed none; communicants, added, new none, by removal 2, died or removed 5, present number 124; marriages 4; burials 5; public services, on Sundays 104, on other days 145, total 249; children catechized, times 12; Sunday Schools, officers and teachers 21, scholars 142; Bible classes, teacher 1, members 11; Church 1, sittings 500; School building 1; parsonage 1; cemetery none; arrears of salary, none; number of free sittings 60.

Money receipts from all sources—Pew rents $2322, Offertory at Holy Communion $122, Collections in Church $360, Subscriptions $1104, Donations $1437, other sources $700; Total $6045.

Expenditures and Appropriations—Current expenses (including salary of Rector), $2725, Repairs and Improvements $978, Payments of debts, $829, Episcopal and Convention

Fund $45, Support of Sunday Schools $122, of Parish Schools none, Parish Library none, Parochial Missions (see St. Paul's), for the Poor $497, to Missions, Foreign none, Domestic $220, Home Mission for Colored People none, Diocesan $264, for the Jews $37, Church Building $106, Bibles, Prayer Books and Tracts none, Book Societies none, Christian or Theological Education $154, Disabled Clergymen 68; Total $6045.

Financial condition.—Aggregate value of property of the Parish, real and personal, $50,000; Encumbrances, none; other indebtedness $1400.

Congregational attendance ordinarily large, and increased interest manifested in the public services. Active societies connected with the Parish, are the Ladies Sewing Circle, Ladies Sinking Fund Society, and Busy Bee Society. The Ladies Sinking Fund Society collected last year $1000 in small monthly contributions towards liquidating debt on the Lecture room. In last year's Report this was made to read $100. In justice to the ladies I correct this error in figures. These societies continue in full and healthful operation. The Rector has ever been kindly remembered by his people since he has been connected with the Parish, but especially during the past year, he has been the recipient of very handsome and liberal expressions of their Christian love and good-will, and hereby makes grateful acknowledgment of the same.

St. Paul's Church, Harrisburg. Admitted, 1859. John B. Cox and Thomas Fitzsimmons, Wardens.

Baptisms, adults 2, infants 9, total 11; burial 1; public services, on Sundays 29, on other days 47, total 76; average attendance on Sundays 40; children catechized, times 25; Sunday Schools, officers and teachers 20, scholars 165; Church 1, sittings 200.

Money receipts from all sources—Collections in Church $14.63.

Expenditures and Appropriations—Episcopal and Convention Fund $5; Support of Sunday Schools $200.

Financial condition.—Aggregate value of property of the Parish, real and personal, $6000; Encumbrances, none; Ground Rents none; other indebtedness $100.

DELAWARE COUNTY.

St. Paul's Church, Chester, Rev. Henry Brown, Rector. Admitted 1786. John Larkin and J. B. McKeever, Wardens.

Baptisms, adults 3, infants 28, total 31; confirmed 36; communicants, added, new 40, died or removed 10, present number 224; marriages 14, burials 16; public services, on Sundays 156, on other days 115, total 271; average attendance on Sundays 350; children catechized, times 12; Sunday Schools, officers and teachers 34, scholars 300, Bible classes, teachers 2, members 28; Church 1, sittings 350, Chapels, (the statistics of which are included in this report) 1, sittings 300, parsonage 1, cemetery 1; salary of Rector $1700 per annum.

Money receipts from all sources—Offertory at Holy Communion $110, collections in Church $1200, other sources $500, total $3400.

Expenditures and Appropriations—Repairs and Improvements $900, Episcopal and Convention fund $50, support of Sunday Schools $250, for the Poor $95, Parochial Missions $150, to Missions, Foreign $50, Domestic $85, Diocesan $75; Episcopal Hospital $31; Bibles, Prayer Books and Tracts $23; Disabled Clergymen $17, total $3403.

St. Martin's Church, Marcus Hook. Admitted 1786. Rev. J. Sturgis Pearce, Rector.

Baptisms, adult 1, infants 15, total 16; confirmed 6*; communicants present number 90; burials 9; Sunday Schools, officers and teachers 9, scholars 90; Bible class, teacher 1, members 10; Church 1, sittings 450.

Money receipts from all sources—Alms-box $11 07; a lot and about $1500 towards the erection of a parsonage has been donated.

Expenditures and Appropriations—Repairs and Improvements $425; Episcopal and Convention Fund $20; Board of Missions (mite chests) $40; Sunday School from Jan. 1, 1870, to Jan. 1, 1871, $64 36.

---

*Before reported,

St. David's, commonly called Radnor Church. Admitted 1786. Rev. W. F. Halsey, Rector. Mark Brooke and Joseph W. Sharpe, Wardens.

Baptisms, infants 3; communicants, present number 48; marriage 1, burials 10; public services, on Sundays 51, on other days, chiefly festivals and fasts; children catechised, times 12; Sunday Schools, officers and teachers 4, scholars 30, Church 1, sittings 250; parsonage 1, cemetery 1; salary of Rector $1000 per annum.

Money receipts from all sources—Offertory at Holy Communion $40 86.

Expenditures and Appropriations—Episcopal and Convention Fund $25, Kennet Square Mission $10, to Missions, Foreign $20 85, Domestic $21 24, Home Mission for Colored People $16, for the Jews $2 10, Episcopal Hospital $8 36, Miscellaneous $15, for Bishop Morris, Oregon, $28 77; Church Home for Children $13 79.

The above embraces services held in St. David's Church. Other services have been held in New Town Square, and other adjacent places.

St. John's Church, Concord. Admitted 1786. Rev. John B. Clemson, D.D., Rector. Robert M'Call and Henry L. Paschal, Wardens.

Baptisms, infants 8; communicants, died or removed, 9 present number 85; marriage 1; burials 4; public services on Sundays, and prominent festivals and fasts; Sunday Schools, officers and teachers 6, scholars 30; Church sittings 250; parsonage $1500; cemetery 1; salary of Rector $400 per annum, arrears of salary, none.

Money receipts from all sources—Collections in Church $75, Investments $1500 for parsonage.

Expenditures and Appropriations—Repairs and Improvements $10, Episcopal and Convention Fund $10, Parish Library $8.38, to Missions, Foreign $3.08, Domestic $4.66, Episcopal Hospital $4.85, Bibles, Prayer Books and Tracts $8, Disabled Clergymen $8.22.

Financial condition.—Encumbrances, none; Ground Rent none; other indebtedness, none.

Calvary Church, Rockdale. Admitted 1835. Rev. William Ely, Rector. Richard S. Smith and Samuel K. Crozier, Wardens.

Baptisms, adults 4, infants 31, total 35; confirmed 10; communicants, added, new 11, by removal 10, died or removed 8, present number 91; marriages 2; burials 23; public services, on Sundays 82, on other days 20, total 102; average attendance on Sundays good; children catechized, times 12; Sunday Schools, officers and teachers 12, scholars 207; Bible classes, teacher 1, members 15; Church 1, sittings 325, Chapel (the statistics of which are included in this report) 1, sittings 100; parsonage 1, cemetery 1; salary of Rector $800 per annum; arrears of salary, $240.

Money receipts from all sources—Pew Rents $600, Offertory at Holy Communion $60, Collections in Church for current expenses $278.63, Subscriptions $300, for purchase of Sexton's House; Investments $400, interest $24 per annum; total $1262.63.

Expenditures and Appropriations—Current Expenses (including salary of Rector) $762.84, Purchase of Sexton's house $300, Payment of Debts $60, Episcopal and Convention Fund $21, Library of Sunday Schools $31, for the Poor $27, to Missions, Foreign $21, Domestic $72, Diocesan $75 (Convocation Mission at Kennett Square, Pa.), Episcopal Hospital $22.50, Disabled Clergymen $25.60; Total $1417.94.

Financial condition.—Aggregate value of property of the Parish, real and personal, $18,000; Encumbrances, Mortgages on Church edifice, none; on other buildings, $2000; Ground Rent on buildings or lands, none; floating debt, $110.

Christ Church, Media. Rev. Samuel W. Hallowell, Rector. H. Jones Brooke and Edward A. Price, Wardens.

Baptisms, adults 2, infants 11, total 13; confirmed 12, 10 of whom last year, after Convention, and not reported; communicants, added 26, new 12, by removal 14, died or removed 13, present number 83; marriages 4; burials 10; public services, on Sundays 95, on other days 8, total 103; average attendance on Sundays 240; Sunday Schools, officers and teachers 20, scholars 127; Church 1, sittings 300, Chapel (the statistics of which are included in this Report) 1, sittings 200; salary of Rector $900 per annum and parsonage; arrears of salary, none.

Money receipts from all sources—Pew Rents $709.81, Offertory at Holy Communion $112.11, Collections in Church $255.54, Subscriptions $477.40, Donations $5, other sources $291.86; Total $1851.72.

Expenditures and Appropriations—Current Expenses (including salary of Rector) $1259.74, Repairs and Improvements $26.74, Payment of Debts $334.12, Episcopal and Convention Fund $25, support of Sunday Schools $25, for the Poor $10.50, to Missions, Foreign $27.25, Domestic $13.92, Diocesan $13.92, for the Jews $5, Episcopal Hospital $18.18, Book Societies $10, Disabled Clergymen $27.68, Miscellaneous $54.67 ; Total $1851.72.

Financial condition.—Aggregate value of property of the Parish, real and personal, $15,000; Encumbrances, none; Ground Rent, none; other indebtedness, about $1100.

In consequence of the Bishop's visitation, last year, being subsequent to the Convention, no candidates for confirmation were reported. A class of 10 were afterwards confirmed, which, with 2 in the present year, makes the number 12. The prospects of the Church are still encouraging. There is a marked spirit of enterprise in the town at present, and with the prospect of increased building, population, &c., the Episcopal Church, under God's blessing, may hope that the hold it has already taken upon the community will be increased; and should her members prove faithful to their responsibilities, that not only outwardly but spiritually she will continue to prosper. In addition to my services at the Church, I officiate once a month at the County jail.

Church of the Good Shepherd, Radnor. Admitted 1871. Rev. Henry P. Hay, D. D., Rector. Charles W. Cushman and Gorham P. Sargent, Wardens.

Baptisms, adults 2, infants 9, total 11 ; communicants, added, new 1, by removal 9, died or removed 2, present number 21;

marriages 5, burials 7; public services, on Sundays and on other days 223 ; sermons 197 ; children catechized, times 54 ; Sunday Schools, one at Morgan's Corner and one at Paoli, officers and teachers 11, scholars 75; Bible classes, teachers 2, members 18. Church not erected ; salary of Rector $600 and the offertory per annum; arrears of salary, none.

Money receipts from all sources—Offertory $470.09, paid subscriptions $2197, donations $661, investments $61.60; Total $3389 69.

Expenditures and Appropriations—Current expenses (including salary of Rector) $906.86, Support of Sunday Schools, $28.40, Domestic Missions $50, for the Jews $4.27, Episcopal Hospital $12.25, Church building $800, Tracts $2.60, Disabled Clergymen $8.30, Families deceased clergy $10, Indian Mission $2, St. Peter's, Rancocas, $25, St. John's, Ashwood, Tenn. $1, St. Paul's, Fayetteville, Ark. $1; Total $1851.69.

Financial condition.—No encumbrances.

The Parish owns two lots valued at $1000 each ; one for Church edifice, school, chapel, &c., half of it the gift of Mrs. Lyons, the widow of the Rev. Dr. Lyons ; the other lot, for parsonage, is the gift of J. Howard Supplee, a member of the vestry

FRANKLIN COUNTY.

Trinity Church, Chambersburg. Admitted 1869 Rev. Wm. George Hawkins, Rector. Charles H. Taylor and C. C. Tilghman, Wardens.

Baptisms, infants 7: confirmed, no confirmation; communicants, added, new 5, by removal 2, died or removed 1, present number 24; marriage 1; burials 7; public services, on Sundays, two on each Sunday, on other days, daily during Passion Week; average attendance on Sundays 40; children catechized, times monthly; Sunday School 1, officers and teachers 8, scholars 60; Bible class, teacher 1, members 8; other Parish agencies, 1 Ladies' Mite Society, 1 Children's Mite Society. Church, worshipping in rented Hall ; parsonage 1; salary of Rector $750 per annum, arrears of salary, none.

31

Money receipts from all sources—Offertory at Holy Communion $26.05, Collections in Church $36.89, Subscriptions within the Parish $2201.60, other sources, Children's Mite Society $25.02, Ladies' Mite Society $82.50; Total $2382.04.

Expenditures and Appropriations—Current Expenses (including salary of Rector) $320.46, building Church to date $5856.60, Episcopal and Convention Fund $5, support of Sunday Schools $60, Parochial Missions $15.50, Domestic Missions $18.50; Total $6284.06.

. Financial condition.—Aggregate value of property of the Parish, real and personal, $16,000 ; Encumbrances, nothing; on other buildings, Parsonage less than $1800.

NOTE.—Subscriptions from other sources outside the parish towards parsonage and Church $9555.60. This includes $5600 reported paid on Parsonage last year; Total $11,927.60.

CHAMBERSBURG.

As intimated in my last Report, that the great hindrance to the rapid progress of the Church in this place was the absence of any suitable Church building, our present hall being unattractive, the year past has been devoted mostly to the solicitation of funds and the erection of a Church. The purchase, in the first instance, of a parsonage and lot was necessary, to give the Church and Missionary a local habitation—the cost of which was $7500. This has proved a good investment, the estimated value at the present time being over $9000. On the 6th of July last the corner-stone of a neat stone Gothic Church was laid. The services were conducted by the Rev. M. A. DeWolfe Howe, D. D., in the absence of the Bishop, assisted by a large attendance of the Clergy from other portions of the Diocese. The meeting of the South Central Convocation at the same time, in Chambersburg, added much interest to the services.

The work is being prosecuted with vigor, and it is now earnestly hoped the Church will be completed by July next, as its consecration is dependent upon its being free from debt.

The Rector is especially desirous that no effort shall be spared to accomplish this object.

The generosity of the Churches in Philadelphia has been already nobly illustrated by the large gifts of the past year, as will be seen by the above report—over $9555 has been collected outside of this Parish. A large part of this sum has come from the Churches in Philadelphia, our brethren in New York have also contributed. It is estimated that the building will seat comfortably 320 persons; it is 62 x 41ft., is built of limestone, and trimmed with Hummelstown sandstone. The Rector hereby desires to make especial acknowledgments to the ladies' Sewing Society of St. Andrew's, and lately from the Sewing Society of St. James' Church, for their liberal contributions to the comfort of the Missionary and his family.

GETTYSBURG.

No progress has yet been made towards securing a Clergyman for this important place. More frequent services have been held during the past year, always with good attendance. The thanks of the Church are due to the Rev. Dr. Clerc, Messrs. Fischer, Douglass, Nock, Cathell, and others for efficient aid.

SHIPPENSBURG.

I am in frequent communication with persons resident in this town. It is hoped that before another year a settled Missionary will be established in this place—already $300 have been subscribed. An effort is now being made to increase this to $500, which, with the missionary stipend, will enable them to procure a Minister.

MECHANICSBURG.

Regular services by members of the South Central Convocation are being maintained in this place on the second and fourth Sundays in each month. The attendance in the morning is usually 50; in the afternoon over 200. The prospect is exceedingly encouraging.

MONT ALTO.

This place is still without services. The handsome stone Church is every Sunday filled with Sunday School children, maintained by all denominations. Much is due to Col. Wiestling, the Superintendent of the Iron Works, and to Mr. Hughes, through whose efforts the Chapel was built.

HUNTINGDON COUNTY.

St. John's Church, Huntingdon. Admitted 1820.

No report.

LANCASTER COUNTY.

St. James' Church, Lancaster. Admitted 1785. Rev. Edward Shippen Watson, Rector. John L. Atlee and Thomas E. Franklin, Wardens.

Baptisms, adults 15, infants 30, total 45; confirmed 42; communicants, added 40, died or removed 3; marriages 8, burials 14; public services on Sundays, morning, evening and night, all Holy days, daily in Lent, morning and evening in Holy week; children catechized monthly; Sunday Schools, officers and teachers 20, scholars 215, Bible classes, teachers 2, members 40; Parish School, teachers 2, scholars 120; other Parish agencies, Sewing Society 35, Mothers' meeting 25; Church sittings 600, Chapel (the statistics of which are included in this report) 1, sittings 250, school building 1, parsonage 1, cemetery 1; salary of Rector $1500 per annum; number of free sittings 400; extra Sunday services, free to all, 52.

Money receipts from all sources—Offertory at Holy Communion $175, collections in Church $20, Subscriptions $350, Donations $200, improvements $2000.

Expenditures and Appropriations—Episcopal and Convention Fund $75; Christian or Theological Education $75.

St. John's Church, Lancaster. Admitted 1854. Rev. Thomas B. Barker, Rector. Isaac Diller and Henry P. Carson, Wardens.

Baptisms, adults 5, infants 41, total 46; confirmed 35; communicants, added, new 35, died or removed 2, present number 186; marriages 11, burials 16; public services, on Sundays

104, on other days 80, total 184; Sunday Schools, officers and teachers 26, scholars 235, Bible class, teacher 1, members 25; Church 1, sittings 500, parsonage 1, salary of Rector $1000 per annum, arrears of salary, none; number of free sittings, all.

Money receipts from all sources—Offertory at Holy Communion $70, Investments $3000.

Expenditures and Appropriations—Repairs and Improvements $2500, Episcopal and Convention Fund $25, for the Poor $70, for the Jews $10.

Financial condition.—Encumbrances, Mortgage on Church edifice, none.

Bangor Church, Churchtown. Admitted 1810. Rev. Henry R. Smith, Rector. Jacob R. Byler and Barton Whitman, Wardens.

Communicants, new 6, present number 22; burials 3; public services on Sundays 32, on other days 8, total 40; average attendance on Sundays 70; Sunday Schools, officers and teachers 10, scholars 76; Church 1, sittings 250; school building 1, cemetery 1, salary of Rector $125 per annum, arrears of salary, none; number of free sittings, all.

Money receipts from all sources—Collections in Church $27.37, Subscription $166, Investments $50; Total $243.37.

Expenditures and Appropriations—Current Expenses (including salary of Rector) $153, Episcopal and Convention Fund $5, support of Sunday Schools $63, to Missions, Foreign $2.32, Domestic $15.44, Episcopal Hospital $2.39, Disabled Clergymen $2.22; Total $243.37.

The contribution to Domestic Missions was made to the American Church Missionary Society, and was given in part by the children of the Sunday School.

Financial condition.—Aggregate value of property of the Parish, real and personal, $5000; Encumbrances none; other indebtedness none.

Christ Church, Leacock. Admitted 1819. Rev. Henry. R. Smith, Minister. William Bender, Warden.

Baptisms, adults 5, infants 3, total 8; confirmed 10; communicants, added, new 6, by removal 2, died or removed 4, present number 40; marriage 1, burials 5; public services, on Sundays 26, on other days 2, total 28; average attendance 65; Sunday School, officers and teachers 4, scholars 30; Church 1, sittings 150; cemetery 1; salary of Rector $200 per annum, arrears of salary, none; sittings all free.

Money receipts from all sources—Collections in Church $51.17; Subscriptions $215; Investments $42, other sources $75; Total $383.17.

Expenditures and Appropriations—Current Expenses (including salary of Rector) $270, Repairs and Improvements $75, support of Sunday Schools $20, to Foreign Missions $10 47, Episcopal Hospital $4 49, Disabled Clergymen $3 21; Total $383.17.

Aggregate value of property of the Parish, real and personal, $1800; no indebtedness.

All Saints' Church, Paradise. Admitted 1842.

No report.

St. Paul's Church, Columbia. Admitted 1849. Rev. George H. Kirkland. Rector.
D. J. Bruner and George H. Richards, Wardens.

Baptisms, adult 1, infants 8, total 9; communicants, added, by removal 2, removed 1, present number 56; burials 4; public services, on Sundays 70, on other days 31, total 101; average attendance on Sundays 90; children catechized, monthly; Sunday Schools, officers and teachers 16, scholars 100; other Parish agencies, Society for the relief of the Poor. Church 1, sittings 180; salary of Rector $800, arrears of salary none; number of free sittings, all.

Money receipts from all sources—Pew Rents $699.75, Offertory at Holy Communion $51.13, Collections in Church $345.27, Subscriptions $96.60, Donations $60.91, Investments, for parsonage $3500, other sources $111; Total $4864.66.

Expenditures and Appropriations—Current Expenses (including salary of Rector) $945.58, Payment of debts $110, Episcopal and Convention Fund $15, support of Sunday Schools $116.60, for the Poor $51.13, to Missions, Foreign

$27.95, Domestic $32, Diocesan $10, (Convocation); for the Jews $7.40, Episcopal Hospital $9.50, Theological Education $25, Disabled Clergymen $13.50 ; Total $1364 66.

Financial condition.—Aggregate value of property of the Parish, real and personal, $7000; other indebtedness $50.

I took charge of the Parish on the 13th Sunday after Trinity, 11th September, 1870. Up to that time I was Assistant to the Rev. Dr. Paddock of St. Andrew's Church, Philadelphia. The growth of the Parish is steadily going on. On the 1st of April, the system of Pew Rents was abolished, and the Free-Church system on the basis of subscription adopted. This change has already worked good to the Parish. The revenue of the Church has been much increased in this way. A class of eight or ten members is now being prepared for confirmation.

<hr>

St. John's Church, Marietta. Admitted 1849. Rev. Charles H. Mead, Rector.
E. Haldeman and Abram Cassell, Wardens.

Baptisms, infants 3, total 3 ; communicants, added, new 1, by removal 1, died or removed 6, present number 30; marriages 3, burials 3; public services, on Sundays 92, on other days 32, total 124; children catechized monthly; Sunday Schools, officers and teachers 13, scholars 116 on the roll. Church sittings 250 ; salary of Rector $800, arrears of salary, none.

Money receipts from all sources—Pew rents $712.50, Offertory at Holy Communion $116.93, Collections in Church $111.22, other sources $1116.92; Total $2058.57.

Expenditures and Appropriations—Current expenses (including salary of Rector) $881.40, Repairs and Improvements $130, Payments of debts $840, Episcopal and Convention Fund $15; support of Sunday Schools $87.68, for the Poor $31.50, to Missions, Foreign $4.15, Domestic $18.21 ; for the Jews $6.77; Episcopal Hospital $7; Books and Tracts $20; Book Societies $4 26; Disabled Clergymen $12 60, Total $2058.57.

There has been no Episcopal visitation here this year, and

LEBANON COUNTY.

St. Luke's Church, Lebanon. Admitted 1859. Rev. Alfred M. Abel, Rector, Josiah Funck and George Drake, Wardens.

Baptisms, adult 1, infants 24, total 25; confirmed none; communicants, added, new 1, died or removed 5, dropped 1, present number 37; marriage 1, burials 8; public services, on Sundays 68, on other days 78, total 146; children catechized monthly; Sunday School, officers and teachers 10, scholars, about 55; Bible classes, teacher, the Rector, members, male 25, female 12; Church, Chapel 1, sittings 150; parsonage 1; salary of Rector, (including $100 of the amount reported below from Colebrook, and $60 of that reported from Mount Hope,) $1210; but the salary received is usually considerably more than the amount named above. Number of free sittings, all; receipts from regular subscriptions $750, special or occasional gifts or offerings, $139.75. All other receipts below reported, whether for Parochial or extra-Parochial objects, (inclusive of Sunday School offerings), have been offered on some occasion of public service. The two amounts not so presented, ($750, and $139.75), are included in the full statement which follows.

Incidental and current expenses, including salary of Rector from Lebanon only, $1528.93, Episcopal and Convention Fund $15, support of Sunday School $10.50, for the Poor $91.85, Foreign Missions $108.62, Domestic $9.11, Home Missions for Colored People $13.35, Diocesan (including Convocation Missions) $46, for the Jews $11.25, Episcopal Hospital $13.50, Bishop White Prayer Book Society $7.50, Christian or Theological Education $126.42, Disabled Clergy $11, Miscellaneous $54.17; Total $2047.20.

Colebrook Furnace, Lebanon County.

Baptisms, infants 2; communicants 6; public services, on Sundays 8, and one by the Rev. Mr. Ward; contributions to salary $110; Bishop White Prayer Book Society $1.24; Episcopal Hospital $1.36; Christmas Fund $3.34; Episcopal Fund $2.15; Total $118.09.

LEHIGH COUNTY.

Grace Church, Allentown. Admitted 1859. Rev. William R. Gries, Rector. Henry
Colt and Dewees J. Martin, Wardens.

Baptisms, infants 7, total 7; confirmed 15; communicants,
added, new 13, by removal 5, died or removed 2, present
number 60; marriage 1, burials 4; public services, on Sundays 94, on other days 29, total 123; Sunday Schools, officers
and teachers 13, scholars 160. Church 1, sittings 200; salary
of Rector $1200 per annum; arrears of salary, none; extra
Sunday services, free to all every Sunday evening.

Money receipts from all sources—Pew Rents $865, Offer-
tory at Holy Communion $158.70, collections in Church
$299 19; Subscriptions $135; Donations $102, other sources
$55; Total $1614.89.

Expenditures and Appropriations—Current Expenses,)in-
cluding salary of Rector) $1179.60, Episcopal and Conven-
tion Fund $25, support of Sunday Schools $154.97, to Missions, Foreign $11.50, Domestic $20.10, Diocesan $17, for the
Jews $8.50, Episcopal Hospital $20.62, Disabled Clergymen $19, miscellaneous $158.60; Total $1614.89.

Financial condition.—Aggregate value of property of the
Parish, real and personal, $15,000; encumbrance on buildings
$1000.

Church of the Mediator, Allentown. Rev. F. Weston Bartlett, Rector. Henry Colt
and L. H. Gross, Wardens.

Baptisms, infants 10, total 10; confirmed 10; communicants
added, new 9, by removal 1, removed 2, present number 12;
burials 4; public services, on Sundays 56, including Lay
Reading 3 times, on other days 10, total 66; average attendance on Sundays 30; children catechized occasionally; Sunday schools, officers and teachers 6, scholars 50; Church 1,
sittings 175; parsonage 1; salary of Rector $200 per annum
from the parish, besides outside pledges; no arrears due from
this Parish; all the sittings are free.

Money receipts from all sources—Collections in Church,
including Communion Offertories, $95.41, Subscriptions
$1161.88, other sources, say $200; Total $1557.29.

Expenditures and Appropriations—Current Expenses, (including salary of Rector) about $220, Episcopal and Convention Fund $5, support of Sunday schools, say $25, to Missions, Foreign $4.50, Episcopal Hospital $1, Disabled Clergymen $1, Children's Church Home $1.

As to payments of debts, I am unable to give precise figures, as the accounting Warden has reported that some accounts are not settled, &c. I calculate there have been paid in various ways about $1300. The indebtedness has been removed from the rectory, and I include the assumption of a portion thereof by two Churchmen in this estimate. Total $1557.50.

Financial condition.—Aggregate value of property of the Parish, real and personal, $10,000.

CATASAUQUA MISSION.

Services are held weekly on Sunday afternoons and the Holy Communion administered once a month and on the principal Lord's Day Festivals. I have in the past year baptized five children and officiated at one funeral in Catasauqua. Have baptized one child at Siegfried's Bridge, and four children outside my own jurisdiction, by consent or request of their pastors.

LUZERNE COUNTY.

St. Stephen's Church, Wilkesbarre. Admitted 1821.

No Report.

St. Clement's Church, South Wilkesbarre. Admitted 1870.

No Report,

Trinity Church, Carbondale. Admitted 1845. Rev. M. L. Kern, Rector. Rollin Manville and A. O. Hamford, Wardens.

Baptisms, adults 2, infants 7, total 9 ; confirmed 13 ; communicants, added, new 13, died or removed 5, present number 95 ; marriages 7 ; burials 8 ; public services, on Sundays 100, on other days 62, total 162 ; average attendance on Sundays 175 ; children catechized, times 17 ; Sunday Schools, officers and teachers 19, scholars 150 ; Bible clases, teachers 3, members 25; Church, sittings 300, parsonage 1; salary of Rector $1000 per annum.

Money receipts from all sources—Pew rents $1250, Offertory at Holy Communion $38.33, Donations $75, Investments $350.

Expenditures and Appropriations—Current Expenses (including salary of Rector) $1300, Repairs and Improvements $350, Episcopal and Convention Fund $20, Support of Sunday Schools $100, to Missions, Foreign $10, Domestic $10, Diocesan $25, City Missions $10, Episcopal Hospital $17.15, Disabled Clergymen $12.15, Penny Collections $172.93; Total $2143.06.

St. James' Church, Pittston. Admitted, 1852. Rev. C. Hare. Rector. R. J. Wisner, and Thomas Grier, Wardens.

Baptisms, adults 5, infants 43, total 48; confirmed 16; communicants, present number 125; marriages 7; burials 8; public services, on Sundays always twice, and monthly thrice, on other days, on Friday evenings; Sunday Schools, officers and teachers 16, scholars 175; Church 1, sittings 400; parsonage none, cemetery none; salary of Rector $1000 per annum; arrears of salary, none.

Money receipts from all sources—Pew rents $1227.44, Offertory at Holy Communion $68, Charitable Collections in Church $135, other Collections $175.63, From Sunday Schools $100, other sources $840.92; Total $2546.99.

Expenditures and Appropriations—Current Expenses (including salary of Rector) $1422.41, Gift to Rector $300, Episcopal and Convention Fund $25, support of Sunday Schools $197.92, for music $140, sewing societies $100, for the Poor $68, Missions, Foreign 32.64, Domestic $20, Diocesan 16, Episcopal Hospital $6.94, Disabled Clergymen $20, Miscellaneous $200; Total $2548.91.

The Vestry have not yet succeeded in selling at a suitable price, the Church building which is very much injured by the extension of the Lehigh Valley R. R. Until such sale is effected, or in some way a new edifice built, the Church can never do her work in this growing town. The present Rector has been led, from illness in his family the last twelvemonth, to resign the Parish, and expects to remove to Minnesota.

During the eight and a half years of his rectorship, he has received a succession of kindnesses from an affectionate people. Also, with much undone, he can still see signs of unmistakable progress. The communicants have increased in number from fifty to one hundred and twenty. From a Missionary station the congregation has passed into a self-supporting parish, able to help others. The first year the Vestry gave their Rector 300 dollars for a salary; this increased, until the last year he received from them 1300 dollars. The attendance on public worship has quadrupled. A successful parish day-school was maintained for 2½ years, until the Railroad, close by, destroyed it.

During four months of the past year, Sunday afternoon services have been held in North Pittston, in a school house, by the Rector, with an attendance of from 30 to 50 persons. The Tuesday evening services at Tunkhannock have been continued during the year, a parish organized, and they in a fair way to have a parish Church there. In our own parish, this last year, a "Brotherhood" of the young men has been continued, with a Reading-room opened during the winter months. The Brotherhood has a membership of twenty men, meets weekly with an average attendance of twelve members, and has been very useful in stimulating Christian life, and cementing Christian friendliness.

St. Luke's Church, Scranton. Admitted 1853. Rev. A. Augustus Marple, Rector. Henry B. Rockwell and Elisha P. Phinney, Wardens.

Baptisms, adults 9, infants 39, total 48; confirmed 17; communicants 161; marriages 20; burials 34; public services, on Sundays 100, on other days 68, total 168; children catechized, times 15; Sunday Schools, officers and teachers 18, scholars 176; Bible classes, teachers 2, members 24; salary of Rector $2200 per annum.

Expenditures and Appropriations—Episcopal and Convention Fund $30, Support of Sunday Schools $150, to Missions, Domestic $11, Diocesan $20, Episcopal Hospital $22, Church building $8000, Christian or Theological Education $14, Disabled Clergymen $24, Miscellaneous $200.

Financial condition.—Aggregate value of property of the Parish, real and personal, $75,000.

We have just finished (except the tower) a stone Church, at a cost of more than $50,000. We are waiting for the stained glass windows.

———

St. James' Church, Eckley. Admitted 1858. Rev. James Walker, Rector. Richard Sharpe and Francis Weiss, Wardens.

Baptisms, infants 11; confirmed 5; communicants, added, new 5, by removal 2, present number 33; marriages 2, burials 8; public services on Sundays 132, on other days 8, total 140; average attendance on Sundays 90; children catechized, times 6; Sunday Schools, officers and teachers 12, scholars, 100; Bible class, teacher 1, members 6; Church 1, sittings 200, cemetery 1.

Money receipts from all sources—Offertory at Holy Communion $102.94, Collections in Church $67.44, Total $170.38.

Expenditures and Appropriations—Current Expenses (including salary of Rector) $546.14, Episcopal and Convention Fund $12, Parochial Missions $10, to Missions, Foreign $56.11, Domestic $17.80, Diocesan $10, for the Jews $8.51, Episcopal Hospital $26.41, Bibles, Prayer Books and Tracts $5, Christian or Theological Education $9,76, Disabled Clergymen $14.11, Miscellaneous $1.35; Total $171.05.

DRIFTON MISSION.

The Mission is about three miles from Eckley. Service is held in the school house every Sunday, in the afternoon. With very few exceptions, I meet with the children every Sunday.

Connected with the school-house is a large reading-room,

nicely fitted up, and well furnished with books and papers by those who are sustaining the Mission.

Collections and Contributions—For salary $500.

Extra-Parochial—Missions, Diocesan $25, Disabled Clergymen $31.

St. Paul's Church, White Haven. Admitted 1860. Rev. Leighton Coleman, Rector; Mr. Stephen Maguire, Lay-Assistant. Lucius Blakslee and Samuel E. Wallace, Wardens.

Baptisms, infants 2; confirmed, no visitation; communicants, added, new 1, by removal 3, present number 30; burial 1; public services, on Sundays 107, on other days 16, total 123; Sunday Schools, officers and teachers 10, scholars 125; Church 1, sittings 250; salary of Lay Assistant $350 per annum, arrears of salary, none; number of free sittings, *all free.*

Money receipts from all sources—Offertory at Holy Communion, $14,74; contributions of Sunday Schools, $72.53.

Expenditures and Appropriations—Current Expenses (including salary of Lay Assistant) $439.52, Repairs and Improvements $35.55, Episcopal and Convention Fund $10, Support of Sunday Schools $164.32, to Missions, Foreign $8.42, (excluding $10 from the Sunday School), Domestic $5.40, Diocesan $6.75, for the Jews $1.15, Episcopal Hospital $7.10, Disabled Clergymen $13.06, Miscellaneous $23; Grand Total $811.64.

Upon the resignation of the Rev. J. H. H. Millett, I was unanimously requested to resume the charge of this parish, and have since given to it such personal attention as is possible, with the duties devolving upon me in connection with the parishes at Mauch Chunk and Summit Hill. Regular services have been maintained both at White Haven and the Lehigh Tannery (where a number of our most zealous members reside), through the assistance of Mr. Stephen Maguire, a candidate for Holy Orders, and Master of St. Mark's Academy, Mauch Chunk. The condition of the parish is as satisfactory as can be expected in the absence of a resident Minister, the congregations being well maintained, and their interest unflagging. The Sunday School continues to be one of the most promising features of the work. The stability and welfare of the parish are largely owing, under God, to the efficient and generous co-operation of the Vestry, whom I have ever found to be ready and willing to do their utmost in furthering the plans laid before them.

St. Peter's Church, Hazleton. Admitted 1866. Rev. Charles H. Vandyne, Rector. Frederick Lauderburn and Henry Mears, Wardens.

Baptisms, adults 3, infants 6, total 9; confirmed 4; communicants, added, new 3, present number 15; marriages 3; burial 1; public services, on Sundays 93, on other days 41, total 134; average attendance on Sundays 50; children catechized, times 30; Sunday Schools, officers and teachers 8, scholars 45; Church 1, sittings 180; number of free sittings 180

Money receipts from all sources—Offertory at Holy Communion $30.96, Collections in Church $144.05, Subscriptions $482 05; Total $657.06.

Expenditures and Appropriations—Current Expenses (including salary of Rector) $675, Episcopal and Convention Fund $5, Support of Sunday Schools $16, Missions, Diocesan $5, Episcopal Hospital $4.20, Disabled Clergymen $5.50; Total $709.05.

Financial condition.—Aggregate value of property of the Parish, real and personal, $7000.

The services had been discontinued in this Church for about two years prior to June 16, 1870, when the present Rector assumed the charge of the Parish. Since that time the attendance at the services, and the general interest, have shown steady improvement.

Church of the Good Shepherd, Green Ridge. Admitted 1871. Rév. J. H. Hobart Millett, Rector. E. L. Riggs and J. Atticus Robertson, Wardens.

Baptisms, adults 2, infants 9, total 11 ; confirmed 6 ; communicants, added, new 6, by removal 2, died or removed 6, present number 23 ; marriage 1 ; public services, on Sundays 69, on other days 33, total 102 ; average attendance on Sundays 43 ; children catechized weekly ; Sunday Schools, officers and teachers 10, scholars 84 ; Bible class, teacher 1, members 8 ; other Parish agencies, sewing school ; Church 1, sittings 180 ; salary of Rector $600 per annum ; arrears of salary, none ; number of free sittings, all free.

Money receipts from all sources.—Offertory at Holy Communion $53.17, other sources $1883.61 ; Total $1936.78.

Expenditures and Appropriations.—Current Expenses (including salary of Rector) $847.48, Repairs and Improvements $982.95, to Missions, Domestic $3.63, Diocesan $6.80, for the Jews $1.82, Episcopal Hospital $4.25, Christian or Theological Education $8.75, Disabled Clergymen $4.32, Northeastern Convocation $9.81 ; Total $1869.81.

Financial condition.—Aggregate value of property of the Parish, real and personal, $5000 ; Encumbrances, none ; Ground Rent, none ; indebtedness $1000.

The above number of services, extra parochial offertories, etc., is from the first of September, the time when the present Rector first took charge of the Parish.

St. John's Church, Ashley. Rev. J. H. Mac. El'Rey, Rector. E. L. Diffenderfer and Lewis Kind, Wardens.

Baptisms, infants 3 ; total 3 ; communicants, by removal 4, present number 4 ; public services, on Sundays 2, on other days 1, average attendance on Sundays 76 ; children catechized, times 4 ; Sunday School, officers and teachers 15, scholars 140 ; Bible Class, teachers 1, members 8 ; Church 1, sittings 200 ; extra Sunday services free to ALL !

Expenditures and Appropriations—Bibles, Prayer Books and Tracts $18, Disabled Clergymen $3.22 ; total $21.22.

Financial condition.—Aggregate value of property of the Parish, real and personal, $7000.

As appears by record, the first Church service held in what is now the Borough of Ashley, then Coalville. was on the first of May, 1870. This was in a school house, by Rev. John Long, then Missionary at large, in Luzerne county. After service, Messrs. Dr. E. L. Diffenderfer and L. Kind, J. Y. Bossert and W. H. Litzenberg, were appointed a committee to confer with Mrs. Charles Parrish, of Wilkes Barre, soliciting her aid in erecting a Church for the Mission. This was so largely given at once, that contract was immediately made with a builder for erecting a Church.

Deserved mention should here be made of the Donation of two valuable lots, 104 x 300, by Mr. Timpson, President of the Lehigh and Susquehanna Coal Company, one for a Church and the other for a Rectory. This gift was proffered four years ago by Mr. Timpson, but was declined. The same inducement was then made to the Presbyterians, and was immediately accepted, and also the Methodists readily became recipients of a similar favor. They built large Churches, and soon obtained overflowing congregations, "taking the tide at the flow." "The Church," as usual, came in at the ebb.

The corner stone was laid the 14th of August, 1870, by Bishop Stevens.

The present incumbent was appointed by the Bishop to the Mission, January 1st, 1871. The Church was then in a half-finished condition, and every prospect dark. I found four communicants, one male, three female, and a state of things which it would not be edifying, if it were possible, to describe. The Sunday School then numbered 24. It now numbers 140. We have a beautiful wooden structure, capable of seating 200 persons. Basement and gallery, spire and bell, vestry room, study, etc. The chancel furniture was presented by Bishop Stevens, and the bell by Mrs. Charles Parrish, Wilkes Barre. The chancel window, first class quality, emblematical design, was presented by Major Charles M. Conyngham. The Parish of St. Stephen, Wilkes Barre, aided the Mission to the amount of more than $2000. The Church was consecrated on the 21st of April, 1871, by the Rt. Rev. Wm. Bacon Stevens, D. D., of the Diocese of Pennsylvania.

It is only justice to record here, that the Parish of St. John's, Ashley, would not exist to-day, but for the liberality of St. Stephen's Parish, Wilkes Barre.

LYCOMING COUNTY.

St. James Church, Muncy. Admitted 1820. Rev. Abner P. Brush, Rector. Geo. L. L Painter and R. F. Shoemaker, Wardens.

Baptisms, adults 2, infants 8, total 10; confirmed 3; communicants, added, new 2, by removal 8, died or removed 4, present number 106; marriages 4; burials 7; public services, on Sunday 100, on other days 69, total 169; children catechized, times 12; Sunday Schools, officers and teachers 12, scholars 80; Parish Schools, teacher 1; Church 1, sittings 320, school building 1, parsonage 1, cemetery 1; Salary of Rector $800 per annum; number of free sittings, all.

Money Receipts from all sources—Collections in Church $1048.50, Subscriptions $852.97; Total $1901.47.

Expenditures and Appropriations—Current Expenses (including Salary of Rector) $926.09, Repairs and Improvements $726.88, Episcopal and Convention Fund $20, Support of Sunday Schools $30, for the Poor $25, to Missions, Foreign $5, Domestic $118.60, Home Mission for Colored people $4.75, Diocesan $20, Christian or Theological Education $20.50, Disabled Clergymen $5; Total 1901.47.

Christ Church, Williamsport. Admitted 1847. Rev. William Paret, D. D., Rector. Jas. H. Perkins and Wm. F. Logan, Wardens.

Baptisms, adults 6, infants 35, total 41; confirmed 47; communicants, added new 48, by removal 14, died or removed 23, present number 189; marriages 7; burials 13; public services, on Sundays 175, on other days 160, total 335; average attendance on Sundays 250; children catechized, times

52; Sunday Schools, officers and teachers 26, scholars 810; Parish schools, teacher 1, scholars 30; other Parish agencies, sewing school, 35 members, 6 teachers; night school for boys and men, teachers 2, scholars 40; Church 1, sittings 500, Chapel (the statistics of which are included in this Report,) 1, sittings 150, school buildings none, parsonage 1, cemetery none; Salary of Rector, Sunday morning offering, not less than $2000, arrears of salary, none; number of free sittings, *all*. All services free to all.

Money Receipts from all sources.—Pew Rents none, Offertory and Collections in Church $3455.17, Subscriptions $2366.23, balance from sale of old Church $2521.43, from Sunday School $140.04; Total $8482.87.

Expenditures and Appropriations—Current Expenses, (including salary of Rector), $2645.38, Repairs and Improvements $26.60, Payment of Debts $4918.80, Episcopal and Convention Fund $40, Support of Sunday Schools $139.83, Parochial Missions $150, for the Poor $230, to Missions, Foreign $24.40, Domestic $43.50, Diocesan $50, for the Jews $13.45, Bibles, Prayer Books and Tracts $22.25, Christian or Theological Education $22.60, Disabled Clergymen $30, Miscellaneous, Invested for a Church Home $44.11, a Private Communion Service $25; Total $8425.92.

Financial condition.—Aggregate value of property of the Parish, real and personal, $49,000; Encumbrances, Mortgages on Church edifice none, on other buildings $6,200, Ground Rent on buildings or lands none, other indebtedness $11,500.

In addition to Contributions named above, Pledges, amounting to $2,100 have been made in the Parish, for Endowing the Episcopate of the new Diocese.

Trinity Church, Williamsport. Admitted 1866. Rev. Arthur Brooks, Rector. Henry F. Snyder and G. Bedell Moore, Wardens.

Baptisms, adults 5, infants 18, total 23; confirmed 15; communicants, added new 14, by removal 21, died or removed 4, present number 83; marriages 4; burial 1; Sunday Schools, officers and teachers 26, scholars 164; other Parish agencies, sewing school; Ladies Church Missionary Society; Church, sittings 250; salary of Rector $1800 per annum, arrears of salary none; number of free sittings, all.

Money receipts from all sources—Offertory at Holy Communion $169.38, Charitable Collections in Church $299.82, Subscriptions $2000, Donations $200, other sources $10, Collections for support of Church $444; Total $3,123.20.

Expenditures and Appropriations.—Current Expenses, including salary of Rector, $1,684, Repairs and Improvements $380, Episcopal and Convention Fund $30, Support of Sunday Schools $104.21, Parochial Missions $8.75, for the Poor $48.85, to Missions, Foreign $77.04, Home Mission for Colored people $23, Diocesan $33.50, Episcopal Hospital $10, Disabled Clergymen $5; Total $2,404.35.

A barrel of provisions, clothing, etc., sent to Bishop Tuttle by the Ladies' Missionary Society.

Financial condition.—Aggregate value of property of the Parish, real or personal, $6,000.

This report covers a period of a little less than ten months, from July 10th, 1870, to May 1st, 1871. The former date is the one on which the present Rector took charge; there are no records previous to that time from which a full statement could be made.

The subscription for a new Church building is now in progress.

———

Church of Our Saviour, Montoursville. Admitted 1870. Rev. H. M. Jarvis, Rector. James Rawle and R. H. Archer, Wardens.

Baptisms, infants 4, total 4; confirmed 2; communicants, added 1, new 2, died or removed 1, present number 33; burial 1; public services, on Sundays 96, on other days 37, total 133; average attendance on Sundays 35; children catechized, times 50; Sunday Schools, officers and teachers 8, scholars 55; Bible Class, teacher 1, members 6; Church 27 x 65, sittings 250; salary of Rector $600 per annum and a house; arrears of salary, $135.26; number of free sittings, all.

Money receipts from all sources—Collections in Church $404.23, Donations $1470.89, other sources $230.51; Total $2,133.63.

Expenditures and Appropriations—Current Expenses (including salary of Rector) $739.40, Repairs and Improvements $64.54, Payment of Debts $1,288.32, Episcopal and Convention Fund $3.48, Support of Sunday Schools $31.95, Missions, Domestic $5.94; Total $2,133.63.

Financial condition.—Aggregate value of property of the Parish, real and personal, $4,000; Encumbrances—Mortgages on Church edifice none, other indebtedness $195.51.

Rev. J. W. Gibson gave up the charge of the Parish, Nov. 20th, 1870. My first service was held in the Parish Church, January 8th, 1871.

The Church was consecrated on the 13th of October, 1870.

Since this Report was completed, the mite chests have been collected. The sum of their contents amounted to $5.69.

MIFFLIN COUNTY.

St. Mark's Church, Lewistown. Admitted 1832. Rev. Thomas W. Martin, Rector.
E. E. Locke and R. F. Ellis, Wardens.

Baptisms, infants 5; communicants, added, new 1, died or removed 4, present number 29; marriages 2 ; burials 4; public services, on Sundays 93, on other days 48, total 141; average attendance on Sundays 55; children catechized, times 6; Sunday Schools, officers and teachers 15, scholars 97 ; Church 1, sittings 150, parsonage 1, cemetery 1; salary of Rector $750 per annum; extra Sunday services, free to all, 7 at Yeagertown.

Money receipts from all sources—Offertory at Holy Communion $61.77, Collections in Church $179.42, Subscriptions $1170.71, Donations $286, Investments $160, other sources $173; Total $2030.90.

Expenditures and Appropriations.—Current Expenses (including salary of Rector) $900.26, Repairs and Improvements $738.70, payment of debts $5.50, Episcopal and Convention

Fund $10, Support of Sunday Schools $103, to. Missions, Domestic $15 ; Total $1772.46.

Financial condition.—Aggregate value of property of the Parish, real and personal, $11,000, indebtedness, $6.75.

MONTGOMERY COUNTY.

St. James Church, Perkiomen. Admitt-d 1785. Rev. Peter Russell, Rector. Matthias Yost and D. M. Casselberry, Wardens.

Communicants, died 1, present number 75 ; burials 3 ; public services, on Sundays 100, on other days 20, total 120 ; average attendance 150 ; Sunday School 1, officers and teachers 12, scholars 60 ; Church 1, sittings 250, school building 1, parsonage 1, cemetery 1 ; salary of Rector $600.

Money receipts from all sources.—Pew Rents $343.87, Offertory at Holy Communion $26.32, Collections in Church $57.69, Donations $85, Investments $115, other sources $273.50 ; Total $861.38.

Expenditures and Appropriations—Current Expenses (including salary) $713.52, Repairs and Improvements $7.11, Episcopal and Convention Fund $15, Support of Sunday School $55.77, to Missions, Foreign $3.75, Domestic $2, Diocesan $11.25, Episcopal Hospital $6, Disabled Clergymen $3.50; Total $817.90.

Financial condition.—Aggregate value of property of Parish, real and personal, $9000, indebtedness $400.

For a full description of the property and investments of Parish, see Report to Convention of May, 1870.

St. Thomas' Church, Whitemarsh. Admitted 1786. Rev. P. W. Stryker, Rector. Charles Burk and W. H. Drayton, Wardens.

Baptisms, infants 9 ; communicants, present number 100 ; marriage 1 ; burials 11 ; public services, on Sundays 104, on other days 102, total 206 ; children catechized monthly ; Sunday Schools, officers and teachers 6, scholars 50 ; Bible class, teacher 1, members 17 ; Parish school, teacher 1, scholars 16 ; other Parish agencies, a Sunday School in afternoons during summer months, in a distant part of the Parish, and which numbers 5 officers and 34 scholars; Church building not yet completed, services held in Parish school house; school building 1, parsonage 1, cemetery 1; salary of Rector $1200 per annum, arrears of salary, none.

Money receipts from all sources—Free Church, Offertory at Holy Communion $97.04, Collections in Church (special) $517.95; Total $614.99.

Expenditures and Appropriations.—Repairs and Improvements $63, Episcopal and Convention Fund $35, to Missions, Foreign $26.75, Domestic $25, Diocesan $25, for the Jews $15, Episcopal Hospital $86, of which $40 were the offerings of the Sunday School, Christian or Theological Education $10, Disabled Clergymen $30, Miscellaneous $299.24; Total $614.99.

St. John's Church, Norristown. Admitted 1815. Rev. Charles Ewbank McIlvaine, Rector. John McKay and Benjamin E. Chain, Wardens.

Baptisms, adults 7, infants 27, total 34; confirmed 13; communicants, added, new 12, by removal 15, died or removed 8, present number 183; marriages 8; burials 21; public services, on Sundays 101, on other days 56, total 157; children catechized, times 8; Sunday Schools, officers and teachers 30, scholars 244; Bible classes, teachers 2, members 26; sewing school, teachers 15, scholars 92; Church 1, sittings 550, school building 1, parsonage 1, cemetery 1; salary of Rector $1800 per annum, arrears of salary, none.

Money receipts from all sources—Pew Rents $2393.59, Collections in Church $475.83, Ladies' Benevolent Society $84.90, Investments $900, other sources $144, Contributions of Sunday School $199.66, Boyer Legacy, for Church poor, $202.73, 5-cent Subscription Fund $382.80; Total $4783.51.

Expenditures and Appropriations—Current Expenses (including salary of Rector) $2675.40, Repairs and Improvements $516.83, Episcopal and Convention Fund $60, Support of Sunday School $259, Sewing school $30.11, Parochial

34

Missions $228.90, for the poor (exclusive of Boyer Fund) $49.05, to Missions, Foreign $102.24, Domestic $154.93, Home Mission for Colored People $42.59, Diocesan $91.09, for the Jews $14, Episcopal Hospital $85.55, Church building $126.49, Bibles, Prayer Books and Tracts $38.17, Disabled Clergymen $40.32, Miscellaneous $23.25; Total $4537.92.

Financial condition.—Debts owed by the Parish $4683.50.

Christ Church, Pottstown. Admitted 1829. Rev. B. McGann, Rector. Samuel Wells and W. J. Rutter, Wardens.

Baptisms, adults 5, infants 11, total 16; confirmed 10; communicants, added new 10, by removal 4, present number 80; marriage 1; burials 2; public services, on Sundays 94, on other days 49, total 143; average attendance on Sundays 150; children catechized, times 12; Sunday Schools, officers and teachers 14, scholars 90; Bible class, teacher 1, members 13; Church 1, sittings 250, Chapel (the statistics of which are included in this Report) 1, sittings 150; salary of Rector $1000 per annum, $251 for Parsonage; number of free sittings 70; evening services free to all.

Money receipts from all sources.—Pew Rents $960.87, Offertory at Holy Communion, and Collections in Church $578.62, Subscriptions $60, Donations $200, Investments $72, other sources $335; Total $2206.49.

Expenditures and Appropriations—Current Expenses (including salary of Rector) $1232.72, Repairs and Improvements $207.21, payment of debts $200.78, Episcopal and Convention Fund $20, Support of Sunday Schools $87.14, Parochial Missions $20, for the Poor $15, to Missions, Foreign $55.50, Domestic $22.50, Home Mission for Colored People $19.35, Diocesan $14.36, Episcopal Hospital $30, Disabled Clergymen $26, Miscellaneous $204, Missions to Indians $40; Total $2095.56.

Financial condition.—Aggregate value of property of the Parish, real and personal, $16,770, indebtedness $400.

The parish has had a Parsonage until recently, when the

house was sold, with a view to the purchase or erection of another. The money received on this sale, $3500, is reserved for this purpose.

Church of the Redeemer, Lower Merion. Admitted 1852. Rev. Edward L. Lycett, Rector. N. Parker Shortridge and George F. Curwen, Wardens.

Baptisms, adult 1, infants 9, total 10; confirmed 6; communicants, added, new 4, by removal 1, died or removed 13, present number 85; marriages 2; burial 1; public services on Sundays 150, on other days 45, total 195; Sunday Schools, officers and teachers 10, scholars 60; Church, sittings 250, Chapel (the statistics of which are included in this Report) 1, sittings 100; salary of Rector $1500 per annum.

Money receipts from all sources—Pew Rents $1449, Offertory at Holy Communion $188.47, Collections in Church $1625.98, Subscriptions $120, Donations $200, Investments $121.58, other sources $81.25; Total $3786.28.

Expenditures and Appropriations.—Current Expenses (including salary of Rector) $2097.95, Repairs and Improvements $246.38, Episcopal and Convention Fund $50, Support of Sunday Schools $250, Parochial Missions $100, to Missions, Foreign $135.83, Domestic $175.16, Diocesan $100, Kennett Square $40, Episcopal Hospital $150, Disabled Clergy $110, Clergy Daughters $73.51, Children's Church Home $130.05, Proceeds of Missionary Boxes $27.53; Total $3686.41.

Financial condition.—Aggregate value of property of the Parish, real and personal, $17,000.

Church of Our Saviour, Jenkintown. Admitted 1858. Rev. R. Francis Colton, Rector. Charles Hewett and John S. Newbold, Wardens.

Baptisms, adults 7, infants 7, total 14; confirmed 7; communicants, added, new 7, by removal 8, died or removed 6, present number 78; burials 4; public services, on Sundays 104, on other days 43, total 147; children catechized and children's Church, times 7; Sunday Schools, officers and teachers 9; Bible classes 2, teachers 2, members 40; Parish school, teacher 1, scholars 30; Church 1, sittings, 250; school building 1, parsonage 1; salary of Rector $1500 per annum, arrears of salary, none; number of free sittings 250.

Money receipts from all sources—Collections in Church $693.94, Subscriptions $2000, Donations $115.45, other sources about $190.61; Total about $3000.

Expenditures and Appropriations—Current Expenses (including salary of Rector) over $1800, Episcopal and Convention Fund $25, support of Sunday School $50, of Parish school $600, for the Poor $26.61, to Missions, Domestic $13.08, for the Jews $4.97, Episcopal Hospital $267.58, Disabled Clergymen $18.62, Children's Church Home $23.38, Bishop White Prayer Book Society $38, Miscellaneous, about $132.76; Total, about $3000.

In addition to my duties as Rector of the Church of our Saviour, I have discharged, as heretofore, those of Professor of Hebrew in the Philadelphia Divinity School.

Calvary Church, Conshohocken. Admitted 1859. Walter Cresson, Warden.

This Church having been vacant since the resignation of Rev. T. S. Yocum, which took effect at the end of May last, it falls upon me to make the annual Report of the parish.

The services of the Church have been fully maintained on Sundays, and four times on other days. This was done during last summer by such supplies as we could get from week to week, and in the month of September we made an arrangement with Mr. T. W. Davidson, Student of Divinity, who has since acted as lay reader, and taken full charge of the services and the Sunday School, to our very great satisfaction. The school is now in very excellent condition, with 13 attentive teachers, and 95 scholars. Of the general and comparative statistics of the Parish I can say but little, as the late Rector has not left us the records of his ministry. An attempt has been made to get up a list of communicants, and we have reached the number of 45. The attendance on services is generally good.

The cash receipts that have come in my accounts are, from Pew Rents $633.50, Collections $22.97, Payments for Clerical services $676, Convention Fund $5, Episcopal Hospital $22.97, and a small amount for Expenses. The current expenses are paid by a separate organization within the Parish, and there have been one or two collections that did not pass through my hands.

St. Paul's Church, Cheltenham. Admitted 1861. Rev. Edward W. Appleton, Rector. John W. Thomas and Jay Cooke, Wardens,

Baptisms, adults 7, infants 11, total 18; confirmed 12; communicants, added, new 12, by removal 4, died or removed 12, present number 154; marriages 3; burials 6; Sunday Schools, officers and teachers 19, scholars 220; Bible classes, teachers 2, members 155; Church accommodations, edifice 1, sittings 450, parsonage 1, property other than the Church building and lot owned by the Parish, Sunday School house and Library, Hall (400 sittings) and Sexton's house; Clergyman's salary $2500, and use of Rectory.

Collections and Contributions.—Communion Alms $1124.05, Improvements, Repairs and Current Expenses $3031.69, Pew Rents $2344.33, Missions, Diocesan $399, Domestic (per American Church Missionary Society) $542.09, Foreign $206.06, Convention and Episcopal Funds $150, Episcopal Hospital $186.44, Evangelical Educational Society $1672.03, Evangelical Knowledge Society $365.87, Disabled Clergymen $139.08, Sunday School Offerings $750, Jewish Missions $118.70, Miscellaneous $787.44; Total (exclusive of Pew Rents) $9472.45.

St. John's Church, Lower Merion. Admitted 1864. Rev. C. M. Butler, D.D., in temporary charge. David Morgan and Joseph B. Townsend. Wardens.

Baptisms, infants 12; communicants, added, by removal 7, died or removed 3, present number 24; marriages 3; burials 5; public services, on Sundays 90, on other days 10, total 100;

average attendance on Sundays 60; children catechized, times 12; Sunday Schools, officers and teachers 16, scholars 180; Bible classes, teachers 2, members 25; Church, sittings 400, School building 1, parsonage 1.

Money receipts from all sources—Pew Rents $1060, Offertory at Holy Communion $83.44, Collections in Church $250.50, Subscriptions $300, Donations $4000; Total $5693.94.

Expenditures and Appropriations—Current Expenses (including salary of Rector) $2037.98, Repairs and Improvements $4000, Episcopal and Convention Fund $30, Support of Sunday Schools $400, for the Poor $83.44, to Missions, Domestic $229.87; Total $6781.29.

Financial condition.—Aggregate value of property of the Parish, real and personal, $20,000, Ground Rent on buildings or lands $2000.

St. Paul's Memorial Church, Upper Providence. Admitted 1869. Rev. J. Rudderow, Rector. Wm. H. Gumbes and Caleb Cresson, Wardens.

Baptisms, infants 7; confirmed 5; communicants, added, new 4, by removal 3, died or removed 1, present number 22; burials 3; public services on Sundays, morning and evening, on other days, during Lent; average attendence on Sundays 50; children catechized, times 12; Sunday Schools, officers and teachers 7, scholars 82; Bible classes, teachers 3, members 45.

Money Receipts from all sources—Offertory at Holy Communion $23.63, Collection in Church $87.26, other sources, viz., the Sunday School, $123.49; Total $234.38.

Expenditures and Appropriations—Episcopal and Convention Fund $5, support of Sunday Schools $7.50, for the Poor, $38.19, to Missions, Foreign $30.19, Domestic $37.50, Home Mission, for Colored People $8.67, Diocesan $50.50, City Missions $6.92, for the Jews $10.49, Episcopal Hospital $18.39, Bibles, Prayer Books and Tracts $4.02, Disabled Clergymen $10.38, Miscellaneous $6.63; Total $234.38.

Financial condition.—Aggregate value of property of the Parish, real and personal, $6000.

MONTOUR COUNTY.

Christ Church, Danville. Admitted 1834, Rev. J. Milton Peck, Rector. Peter Baldy and Daniel De Long, Wardens.

Baptisms, adults 2, infants 46, total 48; confirmed 3; communicants, added 8, died or removed 3, present number 109; marriages 4; burials 6; public services, on Sundays 96, on all Saints' and Holy days; children catechized, every Sunday; Sunday Schools, officers and teachers 30, scholars 275; Bible Classes 2, members 35; Church 1, sittings 350, parsonage 1, cemetery 1; salary of Rector $1600 per annum, arrears of salary, none; extra Sunday service free to all, once a month a Children's Choral Service.

Money receipts from all sources—Pew Rents, Subscriptions $1066.66, Offertory at Holy Communion $275.19, Collections in Church at Evening Prayer on Sundays $69.68, other offerings and special subscriptions $886.28; Total $2,297.81.

Expenditures and Appropriations.—Current Expenses (including salary of Rector) $1,316.66, Repairs and Improvements $500, on Rectory; Episcopal and Convention Fund $40, Parish Library $20, for the Poor $60, to Missions, Foreign $5, Domestic $70, Diocesan $31.68, for the Jews $8, Christian or Theological Education $140, Disabled Clergymen $25, Church Home $600, Surplices and sundry " Pious and Charitable Uses" $69.89; Total $2,292.23.

Financial condition.—Aggregate value of property of the Parish, real and personal, $25,000; Encumbrances, none; other indebtedness, none.

The above report is for the entire Convention year, although the acts of the present incumbent date only from his Institution in September last.

St. James' Church, Exchange (Derry), Admitted 1849. Rev. A. P. Brush, Rector. Charles Reeder and John Brown, Wardens.

Baptisms, infants 2, total 2; communicants, present number 44; burial 1; public services, on Sundays 12; Church accommodations, 1, edifice sittings 175.

Collections and Contributions—Parochial, Improvements,

Repairs and Current expenses $50, Collections and Subscriptions for salary $88.27; Total $138.27.

Extra-Parochial—Convention and Episcopal Fund $5.

NORTHAMPTON COUNTY.

Trinity Church, Easton. Admitted 1866. Rev. J. Sanders Reed, Rector. Theodore Sitgrave and E. C. Swift, Wardens.

Baptisms, infants 14, total 14; communicants, by removal 3, died or removed 7, present number about 100; marriage 1; burials 2; public services, on Sundays 103, on other days 61, total 164; children catechized, times 8; Sunday Schools, officers and teachers 23, scholars 225; Bible Classes, teacher 1, members 12; Church 1, sittings 500, school building 1; Salary of Rector $1200 per annum.

Money receipts from all sources—Pew Rents $1107, Offertory at Holy Communion $75.77, Collections in Church $301.23, Subscriptions $4550, other sources $300; Total $6355.77.

Expenditures and Appropriations.—Current Expenses (including salary of Rector) $1510.60, Episcopal and Convention Fund $25, Support of Sunday Schools $56.90, to Missions, Foreign $35.50, for the Jews $13.54, Episcopal Hospital $19.64, Disabled Clergymen $17; Total $1,678.18.

Financial condition.—Aggregate value of property of the Parish, real and personal $40,000; Encumbrances, Mortgages on Church edifice $6,000; on other buildings, none; Ground Rent on buildings or lands, none; other indebtedness, none.

While away from my Parish last year during the months of July, August, and September, the Rev. Mr. Boyle ministered to my people. Our Church building is yet incomplete, but, through mortgage and otherwise, having obtained funds sufficient to finish the design, we expect to recommence this month, and I have the promise that we shall occupy it throughout by September. Since January, 1870, we have been regularly worshipping in the *Basement* of the new Edifice. When entire, we shall have one of the most beautiful and commodious Churches in the Diocese. $12,000 are required to finish.

$6,000 we raised on mortgage, the remainder by subscription. Our report will be more full and satisfactory when our Parish arrangements are complete. The report includes the period of time during which Mr. Boyle officiated for me.

Church of the Nativity, South Bethlehem. Admitted 1863. Rev. Cortland Whitehead, Rector. Wm. H. Sayre and Henry Coppée, Wardens.

Baptisms, infants 8, total 8; confirmed 8; communicants, added new 8, by removal 31, died or removed 31, present number 99; burials 8; public services, on Sundays 166, on other days 117, total 283; children catechized, times 12; Sunday Schools, officers and teachers 36, scholars 260; Bible Classes, teacher 1, members 25; other Parish agencies, Parish Association; Ladies Aid Society; Holy Communion administered, times public 17, private 1, total 18; Church 1, sittings 300, Chapel (the statistics of which are included in the Report) 1, sittings 300, parsonage 1; salary of Rector $1800 per annum, arrears of salary, none; number of free sittings, *all;* Extra Sunday services free to all, one.

Money receipts from all sources—Pew Rents, none, Offertory at Holy Communion $154.27, Collections in Church $1445.87, Subscriptions $5312.96, other sources $68.68; Total $6,981.78.

Expenditures and Appropriations—Current Expenses (including salary of Rector) $2206.52, Repairs and Improvements $2710.82, Episcopal and Convention Fund $30, Support of Sunday Schools $366.13, for the Poor $155.11, to Mission Foreign $73.18, Domestic $85.25, Diocesan $300, for the Jews $23.55, Episcopal Hospital $46, Church Building $171.66, Christian or Theological Education $76.69, Disabled Clergymen $39.25, Miscellaneous, Church Home for Children $22.26, other objects $415; Total $6,450.29.

Financial condition—Aggregate value of property of the Parish $40,000; Encumbrances, none; other indebtedness $900.00

For the first six months covered by this Report, the Parish was without a Rector. The present Incumbent entered upon his duties, November 1st, 1870.

35

NORTHUMBERLAND COUNTY.

St. Matthew's Church, Sunbury. Admitted 1827. Rev. Gideon J. Burton, Rector.
Wm. I. Greenough and George W. Smith, Wardens.

Baptisms, adults 6, infants 8, total 14; confirmed 12; communicants, added, new 13, by removal 4, died or removed 3, present number 80; marriages 3; burials 6; public services on Sundays 100, on other days 106, total 206; average attendance on Sundays very good; children catechized nearly every Sunday; Sunday Schools, officers and teachers 19, scholars 170; Bible classes, teachers 2, members 20; private school in Parish school house, teachers 2, scholars 27; other Parish agencies, Rector's week-day Bible class, Mite Society, Night sewing schools; Church 1; school building 1, parsonage 1; salary of Rector $1000 per annum; number of free sittings, all.

Money receipts from all sources—Pew Rents, none, Offertory at Holy Communion $27.62, Collections in Church $1006, Subscriptions $458, Donations $88, Investments, $900, other sources $739, Sunday School Offerings $116.84; Total $3335.46.

Expenditures and Appropriations—Current Expenses (including salary of Rector) $1170.30, Repairs and Improvements $90.23, payment of debts $1450, Episcopal and Convention Fund $12, support of Sunday Schools $100, for the Poor, &c., $27.62, to Missions, Domestic $24.10, Diocesan $15, for the Jews $3.14, Bibles, Prayer Books and Tracts $11.63, Disabled Clergymen $17.60, Midnight Mission, N. Y., $8.75; Total $2918.87.

I am thankful to be able to report that we have succeeded in securing the funds to render our Rectory, built about eighteen months ago, entirely free from debt. We have also a balance on hand, which will be used towards enlarging the Church or Sunday School building, as shall be decided.

The Parish is growing in life and zeal, manifested by the increasing interest in the services; and the enlarged contributions.

St. Mark's Church, Northumberland. Admitted 1848. Rev. Wm. Moore, Rector. John McFarland and Horace Kapp, Wardens.

Baptisms, infants 5; communicants, present number 9; burial 1; public services, on Sundays 42, on other days 13, total 55; average attendance on Sundays 60; children catechized, times 39; Sunday School, officers and teachers 7, scholars 40; Church, sittings 100; salary of Rector $600 per annum, arrears of salary, $196, number of free sittings, all.

Money receipts from all sources—Subscriptions $354, Donations $30, Convocation $161, Domestic Board of Missions $83; Total $628.

Expenditures and Appropriations—Current Expenses (including salary of Rector) $650, Repairs and Improvements $15, Episcopal and Convention Fund $6, to Missions, Foreign $5.16, for the Jews $2, Episcopal Hospital $2.75; Total $658.91.

Financial condition.—Aggregate value of property of the Parish, real and personal, $3500.

———

Trinity Church, Shamokin. Admitted 1866. Rev. A. H. Boyle, Rector. Charles P. Helfenstein, Sr. and John H. Dewees, Jr. Wardens.

Baptisms, infants 46; confirmed 5; communicants, present number 39; burials 3; public services, on Sundays 102, on other days 10, total 112; average attendance on Sundays 75; children catechized, times 12; Sunday Schools, officers and teachers 20, scholars 200; Bible class, teacher 1, members 20; other parish agencies, 2; Church, sittings 150; salary of Rector $800 per annum; number of free sittings, 150.

Money receipts from all sources—Pews free, Offertory at Holy Communion $35, Collections in Church $74.63, Subscriptions $800, other sources $131.51; Total $1140.94.

Expenditures and Appropriations—Current Expenses (including salary of Rector) $869.43, Repairs and Improvements $25, payment of debts $100, Support of Sunday Schools $131.51, to Missions, Domestic $5, Bibles, Prayer Books and Tracts $15, Disabled Clergymen $12.69.

PHILADELPHIA COUNTY.

Christ Church, Philadelphia. Admitted 1785. Rev. Edward A. Foggo, Rector. Rev. G. Woolsey Hodge, Assistant. Edward L. Clark and Joseph K. Wheeler, Wardens.

Baptisms, adults 14, infants 55, total 69; confirmed 19; communicants, added, new 27, by removal 7, died or removed 33, present number 377; marriages 13; burials 31; public services, on Sundays 121, on other days 218, total 339; children catechized, times monthly; Sunday Schools, officers and teachers 33, scholars 349; Bible classes, teachers 3, members 50; Parish schools, teachers 2, scholars 70; other Parish agencies, Mothers' Meeting, members 37; Church 1, sittings 850, school buildings 2, cemetery 1; number of free sittings, 250; extra Sunday services free to all, once on Sunday during the winter.

Money receipts from all sources—Pew Rents $3230.29, Offertory at Holy Communion $439.79, Collections in Church $857.39, Donations $11,200, Investments $2349.30.

Expenditures and Appropriations—Current Expenses (including salary of Rector) $5078.20, Repairs and Improvements $352.50, Episcopal and Convention Fund $140, support of Sunday Schools $232.57, of Parish schools $480.50, Parochial Missions $336.02, for the Poor $1510.75, to Missions, Domestic $208.09, Home Mission for Colored People $10, Diocesan $95.13, City Missions $60.94, for the Jews $20, Episcopal Hospital $16, Church building $50, Bibles, Prayer Books and Tracts $124.86, Book Societies $20.16, Christian or Theological Education $100, Disabled Clergymen $32.62.

The Ladies' Missionary Association has made, in addition, offerings to the amount of $780.20. The regular duty at Christ Church Hospital has been continued. The new Parish building has been completed. The schools entered it on the first Sunday in Lent. The rooms are large, well ventilated and comfortable.

St. Peter's Church, Philadelphia. Admitted 1785. Rev. Thomas F. Davies, Rector.
Rev. Wm. White Bronson, Rev. Robert F. Chase, Assistant Ministers.
John Welsh and Francis Gurney Smith, Wardens.

Baptisms, adults 12, infants 110, total 122; confirmed 63; communicants, added 40, lost by death or removal 24, by revision of list 236, present number 423; marriages 18; burials 19; public services, on Sundays 172, on other days 626, total 798; children catechized, day-school, weekly, Sunday Schools monthly; Sunday Schools, officers and teachers 85, scholars 391; Bible classes, teachers 4, members 110; Parish school teacher 1, scholars 79; sewing school, scholars 95; whole number of pupils 675; school building 1, parsonage 1, cemetery 1; arrears of salary, none; extra free services, free to all, 62.

Expenditures and Appropriations—Current Expenses (including salary of Rector) $8137.07, Repairs and Improvements $777.35, Episcopal and Convention Fund $210, Sunday and Parish schools $1529.48, Parochial Missions $1800, for the Poor $1428.86, to Missions, Foreign $856,47, Domestic $3471.64, Home Mission for Colored People $247.92, Diocesan $944.71, for the Jews $96, Episcopal Hospital $950.76, Theological Education $1810, Disabled Clergymen $283.79, Dorcas $413, Ladies Missionary Aid Society $716, Box for Nashotah $370, for purchase of Rectory $14,000; Total $38,270.43.

The usual services at Christ Church Hospital have been maintained throughout the year, in connection with the Clergy of Christ Church.

The Rev. Franklin L. Bush, after more than two years of untiring labor, has resigned the charge of the Memorial Mission, to seek needed rest in a foreign tour, and is succeeded by the Rev. Robert F. Chase.

St. Paul's Church, Philadelphia. Admitted 1785. Rev. Robert T. Roach, D. D., Rector.
Andrew Jackson Holman, Sr., and Collins West, Wardens.

Baptisms, adults 11, infants 19, total 30; confirmed 13; communicants, added new 41, by removal 3, died or removed 1, present number 150; marriages 6; burials 18; public services, on Sundays 118, on other days 93, total 211; Sunday Schools, officers and teachers 29, scholars 300; Bible Classes, teachers 2, members 25; sittings 1100, school buildings none, parsonage none, cemetery 1; salary of Rector $2000 per annum, arrears of salary, none.

Money receipts from all sources—Offertory at Holy Communion $278.34, other sources $791.09, Christmas offertory for the Poor $62.91.

Expenditures and Appropriations—For the Jews $20, Church Home for Children $32.42.

St. James' Church, Philadelphia. Admitted 1810. Rev. Henry J. Morton, D.D., Rector. George W. Hunter and John T. Lewis, Wardens.

Baptisms, adults 4, infants 19, total 23; confirmed 16; communicants, present number about 200; public services, on Sundays 128, on other days 150, total 278; children catechized, times 30; Sunday Schools, officers and teachers 10, scholars 80; Bible Classes, teachers 4, members 38; Parish schools, teacher 1, scholars 40; sewing school, scholars 30; Church 1, unfinished, sittings 920, school buildings 1, cemetery 1, salary of Rector $3000 per annum, arrears of salary none; assistant $2000.

Money receipts from all sources—Pew Rents $4900, Offertory at Holy Communion $1063.27, Collections in Church $2057.30, Subscriptions $40.379, Donations $2462.70, Investments $204, other sources $220; Total $51,304.27.

Expenditures and Appropriations—Current Expenses (including salaries of Clergy), $8600, Repairs and Improvements $45,620, Episcopal and Convention Fund $150, Support of Sunday Schools $95, of Parish schools $604, for the Poor $1,069.49, to Missions, Foreign $203.30, Domestic $188, Diocesan $176.55, Church for Seamen $100, Church Home $211.42, Episcopal Hospital $410, Disabled Clergymen $222.36, Dorcas Missionary Work $1982.70, Special Missions $120; Total $59,752.77.

Financial condition.—Aggregate value of property of the Parish, real and personal, $200.000, Ground Rent on buildings or lands $3000 per year.

St. Andrew's Church, Philadelphia. Admitted 1823. Rev. William F. Paddock, D.D., Rector. Rev. J. L. Trowbridge, D.D., Assistant. Thomas Robins and Frederick Brown, Wardens.

Baptisms, adults 7, infants 28, total 35; confirmed 26; communicants, added new 26, by removal 21, died or removed 10, present number 814; marriages 4; burials 21; public services, on Sundays 110, on other days 38, total 148; children catechized, times 12; Sunday Schools, officers and teachers 56, scholars 657; Bible Classes, teachers 4, members 122; Sewing School, teachers 12, scholars 138, Mothers' Meeting, officers 3, members 124; Church 1, sittings 900; salary of Rector $3,500, arrears of salary, none.

Money receipts from all sources.—Pew rents $6,955.18, Offertory at Holy Communion $809.08, Collections in Church $7384.99, Subscriptions $2,177.72, Donations $1,050.00, other sources $1,917.60; Total $19,394.66.

Expenditures and Appropriations—Current Expenses, (including salary of Rector) $8,063.50, Episcopal and Convention Fund $210, Support of Sunday Schools $457.40, Young Women's Christian Association $794, Parochial Missions $158.11, for the Poor $684.08, to Missions, Foreign $1,117.11, Domestic $365, News Boys' Home $542.75, Diocesan $538.85, City Missions $370.75, for the Jews $93.80, Episcopal Hospital $400, Church buildings $105, Bibles, Prayer Books and Tracts $81.80, Church Home for Children $228.85, Christian or Theological Education $658.25, Disabled Clergymen $579.50, Bedell Professorships, Gambier, additional $689.65, St. Andrew's Endowment Fund $1,480, Miscellaneous $354,26; Total $19,394.66.

Financial condition—Aggregate value of property of the Parish, real and personal, $70,000; Encumbrance, $100 per year on Chapel; other indebtedness none.

St. Stephen's Church, Philadelphia. Admitted 1823. Rev. Wm. Rudder, D. D., Rector. Rev. Francis F. Clerc, D. D.. Warden of "The Burd Orphan Asylum of St. Stephen's Church." Rev. Alexander Fullerton, Rector's Assistant. Thomas Neilson and Louis Rodman, Wardens.

Baptisms, adults 13, infants 41, total 54; confirmed 23; communicants, added new 18, by removal 3, died or removed 6, present number about 450; marriages 10; burials 9; Sunday Schools 2, officers and teachers 36, scholars 336; Bible Classes 2, teachers 2, members 51; Parish School, teacher 1, scholars 50; other Parish agencies, Sewing Schools 2, teachers 32, scholars 366; Chapels (the statistics of which are included in this Report) 2.

Money receipts from all sources—Pew Rents $11,000, Offertory at Holy Communion $1,405.21, Collections in Church $7,015.28; Total $19,420.49.

Expenditures and Appropriations—Episcopal and Convention Fund $280, Support of Sunday Schools $270.42, to Missions, Foreign $320.75, Domestic $1,302.89, Diocesan $215.39, for the Jews $127.04, Episcopal Hospital $353.77, Disabled Clergymen $328.88, Miscellaneous $1,530.11, Society for Increase of Ministry $237.04, Female Tract Society $88.49, Missionary Box Society $810.56, Church Home Building $350.87, Bishop Neely $75, Bishop White Parish Library Society $224.07, Female Benevolent Society $500; Total $7,015.28.

Deaf Mission of St. Stephen's Church, confirmed 3 (included above); marriages 2; burial 1; communicants 17.

Chapel of "Burd Orphan Asylum of St. Stephen's Church," infant baptisms 3; marriages 3; burials 3; communicants 20; $147.05.

The above includes the Report of St. Stephen's Chapel, West Philadelphia.

————

Grace Church, Philadelphia. Admitted 1827. Rev. William Suddards, D. D., Rector. Rev. John S. Beers, Assistant. Isaac S. Williams and Andrew H. Miller, Wardens.

Baptisms, adults 5, infants 46, total 51; confirmed 17; communicants, added new 17, by removal 8, died or removed 18, present number 477; marriages 20; burials 32; public services, on Sundays 140, on other days 100, total 240 ; children catechized, times monthly ; Sunday Schools, officers and teachers 56, scholars 454 ; Bible Classes, teachers 3, members 91 ; Church 1, sittings 1130 ; salary of Rector $3,500 per annum, arrears of salary, none ; number of free sittings 336 ; extra Sunday services, free to all, evening.

Money receipts from all sources—Pew Rents $6,003, Offertory at Holy Communion $500, Collections in Church $1492.68, Subscriptions $3,725.60, Donations $1,200, Investments $697, other sources $300 ; Total $13,918.28.

Expenditures and Appropriations—Current Expenses (including salary of Rector) $4,550, Repairs and Improvements $5,260.75, Episcopal and Convention Fund $225, Support of Sunday Schools $300, Parish Library $250, Parochial Missions $400, for the Poor $800, to Missions, Foreign $307, Domestic $250, Diocesan $150, City Missions $135, Episcopal Hospital $370, Bibles, Prayer Books and Tracts $100, Christian or Theological Education $300, Disabled Clergymen $163.28, Miscellaneous $357.23 ; Total $13,918.28.

Church of the Epiphany, Philadelphia. Admitted 1836. Rev. Richard Newton, D.D., Rector. Rev. J. Everist Cathell, Assistant. Joshua Cowpland and Wm. G. Boulton, Wardens.

Baptisms, adults 2, infants 38, total 40 ; confirmed 43 ; communicants added new 40, by removal 12, died or removed 11, present number 697 ; marriages 15 ; burials 24 ; public services, on Sundays 104, on other days 66, total 170 ; average attendance on Sundays 500 ; Sunday Schools, officers and teachers 86, scholars 807 ; Bible classes, teachers 4, members 150 ; Church 1, sittings 1,300, Chapel (the statistics of which are included in this Report) 1, sittings 250, school building 1 ; salary of Rector $5,000 per annum, arrears of salary, none ; number of free sittings 275.

Money receipts from all sources—Pew Rents $10,204.86, Offertory at Holy Communion $1,923, Collections in Church $13,935.72, other sources $670 ; Total $25,733.58.

Expenditures and Appropriations—Current Expenses (in-

36

...uding salary of Rector) $10,624.03, Repairs and Improvements $344.79, Episcopal and Convention Fund $275, Support of Sunday Schools $337.58, Parochial Missions $2931.43, for the Poor $2,576, to Missions, Foreign $255, Domestic $1,700, Home Mission for Colored People $50, Diocesan $410, City Missions $428, for the Jews $213.85, Episcopal Hospital $1,588.26, Church building $766, Bibles, Prayer Books and Tracts $337.75, Book Societies $475, Christian or Theological Education $397, Disabled Clergymen $375, Miscellaneous $1,100; Total $24,519.96.

Financial condition.—Aggregate value of property of the Parish, real and personal, $150,000, and Mission Chapel $7,000.

Church of the Ascension, Philadelphia. Admitted 1837. Rev. Robert F. Chase, Officiating. Alfred Zautzinger, and Thomas R. Maris, Wardens.

Baptisms, adults 2, infants 32, total 34; communicants, added new 30, by removal 3, died or removed 7, present number 326; marriages 5; burials 25; Sunday Schools, officers and teachers 13, scholars 90; Bible Classes, teachers 7, members 80; Parish School, teacher 1, scholars 24; other Parish agencies, Infant School, teachers 4, scholars 100; Sewing School, teachers 8, scholars 85; Mothers' Meeting, directresses 2, members 45; Church 1, sittings 600.

Money receipts from all sources—Pew Rents $916.05, Offertory at Holy Communion $208.35, Collections in Church $816.09, Subscriptions $1,981, other sources $179.45, Collections in Sunday School $149.48; Total $4,156.54.

Expenditures and Appropriations.—Current Expenses (including salary of Rector) $2,802.58, Repairs and Improvements $286.20, Episcopal and Convention Fund $25, Support of Sunday Schools $110.91, of Parish Schools $30.63, for the Poor $200.06, to Missions, Foreign $80, Domestic $15, Home Mission for Colored People $10, Diocesan $6.40, City Missions $95.42 Episcopal Hospital $90.65, Bibles, Prayer Books and Tracts $30, Disabled Clergymen $20; Total $3,802.85.

Financial condition.—Aggregate value of property of the Parish, real and personal, $25,000.

This Parish became vacant in December, by the resignation of the Rev. William H. Hare, to whose earnest and faithful labors its present prosperity is, under God, chiefly owing.

St. Luke's Church, Philadelphia. Admitted 1840. Rev. M. A. DeWolfe Howe, D. D., Rector. Rev. Alfred Louderback, Assistant. Geo. L. Harrison, Warden.

Baptisms, adults 6, infants 34, total 40; confirmed 20; communicants, added new 20, by removal 17, died or removed 15, present number 600; marriages 9; burials 32; public services, on Sundays 104, on other days 75, total 179; children catechized, times 6; Sunday Schools, officers and teachers 48, scholars 488; Bible Classes, teachers 7, members 137; Parish Schools, teachers 2; other Parish agencies, Colored Mission, Rector's Bible Class, Mothers' Meeting, Night School for Boys, Sewing School; Church 1, sittings 1300, Chapel (the statistics of which are included in this Report,) 1, sittings 150, parsonage none, cemetery none; salary of Rector $5,000 per annum, arrears of salary, none.

Money receipts from all sources—Pew Rents $9,101.01, Offertory at Holy Communion $900.87, Collections in Church $4,883.08, Subscriptions $3,164, Donations $1,972, other sources $1,020.95, Home for Aged Women, given, cost $15,000; Total $36,041.81.

Expenditures and Appropriations—Current Expenses (including salary of Rector and Repairs and Improvements) $9,000, Episcopal and Convention Fund $225, Support of Sunday Schools $585.56, of Parish Schools $266, Parochial Missions $250, for the Poor $2,244.13, to Missions, Foreign $1,899.69, Domestic $1,251.11, Diocesan $738.99, City Missions $463.47, for the Jews $114.96, Episcopal Hospital $830.13, Church Building $1,170, Bibles, Prayer Books and Tracts $86.37, Christian or Theological Education $274.90, Disabled Clergymen $344.26, Miscellaneous $196.28; Total $35,940.80.

Financial condition.—Aggregate value of property of the

Parish, real and personal, Church lot, building and furniture, cost about 90,000. A Home for Aged Lone Women has been in the past year donated in trust to the vestry of St. Luke's. Cost of the property and furniture about $16,000.

A Sunday School for Colored Children has been maintained in connection with this Church, at a hired hall in the vicinity, for several years. Last autumn a Clergyman was engaged to superintend the work, and also to conduct public worship and to preach in the Hall every Sunday P. M. A congregation highly respectable in numbers and character had been thus gathered. We propose to continue the effort, hopeful that it may grow into the establishment of a new Church for Colored People in a section of the City where they are very numerous, and no adequate accommodation exists for their attendance on Divine Worship.

Church of the Atonement, Philadelphia. Admitted 1847. **Rev. Benjamin Watson, D.D., Rector. Rev. Thos. M. Antrim, Assistant.** Townsend Whelen and Frederick Fairthorne, Wardens.

Baptisms, adults 15, infants 36, total 51; confirmed 35; communicants added new 35, by removal 29, died or removed 29, present number 479; marriages 10; burials 26; public services, on Sundays 100, on other days 84, total 184; Sunday Schools, officers and teachers 49, scholars 395; Bible Classes, teachers 8, members 70; other Parish agencies, Mothers' Meetings, Weekly Cottage Lectures, a female missionary; Church 1, sittings 1100; salary of Rector $3,500. Arrears of salary, none.

Money receipts from all sources—Pew Rents $7,062.46, Offertory at Holy Communion $569.73, Collections in Church $3,044,38, Donations $25, Sunday School Missionary Collections $333.79; Total $11,034.90.

Expenditures and Appropriations—Current Expenses (including salary of Rector), $7062.46, Payment of Debts $443.83, Episcopal and Convention Fund $182, Support of Sunday Schools $437.70, Parochial Missions $201.36, for the Poor $223.04, to Missions, Foreign $418.18, Domestic $342.26,

Diocesan $100, City Missions $131, for the Jews $44.65, Episcopal Hospital $243.58, Christian or Theological Education $241.36, Disabled Clergymen $100, Miscellaneous $333.79; Total $11,074.31.

Financial condition.—Aggregate value of property of the Parish, real and personal, $30,000; Ground Rent on buildings or lands $600, other indebtedness $1,000.

St. Mark's Church, Philadelphia. Admitted. 1848. Rev. Eugene Aug. Hoffman, D. D., Rector. Revs. Robert E. Dennison and Francis D. Canfield, Assistants. Richard R. Montgomery and Isaac Starr, Jr., Wardens.

Baptisms, adults 24, infants 76, total 100; confirmed 51; communicants, added, new or by removal 94, died or removed 26, present number 629; marriages 15; burials 25; public services, on Sundays 186, on other days 626, total 812; average attendance on Sundays 900; children catechized, times 44; Sunday Schools, officers and teachers 31, scholars 302; Bible classes, teachers 3, members 70; Parish schools, teachers 2, scholars 70; other Parish agencies, night-schools 2, scholars 84, industrial school 1, teachers 17, scholars 102; working-women's meeting, members 68; working-men's club 150; Church 1, sittings 900; school buildings 1; parsonage 1; salary of Rector $5000 per annum; arrears of salary, none; number of free sittings 100; extra Sunday services, free to all, 4.

Money receipts from all sources.—Pew rents $11,376.75, Offertory at Holy Communion, and collections in Church and subscriptions $29,140.39; Total $40,338.14.

Expenditures and Appropriations.—Current expenses (including salary of Rector and repairs and improvements) $16,376.75, Episcopal and Convention Fund $300, support of Sunday schools $276.32, of Parish schools $1092.54, Parochial Missions $1907.30, for the Poor $1625.88, Missions, Foreign $145.50, Domestic $2123.29, Home Mission for Colored People $369.25, Diocesan $964.50, for the Jews $126.04, Episcopal Hospital $808.58, Bibles, Prayer Books and Tracts $269.20, Disabled Clergymen $345.33, Miscellaneous $13,607.66; Total $40,338.14.

This parish has been quietly and steadily doing its appointed work during the past year. Six services have been held in the Church every Lord's day during the winter, at four of which all the seats are free. At most of them the attendance had been as large as the building would permit. Through the kindness of some of the neighboring clergy, an instructive course of sermons on the Distinctive Principles of the Church was preached on successive Sunday evenings to large congregations composed mostly of persons not members of our communion.

It is due to the many members of the Parish, who have so earnestly assisted the clergy in every good work, to say that its success, under God, is the result of their untiring devotion. During the past winter, through the zealous efforts of some of the young men, a Working-Men's Club and Institute, under the supervision of the clergy, has been successfully established. Its object is to preserve those for whom it is designed from the temptations which are daily presented in a great city, to provide innocent recreation and instruction for their leisure hours, and to surround them with influences which will conduce to their eternal good. In connection with it there is a good library, well furnished reading and recreation rooms, open every evening but Sunday; a night-school; a Bible class; and a literary or musical entertainment given every fortnight for the families of the members. Already one hundred and fifty working-men have availed themselves of its privileges; and it promises to be a valuable addition to the other useful parochial organizations.

Church of the Mediator, Philadelphia. Admitted, 1848. Rev. Samuel E. Appleton, Rector. Francis A. Lewis and Horace Everett, Wardens.

Baptisms, adults 3, infants 74, total 77; confirmed 17; communicants, added, new 23, by removal 19, died or removed 17, present number 390; marriages 27; burials 35; Sunday Schools, officers and teachers 36, scholars 392; Bible classes, teachers 4, members 64; Church 1, sittings 600; school building 1, salary of Rector $2250 per annum; arrears of salary, nothing.

Money receipts from all sources.—Pew rents $3921.72, Offertory at Holy Communion $339.13, Collections in Church $889.66, Subscriptions $1546.44, other sources $701.14; Total $7398.09.

Expenditures and Appropriations—Current expenses (including salary of Rector) $3912.00, Repairs and improvements $315, Episcopal and Convention Fund $75, Support of Sunday schools $244.67, Missions, Foreign $336.85, Domestic $277.50, Diocesan $278.58, City Missions $403.05, for the Jews $27.83, Episcopal Hospital $53.14, Bibles, Prayer Books and Tracts $58.51, Christian or Theological Education $79.78, Disabled Clergymen $88, Church Home $350, Miscellaneous $89.18; Total $7398.09.

Financial condition.—Aggregate value of property of the Parish, real and personal, $25,000; Encumbrances, on Church edifice none, on other buildings none, ground rent on building or lands none, other indebtedness none.

The past year has been one of uninterrupted harmony and prosperity. More than one thousand dollars was contributed for the cause of Missions by the Men's and Women's Missionary Society of the Parish.

At Easter, some of my parishioners presented me with a generous gift of five hundred dollars.

————

St. Clement's Church, Philadelphia. Admitted. 1855. Rev. Herman G. Batterson, D. D., Rector. Rev. W. H. N. Stewart, Assistant Minister. John Lambert, Accounting Warden. ——— ———, Rector's Warden.

Baptisms, adults 14, infants 46, total 60; confirmed 35; communicants 301; marriages 5; burials 9; Sunday School teachers 20, scholars 200; Church 1, sittings 976, Parish building 1; salary of the Clergy $1500, arrears, none.

Money receipts from all sources—Pew rents $4839.48, Offertory at Holy Communion $765.94; Collections in Church

$3,752.16, Subscriptions $2962.82, Donations $1404.70; Total $13,725.12.

Expenditures and Appropriations—Current expenses (including the salaries of the Clergy) $6243.74, repairs and improvements $1,059.29, Payment of debts $3736.97, Episcopal and Convention Fund $100, Support of Sunday School $146, Parish Library $60, for the Poor $435.11, to Missions, Diocesan $30, Domestic $1386.42, Foreign $10, Episcopal Hospital $163.16, Female Tract Society $12, Bishop White Parish Library Association $25, for the Increase of the Ministry, $151.75, Disabled Clergy $47.63, Church Home for Children $15; Total $13,622.07.

Financial condition.—Estimated value of property held by the corporation $115,000; Incumbrances, ground rent upon Church, principal $23,333.33, annual interest upon the same $1400; Mortgages upon Parish Building $10,000; due on organ $2200; floating debt $2050; Total amount of debt $37,583.33.

The heirs of the late Wm. S. Wilson hold title to pews valued by original appraisement in the sum of $54,600. This amount, though not actually a debt of the Parish, is yet a burden upon it, as the owners are entitled to a stipulated percentage of the amount of rental. Mr. Wilson acquired this title by the surrender of a mortgage upon the Church, amounting to $40,000, and sundry other claims for money loaned and for interest due to him.

Another party holds title to Pews valued at $2,600, the title being acquired by the surrender of claims against the corporation for a like amount.

Supposing the Church, Parish-Building, Organ, and Furniture to have cost $105,000 (which I am assured is in excess of the actual cost), the Parish or corporation has contributed over and above the regular current expenses of the Parish, during the fifteen years of its existence, the sum of $20,216.67·

Church of the Holy Trinity, Philadelphia. Admitted 1857. Rev. Thomas A. Jaggar, Rector. Rev. W. H. Neilson, Jr., Assistant. John Bohlen and Lemuel Coffin, Wardens.

Baptisms, adults 6, infants 12, total 18; confirmed 29; communicants, added new 29, present number 750; marriages 6; burials 13; public services, on Sundays 106, on other days 41, total 147; children catechized, times monthly; Sunday Schools, officers and teachers 67, scholars 756; Bible Classes, teachers 6, members 248; other Parish agencies, Sewing Schools, scholars 230, Night Schools, scholars 75; Church 1, sittings 1,400; Chapel 1, sittings 400, School Building 1; salary of Rector $5,000 per annum, and Rectory; arrears of salary, none; number of free sittings, 150.

Money receipts from all sources—Pew Rents $15,256.50, Offertory at Holy Communion $1,873.09, Collections in Church $9,634.49, Subscriptions $6,228.60, Donations $25,047; Total $58,039.68.

Expenditures and Appropriations—Current Expenses (including salary of Rector) $15,256.50, Episcopal and Convention Fund $300, Support of Sunday Schools $505.25, Parochial Missions $6,613.35, for the Poor $1,873.09, to Missions, Foreign $2,575.30, Domestic $3,742.92, Home Mission for Colored People $417.81, Diocesan $520, City Missions $830.49, for the Jews $150, Episcopal Hospital $805.64, Church Building $7,925, Bibles, Prayer Books and Tracts $125, Christian or Theological Education $715.86, Disabled Clergymen $210.73, Miscellaneous $14,572.74; Total $58,039.68.

Financial condition.—Aggregate value of property of the Parish, real and personal, $300,000; Ground Rent on buildings or lands $37,500, principal, less Sinking Fund, $7,000.

Trinity Chapel, Under the Charge of the Rev. William H. Neilson, Jr., Assistant Minister of the Church of the Holy Trinity.

Baptisms, adults 3, infants 26; confirmed 25; marriages 4; burials 18; communicants, about 175; Sunday Schools, teachers and officers 47, scholars 532; Bible Classes, teachers 3, scholars 102; Sewing School, scholars 260; Night School, scholars 136; Collections and Contributions $562.91.

Church of the Covenant, Philadelphia. Admitted 1858. Rev. Charles E. Murray, Rector. J. A. Kirkpatrick and Jno. P. Rhoads, Wardens.

Baptisms, adults 3, infants 14, total 17; confirmed 9; communicants, present number 425; marriages 18; burials 16; Sunday Schools, officers and teachers 33, scholars 277; Bible Classes, teachers 8, members 35; Total, teachers and scholars 348; Church 1, sittings 800; salary of Rector $2,500 per annum, arrears of salary, none.

Money receipts from all sources—Pew Rents $4,701.45, Offertory at Holy Communion $305.26, Collections in Church $480.04, Subscriptions $1,042.87, other sources $1,390.92; Total $7,920.54.

Expenditures and Appropriations—Current Expenses (including salary of Rector) $5,607.82, Repairs and Improvements $806.31, Episcopal and Convention Fund $70.73, Support of Sunday Schools $307.40, for the Poor $305.26, to Missions, Domestic $508.97, Episcopal Hospital $95.75, Christian or Theological Education $218.60; Total $7,920.54.

St. Thomas' Church, Philadelphia. Admitted 1864. Rev. Wm. J. Alston, Rector. Morris Brown, Sr., and Scipio Sewell, Wardens.

Baptisms, adults 3, infants 11, total 14; communicants, present number 300; marriages 12; burials 20; Church, sittings 500, parsonage 1; salary of Rector $600 per annum, arrears of salary, none; number of free sittings, 100.

Money receipts from all sources—Pew Rents $700, Offertory at Holy Communion $48, Collections in Church $200, Donations $26.40; Total $974.40.

Expenditures and Appropriations—Current Expenses (including salary of Rector), $1,200, Payment of Debts $1,100, Episcopal and Convention Fund $5, for the Poor $50, to Missions, Domestic $26.40, Home Mission for Colored People $10, for the Jews $5, Episcopal Hospital $10, Bible, Prayer Books and Tracts $6.45, Disabled Clergymen $12; Total $1,224.85.

Financial condition.—$1,418.80 the total indebtedness of the Parish.

Trinity Church, Oxford, Philadelphia. Admitted 1785. Rev. Edward Y. Buchanan.
D.D., Rector. William Overington and Harvey Rowland, Wardens.

Baptisms, adults 2, children 8, total 10; confirmed 17; communicants, added new 17, by removal 5, died or removed 5, present number 79; marriages 1; burials 12; public services, on Sundays 83, on other days 17, total 100; Sunday Schools 2, teachers 12, scholars 110.

Contributions—Episcopal and Convention Fund $45, Support of Sunday Schools $93.65, to Missions, Foreign $35.71, Domestic (including a contribution of $53.39, from the boys of Mrs. Crawford's School for Oregon), $423.23, Diocesan Missions $331.77, City Missions $46.69, Episcopal Hospital (including $32.75 from the Chapel) $272.75, Church Building $37, Bishop White Prayer Book Society $34.14, Christmas Fund $101.83, Fund for the relief of French and German sufferers $106 45, Fund for building and furnishing the Chapel $3,558.38, Benches for Basement of Chapel $192.12, of which amount $84.42 were contributed by the Sunday Schools, other purposes including the Rector's salary, $1,615.78; Total $6,899.50.

On Saturday, the 7th day of May of last year, the corner stone of the Chapel above referred to, and which is located at Crescentville, Philadelphia, was laid by the Bishop of the Diocese; and, on Sunday, the 20th of the following November, the building, having been entirely finished, furnished, and paid for, was by him consecrated. Ever since then, with one exception, there has been Divine Service in it on the Lord's day, either in the afternoon or evening. On almost every occasion the attendance has been encouraging. The Chapel is an unusually well-built structure; and as to appearance and convenience, will compare favorably with most of our suburban Churches. The seats are all free; the current necessary expenses (which are only those of heating, lighting, and taking care of the building), being provided for by collections.

During the past year, the grounds of the Church have been greatly improved by the erection, at a cost of between six and seven hundred dollars, of a very beautiful fence of granite and iron, along the western side of the Church yard. For this most ornamental as well as substatial improvement, the Parish is indebted to one of its female members, Mrs. John Lardner. Counting the amount expended on this, the total of our contributions for the year exceeds $7,500.

All Saints' Church, Philadelphia. Rev. E. W. Beasley, D. D., Rector. Rev. W. F. Morsell, Assistant. C. R. King and Alexander Brown. Wardens.

Baptisms, adults 4, infants 16, total 20; confirmed 14; communicants, new 4, died or removed 3, present number 82; marriages 6; burials 13; public services, on Sundays 203, during Lent 2 services each week, one at All Saints', one at Chapel, Eddington. Mr. Morsell will report week day services at Andalusia Chapel. The Rector has also addressed children at Sunday Schools and at Parish Schools on various occasions. Children catechized, at various times; Sunday Schools 3, officers and teachers 20, scholars 170; Parish School 1, scholars 40; Church 1, sittings 450; Chapels, (the statistics of which are included in this Report) 2, sittings 260; school buildings 2, parsonage 1, cemetery 1; salary of Rector $1,600, of Assistant $1,000, arrears of salary, none; number of free sittings 100.

Collections—All Saints' Church, Diocesan Missions $53.50, Special for Hulmeville Church $100, Total $153.50; Foreign Missions $88.60, do $26.75, total $115.35; Domestic Mission, Bishop Clarkson $100, Bishop Morris $31.65, total $131.65; Church of the Crucifixion $50, Prayer Book Societies, Bishop White $15, Female $15, total $30; Episcopal Hospital $29.10, Episcopal and Convention Fund $45, Christmas Fund $16.75, Society for Christianity among the Jews $7.40, for Bishop Tuttle's Mission $23, Sunday Collections $352, Collection for Assistant's salary $675, Improvements and Repairs and current expenses $606.21, Parents' School at All Saints' for Bishop Morris $2.15, Sunday School at All Saints' for Bishop Tuttle $11.45; Total $2,024.55.

Christ's Chapel, Eddington—Diocesan Mission $3, do $4.50, for Bishop Clarkson's Mission $6.50, Bishop Tuttle $6.50, Foreign Missions $4.60, total $25.10; Collections on Sundays for current expenses not reported, for Christmas tree for Sunday School children $85, the Contribution for Sunday School for Missions $17; Total of Collections at Eddington Chapel $77.10.

Pew Rents at All Saints' $1,579.80.

Christ's Chapel $444.75.

Our congregation has suffered much from removals of families from the neighborhood, this has been the case especially at the Chapel at Eddington. A large portion of those who attend at All Saints are with us only for the summer. The Rector has some fifty or sixty families on his Mission list who are visited continuously.

St. John's Church, Northern Liberties, Philadelphia. Admitted 1816. Rev. Charles Logan, Rector. Charles Beamish and Henry Walker, Wardens.

Baptisms, adults 2, infants 35, total 37; confirmed 4; communicants, present number 120; marriages 18; burials 25; public services, on Sundays 104, on other days 34, total 138; children catechized, times 12; Sunday Schools, officers and teachers 25, scholars 275, Bible Classes, teacher 1, members 10, other Parish agencies, Sewing School, teachers 2, scholars 100; Church 1, sittings 1000, parsonage 1, cemetery 1; salary of Rector $800 per annum, arrears of salary, none.

Money receipts from all sources—Pew Rents $837, Offertory at Holy Communion $76.49, Collections in Church $271.11, Subscriptions $24.10, Donations $236, other sources $2,341.07; Total $3,785.77.

Expenditures and Appropriations—Current Expenses (including salary of Rector), $1,151.16, Repairs and Improvements $236, Payment of Debts $2,436, Episcopal and Convention Fund $30, Support of Sunday Schools $66, of Sewing Schools $17, Parochial Missions $28.50, to Missions, Foreign $32, Domestic $50, City Missions $12.50, Episcopal Hospital

$15.09, Church Building $40, Disabled Clergymen $9.01; Total $4,124.26.

Financial condition.—Aggregate value of property of the Parish, real and personal, said to be $75,000; Encumbrances, on other buildings $1,300, other indebtedness $200.

Advent Church, Philadelphia. Admitted 1842. Rev. J. W. Claxton, Rector. Rev. G. L. Bishop, Assistant. Abel Reed and George Remsen, Wardens.

Baptisms, adults 3, infants 27, total 30; confirmed 19; communicants, added, new 19, by removal 17, died or removed 36, present number 361; marriages 14; burials 15; children catechized, times, monthly; Sunday Schools, officers and teachers 34, scholars 436, Bible classes, teachers 5, members 243; Parish Schools, teachers 2, scholars 25; other Parish agencies, Mothers' meeting, Ladies Aid Society, Sewing school.

Salary of Rector $2500 per annum; arrears of salary, none; number of free sittings, ample; extra Sunday services, free to all, every Sunday, A. M.

Money receipts from all sources—Pew Rents $4,353.27, Offertory at Holy Communion $637.05, Collections in Church $1049.53, Subscriptions and Donations $1922.44, Investments none, other sources $2672.18; total $10,634.47.

Expenditures and Appropriations—Current Expenses (including salary of Rector) $5098,79, Payment of Debts $3215.50, Episcopal and Convention Fund $100, Support of Sunday Schools $229.01, Parochial Mission $210, for the Poor $234.54, to Missions, Foreign $341, Domestic $939.55, Home Mission for Colored People $73.14, Diocesan $127.20, for the Jews $16.38, Episcopal Hospital $55, Bibles, Prayer Books and Tracts $33, Christian or Theological Education $37.57, Miscellaneous $102.50; total $10,634.47.

Calvary (Monumental) Church, Northern Liberties   Admitted 1857. The charge of the Clergy of Christ Church.

Baptisms, adults 2, infants 22, total 24; confirmed 19; communicants, added, new 15, by removal 15, removed 3, present number 80; marriages 1; burials 5; public services

on Sundays 104, on other days 63, total 167; children catechised, times monthly; Sunday schools, officers and teachers
14, scholars 105, Bible classes, teachers 2, members 28; other
Parish agencies, Girls' Sewing School, teachers 15, scholars
140; Mothers' meeting, ladies in charge 1, members 40.
Church 1, sittings 350; school building 1; Parsonage fund
$1640; Sexton's house 1; two lots in Franklin cemetery; all
the sittings are free.

Money receipts from all sources—Offertory at Holy Communion $96.22, other Collections in Church $734.58, Donations $250, Investments $329.17, other sources, proceeds of
fair $356.25, raised by the Sunday School $36.84, balance
from previous year $298.83; total $2101.89.

Expenditures and Appropriations—Current Expenses (in-
cluding salaries) $1552.06, Repairs and Improvements $137.66,
Episcopal and Convention Fund $10, support of Sunday
School $118.25, for the Poor 79.28, Domestic Missions, $75.57,
Episcopal Hospital $17.36, Disabled Clergymen $12.85; total
$2003.03.

Financial condition—No encumberances.

Since the last Convention report, the entire property and
control of the Parish has been legally transferred to the Rector, Wardens and Vestrymen of Christ Church, and since the
first of September last, the spiritual affairs of the Parish have
been in the charge of the clergy of that Church. The vestry
of Calvary were actuated in this step solely by a desire to secure the permanence and prosperity of the Parish. The
transfer has been happily accomplished, apparently, to the
satisfaction of all, and the statistics of the present report show
that, so far at least, the change has been advantageous.

Trinity Church, Southwark. Admitted 1821. Rev. J. Y. Burk, Rector. C. M. Peterson and Henry Green, Wardens.

Baptisms, adults 3, infants 29, total 31; confirmed 15; communicants, added, new 15, by removal 4, died or removed 10,
present number 234; marriages 6; burials 49; public services,
on Sundays 118, on other days 74, total 188; children cate-

chized, times 10; Sunday Schools, officers and teachers 32, scholars 297; Church 1, sittings 800; school buildings 1, cemetery 1; salary of Rector $1800 per annum; arrears of salary, none.

Money receipts from all sources—Pew Rents $2731.55, Offertory at Holy Communion $220 06, Collections in Church $855.51, Subscriptions $852.17, Donations $1220, Investments $127.25, other sources $584; total $6,590.54.

Expenditures and Appropriations—Current Expenses (including salary of Rector) $2764.02, Repairs and Improvements $522.51, Payment of Debts $120, Episcopal and Convention Fund $60, support of Sunday Schools $264.70, for the Poor $264.79, to Missions, Foreign $20.15, Domestic $20.15, Home Mission for Colored People $44, Diocesan, $30, City Missions $51.26, for the Jews $17.10, Episcopal Hospital $130, Church Building $65, Bibles, Prayer Books and Tracts, $24, Christian or Theological Education $50, Disabled Clergymen $37.50, Miscellaneous 439.58; total $4924.76.

The semi-centennial anniversary of this Church was celebrated on the 25th of April, 1871, many of the clergy of the city and very large congregations participating in the services.

———

Church of the Evangelists. Admitted 1842. **Rev. Jacob Miller, Rector.** Richard N. Sommers and James Welsh, Wardens.

Baptisms, adults 6, infants 114, total 120; confirmed 20; communicants, added, new 20, by removal 2, died or removed 17, present number, about 390; marriages 14; burials 44; public services on Sundays 116, on other days 70, total 186; children catechized monthly; Sunday Schools, officers and teachers 40, scholars 503, Bible classes, teachers 2, members 18; other Parish agencies, Missionary Society, Relief Committee, Union Association. Church 1; sittings 1000, parsonage none, salary of Rector $1500 per annum; arrears of salary, none.

Money receipts from all sources—Pew Rents $1978.65, Offertory at Holy Communion $203.06, Collections in Church

$463.01, Subscriptions $25, Sunday School offerings $211.22, other sources $1593.64; total $4,474.58.

Expenditures and Appropriations—Current Expenses (including salary of Rector) $3839.37, Repairs and Improvements $494.26, Episcopal and Convention Fund $30, support of Sunday Schools $158.39, for the Poor (by relief Committee) $131.42, for the Jews $7.08, Episcopal Hospital $14.25, Disabled Clergymen $15.20, City Missions 93.22; total $4,783.19

Financial condition—Aggregate value of property of the Parish, real and personal, $35,000; encumberances, mortgage on Church edifice none, on other buildings none; Ground Rent on buildings or lands (per year) $440, other indebtedness $3233.74.

The present Rector took charge of this Parish in June, 1870. My duties have been arduous. I have had no assistant; but through the Divine blessing, I have been enabled to hold regular and special services during the current year, besides performing incidental ministerial duties. My time has been fully occupied. The revising of the "Communion List," has demanded much attention; the number of nominal communicants, though very large, embraces the names of many who have either removed to distant localities, or are regular worshippers in the various churches of this city and elsewhere, and do not "come to the Holy Communion" in the Church of the Evangelists. The present number of *bona fide* communicants is about 390. The average attendance at the Communion is 100.

———

Gloria Dei Church, Philadelphia. Admitted 1836. Rev. Snyder B. Simes, Rector. John Redles and George M. Sandgran, Wardens.

Baptisms, adults 10, infants 58, total 68; confirmed 27; communicants, present number about 250; marriages 33; burials 26; Sunday Schools, officers and teachers 30, scholars 500; Bible class, teacher 1, members 25; Church 1, sittings 470; school buildings 2, parsonage 1, cemetery 1; salary of

38

Rector $1500 per annum and parsonage; arrears of salary, none.

Money receipts from all sources—Pew Rents $1029.56, Offertory at Holy Communion $176.26, Collections in Church $539.31, Donations $323.15, other sources $967.40; Total $3035.68.

Expenditures and Appropriations—Current Expenses (including salary of Rector) $2100, Episcopal and Convention Fund $60, Parish Library $120.20, for the Poor $174.54, City Missions $28.35, Episcopal Hospital $26.55, Bibles, Prayer Books and Tracts $12.82, Book Societies $72.50; Total $2594.96.

Financial condition.—Aggregate value of property of the Parish, real and personal, $20,000.

St. John the Evangelist Church, Philadelphia. Admitted 1860. Rev. Charles L. Fischer, Rector. Wm. H. Myers and John Hacket, Wardens.

Baptisms, adults 11, infants 51, total 62; confirmed 19; communicants, added, new 22, by removal 23, died or removed 16, present number 175; marriages 4; burials 24; public services, on Sundays 104, on other days 80, total 184; children catechized, times monthly; Sunday Schools, officers and teachers 33, scholars 450; Church 1, sittings 350; salary of Rector $1100 per annum; arrears of salary, none.

Money receipts from all sources—Pew Rents $587.50, Offertory at Holy Communion $65, Collections in Church $625.27, Donations $5649.01, other sources $2324.62; Total $9186.40.

Expenditures and Appropriations—Current Expenses (including salary of Rector) $1909.38, Repairs and Improvements $76.85, Payment of Debts $5543.90, Episcopal and Convention Fund $20, support of Sunday Schools $130, Episcopal Hospital $12.80, Miscellaneous $688.40; Total payments as above $7,951.33.

Financial condition.—Aggregate value of property of the Parish, real and personal, $37,000; Encumbrances, Mortgages on Church edifice $1600, Ground Rent on buildings or lands $400 per annum.

The work of the Parish has been steadily increasing, and we are happy to state that there is now a bright prospect of the entire completion of the building before the close of the next Conventional year.

————

Church of the Messiah, Philadelphia. Admitted 1870. Rev. George Bringhurst, Rector. M. Mesier Reese and Samuel P. Godwin, Wardens.

Baptisms, adults 10, infants 41, total 51; communicants, added, 58, by removal 7, died or removed 2, present number 99; marriages 35; burials 26; public services, on Sundays 116, on other days 50, total 166; children catechized, times 12; Sunday Schools, officers and teachers 26, scholars 300; Bible classes, teachers 2, members 50; Church 1, sittings 400.

Money receipts from all sources—Offertory at Holy Communion $82 85.

————

Church of the Redemption, Philadelphia. Admitted 1846. Rev. John Pleasonton Du Hamel, Rector. W. H. Eastwood, Rector's, and Alexander Crow, Accounting Wardens.

Baptisms, adults 2, infants 54, total 56; confirmed 21, of which one was presented at St. Luke's Church; communicants, added, new 29, by removal 7, died or removed 5, present number 208; marriages 49; burials 40; public services, on Sundays 100, on other days 63, total 163; children catechized, times monthly; Sunday Schools, officers and teachers 24, scholars 364; Bible classes, teachers 4, members 56; other Parish agencies, the Parish has also a weekly Mothers' meeting and Sewing School for girls, both of which have been well attended; Church 1, sittings 600; rectory 1; salary of Rector $1000 per annum, arrears of salary, none; services free to all, two during the week.

Money receipts from all sources—Pew Rents $1042.08, Offertory at Holy Communion $236.96, Collections in Church $690.03, Donations $50, other sources $279.20; Total $2298.27.

Expenditures and Appropriations—Current Expenses (including salary of Rector) $1398.54, Repairs and Improvements $173.30, Episcopal and Convention Fund $10, for the Poor $35, to Missions, Foreign $47.12, City Missions $22.75, for the Jews $11.20, Episcopal Hospital $22.64, Church Home for Children $28.44, Disabled Clergymen $23.20; addition for Tablet to the Rev. George A. Durborow, $200; Total $1927.19.

Financial condition.—Aggregate value of property of the Parish, real and personal, $50,000.

St. Philip's Church, Philadelphia. Admitted 1841. Rev. Percy Brown, Rector. Rev. Enoch H. Supplee, Assistant. John Agnew and Geo. R. Kellogg, Wardens.

Baptisms, adults 15, infants 13, total 28; confirmed 31; communicants, added new 33, present number 430; marriages 13; burials 17; public services, on Sundays $100, on other days 60, total 160; children chtechized, times 12; Sunday Schools, officers and teachers 60, scholars 575; Bible Classes, teachers 2, members 40; other Parish agencies, Young Peoples Association, Parochial Missionary Society, and Dorcas Society; salary of Rector $4,000 per annum, arrears of salary, none.

Money receipts from all sources—Pew Rents $5,500, Offertory at Holy Communion $550, Collections in Church $1,400, Subscriptions $350, Donations $227, Sunday School $445, other sources $825; Total $8,697.

Expenditures and Appropriations—Current Expenses (including salary of Rector) $5,450, Repairs and Improvements $250, Episcopal and Convention Fund $150, Support of Sunday Schools $350, for the Poor $550, to Missions, Foreign $527.00, Domestic, Diocesan, etc., $370; Total $7,647.

Church of the Nativity. Admitted, 1845. Wm. B. Ridgely and Wm. Hobart Brown, Wardens.

No report.

St. Jude's Church, Philadelphia. Admitted 1848. Rev. W. H. Graff, Rector. Charles R. Taylor and Jacob L. Smith, Wardens.

Baptisms, adults 7, infants 3, total 10; confirmed 16; marriage 1; burial 1; public services, on Sundays 43, on other days 78, total 121; average attendance on Sundays over 200; children catechized, times 16; Sunday Schools, officers and teachers 16, scholars 124; Bible Classes, teachers, 2, members 20; Other Parish Agencies, Pastoral Aid Society Young Ladies Aid Society, and Brotherhood of St. Jude's; Church 1, sittings 460; salary of Rector $1,500 per annum, arrears of salary, none; number of free sittings, all; Services, free to all, all.

Money receipts from all sources—Pew Rents none, the Church is free to all, Offertory at Holy Communion $107 since September, Collections in Church $862, Subscriptions $1,622, Donations $200, Investments $51, other sources $128; Total $2,970.

Expenditures and Appropriations—Current Expenses (including salary of Rector), $2,829, Repairs and Improvements $57, Payment of Debts $50, Episcopal and Convention Fund $35, Parish Library $3.25, for the Poor $85.82, to Missions, Foreign $25, Domestic $217.50, City Missions $10.54, Episcopal Hospital $40.10, Disabled Clergymen $26, Miscellaneous $153; Total $3,525.21.

The Clerical acts include only those that have taken place during my Rectorship, commencing Dec. 18th 1870.

Financial condition.—Encumbrances, Ground Rent on buildings or lands $5,000, other indebtedness $1,158.82.

Church of St. Mathias, Philadelphia. Admitted 1859. Rev. Richard N. Thomas, Rector. Henry S. Godshall and Wm. H. Rhawn, Wardens.

Baptisms, adults 9, infants 21, total 30; confirmed 31, communicants, added new 34, by removal 30, died or removed 6, present number 190; marriages 7; burials 19; children catechized, times monthly; Sunday Schools, officers and teachers 25, scholars 225; Other Parish Agencies, Mite Society; Church 1, sittings 500.

Money receipts from all sources—Pew Rents $3,003.80, Offertory at Holy Communion $263.93, Collections in Church $499.06, Donations $10, other sources $1,674.33, Mite Society Collections $351.96.

Expenditures and Appropriations—Current Expenses (including salary of Rector), $4,675.34, Payment of Debts $100, Episcopal and Convention Fund $43, Support of Sunday Schools $143, for the Poor $170.71, to Missions, Domestic $36.25, Episcopal Hospital $40, Bibles, Prayer Books and Tracts $15.54, Disabled Clergymen $42.50.

Church of the Incarnation, Philadelphia. Admitted 1860. Rev. Joseph D. Newlin, Rector. James W. Patton and John Rapson, Wardens.

Baptisms, adults 16, infants 29, total 45; confirmed 50; communicants, added, new 50, by removal 33, died or removed 27, present number 346; marriages 5, burials 22; public services, on Sundays 102, on other days 93, total 195; children catechized, times, monthly; Sunday Schools, officers and teachers 32, scholars 382; Bible classes, teachers 2, members 51; Church 1, sittings 1000, school building 1.

Money receipts from all sources—Pew Rents $3307.28, Offertory at Holy Communion $488.38, Collections in Church $3562.03, Subscriptions $321.16, Donations $3194.27; Total $10,873.12.

Expenditures and Appropriations—Current Expenses (including salary of Rector) $3976.37, Repairs and Improvements $4559.38, Episcopal and Convention Fund $50, support of Sunday Schools $91.30, of Parish schools $18.25, Parish Library $67.45, for the Poor $205.78, to Missions, Foreign $95, Domestic $176, Diocesan $52.55, for the Jews $26.10, Episcopal Hospital $53, Bibles, Prayer Books and Tracts $40; Total $9411.18.

Financial condition.—Aggregate value of property of the Parish, real and personal, $180,000; Ground Rent on buildings or lands $12,866.67, other indebtedness $61,264.22.

of the Holy Apostles, Philadelphia. Admitted 1868. Rev. Chas. D. Cooper, Rector. Lewis H. Redner and George C. Thomas, Wardens.

tisms, adults 4, infants 37, total 41; confirmed 21; communicants, added 30, present number 125; marriages 4; als 20; public services, on Sundays 104, on other days total 124; Sunday Schools, officers and teachers 36, scholars 400, Bible classes, teachers 2, members 28; Church sittings 1100, Chapel (the statistics of which are included in this Report) 1, sittings 300.

Money receipts from all sources—Total $5900.

The new edifice of the Church of the Holy Apostles was completed in December, 1870. It is built of stone, and will accommodate about eleven hundred persons. Cost of Church and furniture about $50,000. Balance due about $6500.

St. Matthew's Church, Philadelphia. Admitted 1825. Rev. John B. Falkner, Rector. George M. Stroud and Jos. P. Mumford, Wardens.

Baptisms, adults 10, infants 35, total 45; confirmed 30; communicants, added, new 30, by removal 36, died or removed 25, present number about 400; marriages 5; burials 34; public services, on Sundays, morning and evening, on other days 55; children catechized, times 12; Sunday Schools, scholars 465; Bible classes, teachers 5, members 94; other Parish agencies, St. Matthew's Chapel, cor. Ridge Avenue and Columbia, Sunday School, average attendance 50; Divine service every Sunday afternoon, St. Matthew's Young Men's Library Association, 50 members; Church 1, sittings 640, Chapels (the statistics of which are included in this report) 2; salary of Rector $3000 per annum, arrears of salary, none.

Money receipts from all sources—Pew Rents $4610.03, Offertory at Holy Communion $304, Collections in Church $1262.47, Subscriptions $2111.46, other sources $715; Total $9002.96.

Expenditures and Appropriations—Current Expenses (including salary of Rector) $5091.37, Repairs and Improvements $579.84, Payment of debts $643.54, Episcopal and Convention Fund $50, support of Sunday Schools about $300, Parochial Missions $150, for the Poor $402, to Missions, Foreign $156, Domestic $135, Episcopal Hospital $100, Christian or Theological Education $318, Disabled Clergymen $77.21, invested for Building Fund of Chapel $1000; Total $9002.96.

Church of the Good Shepherd, Philadelphia. Admitted 1869. Rev. J. W. Claxton, Rector. Rev. A. H. Rickert, Minister in charge. J. M. Christian and William A. Parke, Wardens.

Baptisms, adults 4, infants 26, total 30; confirmed 16; communicants, added, new 16, by removal 16, died or removed 4, present number 50; marriages 5; burials 15; public services, on Sundays 87, on other days 14, total 101; average attendance on Sundays 100; children catechized monthly; Sunday Schools, officers and teachers 19, scholars 208; Bible class, teacher 1, members 13; other Parish agencies, Sewing School, teachers 9, scholars 120; public hall.

Money receipts from all sources—Offertory at Holy Communion $30.93, Collections in Church $140.97, Subscriptions $605 50, Donations $39, other sources, collections in Sunday School $161.73; Total $978.13.

Expenditures and Appropriations—Current Expenses (including salary of Rector) $780.80, Episcopal and Convention Fund $5, support of Sunday Schools $35.24, of Sewing School $10, for the Poor $41, Domestic Missions, $16, Episcopal Hospital $10.25, Disabled Clergymen $4.51; Total $902.80.

St. Mary's Church, West Philadelphia. Admitted 1827. Rev. Thos. C. Yarnall, D. D. Rector. George A. Wright and Wm. Yarnall, Wardens.

Baptisms, adults 4, infants 17, total 21; confirmed 21; communicants, added, new 20, died or removed 5, present number 145; marriages 6; burials 17; public services, on Sundays 106, on other days 108, total 214; Sunday School, teachers 14, scholars 117.

Money receipts from all sources—Pew Rents $2798.12,

Offertory at Holy Communion $334.13, Collections in Church $837.80, Subscriptions $322, Donations $280, other sources $543.69; Total $5115.74.

Expenditures and Appropriations—Current Expenses (including Salary of Rector) $2549.67, Repairs and Improvements $1086.73, Episcopal and Convention Fund $43, Support of Sunday School $312.31, Foreign Missions $122.44, Domestic $43.19, Diocesan $31.92, City Missions $2, Episcopal Hospital $32.93, Christmas Fund $53.71, Miscellaneous, including disbursement of Communion Alms, $455.15; Total $4733.05.

Estimated value of Church property about $60,000, upon which there is no encumbrance.

St. Andrew's Church, West Philadelphia. Admitted 1852. Rev. Samuel E. Smith, Rector. H. W. Siddall and Henry B. Chapman, Wardens.

Baptisms, adults 5, infants 47, total 52; confirmed 15; communicants, added new 12, by removal 15, died or removed 14, present number 132; marriages 10; burials 23; public services, on Sundays 115, on other days 85, total 200; children catechized, times 12; Sunday Schools, officers and teachers 18, scholars 200; Bible Class, teacher 1, members 11; Church 1, sittings 354; salary of Rector $1,700 per annum; number of free sittings 42; Sunday services, free to all, 55.

Money receipts from all sources—Pew Rents $1,714.64, Offertory at Holy Communion $157.32, Collections in Church $457.72, Subscriptions $532.50, Donations $40, other sources $497.86; Total $3,400.04.

Expenditures and Appropriations—Current Expenses (including salary of Rector), $2,298.85, Repairs and Improvements $88.40, Payment of Debts $862, Episcopal and Convention Fund $15, for the Poor $15, to Missions, Foreign $12, Domestic $15, Diocesan $20, City Missions $11, Episcopal Hospital $20, Christian or Theological Education $46; Total $3,403.25.

Financial condition.—Aggregate value of property of the Parish, real and personal, $26,000; Encumbrances, Mortgage on Church Lot $7,500.

Church of the Saviour, Philadelphia. Admitted 1852. Rev. J. Houston Eccleston, Rector. John D. Taylor and Henry P. Rutter, Wardens.

Baptisms, adults 4, Chapel, infants 22, total 26; confirmed 8; communicants, present number 200, very incomplete; marriages 2; burials 4; public services, on Sundays 100, on other days 15, total 115; Sunday Schools, officers and teachers 39, scholars 488; Church 1, sittings 500; Chapel (the statistics of which are included in this Report), 1, sittings 250; salary of Rector $3,000 per annum.

Money receipts from all sources—Pew Rents $3,475, Offertory at Holy Communion $186.05, Collections in Church $1,462.38, Subscriptions $7,686 87, other sources $485.63; Total $13,295.93.

Expenditures and Appropriations—Current Expenses (including salary of Rector), $3,338.77, Repairs and Improvements $701.83, Payment of Debts $,5820.50, Episcopal and Convention Fund $120, Support of Sunday Schools $171.64, Parochial Missions $682.09, for the Poor $60.25, to Missions, Foreign $67.30, Domestic $191.82, City Missions $192.88, for the Jews $40.29, Episcopal Hospital $612.30, Christian or Theological Education $232.50, Disabled Clergymen $44.22, Miscellaneous $57.84; Total $12,354.03.

Financial condition.—Aggregate value of property of the Parish, real and personal, $42,000; Encumbrances, Ground Rent on buildings or lands, $2,000 on Chapel.

Having been in the Parish but a few weeks, the Rector is unable to make an accurate report. All the adult baptisms and all the confirmations here reported are from the Chapel of the Holy Comforter, now under the charge of Mr. Wm. H. Platt, acting under a license of lay reader.

Emmanuel Church, Philadelphia. Admitted 1837. Rev. William H. Munroe, Rector. Thomas H. Powers and Douglass McFaden, Wardens.

Baptisms, adults 15, infants 65, total 80; confirmed 46; communicants, added new 46, by removal 8, died or removed 4, present number 475; marriages 26; burials 51; public services, on Sundays 102, on other days 78, total 180; children catechized, times 12; Sunday Schools, officers and teachers 40, scholars 626; Bible Classes, teachers 6, members 129; Church 1, sittings 800; Salary of Rector $2,000 per annum, arrears of salary, none.

Money receipts from all sources—Pew rents $2400, Offertory at Holy Communion $195.50, Collections in Church $334.82; Total $2,930.32.

Expenditures and Appropriations—Repairs and Improvements $312.17, Episcopal and Convention Fund $50, Support of Sunday Schools $100, Parochial Missions $150, for the Poor $195.50, to Missions, Domestic $100, City Missions $100, for the Jews $11.05, Episcopal Hospital $20.19, Bibles, Prayer Books and Tracts $40, Book Societies $170, Christian or Theological Education $75, Disabled Clergymen $61.32, Miscellaneous $250; Total $1,635.23.

Church of St. Bartholomew, Philadelphia. Admitted 1849. Rev. James Saul, Rector. George W. Taylor and John C. Mitchell, Wardens.

Baptisms, infants 3, total 3.

Expenditures and Appropriations—Support of Sewing School $47.30, to Missions, Foreign $18, Domestic $3, Law Expenses $264.80; Total $333.10.

Disappointment has attended the efforts made to bring to Trial the Suit for the recovery of the Church property of the Parish, and likewise to obtain the consent to locate a Chapel at a selected point in another quarter of the City. The Sewing School referred to in the last Report is again in session, with undiminished usefulness. It is a means of much religious instruction; many of the anthems in the morning and evening services have been committed to memory by the girls and are well sung by them; thus, and in other ways, it is believed a taste for the service of the Church is being cultivated.

Until Easter I officiated in other Parishes in the city; since then, as Minister in Charge of Christ Church, Waterford, New Jersey, under invitation of the Vestry of that Church, upon the very sudden death of the Rector, the Rev. Wm. Stewart.

All Saints' Church, Philadelphia. Admitted 1836. Rev. Herman L. Duhring, Rector. William Stirling and William Ridings, Wardens.

Baptisms, adults 5, infants 58, total 63; confirmed 21; communicants, present number 375; marriages 13; burials 43; public services, on Sundays 120, on other days 50, total 170; Sunday Schools, officers and teachers 40, scholars 550; Bible Classes, teachers 2, members 60; Church, sittings 800, cemetery 1; Salary of Rector $1,900 per annum, arrears of salary, none.

Money receipts from all sources—Pew Rents $2,995.70, Offertory at Holy Communion $281, Collections in Church $931.85, Subscriptions $600, Donations $250, other sources $300; Total $5,358.55.

Expenditures and Appropriations—Current Expenses (including salary of Rector), $2,900, Repairs and Improvements $400, Episcopal and Convention Fund $40, Support of Sunday Schools $250, for the Poor $281, to Missions, Foreign $100, Domestic $250, Diocesan $100, City Missions $25, Episcopal Hospital $250, Christian or Theological Education $75, Disabled Clergymen $28.45, Miscellaneous $659.10; Total $5,358.55.

Church of the Crucifixion, Philadelphia. Admitted 1847. Thomas R. Maris and W. B. Whitney, Wardens.

Baptisms, adult 1, infants 26, total 27; confirmed, no visitation; communicants, added new 8, died or removed 12, present number 131; marriages 7; burials 19; public services, on Sundays 137, on other days 62, total 199; Sunday Schools, officers and teachers 20, scholars 308; Bible Class, teacher 1, members 92; Other Parish Agencies, Mothers' Meeting, Sewing School, Bible Reader, and "The Temporary Home for the Homeless;" Church 1, school buildings 2; number of free sittings, all.

Money Receipts from all sources.—Pew Rents free, Offertory at Holy Communion $49.70, Collections in Church $114.93, Investments $66.60, other sources $232.85; Total $464.08.

Expenditures and Appropriations—Current Expenses

$181.53, Parochial Missions $225.60, for the Poor $49.70, Book Societies $7.25; Total $464.08.

N. B.—There was subscribed by the friends of the Mission during the year, towards the support of the Church $1,780.68, and to the Home for the Homeless $1,074.70, making a total of $2,855.38.

Financial condition.—Encumbrances, Mortgages, Home for the Homeless Buildings $3,000, Ground Rent on buildings or lands $2,158.33, Lot on which Church stands.

The Rev. Joseph R. Moore resigned the Rectorship of the Parish on the 1st of September last, and as an expression of their appreciation of his services would place on record the following extract from their last Annual Report:

The Vestry deeply regret the cause which led to the resignation of Rev. Mr. Moore, whose unceasing devotion to his labors in this important sphere of Christian duty, has produced visible and lasting effects in saving precious souls, ameliorating the condition of the unfortunate and afflicted, and extending the Redeemer's kingdom, in the most degraded, neglected and abandoned portion of our great city. It is but simple justice to refer with pleasure to his fidelity, conscientiousness, and wise administration, in carrying out the work of both the Church of the Crucifixion and the Home for the Homeless, and since his resignation they have endeavored to secure a successor, though so far without success. This failure, however, has not interfered with any of the public services, as they have all been regularly carried on, including those of the Sunday School, and the *special* service at the Home for the Homeless, on Sunday evenings, which last is conducted by four members of the Vestry alternately.

The Home for the Homeless, one of the many agencies employed by the Church of the Crucifixion for ameliorating the condition of the large class of degraded persons living within the bounds of the Parish, has continued in an unostentatious manner, to carry out the special object of its establishment, viz.: to furnish a *temporary* home for destitute females until permanent homes or situations can be procured for them.

The *dinner for invalids*, to which reference was made in last year's report, has proven itself to be one of the cheapest, and yet at the same time one of the most useful agencies ever devised to assist the worthy poor, saving as it did, in the opinion of physicians, the lives of not a few who were stricken down by the relapsing fever, which raged so fearfully last summer in the Parish. One physician, whose patients enjoyed its benefits, says:

"In no form can charity be more admirably exhibited. The constitutions of the poor are usually enfeebled by hereditary disease, or by want and irregularity of life; and when they are attacked by disease require from the outset a full supply of the strongest nourishment; and I have often felt the mockery of giving tonics to create an appetite when there was no means of gratifying it when created. Even when poverty is not so extreme, the ignorance and apathy of attendants keep them from bestowing the care necessary in preparing food for the sick. *Full and proper diet is more necessary for these miserable ones than medicine; and your institution of more use than a dispensary.*"

The Church of the Saviour. Admitted, 1852.

No report.

St. Luke's Church, Germantown. Admitted 1818. Rev. John Rodney, Rector Emeritus, Rev. Albra Wadleigh, Rector. James M. Aertsen and R. P. McCullagh, Wardens.

Baptisms, adults 4, infants 22, total 26; confirmed 14; communicants, added 34, new 15, by removal 10, died or removed 51, present number 305; marriages 6; burials 15; public services, on Sundays 135, on other days 180, total 315; children catechized, times 26; Sunday Schools, officers and teachers 20, scholars 192; Bible Classes, teachers 4, members 48; Parish Schools, teachers 2, scholars 80; Other Parish Agencies, St. Luke's Guild; Church 1, sittings 500, school building 1, parsonage 1, cemetery 1; Salary of Rector $2,200 per annum;

arrears of salary, none; number of free sittings 48; Extra Sunday Services free to all, 31.

Money receipts from all sources—Pew Rents $5,138.26, Offertory at Holy Communion $496.02, Collections in Church $1,875.82, Subscriptions $1,506.85, Donations $593.40, other sources $837.98; Total $10,448.33.

Expenditures and Appropriations—Current Expenses (including salary of Rector) $5,473.43, Repairs and Improvements $390.63, Payment of Debts $800, Episcopal and Convention Fund $130, Support of Sunday Schools $375.07, of Parish Schools $650, Parish Library $36.70, Parochial Missions $200, for the Poor $762, to Missions, Foreign $82.25, Domestic $1,090.63, Home Mission for Colored People $37.70, Diocesan $210, City Missions $113.31, Episcopal Hospital $141.17, Church Building $217.03, Book Societies $67.86, Christian or Theological Education $299.90, Disabled Clergymen $103, Miscellaneous $100; Total $10,780.68.

Financial condition.—Encumbrances, Mortgages, on Church, none, on other buildings $5,000, other indebtedness $2,200.

Christ Church, Germantown. Admitted 1855. Rev. Theo. S. Rumney, D.D., Rector. Henry H. Houston and Charles Spencer, Wardens.

Baptisms, adults 6, infants 22, total 28; confirmed 30; communicants, added, new 29, by removal 40, died or removed 9, present number 315; marriages 3; burials 12; public services, on Sundays 113, on other days 109, total 222; children catechized, times, monthly; Sunday Schools, officers and teachers 60, scholars 480; Bible classes, teachers 8, members 67; other Parish agencies, Sewing school, Christ Church Mission, Mothers' Meeting, Parish Library, Missionary Society; Church 1, sittings 800; school building 1, parsonage 1; salary of Rector $2500 per annum and rectory, arrears of salary, none.

Money receipts from all sources—Pew Rents $4300, Offertory at Holy Communion $541.59, Collections in Church $5740.93, Donations $2585.40, Investments $690, other sources $285.68; Total $14,143.60.

Expenditures and Appropriations—Current Expenses, (including salary of Rector) $3730, Payment of Debts $764, Episcopal and Convention Fund $175, support of Sunday Schools $200, Parish Library $100, for the Poor $475, to Missions, Foreign $2054.38, Domestic $1495.78, Diocesan $81, City Missions $761, for the Jews $71.09, Episcopal Hospital $232.59, Christian or Theological Education $719.34, Disabled Clergymen $149.48, Miscellaneous $2434.94; Total $13,443.60.

Financial condition.—Aggregate value of property of the Parish, real and personal, about $100,000; Encumbrances, none.

The Rector has been compelled to omit from the Communion list the names of persons who appear to be no longer members of the Parish, which will explain the discrepancy between his report and that of the former Rector.

Church of St. John the Baptist, Philadelphia. Admitted 1858. Rev. Wm. N. Diehl, Rector. Gilbert H. Newhall and Charles W. Cushman, Wardens.

Baptisms, adults 2, infants 8, total 10; confirmed 8; communicants, added, new 11, by removal 5, died or removed 14, present number 72; marriages 3; burials 5; public services, on Sundays 104, other days 44, total 148; children catechized monthly; Sunday School 1, teachers 8, scholars 110; Parish school, teacher 1, scholars 30, night school, during winter and spring, for adults; Church sittings 400; chapel and Sunday School rooms, chapel 200 seats, Sunday School rooms accommodate 200; salary of Rector $600; number of free sittings, all, at all times; free Church.

Collections—Communion Alms and Parish Guild $668.90, Sunday School for Missions $50; Total $718.90.

Calvary Church, Germantown. Admitted 1859. Rev. James DeW. Perry, Jr., Rector. Samuel K. Ashton, and James E. Caldwell, Wardens.

Baptisms, infants 23; confirmed 4; communicants, added, new 4, by removal 12, died or removed 11, present number 121; marriages 2, burials 4; public services on Sundays

117, on other days 48, total 165; average attendance on Sundays good; children catechized, times 20 ; Sunday Schools, officers and teachers 26, scholars 161; Bible classes, teachers 4, members 36; other Parish agencies, Mothers' Meeting, Sewing school, night schools, Guilds, &c.; Church 1, sittings 450, school building 1, parsonage 1 ; salary of Rector $2000 per annum, arrears of salary, none; number of free sittings, 50.

Money receipts from all sources—Pew Rents $2716.40, Offertory at Holy Communion $249.56, Collections in Church $1419.85, Subscriptions $6684.55, Donations $887.14, other sources $504.05 ; Total $12,461.64.

Expenditures and Appropriations—Current Expenses (including salary of Rector) $3678.96, Repairs and Improvements $5193.76, Payment of Debts $2849.64, Episcopal and Convention Fund $100, support of Sunday Schools $124.10, Parish Library $29.44, for the Poor $348.56, to Missions, Foreign $183.70, Domestic $601.84, Home Mission for Colored People $58.30, Diocesan $156.58, for the Jews $24.81, Episcopal Hospital $144.83, Bibles, Prayer Books and Tracts $47.14, Christian or Theological Education $63.99, Disabled Clergymen $94.09, Miscellaneous $753.64: Total $14,453.38.

Financial condition.—Aggregate value of property of the Parish, real and personal, $45,000 ; indebtedness $3500.

The difference between the receipts and expenditures is accounted for, by the fact that certain amounts, reported as receipts last year, have been paid, and reported as expenditures this year.

$175 of the offerings to Domestic Missions were made by the children.

A convenient, well-built stone Rectory will be finished and nearly all paid for this month.

St. Michael's Church, Germantown. Admitted 1860. Rev. John K. Murphy, Rector.
Arthur Wells and S. Harvey Thomas, Wardens.

Baptisms, adults 5, infants 21, total 26; confirmed 10; communicants, added, new 20, by removal 25, died or removed 30, present number 141; marriages 5; burials 20; public services, on Sundays 120, on other days 208, total 328; children catechized, times 13; Sunday Schools, officers and teachers 19, scholars 170; other Parish agencies, Ladies' Parish Aid Association, Library Association for young men, Mothers' Meeting and Sewing School; Church 1, sittings 320, school building 1; salary of Rector $2400 per annum; number of free sittings, all.

Money receipts from all sources—Pew Rents, none, Collections in Church $2676.23, other sources $907.94; Total $3584.17.

Expenditures and Appropriations.—Current Expenses, including salary of Rector) $3158.65, payment of debts $1100, Episcopal and Convention Fund $30, Support of Sunday Schools $59.25, for the Poor $72.45, to Missions, Foreign $14.54, Domestic $56.02, Diocesán $26.50, Episcopal Hospital $41.10; Total $4558.51.

The item for the payment of debts, $1100, was collected previous to the period included in this report.

Financial condition.—Aggregate value of property of the Parish, real and personal, $18,000; Encumbrances, Mortgages on Church edifice $3500, on other buildings $900, Ground Rent on buildings or lands $1875, other indebtedness, none.

The congregation has suffered severely during the past year in the death and removal of many members of the parish, who have been identified with its interests and work from the beginning of its existence. The death of the Rev. Mr. Lambdin was especially felt, as the withdrawal of one who had devoted whatever talents and energy God had given him, to further its usefulness, and to secure its prosperity.

Although the losses we mourn have been more than supplied, in the number of added members, the financial fig-

ures of this report show that we have fallen short of the
past two years in the important matter of revenue. We have
but paid our way with difficulty, and have done nothing towards the extinguishment of our indebtedness.

Emmanuel Church, Holmesburg. Admitted 1844. Rev. D. Caldwell Millett, Rector.
Presley Blakiston and Lewis Thompson, Wardens.

Baptisms, infants 12; confirmed 14; communicants, added,
new 8, died or removed 8, present number 125; marriages 4;
burials 8; public services, on Sundays 104, on other days 88,
total 192; children catechized in Sunday School; Sunday
Schools, officers and teachers 13, scholars 134; Bible class,
teacher 1, members 9; other parish agencies, night school for
boys, about 40; sewing school for girls, about 70; Church 1,
sittings 360; school building 1, parsonage 1, cemetery 1;
salary of Rector $1500 per annum; Sunday services, free to
all, in the evening.

Money receipts from all sources—Pew Rents $1611.14,
Offertory at Holy Communion $159.38, Collections in Church
$424.03, Subscriptions $234.35, Investments $118.20, other
sources $90; Total $2637.10.

Expenditures and Appropriations.—Current Expenses (including salary of Rector) $2095.28, Repairs and Improve-
ments $307.02, Episcopal and Convention Fund $50, support
of Sunday Schools $154.74, of Parish schools $67, Parish
Library $21.55, to Missions, Foreign $31.62, Domestic $40,
City Missions $18.25, for the Jews $5, Episcopal Hospital
$38.13, Bibles, Prayer Books and Tracts $17, Christian or
Theological Education $25.50, Disabled Clergymen $38.43,
Miscellaneous $97.77; Total $3007.29.

St. James Church, Kingsessing. Admitted 1844. Rev. Charles A. Maison, Rector.
Robert Buist, Warden.

Baptisms, adults 4, infants 33, total 37; confirmed 11;
communicants, added, new 7, by removal 8, died or removed
14, transferred to St. George's 13, present number 134; marriages 12, burials 28; public services, on Sundays 102, on

other days 24, total 126; Sunday School, officers and teachers 14, scholars 176; Church 1, sittings 500; school buildings 2, parsonage 1, cemetery 1; salary of Rector $1500.

Expenditures and Appropriations—Repairs and Improvements $141.60, Episcopal and Convention Fund $50, support of Sunday Schools $148.42, of Parish Schools $397.45, for the Poor $94.70, to Missions, Domestic $58.64, Home Missions for Colored People $4.30, Diocesan $45, for the Jews $3.81, Episcopal Hospital $41.54, Bibles, Prayer Books and Tracts $7.54, Book Societies $12.78, Christian or Theological Education $60.67, Disabled Clergymen $20.45; Miscellaneous $19.50, Sufferers in France and Germany $50.87, Church Home $54.62; total $1211.89.

Divine service has been celebrated on several Sunday evenings in the school-house at Boon's Dam, the building being filled with an attentive congregation.

A separate report is made this year for St. George's Church, which is an off-shoot from this parish.

———•———

St. Mark's Church, Frankford.   Admitted 1846.   Rev. D. S. Miller, D. D., Rector, Rev. Samuel Tweedale, Assistant.   John Clayton and Benjamin Rowland, Jr., Wardens.

Baptisms, adults 9, infants 82, total 91; confirmed 44; communicants, added, new 51, died or removed 33, present number 1048; marriages 27; burials 97; public services, on Sundays 201, on other days 62, total 263; children catechized monthly; Sunday Schools and Bible classes, officers and teachers 74, scholars 1533, Parish Day, Night and Sewing Schools, teachers 24, scholars 479; other Parish agencies, Mothers' meetings 2, committee 15, members 340.   These details include the mission work at Aramingo, Frankford.   Church 1; school buildings 1; parsonage 1; salary of Rector $2000 per annum; Sunday services, free to all, four.

Money receipts from all sources—Small Collections in Church $359, Subscriptions $3660.68, Donations $2000.

Expenditures and Appropriations—Current Expenses (including salary of Rector) $4057.21, Repairs and Improvements

$900.95, Payment of Debts $812.68, Episcopal and Convention Fund $75, support of Sunday and Parish schools, Parish library and Parochial Missions $1998.49, for the Poor, including Mothers' Aid and Mothers' Meeting Fund $1470.22, to Missions, Foreign $702.35, Domestic $446, Mormons $219, Oregon $109, Indian $421.02, Home Mission for Colored People $228.74, Diocesan $361, City Missions $60, for the Jews $43, Episcopal Hospital $845.42, Bibles, Prayer Books and Tracts $50, Book Societies $229.38, Christian or Theological Education $976.94, Disabled Clergymen $78.03, Miscellaneous, German and French sufferers $67.47, Church Home for Orphans $30.

Church of the Messiah. Admitted 1847. Rev. Reese C. Evans, Rector. Henry Christian and J. H. Raker, Wardens.

Baptisms, infants 39 ; confirmed 13 ; communicants, added, new 6, died or removed 4, present number 59 ; marriages 14 ; burials 16 ; public services, on Sundays 114, on other days 25, total 139 ; children catechized, times 52 ; Sunday Schools, officers and teachers 6, scholars 80 ; Bible classes, teachers 2, members 21, total 101 ; Church 1, sittings 500 ; parsonage 1, cemetery lot ; arrears of salary, none ; extra Sunday services, free to all, 10.

Money Receipts from all sources—Pew Rents $546, Offertory at Holy Communion $47.77, Collections in Church $112.53, Donations for Church and Rectory, to the value of $245.68, other sources $45.75 ; Total $997.73.

Expenditures and Appropriations—Current Expenses (including salary of Rector) $706.38, Repairs and Improvements $245.68, Episcopal and Convention Fund $5, Episcopal Hospital $9.32, Disabled Clergymen $6.33, Poor and Miscellaneous $51 ; Total $1054.11.

In addition, in support of Missions, Sunday School and Library, contributed by Sunday School scholars and Bible classes $69.

Financial condition.—Aggregate value of property of the Parish, real and personal, $17,000, Ground Rent on Lands $1200, other indebtedness $500.

Zion Church, Philadelphia. Admitted 1849. Rev. C. W. Duane, Rector. Dell Noblit, Jr., and Thomas R. Alexander, Wardens.

Baptisms, adults 6, infants 13 total, 19; confirmed 17; communicants, added new 17, by removal 29, died or removed 16, present number 190; marriages 9; burials 10; public services, on Sundays 100, on other days 39, total 139; children catechized, times 8; Sunday Schools, officers and teachers 20, scholars 270, Bible Classes, teachers 5, members 80; Church 1, sittings 750, parsonage none, cemetery none; salary of Rector $1800 per annum, arrears of salary, none.

Money receipts from all sources—Pew Rents $2208.16, Offertory at Holy Communion $94.94, Collections in Church $1035.30, Subscriptions $1046, other sources $982.39; Total $5416.79.

Expenditures and Appropriations—Current Expenses (including salary of Rector) $3191.72, Repairs and Improvements $1821.17, Episcopal and Convention Fund $25, Support of Sunday Schools $215.44, for the Poor $159.94, to Misssions, Foreign $59.10, Domestic $357.34, Diocesan $96.10, for the Jews $11.30, Episcopal Hospital $46.15, Disabled Clergymen $14.32, Miscellaneous, Church Home for Children $42; total $6039.58.

Financial condition—Aggregate value of property of the Parish, real and personal, $40,000; Encumbrances, mortgage on Church edifice $10,000; Ground Rent on buildings or Lands, none; other indebtedness $2500, temporary loan to cover deficiencies in improvements and other expenses.

St. David's Church, Manayunk, Philadelphia. Admitted 1833. Rev. F. H. Bushnell, Rector. Orlando Crease and Edward Holt, Wardens.

Baptisms, adults 7, infants 52, total 59; confirmed 28; communicants, added, new 12, by removal 1, died or removed 18, present number 240; marriages 12; burials 31; public services, on Sundays 106, on other days 48, total 154; children catechized, times 12; Sunday Schools, officers and teachers 33, scholars 500; Bible classes, teachers 2, members 130; Church 1, sittings 590, school building 1, parsonage 1, cemetery 1; salary of Rector $1300 per annum, arrears of salary, none; number of free sittings 8, Sunday services, free to all, 1.

Money receipts from all sources—Pew Rents, $1518, Offertory at Holy Communion $136, Collections in Church $991.34, Subscriptions $3088.59, Donations $344.15, other sources $57; Total $6135.08.

Expenditures and Appropriations—Current Expenses (including salary of Rector) $1775, Repairs and Improvements $2913.81, Episcopal and Convention Fund $45, support of Sunday Schools $610.65, Parish Library $16.45, Parochial Missions $10, for the Poor $136, to Missions, Foreign $160.88, Domestic $298.48, Home Mission for Colored People $31, City Missions $15, Episcopal Hospital $21.76, Bibles, Prayer Books and Tracts $25, Christian or Theological Education $50, Disabled Clergymen $26.05; Total $6135.08.

Financial condition.—Aggregate value of property of the Parish, real and personal, $40,000.

Church of the Resurrection, Rising Sun, Philadelphia. Admittted 1850. Rev. Thomas J. Davis, Rector.

Baptisms, infants 6; Communicants, died or removed 6, present number 13; Sunday School, teachers 7, scholars, boys 42, girls 44, total 86.

After the election of vestrymen, Easter Monday, 1870, the work of re-erecting the Church of the Resurrection was commenced. The corner-stone thereof was laid on the 2d of June, by the Rev. Dr. Howe. It is now far advanced towards completion. But the work is for the present at a stand, for want of funds sufficient to meet the payment when completed.

The amount contracted for was $4500, to which has been necessarily added the sum of $940 for the improvement of Broad Street. $2000 will now enable us to meet all the payments of both Church and street, which amount it is confidently hoped will be speedily raised, that the Church may be consecrated and the services thereof again regularly celebrated.

Trinity Church, Maylandville, Philadelphia. Admitted 1853. Rev. J. Houston Eccleston, Rector. N. B. Brown and Charles P. B. Jefferys, Wardens.

Public services, on Sundays, P. M.; average attendance on Sundays 25; children catechized, times 1 per month; Sunday Schools, officers and teachers 12, scholars 100; other Parish Agencies, Mothers' Meeting; Church 1, sittings 120.

This report is unavoidedly incomplete, as it is only since March 19th, that the present Rector has been in the parish, and the records are greatly confused. Since January, the Rev. Dr. Goodwin has been supplying the pulpit regularly.

St. Paul's Church, Chestnut Hill, Philadelphia. Admitted 1856. Rev. J. Andrews Harris, Rector. M. Russell Thayer and Richard Norris, Wardens.

Baptisms, adults 3, infants 29, total 32; confirmed 11; communicants, added, new 18, by removal 7, died or removed 15, present number 145; marriages 3; burials 9; public services, on Sundays 128, on other days 96, total 224; average attendance on Sundays varies; children catechized, times 107; Sunday Schools, officers and teachers 9, scholars 100; Bible Class, teacher 1, members about 60; Parish schools, teachers 2, scholars 60; Church 1, sittings 500, Chapels, (the statistics of which are included in this report) 1, sittings 125, free; school building 1, parsonage 1, cemetery none; arrears of salary, none; number of free sittings in Church 96, besides those in the Chapel; extra Sunday service, free to all, 12.

Money receipts from all sources—Pew Rents, $3505.50, Offertory at Holy Communion $452.59, Collections in Church $1518.57, Subscriptions and Donations $2380.45, other sources $67.65; Total $7924.76.

Expenditures and Appropriations.—Current Expenses (including salary of Rector) $3750, Repairs and Improvements, $667.45, Payment of Debts $549.40, Episcopal and Convention Fund $100, support of Sunday Schools $119.93, Parish schools $811.67, Parish Library $17.43, Parochial Missions $181.86, for the Poor $332.45, to Missions, Foreign $41, Domestic $607.71, Home Mission for Colored People $31.38,

Diocesan $41.28, City Missions $5, for the Jews $11.25, Episcopal Hospital $256.45, Christian or Theological Education $399.08, Disabled Clergymen $46.20, Miscellaneous $70,88, Total, part of which in excess of receipts was supplied by balance from last year, $7989.92.

Financial condition.—Aggregate value of property of the Parish, real and personal, $30,000; Encumbrances, on parsonage $5000, other indebtedness $387.41.

Several of the names of those reported last year as communicants have not been included in this year's report, as they are found to be registered in some other city parish; and of those reported as legitimately belonging to this parish, sixteen (16) have not been to the Holy Communion during the year, several of them being temporarily absent from the parish.

St. Timothy's Church, Roxborough, Philadelphia. Admitted 1862. Rev. Wm. Augustus White, Rector.   J. Vaughan Merrick and J. F. Cauffman, Wardens.

Baptisms, adults none, infants 13, total 13; confirmed none; communicants, added new 3, by removal 4, died or removed 15, present number 84; marriages 11; burials 8; public services, on Sundays 140, on other days 55, total 195; average attendance on Sundays 200; children catechized, times 8; Sunday Schools, officers and teachers 11, scholars 100; Bible classes, teachers 2, members 15; Church 1, sittings 250, School building 1, parsonage 1, cemetery 1; salary of Rector $1500 per annum, arrears of salary none; number of free sittings 62; Sunday services, free to all, 88.

Money receipts from all sources—Pew Rents $970.30, Offertory at Holy Communion $129.62, Collections in Church $927.27, Subscriptions $356.28, Donations $53.50, Investments $16.70, other sources $358.11; Total $2811.78.

Expenditures and Appropriations—Current Expenses (including salary of Rector) $2085, Repairs and Improvements $172.36, Episcopal and Convention Fund $20, Support of Sunday Schools $97.69, for the Poor $129.62, to Missions, Foreign $15, Domestic $15, Diocesan $8, Episcopal Hospital

41

$200, Bibles, Prayer Books and Tracts $12, Disabled Clergymen $20, Miscellaneous $38.27 ; Total $2812.94.

Financial condition.—Aggregate value of property of the Parish, real and personal, $19,000 ; Encumbrances, mortgage $2300 on parsonage; Ground Rent on buildings or lands $12.36, annually on Sunday School lot; other indebtedness $1260.

The number of communicants has been much reduced this year, by removals, and some have been stricken from the list who no longer seem to care to claim the privileges of the "Household of Faith."

Without any marked events, during the past year, the Parish has, nevertheless, been steadily growing in strength and grace, we trust. A small class for confirmation will be presented (the Lord willing) on Thursday in Whitsun week.

The Parish night-school was not in operation last winter, it being found impossible to secure the regular attendance of a suitable corps of teachers. The opening of the public school houses for instruction at night, had, however, very much diminished the number of our pupils before the close of the session in April, 1870.

––––––

Church of St. Alban, Roxborough, Philadelphia. Admitted 1862. Rev. John Ireland, Rector. Jacob Casselbery and James L. Rahn, Wardens.

Communicants, added new 1, died or removed 7, present number 25 ; marriages 2 ; burials 4 ; public services, on Sundays 2, on other days 1 ; average attendance on Sundays 100 ; children catechized, times monthly ; Sunday Schools, officers and teachers 8, scholars 70 ; Church 1, sittings 250, school building 1 ; Salary of Rector $800.

Money receipts from all sources—Pew Rents $400, Offertory at Holy Communion $10, Collections in Church $100, Subscriptions $330; Total $840.

Expenditures and Appropriations—Current Expenses (including salary of Rector), $1050, Repairs and Improvements $50, Episcopal and Convention Fund $5.50, Support of Sunday Schools $75, Parish Library $30, for the Poor, offertory ; Total $1280.

Financial condition.—Aggregate value of property of the Parish, real and personal, $15,000.

Memorial Church, St. Luke the Beloved Physician, Bustleton, Philadelphia. Admitted 1861. Rev. J. H. Barnard, Rector.

Baptisms, adult 1, infants 3, total 4 ; communicants, added new 2, by removal 1, present number 32; burial 1; public services, on Sundays 104, on other days 84, total 188; average attendance on Sundays 40; children catechized, times 28 ; Sunday Schools, scholars 50 ; Bible Classes, teachers 5 ; Church 1, sittings 250; Chapel (the statistics of which are included in this Report), 1, sittings 125, parsonage 1, cemetery 1, Salary of Rector $700 per annum, arrears of salary, none.

Money receipts from all sources—Pew Rents $736.85, Offertory at Holy Communion $25.62, Collections in Church $68.58; Total $831.05.

Expenditures and Appropriations—Current Expenses (including salary of Rector), $728.17, Episcopal and Convention Fund $5, for the Jews $1; Total $734.17.

House of Prayer, Branchtown, Philadelphia. Admitted 1861. Rev. A. T. McMurphey, Rector. C. D. Barney and Bennet Medary, Wardens.

Baptisms, adult 1, infants 15, total 16; confirmed 6; communicants, added new 6, by removal 3, died or removed 5, present number 33; marriages 2; burials 3; public services, on Sundays 96, on other days 30, total 130; average attendance on Sundays 75 ; Sunday Schools, officers and teachers 15, scholars 167; other Parish agencies, Sewing School, teachers 7, scholars 70 ; Night School, teachers 8, scholars 60 ; Church 1, sittings 140; salary of Rector $1000 per annum, arrears of salary $150.

Money receipts from all sources—Offertory at Holy Communion $32.41, Collections in Church $188.30, Subscriptions

$918, Donations $125, Sunday School $182.79, Mite Society $80; Total $1526.50.

Expenditures and Appropriations—Current Expenses (including salary of Rector), $1200, Payment of Debts $207, Episcopal and Convention Fund $10, Support of Sunday Schools $20, of Parish Schools $103, for the Poor $60, to Missions, Foreign $25, Domestic $25, Diocesan $10. for the Jews $3.50, Episcopal Hospital $12, Book Societies $5, Christian or Theological Education $15, Disabled Clergymen $3, Children's Home $10; Total $1488.

The Pastoral Aid and Mite Societies, the Sewing and Night Schools, and the Mother's Meeting have been in active operation in the year past. And our Parish, though slowly, is yet we trust steadily progressing.

Our Sunday School under an efficient Superintendent and faithful teachers, has increased in interest and numbers. And I would here acknowledge with gratitude our obligations to the Rector and members of St. Paul's Cheltenham, who still continue to give us valuable assistance in our Parish work, and we believe the seed thus scattered will, with the Divine blessing, result in great good to this community.

And we must be permitted to express our regret in the loss of our late Senior Warden, and the services rendered by himself and his estimable family in the interest of our Church here, and we can assure them that their efforts were appreciated, and though brought to a sudden close by the interposition of an All wise Providence, yet they are remembered by us, and they share largely in our sympathies and prayers. An earnest effort is now being made to provide a suitable building for our Sunday School, and to enable us to carry on more efficiently the other parts of our Parish work.

On behalf of the Vestry I would express our thanks to those friends who by their donations and contributions have aided our truly missionary work.

Grace Church, Mount Airy, Philadelphia. Admitted 1862. Rev. Robt. A. Edwards, Rector. C. M. Bayard, Warden.

Baptisms, adults 2, infants 5, total 7; communicants, present number 70; marriage 1; burials 6; public services, on Sundays 104, on other days 15, total 119; children catechized, times frequently; Sunday Schools, officers and teachers 17, scholars 130; Bible Classes, teachers 3, members 20; Church 1, sittings 240, cemetery, 1 lot; salary of Rector $1500 per annum, arrears of salary, none.

Money receipts from all sources—Pew Rents $1600.

Expenditures and Appropriations—Current Expenses (including salary of Rector) $1953.39, Episcopal and Convention Fund $20, Support of Sunday Schools $184.96, for the Poor $48.76, to Missions, Foreign $122.02, Domestic $72.30, Diocesan $25, Episcopal Hospital $15.59, Book Societies $46.59, Christian or Theological Education $85.65, Disabled Clergymen $30.25, Miscellaneous $300, Mission House $150.56; Total $3055.09.

Financial condition.—Ground Rent on buildings or lands $75.

The Rector desires to record here his thanks to the Vestry and congregation for their kindness and liberality in enabling him to spend five months of the past year on a European tour. During his absence (from July 1st until Dec. 1st) the Parish was in charge of the Rev. Dr. Shiras, whose faithful and efficient services were deeply appreciated by all connected with the Church.

St. John's Free Church, Frankford Road, Philadelphia. Admitted 1864. Rev. E. Solliday Widdemer, Missionary in Charge. Robert Whitechurch and William Ellis, Wardens.

Baptisms, infants 10; communicants, present number 44; burials 4; average attendance 70; Sunday Schools, officers and teachers 10, scholars 151.

My report begins Nov. 1st and ends with the second Sunday in April. By a vote of the Vestry, the Parish has been given in charge of the City Mission. The congregations are much better than they were when the City Mission took charge of it. There is a large field for Mission work in the vicinity, and I doubt not that a large and flourishing Parish will in a few years be raised in this portion of the city.

St. James' Church, Hestonville, Philadelphia. Admitted 1867. Rev. Thomas Poole Hutchinson, Rector. John Halliwell and James Cadmus, Wardens.

Baptisms, adults 2, infants 7, total 9; confirmed 11; communicants, added 14, new 8, by removal 4, present number 31; marriages 8; burials 8; public services on Sundays 106, on other days 40, total 146; average attendance on Sundays 70; children catechized, times 20; Sunday Schools, officers and teachers 12, scholars 105; Bible class, teacher 1, members 6; Church 1, sittings 250; salary of Rector $900 per annum, arrears of salary, $24.50; number of free sittings 250.

Money receipts from all sources—Offertory at Holy Communion $17, Collections in Church $131.07, Subscriptions $836, Donations $28.50, other sources $100; Total $1113.20.

Expenditures and Appropriations—Current Expenses (including salary of Rector) $1345.01, payment of debts $16.30, Support of Sunday Schools $150, for the Poor $108, Episcopal Hospital $3.30, Miscellaneous $40; Total $1662.71.

Financial condition.—Aggregate value of property of the Parish, real and personal, $12,000, Encumbrances, about $2000.

I have also superintended a Sunday School at Hopkinsville, and preached and conducted Divine service every Sunday afternoon in connection with the City Mission. Average attendance 30.

Church of the Holy Innocents, Tacony, Philadelphia. Admitted 1869. Rev. D. Caldwell Millett, Rector. J. Burd Peale and Henry L. Foster, Wardens.

Baptisms, infants 4; confirmed, no visitation; communicants, died or removed 5, present number 25; burial 1; public services, on Sundays 98, on other days 46, total 144; children catechized in Sunday School; Sunday School, officers and teachers 6, scholars 80; Church 1, sittings 180; number of free sittings, all; services free to all.

Money receipts from all sources—Collections in Church $191.65, Donations $150, special Collections $34.68, charitable objects $97; Total $473.33.

Regular services have been maintained during the year.

The morning service has been sustained by the Junior Warden, with great acceptance, and the Rector has been able, in addition to his services in Holmesburg, to officiate in the afternoon of each Sunday, and also on the 3d Sunday morning in the month, when the Holy Communion has been administered.

Church of St. James the Less, Philadelphia. Admitted 1846. Rev. Robert Ritchie, Rector. Ellis Yarnall and Edward S. Buckley, Wardens.

Baptisms, adults 2, infants 18, total 20; confirmed 6; communicants, present number about 50; marriages 2; children catechized, times 52; Sunday Schools, officers and teachers 10, scholars 150; Bible class, teacher 1; Parish school, teacher 1, scholars 40; Church 1, sittings 200, school buildings 2, parsonage 1, cemetery 1; salary of Rector $1500 per annum, arrears of salary, none; number of free sittings, 200.

Clay Mission.

No report.

St. Stephen's Church, Bridesburg. Philadelphia. Admitted 1869. Rev. Wm. Jarrett, Rector. Robert C. Cornelius and Isaac Wilson, Wardens.

Baptisms, adults 10, infants 23, total 33; confirmed 21; communicants, added new 21, by removal, none, died or removed, none, present number 45; marriages, none; burials 2; public services, on Sundays 100, on other days 58, total 158; children catechized, times 13; Sunday Schools, officers and teachers 16, scholars 150; Bible class, teacher 1, members 21; other Parish agencies, Mothers' Meeting, Sewing School; Church, sittings 250, school building, part of Church; salary of Rector $1000 per annum, arrears of salary, none; number of free sittings, all.

Money receipts from all sources.—Pew rents none, Offertory at Holy Communion $37.85, Collections in Church $33.50, Subscriptions $659.37, Donations $340.63; Total $1070.65.

Expenditures and Appropriations—Current Expenses (including salary of Rector) $1360, Episcopal and Convention Fund $5, support of Sunday Schools $203, Episcopal Hospital $12.50, Disabled Clergymen $5, Miscellaneous $11.

Financial condition—Aggregate value of property of the Parish, real and personal, $12,000.

St. George's Church, Philadelphia. Admitted 1870. Rev. Charles A. Maison, Rector Henry S. Henry and Hugh Whitely, Wardens.

Baptisms, infants 14; communicants, added, new 8, by removal 27, died or removed 2, present number 33; marriages 3; burials 3; public services twice on Sundays; average attendance on Sundays 200; children catechized, times monthly; Sunday Schools, officers and teachers 18, scholars 125; Bible class, teacher 1, members 20; Church 1, sittings 300.

Money receipts from all sources.—Pew Rents $340.83, Collections in Church $508.86, Subscriptions $5093, other sources $867.18. Total $6809.87.

Expenditures and Appropriations— Current Expenses $329.30, Episcopal and Convention Fund $5, Church building $6074.47; Total $6408.77.

Financial condition.—Aggregate value of property of the Parish, real and personal, $15,000; indebtedness $6000.

This new parish shows, in its commencement, signs of vigorous life, and promises to be an agency of great good.

The Rector has pleasure in acknowledging the very efficient and acceptable labors of Mr. J. H. B Brooks, a candidate for holy orders, who, for several months has acted as Lay-reader, Parish visitor, and head of the Sunday School of the parish.

St. George's Church, Kenderton, Philadelphia. Admitted 1870. Rev. Jos. R. Moore, Rector. Daniel Hertz and Elijah Wyatt, Wardens.

Baptisms, adults 2, infants 7, total 9; confirmed 9; communicants, added, new 1, by removal 6, present number 25; marriage 1; burials 8; public services, on Sundays 82, on other days 35, total 117 ; children catechized, times monthly ; Sunday Schools, officers and teachers 13, scholars 90 ; Bible class teacher Rector, members, congregation ; Church, none, worship in rented hall ; salary of Rector $1200 per annum, arrears of salary, none.

Money receipts from all sources—Pew Rents $394.83, Offertory at Holy Communion $74.83, Collections in Church $493.39, Subscriptions $629.58, other sources (including Sunday School Offerings of $126.27,) $330,39 ; Total $1923.02.

Expenditures and Appropriations—Current Expenses (including salary of Rector) $1147.80, Repairs and Improvements $176.01, Episcopal and Convention Fund $10, support of Sunday Schools $265.10, for the Poor $9, City Missions $16.50, Episcopal Hospital $25, Church building $246.45, Book Societies $5.18, Disabled Clergymen $12 50 ; Total $1913.54.

Previous to the organization of St. George's P. E. Church, services were held in Tioga Hall (its present place of worship) on Sunday afternoons, by the Rev. James DeW. Perry, of Calvary Church, Germantown ; and after its admission into the Convention, on Sunday mornings, by other clergymen, engaged by the Vestry, until September 1st, when the undersigned entered upon his duties as its first Rector.

At the first celebration of the Holy Communion, eighteen persons communicated, and were enrolled as *original* members.

My official acts as Rector of the Church of the Crucifixion, from May 1st, to September 1st, 1870, will be found in the report of that Church.

Church of the Redeemer, Seamen's Mission, Philadelphia. Founded 1847. Rev. Washington B. Erben, Rector. Joseph Eves Hover and George W. Story, Wardens.

Baptisms, adults 4, infants 45, total 49 ; communicants, present number about 50 ; marriages 21 ; burials 36 ; public services, on Sundays 116, on other days 38, total 154 ; children catechized, times 12 ; Sunday Schools, officers and teachers 14, scholars 150; Church 1, sittings 400, parsonage 1; salary of Rector $1000 per annum, arrears of salary, none; number of free sittings, all free.

Expenditures and Appropriations—Current Expenses (including salary of Rector) $1550, Repairs and improvements $260, support of Sunday Schools $88.50, for the Poor $183.50, to Missions, Domestic $5, Home Mission for Colored People $5, Diocesan $15.39, City Missions $3, Episcopal Hospital $25, Bibles, Prayer Books and Tracts for Seamen $90, Miscellaneous $2 ; Total $2227.39.

Financial condition.—Aggregate value of property of the Parish, real and personal, $36,450.

The Free Church of the Redeemer, for Seamen and their families, is maintained by the " Churchmen's Missionary Association for Seamen of the Port of Philadelphia," and the Association is dependent for support on voluntary contributions from individuals and Churches.

The Bishop's Church, Spring Garden. Admitted 1859. Rev. E. Owen Simpson, Rector. George H. Greenleaf, Treasurer.

Baptisms, adults 8, infants 44, total 52 ; confirmed, no visitation, class prepared ; communicants, added, by removal 45, died or removed 14, present number 180; marriages 2; burials 14 ; public services, on Sundays 105, on other days 52, total 157 ; children catechized, times 10 ; Sunday Schools, officers and teachers 32, scholars 350; Church 1, sittings 1000; salary of Rector $1800 per annum, arrears of salary, none.

Money receipts from all sources—Pew Rents $2039.60, Offertory at Holy Communion $391.08, Collections in Church $1426.56, other sources $615.30 ; Total $4472.54.

Expenditures and Appropriations—Current Expenses, (including salary of Rector) $3472.61, Repairs and Improvements $400, Episcopal and Convention Fund $40, support of Sunday Schools $458.55, to Missions, Foreign $24.39, Domestic $18.87, City Missions $18.02, Episcopal Hospital $20.10 Bibles, Prayer Books and Tracts $20 ; Total $4472.54.

The present Rector took charge May 1, 1870. By vote of the congregation and consent of the Bishop (the owner of the Church property) the *free pew* system has been discontinued and the *pews rented.* The income of the Church during the year has been sufficient to meet all necessary expenses. Forty-five communicants have been added by *transfer.*[*]

A monthly, "The Little Episcopalian," is issued in the interests of the Parish. The Sunday School has increased from 75, teachers and scholars, to 382. A Liturgy for the school has been prepared by the Rector.

Chapel of "Our Merciful Saviour," Philadelphia.   Rev. E. Solliday Widdener, Missionary in charge.

Baptisms, infants 7; marriage 1; burials 2; Sunday School, officers and teachers 25, scholars 125; sittings 400.

Money receipts from all sources—Collections in Church $70, Subscriptions $750; Total $820.

Under the appointment of the City Missions and the approval of the Bishop of the Diocese, I secured an upper room at the N. W. cor. of Norris and Camac streets, and preached the first sermon on Sunday morning, Nov. 20th, the Rev. Samuel Durborow, Supt. of City Missions, and the Rev. Richardson Graham, taking part in the services.

This portion of the City had previously been canvassed under the directions of the City Missions, from 10th street on the east and from Montgomery Avenue on the south, the result of which proved that this new enterprise was a great necessity, proving that many families, both Episcopal and others, went to no regular place of worship.

Soon after we commenced these services, a layman of the Church of the Epiphany, Robert B. Sterling, Esq., generously offered to erect a temporary Chapel, which we entered on the Sunday after Easter. It will seat about 400 persons. The Chapel has been called the Chapel of "Our Merciful Saviour."

[*] Owing to the sickness of the Bishop there has been no visitation—a class of 35 is ready for confirmation.

SCHUYLKILL COUNTY.

Trinity Church, Pottsville. Admitted 1836. Rev. Wm. P. Lewis, Rector. E. O. Parry
and Chas. M. Hill, Wardens.

Baptisms, adults 6, infants 37, total 43; confirmed 29; communicants, added 39, of whom 10 by removal, died or removed 18, present number 311; marriages 6; burials 22; public services, Sundays 144, other days 125, total 269; children catechized 12 times; main Sunday School, teachers 28, scholars 203; Infant School, teachers 3, scholars 107; Bible Class 1, scholars 20; branch School, Fishbach, teachers 12, scholars 125 (including an Infant School of 40 scholars); Mechanicsville, teachers 13, scholars 85; Mt. Carbon, teachers 5, scholars 35, librarians 6; Total, teachers 68, scholars 575. Cottage lectures have been held with very good attendance. Church, sittings 700; chapels (the statistics of which are included in this report) sittings 350; salary $3000 per annum; number of free seats 83, all the pews are free every Sunday evening.

Offerings, Parochial.—Alms for the Poor at Holy Communion $250, Circle of Industry, for payment of Church debt $1482.40, for additions to Organ $687.45, Dorcas Society $206.72, Children's Festival on Innocents' Day $300, Melodeon and building at Mechanicsville $300, Fishbach $70, Organ repairs $77.88, Current Expenses $540.56, Miscellaneous $575; Total $4289.91.

Extra Parochial—Convention Fund $38.07, Bible and PrayerBooks $26·74, Domestic Missions $97.69, Foreign Missions $90.07, Episcopal Hospital $33.40, Christmas Fund $100, Bible Society $24.46, Oregon $70.52, Convocation Missions $75, St. Andrew's Church, Tioga, $50, Society for the Increase of the Ministry $278.51, St. Clair $75, Cressona Sunday School $21, Chambersburg $15, Miscellaneous $200; Total $1195.46.

Sunday School offerings—Mite Chests for six months $165, main Schools, Sunday offerings $198,40, for Missions $77.50, for Sunday School Organ $64.63, branch Schools $38, besides $15 from Mt. Carbon, included in various extra-parochial offertories; Total $543.40. Grand Total $6028.77.

The Memorial Church of St. John, Ashland. Admitted 1857. Rev. D. Washburn, Rector. D. J. McKibben and H. Holbert, Wardens.

Baptisms, total 31; confirmed 14; communicants, added 18, died or removed 3, present number 38; marriages 8, burials 20; public services, on Sundays 127, on other days 73, total 200; children catechized, times 15; Sunday Schools, officers and teachers 7, scholars 100. Besides which I baptized 15 in Centralia up to October, and added to the communicants there, so that they numbered 22; which, with those residing some miles distant, yet attending my services, make a total of over 70. Church, sittings 400, School building and Parsonage being built, number of free sittings, all.

The Sunday Schools at Centralia, superintended by Mr. Thomas R. Stockett, will be therefrom reported.

Money receipts from all sources—Pew Rents, none, Offertory at Holy Communion $30, Collections in Church $50, Subscriptions incomplete.

The Schuylkill and Lehigh Convocation have given $75 towards my missionary expenses, with horse and carriage, &c. between Frackville and Mt. Carmel.

I furnished my own horse and vehicle, costing, in 1867, $300. The annual keeping of a horse here is usually about that figure. These three years past might easily make $1000 expended by me in this missionary service. The Diocesan Board in January appropriated $100 in recognition of the same, for which this acknowledgment is gratefully rendered.

Financial condition.—Aggregate value of property of the Parish, real and personal, $10,000, estimated; Encumbrances, Mortgages on Church edifice, none, on other buildings, none, other indebtedness, balance on unfinished Parsonage building, which includes a wing, three stories, 16 x 36 feet, for schools.

The suspension of coal mining has distressed this community, and hindered our parsonage building very painfully.

The prime object of my taking charge of this field, viz., the building of a Church at Centralia, was consummated in the consecration of the edifice on the 4th of September last. But along with the progress of that enterprise, the making something of St. John's, Ashland, and the extension of our Church ministrations to Mt. Carmel on the west, and to the head of Mahanoy Plane on the east, have been unremitted.

In October last, by your permission, the services of a Deacon, Rev. P. P. Reese, were secured for Centralia; and to him, from November 1st, I voluntarily relinquished my entire support thence derived, though consenting to continue Rector while I am needed to administer monthly the Holy Communion there.

The troubles in the coal region have somewhat involved me, but it rejoices me beyond expression to know that our two Church bells answered each other across Locust Mountain every Lord's day, one of them the only summons to Divine worship in all Southern Columbia County. And at four several points our light has shone where previously unknown.

St. Paul's Church, Minersville. Admitted 1841. Rev. J. Thompson Carpenter, Rector. Robert Patten and Thomas Robinson, Wardens.

Baptisms, infants 15; confirmed 3; communicants, added, new 3, by removal 3, died or removed 3, present number 50; marriages 3; burials 14; public services, on Sundays 109, on other days 10, total 119; average attendance on Sundays 60; children catechized, times 24; Sunday Schools, officers and teachers 20, scholars 187; other Parish agencies, Mite Society, organized October 1869; Church 1, sittings 200, Chapel (the statistics of which are included in this report) 1, sittings 150, parsonage 1; salary of Rector $600 per annum; number of free sittings, all; all Sunday services free to all.

Money receipts from all sources—Offertory at Holy Communion $61.63, Collections in Church $101.09, Subscriptions $860.15, Donations $1964.49, other sources $112.23; Total $3099.59.

Expenditures and Appropriations—Current expenses (including salary of Rector) $584.25, Repairs and Improvements $2606.92, Payment of debts $50.50, Episcopal and Convention Fund $7, Support of Sunday School $131.81, Convocation Missions $20, for the Poor $41.63, to Missions, Domestic $20, for the Jews $2, Episcopal Hospital $4, Disabled Clergymen $10; Total $3478.11.

Financial condition.—Aggregate value of property of the Parish, real and personal, $8000; Encumbrance, indebtedness $100.

During the past year the Church has been thoroughly repaired, at an expense of $1439.35. The greater part of the money for this was contributed by our friends in Philadelphia, and we gratefully acknowledge the gift.

The Mite Society, after paying the debt of the Church, has also refurnished it. Repairs and furniture are all paid for. The only indebtedness of the Church is $100 for curbing done by the Borough.

St. Stephen's Chapel, at Forestville, has also been nicely repaired and furnished, at an expense of $1167.57, which was raised by Mr. and Mrs. A. B. De Saulles, who have taken a very lively interest in the welfare of the Chapel since their removal there. On the 11th of February, the Chapel was consecrated by the Bishop.

As this is the last Report which will be sent from this Parish to this Diocese, I desire to place upon record the fact that the three years I have passed in the Parish have been among the most pleasant of my life. I am strongly attached to the people, and I have good reason to know that this feeling is reciprocated, having received from them several substantial tokens of their regard.

Church of the Holy Apostles, St. Clair. Admitted 1848. George Rodgers and William March, Wardens.

Baptisms, adult 1, infants 8, total 9; confirmed none; communicants. added, by removal 2, present number 34; marriages 4; burials 6; public services, on Sundays 104, on other days 4, total 108; average attendance on Sundays 50; Sunday Schools, officers and teachers 8, scholars 50; Church 1, sittings 200; parsonage 1; salary of Rector $440 per annum, arrears of salary, none; number of free sittings, all; extra Sunday services free to all.

Money receipts from all sources—Offertory at Holy Communion $7.87, Collections in Church $41.58, Subscriptions $627.59, Legacy on interest $890, Investments $26.18, other sources $26,99, Sunday School; Total $748.46.

Expenditures and Appropriations—Current Expenses (including salary of Rector) $512.99, Repairs and Improvements $213, Episcopal and Convention Fund $7, for the Poor $7.87, Episcopal Hospital $8.75, Disabled Clergymen $2.50.

Financial condition —Aggregate value of property of the Parish, real and personal, $7000; indebtedness $87.

During the last two months of the Conventional year, the Parish has been without a Rector; during which time the services have been regularly kept up, partly by supplies from Philadelphia and Pottsville, and the Sunday evenings by the Rev. J. T. Carpenter, Rector of St. Paul's, Minersville, and Good Friday by the Rev. Dr. Lewis, of Pottsville.

St. James Church, Schuylkill Haven. Admitted. 1839. Rev. James Walker, Rector.

No report.

Calvary Church, Tamaqua. Admitted 1849.

No report.

Mahanoy City, Church of Faith. Admitted 1865. Rev. Joseph W. Murphy, Rector. Henry Jackson and Wesley Hammer, Wardens.

Baptisms, infants 23; confirmed 4; communicants, added, new 6, by removal 7, died, withdrawn or removed 9, present number 33; marriages 2; burials 5; public services, on Sundays 133, on other days 135, total 268; average attendance on Sundays 75; children catechized, times 13; Sunday School, officers and teachers 12, scholars 93; Rector's Bible

Class, members 15; other Parish agencies, an active Ladies' Church Aid Society; Church 1, sittings 200; Chapels (the statistics of which are included in this report), Hall in Shenandoah, sittings 75; parsonage 1; salary of Rector $600 per annum; arrears of salary, none.

Money receipts from all sources—Pew Rents $680, Offertory at Holy Communion $23.92, Collections in Church $348.10, Subscriptions $120.41, Donations $150, other sources $2.68; Total $1325.11.

Expenditures and Appropriations—Current Expenses (including salary of Rector) $739.75, Repairs and Improvements, $144.35, Episcopal and Convention Fund $10, Support of Sunday Schools $115.61, Parish Library $2.68, Parochial Missions $74.29, for the Poor $23.92, to Missions, Foreign $3.85, Domestic $36.17, Home Mission for Colored People $2.85, Diocesan $34, for the Jews $3.75, Episcopal Hospital $3.65, Church Building $15.73, Bishop White Prayer Book Society $2 50, Society for the increase of the Ministry $7, Disabled Clergymen $5.43, Miscellaneous $83.06; Total $1308.59.

Of the baptisms reported, 3 were at Shenandoah and 5 at St. Nicholas. Of the communicants, 3 are at or near Shenandoah. The offerings for Parochial Missions, $74.29, were for an organ for the Hall in Shenandoah, where I officiate on two Sundays in each month, the greater part of that amount being contributed by persons there.

SUSQUEHANNA COUNTY.

St. Mark's Church, New Milford. Admitted 1822. Rev. John A. Jerome, Rector. Albert Moss and Henry Burritt, Wardens.

Baptisms, none; confirmed 1; communicants, added, new 1, by removal 2, died or removed 3, present number 39; marriages 7; public services, on Sundays 56, on other days 21, total 77; Sunday Schools, officers and teachers 7, Church 1, sittings 200; parsonage 1; salary of Rector $300 per annum; arrears of salary $40; all the sittings are free at all services.

43

Money receipts from all sources—Offertory at Holy Communion $24.25, Collections in Church $72.41, Subscriptions $303.95, Donations $25, Sunday School offerings $19.63, Church Aid Society $65 ; Total $510.24.

Expenditures and Appropriations—Current Expenses (including salary of Rector) $315.15, Repairs and Improvements $65, Episcopal and Convention Fund $7, Support of Sunday Schools $51.47, for the Poor $1.05, to Missions, Foreign (S. School $5) $14.50, Domestic, American Church Missionary Society (Sunday School $12), $14.50, Diocesan $3, Santee Mission $4.50, Episcopal Hospital $3, Disabled Clergymen $6, Miscellaneous $29 ; Total $518.17.

Financial condition.—Aggregate value of property of the Parish, real and personal, $5,000 ; indebtedness.$67.

St. Paul's Church, Montrose.   Admitted 1832.   Rev. Edward A. Warriner, Rector.
Frederick M. Williams and Wm. H. Cooper, Wardens.

Baptisms, adults 9, infants 11, total 20; confirmed 27 ; communicants, added, new 27, by removal 3, died or removed 16, present number 84; marriages 2 ; burials 7; public services, on Sundays 112, on other days 57, total 169 ; average attendance on Sundays 200; children catechized, times 12 ; Sunday Schools, officers and teachers 10, scholars 50; Bible Class, teacher 1, members 10 ; Church 1, sittings 250 ; parsonage 1 ; salary of Rector $1,000 per annum, and parsonage.

Money receipts from all sources—Pew Rents $1025, Offertory at Holy Communion $68.60, Collections in Church $1137.41, Subscriptions $146.37 ; Total $2377.38.

Expenditures and Appropriations—Current Expenses (including salary of Rector), $1252, Repairs and Improvements $75, Payment of Debts $700, Episcopal and Convention Fund $22, Support of Sunday Schools $90, for the Poor $75, Missions, Diocesan $50.19, for the Jews $7.35, Episcopal Hospital $31.29, Christian or Theological Education $50.19, Disabled Clergymen $24.36; Total $2377.38.

Financial condition.—Aggregate value of property of the Parish, real and personal, $15,000.

Grace Church, Great Bend. Admitted 1860. Rev. John A. Jerome, Rector. Ebenezer Gill and Alanson B. Whiting, Wardens.

Baptisms, adult 1, infants 2, total 3; confirmed 2; communicants, added, new 2, by removal 5, died or removed 3, present number 46; marriages 2; burial 1; public services, on Sundays 70, on other days 33, total 103; Sunday School, officers and teachers 9, scholars 50; other Parish agencies, Church Aid Society, and co-operation in the Young Men's Christian Association; Church 1, sittings 150; cemetery 1; salary of Rector $300 per annum; arrears of salary, not any; number of free sittings 150; services free to all.

Money receipts from all sources—Offertory at Holy Communion $16.75, Collections in Church $74.29, Subscriptions $250.57, Donations $230.56, Investments $30, Sunday School offerings $26.04, other sources $276.83, received from friends outside of the Parish for new Church $1094.08; Total $1999.12.

Expenditures and Appropriations—Current Expenses (including salary of Rector), $365.98, Repairs and Improvements $1400, Payment of Debts $37.79, Episcopal and Convention Fund $5, Support of Sunday Schools $76.35, Parish Library $3.05, Young Men's Christian Association $17.26, for the Poor $12, to Missions, Foreign (Sunday School $7.18,) $17.38, American Church Misssionary Society (Sunday School $10.18,) $18.18, Diocesan $3, Mission House $7.50, Evangelical Educational Society $7.50, Disabled Clergymen $4.20, American Sunday School Union $3, Santee Mission $7.05, Miscellaneous $13.37; Total $1998.61.

Financial condition.—Aggregate value of property of the Parish, real and personal, $4,000; other indebtedness about $200; local subscription for new Church $1400.

St. Andrew's Church, Springville.

No report.

new Church, because they are included in the cost of the Church given below. I have not included in the present number of communicants 15 of the class confirmed, who were admitted to the Holy Communion on the first Sunday in May, but not in time for this report.

As we have now completed our new Church, and as this will be my last report as a member of this Diocese, it may be well to state briefly the work which has been done. Five years ago the present missionary commenced his labors in this small place, no parish being as yet organized, with eight families and ten communicants. I have baptized 66 persons, 32 infants and 34 adults, and presented 55 for confirmation. Admitted to Holy Communion 51, received 9 from other parishes, 8 have removed and 3 entered into rest. Offerings for various purposes have amounted to $2369 ; which, however, does not include some contributions of which no record was made.

The Church, of wood, gothic, recently completed, consisting of nave 60 by 30 feet, chancel 20 by 18 feet, organ chamber, tower and vestry room, seating about 250 persons, is indeed a beautiful structure. The seats are moveable and free to all. The entire interior is finished in ash and oiled, the chancel furniture is of chestnut and rich. The windows with their figures and emblems are exceedingly effective in design, drawing and color. The tower is supplied with a sweet toned-bell of over 1000 pounds, and the organ chamber with a sweet-toned pipe organ, both the munificent gift of Charles E. Smith, Esq., of Philadelphia. The silver Communion set, consisting of two large chalices, the paten and the silver basin for presenting the alms, the plated alms basins, the beautiful portable fine brass font, surplice and parish register, are the gift of Mrs. Margaret S. Wilson, to whose early labors in a Sunday School many years ago, may be traced, perhaps, the beginning of our good work here. The large and commodious lot for the Church and rectory, in the centre of the village, is the generous gift of Joseph P. Morris and wife. The Church is desirably located for constant influence on others besides the congregation, this place being the seat of a State Normal School and a school for Soldiers' Orphans. The Church, including the lot, the organ and bell, has cost about $7500. The Church was consecrated by the Bishop on the 24th of April.

Much is due to the generous liberality of friends abroad, to the fostering care and aid of the Bishop, while our people "have a mind to work." But we recognize above all, the abundant blessing of God on our work. "This is the Lord's doing, and it is marvellous in our eyes."

A guild for promoting systematic parish work is in effective operation.

St. Thomas' Church, Fall Brook.

No report.

St. Andrew's Church, Tioga. Admitted 1861. Rector, since May 2, 1871, Rev. John H. Babcock. Wardens, John W. Guernsey and Francis H. Adams.

Baptisms, adults 7, infants 3, total 10; confirmed 10; communicants, present number 30; Sunday School, teachers 6, pupils 45.

Collections and Contributions—Parochial—Church and Rectory and lot $5100, of which the Sunday School paid $76.25, furniture of Church $310, of which the Sunday School paid $14; Chapel $110, Current Expenses and Insurance $71.82, Christmas Tree $21.70, Sunday School Library $31.36; Total $5644.88.

Extra Parochial—Santee Sioux Indian Mission (fromSunday School) $11.35, Bishop Morris (from Sunday School) $6, Mite Chests, up to January, 1871, $20.09, Convention Fund $15, Fund for Disabled Clergymen $4.56; Total $57.

The baptisms and confirmations are those for the last three years, and the offerings for the Church property were gathered during the past fifteen years. There was no Rector from November, 1868, to May 1, 1871; but during that time the Parish has made eleven attempts to get a Pastor; has bought and paid for a lot, a Rectory, and a building which was made over into a neat and convenient Church; has kept up the Sunday School, and has contributed towards Diocesan expenses and Missions. The Church was finished in November, 1869, and it and the Rectory were burned in February, 1871. Within three weeks after this heavy loss, a Chapel was built, and measures were taken to rebuild the Church and Rectory, which are considered to be absolutely necessary for carrying on the work. With such a record of zeal and perseverance, the parish appeals for the sympathy and help which it fairly deserves.

WAYNE COUNTY.

Grace Church, Honesdale. Admitted 1833. Rev. O. ﬀ. Landreth, Rector. Z. H. Russell and W. R. McClaury, Wardens.

Baptisms, adult 1, infants 4, total 5; confirmed 4; communicants, added, new 5, by removal 7, died or removed 2, present number 110; marriages 2; burials 3; public services, on Sundays 100, on other days 57, total 157; average attendance on Sundays 300; children catechized, times, once a month; Sunday Schools, officers and teachers 16, scholars 86, Bible class, teacher 1, members 9; other Parish agencies, "Ladies' Society;" Church 1, sittings 400, parsonage 1; salary of Rector $1200 per annum, arrears of salary, none; number of free sittings, 40.

Money receipts from all sources.—Pew rents $1163.75, Offertory at Holy Communion $29.40, Collections in Church $191.97, Subscriptions $775, Donations $60; Total $2281.14.

Expenditures and Appropriations—Current Expenses (including salary of Rector) $1896.31, Episcopal and Convention Fund $50, Support of Sunday Schools $200, for the Poor $24.75, to Missions, Foreign $41.02, Domestic $50, Episcopal Hospital $15, Bibles, Prayer Books and Tracts $40, Christian or Theological Education $40, Disabled Clergymen $20, Miscellaneous $200; Total $2577.08.

Financial condition.—Aggregate value of property of the Parish, real and personal, $35,000.

St. Paul's Church, Pleasant Mount. Admitted 1868. Rev. Horatio C. Howard, Rector.
Wm. W. Brown and John Fitz, Wardens.

Baptisms, adults 2, infants 15, total 17; confirmed 6; communicants, added, new 7, died or removed 1, present number 23; marriages 2; burials 6; public services, on Sundays 107, on other days 49, total 156; average attendance on Sundays 53; children catechized, times 12; Sunday Schools, officers and teachers 3, scholars 29, Bible class, teacher Rector, members 6; Church 1, sittings 200; salary of Rector $600 per annum; arrears of salary, none; number of free sittings, none; extra Sunday services, free to all, evenings.

Money receipts from all sources—Pew Rents $308, Offertory at Holy Communion $5.15, Collections in Church $60.82, Subscriptions $275, Donations, $50 to Rector, other sources $41.75, Ladies' Mite Society $306.50; total $1063.22.

Expenditures and Appropriations—Current Expenses (including salary of Rector) $675, Repairs and Improvements $310.75, for bell, &c., Episcopal and Convention Fund $5, support of Sunday Schools $41.75, to Missions, Diocesan $4, Episcopal Hospital $5, Disabled Clergymen $2; Total $1043.50.

Financial condition.—Aggregate value of property of the Parish, real and personal, $3500.

Included in above report of baptisms there are one adult and four children, also four funerals, which belong to the Mission work at the Gates' School-house, about five miles north of the village, established June 29th, 1870. Services are held at this point every Sunday afternoon, excepting the first in the month. There have been 37 services held, with an average attendance of 35. During the winter, in consequence of inclement weather, and heavy snow drifts, the attendance at these services is irregular.

In addition, have held two services at St. James' Church, Dundaff.

Report of Rev. Rowland Hill Brown, Missionary at St. John's, Salem, and Zion Church,
Sterling, for the year ending May 1st, 1871.

Stations added 2, whole number of stations 7.

1st. St. John's, Salem, Wayne Co., Pa.

2d. Zion Church, 6 miles from St. John's.

3d. Catterson's, 4½ " "

4th. Ledgdale, 6 " "

5th. Tinley's, 4 " "

6th. Bidwell's, 4 " "

7th. Hollisterville, 2½ " "

I have also preached, and collected in aid of Missionary work, at Honesdale, Carbondale, Wilkes-Barre and Philadelphia. Most of the time I have preached 3 times every Sunday, traveling from 17 to 24 miles.

YORK COUNTY.

St. John's Church, York. Admitted 1785. Rev. Wm. P. Orrick, Rector. George H Sprigg and H. C. Adams, Wardens.

Baptisms, infants 4; confirmed none; communicants, present number 120; marriages 2; burials 2; public services, on Sundays 98, on other days 55, total 153; children catechized, times, monthly; Sunday Schools, officers and teachers 36, scholars 254; Bible classes, teachers 2, members 12; other Parish agencies, Sewing school, teachers 4, scholars 25; Church, sittings 480, School building 1, parsonage 1.

Money receipts from all sources—Pew Rents $1400, Offertory at Holy Communion $55.72, Collections in Church $1432.73, Subscriptions $600, Investments $300, other sources $100; Total $3888.45.

Expenditures and Appropriations—Current Expenses (including salary of Rector) $1675, Payment of debts $600, Episcopal and Convention Fund $35, Support of Sunday Schools $30, for the Poor $55.72, to Missions, Foreign $350, Domestic $375, Diocesan $50, for the Jews $48, Episcopal Hospital $78.74, Christian or Theological Education $250, Disabled Clergymen $88.20; Total $3435.66.

Financial condition.—Indebtedness $1400.

Report of Rev. F. E. Arnold, Philadelphia.

During the last Conventional year I have conducted services and preached 136 times, baptized 10, married 3, and buried 3.

Report of Rev. John S. Beers.

I respectfully report that my connection with Grace Church, in this city, as assistant minister, has continued unchanged.

Report of Rev. V. Hummel Berghaus, Harrisburg.

Owing to ill health, I have not been able, during the present Conventional year, to take any settled parochial work. The occasional services I have rendered are as follows: Officiated at Divine Service on Sundays 51 times, on other days 15 times, preached 31 times, made 6 addresses and lectures, assisted in the administration of the Holy Communion 6 times, performed one burial and assisted at another; baptized 2 adults and 8 infants. The baptisms took place in the parishes of St. Paul's and St. Stephen's, Harrisburg, and are included in the reports from those parishes.

Report of Rev. Gustavus C. Bird, West River, Maryland.

I would respectfully report to my Diocesan, that since November last, when I resigned my Parish in Honesdale, I have been sojourning at West River in the Diocese of Maryland, and have been constantly engaged in the exercise of my ministry as solicitations for the same have been made to me. I am now officiating temporarily in the "Memorial Church," Baltimore city, but my engagement there will terminate on the first of June.

Report of Rev. Wm. V. Bowers, Itinerating Missionary.

From the 1st of May, 1870, to the 1st of May, 1871, I have done clerical duty as follows, including two engagements a month at the Magdalen Asylum, Philadelphia:

Preached, times 78; performed whole services, times 54; in part, times 13; administered communion, times 7, and assisted on four other occasions; baptisms, infants 2; burial 1; in discharge of ministerial duty travelled about 925 miles, received $205, and incurred $7.44 expense. My voice continues feeble as last reported.

Report of Rev. Franklin L. Bush.

I respectfully report that during the past year I have served as Minister in charge of the Memorial Mission of St. Peter's Church. The details of my work are included in the report of St. Peter's Parish.

Report of Rev. C. M. Butler, D. D., Philadelphia.

I have the honor to report that in addition to my duties as Professor in the Divinity School, I have read prayer and preached in several Churches, generally twice a day, on all the Sundays since the last Convention, with the exception of those which occured during the vacation of the Divinity School. I have also performed infant baptism on six occasions, the record of which has been entered on the Parish registers of the Churches in which the service was performed.

Report of Rev. J. Everist Cathell, Deacon.

I was ordained on the 12th of October, 1870, at Williamsport, Pa., by Bishop Stevens. The remainder of the month of October was spent at Gettysburg, where I preached four times. On the first of November, 1870, I became the assistant Minister of the Church of the Epiphany, Philadelphia, and all my official duties have been recorded in the register of that Parish.

Report of Rev. John A. Childs, D. D.

During the past year I have been engaged in my duties as usual, viz.: as the Secretary of the Bishop, Secretary of the Convention of the Diocese, Secretary of the Trustees and Overseers of the Divinity School, Secretary of the Hospital of the Protestant Episcopal Church in Philadelphia, Secretary of the Board of Missions, and have officiated occasionally in desk and pulpit.

Report of Rev Edmund Christian.

I beg to submit the following report of services performed by me since last Convention. From that time until Feb. 28th, (ten months) full services with sermons at St. Clair 125, baptisms 6, funerals 6, marriages 3, instructed a Bible Class every Sunday afternoon, officiated at other places and assisted in the services 18 times, and preached 6 sermons.

Report of Rev. R. Bethell Claxton, D. D., Philadelphia.

Since the last Convention I have continued to discharge the duties of my Professorship in the Divinity School and the Mission House.

I have also assisted my Clerical brethren in various Parishes, preaching or lecturing 94 times, reading the service in whole or in part 131 times, and administering the Holy Communion on 12 occasions. I have baptized 7 infants, solemnized 7 marriages, and officiated at 2 funerals. These, I presume, are all reported by the Rectors of the Parishes, on whose registers they have been recorded.

Report of Rev. George Alexander Crooke, D. D., D. C. L., Philadelphia.

Dr. Crooke begs leave to report that he has been engaged in the exercise of his Ministry, during the last Conventional year as circumstances would permit. His official acts are included in the reports of the various Churches in which he has officiated.

Report of Rev A. H. Cull.

Although without a Pastoral charge during the last 12 months, yet I have officiated whenever an opportunity presented. Sometimes conducting the entire services, and preaching once or twice on the same days, at other times taking a part in the prayers. I have supplied vacant pulpits, at Lancaster, Chambersburg, and other places in this Diocese, Meadville and several other places in the Diocese of Pittsburgh, and occasionally in other places beyond the limits of Pennsylvania, and desire to acknowledge my obligations to my brethren and other kind friends for their generous hospitality and Christian courtesy.

Report of Benjamin J. Douglass, Philadelphia.

My report of the yearly services ending 1st of May, 1871, are as follows: public services, on Sundays 88, other days 28, total 116; Holy Communion administered, times 8; burial 1; baptism 1.

Not having been employed in regular Parochial duty since the first of August, and not having as yet accepted a charge, the usual parochial items do not appear.

Report of Rev. Samuel Durborow, General Suprintendent of the Philadelphia Protestant Epicopal City Missions.

I beg leave to report that since May 1st, 1870, I have engaged constantly in the duties of the office of General Superintendent of the Philadelphia Protestant Episcopal City Mission, under your appointment. In addition to the usual duties of the Mission I have baptized 10 adults, 29 infants, total 39; married 100 couples; buried 35; preached, on Sundays 87 times, other days 45, total 132; Received for General Fund City Missions $6367.24, Charity Fund $43.19; Total $6805.43.

Report of Rev. J. P. Fugett.

During the past Conventional year I have read prayer and preached upon all Sundays, with the exception of only two, and generally twice a day; and I have, in addition, performed services and delivered lectures several times.

Report of Rev. Alexander Fullerton, Philadelphia.

Having continued in my post as Assistant Priest to St. Stephen's Church, Philadelphia, during the past year I have officiated 221 times, preached or lectured 48 times, assisted in administering the Holy Communion 17 times, baptized 21 children, buried 5 persons, and married 1 couple, which acts are recorded in the Parish Register.

Report of Rev. John G. Furey, Philadelphia.

The Missionary respectfully reports that during the past year he has been fully and regularly occupied in the special work assigned to him, viz.: visiting the sick, needy, and destitute, and officiating in the Public Institutions of this city. He has performed the following duties: special Missionary visits, about 850; services, sermons and addresses on all occasions, about 300; baptisms, adults and children 60; Holy Communion administered, times 10; marriages solemnized 3; funerals attended 50; Bibles, Testaments, Prayer Books and Tracts distributed, about 5000.

These services have been given at all the working hours of day and evening, every day in the week and in every section of the city. The Missionary's work is, of necessity, general and desultory, except that at certain stated times on week days and Sundays, he holds services at about ten (10) places which are scattered widely apart throughout the city. This part of his work involves a large amount of time and labor, (and considerable expense), in going to and from the different places. The Missionary attends, however, cheerfully and regularly to his work from day to day, and feels grateful to a gracious Providence for the measures of health and success vouchsafed to him in the performance of the above named duties.

Report of Rev. Daniel R. Goodwin, D. D., Philadelphia.

During the year past, besides the discharge of my duties as Professor in the Divinity School, in Philadelphia, my ministerial acts have been as follows:

Preached 54 times, officiated in Divine Service 74 times, administered the Holy Communion 7 times, assisted in its administration 7 times, and baptized two infants.

Report of Rev. Richardson Graham, Philadelphia.

I would respectfully report that I resigned the Rectorship of St. John's Church, Concord, Delaware Co., Pa., on the 31st of July, 1870, and was appointed a Missionary under the

Ecclesiastical authority of the Diocese. Since the 1st of August, 1870, I have been supplying and assisting in Parishes in this and neighboring Dioceses.

Report of Rev. G. Emlen Hare.

Throughout the year I have lectured to students of Divinity from six to eight times per week, and on Sundays have sometimes preached or otherwise officiated.

Report of Rev. William H. Hare, D. D.

I beg to say in explanation of my absence from the Convention that my duties here prevented my attendance, and to report that since my resignation of the Rectorship of the Church of the Ascension, in December last, I have been discharging the duties of the office of Secretary, and General Agent of the Foreign Committee of the Board of Missions.

Report of Rev. Samuel Hazlehurst, Philadelphia.

During the year ending May 1st, 1871, I have preached 17 times, officiated at four funerals, baptized 3 children, read service and assisted at the administration of the Holy Communion a number of times.

Report of Rev. G. W. Hodge.

I would respectfully report that I have continued in my position as Assistant Minister of Christ Church, assisting the Rector in that Parish, and also, since September last, in Calvary Church. I have officiated on 302 occasions, celebrated or assisted in the Holy Communion 32 times, preached 128 times; baptisms 23, marriages 2, burials 16. All included in Parochial Reports.

Report of the Rev. John Ireland.

I have been fully employed in ministerial duty during the past year, in the Church of the Holy Apostles, Philadelphia, and in the parish of St. Alban, Roxborough, about eight miles from the city.

Report of Rev. E. N. Lightner.

I am sorry that I have been compelled to report that I have not been able to officiate in the office of the ministry the last year. Nor am I yet able. The same impediments continue, not alleviated, but aggravating me thus by continuance.

Report of Rev. John Long.

From May 1st to September 11th, 1870, I officiated in the Mission field in Luzerne county, as follows: Church of the Good Shepherd, Green Ridge, 17 times; baptisms, infants 5. South Wilkes-Barre, St. Clements, 5 times; Coalville 4 times; other places 30 times, total 56.

The Church of the "Good Shepherd," Green Ridge, was formally opened for public services, on Sunday, June 5th, and the Church of St. Clement, South Wilkes-Barre, was enclosed before I left the field. Amount due on salary from St. Clement's, since March 1st, 1870, $77.17. Since the 11th of September I have been regularly officiating in St. Luke's Church, Cleveland.

Report of the Rev. L. Martin.

The Conventional year just closed is full of pleasing incidents in the Christian life which belong to the Seamen's Mission under my care. Several officers of merchant ships have freely and openly confessed the Saviour through my counsels and prayers, and by corresponding demeanor, proven their translation from darkness to light and from the power of Satan to God. The men before the mast have enjoyed larger kindnesses from such officers as described, who have granted extra time for reading and for worship, recommending the Holy Bible and Book of Common Prayer, as fit companions of daily life, and in not a few instances whole crews have been selected for *personal worth*, or at least of their being clear of drunkenness, swearing and the like; also, a marked improvement in the behaviour of sea-going men is admitted, by agents and

45

others doing business with our merchant marine, these have wished us "God speed" in our moral instruction of seamen.

I herewith present you with an annual summary of statistics as follows: Ships visited, 770, boarding houses 132, Bibles given 144, Prayer Books 455, Tracts (four paged) 13,300, shipping agents 53, visits to Port Richmond 12, barracks, Navy Yard 24, receiving ship, Navy Yard 24, to Fort Mifflin 5, public *week day* services 15, baptisms 16, marriages 4, funerals 7. Monies received from Grace Church, (city) $25, other sources $50, expended for charity and sickness, &c., among seamen.

Report of Rev. Robert C. Matlack, Philadelphia.

As the *Secretary* of "*The Evangelical Educational Society* of the *Protestant Episcopal Church*," I have preached constantly on Sunday, delivered many addresses, carried on extensive correspondence, and attended to all the usual duties of my office.

Report of Rev. A. M. Morrison, West Philadelphia.

I have continued in the regular discharge of my duties, as instructor in the Mission House, until the month of January, 1871, at which time organic changes in the House, transferring to the regular courses of the various established Institutions, the departments, Theological and Academic, previously taught by me, rendered my resignation a matter of course. Since that time I have not been engaged in any settled ministerial work.

Report of Rev. W. F. C. Morsell, Assistant Minister of All Saints' Parish, Lower Dublin.

During the past year, by the grace of God, I have been permitted to perform the following duties:

Services 120, Sermons 112, Addresses 80, Lectures 25, Object Lessons 30, Lessons in Scripture History 20; Total 387. Under my charge last year was a Sunday School, at Eddington, Bucks Co. There have been added 6 pupils and two male teachers. The School now numbers teachers 8, pupils 72. At Andalusia I have organized a new Sunday School which has teachers 6, pupils 30; in all 14 teachers and 102 pupils.

Report of Rev. Robert J. Nevin, Rector of Grace Church, Rome, Italy, for the year ending April 30th, 1871.

Services—Baptisms, infants 3; marriage 1; burials 2; read service 114 times; preached 46; celebrated Holy Communion 24.

Collections—For Current Support of Chapel $3238.07, Domestic and Foreign Missions, and local Charities $337.40, Creche—Day Nursery for the Children of Working Women $855, for Building Fund for new Church within the Walls $5000; Total $9430.47.

Besides the above amount, the Americans this winter in Rome contributed very nearly $3000 for the relief of the sufferers by the terrible overflow of the Tiber, in December last.

I cannot praise too highly the prompt liberality of my fellow countrymen on all occasions where I have had need to call upon their charity. The collections this winter have been larger than ever before, although the number of travellers has been unusually small.

The Chapel services were opened for the season on the 16th of October, and have been well attended up to the present. Average from 300 to 450.

After the Italian Government proclaimed liberty in Rome, in the matter of religious worship, every effort was made to secure a room at once for our service within the city walls. It was found impossible, however, to secure a room large enough for the wants of the congregation.

The Vestry have now resolved to build within the walls at once a Church of our own, which shall be in some measure worthy of our faith and nation. They ask of the Church at large, for it is not a local work, $100,000, for this object; and, God willing, I shall visit the United States this coming summer on this mission. The money given to this work will benefit not only the Church and our own people, who shall hereafter worship in it from every Diocese in our Union, but will help forward the cause and the manifestation of true religious liberty among the Italians more rapidly than anything else that we can do for them. A Protestant Church, and that a distinctive one, openly building in Rome, will make this people understand their rights of conscience more clearly than all the preaching and printing that could be brought to bear upon them for years. *

Our plan of building meets with much countenance from the Government, and finds much sympathy among the people.

In conclusion, I must express my great regret, that during the past two years we have not enjoyed the official visit for confirmation, of yourself or any of our Right Reverend Fathers.

Each year I have had a class of persons anxious for confirmation, and each Easter have been obliged to receive them to the Holy Communion without the strengthening of this rite, in accordance with the rubric which admits thus those ready and desirous to be confirmed, where the Church neglects to afford the opportunity.

Report of Rev. Louis C. Newman, Philadelphia.

Since last Convention I have continued to work in that portion of the Lord's vineyard entrusted to my care. In addition to my duties at home I have also visited Pittsburgh, Chicago, Detroit, London, Hamilton, Toronto, and New York, last autumn, and Pittsburgh, Baltimore, Washington, Newark, New York, Boston, Providence the past winter and spring, In these journeys I have travelled over 7000 miles, and made prayerful efforts to awake a Scriptural interest in the spiritual welfare of God's anciently chosen people.

I am thankful to report the baptism of 4 adults, and 2 infants, children of Israel. I have also baptized two infants of Christian parents. During the past Conventional year I have officiated 86 times, preached 90 times, administered and assisted in the administration of the Holy Communion 15 times, and officiated at two funerals   During the same time I paid 405 visits, including 95 visits paid in the above named cities, and received 190 visits from 35 converts and inquirers after the truth as it is in Jesus. During the same period I distributed the following: 18 Bibles, 16 Pentateuchs with Haphtorath and Messianic Selections of prophecies, 14 Hebrew New Testaments, 31 Parts of New Testaments with Hebrew Commentaries, 5 Books of Common Prayer in Hebrew, 13 Pilgrim's Progress in Hebrew, 6 Old Paths in German and Hebrew, and about 22,000 pages of various Tracts.

Report of Rev. A. Prior.

During the past Conventional year I have exercised the duties of my ministerial office 52 times in connection with St. John's Chapel, Fishbach, and have, in addition, preached and read the service nine times in Parishes unconnected with my field of labor. For a detailed statement of the present condition of the Sunday School to which my labors have been given, I beg leave to refer to the Report of the Rev. Doctor Lewis, Rector of Trinity Church, Pottsville.

Report of Rev. J. W. Robins, Head Master of the "Academy of the Protestant Episcopal Church in the City of Philadelphia."

Since my last Report I have been engaged in the duties of my position at the Academy, officiating occasionally in the Churches of Philadelphia and its vicinity.

Report of Rev. H. J. Rowland.

I would respectfully report that I continued in the discharge of my duties as the assistant minister of St. James' Church, Philadelphia, up to the first of July last; since that time I have been obliged to suspend active work, owing to the feeble state of my health.

Report of Rev. Alex. Shiras, D. D., Philadelphia.

I would respectfully report that since the last Convention, besides continued engagements in several schools, I supplied from June till December the place of the absent Rector of Grace Church, Mount Airy, holding two services each Sunday and one on Thanksgiving Day. Subsequently I officiated, as opportunity was presented me, on nine different occasions, preaching, reading service, or aiding in the administration of the Holy Communion. Since Easter Sunday, I have been engaged in assisting Bishop Lee, of Delaware, at St. Andrew's Church, Wilmington, my engagement there extending to the first Sunday of July next. I regret much my inability to report more continuous clerical work, in which work has always been my highest satisfaction.

Report of Rev. W. H. N. Stewart, Assistant Minister of St. Clement's Church, Philadelphia.

The statistical returns of the services I have rendered will be made by the Rector of St. Clement's Parish, of which I am the assistant minister.

Report of Rev. E. H. Supplee.

In addition to the discharge of my duties in my school, where we have a daily morning service, I have officiated in Divine service as follows: read service in whole or in part 65 times, preached 32 times, lectured 2 times, attended 2 funerals, baptized 2 infants, administered the Holy Communion 1 time, assisted in its administration 12 times.

Report of Rev Charles West Thomson, York.

Since my last report, my services for the Conventional year have been as follows: I have baptized, infant 1, have officiated at one marriage and one funeral, have administered the Communion once, have read the service, or assisted in doing so, eighteen times, and have preached on twenty-two occasions.

Report of Rev. Samuel Tweedale, Deacon, Assisting the Rev. D. S. Miller, D. D., in St. Mark's Church, Frankford.

I have been engaged as usual during the year ending May 1st. I have assisted at service on Sundays 162, on other days 50 times; baptized 38 children, burials 84, marriages 23, visits made 1274, assisted in distributing 7200 Religious papers, and 3000 Tracts. These services are included in the report of the Parish.

REPORT OF CHURCH INSTITUTIONS.

Hospital of the Protestant Episcopal Church, Front and Lehigh Avenue, Philadelphia. Organized 1851.

	1869.	1870.	1871.
No. of inmates,	925	1040	960

Am't of endowment $240,300.

	$9948.62	$9961.99	$13,335.15

and real estate yielding $1600 per annum.

	1869.	1870.	1871.
Income from collections and other sources.	$25,016.40	$30,048.33	$25,470.45

Report of the Divinity School of the Protestant Episcopal Church, West Philadelphia.

	1869.	1870.	1871.
Number of professors and instructors,	6	6	6
" " students	53	51	46
" " graduates,	11	9	9

Amount of Endowment $285,804.66.

Andalusia College, at Andalusia, Pa. Incorporated 1866. Rev. H. T. Wells, President. Rev. Charles Woodward, Chaplain.

Four Professors and twelve teachers. Three courses of study —the Classical, the Scientific Commercial, and a select course. Potter Hall, the primary department, has separate grounds and buildings, and is for boys under fourteen years of age. The professors, teachers and students, mostly reside in the buildings of the two departments. The President and his family reside at Potter Hall. The Professor of Mathematics and his family reside at the college. Number of students and pupils, 85. The buildings are large and commodious, and the grounds ample, embracing a farm of about fifty acres. Value of property $65,000. Annual assistance rendered to some of the clergy and to orphans, $1000. Dr. George Fox, President of Board of Trustees, the Rev. Leighton Coleman, Secretary, and H. S. Cannell, Treasurer. Committee on aid to some of the clergy and to orphans, the Rev. L. Coleman and the Revs. D. C. Millett, H. H. Weld and H. T. Wells.

Report of the Councillors and Managers of the Lincoln Institution, John L. Redner, Secretary of Board of Council. Margaret Y. Clay, Secretary of Board of Managers.

In compliance with a resolution of the Convention of 1869, the Councillors and Managers of the Lincoln Institution present the following report.

The Institution was organized in the year 1866, through the earnest exertions of several benevolent ladies, who collected sufficient funds in a very short time to purchase the house No. 308 South Eleventh Street, where the Institution now is. Since its inception, just five years ago, 155 boys have been the recipients of its benefits; of this number 134 were the children of deceased soldiers, the remainder were the children of destitute parents: the charter of the Institution providing for such cases.

The plan of this Institution is different from that of any one in this or any other country. When a boy arrives at 12 years of age, if he passes a creditable examination in his studies, he is placed in some situation where the work is light; as soon as old enough, he is, if possible, placed at some trade or in a permanent situation. The Institution has authority to bind them. All they earn until 16 years of age, goes towards their support; after that age they pay $3 per week, and simply have to provide their clothes. They can remain until 21 years of age. Boys from 12 to 16 years are obliged to attend the night school, where the instruction is mostly oral and made as attractive as possible. All the inmates are required to adhere to the rules, which are very simple. Sometimes it is asked how can boys at work all day, study at night. The question is readily answered by a visit to the night school, and better still, by a review of the history of some of our most eminent men whose days were devoted to bodily labor and their evenings to study. Sixty-five boys are now at work and 35 different trades are represented by them; they have the satisfaction of knowing that they are contributing to a great extent towards their own support, a feeling which must make every boy with one spark of manliness in him, rejoice.

The result of the religious and moral training of the boys has been very gratifying; 11 were confirmed during the past year. The entire success of the Institution in all its workings and details is a source of constant pleasure and thankfulness, and the managers most heartily commend this work to the Church in the hope, that under the guidance of Providence, its future welfare will be ensured.

CHURCH HOME FOR CHILDREN,

N. E. Corner 22d and Pine Streets, Philadelphia.

Organized January, 1856.

	1869.	1870.	1871.
Number of Inmates......	52.	61.	66.

Property belonging to Church Home for Children—Lot and buildings 22d and Pine, 44 x 142; Lot 25th Ward, 100 x 250; Lot 25th Ward, 25 x 103; value about......... $5,000

Ground Rent and Principal....... 1,050

"   "   1,300

City 6's....... 8,600

	1869.	1870.
Annual Income from Endowment......	$ 267.22	$ 278.55
" Charity for Current Expenses only.	5,536.26	4,673.38
Total Income......	$5,803.48	$4,951.93

Of the New Home at Angora Station, Media Railroad. That account stands, viz. :

Total Receipts, cash...... $38,626.57

20 "Shares Pennsylvania Lath Manufacturing Co.," worth...... 1,000.00

$39,626.57

Payments on account of building......$23,027.76

Bill of Printing...... 9.50   23,037.26

In hands of Treasurer...... $16,589.31

APPENDIX E.

REPORT OF TREASURER OF CHRISTMAS FUND FOR DISABLED CLERGYMEN.

CR.   *Christmas Fund in Acc't with R. P. McCullagh, Treasurer.*

1870   *Contributions since May 1st,* 1870:

County	Town	Church	Amount
BERKS,	Reading,	St. Barnabas..........	$5 50
BLAIR,	Altoona,	St. Luke	2 64
	"	" 1869...........	27 60
BRADFORD,	Pike,	St. Matthew.	2 50
	"	" 1869........	3 25
	Towanda,	Christ.............	50 00
	"	Sunday School of do...	25 00
BUCKS,	Bristol,	St. James........	22 00
	Centreville,	Trinity	4 20
	Doylestown,	St. Paul..............	13 53
	Newtown.	St. Luke.............	2 40
	Yardleyville,	St. Andrew.........	3 00
CARBON,	Mauch Chunk,	St. Mark	59 04
	Summit Hill,	St. Philip.............	5 32
CENTRE,	Bellefonte,	St. James.............	16 10
CHESTER,	Coatesville,	Trinity	20 82
	Downingtown,	St. James...........	7 00
	Kennett Square and	New London Missions.	5 00
	Phœnixville,	St. Peter.............	10 53
	Pequea,	St. John.	14 72
	West Chester,	Holy Trinity..........	18 00
CUMBERLAND,	Carlisle,	St. John	25 86
DAUPHIN,	Harrisburg,	St. Stephen...........	67 54
DELAWARE,	Burd Orphan Asylum.		5 00
	Concord,	St John.............	8 22
	Media,	Christ..........	27 68
	Radnor.	Good Shepherd........	8 30
	Rockdale,	Calvary..............	25 60
LANCASTER,	Columbia,	St. Paul..........	13 50
	Churchtown,	Bangor..........	2 22
	Lancaster,	St. John.	5 13
	Leacock,	Christ............	3 21
	Manheim,	St. Paul	8 14
	Marietta,	St. John.	13 00
	Mount Hope,	Hope, 1869............	1 36
LEBANON,	Colebrook,	Church...........	3 34
	Lebanon,	St. Luke............	11 00
LEHIGH,	Allentown,	Grace...., ...	19 00
	"	Mediator............	1 00
LYCOMING,	Muncy,	St. James...........	5 00
	Williamsport,	Christ.........'..	30 00
LUZERNE,	Carbondale,	Trinity.........	12 35
	Drifton Mission,		31 00
	Eckley,	St. James	14 11
	Hazleton,	St. Peter.............	4 50
	Pittston,	St. James.............	20 05
	Scranton,	St. Luke.............	24 00
	"	Good Shepherd........	4 32
	Wilkes-Barre,	St. Stephen...........	114 10
	White Haven,	St. Paul.	13 06
MONTGOMERY,	Bridgeport,	Swedes..............	15 00
	Cheltenham,	St. Paul	139 08
	Jenkintown,	Our Saviour...........	18 62
	Lower Merion,	Redeemer.............	110 00
	"	St. John..............	5 42
	Pottstown,	Christ	26 00
	Perkiomen,	St. James.............	3 50
	Norristown.	St. John..............	46 32
	Upper Providence,	St. Paul's Memorial..	10 40
	Whitemarsh,	St. Thomas............	30 00
MONTOUR,	Danville,	Christ.............	25 00
NORTHAMPTON,	Bethlehem,	Nativity............	39 25
	Easton,	Trinity..............	17 00
	"	" 1869	10 00
NORTHUMBER'D,	Sunbury,	St. Matthew...........	17 60
PHILADELPHIA,	Philadelphia,	Ascension	20 00
	"	Atonement............	100 00
	"	Christ..............	32 62
	"	Epiphany.	300 00
	"	Good Shepherd.......	4 51

     Carried forward.............................. $1804 06

Christmas Fund in Acc't with R. P. McCullagh, Treasurer. CR.

1870				
		Brought forward	$1804	08
PHILADELPHIA,	Philadelphia,	Grace.............	163	28
	"	Holy Apostles........	13	50
	"	Holy Trinity..........	210	73
	"	Mediator..............	88	00
	"	St. Andrew...........	200	00
	"	St. Clement...........	47	63
	"	St. James.............	213	61
	"	St. Luke..............	344	26
	"	St. Mark..............	345	35
	"	St. Peter.............	283	79
	"	St. Stephen...........	328	88
	"	St. Thomas...........	12	00
	Branchtown,	House of Prayer......	3	00
	Bridesburg,	St. Stephen..........	5	00
	Chestnut Hill,	St. Paul	46	20
	Francisville,	St. Matthew..........	60	00
	Frankford,	St. Mark.............	78	03
	Germantown,	Calvary..............	94	09
	"	Christ	149	48
	"	St. Luke.............	103	00
	" A family	Christmas Offering, do.	100	00
	Holmesburg,	Emmanuel.............	33	43
	Kenderton,	St. George...........	12	50
	Kensington,	Chapel Epis. Hospital.	18	10
	Kingsessing,	St. James............	20	50
	Lower Dublin,	All Saints...........	16	75
	Manayunk,	St. David............	26	05
	Mount Airy,	Grace................	30	25
	Moyamensing,	All Saints...........	28	45
	Northern Liberties,	Calvary..............	12	85
	"	St. John.............	9	01
	Oxford,	Trinity..............	101	83
	Port Richmond,	Messiah..............	6	73
	Roxborough,	St. Timothy..........	20	00
	"	" 1869........	17	62
	South Penn,	Zion.................	15	00
	Southwark,	Evangelists...........	15	20
	"	Trinity..............	37	50
	Spring Garden,	Bishop's Church......	6	84
	"	Redemption	23	20
	"	St. Jude.............	26	00
	"	St. Matthias.........	42	50
	Tacony,	Holy Innocents.......	12	08
	West Philadelphia,	St. Mary.............	53	71
SCHUYLKILL,	Mahanoy City,	Faith...............	5	43
	Minersville,	St. Paul	10	00
	Pottsville,	Trinity..............	100	00
	St. Clair,	Holy Apostles........	2	50
SUSQUEHANNA,	Great Bend,	Grace.............	4	20
	Montrose,	St. Paul.............	24	36
	New Milford,	St. Mark.............	6	00
TIOGA,	Wellsboro,	St. Paul.............	11	31
	Tioga,	St. Andrew...........	4	56
WAYNE,	Honesdale,	Grace.............	20	00
	Mount Pleasant,	St. Paul.............	2	00

1871 May 3	Twelve months' interest on $2650 U. S. Six per cent. 5-20's of 1867............................. $159 00		
	Premium on gold, July 1, 1870, 12 per cent.....$9 54		
	" " Jan. 4, 1871, 10½ " 8 35		
	$17 89		
	Interest on balances in the Philadelphia Trust, Safe Deposit and Ins. Co., for 1 year to date................ 109 69		
		$5470	35
		286	58
	Balance rec'd May, 1870, from T. H. Montgomery, Esq., late Treasurer, as per his last Report to the Convention......	2792	05
		$8548	98
May 3	To Balance brought down..............................	$3537	15

E. E.   R. P. McCULLAGH. *Treasurer.*

Philadelphia, May 3d, 1871.

DR.   *Christmas Fund in Acc't with R. P. McCullagh, Treasurer.*

1871	Appropriations paid to Beneficiaries during the year ending May 1, 1871, viz.:		
	Annual to four clergymen..............................$1541 67		
	" six widows of do........................... 1645 83		
	" children of three do....................... 650 00	$3837 50	
	Special to three clergymen........................... $450 00		
	" five widows of do......................... 500 00		
	" children of two do....................... 200 00	1150 00	$4987 50
	Cash paid bills, &c., as follows, viz:		
	McLaughlin Bros., printing Treasurer's receipts..............	3 50	
	Edmund Allen, printing Christmas Circulars................	3 50	
	" Episcopal Register," publishing acknowledgment..........	7 50	
	Postage and Check Stamps, &c., &c...........................	9 83	24 33
	Balance of Cash on hand in the Philadelphia Trust, Safe Deposit and Insurance Co., to the credit of the Treasurer, on interest at 4 per cent.................................		3537 15
			$8548 98

We have examined the foregoing account, compared it with the vouchers, and found it correct, leaving a balance to the credit of the Treasurer in the Philadelphia Trust Safe Deposit and Insurance Company of Thirty-five hundred and Thirty-seven Dollars and Fifteen Cents ($3537.15), together with the investment of Twenty-six Hundred and Fifty ($2650) Dollars in U. S. Six per cent. Loan of 1867.

THOMAS ROBINS,   } *Committee.*
JOHN S. NEWBOLD,

PHILADELPHIA, May 9, 1871.

APPENDIX F.

ACCOUNT

OF

TREASURER OF CONVENTION AND EPISCOPAL FUNDS.

CR.　　*Convention Diocese Pa. in Acc't with B. G. Godfrey, Treasurer.*

Assessments. 1870					Epis. F.	Con. F.
May 4		To balance received from late Treasurer, as per last Report.........			$2501 34	$ 835 49
		From Parishes.				
		ADAMS,	Huntingdon,	Christ...........		
		BEDFORD,	Bedford,	St. James		
1871						
April	$10 00	BERKS,	Douglasville,	St. Gabriel......	6 00	4 00
May, 1870	80 00		Reading,	Christ 1869......	49 52	30 48
Apr. 1871	80 00		"	" 1870......	51 00	29 00
May, 1871	5 00		"	St. Barnabas....	3 00	2 00
	5 00		Morgantown,	St. Thomas, 1867.	3 30	2 00
Feb. 1871	5 00		Birdsboro,	St. Michael......	3 00	2 00
Dec. 1870	12 50	BLAIR,	Altoona,	St. Luke........	9 00	3 50
Dec. 1870	5 00	BRADFORD,	Pike,	St. Matthew.....	3 00	2 00
Oct. 1870	50 00		Towanda,	Christ.	30 00	20 00
Jan. 1870	6 50		Troy,	St. Paul........	4 50	2 00
	6 00		Athens,	Trinity.........		
Nov. 1870	40 00	BUCKS,	Bristol,	St. James........	25 00	15 00
Mar. 1871	5 00		Newtown,	St. Luke........	3 00	2 00
Mar. 1871	5 00		Yardleyville,	St. Andrew.....	3 00	2 00
Apr. 1871	5 00		Hulmeville.	Grace..........	3 00	2 00
Dec. 1870	5 00		Centreville,	Trinity.........	3 00	2 00
Dec. 1870	15 00		Doylestown,	St. Paul.........	9 00	6 00
Apr. 1871	50 00	CARBON,	Mauch Chunk,	St. Mark.......	32 00	18 00
	5 00		Summit,	St. Philip	3 00	2 00
Nov. 1870	12 00	CENTRE,	Philipsburg,	St. Paul........	7 00	5 00
May 1871	20 00		Bellefonte,	St. John 1870....	7 00	4 10
	10 00		"	" 1869....	9 00	6 00
Dec. 1870		CHESTER,	Great Valley,	St. Peter.......	6 00	4 00
Apr. 1871	5 00		New London,	St. John........	3 00	2 00
	5 00		Warwick,	St. Mary........	12 00	6 77
May 1871	17 00		Pequea,	St. John, 1869....	10 00	7 00
Dec. 1870	7 00		West Whiteland,	St. Paul	4 00	3 00
Oct. 1870	5 00		West Vincent,	St. Andrew......	3 00	2 00
	5 00		Honeybrook,	St. Mark........		
May 1871	50 00		West Chester,	Holy Trinity....	32 00	18 00
Oct. 1870	20 00		Phoenixville.	St. Peter.......	12 50	7 50
May 1870	20 00		Downingtown,	St. James.	13 00	7 00
	10 00		West Marlboro,	Trinity.........		
May 1870	30 00	CLINTON,	Lock Haven,	St. Paul. 1869....	19 00	11 00
	35 00	COLUMBIA,	Bloomsburg,	St. Paul.........		
	5 00		Centralia,	Holy Trinity 1869	3 00	2 00
			"	" 1870	3 00	2 00
Apr. 1870	40 00	CUMBERLAND,	Carlisle,	St. John........	28 00	12 00
	45 00	DAUPHIN,	Harrisburg,	St. Stephen......	29 00	16 00
May 1870	5 00		"	St. Paul, 1869....	3 00	2 00
Dec. 1870			"	" 1870....	3 00	2 00
May 1870	50 00	DELAWARE,	Chester,	St. Paul, 1869....	25 00	15 00
	20 00		Marcus Hook,	St. Martin......		
Dec. 1870	25 00		Radnor,	St. David........	16 00	9 00
May 1870	10 00		Concord,	St. John, 1869....	6 00	4 00
Nov. 1870	10 00		Rockdale,	Calvary.	6 00	4 00
Oct. 1870	25 00		Media,	Christ..........	16 00	9 00
		FRANKLIN,	Mont Alto,	Emmanuel......		
Oct. 1870	5 00		Chambersburg,	Trinity..........	3 00	2 00
	5 00	HUNTINGDON,	Huntingdon,	St. John		
Mar. 1871	75 00	LANCASTER,	Lancaster,	St. James........	48 00	27 00
Dec. 1870	25 00		"	St. John........	16 00	9 00
	5 00		Churchtown,	Bangor..........		
	5 00		Leacock,	Christ..........		
	10 00		Paradise,	All Saints		
Feb. 1871	15 00		Columbia,	St. Paul..	9 00	6 00
Dec. 1871	15 00		Marietta,	St John........	9 00	6 00
May 1870			Mt. Hope,	Hope............	1 00	64
Apr. 1871			"	"	1 44	
Apr. 1871	5 00		Colebrook Furnace	....	2 15	
	5 00		Gap Mines,	Grace..........		
Dec. 1870	5 00		Manheim,	St. Paul	3 00	2 00
	$1056 50			Carried forward...............	$3112 75	$1194 48

Convention Diocese Pa. in Acc't with B. G. Godfrey, Treasurer. CR.

Assessments.				Epis. F.	Con. F.
$1056 50		Brought forward..................		$3112 75	$1194 48
Apr. 1870	15 00	LEBANON,	Lebanon,	St. Luke.........	9 50	5 50
Dec. 1870	25 00	LEHIGH,	Allentown.	Grace.........	16 00	9 00
Oct. 1870	5 00		Allentown Furnace.	Mediator......	3 00	2 00
Nov. 1870	60 00	LUZERNE,	Wilkesbarre,	St. Stephen	35 00	25 00
	5 00		"	St. Clement......		
Mar. 1871	20 00		Carbondale,	Trinity.........	13 00	7 00
May 1870	25 00		Pittston,	St. James, 1868....	16 00	9 00
			"	" 1869	16 00	9 00
Apr. 1871			"	" 1870..	17 00	8 00
	30 00		Scranton,	St. Luke......		
Jan. 1871	12 00		Eckley,	St. James	8 00	4 00
Apr. 1871	10 00		White Haven,	St. Paul......	6 00	4 00
			Plymouth,	St. Peter.........		
Apr. 1871	5 00		Hazleton,	St. Peter.........	3 00	2 00
	20 00	LYCOMING,	Muncy,	St. James......		
Apr. 1870	40 00		Williamsport,	Christ.........	25 00	15 00
Feb. 1871	20 00		"	Trinity, 1869..	7 00	3 00
			"	" 1870	14 00	6 00
May 1870	5 00		Montoursville,	Our Saviour.....	2 20	1 20
Dec. 1870	10 00	MIFFLIN,	Lewistown,	St. Mark......	6 00	4 00
Oct. 1870	35 00	MONTGOMERY,	White Marsh,	St Thomas......	22 00	13 00
	15 00		Perkiomen,	St. James, 1868..	4 75	2 75
May 1870			"	" 1869..	11 00	7 00
Nov. 1870	15 00		"	" 1870..	9 00	6 00
	60 00		Norristown,	St. John......	38 00	22 00
May 1870	20 00		Pottstown,	Christ, 1869......	13 00	7 00
Apr. 1871	20 00		"	" 1870......	13 00	7 00
Apr. 1871	25 00		Bridgeport,	Swedes'.'......	17 00	8 00
Apr. 1871	50 00		Lower Merion,	Redeemer.......	32 00	18 00
	25 00		Jenkintown,	Our Saviour......		
Apr. 1871	5 00		Conshohocken,	Calvary, 1869....	3 00	2 00
			"	" 1870....	3 00	2 00
Apr. 1871	75 00		Cheltenham,	St. Paul.........	48 00	27 00
Nov. 1870	30 00		Lower Merion,	St. John......	18 00	12 00
May 5	5 00		Upper Providence,	St. Paul, 1869....	3 49	1 42
Jan. 1871	5 00		"	" 1870....	3 00	2 00
			Gwynnedd,	Messiah.........		
Dec. 1870	40 00	MONTOUR,	Danville,	Christ.........	25 00	15 00
	5 00		Derry,	St. James......		
	25 00	NORTHAMP'N,	Easton,	Trinity.........		
	30 00		Bethlehem,	Nativity.........		
May 1870	12 00	NORTHUMB'D,	Sunbury,	St. Matthew, 1869	5 34	3 26
			"	" 1871	7 00	5 00
Nov. 1870	6 00		Northumberland,	St. Mark........	4 00	2 00
			Milton,	Christ........		
	8 00		Shamokin,	Trinity. ...		
Feb. 1871	140 00	PHILADELPHIA,	Philadelphia,	Christ......... ...	90 00	50 00
April	210 00		"	St. Peter.......	134 00	76 00
Dec. 1870	80 00		"	St. Paul.......	51 00	29 00
Dec. 1870	150 00		"	St. James.......	95 00	55 00
Nov. 1870	280 00		"	St. Stephen	180 00	100 00
Apr. 1870	210 00		"	St. Andrew......	125 00	70 00
Mar. 1870	225 00		"	Grace......	143 00	82 00
Mar. 1870	275 00		"	Epiphany.......	175 00	100 00
	25 00		"	Ascension......		
Dec. 1870	225 00		"	St. Luke.......	143 00	82 00
May 1870	180 00		"	Atonement.......	115 00	65 00
Dec. 1870	300 00		"	St. Mark.......	191 00	109 00
Oct. 1870	60 00		"	Covenant......	35 00	25 00
	5 00		"	St. Thomas.....		
Mar. 1871	25 00		"	Holy Apostles...	17 00	8 00
	5 00		"	Holy Commun'n		
	5 00		"	Good Shepherd..		
Nov. 1870	10 00		"	Messiah.........	6 00	4 00
May 1870	75 00		"	Mediator........	47 00	28 00
Apr. 1871	150 00		"	St. Clement.....	64 00	36 00
Dec. 1870	300 00		"	Holy Trinity....	191 00	109 00
Nov. 1870	45 00		Oxford,	Trinity.........	28 50	16 50
$4854 50			Carried forward...................		$5419 51	$2515 11

	Epis. F.	Con. F.
......	$5419 52	$2515 11
All Saints.......	29 00	16 00
..erty, St. John, 186....	9 00	6 00
" 1870....	9 00	6 00
Advent.........	70 00	30 00
Calvary..........	6 00	4 00
Trinity...........	38 00	22 00
Evangelist.......	19 00	11 00
Gloria Dei.......	38 00	22 00
St. John Ev. 1869	13 00	7 00
St. Luke.........	83 00	47 00
Christ...........	111 00	64 00
St. John Baptist		
Calvary.........	64 00	36 00
St. Michael.....	19 00	11 00
-. .ur:phia, St. Mary........	27 00	16 00
St. Andrew.....	9 00	6 00
Our Saviour.....	76 00	44 00
Good Shepherd.	3 00	2 00
-- -.1:, St. Matthew,1869	32 00	18 00
" 1870	32 00	18 00
Emmanuel......	32 00	18 00
.. .arden, St. Phillp........	95 00	55 00
Nativity.........	64 00	36 00
st. Jude.........	22 00	13 00
Bishop's Ch. 1869	13 00	7 00
" 1870	13 00	7 00
. Redemption,1869	6 00	4 00
" 1870	6 00	4 00
. St. Matthew,1869	27 00	16 00
" 1870	27 00	16 00
Incarnation.....	32 00	18 00
. ..sburg, Emmanuel......	30 00	20 00
...ssing, St. James.......	30 00	20 00
St. George......	3 00	2 00
...ayunk, St. David, 1869..	16 86	9 07
" 1870..	29 00	16 00
...nut Hill, St. Paul.........	64 00	36 00
a. ..uensing, All Saints.......	25 00	15 00
" Our Saviour.....		
" Crucifixion.....		
..kford, St. Mark........	50 00	25 00
.. .h Penn, S.James theLess	16 00	9 00
...h Penn. Zion..............	16 00	9 00
..rt Richmond, Messiah........	3 00	2 50
...borough, St. Timothy....	13 00	7 00
" St. Alban, 1869..	3 50	2 00
" 1870..	3 00	2 50
..stleton, St. Luke.........	3 00	2 00
..anchtown, House of Prayer	7 00	3 00
..: Alry, Grace............	13 00	7 00
...nkford Road, St. John..........		
t..stonville, St. James.		
..nderton, St. George	7 00	3 00
..sing Sun, Resurrection....		
..cony, Holy Innocents..	3 00	2 00
..ridesburg, St. Stephen......	3 00	2 00
..ttville. Trinity, balance.	50 00	30 00
..inersville, St. Paul.........	4 00	3 00
..t. Clair, Holy Apostles...	4 50	2 50
..chuylkill Haven, St. James........		
..lahanoy, Faith, acct. 1869.	3 00	2 00
" 1870....	3 00	2 00
..amaqua, Calvary.........		
..ressona, Grace...........		
..shland. St. John, 1870....	4 00	3 00
..ew Milford, St. Mark........	4 00	3 00
..lontrose, St. Paul.........	14 00	8 00
..reat Bend, Grace........	3 00	2 00
Carried forward..................	**$6871 39**	**$3344 18**

Convention Diocese Pa. in Acc't with B. G. Godfrey, Treasurer. CR.

Assessments.					Epis. F.	Con. F.
	$7145 50		Brought forward..................		$6871 39	$3344 18
Nov. 1870	5 00	SUSQUEHANNA,	Springfield,	St. Andrew......	3 00	2 00
			Dundaff,	St. James.......		
May 1871	10 00	TIOGA,	Wellsboro,	St. Paul.........	6 00	4 00
Jan. 1871	5 00		Tioga,	St. Andrew...	3 00	2 00
Oct. 1870	5 00		Blossburg,	St. Luke........	3 00	2 00
May 1870	5 00		Mansfield,	St. James.......	2 50	1 50
Jan. 1870	50 00	WAYNE,	Honesdale,	Grace...........	32 00	18 00
Dec. 1870	5 00		Pleasant Mount,	St. Paul........	3 00	2 00
	3 00		Salem,	St. John........		
	3 00		Sterling,	Zion............		
Mar. 1871	35 00	YORK,	York,	St. John........	23 00	12 00
	$7271 50					

		Epis. F.	Con. F.
1870 **May**	A. DOZ LEGACY—Interest 6 months' ground rent from John Laws. due 1st inst., in coin ....$12 00 Premium..................... 1 72		
		13 72	
July	GENERAL FUND—6 months' interest on $2000 5-20's U. S. loans, 1881................. ....$60 00 Premium 11-29............................. 6 90		
		66 90	
July	Returned from Philadelphia Safe Deposit and Trust Co....	2 50	
August	Through G. W. Taylor, Esq., Treasurer, 6 months' interest on $100 Philadelphia 6 per cent. loan.........	3 00	
	6 mos. int. on $8128 29 Pennsylvania 6 per cent loan....	243 85	
	HUTCHINS LEGACY—$1888 35 Pennsylvania 6 per cent. loan	56 65	
	PILMORE LEGACY—$7983 36, interest on Pennsylvania 6 per cent. loan...............................	239 50	
	Returned by J. H. Nichols..........	2 33	
Sept.	GENERAL FUND—6 months' interest on $25,350 Pennsylvania 6 per cent loans.....	760 50	
	KOHNE LEGACY—$150 6 per cent. loan.............	4 50	
	A. DOZ LEGACY—$2000 6 per cent. loan.............	60 00	
	GENERAL FUND—$1000 5 per cent. loan.............	25 00	
	Premium, 13⅜%.................	3 34	
1871 **Jan.**	GENERAL FUND: U. S. 10-40's Sept. 1st....................$25 00 " 5-20's. Nov. 1st..................... 30 00 " 5-20's. Jan. 1st..................... 60 00 Premium 10⅛%....................... 12 22		
		127 22	
	FUND FOR SUPPORT OF EPISCOPATE—Through G. W. Taylor, Esq., Treas., 6 months' int. $100 6 per cent. loan.......	3 00	
	GENERAL FUND—6 months' interest on $2400 Philadelphia City Loan.........................$72 00 Less State Tax. .... 3 60 ————$68 40		
	KOHNE LEGACY—$4600 Philadelphia City loan.$138 00 Less....................... 6 90 ————$131 10 Premium, gold..................... 20 95		
		220 45	
Feb.	GENERAL FUND—6 months' interest on $25,350 Pennsylvania 6 per cent. loan......................	760 50	
	KOHNE LEGACY—$150 Pennsylvania 6 per cent. loan...	4 50	
	A. DOZ LEGACY—$2000 " " "	60 00	
Feb. 2	GENERAL FUND—$1000 5 per cent. loan.............$25 00 Premium, 11½ per cent............................. 2 87		
		27 87	
	Fund for the Support of the Episcopate, through G. W. Taylor, Esq., Treasurer, 6 months' interest on $8128 29 Pennsylvania 6 per cent. loan......................	243 85	
	HUTCHINS LEGACY, through G. W. Taylor, Esq., Treasurer, $1886 Pennsylvania 6 per cent. loan......................	56 65	
	PILMORE LEGACY, through G. W. Taylor, Esq., Treasurer, $7983 35 Pennsylvania 6 per cent. loan..................	239 50	
	Carried forward.................................	10172 22	$3337 68

... with B. G. Godfrey, Treasurer.

	Epis. F.	Con. F.
....	$10,172 22	$3387 68
..... due July 1st, 1869, on		
... loan........$72 00		
.... 3 69		
——— 68 40		
...ivania 6 per		
...............$138 00		
.... 6 90		
———131 10		
... . 25 94		
	$225 44	
round rent from Mrs. M. E.		
....	144 00	
...und rent from John Law-		
...................$12 00		
...remium 6 per cent.... 72		
	12 72	
...nd rent from Mrs. M.		
.....................$36 00		
...xes................... 10 00		
	26 00	
...terest on $1000 U. S.		
...................$25 00		
...ent................... 30 00		
.... 6 05		
	61 05	
....	8 75	
....	2 66	
...ust Co., to date...........	64 52	
...................$ 26		
.... 8		
		34
	$10,717 36	$3388 02
....	$2408 07	$919 42

Convention Diocese Pa. in Acc't with B. G. Godfrey, Treasurer.   DR.

		Epis. C.	Con. F.
1870 May	Paid travelling expenses of the following named Clergymen in attendance on the Annual Convention of 1870:		
	Rev. George P. Hopkins.....................................		15 00
	" G. W. Shinn..		12 00
	" M. L. Kern..		8 00
	" E. L. Lightner.......................................		6 50
	" R. H. Brown..		2 50
	" J. L. Heysinger......................................		2 00
	" R. H. Brown..		8 25
	" W. C. Leverett.......................................		7 00
	" F. Byllesby..		14 50
	" John Long...		7 50
	" Peter Russell..		2 70
	" W. R. Stockton.......................................		1 00
	" C. Hare..		9 50
	" W. S. Heaton..		14 20
	" J. H. Jerome..		10 65
	" D. Washburn...		8 00
	" Edmund Leaf...		1 50
	" Samuel H. Meade.....................................		9 90
	" R. Graham...		1 50
	" W. R. Gries...		4 00
	" J. Thompson Carpenter		3 00
	" E. A. Warriner......................................		10 85
	" A. A. Marple..		8 00
	" J. H. Millett.......................................		3 30
	" Thomas W. Martin....................................		7 00
	" James Walker..		5 50
	" J. Karcher..		1 80
	" G. C. Bird..		15 00
	" G. J. Burton..		8 40
	" W. G. Hawkins.......................................		9 70
	" C. W. Thomson.......................................		4 00
	" William Paret.......................................		12 00
	" H. Baldy..		2 00
	" M. Barrows..		21 82
	" L. W. Gibson..		12 90
	" A. P. Brush...		12 00
	" B. J. Douglass......................................		3 00
	" W. P. Orrick..		6 00
	" Thomas H. Cullen....................................		6 20
	" F. W. Bartlett......................................		3 30
	" Thomas Barrows......................................		2 00
	" Henry R. Smith......................................		3 10
	" J. S. Reed..		4 00
	" W. P. Lewis...		2 80
	" E. Christian..		2 90
	" L. Coleman..		3 30
	" J. P. Hammond.......................................		1 80
	Paid Salary of the Bishop of the Diocese to July 1st, 1871..	$6500 00	
	Paid Salary Rev. J. A. Childs, D. D., Bishop's Secretary..	500 00	
	Rev. J. A. Childs, D.D., postage..........................	20 00	
	Paid James Erickson, Desk for Convention.................		3 65
	Paid Wm. Anderson, Sexton................................		29 25
June 3	Tax Episcopal Residence, by order of the Convention, City and State, 1870................................		325 45
	Paid John Short, attending Standing Committee............		15 00
	Paid J. H Nichols, " "		8 75
	Paid James Hogan, Stationery for Convention..............		19 43
	Paid W. W. Carter, repairing Episcopal Residence........		36 20
	Paid Philadelphia Trust and Safe Deposit Company, use of Vault...............................$15 00		
	Use of Tin Box....................... 2 25		
	Deposit papers....................... 1 00		
		18 25	
	Paid Rent of Episcopal Rooms, 12 mos. rent, June 1871....		250 00
	Paid Water Rent Episcopal Residence, 1870....		17 25
	Paid A. H. Nichols, postage of Convention................		6 75
	Paid Rev. J. A. Childs, D.D., postage,....................		15 00
	Carried forward................................	$7038 25	$1048 60

DR.   *Convention Diocese Pa. in Acc't with B. G. Godfrey, Treasurer.*

1870		Epis. F.	Con. F.
	Brought forward..................................	$7038 25	$1048 60
June 3	Paid Rev. J. A. Childs, postage of Diocese.................		15 00
	Paid Rev. J. A. Childs, postage of Convention............		20 00
Oct. 6	Paid M. B. Helmuth 6 months' ground rent, gold..$180 00		
1871	Premium, 1.13...................................	23 40	203 40
April 8,	Paid M B. Helmuth, ground rent, gold...........$180 00		
	Premium...................................	20 25	200 25
	Paid J. H. Hover, stationery...............................		8 35
	Paid King & Baird, Standing Committee................		2 50
Oct. 1870	Paid John Short, Historical Committee.................		30 00
Jan. 6, '71	Paid M'Calla & Stavely, printing Journal of Convention..		1155 50
Nov. 1870	Paid travelling and incidental expenses of Bishop to		
	date...	175 00	133 67
May 1871	Paid Enterprise Insurance Co., for $4000 insurance on		
	furniture of Episcopal Residence..................	40 00	
Nov 30,'70	Paid Mary B. Reed, written copy of Convention Journal,		
	1870......................................		25 00
July 1, '70	Paid William Anderson, Sexton.....................		6 00
Dec. 9, '70	Paid Bishop Stevens for repairs made on Episcopal Resi-		
	dence...................................	279 99	
	Paid James Hogan, sundries...................		13 48
Apr.7, '71	Paid John Clayton, Secretary Standing Committee, as		
	per order...........................		10 50
Apr.8, '71	Paid Tax on Episcopal Residence, No. 1633 Spruce Street		
	(for 1871)...........................$357 40		
	Water rent.............................	15 00	
		372 40	
	Balance for support of the Episcopate....................	2408 07	
	Balance for expenses of the Convention.................		919 42
		$10,717 36	$3388 02

The Episcopal Fund of the Diocese of Pennsylvania amounts to Thirty-seven Thousand Five Hundred (37,500) Dollars, namely: for the GENERAL FUND, $32,750, and for the KOHNE LEGACY $4750, as follows:

```
·  Pennsylvania Six per cent. Loan......$25 350
        "        Five        "      ......   1000
   Philadelphia Six          "      ......   2400
   U. S. Six per cent. Loan, 1881..........   2000
    "    "         "    1865-1885.....   1000
    "    Five      "    1864-1904.....   1000
                                        ------- $32,750
   Philadelphia Six per cent. Loan.......   4600
   Pennsylania   "        "      ........    150
                                        -------   4750
```

Total (exclusive of cash balance, $2408 07) $37,500

Say, Thirty-seven Thousand Five Hundred Dollars, exclusive of Twenty-four Hundred and Eight Dollars and Seven cents in money.

Convention Diocese Pa. in Acc't with B. G. Godfrey, Treasurer.

The undersigned, appointed by the Standing Committee to audit the accounts of the Treasurer of the Convention, have examined the same, compared the vouchers with the various entries, and find them correct, leaving a balance in his hands of Three Thousand Three Hundred and Twenty-seven Dollars and Forty-nine Cents ($3327 49), of which sum Two Thousand Four Hundred and Eight Dollars and Seven Cents $2408 07) is deposited in the Philadelphia Trust and Safe Deposit Company to the credit of the Episcopal Fund, and Nine Hundred and Nineteen Dollars and Forty-two Cents ($919 42) in the Philadelphia National Bank for the Expenses of Convention.

They have also examined the securities in which the funds of the Episcopate are invested, and find Certificates of Loans, namely: Twenty-seven Thousand Five Hundred (27,500) Dollars of the Six per cent. Loan, and One Thousand (1000) Dollars of the Five per cent. Loan (due July 1st, 1870), all of the State of Pennsylvania; Seven Thousand (7000) Dollars of Philadelphia City Six per cent. Loan (taxable); Two Thousand (2000) Dollars United States Six per cent. Loan, due 1881; One Thousand (1000) Dollars U. S. Six per cent. Loan, May 1865-85, and One Thousand (1000) Dollars Five per cents Loan, Ten-Forty; making a total of Thirty-nine Thousand Five Hundred (39,500) Dollars. All of this sum composes the GENERAL FUND, with the exception of $4600 Philadelphia City Loan, and $150 Penna. Six per cent. Loan, which constitute the KOHNE LEGACY, and $2060 Penn. Six per cent. Loan, which forms part of the ANDREW DOZ TRUST.

RECAPITULATION:

GENERAL FUND:

Pennsylvania Six per cent. Loan,	$25,350	
" Five "	1000	
Philadelphia Six " (taxable)	2400	
U. S. Loan, Six per cent., 1881,	2000	
" " 1865–1885.	1000	
" Five " 10-40,	1000	
		32,750

KOHNE LEGACY:

Philadelphia Six per cent. Loan, taxable,	$4600	
Pennsylvania Six per cent. Loan,	150	
		4750

ANDREW DOZ TRUST:

Pennsylvania Six per cent. Loan,	2000
	$39,500

Philadelphia, May 6th, 1871.

THOMAS ROBINS,
WM. F. GRIFFITTS.

ASSESSMENTS UNPAID MAY, 1871.

				1868	1869	1870
BEDFORD.	Bedford,	St. James,	Rev. Wm. Jarrett.			5 00
BRADFORD,	Athens	Trinity,			$ 5 00	6 00
CHESTER,	Honeybrook,	St. Mark,	Vacant.			5 00
CLINTON,	Lock Haven,	St. Paul,	Rev. Geo. S. Teller.	$ 5 50	5 00	30 00
COLUMBIA.	Bloomsburg,	St. Paul,	Rev. John Hewitt.			35 00
HUNTINGDON.	Huntingdon,	St. John,	vacant	5 50	5 00	5 00
LANCASTER,	Leacock,	Christ,	Rev. H. R. Smith.			5 00
MONTGOMERY,	Jenkintown,	Our Saviour,	Rev. R. F. Colton.			25 00
NORTHAMPTON,	Easton,	Trinity,	Rev. J. S. Reed.			25 00
NORTHUMBERL'D,	Shamokin,	Trinity,	Rev. A. H. Boyle.	4 80	8 00	8 00
PHILADELPHIA,	Hestonville,	St. James,	J. M. Cadmus, Warden			7 00
	Frankford Rd.,	St. James,	Rev. Jos. A. Nock.	11 00	5 00	5 00
SCHUYLKILL,	Tamaqua,	Calvary.		20 00	10 00	10 00
	Cressona	Grace,	vacant.	5 00		10 00
SUSQUEHANNA,	Springville,	St. Andrew,	vacant.	11 00	5 00	
WAYNE,	Salem,	St. John,	Rev. R. H. Brown.			3 00

APPENDIX G.

REPORT OF TRUSTEES OF CHRISTMAS FUND FOR DISABLED CLERGYMEN, AND THE WIDOWS AND CHILDREN OF DECEASED CLERGYMEN.

The Trustees of the Christmas Fund for Disabled Clergymen, and the Widows and Children of Deceased Clergymen, respectfully report—

That the receipts from the Offertory at the celebration of the Holy Communion upon Christmas Day, amounted to five thousand four hundred and Seventy dollars and thirty-five cents ($5470.35), being an increase from last year of five hundred and ninety-three dollars and fifty-six cents ($593.56), and from interest received from the reserve fund and from deposits, two hundred and eighty-six dollars and fifty-eight cents ($286.58), making the total of receipts, five thousand seven hundred and fifty-six dollars and ninety-three cents ($5756.93).

The appropriations made so far for the year, amount to four thousand nine hundred and eighty-seven dollars and fifty cents ($4987.50), being for the regular stipends to four (4) Clergymen, to six (6) widows of Clergymen, and to three (3) families of deceased Clergymen; and for special appropriations made in ten instances.

In presenting this report of the operations of the Trust, the Trustees can only reiterate their already often expressed opinion of the great value of this charity of the Church, and of the vast amount of good it has been the means of doing to those, who, but for its care, would have been left to contend alone with the sickness and poverty and sorrow of their lot.

By order of the Board.

JOHN S. NEWBOLD, Sec'y.

Philadelphia, May 9, 1871.

48

APPENDIX H.

ASSESSMENT OF CHURCHES FOR THE CONVENTION FUND, EMBRACING THE SUPPORT OF THE EPISCOPATE, AS WELL AS THE EXPENSES OF THE DIOCESAN AND GENERAL CONVENTIONS, FOR THE YEAR 1871, PAYABLE ON OR BEFORE DECEMBER 31, 1871, TO BENJAMIN G. GODFREY, TREASURER, 245 MARKET ST.

COUNTY.	CHURCH.	PLACE.	RECTOR OR WARDEN.	AM'T.
Adams........	Christ.............	Huntingdon ..		$ 6 00
Bedford..........	St. James........	Bedford........	Rev. Mr. Jarrett........	
Berks...........	St. Gabriel........	Douglassville..	" J. Karcher........	12 50
"	Christ..........	Reading........	" J. P. Hammond....	100 00
"	St. Barnabas....	"	" J. Karcher.........	6 00
"	St. Thomas......	Morgantown ..	" H. R. Smith.......	6 00
"	St. Michael......	Birdsboro......	" E. Leaf..........	6 00
Blair............	St. Luke.........	Altoona........	" J. J. A. Morgan....	15 00
Bradford........	St. Matthew......	Pike		6 00
"	Christ...........	Towanda......	" Wm. McGlathery..	60 00
"	St. Paul.........	Troy	" G. P. Hopkins.....	8 00
"	Trinity..........	Athens		7 50
Bucks...........	St. James........	Bristol.........	Rev. J. H. Drumm, D.D.	50 00
"	St. Luke........	Newtown.......	G. W. Jenks, Warden...	6 00
"	St. Andrew......	Yardleyville..		6 00
"	Grace..........	Hulmeville	Rev. T. Burrows.......	6 00
"	Trinity.........	Centreville....	" H. Baldy........	6 00
"	St. Paul........	Doylestown....	" "	20 00
Carbon..........	St. Mark.......	Mauch Chunk..	" L. Coleman........	62 00
"	St. Philip.......	Summit........	" "	6 00
Centre...........	Trinity..........	Phillipsburg....	" S. H. Meade........	16 00
"	St. John........	Bellefonte.....	" H. J. W. Allen.....	25 00
Chester..........	St. Peter	Great Valley..	" E. A. Tortat.......	12 00
"	St. John........	New London..	Thos. M. Charlton, Wrdn	6 00
"	St. Mary........	Warwick.......	D. B. Mauger, Warden..	6 00
"	St. John........	Pequea........	Rev. H. R. Smith.......	21 00
"	St. Paul........	W. Whiteland.	" A. E. Tortat.......	9 00
"	St. Andrew......	W. Vincent...		6 00
"	St. Mark.......	Honeybrook ..		6 00
"	Holy Trinity.....	West Chester..	Rev. John Bolton......	62 00
"	St. Peter.......	Phœnixville..	" W. R. Stockton....	25 00
"	St. James........	Downingtown.	" R. F. Innis........	25 00
"	St. James........	W. Marlboro..		
"	Trinity..........	Coatesville	Rev. G. G. Field.......	15 00
Clinton..........	St. Paul........	Lock Haven...	" George S. Teller....	37 00
Columbia........	St. Paul........	Bloomsburg....	" John Hewitt	44 00
"	Holy Trinity......	Centralia......	" D. Washburn	6 00
Cumberland.....	St. John........	Carlisle.......	" W. C. Leverett....	50 00
Dauphin.........	St. Stephen.......	Harrisburg	" R. J Keeling, D.D.	55 00
"	St. Paul........	"	Thos. Fitzsimmons, Wdn	6 00
Delaware........	St. Paul........	Chester........	Rev. H. Brown.......	62 00
"	St. Martin	Marcus Hook.	" J. S. Pearce........	25 00
"	St. David	Radnor........	" W. F. Halsey......	30 00
"	St John........	Concord	" J. B. Clemson, D.D.	12 00
"	Calvary..........	Rockdale......	" Wm. Ely..........	12 00
"	Christ..........	Media........	" S. W. Hallowell....	30 00
Franklin........	Emmanuel.......	Mont Alto..		
"	Trinity..........	Chambersburg	Rev. W. G. Hawkins....	6 00
Huntingdon.....	St. John.........	Huntingdon..		6 00
Lancaster........	St. James........	Lancaster.....	Rev. E. Shippen Watson	95 00

| | | | | $1105 00 |

Assessment of Churches for the Convention Fund, 1871.

COUNTY.	CHURCH.	PLACE.	RECTOR OR WARDEN.	AM'T.
			Amount forward........	$1105 00
Lancaster......	St. John.........:	Lancaster......	Rev. T. B. Barker......	30 00
"	Bangor.........	Churchtown...	" H. R. Smith......	6 00
"	Christ.........	Leacock......	Wm. Bender, Warden...	6 00
"	All Saints........	Paradise......	E. W. Eshleman, Warden	12 00
"	St. Paul.........	Columbia.....	Rev. Geo. H. Kirkland...	20 00
"	St. John.........	Marietta......	S. F. Eagle, Warden....	20 00
"	Hope.........	Mt. Hope......	Rev. A. M. Abel......	
"	Grace.........	Gap Mines.....		6 00
"	St. Paul.........	Manheim......	Rev. W. S. Heaton.....	6 00
Lebanon......	St. Luke........	Lebanon......	" A. M. Abel......	20 00
Lehigh.........	Grace.........	Allentown.....	" W. R. Gries......	30 00
"	Mediator.........	"	" F. W. Bartlett......	6 00
Luzerne......	St. Stephen........	Wilkesbarre..	" R. H. Williamson..	75 00
"	St. Clement......	S. Wilkesbarre	E. W. Sturdevant, Wrdn	6 00
"	Trinity.........	Carbondale....		25 00
"	St. James........	Pittston......		30 00
"	St. Luke.........	Scranton.....	Rev. A. A. Marple....	37 00
"	St. James........	Eckley......	" James Walker.....	15 00
"	St. Paul.........	White Haven..	" L. Coleman.....	12 00
"	St. Peter.........	Plymouth......		
"	St. Peter.........	Hazleton......	" C. H. Van Dyne..	6 00
Lycoming......	St. James........	Muncy........	" A. P. Brush.....	25 00
"	Christ.........	Williamsport..	" W. Paret, D. D...	50 00
"	Trinity.........	"	" Arthur Brooks...	25 00
"	Ch. of our Saviour.	Montoursville,.	James Rawle, Warden..	6 00
Mifflin......	St. Mark.........	Lewistown.....	Rev. T. W. Martin.....	12 00
Montgomery....	St. James.........	Perkiomen.....	" P. Russell......	20 00
"	St. Thomas......	Whitemarsh...	" P. W. Stryker....	45 00
"	St. John.........	Norristown....	" C. E. McIlvaine...	75 00
"	Christ.........	Pottstown.....	" B. McGann......	25 00
"	Redeemer......	Lower Merion.	" E. L. Lycett......	62 00
"	Our Saviour......	Jenkintown....	" R. Francis Colton...	30 00
"	Calvary.........	Conshohocken.	" T. W. Davidson...	6 00
"	St. Paul.........	Cheltenham....	" E. W. Appleton...	90 00
"	St. John.........	Lower Merion.	David Morgan, Warden.	37 00
"	St. Paul.........	L. Providence.	Rev. J. E. Kudderow....	6 00
Montour......	Christ.........	Danville.......	" J. Milton Peck.....	50 00
"	St. James........	Exchange......	" A. P. Brush......	6 00
Northampton...	Trinity.........	Easton.........	" J. S. Reed........	25 00
"	Nativity.........	Bethlehem.....	" C. Whitehead.....	37 00
Northumberland	St. Matthew......	Sunbury......	" G. J. Burton......	15 00
"	St. Mark.........	Northumberl'd	" Wm. Moore........	7 00
"	Christ.............	Milton......		
"	Trinity.........	Shamokin......	Rev. A. H. Boyle......	10 00
Philadelphia ...	Christ.........	Philadelphia...	" E. A. Foggo, D.D...	125 00
"	St. Peter......	"	" T. F. Davies, D.D...	250 00
"	St. Paul......	"	" R. T. Roach, D.D....	75 00
"	St. James........	"	" H. J. Morton, D. D.	200 00
"	St. Stephen......	"	" Wm. Rudder, D.D...	325 00
"	St. Andrew......	"	" W. F. Paddock, D.D	250 00
"	Grace......	"	" W. Suddards, D.D...	250 00
"	Epiphany......	"	" R. Newton, D. D..	300 00
"	Ascension........	"	Alfred Zantzinger, Wrdn	30 00
"	St. Luke........	"	" M.A.DeWHowe,DD.	300 00
"	Atonement......	"	" B. Watson, D.D....	200 00
"	St. Mark........	"	" E. A. Hoffman, DD.	350 00
"	Mediator........	"	" S. E. Appleton....	100 00
"	St. Clement......	"	" H. G. Batterson,DD	125 00
"	Holy Trinity......	"	" T. A. Jaggar......	350 00
"	Covenant........	"	" C. E. Murray.......	75 00
"	St. Thomas......	"	" W. J. Alston.......	6 00
"	Trinity.........	Oxford......	" E. Y. Buchanan,DD	50 00
"	All Saints........	Lower Dublin..	" F. W. Beasley, DD.	50 00
"	St. John........	Phila. N. L...	" Charles Logan.....	20 00
"	Advent........	"	" J. W. Claxton......	125 00
"	Calvary.........	"	" E. A. Foggo, D.D...	12 00
"	Trinity.........	Southwark	" J. Y. Burk........	75 00
"	Evangelists........	"	" Jacob Miller.......	30 00
"	Gloria Dei........	"	" S. B. Simes........	60 00
				$5850 00

Assessment of Churches for the Convention Fund, for 1871.

COUNTY	CHURCH	PLACE.	RECTOR OR WARDEN.	A'MT.
			Amount forward........	$5850 50
Philadelphia....	St. John Evng'lst	Southwark....	Rev. C. L. Fischer......	12 00
"	Redemption.......	Fairmount....	" J. P. Du Hamel..	12 00
"	St. Philip.........	Spring Gard'n	" Percy Brown......	150 00
"	Nativity.........	"	" Wm. Newton......	125 00
"	St. Jude..........	"	" Wm. H Graff.....	50 00
"	Intercessor.......	"	" Owen E. Simpson..	25 00
"	St. Matthias......	"	" R. N. Thomas.....	50 00
"	Incarnation......	"	" J. D. Newlin.....	60 00
"	St. Matthew.......	Francisville..	" J. Blake Falkner.	60 00
"	St. Mary.........	West Phila....	" T. C. Yarnall, D. D.	50 00
"	St. Andrew......	"	" S. E. Smith.....	20 00
"	The Saviour.....	"	" J. H. Eccleston....	150 00
"	St. James.........	Hestonville....	Jas. M. Cadmus, Ward'n	8 00
"	Emmanuel......	Kensington....	Rev. W. H. Monroe....	60 00
"	All Saints........	Moyamensing..	" H. L. Duhring.....	50 00
"	Crucifixion		" W. H. Josephus....	
"	St. Luke.........	Germantown..	" Albra Wadleigh..	150 00
"	Christ...........	"	" T. S. Rumney, D. D	200 00
"	St. John Baptist ..	"	" W. N. Diehl.....	6 00
"	Calvary.........	"	" J. DeW. Perry....	125 00
"	St. Michael.......		" J. K. Murphy....	50 00
"	Emmanuel......	Holmesburg..	" D. C. Millett, D. D.	60 00
"	St. James	Kingsessing....	" C. R. Matson......	60 00
"	St. James, Less....	North Penn..	" Robert Ritchie...	30 00
"	St. Mark.........	Frankford ...	" D. S. Miller, D. D..	100 00
"	Messiah..........	Pt. Richmond..	" R. C. Evans........	6 00
"	Zion............	South Penn....	" C. W. Duane.....	20 00
"	St. David........	Manayunk....	" F. H. Bushnell.....	60 00
"	Resurrection......	Rising Sun....	" T. J. Davis......	
"	Trinity..........	Maylandville..	" J. H. Eccleston...	5 00
"	St. Paul.........	Chestnut Hill..	" J. A. Harris......	125 00
"	St. Timothy......	Roxborough...	" W. A. White.....	25 00
"	St. Alban.........	"	" Richardson Graham	6 00
"	St. Luke.........	Bustleton....	John Willian, Warden.	6 00
"	House of Prayer..	Branchtown..	Rev. A. T. McMurphey.	12 00
"	Grace..........	Mt. Airy......	" R. H. Edwards....	25 00
"	St. John........	Frankford Rd.	" J. A. Nock......	6 00
"	Holy Apostles....	Philadelphia..	" C. D. Cooper....	40 00
"	Holy Innocents...	Tacony......	" C. D. Millett, D.D..	6 00
"	St. Stephen......	Bridesburg...	" I. Martin......	6 00
"	Good Shepherd....	Philadelphia..	" J. W. Claxton.....	6 00
"	St. George........	Kenderton...	" J. R. Moore.....	15 00
"	Messiah..........	Philadelphia..	" Geo. Bringhurst...	12 00
"	St George........	"	" Chas. A. Maison...	6 00
Schuylkill......	Trinity	Pottsville....	" W. P. Lewis, D.D.	125 00
"	St. Paul.........	Minersville....	" J. T. Carpenter...	10 00
"	Holy Apostles.....	St. Clair....	George Rodgers, Ward'n	8 00
"	St. James.........	Schuylk'l H'n.		
"	Faith...........	Mahanoy......	Rev. J. W. Murphy.....	12 00
"	Calvary.........	Tamaqua......	....	5 00
"	Grace...........	Cressona......		
"	St. John.........	Ashland.......	Rev. D. Washburn.....	8 00
Susquehanna....	St. Mark..........	New Milford..	" J. A. Jerome....	8 00
"	St. Paul.........	Montrose......	" E. A. Warriner.....	25 00
"	Grace...........	Great Bend....	" J. A. Jerome....	6 00
"	St. Andrew......	Springville.....	B. Parke, Warden....	6 00
"	St. James........	Dundaff.....	Rev. H. C. Howard....	5 00
Tioga.........	St. Paul.........	Wellsboro	" J. K. Karcher....	20 00
"	St. Andrew......	Tioga......	" J. H. Babcock....	6 00
"	St. Luke.........	Blossburg....	" B. Hartley........	6 00
"	St. James........	Mansfield....	" N. Barrows.....	6 00
Wayne.........	Grace...........	Honesdale....	" O. W. Landreth...	60 00
"	St. Paul.........	Pleasant Mt...	" H. C. Howard....	6 00
"	St. John.........	Salem.........	" R. H. Brown......	4 00
"	Zion............	Sterling.......	" " "	4 00
York..........	St. John.........	York........	" W. P. Orrick......	42 00
				$8277 00

STATEMENT OF ACCOUNT

OF THE

...r of the Trustees of the Clergy Daughters' Fund.

.. on hand 18th of April, 1870.............................$434 82

... EIPTS for year.

... ne from Permanent Fund....................	$675 60	
...ium on Gold sold	70 19	
...rah Moorhead " Scholarships.................	600 00	
...nual Subscriptions...........................	230 00	
Collections in Churches..........................	;89 55	
Interest on Deposits...........................	11 70	
	———	$1777 04
		$2211 36

PAYMENTS.

For Board and Tuition of 10 Beneficiaries, Daughters of Clergymen of this Diocese................................. $1523 51

Balance on deposit with Pennsylvania Company for Insurance
on Lives, &c., April 10, 1871......................... $687 85

The PERMANENT FUND is invested as follows :

U. S. 5–20 Bonds 1862, Coupon.............................	$ 500	00
" " 1864, Registered............................	4000	00
U.S. 10–40 " Registered............................	1500	00
Philadelphia City Loan.......................................	4000	00
Chesapeake and Delaware Canal Co.'s Mortgage Loan........	1600	00
	$11,600	00

E. E.   *Philadelphia, April 10th, 1871.*

CHARLES W. CUSHMAN,

Treasurer.

⸱ PENNSYLVANIA.

⸱⸱⸱ Stevens, D. D., LL. D., Bishop.

⸱ THE TRIENNIAL REPORT.

⸱dates for Holy Orders.

	1869.	1870.	1871.	Total.
⸱⸱itted......	20	27	13	
....				49
....	14	13	10	37
....	4	5	7	16
....	6	6	3	15
....		1	1	2
....	16	6	12	34
....	6	15	11	32
....	16	23	21	60
....	14	20	18	52
....	5	4		9
....	208	217	217	
....	214	223	229	
....	9	8	4	21
⸱⸱th Convention..	8	8	4	21
....				198
⸱⸱⸱ and............	6	5	4	15
....	4	5	6	15
....				168
....				64,975
....				84
....	3244	3042	3031	9317
....	531	562	685	1778
....	3775	3604	3716	11,095
....	1795	1665	1905	5275
....	1017	967	973	2957
....	1772	1979	1833	5584
....	1677	1567	1900	
....	845	814	853	
....	2522	2381	2753	7656
....	938	1087	1230	3255
....	20,196	22,035	23,024	
....	2808	2899	3192	
....	30,676	29,923	31,336	
....	178	203	222	
....	3106	2429	3997	

DIOCESAN FINANCIAL REPORT.

	1869.	1870.	1871.	Total.
Episcopal Fund, capital...	$57,600 00	$60,131 34	$60,008 07	
Income...............	3625 62	3778 86	3706 06	$11,110 54

	ANNUAL INCOME.			
Expenditures of Convention, contingent expenses and Bishop's salary.	$11,042 76	$ 6606 34	$10,331 57	$ 27,981 17
Diocesan Missions.......	8821 04	7965 91	6870 23	23,657 18
Domestic "	24,087 56	27,915 57	28,578 79	80,521 72
Foreign "	19,600 62	15,717 86	15,762 64	51,081 12
Education for the Ministry	15,714 93	19,386 67	12,460 79	47,562 39
Aged and Infirm Clergy..	4841 02	4876 79	5736 93	15,274 74
Miscellaneous and Unspecified.........	367,916 23	513,935 61	545,714 19	1,427,566 03
Number of Parishes not reported to Convention.	29	7	21	

Aggregate Salaries of Clergy................................$ 239,468
  "   Value of Church Property...................... 5,474,200
Average Salary of Clergy................................   1,200

INDEX.

49

JOURNAL OF 1871.

NOTICE.

The next annual Convention of the Church in this Diocese, held in St. Andrew's Church, Philadelphia, on the second Tues. May, 1872, at 5 o'clock, P. M.

JOHN A. CHILDS, *Secretary,*
No. 708 *Walnut Street, Phila*

OFFICERS OF CHURCH INSTITUTIONS IN PHILADF

Treasurer of Episcopal and Convention Fund.
BENJ. G. GODFREY, 245 Market Street.

Treasurer of Christmas Fund,
R. P. McCULLAGH, 421 Chestnut Street.

Treasurer of Board of Missions of Diocese of Pennsylv.
JAMES S. BIDDLE, 1714 Locust Street.

Secretary of Hospital of the Protestant Episcopal Church, of B. Diocese of Pennsylvania, and of the Trustees and Overseers of
Rev. JOHN A. CHILDS, D.D., 708 Walnut

Treasurer of Hospital of Protestant Episcopal Cy.
GEORGE L. HARRISON, 101 S. Front F

Secretary of Bishop White Prayer Book Soch
JAMES S. BIDDLE, 1714 Locust St

Treasurer of Corporation for Relief of Widows and Children
J. SOMERS SMITH, 212 S. Fourth

Registrar of the Diocese, and Head Master of the Academy Church in Philadelphia,
Rev. J. W. ROBINS, 1821 De La

Treasurer of Clergy Daughters'
CHARLES W. CUSHMAN, 128 South

Treasurer of Evangelical Educatic
WM. C. HOUSTON, 1224 Ches

General Agent of Evangelical Educ
REV. R. C. MATLACK, 1224 C

Treasurer of Society for the Advancement of Cr
GEORGE W. TAYLOR, Fift!.

Corresponding Secret
Rev. E. A. FOGGO, D.D., 268

Treasurer of Society for the Promoting Ch
ZEBULON LOCKE, 1010

G,

mery.

JOURNAL

OF THE

PROCEEDINGS

OF THE

EIGHTY-EIGHTH CONVENTION

OF THE

Protestant Episcopal Church,

IN THE

DIOCESE OF PENNSYLVANIA,

HELD IN

ST. ANDREW'S CHURCH, PHILADELPHIA,

Commencing Tuesday, May 14, and ending Thursday, May 16, 1872.

PUBLISHED BY ORDER OF THE CONVENTION.

PHILADELPHIA:
M'CALLA & STAVELY, PRINTERS, N. E. COR. SIXTH AND COMMERCE STS.
1872.

Officers of the Convention.

BISHOP OF THE DIOCESE AND PRESIDENT EX-OFFICIO,
RT. REV. WM. BACON STEVENS, DD., LL.D.

SECRETARY AND PRIV. SECRETARY TO THE BISHOP,   ASSISTANT SECRETARY,
REV. JOHN A. CHILDS, D.D.,   DR. CHARLES R. KING,
708 Walnut Street.   Andalusia.

TREASURER OF THE EPISCOPAL AND CONVENTION FUNDS,
BENJAMIN G. GODFREY,
245 Market Street.

TREASURER OF THE CHRISTMAS FUND,
R. P. McCULLAGH,
421 Chestnut Street.

REGISTRAR,
REV. JAMES W. ROBINS.

STANDING COMMITTEE.
Rev. D. R. Goodwin, D. D., President.

Rev. G. Emlen Hare, D.D.,	Mr. Thomas Robins,
" H. J. Morton, D.D.,	" Richard S. Smith,
" B. Watson, D.D.,	" William F. Griffitts,
" J. H. Eccleston, D.D.,	" John Bohlen,

Mr. John Clayton, Secretary.

DEPUTIES TO THE GENERAL CONVENTION.

Rev. G. Emlen Hare, D.D.,	Mr. George L. Harrison,
" D. R. Goodwin, D.D.,	" Lemuel Coffin,

Mr. William Welsh.

TRUSTEES OF THE EPISCOPAL FUND.

Mr. Thomas Robins, ·	Mr. Isaac Hazlehurst,
" P. McCall,	" George Whitney,

Mr. John Welsh.

TRUSTEES OF CHRISTMAS FUND.

Mr. Thomas Robins,	Mr. John S. Newbold,
" John Welsh,	" Thomas H. Montgomery.

TRUSTEES OF FUND FOR EDUCATION OF SONS OF THE CLERGY.

Mr. Charles R. King,	Mr. H. H. Houston.

COMMITTEES

TO REPORT AT THE NEXT CONVENTION.

----:o:----

COMMITTEE ON CANONS.

REV. G. EMLEN HARE, D.D.,
" E. A. HOFFMAN, D.D.,
" B. WATSON, D.D.,

MR. R. R. MONTGOMERY,
" GEORGE W. HUNTER,
" JOHN BOHLEN.

----:o:----

COMMITTEE ON FEDERATE CONVENTION.

REV. G. EMLEN HARE, D.D.,
" E. A. HOFFMAN, D.D.,
" B. WATSON, D.D.,

MR. R. R. MONTGOMERY,
" GEORGE W. HUNTER,
" JOHN BOHLEN.

----:o:----

COMMITTEE ON CENTENNIAL CELEBRATION.

REV. T. F. DAVIES, D.D.,
" E. A. FOGGO, D.D.,
" R. B. CLAXTON, D.D.,

MR. FREDERICK FRALEY,
" CHARLES R. KING,
" JAMES M. AERTSEN.

----:o:----

COMMITTEE ON BISHOP POTTER MEMORIAL HOUSE.

REV. J. ANDREWS HARRIS,
" D. S. MILLER, D.D.,
" S. F. DAVIES, D.D.,

MR. LEMUEL COFFIN,
" CHARLES R. KING,
" ANDREW WHEELER.

----:o:----

COMMITTEE ON PARSONAGES.

REV. WM. RUDDER, D.D.,
" ALBRA WADLEIGH,

MR. S. K. ASHTON.

----:o:----

COMMITTEE ON PAROCHIAL HISTORY.

REV. JAMES W. ROBINS,
" J. ANDREWS HARRIS,
" JOHN BOLTON,
" E. Y. BUCHANAN, D.D.,

MR. FRANCIS C. YARNALL,
" THOMAS LATIMER,
" THOMAS H. MONTGOMERY,
" CHARLES WILLING.

·Clergymen of the Diocese of Pennsylvania,

AND OF THE

LAY DEPUTIES,

COMPOSING THE CONVENTION OF 1872.

Those printed in *Italic* were not members of the Convention.
Not present during the Convention, *
Removed from Diocese since Convention, †

CLERGY.

The Rt. Rev. WM. BACON STEVENS, D.D., LL.D., Bishop, 708 Walnut Street, Philadelphia.

Ashton, Rev. James W., Deacon, officiating, Philadelphia.

ALSTON, WM. J., Rector of St. Thomas' (African) Church, Philadelphia.

*ANTRIM, THOMAS M., Deacon, Philadelphia.

APPLETON, EDWARD W., Rector of St. Paul's Church, Cheltenham; P. O. Shoemakertown, Montgomery County.

APPLETON, SAMUEL E., Rector of the Church of the Mediator, Philadelphia.

BALDY, H., Rector of St. Paul's Church, Doylestown, and Trinity Church, Centreville, Bucks Co.

Batterson, H. G., D. D., Philadelphia.

Benedict, Charles E., Deacon.

BEASLEY, FREDERICK W., D. D., Rector of All Saints' Church, Lower Dublin; and Christ Chapel, Oak Grove; P. O. Eddington.

Bird, Gustavus C., Rector of St. Martin's Church, Marcus Hook, Delaware Co.

BOLTON, JOHN, Rector of the Church of the Holy Trinity, West Chester.

BISHOP, G. LIVINGSTONE, Rector of St. James' Church, Hestonville, Philadelphia.

Bowen, Robert James, Deacon.

BOWERS, WM. V., Philadelphia.

BRINGHURST, GEORGE, Rector of the Church of the Messiah, Philadelphia.

BRONSON, W. W., Assistant in St. Peter's Church, Philadelphia.

BROOKS, JAMES H. B., Deacon, Minister of St. George's Church, Philadelphia.

BROWN, HENRY, Rector of St. Paul's Church, Chester; and St. Luke's, South Chester.

BUCHANAN, EDWARD Y., D. D., Rector of Trinity Church, Oxford; and Chapel, Crescentville; P. O. Oxford Church.

Brinckloe, W. G. P., Deacon, Minister Grace Church, Hulmeville.

BURK, JESSE Y., Rector of Trinity Church, Southwark, Philadelphia.

Burton, John Henry, Deacon, Assistant in the Church of the Saviour, West Philadelphia.

Bush, Franklin L.

BUSHNELL, F. H., Rector of St. David's Church, Manayunk.

BUTLER, C. M., D.D., Professor in the Divinity School, West Philadelphia.

CANFIELD, FRANCIS D., Assistant Minister in St. Mark's Church, Philadelphia.

CHASE, R. F., Memorial Mission of St. Peter's Church.

CHILDS, JOHN A., D. D., Secretary of the Bishop; of the Board of Missions of the Diocese; of the Managers of the Episcopal Hospital; and of the Overseers of the Divinity School, Philadelphia.

Christian, Edmund.

CLAXTON, J. W., Rector of the Church of the Advent, Philadelphia.

CLAXTON, R. BETHELL, D. D., Professor in the Divinity School, Philadelphia.

*CLEMENTS, SAMUEL, Principal of Cheltenham Academy; P. O. Shoemakertown, Montgomery County.

*COLEMAN, JOHN, JR., Assistant Minister in St. Mark's Church, Philadelphia.

Colton, Chauncey, D. D., Philadelphia, residing at Jenkintown.

COLTON, RICHARD F., Professor in the Divinity School, Philadelphia; and Rector of the Church of Our Saviour, Jenkintown, Montgomery Co.

CONNOLLY, PIERCE, Rector of American Episcopal Chapel, Florence, Italy.

COOPER, CHARLES D., Rector of the Church of the Holy Apostles, Philadelphia.

Cull, Alexander H., Philadelphia.

Cummins, Alexander H.

†DAVIDSON, T. WILLIAM.

DAVIES, THOMAS F., D. D., Rector of St. Peter's Church, Philadelphia.

DAVIS, THOMAS J., Rector Emeritus of the Church of the Resurrection, Nicetown, Philadelphia.

*DIEHL, WILLIAM N., Rector of the Church of St. John the Baptist, Germantown, Philadelphia.

DOUGLASS, JACOB M., Philadelphia.

DRUMM, JOHN H., D. D., Rector of the Church of St. James the Greater, Bristol.

DUANE, CHARLES W., Rector of Zion Church, Philadelphia.

DU HAMEL, J. PLEASANTON, Rector of the Church of the Redemption, Philadelphia.

DUHRING, H. L., Rector of All Saints' Church, Philadelphia.

*DUPUY, CHARLES M., Philadelphia.

Durant, N. Joseph, Barbadoes, W. I.

DURBOROW, SAMUEL, General Superintendent of Protestant Episcopal City Missions, Philada.

Eastman, Rush S., Deacon.

ECCLESTON, JOHN H., D. D., Rector of the Church of the Saviour, West Philadelphia.

EDWARDS, ROBERT A., Rector of Grace Church, Mt. Airy, Philadelphia.

ELLIS, JAMES S., Assistant to the Rector of Grace Church, Philadelphia.

ELWYN, ALFRED, West Chester.

ELY, WILLIAM, Rector of Calvary Church, Rockdale; P. O. Lenni, Delaware Co.

ERBEN, WASHINGTON B., Rector of the Church of the Redeemer, for Seamen, Philadelphia.

EVANS, REES C., Rector of the Church of the Messiah, Port Richmond, Philadelphia.

FALKNER, J. BLAKE, Rector of St. Matthew's Church, Francisville, Philadelphia.

Fessenden, Charles E., Deacon.

FIELD, GEORGE G., Rector of the Church of the Trinity, Coatesville, Chester Co.

FISCHER, CHARLES L., Rector of St. John's Church, Lower Merion, Montgomery Co.

FOGGO, E. A., D. D., Rector of Christ Church, Philadelphia.

Fugett, J. P., Philadelphia.

Fullerton, Alexander, Philadelphia.

FUREY, JOHN G., City Missionary, Philadelphia.

GIBSON, L. W., Assistant Minister in St. James' Church, Philadelphia.

Goodfellow, John A., Rector of the Church of the Good Shepherd, Philadelphia.

GOODWIN, DANIEL R., D. D., LL.D., Professor in the Divinity School. Philadelphia.

GRAFF, W. HENRY, Rector of St. Jude's Church, Philadelphia.

GRAHAM, RICHARDSON, Philadelphia.

*HALL, RICHARD D.

HALLOWELL, SAMUEL D., Rector of Christ Church, Media (deceased).

HALSEY, WILLIAM F., Rector of St. David's Church, Radnor; P. O. Spread Eagle, Chester Co.

*HARD, ANSON B., Chester.

HARE, G. EMLEN, D. D., Professor in the Divinity School, Philadelphia.

*HARE, WM. HOBART, Secretary and General Agent of the Foreign Committee of the Board of Missions, New York.

HARRIS, J. ANDREWS, Rector of St. Paul's Church, Chestnut Hill.

HAY, H. P., D. D., Rector of the Church of the Good Shepherd, Radnor.

HAZLEHURST, SAMUEL, Philadelphia.

HENING, ED. W., in the service of the Committee of Foreign Missions, Philadelphia.

HEYSINGER, J. D., Rector of St. Timothy's Church, Philadelphia.

Hirst, Marmaduke, Norristown.

HODGE, GEORGE W., Assistant Minister of Christ Church, Philadelphia.

HOFFMAN, EUGENE A., D. D., Rector of St. Mark's Church, Philadelphia.

HUTCHINSON, THOMAS P., Assistant to the Rector of St. Peter's Church, Philadelphia.

INNIS, ROBERT F., Rector of St. James' Church, Downingtown.

JACKSON, W. F. B., Rector of the Church of St. John the Evangelist, Philadelphia.

JAGGAR, THOMAS A., Rector of the Church of the Holy Trinity, Philadelphia.

Jones, Pierre E., Deacon.

JOSEPHUS, WM. H., Minister of the Church of the Crucifixion, Philadelphia.

Keith, Ormes B. •

LOGAN, CHARLES, Rector of St. John's Church, Northern Liberties, Philadelphia

Louderback, Alfred, Philadelphia.

LYCETT, EDWARD L., Rector of the Church of the Redeemer, Lower Merion; P. O. Cabinet, Montgomery county.

MACKIE, ROBERT, City Missionary, Philadelphia.

MAISON, CHARLES A., Rector of St. James' Church, Kingsessing, Philadelphia.

MARTIN, ISAAC, Rector of St. Stephen's Church, Bridesburg.

MATLACK, R. C., General Secretary of the Evangelical Education Society, Philadelphia.

McGANN, BYRON, Rector of Christ Church, Pottstown.

McILVAINE, CHARLES E., Norristown.

McMURPHY, A. T., Rector of the House of Prayer, Branchtown, Philadelphia.

MIEL, CHARLES F. B., Rector of the French Church, St. Sauveur.

MILLER, DANIEL S., D. D., Rector of St. Mark's Church, Frankford, Philadelphia.

MILLER, JACOB, Rector of the Church of the Evangelists, Philadelphia.

MILLER, JOSEPH L., Assistant Minister of the Church of the Holy Trinity, Philadelphia.

MILLETT, D. C., D. D., Rector of Emmanuel Church, Holmesburg.

MOMBERT, J. ISADOR, D. D., Rector of St. John's Church, Dresden, Germany.

MOORE, JOSEPH R., Rector of the Church of the Resurrection, Nicetown, Philadelphia.

Morrison, A. M., West Philadelphia.

MORSELL, WM. F. C., Assistant to the Rev. Dr. Beasley, P. O. Torresdale.

MORTON, ALGERNON, Assistant Minister at St. Luke's Church, Philadelphia.

MORTON, HENRY J., D. D., Rector of St. James' Church, Philadelphia.

MUNROE, WM. H., Rector of Emmanuel Church, Kensington, Philadelphia.

MURPHY, JOHN K., Rector of St. Michael's Church, Germantown, Philadelphia.

*MURRAY, CHARLES E., Rector of the Church of the Covenant, Philadelphia.

NEILSON, WM. H., JR., Minister of the Holy Trinity Chapel, Philadelphia.

NEVIN, ROBERT J., Rector of St. Paul's Church, Rome, Italy.

NEWLIN, JOSEPH D., Rector of the Church of the Incarnation, Philadelphia.

NEWMAN, LOUIS C., Missionary to the Jews, Philadelphia.

NEWTON, RICHARD, D. D., Rector of the Church of the Epiphany, Philadelphia.

NEWTON, WILLIAM, Rector of the Church of the Nativity, Philadelphia.

NOCK, JOSEPH A., Minister of St. John's Free Church, Frankford Road, Philadelphia, and Missionary.

*PADDOCK, WM. HEMANS, Philadelphia (deceased).

PADDOCK, WILBUR F., D. D., Rector of St. Andrew's Church, Philadelphia.

PARKER, HENRY A., Rector of the Church of St. Luke the Beloved Physician, Bustleton.

*PERINCHEIF, O., Rector of Christ Church (Swedes), Bridgeport, Montgomery Co.

Perkins, W. S., Bristol.

PERRY, JAMES DeWOLFE, Rector of Calvary Church, Germantown, Philadelphia.

Platt, Wm. Henry, Deacon, officiating in Chapel of Holy Comforter, West Philadelphia.

QUICK, CHARLES W., Rector of the Church of Our Saviour, Philadelphia.

RICKERT, A. A., Philadelphia.

Ridgely, G. W., New York.

RITCHIE, ROBERT, Rector of the Church of St. James the Less, Falls of Schuylkill.

ROACH, ROBERT T., D. D., Rector of St. Paul's Church, Philadelphia.

ROBINS, JAMES W., Head Master of the Academy of the Protestant Episcopal Church, Philada.

RODMAN, WASHINGTON, Philadelphia.

RODNEY, JOHN, Rector Emeritus of St. Luke's Church, Germantown, Philadelphia.

*ROWLAND, HENRY J., Philadelphia.

RUDDEROW, JOEL, Rector of St. Paul's Memorial Church, Lower Providence; P. O. Oaks, Montgomery Co.

RUDDER, WM., D. D., Rector of St. Stephen's Church, Philadelphia.

RUMNEY, THEODORE S., D. D., Rector of Christ Church, Philadelphia.

RUSSELL, PETER, Rector of St. James' Church, Perkiomen; P. O. Lower Providence, Montgomery, Co.

SAUL, JAMES, Rector of St. Bartholomew's Church, Philadelphia.

SHIRAS, ALEXANDER, D. D., Philadelphia.

SIMES, SNYDER B., Rector of Gloria Dei Church, Philadelphia.

SIMPSON, E. OWEN, Rector of the Bishop's Free Church, Philadelphia.

*SMITH, SAMUEL E., Rector of St. Andrew's Church, West Philadelphia.

SPACKMAN, HENRY S., Chaplain of the Episcopal Hospital, West Philadelphia.

Spear, J. Newton, West Vincent, Chester Co.

Spear, Wm. W., D. D., Rector of St. Andrew's, West Vincent; St. Mary's, Warwick; and St. Mark's, Honeybrook. P. O., West Vincent.

STEWART, W. H. N., LL. D., Assistant Minister of St. Clement's Church, Philadelphia.

STOCKTON, WM. R., Rector of St. Peter's Church, Phœnixville.

Stout, C. B., Jr., Minister of Trinity Chapel, Maylandville, Philadelphia.

Stryker, P. W., Rector of St. Thomas' Church, White Marsh, Montgomery Co.

Stuart, Henry M., Rector of the Church of the Ascension, Philadelphia.

Suddards, Wm., D. D., Rector of Grace Church, Philadelphia.

Supplee, Enoch H., Principal of an Institute for Young Ladies, Philadelphia.

Tetlow, John, Philadelphia.

Thomas, Richard N., Rector of St. Matthias' Church, Philadelphia.

*Tortat, A. E., P. O. Newtown Square, Delaware Co.

*Trowbridge, Isaac L., Philadelphia.

Tweedale, Samuel, Assistant Minister of St. Mark's Church, Frankford, Philadelphia.

*Vanpelt, Peter, D. D., Philadelphia.

Wadleigh, Albra, Rector of St. Luke's Church, Germantown, Philadelphia.

*Ward, Chas. H., Assistant to the Rector of St. Stephen's Church, Philadelphia.

Ward, Henry Dana, Philadelphia.

Watson, Benjamin, D. D., Rector of the Church of the Atonement, Philadelphia.

White, Wm. A., Rector of St. Timothy's Church, Roxborough; P. O. Leverington.

Widdemer, Ephraim S., Rector of the Church of the Merciful Saviour, Philadelphia.

Williams, Jesse M., Deacon.

Winslow, Frank W., Assistant at the Church of the Advent, Philadelphia.

Windeyer, Walter, Minister of Trinity Church, Falls of Schuylkill.

Yarnall, Thomas C., D. D., Rector of St. Mary's Church, West Philadelphia.

LAY DEPUTIES.

BUCKS COUNTY.

BRISTOL, *St. James Ch.*—H. L. Gaw, *Burnet Landreth, John Ward, M. D.

NEWTOWN, *St. Luke.*—*Geo. A. Jenks, *Alex. Chambers.

YARDLEYVILLE, *St. Andrew.*—*Thomas Heed, *James Paff.

HULMEVILLE, *Grace.*—Edmund G. Harrison, *Joseph K. Vanzandt, John P. Thompson.

CENTREVILLE, *Trinity.*—William Stavely, George G. Maris, Albert S. Paxson.

DOYLESTOWN, *St. Paul.*—*Nathan C. James, Geo. E. Donaldson, W. H. H. Davis.

CHESTER COUNTY.

GREAT VALLEY, *St. Peter.*—John L. Phillips, *Wm. Sullivan.

NEW LONDON, *St. John.*—Thos. M. Charlton, *John C. McDonald, *Benj. F. McDonald.

WARWICK, *St. Mary.*—Thos. K. Bull.

PEQUEA, *St. John.*—*Joseph Hamilton, Henry W. Worrest, *J. H. Clark.

W. WHITELAND, *St. Paul.*—*Geo. W. Jacobs, John W. Stone.

W. VINCENT, *St. Andrew.*—Nathan G. Grimm, *John Strickland.

HONEYBROOK, *St. Mark.*—No Deputies.

WEST CHESTER, *Holy Trinity.*—James H. Bull, W. B. Brinton, *F. C. Hooton.

PHŒNIXVILLE, *St. Peter.*—*John Griffen, *Carroll S. Tyson, *L. B. Hawley.

DOWNINGTOWN, *St. James.*—Charles L. Wells, Joseph B. Baker, William Edge.

W. MARLBORO, *St. James.*—No Deputies.

COATESVILLE, *Church of the Trinity.*—*John L. Martin, *James S. Scott, *Horace A. Beale.

PARKESBURG, *Grace.*—Geo. W. Worrest, *Philip Hardwick.

DELAWARE COUNTY.

CHESTER, *St. Paul.*—John Larkin, Jr., Robert Hall, Joseph R. T. Coates.

MARCUS HOOK, *St. Martin.*—*David Trainer, *Abner Vernon, William Trainer.

RADNOR, *St. David.*—*John B. Thayer, *Benjamin Brooke.

*   *   *Church of the Good Shepherd.*—*Gorham P. Sargent, Chas. W. Cushman, Edward S. Lawrance, —— ——.

CONCORD, *St. John.*—Joseph H. Cloud, *Henry L. Paschall, *George Rush.

ROCKDALE, *Calvary.*—Richard S. Smith, Samuel K. Crozier, *Robert L. Martin.

MEDIA, *Christ.*—H. Jones Brooke, *Samuel B. Thomas, Edward A. Price.

MONTGOMERY COUNTY.

WHITEMARSH, *St. Thomas.*—W. H. Drayton, Jesse Shay.

PERKIOMEN, *St. James.*—Charles P. Shannon, *William Fronefield, Isaac Casselberry.

NORRISTOWN, *St. John.*—*Wm. Wills, *Samuel S. Smith, John McKay.

POTTSTOWN, *Christ.*—*Samuel Wells, *Wm. J. Rutter, *R. M. Cooper.

LOWER MERION, *Redeemer.*—*Geo. F. Curwen, *James C. Booth, Francis C. Yarnall.

LOWER MERION, *St. John.*—Isaac Hazlehurst, David Morgan, *Albert H. Franciscus.

JENKINTOWN, *Our Saviour.*—Charles Hewitt, John Glenn, *Henry C. Davis.

CONSHOHOCKEN, *Calvary.*—*Walter Cresson, *Theodore Trewendt, *Charles Lukens.

CHELTENHAM, *St. Paul.*—Thomas T. Lea, John W. Thomas, *Samuel G. Ogilby.

UPPER PROVIDENCE, *St. Paul's Memorial.*—*Chas. Davis, Caleb Cresson, C. W. Gumbes.

GWYNEDD, *Messiah.*—*Rodolphus Kent, William J. Smith.

PHILADELPHIA COUNTY.

PHILADELPHIA, *Christ.*—*Samuel Wagner, Joseph K. Wheeler, George E. Hoffman.

St. Peter.—Jas. S. Newbold, Chas. Willing, Geo. C. Morris.

St. Paul.—Thomas Latimer, Eleazer Fenton, William Cummings.

St. James.—*Geo. W. Hunter, William J. Griffitts, Frederick Fraley.

St. Stephen.—Thomas Neilson, Ludovic C. Cleeman, Oliver A. Judson.

St. Andrew.—Thomas Roberts, A. G. Coffin, Frederick Brown.

Grace.—Isaac S. Williams, Andrew H. Miller, M. J. Mitcheson.

Epiphany.—Robert B. Sterling, Charles E. Lex, Wm. S. Lane.

Ascension.—Alfred Zantzinger, Thomas R. Maris, Clement H. Smith.

St. Luke.—Geo. L. Harrison, Andrew Wheeler, Wm. W. Frazier, Jr.

Atonement.—Samuel F. Ashton, Lafayette Baker, William C. Houston.

St. Mark.—Richard R. Montgomery, Edward S. Buckley, David Pepper.

Mediator.—John Ashhurst, Jr., Francis Hoskins, *Charles Wirgman, Sr.

St. Clement.—Walter H. Tilden, Chas. B. Stewart, Elias L. Boudinot.

Holy Trinity.—John Bohlen, Lemuel Coffin, Wm. P. Cresson.

Covenant.—John P. Rhoads, James A. Kirkpatrick, James C. Allen.

St. Thomas.—U. P. Vidal, Morris Brown, Sr., John C. Bowers.

OXFORD, *Trinity.*—Wm. Overington, Harry Ingersoll, John Cooke.

LOWER DUBLIN, *All Saints.*—Alex. Brown, James Hall, Chas. R. King.

NORTHERN LIBERTIES, *St. John.*—Henry Walker, Charles Beamish, John B. Lever.

Advent.—Abel Reed, George Remsen, *Daniel Fitler.

Calvary.—Geo. B. Bonnell, Geo. Elkington, *Henry H. Haines.

SOUTHWARK, *Trinity.*—Wm. S. Price, Joseph W. Flickwir, Charles M. Peterson.

Evangelist.—William J. Mullen, *Henry Nicholl, *Samuel G. Finley.

Gloria Dei —Geo. M. Sandgran, Richard Sharp, Robert B. Salter.

St. John the Evangelist.—Wm. H. Myers, Geo. G. Roberts, A. J. Baton.

Ch. of Messiah.—*M. Mesier Reese, *Wm. Jordan, Doctor Hart.

FAIRMOUNT, *Redemption.*—*Alexander Crow, Wm. H. Eastwood, Geo. Drew Phelan.

SPRING GARDEN, *St. Philip.*—John Agnew, *Joseph R. Rhoads, Mifflin Wister.

Nativity.—*Wm. H. Brown, Lewis Thompson, *J. N. Collins.

St. Jude.—Jacob S. Miller, *B. L. Middleton, Wm. M. Abbey.

St. Matthias.—Wm. H. Rhawn, Henry S. Godshall, Joseph M. Cardeza.

Incarnation.—Geo. Williams, W. J. Philips, C. M. Husbands.

Holy Apostles.—Lewis H. Redner, *Geo. C. Thomas, Wm. D. Thomas.

FRANCISVILLE, *St. Matthew.*—Lewis D. Vail, Thomas Cain, Samuel R. Marshall.

Ch. of Good Shepherd —Joseph M. Christian, *William Tardif, Jr., *Horace J. Subers.

WEST PHILADELPHIA, *St. Mary.*—Ed. R. Thompson, *Henry C. Townsend, Wm. Yarnall.

St. Andrew.—Wm. H. Wilson, J. R. Sypher, H. W. Siddall.

The Saviour.—John D. Taylor, A. J. Drexel, Henry P. Rutter.

MANAYUNK, *Trinity.*—Robert D. Work, C. P. B. Jeffreys, *Robert Craven.

KENSINGTON, *Emmanuel.*—Douglas McFadden, John Scanlin, *Chas. S. Howe.

MOYAMENSING, *All Saints.*—Wm. Stirling, Wm. Riding, James Kidd.

Crucifixion.—Peter C. Williams, Dennis Green, *Joseph Stewart.

Our Saviour.—No Deputies.

GERMANTOWN, *St. Luke.*—James M. Aertsen, R. P. McCullagh, *Thos. H. Montgomery.

Christ.—Chas. Spencer, A. Miskey, Joseph M. Lewis.

St. John the Baptist.—Wm. A. James, *John J. Crout.

Calvary.—J. E. Caldwell, Samuel K. Ashton, A. R. Potter.

St. Michael.—S. Harvey Thomas, Arthur Wells, *Alfred C. Lambdin.

Holmesburg, *Emmanuel.*—Presley Blakiston, Henry Dewees, John Lardner.

Kingsessing, *St. James.*—D. Henry Flickwir, Thomas Sparks, Isaac T. Jones.

Frankford, *St. Mark.*—John Clayton, *Benjamin Rowland, Jr., William Welsh.

Port Richmond, *Messiah.*—*Henry Christian, Wm. A. Rogers, *Adam Rutherford.

South Penn, *Zion.*—*Dell Noblit, Jr., Thos. R. Alexander, *M. C. Thackray.

Manayunk, *St. David.*—*Wm. B. Stephens, *Orlando Crease, *S. T. Auge.

Rising Sun, *Resurrection.*—George Blight, *Joseph Thorp.

Chestnut Hill, *St. Paul.*—M. Russell Thayer, Franklin H. Bowen, Wm. C. Mackie.

Roxborough, *St. Timothy.*—J. Vaughan Merrick, T. F. Cauffman, *Wm. H. Merrick.

St. Alban.—*E. O. Abbott, James L. Rahn.

Bustleton, *St. Luke.*—David Saul, *John Willian.

Branchtown, *House of Prayer.*—*Bennett Medary, Jr., James Lowe.

Mount Airy, *Grace.*—*George M. Stroud, *C. M. Bayard, Doctor Shellenburgh.

Frankford Road, *St. John.*—*James Hamilton, John S. Powell, Cornelius Stephens.

Hestonville, *St. James.*—*J. Halliwell, *H. Brooks, Jas. M. Cadmus.

Tacony, *Holy Innocents.*—Edward E. Chamberlain, H. L. Foster, *Jacob Titus.

Falls of Schuylkill, *St. James the Less.*—Ellis Yarnall, *Benjamin J. Ritter, George M. Conarroe.

Clay Mission.—No Deputies.

Bridesburg, *St. Stephen.*—*S. J. Treadwell, *J. S. Rulon, W. R. Pigott.

St. George.—Hugh Whiteley, *Wm. N. Marcus, *H. S. Henry.

Kenderton, *St. George.*—*Thos. Maddock, Percy Lauderdale, *Elijah Wyatt.

St. Timothy.—*Samuel F. Flood, M. Clover, *F. M. Lorrillier.

JOURNAL.

Philadelphia, St. Andrew's Church,
TUESDAY, May 14th, 1872, 5 O'CLOCK, P. M.

This being the day appointed for the meeting of the Convention of the Protestant Episcopal Church in the Diocese of Pennsylvania, a number of Clergymen and Lay Deputies attended at St. Andrew's Church, Philadelphia.

Before the organization of the Convention, Evening Prayer was read by the Rev. John Bolton and the Rev. Jos. D. Newlin.

The Rt. Rev. Wm. Bacon Stevens, D. D., LL.D., took the Chair.

The Secretary proceeded to call the names of the Clergy entitled to seats, from a list prepared by the Bishop, when 98 answered to their names.

The Secretary then called the names of the Lay Deputies, as recorded by him, from the certificates presented in the form prescribed by the Canon, when 132 answered and took their seats.

The Convention then proceeded to the election of a Secretary and Assistant Secretary.

The Rev. Dr. Childs was nominated for the office of Secretary: there being no other nomination, the balloting was dispensed with, and he was thereupon duly elected *viva voce*.

Mr. Chas. R. King, a Lay Delegate from All Saints' Church, Lower Dublin, was then nominated for the office of Assistant Secretary, and there being no other nomination, he was in a like manner duly elected Assistant Secretary.

The Secretary reported the following business as unfinished at the last Convention, and referred to appropriate Committees:

On Alterations of Canons of the Diocese.
On Parsonages.
On Funds of the Diocese.
On Minority Representation.
On City Missions.

The President appointed the following Standing Committees:

COMMITTEE ON CHARTERS.

Rev. R. B. Claxton, D.D.,   Rev. J. A. Harris,   Mr. Jas. H. Bull,
Rev. D. C. Millett, D.D.,   Mr. M. J. Mitcheson,   Mr. Wm. S. Price.

COMMITTEE ON CLAIMS OF CLERGYMEN TO SEATS.

Rev. B. Watson, D.D.,   Rev. T. C. Yarnall, D.D.,   Rev. H. S. Spackman, D.D.

COMMITTEE ON CLAIMS TO SEATS AS LAY DEPUTIES.

Mr. L. D. Vail,   Mr. L. H. Redner,   Mr. Geo. Blight.

COMMITTEE ON CANONS.

Rev. G. E. Hare, D.D.,   Mr. Isaac Hazlehurst,   Mr. Jas. C. Booth,
"   E. A. Hoffman, D.D.,   "   John Bohlen,   "   Geo. W. Hunter,
"   D. R. Goodwin, D.D.,   "   R. R. Montgomery,   "   S. F. Appleton.
"   B. Watson, D.D.,

COMMITTEE ON PAROCHIAL HISTORY.

Rev. Jas. W. Robins,   Rev. E. Y. Buchanan, D.D.,   Mr. Chas. Willing,
"   J. A. Harris,   "   T. C. Yarnall, D.D.,   "   Thos. H. Montgomery.
"   J. Bolton,   Mr. Thos. Latimer,

Mr. Ingersoll, a Deputy from Trinity Church, Oxford, laid the following resolution on the table, with the consent of the Convention:

Resolved, That the Churches in union with this Convention will contribute annually for the two years next ensuing, toward the support of the Episcopate of Central Pennsylvania, the same amount that is annually paid by them to the fund for the support of the Episcopate of this Diocese; to be assessed and collected in the same manner, and paid over annually, for the two years specified, by the Treasurer of the Episcopal Fund of this Diocese to the Treasurer of the Episcopal Fund of the Diocese of Central Pennsylvania.

The Rev. Washington B. Erben offered the following, which was adopted:

Whereas, The Bishop of this Diocese, at the request of a number of the Clergy, has consented to deliver an address, giving an account of his recent visitation of the Churches in Europe, which are under the auspices of the General Convention; and has named this evening, and St. Andrew's Church, as the time and place for such address; therefore

Resolved, That the Convention unites in the request for the delivery of said address, in this Church, this evening, at eight o'clock.

Nominations for the Standing Committee of the Diocese were made as follows:

By the Rev. F. J. Clerc, D.D.:

STANDING COMMITTEE.

Rev. H. J. Morton, D. D.,
" G. Emlen Hare, D. D.,
" E. A. Hoffman, D. D.,
" Thos. F. Davies, D. D.,

Rev. E. A. Foggo, D. D.,
Mr. Thos. Robins,
" Richard S. Smith,

Mr. Wm. F. Griffitts,
" R. R. Montgomery,
" G. W. Hunter.

By Rev. Chas. D. Cooper:

CLERGY.

Rev. G. Emlen Hare, D.D.,
" D. R. Goodwin, D.D.,

Rev. B. Watson, D.D.,

Rev. J. H. Eccleston, D.D.

. LAY.

Mr. Thomas Robins,
" Richard S. Smith,

Mr. John Bohlen,
" William F. Griffitts,

Mr. John Clayton.

By Rev. J. W. Claxton:

Rev. Dr. Morton,
" Hare,
" Watson,
" Davies,

Rev. Dr. Yarnall,
Mr. R. S. Smith,
" Wm. F. Griffitts,

Mr. Thos. Robins,
" John Bohlen,
" T. H. Montgomery.

By Rev. Chas. Logan:

Rev. Dr. Morton,
" Davies,
" Hoffman,
" Childs,

Rev. Dr. Eccleston,
Mr. Thos. Robins,
" W. F. Griffitts,

Mr. John R. Whitney,
" R. S. Smith,
" W. S. Price.

By Rev. James Saul:

Rev. Dr. Goodwin,
" Watson,
" Hare,
" Eccleston,

Rev. Dr. Morton,
Mr. R. S. Smith,
" Thos. Robins,

Mr. Wm. F. Griffitts,
" John Bohlen,
" Geo. W. Hunter.

The following nominations were made for Deputies to the General Convention:

By Mr. George M. Conarroe, a Deputy from the Church of St. James the Less:

Rev. Edw. Y. Buchanan, D.D.,
Rev. J. A. Harris,
Rev. Wm. Rudder, D.D.,

Rev. Thos. C. Yarnall, D.D.,
Mr. William Welsh,
Mr. J. Vaughan Merrick.

Mr. R. M. Lewis,
Mr. W. Russell Thayer.

By Mr. Edward S. Lawrance, a Deputy from the Church of the Good Shepherd, Radnor:

Rev. Dr. Hare, Rev. Dr. Rumney, Mr. Lemuel Coffin,
Rev. Dr. Rudder, Mr. William Welsh, " M. R. Thayer.
Rev. Dr. Foggo, " Isaac Hazlehurst,

By Rev. R. Newton, D.D.:

Rev. Dr. Hare, Rev. Dr. Miller, Mr. Charles Gibbons,
" Henry Brown, Mr. Lemuel Coffin, " George L. Harrison.
" Dr. Goodwin, " James H. Bull,

Mr. Thomas Robins nominated Mr. B. G. Godfrey as Treasurer of the Convention Fund, and Mr. R. P. McCullagh as Treasurer of the Christmas Fund.

Mr. G. M. Conarroe nominated the Rev. J. W. Robins as Registrar of the Diocese.

On motion of the Rev. Dr. Paddock, it was

Resolved, That the Secretary of the Convention prepare and distribute ballots containing the names of each nominee, for the several Offices to be voted for by this Convention.

On motion of the Rev. Dr. Pratt, the Revised Regulations were suspended for the purpose of introducing the following, which was adopted:

Resolved, That the operation of the fifth of the Revised Regulations (which concerns the Order of Business of the Convention) be, and the same is hereby, so far suspended as to admit the Report of the Board of Missions, and the discussion incident thereto, as the order of the day for Thursday next, at 10 o'clock A. M., provided that the elections shall have been then concluded.

The Secretary read the following Report of the Standing Committee, on Charters submitted to them for their approval:

The Standing Committee herewith present the Charter of the Church of "Saint Sauveur," with the information that it agrees with the form prescribed by the Convention, except that in providing for the services, it directs that they may be conducted in the French and English languages, which the Committee consider not opposed to the spirit and sense of the prescribed form of Charter, and therefore approve of the same.

The Charters of the Church of the Good Shepherd, Milford, Pike County, and of St. John's Church, Hanover, Luzerne County, have also been approved.

JOHN CLAYTON, Secretary.

PHILADELPHIA, May 14, 1872.

On motion of Mr. Bohlen, the Charter of the Church of St. Sauveur was referred to the Committee on Charters.

On motion of the Rev. Dr. Hoffman, it was

Resolved, That Clergymen belonging to this Diocese, but not entitled to seats in this Convention, Clergymen of other Dioceses, Clergymen of other Churches in communion with this Church, and candidates for Holy Orders, in the Protestant Episcopal Church, be admitted to the sittings of this Convention.

The Secretary read invitations for the members of the Convention to visit the new Hall of the Pennsylvania Historical Society, and also, the Hall of the Union League.

On motion, adjourned.

JNO. A. CHILDS,
Secretary.

PHILADELPHIA, MAY 15TH, 1872.

The Convention met pursuant to order.

Morning Prayer was read by the Rev. T. F. Davies, D. D., the Rev. R. Newton, D. D., and the Rev. B. McGann.

The Communion Service was conducted by the Bishop of the Diocese, assisted by the Bishop of Central Pennsylvania, the Rev. Dr. Buchanan, the Rev. Dr. Morton and the Rev. Henry Brown. The Post Communion Service by the Rev. Thomas A. Jaggar, and the Benediction pronounced by the Rt. Rev. Charles P. McIlvaine, D. D., D. C. L., Bishop of Ohio.

The Sermon was preached by the Rev. J. W. Claxton, Rector of the Church of the Advent, Philadelphia, from the third chapter of the Book of the Revelation of St. John, and 11th verse: "Hold fast that which thou hast, that no man take thy crown."

At the conclusion of Divine Service, Bishop Stevens called the Convention to order.

The minutes of yesterday's proceedings were read and approved.

3

The Secretary then called the names of such clergymen and laymen as were not present yesterday, when 19 clergymen and 47 laymen answered.

The Bishop then introduced the Rt. Rev. the Bishop of Ohio, and the Rt. Rev. the Bishop of Central Pennsylvania, who were received by the Convention rising.

After a few remarks by the Bishop of Ohio, on motion of the Rev. Dr. Davies—

Resolved, That the members of the Convention of the Diocese of Pennsylvania desire to express their pleasure in the presence of the Rt. Revs. the Bishops of Ohio and Central Pennsylvania, and to offer to them their filial and respectful salutation.

The Bishop proceeded to read his Annual Address:

Dear Brethren of the Clergy and Laity:

I greet you with a glad and thankful heart as you come up to this Annual Convention. These milestones of our progress, tell us how rapidly our Ministry is passing away, and how soon we shall be called to give an account of our stewardship. At the last Convention, I was able to be with you only about two hours, in consequence of sickness, and consequently I could take no part in your interesting discussions. I thank God that I am here to-day, well and strong.

On the Sunday following the last Convention, the 14th of May, 1871, I went to the Church of the Messiah, and confirmed 25 persons; but was too ill to make an address, or remain through the whole service. P. M., I baptized my grandchild, Julia Stevens, daughter of Edward C. Mitchell, Esq.

Monday, 15. I left for Geneva, New York, to take, by direction of my physician, a rest of two weeks.

On Thursday, 1st of June, I united in marriage, in the Church of the Holy Trinity, Philadelphia, John Struthers and Virginia Moylan Bird.

Sunday, 4. In the Morning I visited St. Timothy's, Roxborough, confirmed 8, and addressed them. Evening, in the "Bishop's Church," I confirmed 36, and made an address.

Thursday, 8. Lebanon. In St. Luke's Church in the evening, after an address to the congregation, I confirmed 13 persons.

Friday, 9. Manheim. Evening, in St. Paul's, I preached, and confirmed 1 person.

Saturday, 10. A. M., I confirmed a sick person in private, in Manheim. Evening, in Columbia. I met the class preparing for confirmation, and addressed them.

Sunday, 11. Columbia. In St. Paul's Church I preached, and confirmed 12 persons. Evening, in Marietta, St. John's Church, I preached and confirmed 10 persons.

Tuesday, 13. Altoona. In St. Luke's Church, I admitted to Priest's Orders the Rev. J. J. A. Morgan. I preached the sermon and administered the Lord's Supper. Evening, in the same Church, I confirmed 30 persons, and addressed them.

Thursday, 15. Coatesville. Evening, in the Church of the Holy Trinity, I preached, and confirmed 13 persons.

Friday, 16. York. Evening, in St. John's, I preached, and confirmed a class of 24.

Sunday, 18. A. M., in St. James', Kingsessing, I preached, and confirmed 10. Afterwards confirmed a sick person in private. P. M., in St. George's Church, Cardington, I preached, and confirmed 19. Afterwards confirmed a sick person in private.

Thursday, 22. Bethlehem. Attended, as President of the Board of Trustees of the Lehigh University, the Commencement Exercises in Packer Hall.

Friday, 23. A. M., in the Church of the Saviour, West Philadelphia, and in the presence of the Bishop of Delaware and the Rev. Dr. Childs, I received the Rev. Charles Francois Bonaventure Miel, formerly a Priest of the Roman Church (who had been transferred to my jurisdiction by the Bishop of Illinois) into the Priesthood of the Protestant Episcopal Church, according to the provisions of Canon 9, Title I. of the Digest. At the same time and place, I ordained to the Diaconate, T. William Davidson, Joseph L. Miller, John G. Rawn, Wm. H. Josephus; and acting for the Bishop of Rhode Island, Eben Thompson. At the same time and place, I advanced to the Priesthood, the Rev. Ezra Isaac, Rev. G. Livingstone Bishop, J. Everist Cathell. The same evening, in Calvary Church, Rockdale, I preached, and confirmed 15 persons.

Sunday, 25. In Grace Church, Mount Airy, I preached, and confirmed 3 persons. P. M., in the Church of Our Saviour, Jenkintown, I preached, and confirmed 10.

July 2d, Sunday. Scranton. I was present at the opening of the new Church of St. Luke. Preached the sermon and administered the Holy Communion. In the evening, in the same Church, after an address to the congregation, I confirmed 6.

Monday, 3. Bethlehem. Presided at a meeting of the Trustees of the Lehigh University. At this meeting, its generous founder, the Hon. Asa Packer, assumed all the annual expenses of the University, and declared it to be a Church institution under the patronage of the Protestant Episcopal Church.

Thursday, 6. In Philadelphia, and in the presence of the Rev. Dr. Childs and the Rev. R. Graham, I deposed from the Ministry, at his own request, Mr. P. Quick Wilson, Deacon.

Sunday, 9. Wilkesbarre, A. M., I read the service and preached in St. Stephen's Church.

Tuesday, 11. I consecrated St. Clement's Church, South Wilkesbarre. Evening of the same day, in St. Mark's Church, Mauch Chunk, I confirmed 5, and made an address.

Wednesday, 12. In the morning, in St. Mark's, Mauch Chunk, at the request of the Bishop of New York, I ordained Mr. P. H. A. Brown, and at the request of the Bishop of Delaware, Mr. John Coleman, to the Diaconate.

Thursday, 13. Shamokin. Evening, in Trinity Church, I preached and confirmed 8.

Friday, 14. P. M., in St. Mark's, Northumberland, I preached. No confirmation, as Minister was absent. Evening, in St. Matthew's, Sunbury, I preached, and confirmed 10.

Saturday, 15. Williamsport. P. M., I laid the corner-stone of the New Trinity Church, and made an address.

Sunday, 16. A. M., I preached in Trinity Chapel, Williamsport, and confirmed 8. Evening, in Christ Church, Williamsport, I preached, and confirmed 36.

Monday, 17. A. M., In Williamsport, I confirmed a sick woman in private. The same evening, in Lock Haven, I preached, and confirmed 4.

Sunday, 23. Bedford. A. M., I preached in the Court House (as St. James' was not completed), and in the evening in the Presbyterian Church.

Tuesday, 25. P. M., I laid the corner-stone of the Church of the Good Shepherd, Radnor; made an address.

Wednesday, 26. A. M., I consecrated the Church of the Trinity, Coatesville, and preached and confirmed two persons.

Sunday, 30. A. M., I read the service and preached in St. Clement's, South Wilkesbarre. Evening, in St. John's, Ashley, I preached; confirmed 21; made an address.

Sunday, August 6. Wilkesbarre. I preached morning and evening in St. Stephen's Church.

Thursday, 10. P. M., laid the corner-stone of the Church of the Messiah, Gwynedd, and made an address.

Sunday, 13. A. M., I preached in Trinity Church, Athens, and confirmed 1 person. Evening in Christ Church, Towanda, I preached, and confirmed 12.

Sunday, 20. A. M., I preached in the Lutheran Church, Catawissa, and confirmed 4. Evening, in St. Paul's, Bloomsburg, I preached, and confirmed 9.

Sunday, September 3. A. M., I preached in Grace Church, Newton, Mass., and administered the Holy Communion. P. M., I preached in the Unitarian Meeting House, West Newton. Evening, I again preached in Grace Church.

Sunday, 10. Evening, I preached in Grace Church, Newton.

Sunday, 17. A. M., I preached in the Swedes' Church, Bridgeport, confirmed 27, and addressed them.

Wednesday, 20. I laid the corner-stone of St. Paul's Memorial Church, Upper Providence, and made an address.

Sunday, 24. Bethlehem. A. M., I preached in the Church of the Nativity, confirmed 10 and addressed them.

Monday, 25. Carlisle. Evening, in St. John's Church, I preached, and confirmed 5.

Tuesday, 26. Chambersburg. A. M., I consecrated Trinity Church and preached; also in the Church, I baptized Mary Powlee, daughter of Charles Taylor. Evening, in Mechanicsburg, I preached in the Lutheran Church.

Thursday, 28. I visited St. John's, Concord, Delaware Co., preached, and confirmed 3. P. M., I again addressed the congregation.

Sunday, October 1. A. M., officiated in St. John's, Lower Merion, preached, and administered the Holy Communion.

Wednesday, 4. Baltimore. At the opening of the General Convention, in Emmanuel Church, I took part in the service of the Holy Communion.

Friday, 6. Evening in Emmanuel Church, Baltimore, at the Semi-Centennial Missionary Meeting, I made an address.

Sunday, 8. A. M., I preached in the Church of the Ascension, Baltimore. Evening, I preached in St. Peter's, Baltimore.

Wednesday, 11. In Grace Church, Baltimore, at a meeting in behalf of the Italian Reformation Movement, I made an address.

Thursday, 12. Took part in the Missionary Memorial Service in Emmanuel Church.

Sunday, 15. Philadelphia. At St. Andrew's Church, I made an address in behalf of the Endowment Fund of said Church. P. M., at a Missionary Meeting in the same Church, to take farewell of the Rev. Elliott H. Thompson and wife, Missionaries to China, I made an address.

Tuesday, 17. Evening, I preached in the Church of Our Saviour, Broadway, Baltimore.

Sunday, 22. A. M., in Trinity Church, Oxford, Philadelphia, I preached, and confirmed 6 persons. P. M., in the Chapel of Trinity Church, Oxford, I preached, and confirmed 5.

Sunday, 29. Easton. A. M., preached on the occasion of the opening of the new Trinity Church. P. M., I made an address to the Sunday School. Evening, I again preached, confirmed 9, and addressed them.

Wednesday, November 1. Married Dr. Edward R. Mayer and Mrs. Elizabeth G. Monroe, in Philadelphia.

Sunday, 5. A. M., in Christ Church, Philadelphia, I advanced the Rev. John Coleman to the Priesthood; afterwards confirmed 18, and administered the Holy Communion. P. M., in the Chapel of the Episcopal Hospital, I preached, confirmed 28, and addressed them, and afterwards, in two separate services, in two wards, confirmed 2 patients.

Monday, 6. Evening, presided at a Missionary Meeting in St. Luke's Church and made an address. The Lord Bishop of Lichfield, the Dean of Chester (Dr. Howson) and the Rev. Mr. Iles, of Wolverhampton, also made addresses.

Tuesday, 7. I presided at a Complimentary Breakfast given by the Clergy and Laity to the Lord Bishop of Lichfield and the Very Rev. the Dean of Chester, at the Union League House, and made an address of welcome to the distinguished guests.

Wednesday, 8. Harrisburg. This being the day for the meeting of the Primary Convention of the New Diocese, the Clergy and Laity assembled for Divine Service in St. Stephen's Church. The Bishop of Lichfield preached at my request the Convention Sermon. After the administration of the Holy Communion, the Convention was organized under my Presidency. In the evening, a public meeting was held in St. Stephen's Church, for the purpose of hearing addresses from Bishop Selwyn and Dr. Howson, at which I presided.

Thursday, 9. The Convention of the new Diocese of Central Pennsylvania elected the Rev. M. A. De W. Howe, D. D., Bishop, and adjourned at 7 P. M.

Saturday, 11. I sailed from New York, with Mrs. Stevens, in the Steamship "City of Paris," for Europe, to make an official visitation of the Protestant Episcopal Churches in union with the General Convention, and which had been committed to my care by the Presiding Bishop for three years.

Sunday, 12. At sea. I preached in the saloon of the ship.

Tuesday, 21. We landed at Queenstown, in Ireland, and proceeded at once to Dublin. We were the guests for several days of His Grace, the Archbishop of Dublin, whose name and writings, as Dr. Trench, are so familiar to you all.

Saturday, 25. I went to Armagh, and presented to the Most Rev. the Archbishop of Armagh and Primate of Ireland, the letter and address from the General Convention of the Church in America to her Sister Church of Ireland.

The next day, Sunday, 26, at the request of the Lord Primate, I preached in the Cathedral of Armagh, being, I believe, the first American Bishop who has preached in that venerable Church.

On Tuesday, 28, in the Parish Church of Ballymoney, County Antrim, I baptized the infant son of J. Leslie Beers, Esq.

Thursday, 30. At the earnest request of the Bishop and Rector, and others, I preached in All Saints' Church, Cloony, near Derry. The Bishop of Derry and the Bishop of Tuam were present.

Sunday, December 3. I spent in Oxford, England, where I had the pleasure of hearing the first of a series of Advent Sermons by the Dean of Norwich, the Rev. Dr. Goulbourn. At the request of the Rev. John W. Burgon, author of Plain Commentary, the Vicar of St. Mary's (commonly called the University Church, because the University Sermons delivered by select Preachers and the celebrated Bampton Lectures are delivered there), I took part in the Morning Service, and consecrated the elements and assisted in the administration of the Lord's Supper. There is something very striking in the congregation which gathers in this University Church. It consists of the Vice-Chancellor, Heads of Colleges, Professors, Proctors, Fellow-Tutors and Undergraduates of all the 24 Halls and Colleges which make up the University of Oxford, dressed in their various robes of office, and, with the insignia of their several degrees. Probably no place in England, I might almost say in the world, present such a concentration of learning, talent and authorship as gathers to these Select Sermons in St. Mary's, Oxford.

On Sunday, the 10th, by invitation of Dean Stanley, I attended the Morning Service in Westminster Abbey, and in the afternoon the Dean of St. Paul's kindly assigned me a privileged seat where I had the pleasure of hearing Canon Liddon preach to one of his great congregations, gathered under the dome of the Cathedral.

On Saturday, 16. I reached Dresden, in Saxony.

The next day, Sunday, 17, in the Hall fitted up by the congregation of St. John's Church, I took part in the service, and preached an Advent Sermon. In the evening, in the same place, after Evening Prayer, in which the Rev. Dr. Mombert was assisted by the Rev. Mr. Gilderdale, Rector of All Saints' (Church of England) Church, Dresden, I made an address to the congregation, and then administered the rite of confirmation to 11 persons; 8 being for St. John's, and 3 for All Saints' Church. I also addressed a few words of counsel to the candidates.

In order to give me an early opportunity to become acquainted with his Parishioners, Dr. Mombert invited them to meet me at a Reception which he appointed at his house, Villa Emma Strehlen, on Monday afternoon, the 18th. A large number of persons called and I was most cordially welcomed by the whole congregation.

The following Sunday, 24, I visited, by request of the Superintendent, the American Sunday School, held in a club room, and made an address. After visiting the School, I read part of the service, and preached to St. John's congregation.

In the evening, Dr. Mombert accompanied me to the English Church, All Saints, where, at the request of the Rector, the Rev. Mr. Gilderdale, I preached; Dr. Mombert also taking part in the service.

The next day was Christmas; clear and bright, but very cold. I officiated in St. John's Parish, by preaching and administering the Holy Communion to nearly 70 persons. This completed my visitation to this Church.

The Parish of St. John's, Dresden, was founded Easter Monday, April 29, 1869, by the Rev. John Anketell, A. M., Presbyter of the Diocese of Western New York, then temporarily sojourning in that city. Mr. Anketell thus details its history: Took charge of the enterprise for several months; but September 10, 1869, the Vestry having given an unanimous call to the Rev. J. Isidor Mombert, D. D., formerly Rector of St. James' Church, Lancaster, Pennsylvania, then in Dresden, he accepted the same and entered at once upon his duties. Dr. Mombert has been very diligent and zealous in his work, and his efforts have been rewarded with a great measure of success. The Parish, though organized, labored under several difficulties which are thus described by Dr. Mombert: "Under the laws of Saxony, the congregation was viewed and treated as a private assembly, while its minister could not *legally* perform ecclesiastical acts. The present Rector immediately took steps towards the removal of this disability and his efforts proved successful. The Parish and its minister were duly recognized by the Saxon Government and the minister received regulations framed for the full and free exercise of all ecclesiastical functions and acts belonging to him as a Presbyter of this Church. The effect of this action on the part of the Saxon Government being, that Baptisms, Marriages and Funerals solemnized by the American Clergyman are held legally valid in Saxony and nothing being wanting to render them valid in any Court of the Union, except the certificate of the resident United States Consul.

" The second difficulty has respect to a place of worship. Public halls used for secular purposes had to be hired, and although by the courtesy of the local government, the use of a Church edifice has now been granted ; the circumstance that it cannot be heated, compels us to hire a hall during the winter months. This is greatly to be deplored for the repeated change from place to place gives to our venture an air of instability and uncertainty, which cannot be effectually removed until we own, or at least have the use of, a worthy edifice, in which our services may be conducted throughout the entire year."

I found the congregation worshipping in a new hall which had been fitted up in quite a churchly style, and in which they might be permitted to remain at least for a season. Still the permission might be withdrawn, and then the flock would be without a fold. Under these circumstances, at a meeting of the Vestry, called to confer with me, I urged them to take immediate steps looking to the erection of a good and substantial Church edifice. My views met their full approbation, and though the plan may not be immediately carried out, yet, having been broached and endorsed, it will more and more commend itself to the thoughtful consideration of both residents in and visitors to Dresden ; and I fully believe that it will soon result in the desired end.

There are two congregations of the Church of England there ; and one Parish, " All Saints," occupies a most beautiful stone Church, built as a memorial by an English lady, and which is at once an ornament to the city and a monument of her Faith. If the Parish of St. John's had an appropriate Church, known and recognized as the American Episcopal Church, with all proper Church appointments and Church provisions, I feel sure that the congregation would soon be greatly enlarged, and permanence and success be thus fully secured. I sincerely hope that the effort which was inaugurated last December may, by the liberality of the American residents in Dresden and the American visitors, be soon accomplished. It is the only Church of our Communion in the whole German Empire. It has received the recognition and sanction of the Saxon Government. It is the Common Home of American Christians, visiting or residing, in one of the Art Capitals of Europe. It stands in the highway of Continental travelers, and many hundreds pass through Dresden every year, to whom the services of the Church would be specially attractive in a foreign land.

My next Ministerial act was the Baptism of the infant son of Dr. Copley Green, in Vienna, Austria, on Wednesday, the 27th of Dec.

We arrived in Florence, Saturday evening, the 30th of Dec.; and the next morning, Sunday, the 31st, I went to the Chapel occupied by the Protestant Episcopal Church, in the Piazza del Carmine, where, after taking part in the service with the Rev. Pierce Connolly, the Rector, I preached an Advent Sermon.

Monday, January 1st, 1872, the Feast of the Circumcision, I took part in the Church services with the Rev. Mr. Connolly, and he preached. For four days I was confined to the house by sickness. The following Sunday, I again preached and administered the Holy Communion.

I officiated in Rome on two Sundays :

The first Sunday, 14th of January, I preached in St. Paul's American Episcopal Church, the Rev. M. Nevin reading the service. In the afternoon, I made an address from the Chancel in the same Church.

The second Sunday, January 21st, I preached in the morning in St. Paul's Church, and then confirmed 5 persons and administered the Holy Communion. In the afternoon, at the request of Rev. M. Shadwell, the incumbent, I preached for the Church of England congregation in the English Church.

On Sunday, 28th of January, at the request of the Rev. M. Childers, I preached in the English Church of the Holy Trinity, Nice, France.

On Sunday, 4th of February, I preached both morning and afternoon in the Church of the Holy Trinity (American), Paris. The following Sunday, the 11th, I again preached all day in the same Church, and in the afternoon confirmed a class of 6 persons. In the evening, at the request of the incumbent, the Rev. Mr. Forbes, I preached in the English Church, Rue d' Agessau.

Ash Wednesday, Feb. 14, I preached in the American Episcopal Church (Holy Trinity).

Sunday, 18. In the morning, in the same Church, I preached and administered the Holy Communion, and in the afternoon again preached.

At all these services in Paris, except that in the English Church, the Rev. W. O. Lamson, the then Rector of the Parish, read the service, assisted on several occasions by the Rev. Edward N. Mead, D. D., of the Diocese of New York.

My last official act in Europe was being present, by invitation, in St. Paul's Cathedral on the occasion of the National Thanksgiving for the Recovery of the Prince of Wales, on Tuesday, February 27.

Through the good hand of our God upon us, I was permitted to get back to my Diocese, Friday, March 15.

We left England in the Cunard steamship, Abyssinia, and both Sundays at sea I took part in Divine Service.

Sunday, A. M., 17. I visited St. John's Church, Frankford Road, preached, confirmed 16, and addressed them.

Friday, 22. I preached in the evening in the "Bishop's Church," Spring Garden Street.

Sunday, 24. I confirmed 48 in the morning, in St. Peter's Church; 24 in the afternoon, in St. Andrew's Church; 8 publicly and one in private for St. George's, Kenderton. Owing to a severe cold, I was unable to make any address except a few words in St. George's, Kenderton.

Tuesday, 26. In the evening I preached in the Church of the Nativity, and confirmed 18.

Wednesday, 27. In the Church of the Saviour, West Philadelphia, I preached and confirmed 43, seven of whom were for the Parish of St. Mary's, temporarily worshipping in that Church during the rebuilding of St. Mary's.

Thursday, 28. In the evening, in St. Jude's Church, I confirmed 8, and addressed them.

Good Friday morning, I was at St. James' Church, confirmed 30, and made an address. In the evening, I preached in Grace Church, and confirmed 51.

Easter Eve, I visited St. Mark's Church, and after preaching, I confirmed 35.

Easter. In the morning, I confirmed 30 in Christ Church, and addressed them, and in the evening, I preached in St. Matthias' Church, and confirmed 29.

April 5, Friday. In Gloria Dei Church, I preached, and confirmed 14.

Sunday, 7. In the morning, in Ascension Church, after preaching, I confirmed 17. In the afternoon, I confirmed 42 in St. Matthew's Church, and addressed them; and in the evening, in St. Mark's, Frankford, I confirmed 29, and made an address.

Monday, 8. In the Church of the Holy Comforter, I preached, and confirmed 4.

Tuesday, 9. I officiated at a wedding in St. Luke's Church.

Wednesday, 10. In St. James', Bristol, I preached, and confirmed 14.

Thursday, 11. In the evening, in the Church of the Redeemer, I preached, and confirmed 7.

Friday, 12. In the Church of the Evangelists, I preached, and confirmed 25.

Sunday, 14. A. M., in the Church of the Incarnation, I preached, and confirmed 18. In the afternoon, in St. Thomas', Whitemarsh, I preached, and confirmed 14; and in the evening, in St. Paul's, Cheltenham, I confirmed 15, and made an address.

Wednesday, 17. In Calvary Church, Germantown, I preached, and confirmed 14.

Thursday, 18. In the afternoon, I preached in the Church of the Good Shepherd, Radnor, and confirmed 8.

Friday, 19. I preached in the evening in St. Thomas' (African) Church, and confirmed 7.

Saturday, 20. I assisted in the Burial Service.

Sunday, 21. In the afternoon, in the Church of St. James the Less, I confirmed 12, and addressed them. At the Church of the Atonement, in the evening, I preached, and confirmed 13.

Tuesday, 23. In Grace Church, Mount Airy, I preached, and confirmed 5.

Wednesday, 24. In St. Timothy's Church (8th and Reed), in the evening, I preached, and confirmed 12.

Thursday, 25. In St. Paul's, Doylestown, I preached, and confirmed 12.

Friday, 26. Evening, in Holy Trinity Chapel, I confirmed 30, and addressed them.

Sunday, 28. A. M., in Holy Trinity Church, I preached, and confirmed 16. Evening, in the Church of the Epiphany, I preached, and confirmed 29.

Wednesday, May 1. A. M., I delivered an address to the Students of the Philadelphia Divinity School, in Spencer Hall. Evening, in Emanuel Church, I preached, and confirmed 27.

Friday, 3. Evening, in St. Michael's, Germantown, I preached, and confirmed 9.

Sunday, 5. A. M., in the Church of the Advent, I preached, confirmed 37, and made an address. Evening, in All Saints' Church, I preached, and confirmed 29.

Tuesday, 7. A. M., I opened the Session of the American Medical Association, with Prayer, in Horticultural Hall. Evening, in Holy Trinity, West Chester, I preached, and confirmed 10.

Wednesday, 8. Downingtown, A. M., in St. James' Church, I admitted the Rev. Robert F. Innis to the Priesthood. Evening, in same Church, I preached, confirmed 18, and addressed them.

Ascension Day, 9. In the evening, in St. Paul's, Philadelphia, I preached, and confirmed 16.

Friday, 10. I went to Pottstown, and at half past five in the afternoon, laid the corner-stone of the new Church (Christ Church), and made an address. In the evening, I preached in the Chapel of this Church, confirmed 14, and made an address.

Sunday, 12. A. M., St. John's, Norristown, I preached, confirmed 9, and an made address. Evening, in St. David's, Manayunk, I preached, confirmed 36, and made an address.

Summary for Conventional year:

Number of Confirmation Services..	91
" " Persons confirmed...	1382
Sermons..	102
Addresses..	49
Marriages..	3
Funerals...	1
Baptisms...	4
Ordinations to Diaconate..	7
" " Priesthood...	6
Churches Consecrated...	3
Corner-stones laid...	5

CLERICAL CHANGES.

In addition to those Clergymen who had ceased to be members of this Convention, by reason of their territorial connection with the new Diocese of Central Pennsylvania, 13 have removed to Dioceses outside of Pennsylvania, and 2 have been taken away by death.

The first of these in order of time, was the Rev. J. Irving Forbes, who died in June last. This dear Brother was one of the most earnest and faithful workers in the ministry. He had endeared himself in an eminent degree to the hearts of all those who were brought in contact with him. He was a man of clear and well defined views—of deep religious convictions—of plain, outspoken earnestness; and his ministry in Bethlehem was productive of blessed fruits. He lingered long on a sick bed, enduring much bodily suffering and affliction, but his bed became his pulpit, and its silent lessons of patience and resignation, and hope, and faith, spoke feelingly to the hearts of all visitors; and his daily life as he gradually sunk to rest, was a daily sermon on holiness of life and preparedness for Heaven. His sun went down while it was yet day, but his influence will long survive, and his memory will be lovingly cherished.

The other Brother taken from us, was the Rev. H. T. Wells, LL. D., President of Andalusia College. As the founder of this excellent Boys' School and its energetic supporter, Dr. Wells labored beyond his strength, and brought upon himself that disease which laid him in the grave. So devoted was he to the interest of this institution, that he labored for it night and day with unsparing exertion, and succeeded in establishing two schools, both of which will, I hope, be continued, as much needed to the educational apparatus of this Diocese.

Dr. Wells deserves a remembrance by reason of his industry, courtesy, and successful work in the special field to which he seems to have consecrated his life.

One Clergyman, the Rev. Peter Quick Wilson, a Deacon, recently received into this Diocese, was, at his own request, deposed from the Ministry of this Church, on Thursday, July 6, in the presence of the Rev. Dr. Childs and the Rev. R. Graham.

The Rev. Thomas M. Antrim, in consequence of ill-health, has ceased to be the Assistant to the Rector of the Atonement. The Rev. H. G. Batterson, D.D., has resigned the Rectorship of St. Clement's. The Rev. John S. Beers, has removed to Connecticut. The Rev. Franklin L. Bush, has resigned the position of Assistant to the Rector of St. Peter's Church, and in consequence of ill-health, is temporarily residing in Europe. The Rev. J. Everist Cathell, has removed to New Jersey. The Rev. Francis J. Clerc, D.D., has resigned the Wardenship of the Burd'Asylum, and has been chosen President of Burlington College, New Jersey. The Rev. Thomas J. Davis has resigned the charge of the Church of the Resurrection, Rising Sun, and become " Emeritus Rector " of the same. The Rev. R. E. Dennison has removed to New Jersey. The Rev. Charles L. Fischer has resigned the Church of St. John the Evangelist and become Rector of St. John's, Lower Merion. The Rev. R. Graham has temporary charge of St. Alban's, Roxborough. The Rev. A. Louderback has ceased to be Assistant at St. Luke's. The Rev. Isaac Martin has been elected Rector of St. Stephen's, Bridesburg. The Rev. Joseph R. Moore, in consequence of the fusion of St. George's, Kenderton, with the Church of the Resurrection, has become Rector of the latter Church. The Rev. Algernon Morton is Assistant Minister of St. Luke's Church. The Rev. Jno. A. Nock has become Rector of St. John's, Frankford Road. The Rev. J. Sturges Pearce has resigned Marcus Hook and gone to Massachusetts. The Rev. Dr. Pratt has been elected Rector of St. Philip's Church. The Rev. A. A. Rickert has resigned the Church of the Good Shepherd, on account of illness, and has just returned from the West Indies. The Rev. Robert F. Innis has become Rector of St. James', Downingtown. The Rev. H. A. Parker has taken charge of St. Luke's, Bustleton. The Rev. W. G. P. Brinckloe, of Hulmeville. The Rev. Jno. Coleman is Assistant to the Rector of St. Mark's. The Rev. Dr. William Spear and Rev. J. Newton Spear have under their care St. Mary's, Warwick ; St. Andrew's, West Vincent ; and St. Mark's, Honeybrook. The Rev. C. F. Miel has become Pastor of the French Church of St. Sauveur. The Rev. James H. Brooks has St. George's Church, Cardington. The Rev. Mr. Davidson has Calvary Church, Conshohocken. The Rev. Mr. Goodfellow has the Church of the Good Shepherd. The Rev. W. F. B. Jackson has become Rector of St. John the Evangelist. The Rev. W. H. Josephus has the Church of the Crucifixion. The Rev. Jos. L. Miller is Assistant at Holy Trinity Church. The Rev. Mr. Stout is Assistant of the Church of Our Saviour, West Philadelphia. The Rev. Mr. Prescott is Assistant at Christ Church. The Rev. W. Rodman has become the Principal of the Mission House. The Rev. H. M. Stuart has become Rector of Ascension Church. The Rev. F. A. Winslow is Assistant at the Church of the Advent. The Rev. Robert F. Chase has charge of St. Peter's Mission.

There are but four Churches unsupplied with Rectors. Two of these, St. Luke's and St. Clement's, have Assistant Ministers in charge. St. James', Hestonville, has a temporary supply, and a Missionary will soon be appointed to St. John's, New London Township, Chester County.

Thirty Clergymen are unemployed; twenty of whom are laid aside by ill-health or old age. The remaining ten are occasionally occupied in ministerial duty.

EPISCOPAL VISITATION TO SUNDAY SCHOOLS.

It is my purpose, during the next fall and winter, should God spare my life, to organize a system of Episcopal Visitation of the Sunday Schools of this Diocese. I have long thought of the desirableness of such a plan, but the size of the Diocese has hitherto prevented me from carrying it into execution. In consequence of the vast amount of work devolving on your Bishop, it has been impossible to give to the Lambs of his flock that supervision which he felt, that, as Baptized members of the Church, over which the Holy Ghost had made him overseer, they ought to have.

The same argument which sustains the propriety of making the Rector of the Parish the head of the Sunday School of his Parish, sustains the propriety of recognizing the Bishop as the head of all the Sunday Schools in the Diocese. I fully acknowledge the distinction between the two: the Church, established by Christ and officered by Divine appointment, and the Sunday School, a voluntary institution, resting entirely on unordained agencies. Nor would I, in the least, encourage anything like that Episcopal absolutism, which would centre the whole Sunday School system in the Bishop, so as to make him the chief and controlling power in its operations; far from it; it is much better that it should be as it now is, a system mutable to suit the age; adjustable to suit the peculiarities of the clergy and parishes, and free from all ecclesiastical legislation as to its internal management or machinery.

The two points which are aimed at by my plan are, 1st: That the Bishop shall be brought face to face with the Children, whom he is commissioned to oversee, that he may meet them, have special service with them, address them, and show to them and to their Parents and Teachers, that he regards them as an integral and most important part of his Diocese; and that he is not to wait until they become adults, before he is to watch for their souls, but that by the very fact of the charge which is made to sponsors at the end of the Baptismal Office, they come under his spiritual oversight, and should receive a portion of his fatherly care.

The 2d point which I hoped thereby to secure, is to awaken in the minds of the children of the Diocese an early interest in a Bishop's office and work. To let them see him, hear him, know him; not merely on the occasion of his Confirmation Visits, but as making a special visitation to them, that the precious lambs may gather around the chief shepherd of this fold; and that they may be taught to love and reverence, and show an interest in and for the Holy Office of a Bishop in the Church of God. I need not go into the various arguments and statements which have come up to my mind, as this scheme has been gradually maturing there, for I believe that all the clergy, and all the superintendents and teachers, and, I may add, all the children, will be glad to be thus specially visited and addressed by the head of the Diocese.

Where a Parish has several Sunday Schools, numbering enough to fill the Church, I shall give a visitation to that Parish by itself. Where there are several neighboring Churches, with smaller schools, I shall then ask a certain District, to meet in a certain Church; changing the Church in the District year by year. In the country, where it will not be possible to group together Sunday Schools, I shall try and make special arrangements to meet the several cases. Thus I hope to be able to report to the next Convention, that I have visited or had gathered before me every Sunday School in the Diocese. In carrying out this plan, I shall of course do it in conference with the clergy; nor shall I attempt to force it upon any Brother or parish who may object. I firmly believe that such a series of visitations will impart a fresh impulse to these schools; attach the children more firmly to the Church, and bind together, in a more compact and better handled system, the public religious education of the young on the Lord's Day.

CENTENNIAL CELEBRATION OF AMERICAN INDEPENDENCE.

It is known to all of you that extensive preparations are being made by the General Government, the State and the City, for celebrating in a becoming way the One Hundredth Anniversary of the day when we became a Free and Independent Nation. It is true that four years will pass before this Centennial occasion, but I deem it best to call your attention to it now, so that whatever action you may take, either by yourselves, or in conjunction with others, may be well considered and digested.

It seems to me that there are reasons which make it especially proper why this Diocese should take part in this celebration :

The fact that we are living in the city where the Declaration of Independence was first proclaimed;

The fact that the first prayer in the Continental Congress was offered by a Churchman ;

The fact that the President and several of the most prominent members of that Congress were Episcopalians ;

The fact that the first ecclesiastical act under that "Declaration," was taken by the united Vestries of Christ Church and St. Peter's, on the very day, when the Declaration was made, the 4th of July ;

The fact that Bishop White was one of the warm supporters and public upholders of the New Government;

The fact that he was for years the Chaplain of Congress ;

The fact that Washington and Franklin were worshippers in old Christ Church, and the fact that in accepting the altered condition of things, our Church was subjected to more 'trials and sacrifices than any other body of Christians, renders it expedient in my judgment, that we should, before the occurrence of that Anniversary, take some measures for the due commemoration of an event so important to us as a Church, and as citizens of a land where we enjoy civil and religious liberty.

My own opinion is, that in view of the attack made upon freedom of conscience in religious affairs, by the "Syllabus" and "Encyclical" of the Pope,—whose teaching on that subject, has, by the dogma of Infallibility, been declared to be the voice of God,—this Anniversary should be made the occasion for drawing out from all religious bodies a simultaneous and concentrated re-assertion and re-enforcement of this fundamental principle; and as far as possible not only rebutting and rebuking such arrogant claims and such soul-enslaving dogmas as are set forth by the Papal Church, but of maintaining the right and the duty of cherishing religious liberty, as one of the essential elements of civil liberty, and without which, our own political liberty is of but little value. I want to see nothing that will in any way compromise us with the State, but I want to see the principle of religious liberty, of freedom of conscience, of ecclesiastical toleration, set out before the American mind with a clearness and force, that shall show to the world that we can never yield belief in dogmas that take from man his right of conscience, or endanger his religious liberty.

THE AUXILIARY COMMITTEE OF THE BOARD OF MISSIONS.

Last month, the members of the Board of Missions of the Protestant Episcopal Church in the United States, elected by the last General Convention from the Diocese of Pennsylvania, desiring to carry into effect the recommendations of the Board and of the General Convention, last October, met and organized themselves, under the title of "The Pennsylvania Auxillary Committee of the Board of Missions of the Protestant Episcopal Church." Their plan of organization was a simple one, and their aim is to create a deeper missionary spirit, by diffusing missionary information, by having meetings, and sermons and addresses; by securing the co-operation of the laity, and, on all proper occasions, to exert their official and personal influence to aid the operations of the Board and its authorized representatives. I cannot but testify that, as at present administered, the operations of the several Committees of the Board of Missions are admirably and judiciously conducted. Many objections which existed in former days have been removed. Earnest men, full of zeal and self-sacrificing devotion, are found in many far-off fields of labor. The affairs of the Board are administered in no narrow or partisan spirit, and the time has come when all the loyal sons of the Church should unite as one man to sustain these legally constituted agencies as the best channels by and through which to spread the Gospel to the destitute in our own land and to the regions beyond.

The happy and harmonious manner in which our Board of Diocesan Missions has worked for the last ten years, shows what can be done when brethren of the same household of faith are willing to forego and forget mere party drill and organization, and unite in the common cause of our common Lord and Master Jesus Christ. Let the spirit of conciliation, of peace, of unity, which has characterized the meetings of this Diocesan Board be carried out in the general operations of the Church as organized by the action of the General Convention, and there will be given a new impetus to all work, and means will flow into the treasury, and men will offer themselves willingly to the Lord, saying, " Here are we : send us ! "

THE HOSPITAL.

The Protestant Episcopal Hospital continues to do its quiet yet most beneficial work. Its ability to do more good is restricted by the unfinished state of the building, which needs another wing to give it completeness and symmetry.

No work in which the Diocese has been engaged has been productive of greater bodily and spiritual blessings than this Hospital. It can be estimated by no statistics, however carefully prepared; because, in addition to the good done to each patient in the wards or the dispensaries—in addition to the instruction given in its chapel, its Bible classes, its Sunday

Schools—in addition to the benefits imparted to multitudes through its Mothers' Meetings, its Night-classes, its District Visitations, there is to be added the untold influence for good which the very existence of such an institution produces in a community, bodying forth, as it does, in this tangible form, the great love-principle of our holy religion, and thus linking together in the indissoluble bonds of Christian benevolence, soul-healing and body-healing, so touchingly incorporated in the living Christ, and so markedly made the duty of the Church by the example especially of the holy Apostles and of our Blessed Lord.

Our Presbyterian brethren have established a Hospital under their denominational care, but open, like ours, I believe, to all, without regard to class, creed or color. We bid them God speed in this work of charity; and hope that, like ours, it may prove a Bethesda, a house of mercy to many a weary, sin-sick soul. The medical profession of this city are also engaged in organizing another Hospital, in connection with the new buildings of the University of Pennsylvania, in West Philadelphia. Their prospects are bright, and we trust that complete success may crown their efforts. But when all these shall be builded, there will still be a lack of Hospital accommodation. The supply of beds or wards will not equal the demand of this great manufacturing and railroad city, where the very machinery and agencies which give us our wealth and numbers, create the casualties which demand our aid. In the canvassing that is now going on in this community for money to erect these new Hospitals, I implore you not to forget our present unfinished one. Let it not stand any longer in its one-sided imperfection, and in its incomplete endowment, restrained from the fuller exercise of its benevolence because it lacks wards and money; but, considering what it has done in the past as its strongest claim upon your present liberality and future testamentary remembrance, I cannot but indulge the hope that our defective building will soon be pefected, and our limited accommodation be enlarged, and our comparatively small endowment—small in proportion to our needs—be increased, so that the Hospital may stand before the Church in the completeness of its original design, and with its full working power.

THE ORGANIZATION OF THE NEW DIOCESE.

Two circumstances conspire to give special interest to this Convention. One arises from the fact, that since we last met, a new Diocese has been organized within the limits of our former boundaries.

This has taken from us, 37 Counties, 68 Clergy, and 79 Churches, and a million and a-half of People. It thus ranks 5th in the list of the 40 organized Dioceses of our Church; 14th in the same list as to the number of organized Parishes, and 15th in the same list as the number of Clergy. Thus it starts in its Diocesan work, not as a child needing to hold on for guidance and support to the parent's hand, but with a well developed strength and capability.

It is a cause of congratulation that it commences under such unusually favorable auspices, and especially that the Clergy and Laity have chosen one to preside over them, whose long record of faithful services in this Diocese won for him our highest respect; and whose long services in the General Institutions of the Church, secured the confidence and approbation of our entire communion. I feel quite sure, that in the high position to which God has called him, he will give satisfaction to every reasonable mind, and discharge, with exemplary ability, and dignity, and zeal, the solemn responsibilities which weigh upon him, as a Bishop of such a noble Diocese.

It is also an interesting fact in connection with the launching and equipping of this new Diocese, that there were present with us that day, two such men of mark and worth, as the Lord Bishop of Lichfield and the Dean of Chester. Bishop Selwyn had for thirty years been a noble standard-bearer of the Cross in the South Pacific,—the founder of Dioceses, and the leader in the great mission work of the Church of England in New Zealand.

The vigor, sagacity, breadth of view, and whole-souled consecration to his work, which he had displayed in New Zealand, led the Queen to nominate him to the vacant see of Lichfield. This was the first time that a Colonial Bishop had ever been translated to a Home Diocese, and his selection therefore, was the endorsement of the Government to his extraordinary capacity and fitness to labor and guide, not merely such a vast Diocese as Lichfield, with its great array of Church work and Church instrumentalities, ramifying into all departments of Church life; but to take his seat in the House of Lords and participate as a member of Parliament in setting forward those educational, ecclesiastical and reformatory measures, which so engross the English mind and heart. Bishop Selwyn preached the opening Sermon of this Primary Convention, giving great satisfaction to all, and adding deeply to the interest of the occasion.

The presence of Dr. Howson, the Dean of Chester, was also regarded by all as a happy augury. His ripe scholarship, his extended fame, his special advocacy of Woman's work, his genial manners, and his readiness to impart information on the many topics with which he is conversant, made him extremely popular, and bespoke for him what he so well deserved by his books and his labors,—the respect and esteem of all sound Churchmen.

It will always be a satisfaction to the Diocese of Central Pennsylvania to have on the page of its history, which tells of its primary council, written there such bright names as George Augustus Selwyn, the Bishop of Lichfield, and John Howson, the Dean of Chester.

THE FIRST DECADE OF MY EPISCOPATE.

The other circumstance to which I refer, is the fact, that this year completes the tenth year of my Episcopate.

I can scarcely believe, that more than ten years have passed, since I took upon myself the vows, and was consecrated to the office, of a Bishop in the Church of God.

In this Church (St. Andrew's), where I had ministered as its Rector for over thirteen years, I was elected to my present

·5

office by the suffrages of the Convention, on the 24th October, 1861. In this Church, and at this chancel, on the 2d day of January, 1862, I was solemnly set apart for my new work. And now, to-day, after ten years have rolled away, I am permitted to stand in the same Church and deliver from the same chancel, this, my tenth annual address. Many reflections crowd upon my mind as I turn back to the scene of my consecration. Of the seven Bishops who then laid their hands on my head as I kneeled at this chancel, two (Bishops Hopkins and A. Potter) have been removed by death. Of the 121 Clerical names signed to my testimonials, 25 have gone to their rest.

These are solemn warnings, and I trust will not prove unheeded by either you or myself.

It may not be improper at this time to review the progress of the Church during this decade, as it will furnish us much to be thankful for, and valuable materials for future use. At that time, Bishop Alonzo Potter had administered the Diocese for sixteen years. He entered upon his duties in 1845, in the full vigor of a ripe manhood, with mental powers thoroughly trained, and of commanding force. For ten years his career was one of remarkable influence and effectiveness. He impressed himself on the Church at large, as well as on the Diocese, as a Bishop thoroughly furnished unto every good work. In his decennial address, however, he called the attention of the Convention to the beginning of a failing health, which culminated in that sad stroke which made it necessary to elect an Assistant, which was, as you know, done in 1857. Thus, helped by the election of Bishop Bowman, he rallied again, though never to his former working power, when, in 1861, God called Bishop Bowman away; and the whole burden was again laid on Bishop Potter. When I entered on my duties as Assistant Bishop, I found Bishop Potter much improved in health, though unable to discharge all his duties. He, however, seemed as mentally strong as ever, and all the head-work of the Diocese was done by him, until he sailed for California, in February, 1865. When I took the Diocese under my sole control it had, therefore, an impetus given to it by him, which carried it on with much force; and hence, in speaking of Church growth during these ten years, you will bear in mind, that nearly all the instrumentalities now so actively employed, were of his devising and moulding; and to myself belongs the honor of simply endeavoring to carry out what he planned, and give accelerated motion to that which he had started into action.

He labored, and I have entered into his labors. Ten years ago, the Diocese of Pennsylvania was co-terminous with the State of Pennsylvania. Since then, two Dioceses have been carved out of it, while yet the reduced Diocese of Pennsylvania, in clergy and Church influence, remains as strong nearly as it was when the first division was made, in 1865. This fact illustrates at once the necessity of the division and the wonderful growth of our Church in this State.

Of the 179 clergymen who were entitled to seats in the Convention which elected me Bishop, 37 have died; 32 have been cut off by the severance of the new Dioceses; 4 have become Bishops; 42 have gone to other Dioceses; leaving only 64 of the clergy now connected with this Diocese who were then entitled to a seat and vote. The present number of clergy in this Diocese is 166; in the Diocese of Pittsburgh, there are 51, and in the Diocese of Central Pennsylvania, 65; making a total of 282.

It is known to most of you that, owing to severe illness, (which at one time laid me aside for fifteen months), and other disabilities resulting from painful accidents, and attacks of acute disease, I have been incapacitated for the discharge of my duties more than twenty-four months of my Episcopate. Notwithstanding this serious interruption, I have administered the rite of Confirmation on 902 occasions; have confirmed 11,563 persons; have delivered 2,160 sermons and addresses; have consecrated 28 Churches; have laid 33 corner-stones; have ordained 71 to the Diaconate, and 63 to the Priesthood; have superintended and carried through the Organization of two Dioceses; and have made a Visitation of the Church on the Continent of Europe, under the direction of the General Convention. During this period, over 30 Churches have been enlarged and repaired, and 64 new Churches or Chapels have been built, or are now in process of being erected. In addition to these numbers, 7,378 have been confirmed within the past ten years, by Bishop Potter and various Bishops, acting for him and for myself. 33 persons have by them been ordained Deacons; 37 have been advanced to the Priesthood; 11 Churches have been consecrated, and 2 corner-stones have been laid. Making a total, in ten years, of 18,941 persons confirmed; 39 Churches consecrated; 104 candidates ordained Deacons; 100 ordained Priests; 35 corner-stones laid.

In 1862, when the whole State was one Diocese, there were 2,393 Sunday School teachers, and 25,000 scholars. In 1872, before the present Diocese of Central Pennsylvania was cut off, and after the Diocese of Pittsburgh had been erected, there were 3,414 teachers, and 35,333 pupils; showing an increase of over 1,000 teachers, and 10,000 pupils, notwithstanding the decrease of territory and Churches by the organizing of the Diocese of Pittsburgh; and this excludes 21 Parishes which made no report.

The contributions reported for the three years of 1860, '61, '62, amounted to a grand total of $619,000. The contributions of 1869, '70, '71, exclusive, of course, of the Diocese of Pittsburgh, reached the sum of $1,670,000, or over a million of dollars more than was given ten years ago by the whole Episcopal Church in the State.

The number of communicants represented in the undivided Diocese, in 1862, was 13,523; in 1872, with the Diocese of Pittsburgh cut off, 23,024; showing an increase of nearly 10,000 communicant members.

These are evidences of growth which cannot but give us great satisfaction. Yet these evidences of figures are, after all, not so striking as the evidence everywhere apparent of the practical extension of the Church's work, and the daily increasing hold which it is taking on the people. Never has there been more activity in all species of Church labor, and never so many appliances for reaching all classes, as exist now. Nearly every City Parish has its Chapel, or Mission School, and its local organization for Mission work; and I feel sure that if we could have laid before us an exact amount of what is being really done by the several Parishes, we should be ourselves astonished at the life and zeal and labor displayed, and at the number of people brought thus, directly or indirectly, under the Church's eye and hand and teaching.

As I move about from Parish to Parish, and see the interior working of each, and the several agencies employed by each, I am penetrated with a feeling of thanksgiving that our beloved Church, which has been so long stigmatized as only The Rich Man's Church, as being the Aristocratic Church, is, in her sphere, doing more among the lower and degraded classes for their temporal benefit, their mental culture, and their spiritual welfare, than any other body of Christians. Yet I am far from being satisfied. There are undeveloped powers of the Church which need to be evoked; there are Churches which have not yet put on all their working force into the fields around them; there are new avenues in which to work, and new methods of doing the work, which must all be used if we would come up to the full measure of our duty. Much as I find occasion of joy, I find no occasion of boasting; for were I to begin to point to this or that institution or agency with any degree of Diocesan pride, I should find myself checked by a voice within, saying: Look not on the little that has been done in proportion to the amount of mind and wealth and physical and social power lodged in your Church; but on the vast amount that has been left undone—the ignorance untaught—the misery unrelieved—the spiritual wastes uncultivated—the souls, by scores of thousands, still uncared for, and for whom no Church of Christ opens its doors, and to whom no minister of Christ offers the Gospel. Let us rather use what we have done as a stimulus to do more, and make the past but an incentive to greater activity in the future.

THE BISHOP POTTER MEMORIAL HOUSE.

During these ten years of my Episcopate there has grown up, out of seed planted by my revered predecessor, Bishop Potter, the Memorial House which bears his name. This admirable institution has been doing a quiet but most useful and spiritually remunerative work.

In the five years, which are just completed, since it was formally opened, 37 women have been inmates of the House, for a longer or shorter period. Three of them were sent by the Foreign Committee to be trained for Missionary work in Africa.

Two of the Sisters are actively at work among the Indians, one in the Santee, the other in the Yankton Mission; another has been doing, for two years, the work of a Parochial Deaconess in Bridesburg and Whitehall; where, mainly through her instrumentality, a beautiful Church has been built, in communication with which are flourishing Sunday Schools, Bible Classes, a Mother's Meeting, and all other instrumentalities for successful Parish work.

Another lady is in charge of a Hospital in Detroit.

Yet another is resident in a Mission House in one of our large cities. Several have returned to work in their own Parishes, encouraged and strengthened by their residence in the Memorial House.

A successful Mission has been inaugurated at Aramingo, between the Hospital and Frankford, by another Sister, who labored faithfully there during parts of two years, and who has been called to her home, temporarily, by sickness in her family. Her work has, however, been taken up by another, and is going on vigorously. Of the eight inmates of the Memorial House at this time, one has been engaged for three years in faithful work in the Women's Ward of the Episcopal Hospital. A second is engaged in mission work at Aramingo, giving certain hours in each week to attendence at the Church Dispensary in Frankford, where she is learning to put up prescriptions, and is thus in training for a mission among the Indians. A third will probably take the position of nurse in a Children's Hospital about to be opened at one of the bathing places on our own coast, having proved her peculiar fitness for such work by her skilful nursing of the sick in the Mission connected with the Episcopal Hospital. Another is a returned Missionary from Africa. Yet another will be assigned to a new department of work in connection with the House, hereafter to be noted. Two are in training for Parochial Missions, and one other has recently been sent by the Foreign Committee, through its Secretary, to be tested and trained for China.

In view of these and other facts, I venture to ask: Has not the time come for the Diocese to take up and carry on this work? Thus far the burden, or, as the generous Donor would regard it, the privilege of supporting it, has fallen upon one person, who has done as much by his personal labors to introduce Sisterhoods in our Church as any other member of it. The Diocese needs just such a training agency if it would successfully do Christ's work. Experience proves its untold worth. Shall it be left any longer to be supported by one layman? or shall the Diocese put underneath it its broader, stronger shoulder, and lift it up into greater prominence and usefulness? This Memorial House is necessary to the effective working apparatus of this Diocese. The Diocese would be incomplete without it, we shall be going backward if we pass it by, or suffer it to decline.

Every consideration weighs upon us to take it up, enlarge, endow, sustain it. What it has done in the past, what it is doing now, what it can do in the future, all plead to this end. Already has it proved itself a hive of Christian industries and busy toil. We want to make it more busy still,—to enlarge the work on all sides, to minister to new forms of helplessness and suffering,—to keep pace with the diversified out-croppings of humanity on its darker side,—and to give to our Church, in the eyes of the laboring classes, a suppleness and flexibility, which will fit it for all forms of degradation and sin.

But this can be done only by those who are *taught* to do it. The knowledge required for this work does not come by intuition, it is *an art to be learned*, a profession for which one has to be schooled and drilled, and unless thus prepared by patient toil and a daily ripening experience, the largest-hearted sympathy and the most untiring native energy, will be all but wasted or misused. In this Memorial House, sympathy is harnessed to action, and not suffered to foam itself out in mere emotional sentimentalism. Love is here educated to organize its affection into wisely planned methods, and not left to waste itself in the vain attempt to do impossibilities; and Christian energy is here disciplined to order, and guided into channels where all its power is economized, and where but little is lost by misdirection or ignorance.

This is what is needed to give greater efficiency to this "Memorial House." This is what is wanted to bring out into untold usefulness hundreds of Christian women, who have the mind to work, and the hands to work, but know not the true methods of labor, or how to use the tools which God has put into their hands.

Will the Diocese take up this subject and give it prayerful thought? There is no time to lose. The day of work and action has come; God grant that the workers may be provided, and that the work may be wisely done.

LEHIGH UNIVERSITY.

Another institution which has been founded and successfully organized, within these ten years, is the Lehigh University, at Bethlehem.

This enterprise, the sole result of the gift by the Hon. Asa Packer, of Mauch Chunk, of over $500,000, was, at his request, planned in the main features by myself, and at its head I have continued to this time, though now, that it falls within the limits of the Diocese of Central Pennsylvania, I shall resign my position as President of the Board of Trustees next month.

But there the University stands, the finest college building in this State; with an accomplished and competent corps of Professors, with all the means and appliances of imparting the highest literary, or scientific education. It is free to all who choose to avail themselves of its offered privileges; and last summer, by the fresh liberality of its generous founder, he undertook to pay all its yearly expenses; and declared his desire, which the Trustees embodied into an unanimous resolution, that it should, thenceforth, be regarded as a Church Institution.

As this is the first University of the kind given to the Church and placed under its sole control, and the first where tuition is free in all branches, and to all well disposed comers,— and as it was the outgrowth of Christian love, opening the heart of one, to whom God had entrusted a large stewardship,— it deserves to be noted as one of the signs and evidences of growth, both in liberality and in Church feeling and extension. Though this Diocese must now give it up to our younger sister, yet we can rejoice, that such a noble educational charity was born and baptized, and signed with the sign of the cross, while yet under our jurisdiction. May the rich dews of God's grace ever fall upon the Founder and upon the University!

PHILADELPHIA DIVINITY SCHOOL.

During these ten years, another important institution has been planted in our midst: I refer to the Philadelphia Divinity School, chartered in 1863. This school of the Prophets, with a faculty, which for sound learning and professional ability, is second to none in the Church, has been the means of doing a vast amount of good. Young men have graduated from it, who have gone almost everywhere, preaching the Word, and are now occupying important posts in 20 different Dioceses. The undergraduates are each and all, according to their several abilities and opportunities, doing Mission work in a variety of Parishes, and others learning practically the duties which they are, by and by, to discharge in a higher sphere; and so while they are watering others, they are being watered also themselves. This was one of Bishop Potter's well planned schemes, and I well remember with what diligence and care he elaborated its constitution and laws, so as to give it breadth and depth, and make it a place where thorough scholarship and thorough practical training should go hand in hand. This is not, strictly speaking, a Diocesan Institution, but as an institution *in* the Diocese, mainly supported by the means which it has contributed, and giving back in return a goodly number of efficient Ministers to serve in our Parishes, it deserves notice and commendation in this address.

BOARDING HOMES FOR YOUNG WOMEN.

Within these ten years, also, have been established two Boarding Homes for Young Women, for the reception, protection and care of those who come to the city to seek employment in stores and offices, or for the purpose of preparing themselves for becoming teachers. Both of these Homes, originated by the holy zeal and liberality of one Christian woman, are under the management of ladies of the Protestant Episcopal Church, and are doing a much needed work with great efficiency and satisfaction. As a means of providing this class of young women with Christian Homes, under Church influences, and as a precautionary measure, whereby much evil is averted, these unpretending institutions are entitled to a liberal support and to your warmest sympathy.

THE CHURCH HOME FOR CHILDREN.

The Church Home for Children, which I brought to your special notice two years ago, is progressing most favorably. The new building will soon be ready for its little inmates. All its enlarged accommodations will be at once needed, and if the liberality of Churchmen would only permit us to double our capacity, there would still be a demand unsupplied. At a recent confirmation, I administered that Apostolic rite to 8 children of the " Home;" thus showing, that not the bodies only, but the hearts of the children are watched over and trained up for Christ. In this way it pays back to the Church what it gives to support its material interest; and so the streams of human benevolence and Divine grace beautifully blend, and leave behind choicest blessings for body and soul, for time and for eternity.

THE LINCOLN INSTITUTION.

Another remarkably useful institution, established in this Diocese within this decade, is "The Lincoln Institution," chartered in 1866.

This was incorporated for the purpose of providing a home for the care and training of friendless white boys and youths, and for the orphan sons of soldiers and sailors of the United States. This benevolent purpose has been admirably well carried out. Already has the building been once enlarged, and its capacity is still below the demand made upon it. Here between one and two hundred boys receive a fair education, are taught good habits of body and mind, are drilled with severe military precision, and their spiritual interests are carefully watched over and provided for, so that it is a well ordered school and home for a most interesting class of children. Eleven pupils of this Institution were confirmed by me in Epiphany Church. As the time is fast approaching when it will necessarily cease to be a Soldiers' Orphans Home, the Board of Council and Managers are already making arrangements to continue its benefactions to orphan boys, both as a training school and where they can find a home until old enough to go to work, and where their characters can be moulded in truth and honesty. Thus will very many boys be trained up in the ways of virtue and be made useful men and citizens, who, but for this Institution, would furnish recruits to the swarms of vagrants, who now roam our streets, and grow up hardened in sin and crime, at once an expense and a disgrace to the city.

CITY MISSIONS.

One more work has been inaugurated and established during these ten years, to which I must call your attention: I refer to the City Mission work.

Until recently, the whole plan (if that could be called a plan which had no plan) of doing this work was lamentably defective. Several efforts were made to interest the city Rectors and effect a city organization, but they failed. It was then undertaken by your Diocesan; a Superintendent was appointed, Missionaries were set to work, a house was taken, halls and rooms were rented, services were 'commenced in various places and money was collected. After being on my hands long enough to show that it could be done,—that it ought to be done, and that the machinery and the money for doing it could be commanded,—I again made an effort to put it into the hands of responsible parties, and, fortunately, have fully succeeded.

A "Board of Council" was appointed, representing the various Churches, and to that Board has been transferred the whole work. This work has assumed a magnitude beyond what I had anticipated; and what it has accomplished already, in the way of starting new Parishes and helping feeble ones, and preaching to those who will not go inside Churches; of sewing schools, night schools, Sunday Schools; of District Visiting; of relief to the souls and to the bodies of thousands; all this has shown the need of such a work, and that it will expand just as fast and as far as the money and the men shall be forthcoming to occupy the opening fields, and furnish the desired relief. This has been one of the most cheering signs of Church life, and has furnished a model of action which has been copied in other Dioceses.

I will not weary you with any further suggestions. There are many things, which, during the year, arise before me as proper subjects on which to speak at our Annual Conventions, and which I note down for presentation. But time would fail to bring them all out and lay them before you.

I congratulate you that, as a Diocese, we are healthful and prosperous. Work is going on everywhere, and gratifying results are visible on all sides. The tone of feeling and harmony of action of the last General Convention has had a most salutary effect in broadening narrow views, removing prejudices, harmonizing differences and consolidating our working power. I trust that this spirit may more and more pervade the hearts of our Clergy and our Laity.

One thought more, and I have done.

We are wandering mid-way between "Expectation Sunday," as the ancients named the last Lord's Day (because the Disciples were then tarrying in Jerusalem and waiting "for the promise of the Father"), and the festival of Whit-sunday. That day inaugurated the dispensation of the Spirit under which we are now, as a Church, living. That day the Ascended Lord, having received "Gifts for men," distributed them in the Pentecostal Blessings of that first Whit-sunday in Jerusalem.

Then, the Disciples of Jesus were in unity and peace, for they "were all with one accord in one place." Then they were in a waiting and expectant state, prepared in heart and mind for the promised Comforter, for "they continued with one accord in prayer and supplication." May we, Brethren, imitate them in these respects. Let us take this waiting posture, let us cherish this praying frame of mind, let us cultivate this unity and brotherly love. Then, and then only, may we confidently look for a fresh unction from the Holy One; and how much do we need this Baptism of the Holy Ghost, on all our congregations, on all our schools, on all our Parish work, on all our Missionary organizations, and especially on our hearts and minds, that we may be taught by the Spirit of Truth, and be preserved from the assaulting errors of the age, and be "guided into all truth," even the full and loving knowledge and apprehension of Him, who says of Himself, "I am the Way, the Truth, the Life." With these aspirations, let us anticipate next Sunday's Collect, and say: "O God, who didst teach the hearts of thy faithful people by sending to them the light of Thy Holy Spirit, grant us, by the same Spirit, to have a right judgment in all things, and evermore to rejoice in His holy comfort, through the merits of Christ Jesus our Saviour, who liveth and reigneth with Thee in the unity of the same Spirit, one God, world without end. Amen."

After the Address, on motion, adjourned to meet at 5 o'clock, P. M.

Philadelphia, St. Andrew's Church,

Wednesday, 5 o'clock, P. M.

The Convention assembled pursuant to order; the Bishop of the Diocese presiding.

The President stated that the order of the day was the election of the Standing Committee, and appointed the Rev. J. W. Claxton and Rev. Byron McGann, tellers of the Clerical vote, and Messrs. H. L. Gaw and J. Vaughan Merrick, tellers of the Lay vote.

While the tellers were counting the votes,

The Rev. Dr. Hare, on behalf of the Committee on Alteration of Canons, moved that the Convention take up the Report of the Committee on Alteration of Canons made to the last Convention, which was agreed to.

The first resolution, appended to the Report, was adopted, as follows:

1. That in Section 1, of Canon VI., the passage beginning, "and to entitle him to such testimonial," and ending, "to the Standing Committee thereof," be stricken out, as conflicting with Title 1, Canon XII., Section 7, of the Digest.

The second resolution was adopted, as follows:

2. That Canon VII., Section 1, be amended to read, as follows: "At every Stated Convention a Standing Committee to consist of five of the Clergy and five of the Laity, shall be chosen by ballot, by the concurrent vote of the members of each order; provided, that the balloting may be dispensed with, in cases where only five Clergymen and five Laymen are nominated. And vacancies occurring by death or otherwise, in said Committee, shall be supplied by the concurrent vote of the remaining Clerical members and Lay members of the Committee."

The third resolution was adopted, as follows:

3. That in Canon XIV., the title be amended so as to read, "of Vacant Parishes," and that the first section be omitted.

The fourth resolution was adopted, as follows:

4. That Canon XV., Section 1, be amended to read as follows: "At every Stated Convention this Diocese, there *may*, and at the Stated Convention immediately preceding the Stated General Convention, there *shall* be chosen, by the concurrent ballot of the Clerical and Lay votes, Deputies the General Convention, whose appointment shall continue until the next Stated Convention, and until others are chosen in their places; provided, that the balloting may be dispensed with, in cases where only four Clergymen and four Laymen are nominated.

Mr. Elias P. Boudinot moved that the consideration

of the fifth Resolution be postponed until after the presentation of the Report of the Committee on Minority Representation.

The President decided that the resolution was carried, but a division being called for, it was adopted by a vote of 95 ayes, and 54 nays.

Pending the consideration of these resolutions, the tellers of the Clerical vote presented the following report:

Whole number of votes cast.. 105
Necessary to a choice... 53

CLERICAL MEMBERS.

Rev. Dr. Hare received.. 88
"   "   Morton   " 62
"   "   Goodwin " 60
"   "   Watson   " 60
"   "   Eccleston " 60
"   "   Davies   " 51
"   "   Hoffman " 41
"   "   Foggo   " 33
"   "   Yarnall " 30
"   "   Childs   " 19

LAY MEMBERS.

Mr. R. S. Smith received.. 99
"   Thomas Robins   " 97
"   Wm. F. Griffitts " 85
"   John Bohlen   " 72
"   John Clayton   " 66
"   G. W. Hunter   " 39
"   R. R. Montgomery " 38
"   John R. Whitney " 18
Scattering.. 7

The tellers of the vote of the Laity presented the following report:

Whole number of votes cast.. 77
Necessary to a choice... 39

Rev. Dr. Hare received.. 71
"   "   Watson   " 50
"   "   Morton   " 49
"   "   Goodwin " 49
"   "   Eccleston " 44
"   "   Davies   " 30
"   "   Foggo   " 23
"   "   Hoffman " 22
"   "   Yarnall " 22
"   "   Childs   " 14

LAY MEMBERS.

Mr. Thomas Robins received... 73
" R. S. Smith　　　　"　.. 71
" Wm. F. Griffitts　　"　.. 62
" John Bohlen　　　　"　.. 50
" John Clayton　　　　"　.. 48
" G. W. Hunter　　　　"　.................................:............................ 24
" R. R. Montgomery　"　.. 24
" J. R. Whitney　　　　"　.. 13
Scattering... 7

The President announced that the Rev. Dr. Hare, Rev. Dr. Morton, Rev. Dr. Goodwin, Rev. Dr. Watson and Rev. Dr. Eccleston, and Mr. Richard L. Smith, Mr. Thomas Robins, Mr. Wm. F. Griffitts, Mr. John Bohlen and Mr. John Clayton, having received a majority of the votes of both orders, were duly elected the Standing Committee.

The consideration of the resolutions appended to the Report of the Committee on Alteration of Canons, was then resumed, and the sixth resolution was adopted, as follows:

6. That Canon XVI. (respecting the repeal of former Canons) be omitted.

The seventh resolution was adopted, as follows:

7. That resolutions of a permanent nature, which have been passed by former Conventions, viz.: the Resolutions concerning the Establishment of the Diocesan Board of Missions: concerning the Convention, the Episcopal and the Christmas Funds; concerning drafts upon the funds by the Bishop and the Standing Committee; be incorporated with the Canons, after striking out therefrom so much as requires the election of the Treasurer of the Convention to be made by ballot, and making such merely verbal changes as may be necessary.

Before proceeding to the consideration of the eighth resolution, the Committee on Charters asked for permission to retire, which, on motion, was granted.

The eighth resolution was then adopted, as follows:

8. That Revised Regulations I., 1, be amended so that it shall read simply, " The Convention shall meet at five o'clock, P. M., on the day appointed."

I. 2, So the section shall be without the words, " it shall proceed in the dispatch of business."

I. 4, 4, Omit " without advancing "

I. 4, 13, Omit the whole.

Insert the order of I., 4 and I., 5.

Change I., 5. 3, so as to read, " Appointments of Committees, viz.: Committee on Charters, Committee on Claims of Clergymen to Seats, Committee on Claims of Deputies to Seats, Committee on Canons, Committee on Parochial History."

Add to I., 5, the following:

" 3. The above Order of Business and Rules of Order may be suspended by a vote of two-thirds of the members present, but not otherwise."

Omit Revised Regulations IV.

Make Revised Regulations V. a foot note to Canon XIII.

Omit Revised Regulations VI., 1, 2, 3, also VII.

The ninth resolution was adopted, as follows:

9. That in the Form of Charter, in the third paragraph, the phrase, "State of Pennsylvania," be exchanged for the phrase, "Diocese of Pennsylvania."

The tenth resolution was adopted, as follows:

10. That the Revised Regulations, amended as above, shall be incorporated with the Canons.

The eleventh resolution was adopted, as follows:

11. That the order of the Canons be so changed, that such incongruities as the precedence now given to penal matters may be avoided.

The twelfth resolution was adopted, as follows:

12. That there be prefixed to the Act of Association, Constitution and Canons, a Table of Contents.

The thirteenth resolution was adopted, as follows:

13. That one thousand copies of the Act of Association, the Constitution and the Canons (the last as by the above resolution amended), be printed under the direction of this Committee.

The fourteenth resolution was adopted, as follows:

14. That the following words in the Sixth Article of the Constitution of the Protestant Episcopal Church in the Diocese of Pennsylvania, viz.: "To preserve their journals and records," be stricken out, provided the next Convention of the Diocese shall so decide.

Rev. Dr. Hare, from the same Committee, moved to insert in Canon IX., Section 4, line 1, after the word "Diocese," "except in the City of Philadelphia," which resolution was, on motion, postponed.

Rev. Dr. Hare, from the same Committee, offered the following resolution, to be adopted as Section III., in Canon X.: *

1. The Christmas Fund shall consist of the avails of collections made in the Churches of the Diocese on Christmas Day, and sums of money otherwise contributed. It shall be managed by a Committee of Five Laymen, who shall be appointed annually by the Convention, of which Committee the Treasurer of the Fund shall be one. They shall have power and authority to receive and hold all moneys or other property contributed to the Fund either by bequest or otherwise, and

---

* The original paper containing this resolution was destroyed by the fire which consumed the office of the Printer. The substance is here given.

to appropriate the same, from time to time, in accordance with the provisions of this Canon. And any surplus of funds which may remain in their hands shall be invested by them in safe and productive securities, to be realized from, when, in the judgment of the Committee, the funds are needed to meet the appropriations made or to be made.

2. All appropriations from this Fund shall be made by the Committee, first, to Clergymen who shall be entitled to seats in the Convention of this Diocese, and shall at the time of the application be disabled by age or infirmity from performing the duties of their office; and, second, to the widows and orphans of Clergymen who, at the time of their death, were entitled to seats in the Convention. No appropriation to any beneficiary shall exceed $500 per annum.

3. If from any cause the Convention shall fail to appoint the Committee, then the old Committee shall hold over until a new one is regularly appointed. If, during the year, two or more of the Committee die or resign, the Standing Committee shall, upon being notified of the vacancies, appoint suitable persons to fill them.

4. The Convention shall, at every annual meeting, appoint a Treasurer of the Christmas Fund.

Rev. Dr. Buchanan moved the following amendment:

Resolved, That the words in paragraph 2, " shall be entitled to seats in the Convention," be stricken out, and the words, " has been received as a clergyman," be inserted in their place.

The amendment was lost.

The resolution was then adopted.

Rev. Dr. Hare offered, from the same Committee, the following resolution, to be adopted as Section 4, of Canon X.: *   :

" That Trustees be appointed by the Convention to receive any moneys which may be given, either for a permanent fund or for immediate distribution, for the education of the sons of the Clergy of this Diocese; the distribution to be made under the direction of the Bishop, who shall have the designation of the incumbents of all scholarships which may be created; except in the case of annual contributors to the Fund of not less than two hundred dollars, who shall have the right to nominate the incumbents to the scholarships created by them, during the continuance of their contributions."

The resolution was adopted.

The Rev. Mr. Wadleigh, on behalf of Mr. Aertsen, laid the Annual Report of the Trustees of the Christmas Fund on the table.

REPORT OF THE TRUSTEES OF THE CHRISTMAS FUND.

The Trustees of the Christmas Fund for Disabled Clergymen, and the Widows and Children of Deceased Clergymen, respectfully report:

That the receipts from the offertory, at the celebration of

---

* The original paper containing this resolution was destroyed by the fire which consumed the office of the Printer. The substance is here given.

the Holy Communion upon Christmas Day, amount to $3,395.28; from interest upon the Reserved Fund, and from interest upon temporary deposits, $297.40; making a total of receipts from all sources, $3,792.68.

The expenditures during the year have been $4,425 to beneficiaries, including special contributions to the same, there being now upon the list four Clergymen, six widows of Clergymen, and three Clergymen's families, all regular stipendaries. The number of these beneficiaries will, however, the coming year, be diminished by removal from the Diocese, and from the reach of the benefactions of the trust.

The Reserved Fund in the hands of the Treasurer amounts to $2,650, invested in United States Bonds. In addition to this fund, the Trustees will, in the course of the present year, be put in possession of a legacy of $5,000 from the estate of Mrs. Ann D. Ducachet, the widow of the Rev. H. W. Ducachet, D. D., the principal sum of which legacy is to be held intact, and the interest only to be applied to the purposes for which this trust was created.

Since the last meeting of the Convention, the division of the Diocese, then consented to, has become an accomplished fact, and the attention of the Trustees has been called to what seemed to them an equitable claim, of the Diocese of Central Pennsylvania to a part of the Reserved Fund of the trust.

The Parishes comprised within the circuit of the new Diocese have regularly contributed to the Christmas Fund, while the disbursements therein have been very small; at the time of the separation but one beneficiary upon our list residing there. As the Convention of the Diocese of Central Pennsylvania has established a similar trust to ours, it seems but just to ask that that trust should enjoy the benefits of the accretion of former years, the result, in part, of the contributions of those whom it represents; and we would recommend that our Treasurer be empowered to pay over to the Treasurer of the Christmas Fund of the Diocese of Central Pennsylvania, fifteen hundred dollars of Bonds of the United States, being part of the Reserved Fund now held by this trust.

The Trustees cannot close their report without recording their sense of the great loss sustained by them in the death of Mr. Edward L. Clark, since the year 1861, a member of their Board, and always zealous and active in promoting the objects had in view in its creation, and ever assisting in its deliberations with wise and liberal counsel.

By order of the Board.

JOHN S. NEWBOLD,

Secretary.

Rev. Mr. Wadleigh, on behalf of the Trustees of the Christmas Fund, offered the following resolution, which was adopted:

Resolved, That the Treasurer of the Christmas Fund for Disabled Clergymen and the Widows and Children of Deceased Clergymen be, and he is hereby, instructed to hand over to the Treasurer of the Christmas Fund of the Diocese of Central Pennsylvania fifteen hundred dollars, in Bonds of the United States, being part of the Reserved Fund now in the hands of the Trustees.

Rev. Mr. Wadleigh nominated the following Trustees of the Christmas Fund:

Mr. Thomas Robins,	Mr. John S. Newbold,
" John Welsh,	" Thomas H. Montgomery.

There being no other nominations, they were duly elected.

Mr R. P. McCullagh having been nominated as Treasurer of the Christmas Fund, and there being no other nominations, he was duly elected.

The Report of the Treasurer of the Convention Fund was laid upon the table.

Mr. Benjamin G. Godfrey having been nominated as Treasurer of the Convention Fund, and there being no other nominations, he was duly elected.

Rev. Dr. Claxton, from the Committee on Charters, reported favorably on the Charters of "the Church of Our Merciful Saviour," and of the "Eglise du St. Sauveur," and, on motion, they were admitted into union with the Convention.

Rev. Dr. Watson, from the Committee to take into consideration verbal changes in the Constitution, made a report, by which the Preamble to the Constitution shall read as follows: *

WHEREAS, By an Act of Association, agreed to and adopted in Convention, on the 24th day of May, 1785, sundry of the Protestant Episcopal Churches within this Commonwealth were united under the name of "The Protestant Episcopal Church in the State of Pennsylvania;" which Association embraced all those Clergy and Congregations who did at that time, or subsequently, assent to the same;

AND WHEREAS, Since that time, in General Conventions of the Protestant Episcopal Churches within the United States, a Constitution and Canons were formed for the government and discipline of the same, which recognized each State as constituting a District or Diocese, with the right to the Churches within the same to exercise a local government over themselves; which right has been accordingly exercised by the Protestant Episcopal Churches within the State of Pennsylvania, associated as aforesaid;

AND WHEREAS, By the action of subsequent General Conventions, two new Dioceses have been erected within the State of Pennsylvania, whereby the limits of the parent Diocese have been lessened, and its boundaries made different from the boundaries of the State;

AND WHEREAS, It is now deemed expedient more expressly to set forth the system of local government to be exercised within this Diocese,

The following, with the Act of Association, is declared to be the Constitution of the Protestant Episcopal Church in the Diocese of Pennsylvania:

Also proposing to substitute the word "Diocese" for the word "State," viz: in Sections II. and IV. of the Constitution.

On motion, the resolution appended to the report was adopted.

Dr. Hoffman, from the Committee on City Missions, read a report, with a resolution proposing a Canon appended.

On motion, the resolution was laid upon the table for the present.

Rev. Mr. Harris read a report from the Committee on Parochial History, with a resolution, recommending that the same amount should be appropriated as last year for the purposes of the Committee; which was adopted.

On motion, adjourned.

---

* Original destroyed. As before, the substance is given.

Philadelphia, St. Andrew's Church,

May 16th, 1872, 9 O'CLOCK, A. M.

The Convention met pursuant to order.

Morning Prayer was read by Messrs. DuHamel and R. A. Edwards.

The President having taken the Chair,

The Secretary read the minutes of the proceedings of yesterday's sessions, which, on motion, were adopted.

The President, in a few feeling remarks, called attention to the sudden death of Mr. Charles E. Lex, a Lay Deputy to this Convention.

Rev. Dr. Goodwin offered the following preamble and resolution, which were seconded by the Rev. Dr. Newton, and were unanimously adopted, after a number of addresses made by members of the Convention, the vote having been taken standing :

WHEREAS, This Convention has just heard of the sudden demise of Charles E. Lex, Esq., one of its prominent Lay Members ; therefore,

Resolved, That in the Christian character of Mr. Lex, and in his noble work for Christ, we recognize an admirable example for ourselves, while in his cheerful trust in the Redeemer, we have seen the wisdom of his preparation for his departure. We desire to place on record this expression of our high estimate of his personal qualities, as well as of the value of his services to the Church, particularly as a member of this Convention and, for several years, of the Standing Committee of the Diocese. With the expression of our own profound grief and sorrow, we hereby tender to his family and friends the assurance of our most heartfelt sympathy; and will join in humble prayers to Almighty God, that He will grant them His heavenly support and consolation.

The Bishop then invited the Convention to join with him in prayer, for the family and friends of Mr. Lex, and for ourselves.

Rev. Mr. Matlack moved that a Committee be appointed to present these resolutions to the family of Mr. Lex.

The President appointed Rev. Drs. Goodwin and Newton, Rev. Mr. Matlack, and Messrs. M. Russell Thayer, Isaac Hazlehurst, and R. R. Montgomery, the Committee.

Rev. Dr. Stewart moved the following resolution:

Resolved, That the name of H. G. Batterson, D. D., be referred to the Committee on Claims of Clergymen to Seats.

Which was lost.

The Secretary called the names of the Deputies from the Church of the Merciful Saviour.

The order of the day, the Report of the Board of Missions in the Diocese, was then called for.

Rev. J. W. Claxton read the Report of the Board (see Appendix), to which was appended a Report of the Southeastern Convocation, and, also, the following resolution, viz.:

Resolved, That it be recommended to the Convention of this Diocese to rescind its action by which the City of Philadelphia was withdrawn from its field of labor in order that the Board may take entire charge of Missions in this Diocese.

Judge Thayer moved that the resolution of the Board be laid upon the table, but withdrew the motion temporarily for the purpose of discussion.

Mr. J. R. Sypher offered the following resolution:

Resolved, That the Bishop in consultation with the Board of Diocesan Missions may appoint a Board of Council on Missionary Work in the City of Philadelphia, to have charge of such special work in the City as may be assigned to it, by the Board of Diocesan Missions.

Judge Thayer made the point of order that this resolution contemplated a fundamental change in the Canon and must therefore go through the regular course prescribed in such cases.

He afterwards withdrew the point of order.

Rev. Dr. Hay moved the following, as a substitute for Mr. Sypher's resolution:

Resolved, That the Board of Missions be instructed to carry on the charitable and religious work in the City of Philadelphia as a distinct department in the work entrusted to the Board.

Mr. William Welsh offered a resolution, which was accepted by the Rev. Dr. Hay, as a substitute for his substitute:

Resolved, That it be recommended to the Board of Missions to continue a Board of Council for City Missions, in accordance with the recommendation of the Bishop in his address to the Convention.

The resolution, as substituted, was, on motion, adopted.

The President announced that the Rt. Rev. the Bishop of Central Pennsylvania was present, and as the Convention was upon the subject of Diocesan Missions, he would, with its consent, ask him to address to the Convention any remarks he might have to make.

In accordance with the request, the Bishop of Central Pennsylvania addressed the Convention, earnestly appealing to it to instruct the Board of Missions to continue a longer assistance than that already promised to the support of Missions in Central Pennsylvania.

Rev. Mr. Matlack offered the following resolution:

Resolved, That it be recommended to the Board of Missions of this Diocese, and said Board is hereby authorized, to extend to the Missionary stations now under its care in Central Pennsylvania such aid in the future as it may think wise and expedient.

Mr. Fred. Fraley offered the following amendment:

That the Bishop of this Diocese be respectfully requested to name some Sunday in each of the next three years, on which a collection may be taken in each of the Churches of this Diocese for Missions in Central Pennsylvania.

Which was lost.

Dr. Pratt offered a substitute:

Resolved, That the Board of Missions be authorized to notify the Diocese of Central Pennsylvania, that after the 1st of November they will appropriate to the Missions in that Diocese the amount appropriated for the current year, less twenty-five per cent.

Which was lost.

Mr. Matlack's resolution was adopted.

On motion, adjourned.

Philadelphia, St. Andrew's Church,

THURSDAY, 5 O'CLOCK, P. M.

The Convention assembled, and was called to order by the President.

The Secretary read the Report of the Standing Committee of the Diocese, as follows:

REPORT.

The Standing Committee report that they organized on the 1st of June, 1871, by electing Rev. Dr. Morton, President, and John Clayton, Secretary. On the 7th of December, 1871, Rev. Dr. Howe resigned as a member of the Committee, and on the 1st of February, 1872, Rev. James Houston Eccleston was elected to fill the vacancy occasioned by his resignation.

December 7, 1871, consent was given to the Consecration of Rev. Mark Antony DeWolfe Howe, D. D., as Bishop of Central Pennsylvania.

During the official year they have recommended for ordination to Priest's Orders:

Rev. J. Everist Cathell,	Rev. R. K. Innes,
" J. J. A. Morgan,	" Algernon Morton,
" Gilbert L. Bishop,	" Joseph Lyons Miller,
" John S. Beers,	" William H. Josephus,
" Ezra Isaac,	" Robert Mackie.
" John Coleman,	

They have received and accepted Certificates of Examination of the following Candidates for Priest's Orders:

Albert Clark Abrams,	Charles E. Benedict,
William B. Burk,	Rev. Joseph Lyons Miller,
Henry C. Pastorius,	" William H. Josephus,
Rev. T. William Davidson,	" Robert Mackie.
" Algernon Morton,	

They have recommended for ordination to Deacon's Orders:

Joseph Lyons Miller,	Rush S. Eastman,
William H. Josephus,	Wm. Henry Platt,
T. William Davidson,	Robert James Bowen,
John G. Bawn,	William B. Burk,
William G. P. Brinckloe,	Thomas Reed List,
Henry G. Pastorius,	Peter E. Jones,
William Simonton Cochran,	Charles E. Benedict.

8

And have recommended as candidates for the Holy Order of Deacons:

Henry Morton Reed,	Rodney Rush Swope,
Everard Patterson Miller,	Wm. Jones Skerrett,
Marcellus Karcher,	J. Chalice Craven,
James W. Ashton,	Geo. O. Eddy.

On the 2d of November, 1871, the Bishop notified the Committee, that on the 11th inst., he proposed leaving for Europe on an official visitation to the Churches and congregations there connected with our Church, to be absent until March, 1872, and authorized the Committee to act as the Ecclesiastical authority of the Diocese during his absence.

In pursuance of the authority so vested in them, the Committee granted Letters Dimissory as follows:

Rev. F. E. Arnold, to Diocese of Delaware, December 4th, 1872.
" Benj. J. Douglas, " " " "
" John Ireland, " New Jersey, " "
" Wm. Temple Bowen " Central Penn'a, " "
" Thos. Burrows, " Maryland, February 14th, 1872.

The following Letters Dimissory were recieved:

Rev. W. W. Spear, D. D., from Diocese of New Jersey, March 3d, 1872.
" J. Newton Spear, " " " " "
" Henry A. Parker, " " New York " 5th, 1872.

On the 7th of September, 1871, consent was given to the Church of the Holy Apostles, Philadelphia, mortgaging their Church edifice and ground for the sum of $18,000, of which $10,000 was to be applied to the extinguishment of a ground rent thereon, and the balance to the payment of debts against the Church building. December 7th, 1871, Committee assented to the Church of the Resurrection, Rising Sun, Philadelphia, mortgaging their Parsonage and piece of ground for $3,000, a debt incurred in rebuilding their Church edifice. January 4th, 1872, St. Luke's Church, Germantown, was authorized to mortgage certain property for $7,000, and to sell certain other property, and on the 4th of April, 1872, authority was given St. Andrew's Church, West Philadelphia, to sell a certain lot of ground.

The Committee have, during the year, consented to the establishment of the following new Churches in Philadelphia: One at Falls of Schuylkill, another at Norris and Camac Streets, and a third at Nineteenth and Titan Streets.

On the 1st of June, 1871, the following gentlemen were elected members of the Board of Missions, to serve for three years:

Rev. M. A. De Wolfe Howe, D. D.,	Rev. E. A. Warriner,
" T. F. Davies,	Mr. John Welsh,
" W. P. Orrick,	" J. S. McCalla,
" S. E. Appleton,	" Edw'd L. Clark,
" Percy Browne,	" Frederick Fraley.

And subsequently Rev. D. S. Miller, D. D., Rev. J. B. Faulkner, and Mr. George Hoffman were elected in the place of Rev. Dr. Howe and Rev. Mr. Browne, removed, and Mr. E. L. Clark, deceased.

The following disbursements have been made by the joint direction of the Bishop and Standing Committee, by drafts on the Treasurer of the Convention and Episcopal Funds:

John Short, services...$15 00
Payment of 2d Vol. Historical Collections of American Colonial Church...... 10 75
    "   Atlas of Pennsylvania in Counties............................... 12 00

The following official acts were performed by the Rt. Rev. Bishop Howe, of Central Pennsylvania, during the absence of Bishop Stevens:

January 5th. Confirmed one person, in private, for St. Mark's, Philadelphia.
January 7th. Confirmed 16, at St. Andrew's Church, West Philadelphia.
January 21st. Ordained to the Diaconate, W. G. P., Brinckloe, at Church of Annunciation.
Same day. Evening, Confirmed 17, at Church of the Merciful Saviour, Philadelphia.
January 22d. Confirmed 10, at Grace Church, Hulmeville.
January 28th. Confirmed 25, at Church of the Redemption. Philadelphia.
February 12th. Confirmed 21, at St. James' Church, Downingtown.
February 25th, A. M. Confirmed at Church of the Mediator 14. P. M., confirmed at St. George's, Cardington, 22. Evening, Church of Messiah, Philadelphia, 18.
March 6th. Evening, confirmed at Zion Church, Philadelphia, 15.
March 7th. Consecrated Church of Good Shepherd, Radnor.
March 8th. Consecrated Church of the Resurrection, Rising Sun, and confirmed 14. Evening, at Episcopal Hospital, confirmed 11.
April 21st. Confirmed at St. Luke's, Philadelphia, 42.
April 26th. Confirmed in St. John's, Pequea, 14.
Total confirmed, 240, on 13 occasions ; ordained 1 ; consecrated 2 Churches.

The Committee herewith present the account of the Treasurer of the Convention and Episcopal Funds, together with the account of Benjamin G. Godfrey, Treasurer of the Diocese, as to the collections and contributions in response to the Pastoral Letter of Bishop Stevens, of October 10, 1871, in behalf of the suffering people of Chicago; which several accounts have been examined, and are correct.

JOHN CLAYTON,

Philadelphia, May 15, 1872.   *Secretary.*

Mr. Harry Ingersoll offered the following resolution:

Resolved, That the Bishop of the Diocese is hereby requested to appoint six Clergymen and six Laymen, as representatives of this Convention, to attend the funeral of our late fellow-member, Charles E. Lex.

Which was adopted.

The President appointed the following gentlemen to act under the resolution:

Messrs. H. Ingersoll, G. W. Stroud, Isaac Hazlehurst, John Bohlen, M. Russell Thayer, L. H. Redner, Rev. Drs. Goodwin, Morton, Claxton, Suddards, Rev. J. P. DuHamel and Rev. Dr. Yarnall.

Dr. Hare called up the Report of the Committee on Minority Representation to the last Convention, and moved the adoption of the resolution appended to the Report.

The motion was lost.

Dr. Hare moved that the matter which had been postponed until after this Report had been acted upon, be the fifth resolution of the Committee on Alteration in Canons, and moved the passage of the Canon as Canon XXII., which was adopted.

Dr. Hare asked permission to leave out certain objectionable expressions in the Canon respecting the Christmas Fund, which was granted.

Dr. Childs moved the reconsideration of the adoption of Letter H. in the Order of Business on the Second Day, p. 167, Journal 1871, which was agreed to.

Dr. Childs then moved to transfer Letter H., p. 161, to Letter A., on the same page, on the third day, so as to read as follows:

"The Report of the Board of Missions and the discussion incident thereto, at 10 o'clock, A. M.: *Provided,* That the elections shall have been then concluded."

On motion, the Canons, as amended, were adopted.

The Rev. Dr. Drumm renewed the resolution offered by him at a former Covention :

Resolved, That the religious services of the Convention be held in a Church, and the business meetings elsewhere.

The motion was lost.

The Rev. Dr. Claxton offered the following resolution:

Resolved, That the Secretary be requested to acknowledge the polite invitations of the Historical Society of Pennsylvania and the Union League of Philadelphia, and to tender to these Societies respectively, the thanks of this Convention.

Which was adopted.

Mr. Richard R. Montgomery moved the appointment, by the President, of the Committee on Canons called for by the Canons now adopted, as if it had been made on the first day of the Convention, which was ageed to.

The Rev. Dr. Drumm offered the following :

Resolved, That the thanks of this Convention be and are hereby given to the Bishop of the Diocese for his very interesting and instructive account of his visit to the Churches of our Communion on the Continent of Europe, and that the Bishop be requested to furnish the Convention with a copy of the Address for publication.

Which was carried unanimously.

The President named as the Committee on Canons : Rev. Drs. Hare, Hoffman and Watson, and Messrs. R. R. Montgomery, George W. Hunter, John Bohlen.

The Rev. William Newton offered the following:

Resolved, That so much of the Bishop's Address as relates to the celebration of the Centenary of our National Independence, be referred to a Committee of six persons, to report at the next Convention.

Which was adopted.

The President appointed the Rev. Drs. Davies, Foggo and Claxton, Messrs. Frederick Fraley, Charles R. King, James M. Aertsen.

Mr. William Welsh offered the following :

Resolved, That so much of the Bishop's Address, as relates to the Bishop Potter Memorial House, be referred to a Committee of three Clergymen and three Laymen to co-operate with the Bishop in carrying his suggestions into effect, and to report their action to the next Convention.

Which was adopted.

The President appointed the Rev. J. Andrews Harris, the Rev. Dr. Miller, the Rev. Dr. Davies, Messrs. Lemuel Coffin, Charles R. King, Andrew Wheeler.

The Rev. Dr. Hoffman moved that a Canon brought in by the Committee on City Missions, on the organization of new Parishes, and the establishment of Missionary Stations, be referred to the Committee on Canons; which was adopted.

On motion of Mr. George W. Hunter:

Resolved, That the next Annual Convention of this Diocese be held in St. Andrew's Church, Philadelphia, on the second Tuesday in May, 1873.

Mr. Hazlehurst read the Report of the Committee on the subject of the Distribution of the Episcopal Fund of the Diocese, as follows, and asked that the Committee be discharged:

REPORT.

At the Annual Convention of this Diocese, held in May, 1871, it was

Resolved, That the whole subject relating to a division of the "Episcopate Fund," for the support of the new Diocese proposed to be set off, be referred to a Committee of Seven, to report at the next Convention.

In conformity with the requirements of that resolution, your Committee respectfully beg leave to make the following report:

The only subject to which the attention of the Committee has been called is that of the "*Episcopal Fund*" of this Diocese; and the sole question before them for consideration was, Whether the Diocese of Central Pennsylvania has any legal or equitable claim to any portion of said Fund.

The history of the Episcopal Fund may thus be stated: On the 31st day of May, A. D. 1809, Bishop White, in his Address to the Convention of the Diocese, made the following communication:

"It becomes my duty to make known to this Convention, that some years ago, the late Mr. Andrew Doz devised the greater part of his estate to be divided, after the decease of his then wife and daughters, and applied to seven public uses; among which was a provision for the Bishop of the Protestant Episcopal Church and his successors, who shall have the City of Philadelphia within his Diocese. In consequence of the late decease of Mrs. Margaret McGaw, daughter of Mr. Doz, the three Trustees under the will, of whom I am one, are taking measures for the sale and distribution of the property; of which $2,000 have been paid this morning, and are now ready to be appropriated as a Fund for your Bishop for the time being."

The Journal then proceeds as follows, after the close of the Bishop's Address :

" In consequence of the information laid before this Convention by the Bishop, of a legacy bequeathed by the late Mr. Andrew Doz, it was

" *Resolved,* That the Standing Committee and Council of Advice be authorized to consider of and direct proper measures for the vesting of the said legacy, and further securing of it in Trustees."

On the 19th of June, 1810 (26th Convention), Bishop White, in his address to the Convention, referred to the same subject in the following words:

" Having noticed to the last Convention the legacy of the late Mr. Andrew Doz, and informed them that the sum of Two Thousand Dollars had been recently paid, I think it proper to mention now that the said Fund has been laid out by the Council of Advice in a ground rent, which is vested in two Trustees, and made payable to the Bishop of this Church for the time being. The Trustees, under the will of Mr. Doz, are proceeding in the sales of different parts of his estate, and it is probable that another sum will be received shortly."

On the 11th of June, 1811, Bishop White, in his address to the 27th Convention, alluded again to the Doz legacy, in the following words:

" In my last annual communication there was held out the expectation of another payment from the estate of the late Mr. Andrew Doz. Accordingly it may be proper to mention that there has been a payment of two thousand dollars, of which thirteen hundred and thirty-three dollars and thirty-three cents are on a bond, secured by mortgage, and the remainder in money. The Council of Advice have taken means for the realizing of the latter sum, agreeably to the directions of a former Convention."

At this Convention, on motion of the Hon. James Wilson, it was

Resolved, That a Committee be appointed to devise a plan for instituting a Fund for the Support of the Episcopate in this State, to report to the next Convention.

On May 26th, 1812, that Committee made a report to the 28th Convention, in which reference is made to the legacy of A. Doz, Esq., towards a Fund for the support of the Bishop in the State of Pennsylvania, and proposed "a plan for completing the Fund, of which he has so generously laid the foundation;" which was, in brief, that each settled Clergyman should once a year preach a sermon on the Apostolic Succession, and that a collection shall then be made for the support of the Episcopate; and that such collections, and the interest thereon, shall be made an increasing fund, until a future Convention shall think it expedient to apply the proceeds thereof to the proposed object. This Report "was considered by sections, and unanimously adopted." In 1814, the Canons and Regulations were revised and confirmed. Of the Regulations, the following plan was one, and the 13th Regulation is as follows: "The Standing Committee and Council of Advice are hereby authorized to consider of and direct proper measures for the vesting of the legacy of Andrew Doz, Esq., to the Bishop of the Protestant Episcopal Church, and his successors, who shall have the City of Philadelphia within his Diocese." On May 8th, 1816, the following declaration was unanimously adopted:

"Whereas, The bequest of the late A. Doz, Esq., to the Bishop of the Protestant Episcopal Church, and his successors, is by the terms thereof given to such Bishop as shall have the City of Philadelphia within his Diocese;

And whereas, In pursuance of certain resolutions, adopted by the Convention on the 26th of May, 1812, and confirmed by the Convention of 1814, a considerable sum of money has been contributed by members of the Churches in this State, eastward of the Allegheny Mountains, for completing the Fund of which he has so liberally laid the foundation;

And whereas, It is intended, and implied, by the said resolutions, although not so expressed, that the money so raised, and to be raised, shall, when in the opinion of a future Convention it shall be thought expedient, be applied to the same purpose which was contemplated by the donor of the foundation of the Fund of which it formed a part; and it is expedient to prevent any misapprehension which a change of circumstances might give rise to on this subject;

It is therefore hereby declared, That the sums of money heretofore raised, and all such as shall hereafter be raised, by virtue and in pursuance of the resolution before mentioned, shall be exclusively appropriated to the Bishop of the Protestant Episcopal Church and his successors, who shall have the City of Philadelphia within his Diocese."

On the 23d of May, 1829, the VI. Revised Regulation of the Fund for the Support of the Episcopate, as it now stands, was adopted. It is substantially the same as it was before, with the addition of the declaration of 1816, as its 5th Article, that the income of the said Fund shall be exclusively appropriated for the use of the Bishop who shall have the City of Philadelphia within his Diocese."

Since this declaration, the Episcopal Fund has increased by contributions from numerous individual donors and the accumulations thus received, amounting in all to $39,500, have been invested for that Trust.

. To a portion of that Fund the new Diocese of Central Pennsylvania now lays claim.

While the Committee have not been favored with any argument in support of this claim, beyond the documents submitted to this Convention, at its last session, they have considered the whole subject with great care and thought, and have called to their aid the experience and action of other Dioceses under similar circumstances. The argument, that whenever a Diocese is divided, the parts set off retain their rights to the property of the undivided Diocese, is without weight. The case of the division of a Diocese is the same as the division of a parish or a county. If an outlying portion of a Parish divide from the Mother Church, and form a new Parish, in the absence of agreements to the contrary, it retains no right to the property of the old one. Though the individuals who withdraw may be the very ones who have contributed most largely to the old Church and its support, they can reclaim nothing, and as the same rule holds good in the division of a county, it must apply to the division of a Diocese.

But the Diocese of Central Pennsylvania, through its Committee to Secure an Endowment of its Episcopate, ask: *First.*

9

That all the Diocesan Funds now belonging to the present Diocese of Pennsylvania, be *equitably* divided; and, *Secondly.* That all the funds now belonging to the present Diocese of Pennsylvania, which are not restricted from alienation, be given to the new Diocese, provided the same do not exceed one-half the entire amount of such Fund. The Committee have not been favored with any argument in favor of the resolution. It is true that the Committee say: "That they have labored under constant embarrassment in obtaining subscriptions and pledges from what may with propriety be termed the general response of the Church within those limits, viz., of the proposed division of the Diocese. Without an equitable division of the several Diocesan Funds now belonging to the Diocese of Pennsylvania, it would be an act of injustice; as they have hitherto contributed to the funds now in the custody and control of the present Diocese of Pennsylvania, they consider themselves entitled to a just proportion of said funds to be appropriated in aid of the endowment of the new Diocese."

In the judgment of your Committee, the application for a division of the Fund has no foundation in equity, and it is a conclusive answer to it, that there is *no fund which the Convention can divide or alienate without violating a fundamental condition of the Trust upon which it was created and is held.*

The Churches not embraced within the five counties, when they took measures for a Diocese of their own, knew that this would involve expense, in a special pecuniary burden incident to the division, and to their having an Episcopate of their own. If any expectation had existed on the part of any of the brethren in the new Diocese that the Episcopal Fund would be divided, such expectations could only have arisen out of a very imperfect knowledge of the facts.

Your Commiitee are, therefore, satisfied that the Diocese of Central Pennsylvania has no legal or equitable claim whatever to any part of the Episcopal Fund of the Diocese of Pennsylvania, and they are also satisfied that the Convention of this Diocese has no power to direct the division of, or to alienate any portion of it. The Committee ask to be discharged from the further consideration of the subject.

ISAAC HAZLEHURST,
GEO. W. HUNTER,
M. RUSSELL THAYER,
THOMAS ROBINS.

Mr. Sypher moved that the Report be recommitted, with instructions to investigate the matter more fully, and report to the next Convention, which was lost.

On motion, the Committee was discharged.

The Rev. Dr. Hare stated that the matter of the formation of a Federate Council had been referred to a Committee.

The Rev. Dr. Watson thereupon read the following report:

WHEREAS, At the General Convention of the Protestant Episcopal Church, in the year 1868, a Canon was passed (viz., Canon VIII. Title 3) empowering the several Dioceses within the limits of a single State or Commonwealth, where such may be formed, "to establish for themselves a Federate Convention or Council, representing such Dioceses, which may deliberate and decide upon the common interests of the Church within the limits aforesaid," with the following proviso: " But before any determinate action of such Convention or Council shall be had, the powers proposed to be exercised thereby shall be submitted to the General Convention for its approval;"

AND WHEREAS, There are now within the limits of the Commonwealth of Pennsylvania three Dioceses, to wit: the Diocese of Pennsylvania, the Diocese of Pittsburgh, and the Diocese of Central Pennsylvania, therefore

Resolved, That it is expedient that steps be taken by this Convention to inaugurate action under said Canon, looking to the formation of a Federate Council of the Dioceses above named.

Resolved, That a Committee of Six be appointed to confer with the authorities of the Dioceses of Pittsburgh and Central Pennsylvania, proposing the formation of such Federate Council, and uniting with them (agreeing to such a measure) in arranging the preliminaries which shall be necessary to its consummation.

Resolved, That said Committee report its proceedings and final acts to the next Convention of the Diocese.

The resolutions were adopted.

The President, with the consent of the Convention, named the Committee on Canons as the Committee.

The Rev. Dr. Pratt offered the following:

Resolved, That this Convention listened with great interest to the statement and appeal of Bishop Howe, of the Diocese of Central Pennsylvania, and hereby assures him of its deep sympathy in his work, and of its earnest desire to aid him in all suitable ways, in his efforts to establish the Church in his important Diocese.

Which was adopted.

The Rev. Dr. Hare, from the Committee on Canons, reported back the Canon of the Organization of New Parishes and the Establishment of Mission Services in the City of Philadelphia.

The Rev. Dr. Goodwin moved that the consideration of the Canon be postponed until the next Convention, which was lost on a division—ayes 53, nays 57.

On motion of the Rev. Robert Ritchie, the Canon reported by Dr. Hare, was amended so as to remove the right of appeal from the five nearest Rectors.

The Rev. Dr. Davies moved a re-consideration of the vote against postponement, which was agreed to :

And, on motion, it was

Resolved, That the further consideration of the Canon be postponed until the next Convention.

On motion of Mr. Welsh, it was ordered, that 750 copies of the Journal of the Proceedings be printed for the use of the Convention.

On motion, it was

Resolved, That after reading the rough minutes of this day's Session, the Convention adjourn

The minutes were then read, and approved.

After religious exercises, which, at the request of the Bishop of the Diocese, were conducted by the Bishop of Central Pennsylvania, the Convention adjourned *sinc die*.

JOHN A. CHILDS,

Secretary.

CHURCHES IN UNION

WITH THE

CONVENTION.

	Admitted.
BUCKS COUNTY.	
Church of St. James the Greater, Bristol..........................	1785
St. Andrew's Church, Yardleyville.............................	1835
St. Luke's Church, Newtown..................................	1835
Grace Church, Hulmeville.....................................	1837
Trinity Church, Centreville...................................	1840
St. Paul's Church, Doylestown................................	1847
CHESTER COUNTY.	
St. Peter's Church, Great Valley..............................	1785
St. John's Church, New London...............................	1793
St. Mary's Church, Warwick Township.........................	1808
St. John's Church, Pequea....................................	1810
St. Paul's Church, West Whiteland Township...................	1828
St. Andrew's Church, West Vincent............................	1834
St. Mark's Church, Honeybrook...............................	1837
Church of the Holy Trinity, West Chester......................	1838
St. Peter's Church, Phœnixville...............................	1840
St. James', Downingtown.....................................	1844
St. James', West Marlboro'...................................	1849
Church of the Trinity, Coatesville............................	1869
Grace Church, Parkesburg...................................	1871
DELAWARE COUNTY.	
St. Paul's Church, Chester...................................	1786
St. Martin's Church, Marcus Hook............................	1786
St. David's (Radnor) Church, Newtown Township...............	1786
St. John's Church, Concord Township.........................	1786
Calvary Church, Rockdale....................................	1835
Christ Church, Media.......................................	1858
Church of the Good Shepherd, Radnor........................	1871
MONTGOMERY COUNTY.	
St. James' Church, Perkiomen................................	1785
St. Thomas' Church, Whitemarsh.............................	1786
St. John's Church, Norristown...............................	1815
Christ Church, Pottstown....................................	1829
Church of the Redeemer, Lower Merion.......................	1852
Church of Our Saviour, Jenkintown..........................	1858
Calvary Church, Conshohocken..............................	1859
St. Paul's Church, Cheltenham..............................	1861
St. John's Church, Lower Merion..............................	1863
Church of the Messiah, Gwynedd.............................	1868
St. Paul's Memorial Church, Upper Providence................	1869

PHILADELPHIA COUNTY.	Admitted.
Christ Church..	1785
St. Peter's Church....................................	1785
St. Paul's Church......................................	1785
Trinity Church, Oxford...............................	1785
All Saints', Lower Dublin............................	1786
St. James' Church......................................	1810
St. John's Church, Northern Liberties..............	1816
St. Luke's Church, Germantown.....................	1818
Trinity Church, Southwark...........................	1821
St. Stephen's Church..................................	1823
St. Andrew's Church..................................	1823
St. Matthew's, Francisville..........................	1825
Grace Church..	1827
St. Mary's, West Philadelphia.......................	1827
St. David's Church, Manayunk.......................	1833
Church of the Epiphany...............................	1834
Church of the Ascension..............................	1837
Emmanuel Church, Kensington......................	1837
All Saints' Church, Moyamensing....................	1838
St. Luke's Church	1839
St. Philip's Church, Spring Garden..................	1841
Church of the Advent, Northern Liberties..........	1842
Church of the Evangelists, Southwark..............	1842
Emmanuel Church, Holmesburg.....................	1844
St. James' Church, Kingsessing......................	1844
Gloria Dei Church, Southwark.......................	1845
Church of the Nativity, Spring Garden..............	1845
Church of the Redemption, Spring Garden..........	1846
Church of St. James the Less, North Penn Township....	1846
St. Mark's Church, Frankford........................	1846
Church of the Crucifixion, Moyamensing...........	1847
Church of the Messiah, Port Richmond.............	1847
Church of the Atonement............................	1847
St. Mark's Church.....................................	1848
Church of the Mediator..............................	1848
St. Jude's Church, Spring Garden...................	1848
Zion Church, South Penn Township.................	1849
St. Bartholomew's Church, Kensington.............	1849
Church of the Resurrection, Rising Sun............	1851
St. Andrew's, West Philadelphia....................	1852
Church of the Saviour, West Philadelphia..........	1852
Christ Church, Germantown..........................	1853
Trinity Church, Maylandville........................	1853
Church of Our Saviour, Moyamensing..............	1854
St. Clement's Church.................................	1855
St. Paul's Church, Chestnut Hill....................	1856
Church of the Holy Trinity...........................	1857
Calvary Monumental Church, Northern Liberties....	1857
Church of the Covenant..............................	1858
Church of St. John the Baptist, Germantown.......	1858
Calvary Church, Germantown........................	1859
Church of the Intercessor, Spring Garden..........	1859
Church of St. Matthias, Spring Garden.............	1859
Church of the Incarnation, Spring Garden..........	1860
Church of St. John the Evangelist, Southwark......	1860

PHILADELPHIA COUNTY.	Admitted.
St. Michael's Church, Germantown	1860
St. Luke's the Beloved Physician, Bustleton	1861
The House of Prayer, Branchtown	1861
St. Timothy's Church, Roxborough	1861
St. Alban's Church, Roxborough	1862
Grace Church, Mount Airy	1862
Free Church of St. John, Frankford Road	1864
African Church of St. Thomas	1864
St. James' Church, Hestonville	1867
Church of the Holy Apostles	1868
Church of the Good Shepherd	1869
Clay Mission Chapel	1869
St. Stephen's Church, Bridesburg	1869
Church of the Holy Innocents, Tacony	1869
St. George's, Kenderton	1870
St. Paul's, Aramingo	1870
The Church of the Messiah	1870
St. George's Church	1870
St. Timothy's Church	1871
St. Sauveur's Church	1872
Church of the Merciful Saviour	1872

APPENDIX A.

PAROCHIAL REPORTS.

BUCKS COUNTY.

St. James' (the Greater) Church. The Rev. John H. Drumm, D.D., Rector. Admitted 1785.
A. Murray McIlvaine and Henry L. Gaw, Wardens.

Baptisms, adults 7, infants 24, total 31; confirmed 17; communicants, present number about 130; public services, on Sundays 150, on other days about 50, total 200; average attendance on Sundays about 300; children catechized once a month; Sunday Schools 2; officers and teachers principal school, 19; scholars about 170; in Bensalem, 3 teachers and about 25 scholars; Bible Classes 2, teachers 2, members 25; Church 1; sittings about 400; Sunday School building 1; parsonage 1; cemetery 1; salary of Rector $1200 per annum, arrears of salary none, number of free sittings about 30.

Money Receipts from all sources.—Pew rents about $1500, offertory at Holy Communion $84.13, collections in Church for current expenses $160, for other purposes see below, other sources $300, cemetery lots sold. Total, 2666.13.

Expenditures and Appropriations.—Current expenses (including salary of Rector), $1655, repairs and improvements $300, payment of debts $70 interest, Episcopal and Convention Fund, extra assessment $50, support of Sunday Schools $120, melodeon $125, Christmas festival $108, for the poor $84.13, to Missions, Foreign $49.50, Domestic, California, Oregon and Florida $122, Diocesan $125, mite boxes $25.84, for the Jews $6.70, Episcopal Hospital $41.50, Disabled Clergymen $17. Miscellaneous—Chicago and Wisconsin sufferers $155.50; Collected privately for objects within the Parish $400. Total, $3454.77.

Financial Condition—Aggregate value of property of the

10

Parish, parsonage $5000, Encumbrances—Mortgage $1000 on parsonage.　Other indebtedness, none.

The Rector is glad to report that the parish is in a prosperous and promising condition.　The Borough has increased considerably in business and population during the past year, but other religious bodies have gained much more by the influx of strangers than we have, nevertheless this year has been one of the best the Parish of St. James has ever known. The contributions have been greatly more than in former years, and amount to a sum nearly, if not quite, as large as the Parish gave for *all* purposes during the first century of its existence.

The Missionary services at Emilie and Tullytown have been kept up regularly for 14 months, but it is not possible for the Rector to give to those localities the attention they require. It is earnestly hoped that the Board of Missions will soon find a proper person to undertake this work.

————

Grace Church, Hulmeville.　Admitted 1837.　The Rev. W. G. P. Brinckloe, in charge.　Edmund G. Harrison and Jos K. Vanzandt, Wardens.

Baptisms, adults 4, infants 7, total 11; confirmed 10; communicants, added, new 7, by removal 9, died or removed 1, present number 72; marriages 4; burials 7; public services, on Sundays 106, on other days 2, total 108; average attendance, on Sundays 100; Sunday Schools, officers and teachers 10, scholars 116; Bible Classes, teacher 1, members 50; Church 1; sittings 200; parsonage 1; cemetery 1; salary of Rector $800 per annum.

Money Receipts from all sources.—Pew rents $400, collections in Church $50, other sources $400.

Expenditures and Appropriations.—Current expenses (including salary of Rector), $850, repairs and improvements $20, Episcopal and Convention Fund $5.

Financial Condition.—Aggregate value of the property of the Parish, real and personal, $6300, Encumbrances, ground rent on buildings or lands $1000.

The Rev. Thomas Burrows having resigned the Parish on February 1st, 1872, on the request of the Vestry, and with the consent of the Standing Committee (the Bishop being absent), I assumed the charge of the Parish for three months. The foregoing report is mainly of the services rendered by the Rev. Thos. Burrows, of which there has been no other report rendered.

Since February 1st, I have resided in the Parish, have read 20 sermons, and delivered 4 addresses, performed 1 marriage. Have held service, at stated times, at Attleboro', Fallsington, Oxford Valley; have held a Congregational Bible Class on every Sunday evening at Grace Church, Hulmeville, which has been well attended.

This is a large and promising field. The people are anxious for the privilege of religious services, and attend well. There is, however, much to be done, which only prayer and patient waiting will accomplish.

Trinity Church, Centreville. Admitted 1840. Rev. H. Baldy, Rector. William Stavely and William Biles, Wardens.

Communicants, added by removal 1, died 1, present number 28; burials 4; public services on Sunday 45; average attendance 50; Sunday Schools, officers and teachers 17, scholars 100; Bible Classes 3; Church sittings 125; salary of Rector $282.

Money Receipts from all sources.—Pew rents $104, offertory at Holy Communion $13.87, collections in Church $60.72, Donations $305.28. Total $483.87.

Expenditures and appropriations—Salary of Rector $282, Episcopal Fund $6, support of Sunday School $100, Diocesan Missions $1.87, Book Societies $6, Miscellaneous $88. Total $483.87.

St. Paul's Church, Doylestown. Admitted 1847. Rev. H. Baldy, Rector. John Brock and Lewis P. Worthington, Wardens.

Baptisms, adults 6, infants 12, total 18; confirmed 8; communicants, added, new 8, by removal 3, died or removed 1, present number 54; marriages 3; burials 2; public services, on Sundays 72, on other days 34, total 106; average attendance on Sundays 95; children catechized frequently; Sunday Schools, officers and teachers 12, scholars 75; Church 1, sittings 230; parsonage 1; salary of Rector $532 per annum; extra Sunday services, free to all.

Money Receipts from all sources.—Pew rents $598.23; offertory at Holy Communion $131.02, collections in Church $299, donations $100, other sources $311.82, total $1490.07.

Expenditures and Appropriations.—Current expenses (including salary of Rector) $811, repairs and improvements $318.93, Episcopal and Convention Fund $20, support of Sunday Schools $45.37, to Missions, Foreign. $10, Domestic $10.50, Diocesan 11, Episcopal Hospital $12, Bibles, Prayer Books and Tracts $13.30, Book Societies $23.75, Disabled Clergymen $15, Miscellaneous $197.11. Total $1470.85.

CHESTER COUNTY.

St. Andrew's, West Vincent; St. Mary's, Warwick, and St. Mark's, Honeybrook. Rev. William W. Spear, D. D.. Rector. R. J. Newton Spear, Assistant.

These Parishes have been for a long time without regular services, owing to the difficulty of obtaining and supporting a minister suited to their needs. They have become, therefore, very much scattered, besides being greatly reduced by removals and deaths. They were even supposed by many to be hopelessly disorganized. But in January last, I was induced to visit them, and endeavor to save them from extinction and their Church buildings from alienation. I officiated for each of them during the winter, as often as possible, and, though the season was very unfavorable to the effort, I was so much encouraged by the results as to be willing to take charge of them, with the promise of liberal aid from the Board of Missions, so as to enable me to have the services of an assistant. I expect to remove to the neighborhood as soon as the parsonage at St. Andrew's can be repaired. Many difficulties have attended the effort to reorganize and revive these Parishes, and I cannot yet report the statistics of their condition, but hope during the year to bring them once more to some degree of order and activity. They have already shown a degree of zeal and liberality beyond that of many years past.

May 1, 1872.

St. John's Church, Pequea. Admitted 1810. Rev. Henry R. Smith, Rector. Joseph Hamilton and Henry W. Worrest, Wardens.

Baptisms, adults 7, infants 3, total 10; confirmed 14; communicants, added, new 5, died or removed 3, present number, 35; marriages 7; burials 9; public services, on Sundays 53, on other days 40, total 93; average attendance on Sundays 83; children catechized frequently; Sunday Schools, officers and teachers 7, scholars 55; Church 1, sittings 260; parsonage 1; cemetery 1; salary of Rector $800 per annum; arrears of salary, none; number of free sittings 100.

Money Receipts from all sources.—Pew rents $213.50, collections in Church $123.43, subscriptions $589.05, investments $390.50, other sources $263.69. Total $1580.17.

Expenditures and Appropriations.—Current expenses (including salary of Rector) $654.82, repairs and improvements $783.68, Episcopal and Convention Fund $21, support of Sunday Schools $22.05, Domestic Missions $3.93, Diocesan $35, Episcopal Hospital $14.25, Disabled Clergymen $13.35, Wisconsin and Chicago sufferers $30.09. Total $1580.17.

Financial Condition.—Aggregate value of property of the Parish, real and personal, $13,700. Encumbrances—Mortgages on Church edifices none, other indebtedness none.

During the past year I have traveled, in the actual work of my Ministry, 3372 miles, mostly in the saddle; officiated in Divine service 191 times, preached 168 times, delivered 27 addresses, baptized 7 adults and 8 infants, solemnized 8 weddings, officiated at 16 funerals, made 137 pastoral visits, and presented 14 persons for confirmation. Although suffering grievously, at times, from the exposure incident to my work, I have not intermitted my duties for a single Sunday; averaging 30 miles and 3 services every Sunday, and on alternate Sundays holding service in 3 different counties.

Since my last report, our Church building has been completely renovated, at a large outlay, and is now one of the neatest and most comfortable in the country. There has been a marked increase in the average attendance for the past year, which is especially gratifying, from the fact that it is coupled with a spirit of unity and a hearty desire to co-operate with me in every good work.

Holy Trinity Church, West Chester. Admitted 1838. Rev. John Bolton, Rector. Henry Buckwalter and James H. Bull, Wardens.

Baptisms, adults 3, infants 4, total· 7; confirmed 10; communicants, added 13, new 10, by removal 2, died or removed 25, present number 200; marriages 20; burials 4; public services, on Sundays 3, on other days 2, total 5; average attendance on Sundays 400; children catechized, times 12; Sunday Schools, officers and teachers 27, scholars 250; Bible Classes, teachers 2, members 38; Church 1, sittings 600; School building 1; parsonage 1; salary of Rector $1800 per annum; arrears of salary, none; number of free sittings 100; extra Sunday services, free to all, 1.

Money Receipts from all sources.—Pew rents $3120, offertory at Holy Communion $251, collections in Church $100, other sources $1500,

Expenditures and Appropriations.—Current expenses (including salary of Rector) $3200, repairs and improvements $1500, payment of debts $1388, Episcopal and Convention Fund $62, support of Sunday Schools $140, Parish Library, $50, Parochial Missions $60, for the Poor $300, to Missions, Foreign $344, Domestic $118, Home Mission for Colored People $50, Diocesan $150, Episcopal Hospital $41.92, Church building $1000, Bibles, Prayer Books and Tracts $40, Christian or Theological Education $143.25, Disabled Clergymen $23.90.

Financial Condition.—Aggregate value of property of the Parish, real and personal, $50,000. Encumbrances—Mortgages of Church edifice none, on other buildings $7000. Other indebtedness, none.

St. Peter's Church, Phœnixville. Admitted 1840. Rev. W. R. Stockton, Rector. John Griffen and Ellis Reeves, Wardens.

Baptisms, adults 5, infants 9, total 14; confirmed 12; communicants, added, new 12, by removal 10, died or removed 8, present number 136; marriages 2; burials 7; services on Sabbath, 3 each Sabbath part of the year, 2 each Sabbath the remainder of the year; the evening service is for the study of the Holy Scriptures; services on other days 16; Sunday School officers and teachers 20; scholars 175; Church 1; sittings 250; parsonage 1.

Money Receipts.—Pew rents $550 per annum, every pew rented; offertory at Holy Communion $62.75; collections in Church for current expenses, say, $225; collection for coal, &c., $50; collections for Sunday School Library, Papers, &c., $125.

Expenditures and Appropriations.—Rector's salary (pew rents $550; subscription to Rector by Mr. Samuel J. Reeves $300), $850 per annum; current expenses (Sexton, music, coal, and repairs,) $200; collection for Episcopal and Convention Fund $20; Chicago sufferers $16; Philadelphia City Missions $20; Bible Society $12.50, &c., &c.

Financial Condition.—Aggregate value of property — Church lot valued at $5000; Rectory lot $2000; Church building, estimated at $12,000; Rectory buildings, worth $7000; amount of indebtedness $1,000.

St. James' Church, Downingtown. Admitted 1844. The Rev. R. F. Innes, Rector.
Charles L. Wells, Warden.

Baptisms, adults 21, infants 44, total 65; confirmed 39; communicants, added, new 20, by removal 2, died or removed 2, present number 80; burials 11; public services, on Sundays 147, on other days 64, total 211; average attendance on Sundays 125; children catechized frequently; Sunday Schools, officers and teachers 18, scholars 110; Bible Classes, teacher 1, members 15; Church 1; sittings 250; Chapel (the statistics of which are included in this report) 1; sittings 100; parsonage 1; cemetery 1; salary of Rector $1000 per annum; arrears of salary none; number of free sittings 20; extra Sunday services free to all.

Money Receipts from all sources. — Pew rents $873.50; offertory at Holy Communion $62.27; collections in Church $320.57; subscriptions $126.84; donations $124; other sources $440; collections in Sunday School $64.44. Total $2011.62.

Expenditures and Appropriations.—Current expenses (including salary of Rector) $1107.77 ; payment of debts $500; Episcopal Convention Fund $25 ; support of Sunday Schools $62 ; Parochial Missions $21 ; for the Poor $62.27 ; to Missions, Foreign $25.11, Domestic, Rev. Mr. Cook's Indian Mission $45.56; Diocesan, Southeastern Convocation $50 ; for the Jews $6.05 ; Episcopal Hospital $13 ; Disabled Clergymen $6.20 ; Sunday School for Rev. Mr. Cook's Indian Mission $64.44; Chicago sufferers $54.50 ; a Parochial sufferer $24. Total $2,066.90.

Financial Condition.—Aggregate value of property of the Parish, real and personal $15,000. Encumbrances—mortgages on Church edifices $500.

The Church of the Trinity, Coatesville.   Admitted 1869.   Rev. George G. Field, Rector.
Horace A. Beale and John L. Martin, Wardens.

Baptisms, infants 10 ; confirmed upon two occasions 15 ; communicants, added, 13, removed 2, present number 48 ; burials 4; public services, Sundays 96, other days 37, total 133 ; Sunday School children 45 ; teachers 5 ; Bible Class, teacher 1, members 4 ; salary $800 ; no arrears, paid punctually ; Church sittings 180, all free ; value of Church property $6000 ; mortgage on parsonage lot adjoining the Church $900 ; current expenses $180 ; improvements $250 ; Chicago Relief $56.72 ; Convention Fund $15 ; Church Hospital $12 ; Domestic Missions $14.21 ; Christmas Fund $5.44 ; Convocation $7.39 ; Foreign Missions $12.

During the past year, the lot having been given by a parishioner and the remaining debt discharged, the Church was consecrated. It has been enclosed, and, with pavements, additional furniture, carpet and gas, has been made much more comfortable and attractive.

The salary, with its arrears removed, and paid punctually ; and the Missionary stipend to be voluntarily relinquished during the year, the congregation increased, and more compact and stable ; and with the prospect of a parsonage, the ground offered by the same liberal hand which gave the Church lot—these, it is humbly conceived, are some evidences of improvement, growth and stability to be thankful for.

Grace Church, Parkesburg. Admitted 1871. The Rev. Henry R. Smith, Rector. Thomas W. Henderson and George W. Worrest, Wardens.

Confirmed, a class awaiting; communicants 13; public services, on Sundays 96, on other days 4, total 100; average attendance on Sundays 90; children catechized 3 times; Sunday Schools, officers and teachers 5; scholars 51; Church 1; sittings 300; salary of Rector paid by Southeastern Convocation; number of free sittings, all.

Money Receipts from all sources.—Collections in Church $47.25; subscriptions $135.16. Total $182.41.

Expenditures and Appropriations.—Current expenses (including salary of Lay reader) $180.91; Disabled Clergymen $1.50. Total $182.41.

Financial Condition.—Aggregate value of property of the Parish, real and personal $5,000. Encumbrances—mortgages on Church edifices $700; other indebtedness $800.

This Parish has been adopted by the Southeastern Convocation of the Diocese, and since April 1st has been under the care of its Missionary, the Rev. J. Thompson.Carpenter.

DELAWARE.

St. Paul's Church, Chester. Admitted 1786. Rev. Henry Brown, Rector. John Larkin, Jr., and Jno. B. McKeever, Wardens.

Baptisms, adults 3, infants 27, total 30; communicants, added 8, new 4, by removal 4, died or removed 6, present number 220; marriages 14; burials 16; public services, on Sundays 150, on other days 90, total 240; average attendance on Sundays 350; children catechized 12 times; Sunday Schools, officers and teachers 32, scholars 300; Bible Classes, teachers 2, members 30. Other Parish agencies—Ladies' Sewing Society, Tract Society. Church 1, sittings 350; Chapels (the statistics of which are included in this report) 1, sittings 300; parsonage 1; cemetery 1; arrears of salary none; extra Sunday service, free to all, Sunday P. M. and night service.

Money Receipts from all sources.—Offertory at Holy Communion $108.

Expenditures and Appropriations.—Current expenses (including salary of Rector) $2,000, repairs and improvements

11

$200, Episcopal and Convention Fund $55, support of Sunday Schools $200, Parish Library $100, Parochial Missions $150; for the Poor $78, to Missions, Foreign $60, Domestic $50, Home Mission for Colored People $10, Diocesan $80, City Missions $15, Episcopal Hospital $20, Church building $8500. Bibles, Prayer Books and Tracts $15. Total $11,533.

Our Church building is about to be enlarged, room being needed for others who desire to come in. For this purpose the Rector asked an offering of the congregation. On Easter the call was responded to by collection and pledges to the amount of $5000. Since then the ladies, as the result of their efforts, have realized $2200. The work is to be commenced forthwith. It will cost about $10,000. The amount is nearly all in hand.

St. Martin's Church, Marcus Hook. Admitted 1786. The Rev. Gustavus C. Bird, Rector. William Trainer and Frank Smith, Wardens.

Baptisms, adults none, infants 12, total 12; confirmed none, on account of vacancy in the Rectorship since September last; communicants, died 2, present number about 50; marriages none; burials 8; public services, on Sundays 32, on other days about 20; children catechized, times, occasionally; Sunday School 1, officers and teachers 8, scholars 60; Church 1; sittings 450; parsonage 1; cemetery 1; salary of Rector $1000 per annum and parsonage free; the pews are free.

Money Receipts from all sources.—About $2371.23; Sunday School collections about $40; a valuable lot has been donated, and during the past year a handsome and comfortable parsonage has been erected at a cost of $3000; paid assessment for Episcopal and Convention Fund $25.

The present Rector took charge of the Parish on Sunday, May 12th, and owing to a long vacancy in the Rectorship, this report of work done and of money expended is necessarily inaccurate.

St. David's, commonly called Radnor, Church. Admitted 1786. The Rev. William F. Halsey, Rector. Mark Brooke and Joseph H. Sharp, Wardens.

Baptisms, adults 4, infants 6, total 10; confirmed none; communicants, present number 44; marriage 1; burials 9;

public services, on Sundays 51, and on other festival and fast days; children catechized 12 times; Sunday Schools, officers and teachers 4, scholars 30; Church 1; sittings 250; School buildings 1; parsonage 1; cemetery 1; salary of Rector $1000 per annum; arrears of salary $270; number of free sittings 40; extra Sunday services, free to all 8.

Money Receipts from all sources.—Offertory $86.27.

Expenditures and Appropriations.—Current expenses, building Sunday School room, repairs and improvements $900; Episcopal and Convention Fund $30; to Missions, Foreign $16.40; Domestic $20; Home Missions for Colored People $14.60; Episcopal Hospital $8; Bishop White Prayer Book Society $5; for Bishop Morris, Oregon, $25.

Financial Condition.—Encumbrances none.

St. John's Church, Concord Township. Rev. John B. Clemson, D.D., Rector. Robert McCall and Henry L. Paschall, Wardens.

Baptisms, adults 2, infants 10, whole number 12; confirmed 3; communicants added 5, died or removed 8, whole number 38; marriage 1; burials 5.

Expenditures and Appropriations.—Alms $39.34, for Chicago $12.25, City Missions $19.31, Episcopal Hospital $5.54, Children's Home $6.82, Jews 70 cents, Domestic Missions $11, Parish Library $7.10, Church Repairs $92.25.

The Church has been undergoing extensive repairs; not yet completed. An effort is being made to renew the fence around the cemetery in a substantial and creditable manner, and to increase the Parsonage Fund, which has reached $1600. The Parish is believed to be in a healthy and growing condition.

Calvary Church, Rockdale. Admitted 1835. Rev. William Ely, Rector. Richard S. Smith and Samuel K. Crozier, Wardens.

Baptisms, adults 3, infants 21, total 24; confirmed 15; communicants, added, new 15, by removal 8, died or removed 14, present number 100; marriages 6; burials 9; public services, on Sundays 98, on other days 20, total 118; average attendance on Sundays good; children catechized 12 times; Sunday

Schools, officers and teachers 12, scholars 200; Bible Classes, teacher 1, members 15; Church 1, sittings 325; Chapel (the statistics of which are included in this report) 1, sittings 100; parsonage 1; cemetery 1; salary of Rector $800 per annum.

Money Receipts from all sources.—Pew rents $567.75, offertory at Holy Communion $81.28, collections in Church $335.81, subscriptions $50, donations $118.27, investments $12, offerings of Sunday School children $90.54. Total $1255.65.

Expenditures and Appropriations.—Current expenses (including salary of Rector) $791.96, repairs and improvements $40, Episcopal and Convention Fund $21, Library of Sunday Schools $57, for the Poor $26.25, to Missions, Foreign $81.68, Domestic $106.26, Convocation $75, Episcopal Hospital $34, Disabled Clergymen (Christmas Fund) $22.50. Total $1255.65.

Financial Condition.—Aggregate value of property of the Parish, real and personal $18,000. Encumbrances—Mortgages on Church edifice none, on other buildings $2000.

Christ Church, Media. Admitted 1858. Rev. Samuel W. Hallowell, Rector. H. Jones Brooke and Edward A. Price, Wardens.

Baptisms, adults 2, infants 5, total 7; communicants, by removal 6, died 1, removed 14, present number 75; marriages 9; burials 11; public services, on Sundays 97, on other days 9, total 106; average attendance on Sundays 240; children catechized occasionally in Sunday School; Sunday Schools, officers and teachers 15, scholars 118; Church 1, sittings 300; Chapel (the statistics of which are included in this report) 1, sittings 200; salary of Rector $900 per annum and parsonage; arrears of salary none.

Money Receipts from all sources.—Pew rents $620.67, offertory at Holy Communion $112.76, collections in Church $484.25, subscriptions $252.34, donations $62, other sources $414.10.

Expenditures and Appropriations.—Current expenses (including salary of Rector) $1071.54, repairs and improvements $41.63, payment of debts $349.15, Episcopal and Convention Fund $30, support of Sunday Schools $29.93, for the Poor

$25, to Missions, Foreign $43.57, Domestic $10, Diocesan $10, for the Jews $5, Episcopal Hospital $15.24, Bibles, Prayer Books and Tracts $10, Disabled Clergymen $9.09, miscellaneous $113.01.

Financial Condition.—Aggregate value of property of the Parish, real and personal $15,000, other indebtedness about $800.

The Bishop's visitation not taking place until after the Convention, I am not able to report those confirmed. The attendance in the Sunday morning services is good. The town continues to improve, and the Church may calculate upon an increase in her numbers. Through the munificence of a lady communicant, a parsonage will probably be erected in another year.

Church of the Good Shepherd, Radnor. Admitted 1871. Rev. Henry Palethorp Hay, D. D., Rector. Gorham P. Sargent, M. D., and Charles W. Cushman, Wardens.

Baptisms, adults 6, infants 7, total 13; confirmed 8; communicants, added, new 6, by removal 5, died or removed 7, present number 25; marriages 2; burials 4; public services, on Sundays and on other days, total 204; sermons and addresses 203; children catechized 32 times; Sunday Schools, officers and teachers 7, scholars 40; Bible Class, teacher 1, members 7; Church 1, sittings 200; salary of Rector $660 per annum and the offertory; number of free sittings all.

Money Receipts from all sources.—Offertory $591.63, paid subscriptions $7026.49, donations $745, investments $135.56. Total $8498.68.

Expenditures and Appropriations.—Current expenses (including salary of Rector) $976.92, Domestic Missions $39.18, for the Jews $12.55, Episcopal Hospital $12.75, Church building $9799.63, Disabled Clergymen $6.66, Families of Deceased Clergy $20, sufferers by Chicago fire $16.32. Total $10,884.01.

Financial Condition.—Aggregate value of property of the Parish, real and personal $13,000. No encumbrances.

The corner-stone of the Church edifice was laid on St. James' Day, 1871, by the Rt. Rev. Wm. Bacon Stevens, M. D.,

D. D., LL.D., Bishop of the Diocese of Pennsylvania. The first service was held in the Church on the Feast of the Epiphany, 1872. The Church was consecrated by the Rt. Rev. M. A. DeWolfe Howe, D. D., Bishop of the Diocese of Central Pennsylvania, on March 7, 1872.

MONTGOMERY COUNTY.

St. James' Church, Perkiomen. Admitted 1785. Rev. Peter Russell, Rector. Matthias Yost and M. D. Casselbery, Wardens.

Baptisms, infant 1; communicants 75; marriage 1; burial 1; public services, on Sunday, 102, other days 35, total 137; Sunday School 1, officers and teachers 10, scholars 60; Church sittings 250; School building 1; parsonage, with 3 acres of ground; cemetery 1; salary of Rector $600.

Money Receipts from all sources.—Pew rents $361, offertory at Holy Communion $23.30, collections in Church $61.84, donations 73.60, investments $18, Shannon Fund $100, ground rents $300, other sources $115.72. Total $1053.40.

Expenditures and Appropriations.—Current expenses (including salary of Rector) $753, repairs and improvements $38.38, Episcopal and Convention Fund $20, support of Sunday School $113, to Missions, Foreign $14, Domestic $12, Diocesan $11.25, Episcopal Hospital $8.50, Disabled Clergymen $3.55, Chicago $10.24, Miscellaneous $855. Total $991.47.

This is one of the oldest rural Parishes of the Diocese of Pennsylvania, and has connected with it a Sunday School which celebrated its fiftieth anniversary the Sunday after Easter, the Rev. Richard M. Morgan, D. D., of New Rochelle, preaching the sermon.

The School was commenced under the Rectorship of the late Rev. Jehu C. Clay, D. D., the first Sunday of April, 1822.

St. Thomas' Church, Whitemarsh. Admitted 1786. Rev. P. W. Stryker, Rector. Charles Burk and W. H. Drayton, Wardens.

Baptisms, adults 7, infants 14, total 21; confirmed 14; communicants about 100; marriages 3; burials 14; public services, on Sundays 104 on other days 103, total 207; children catechized, monthly; Sunday Schools, officers and teachers 8, scholars 61 ; Bible Classes, teachers 2, members 37 ; Parish school, teacher 1, scholars 23. Other Parish agencies—A Sunday School in the afternoon during the summer months, in a distant part of the Parish, and which numbers 5 officers and 34 scholars. Church building not yet completed, services held in Parish school-house. School building 1 ; parsonage 1 ; cemetery 1 ; salary of Rector $1200; arrears of salary, none.

Money Receipts from all sources.—Offertory at Holy Communion $86.88, collections in Church (special) $638.44. Total $725.42.

Expenditures and Appropriations.—Repairs and improvements $45, Missions, Foreign $27, Domestic $20, for the Jews $10.50, Episcopal Hospital $89.21, of which $47.21 were the offerings of the Sunday School; Disabled Clergymen $18, Chicago sufferers $75, Church Home for children $5, Bureau of Relief $41.16, Miscellaneous $173.07, for the Poor $86.98. Total $725.42.

St. John's Church, Norristown. Admitted 1815. The Rev. Chas. E. McIlvaine, Rector. John McKay and Benj. E. Chain, Wardens.

Baptisms, adults 4, infants 15, total 19; confirmed 9; communicants, added, new 9, by removal 18, died or removed 21, present number 195; marriages 9; burials 14; public services, on Sundays 100, on other days 52, total 152; children catechized 3 times; Sunday Schools, officers and teachers 32, scholars 240; Bible Classes, teachers 2, members 24; sewing school, teachers 15, scholars 85. Other Parish agencies—Sewing Society 1; District Visitors, officers 2, visitors 10. Church 1, sittings 550; school building 1 ; parsonage 1 ; cemetery 1 ; salary of Rector $1800 per annum; arrears of salary none.

Money Receipts from all sources.—Pew rents $2502.24, collections in Church $800.27, investments $900, other sources $75, Five Cent Parochial and Missionary Fund $585.40, Boyer Poor Fund $207.51, Sunday School contributions $219.61. Total $5290.03.

Expenditures and Appropriations.—Current expenses (including salary of Rector) $2546.96, repairs and improvements

$275.81, payment of debts $310, Episcopal and Convention Fund $75, support of Sunday School $250, of Sewing School $23, Parochial Missions $180.23, for the Poor $172.40, Missions, Foreign $188.60, Domestic $330.64, Home Mission for Colored People $67.05. Diocesan $137.83, for the Jews $15, Episcopal Hospital $42.78, Disabled Clergymen $32.24. Miscellaneous $99.93, Home for Friendless Children 59.67, Chicago sufferers $207, Poor Children's Shoe Fund $50. Total $5064.14.

Financial Condition.—Indebtedness $4373.50.

___

Christ Church, Pottstown. Admitted 1829. B. McGann, Rector. Samuel Wells and W. J. Rutter, Wardens.

Baptisms, adults 5, infants 9; confirmations 14; communicants added 14, present number 92; marriage 1; burials 14; public services, on Sundays 102, on other days 42, total 144; children catechized 12 times; Sunday Schools, officers and teachers 20, scholars 100; Chapel 1, sittings 200; salary of Rector $1000 per annum, for parsonage $250.

The Parish is now engaged in building a new Church, the cost of which is already provided for by subscription.

Money Receipts from all sources.—Pew rents $876.25, offertory at Holy Communion and collections in Church $604.29. investments $282, other sources $85.50. Total $1848.04.

Expenditures and Appropriations.—Current expenses (including salary of Rector) $1440.32, payment of debts $122.26, Convention Fund $25, support of Sunday Schools $85.50, to Missions, Foreign $82.44, Domestic $38.10, Home Mission for Colored People $15, Diocesan Missions $30, Mission to Indians $15, Episcopal Hospital $15.58, Christmas Fund $15.56, Theological Education $15, Bible Society $9.75, for Chicago Sufferers $73.84, Miscellaneous $30.25. Total $2013.60.

There is in hand a fund of $3500, received from sale of parsonage, and reserved for the erection of another.

___

Church of the Redeemer, Lower Merion. Admitted 1852. Rev. Edw. L. Lycett, Rector. N. P. Shortridge and Geo. F. Curwen, Wardens.

Baptisms, adults 2, infants 6, total 8; communicants, added, new 1, by removal 5, died or removed 15, present number 75;

marriages 2; burials 7; public services, on Sundays 150, on other days 45, total 195; Sunday Schools, officers and teachers 10, scholars 70; salary of Rector $1500 per annum.

Money Receipts from all sources.—Pew rents $1567, offertory at Holy Communion $180, collections in Church $1571.48, subscriptions $14,000, investments $141.50. Total $18,459.98.

Expenditures and Appropriations.—Current Expenses (including salary of Rector) $2048.38, repairs and improvements $215.12, Episcopal and Convention Fund $62, support of Sunday Schools $100, Parochial Missions $200, to Missions, Foreign $173.83, Domestic $185.07, Episcopal Hospital $60, Disabled Clergymen $60, Chicago $139.10, Church Home for Children $53.21. Total $3296.62.

Financial Condition.—Aggregate value of property of the Parish, real and personal $32,500. Encumbrances on buildings $3000.

The fluctuations of this Parish make it difficult to give a correct report. For two or three years the Parish has declined in point of numbers, and yet its prospects for the future were never more encouraging. The Vestry have already erected a commodious and handsome building as a Rectory, and repurchased five acres of ground, making a lot of ten acres, beautifully situated near Bryn Mawr, upon which they purpose (D. V.) to build a Church and School House. Upon this lot the Rectory stands, which I expect to occupy sometime in the ensuing month of June.

Church of Our Saviour, Jenkintown. Admitted 1858. The Rev. R. Francis Colton, Rector. Charles Hewett and John S. Newbold, Wardens.

Baptisms, adult 1, infants 2, total 3; confirmed 10; communicants, added, new or not previously included 15, by removal 1, died, removed or habitually neglectful, present number 80; marriage, 1; burials 5; public services on Sundays 104, on other days 42, total 146; Sunday Schools, officers and teachers 9, scholars 112; Bible Classes 3; teachers 3; Parish schools, teacher 1, scholars 30. Other Parish agencies—Church Aid Society, Sewing School, Mothers' Meeting. Church 1, sittings 250; school building 1; parsonage 1; salary of Rector, $1500 per annum; arrears of salary none; number of free sittings 250.

Money Receipts from all sources.—Collections in Church $1281; subscriptions $2175; donations $411; other sources $85.15. Total $3952.15.

Expenditures and Appropriations.—Current expenses (including salary of Rector) $2000; repairs and improvements $162.38; Episcopal and Convention Fund $55; support of Sunday Schools $79.37; Parish schools $600; for the Poor $32; Missions, Foreign $21.70; Domestic $21.70; Diocesan $84; for the Jews $447; Episcopal Hospital $139.20; Disabled Clergymen $27.44; miscellaneous $29,50; Chicago sufferers $331.71. Total $3588.97.

Calvary Church, Conshohocken. Admitted 1859. Rev T. William Davidson, Rector. Walter Cresson and T. K. Reid, Wardens.

Baptisms, infants 5, total 5; communicants, present number 45; burials 3; public services on Sundays 43, on other days 13, total 56; average attendance on Sundays 70; children catechized or addressed, every Sunday; Sunday Schools, officers and teachers 17; scholars 131; Church 1; sittings 240; salary of Rector $800 per annum; arrears of salary none.

Money Receipts from all sources.—Pew rents $728.75; other sources $153.20.

Expenditures and Appropriations.—Episcopal Convention and Fund $11; support of Sunday Schools $230.45; Episcopal Hospital $19.76; Disabled Clergymen $16.63; Church Home $5.56; Chicago sufferers $56.06. The current expenses are met by an organization known as the "Parish Aid Society."

During August, September and part of October the carpenters, plasterers and fresco-painters in whose hands the Church had been placed, completely changed its internal appearance, and have made it one of the most beautiful and comfortable Churches of the size in the Diocese. The exact cost of the improvements I am unable to learn, but judge the sum to be about $1200; all of which has been paid, leaving the Church free from all indebtedness.

I regret that I am obliged to present so meagre a report, but this is owing to circumstances beyond my control.

St. Paul's Church, Cheltenham. Admitted 1861. Rev. Edward W. Appleton, Rector. John W. Thomas and Jay Cooke, Wardens.

Baptisms, adults 6, infants 14, total 20; confirmed 15; communicants, added, new 14, by removal 2, died or removed 6, present number 162; marriages 4; burials 5; Sunday Schools, officers and teachers 18, scholars 216; Bible Classes, teachers 2; members 155; sewing school, teachers 6; scholars 70; Church accommodations, edifice 1, sittings 450; parsonage 1. Property other than the Church building and lot owned by the Parish—Sunday School house and Library; Parvin Hall (400 sittings) and sexton's house. Clergyman's salary $2500 and use of rectory.

Collections and Contributions.—Communion alms $1143.58, improvements, repairs and current expenses $2937.22, pew rents $2926, Missions, Diocesan $363.29, Domestic (per American Church Missionary Society) $667.47, Foreign $631.74, Convention and Episcopal Funds $165, Episcopal Hospital $300, Evangelical Educational Society $2639, disabled Clergymen $153.09, Sunday School offerings $1436.51, Jewish Missions $112.75. Miscellaneous $1213.87. Total (exclusive of pew rents) $11763.52.

St. John's Church, Lower Merrion. Admitted 1864. Rev. C. L. Fischer, Rector. David Morgan and Joseph B. Townsend, Wardens.

Baptisms, infants 5, adults 5, total 10; communicants, added 3, removed 4, present number 24; marriages 2; burials 2; public services, on Sundays 100, other days 20, total 120; Sunday Schools, officers and teachers 20, scholars 200; children catechized monthly; Church accommodations, edifice 1; sittings 400; school building 1; parsonage 1; salary of Rector $2000; arrears of salary none.

Money Receipts from all sources.—Pew rents $1060, sub-

scriptions $1008.30, collections in Church $300, Donations
$1161.05, offertory at Communion 26.53.   Total $3555.88.

Expenditures and Appropriations.—Current expenses (including Rector's salary) $2391.21, support of Sunday Schools
$552.89, Domestic Missions, $200, Convention Fund $30,
Chicago sufferers $355.25, alms for Poor $26.53.   Total
$3555.88.

Financial Condition.—Aggregate value of property of the
Parish, real and personal $20,000, amount of indebtedness
$2000.

The above report is for the entire Conventional year, although
the present Rector began his duties in December last.   The
work of the Parish is opening up in a very encouraging way,
and at the present a class is awaiting confirmation by the
Bishop.

St. Paul's Memorial Church, Upper Providence. Admitted 1869. The Rev. Joel Rudderow,
Rector. Wm. H. Gumbes and Caleb Cresson, Wardens.

Baptisms, infants 10 ; communicants, added, new 3, by removal 1, died or removed 1, present number 26; marriages
2 ; burial 1 ; public services, on Sundays, twice a day, on
other days, during Lent ; average attendance, on Sundays 50 ;
children catechized once per month ; Sunday Schools, officers
and teachers 10, scholars about same as last year ; Church
now building ; services free to all.

Money Receipts from all sources, except for Building Fund
and Contribution in Sunday School.—Offertory at Holy Communion $51.18, collections in Church $139.44, donations $19.
Investments—Residue unpaid on the unfinished building.

Expenditures and Appropriations.—Episcopal and Convention Fund $6; for the Poor $108.50; Missions, Foreign $22.07,
Domestic $47, Home Mission for Colored People $8.12, Diocesan $35.20, for the Jews $12.13, Episcopal Hospital $21.19,
Bibles, Prayer Books and Tracts $34.83, Christian or Theo-
logical Education $9.25, Disabled Clergymen $18.91.   Total
$323.13; of which $122.42 was contributed by the Sunday
School.

Financial Condition.—Aggregate value of property of the Parish, real and personal about $10,000.

The corner-stone of the new Church edifice was laid by the Rt. Rev. Bishop Stevens on the 20th of September, 1871. The building, which was roofed in for the winter, is now rapidly approaching completion. It is being constructed after a plan of Mr. J. C. Sidney, of Philadelphia, Architect, of the light gray sand stone of this region, with Hummelstown trimmings, is of the composite order of architecture, and will cost near $10,000.

It is proposed to have it consecrated early in the fall.

PHILADELPHIA COUNTY.

Christ Church, Philadelphia. Admitted 1785. Rev. Edward A. Foggo, D.D., Rector. Rev. G. Woolsey Hodge, Assistant. G. Washington Smith and Jos. K. Wheeler, Wardens.

Baptisms, adults 18 infants 42, total 60; confirmed 40; communicants, added, new 37, by removal none, died or removed 42, present number 372; marriages 18; burials 37; public services, on Sundays 121; on other days 214, total 335; children catechized monthly, Sunday Schools, officers and teachers 28, scholars 311; Bible Classes, teachers 2, members 48; Parish Schools, teachers 2, scholars 72; Church 1, sittings 850; school buildings 2; cemetery 1; arrears of salary none; number of free sittings 250; extra Sunday services, free to all, once every week during the winter.

Money Receipts from all sources.—Pew rents $3167.74; offertory at Holy Communion $507.20; collections in Church $6846.77; subscriptions $851.58; investments $2445.08.

Expenditures and Appropriations.—Current expenses (including salary of Rector) $5914.30; Episcopal and Convention Fund $125; support of Sunday Schools $70; of Parish Schools $696.66; for the Poor $1464.01; to Missions, Domestic $254.60; Home Mission for Colored People $60; City Missions $120; for the Jews $5; Episcopal Hospital $5081.04; Church buildings $105; Christian or Theological Education $204.23. Miscellaneous—Chicago sufferers $471.44; Church Home for Children $135.21.

The Ladies' Missionary Association has made, in addition, offerings to the amount of about $700.

On every alternate month I have performed the Chaplain's duty at Christ Church Hospital.

Through the aid of the Rev. John H. Prescott, Deacon, the Mission on Belmont Avenue has been continued. Regular Sunday Evening Service has been held. The Sunday School numbers 5 teachers and 35 scholars. Three of the persons confirmed were from the Mission, and there have been six baptized.

St. Peter's Church, Philadelphia. Admitted 1785. Rev. Thomas F. Davies, D. D., Rector. Rev. Wm. White Bronson and Rev. Robert F. Chase, Assistant Ministers. Rev. Thomas Poole Hutchinson, Rector's Assistant. John Welsh and Francis Gurney Smith, Wardens.

Baptisms, adults 13, infants 118, total 131; confirmed 48; communicants, added, new 44, by removal 9, died or removed 19, present number, as near as can be ascertained, including those of the Memorial Chapel, 665; marriages 31; burials 50; public services on Sundays 212; on other days 668, total 880. Children catechized—Day Schools, weekly; Sunday Schools, monthly. Sunday Schools, including Chapel 453; Bible Classes, teachers 7, members 81; Mission School 30; Parish Schools 2, scholars 164; Sewing School 100; Church 1; Chapel 1; school building 1; parsonage 1; cemetery 1; Mission House 1; arrears of salary none; extra Sunday services, free to all, 2.

The new Memorial Chapel of St. Peter's Church was completed and opened for Divine Service in January last. It is under the charge of the Rev. Robert F. Chase, and its statistics are included in the above report.

Among the Parish Agencies, in addition to St. Peter's House, a Home for Poor Women which has been generously maintained by a member of the Parish for many years; the Parish Mission House in Mead Street deserves a prominent mention. Here under the supervision of Christian ladies, a free Day-School is regularly maintained. Cottage services are held on Sundays and during the week. There is a largely attended

Club of Working Women, and also one of Men, which meet weekly.

Expenditures and Appropriations.—Current expenses (including salaries, repairs, &c.) $9790; Episcopal and Convention Fund $210; support of Sunday and Day Schools $694.84; Parochial and City Missions $3800; for the Poor $1028.59; daily and free night services $564.71; Christian or Theological Education $1189; Domestic Missions, including those to Indians and Colored People $5694.72; Foreign Missions $1024.44; Diocesan Missions $756.86; Bibles, Prayer Books, &c. $305.92; sufferers by fire in Northwest $878.20; Episcopal Hospital $909.78; Disabled Clergy $226.69; Jews $79.70; Church Home $651.05; Miscellaneous Charities $2435.70; Ladies' Missionary Aid Society $1147.50; Dorcas $317.84; Offerings in Memorial Chapel $538.70. Total $32,244.24.

St. Paul's Church, Philadelphia. Admitted 1785. Rev. Robert T. Roach, D.D., Rector. William Kennedy and Collins West, Wardens.

Baptisms, adults 12, infants 22, total 34; confirmed 17; communicants, added, new 29, by removal 7, died or removed 5, present number 152; marriages 13; burials 22; public services, on Sundays 104, on other days 86, total 190; children catechized 12 times; Sunday Schools, officers and teachers 29, scholars 300; Bible Classes, teachers 2, members 27; Church 1; sittings 1100; cemetery 1; salary of Rector $2000 per annum.

Money Receipts from all sources.—Pew rents $1877.50 offertory at Holy Communion $442.26; collections in Church $306.99; subscriptions $368.59; donations $25; Chicago sufferers $159.56; Thanksgiving Day $38.68. Total $4210.58.

Expenditures and Appropriations.—Current expenses (including salary of Rector $3671.27; Episcopal and Convention Fund $75; for the Poor $336.92; City Missions $58.75; for the Jews $16.77; Episcopal Hospital $30.68; Disabled Clergymen $10.72. Total $4200.11.

Financial Condition.—Aggregate value of property of the Parish, real and personal $75,000.

The attendance at all the services is good, but largely made up of such transient residents in the neighborhood, that great difficulty is experienced in persuading them to take pews, and so lighten the burden which now presses heavily upon the established members of this venerable Church.

I sincerely trust that a plan, for the permanent support of this Parish, proposed by our good Bishop, and approved by Mr. Jay Cooke, and other well-wishers to old St. Paul's, may be carried out by the corporation; for, short of endowment, or rental of a range of offices, which might be constructed contiguous to the Church, it will be difficult to solve the problem of support.

———

Trinity Church, Oxford, Philadelphia (with its Chapel at Crescentville, Philadelphia). Admitted 1785. Rev. Edward Y. Buchanan, D.D., Rector. William Overington and Harvey Rowland, Wardens.

Baptisms, adults 5, children 12, total 17; confirmed 11; communicants, added, new 11, by removal 1, died or removed 8, present number 83; marriages 3; burials 12; public services, on Sundays 105, on other days 17, total 122; children catechized times unknown, but frequently; Sunday Schools 2, teachers 10, scholars 110; Church 1, sittings 250; Chapel 1, sittings 200; parsonage 1; cemetery 1; salary of Rector $1200 per annum, with parsonage; arrears of salary none.

Expenditures and Appropriations.—Repairs and improvements $416.43, Episcopal and Convention Fund $50; support of Sunday Schools $131.49; to Missions, Foreign $277.59, Domestic and Spirit of Missions $590.13, Home Mission for Colored People $23.31, Diocesan $105, City Missions $250, Episcopal Hospital $281.52 (of which $30 from the Chapel), Bishop White Prayer Book Society $45, Christmas Fund $186, Chicago sufferers $203.59 (of which from the Chapel $22.97), Northwestern sufferers $120, Church Home for Children $205.95, Bell for Chapel $410.04, other purposes (including salary of Rector and current expenses of Church and Chapel) $2250. Total $5596.05.

All Saints' Church, Philadelphia. Admitted 1786. Rev. F. W. Beasley, D. D., Rector. Rev.
W. F. C. Morsell, Assistant. C. R. King and Alexander Brown, Wardens.

Baptisms, adults 3, infants 19, total 22; communicants, new
7, died 5, removed 6, present number 78; marriages 7, burials
23; public services, on Sundays 209, during Lent 2 services
each week. During a large portion of the year Mr. Morsell
had week-day services at Andalusia Chapel. I held a few
cottage services at the upper end of the Parish, and one service Sunday evening at a school house at Mechanicsville.
Sunday Schools 3, scholars 170; Parish School scholars 40
or more; Church 1, Chapels 2, sittings in Church 450, in
Chapels 260; School buildings 2; parsonage 1; cemetery 1:
salary of Rector $1600, of Assistant $1000; arrears of salary
none; free sittings 100.

Money Receipts from all sources.—ALL SAINTS', Church of
Crucifixion $15, Episcopal Hospital $40, for Sunday School
at All Saints' $16.05, Building Fund Church Home $75, Domestic Missions $65.50, Bishop Morris, for Mission Work
$47.85, Diocesan Missions, special for Hulmeville $75, sufferers at Chicago fire $112.68, Bishop White Prayer Book So-
ciety $16, Female Prayer Book Society $16.50, Christmas
Fund $11.60, Convention and Episcopal Fund $50, Sunday
School All Saints', for Bishop Tuttle $15, Oak Grove Chapel
for sufferers at Chicago fire $9.70, Children in the Sunday
School for charitable purposes $31, for Christmas tree for Sun-
day School children at Oak Grove $30, for Christmas greens
at Oak Grove $11, for Festival for Sunday School $15. Mr.
Morsell collected for Festival at Andalusia $13, Oak Grove
Chapel for Missions $8.47. A few gentlemen, at the request
of the Rector, paid $500 for a new Vestry-room at All Saint's
Church. Sunday collections in the Parish $346.84, for salary
of Assistant $525, special $150, pew rents at All Saints'
$1406, Chapel at Oak Grove $324.25. Total $3929.12.

Those who reside among us merely during the summer,
and are communicants of the Church, are not reported in the
number above stated. The services of the Rev. Mr. Morsell
have been very acceptable to our people. Our Sunday
Schools at Oak Grove and Andalusia bear witness, in their

13

flourishing condition, to the labor which he has bestowed upon them, and to his ability to convey instruction to the young. I am also very grateful for the zeal of those who are teachers of the Sunday School at All Saints' Church.

St. James' Church, Philadelphia. Admitted 1810. Rev. Henry J. Morton, D. D., Rector Rev. Lewis W. Gibson, Assistant. George W. Hunter and John T. Lewis, Wardens.

Baptisms, infants 17, total 17; confirmed 32; communicants, present number 300; marriages 7; burials 5; public services, on Sundays 126, on other days 144, total 270; children catechized 5 times; Sunday Schools, officers and teachers 12, scholars 83; Bible Classes, teachers 4, members 46; Parish School, teacher 1, scholars 74; other Parish agencies, Dorcas, and Missionary Dorcas Sewing School; Church 920 sittings; School building 1; parsonage none; cemetery 1; salary of Clergy $5000 per annum; arrears of salary none; number of free sittings 120; extra Sunday services, free to all 17.

Money Receipts from all sources.—Pew rents $14,200, offertory at Holy Communion $1623, collections in Church $3270, subscriptions $2124, donations $2012.50, other sources $19,000, balance on hand $33,705.50. Total $75,934.

Expenditures and Appropriations.—Current expenses (including salary of Clergy) $13,518, repairs and improvements $53,368, payment of debts $5000, Episcopal and Convention Fund $200, support of Parish Schools $1000, for the Poor $1100, to Missions, Foreign $296, Domestic $311, Diocesan $382, Episcopal Hospital $742, Disabled Clergymen $243, Chicago sufferers $627, Church at Tioga $147. Total $76,934.

Financial Condition.—Aggregate value of property of the Parish, real and personal, $200,000. Ground rent on buildings or lands, $3000 per annum. Other indebtedness $5000.

The number of communicants here given is not perfectly accurate, many names requiring to be obtained and added. The number 300 represents the number communing at one time on Festival Sundays.

St. John's Church. Admitted 1816. The Rev. Charles Logan, Rector. Charles Beamish and Henry Walker, Wardens.

Baptisms, adults 2, infants 36, total 38; confirmed 1; communicants, present number 120; marriages 14; burials 19; public services, on Sundays 98, on other days 37, total 135; children catechized 10 times; Sunday Schools, officers and teachers 20, scholars 175; Bible Class, teacher 1, members 10; Sewing School, teacher 1, scholars 50; Mothers' Meeting, members 18; Church 1, sittings 1000; parsonage 1; cemetery 1; salary of Rector $800 per annum; arrears of salary none.

Money Receipts from all sources.—Pew rents $932.60, offertory at Holy Communion $65.78, collections in Church $270.21, subscriptions $194.98, other sources $56.15. Total $1519.72.

Expenditures and Appropriations.—Current expenses (including salary of Rector) $1164.09, repairs and improvements $600, payment of debts $200, Episcopal and Convention Fund $20, support of Sunday Schools $37.20, Parochial Missions $65, Missions, Domestic $5, City Missions $5, for the Jews $5.84, Episcopal Hospital $19, Disabled Clergymen $10.73, Relief of Chicago $95. Total $2236.86.

Financial Condition.—Aggregate value of property of the Parish, real and personal $75,000,; encumbrances on other buildings $1300.

St. Luke's Church, Germantown. Admitted 1818. The Rev. John Rodney, Emeritus Rector: Rev. Albra Wadleigh, Rector. James M. Aertsen and R. P. McCullagh, Wardens.

Baptisms, adults 3, infants 19, total 22; confirmed 9; communicants, added, new 8, by removal 16, died or removed 22, present number 307; marriages 7; burials 7; public services, on Sundays 133, on other days 183, total 316; children catechized 25 times; Sunday Schools, officers and teachers 21, scholars 220; Bible Classes, teachers 4, members 51; Parish Schools, teachers 2, scholars 104. Other Parish agencies—St. Luke's Guild, Mothers' Meeting, Parish Library. Church 1, sittings 500; school building 1; parsonage 1; cemetery 1; salary of Rector $2200 per annum; arrears of salary none;

number of free sittings 48; extra Sunday services, free to all 29.

Money Receipts from all sources.—Pew rents $4860.04, offertory at Holy Communion $521.20, collections in Church $3457.15, subscriptions $1064.49, donations $760, other sources $182.97. Total $10,845.94.

Expenditures and Appropriations.—Current expenses (including salary of Rector) $6001.37, Episcopal and Convention Fund $150, support of Sunday Schools $334.95, Parish Schools $620, Parish Library $96, Parochial Missions $100, for the Poor $621.29, Missions, Foreign $34.50, Domestic $1195.29, Indian Mission $78.80, Diocesan $82.17, City Missions $29.05, Episcopal Hospital $81.22, Bibles, Prayer Books and Tracts $38.87, Christian or Theological Education $516.63, Disabled Clergymen $75. Miscellaneous $469.48. Total $10,524.62.

Financial Condition.—Aggregate value of property of the Parish, real and personal $80,000, encumbrance on Church edifice none, on other buildings $5000, other indebtedness $1500.

Trinty Church, Southwark. Admitted 1821. The Rev. Jesse Y. Burk, Rector. Charles M. Peterson and Henry Green, Wardens.

Baptisms, adults 7, infants 33, total 40; communicants, added, new 4, by removal 7, died or removed 19, present number 226; marriages 14; burials 46; public services, on Sundays 116, on other days 61, total 177; children catechized 10 times; Sunday Schools, officers and teachers 23, scholars 280; Church 1, sittings 800; school building 1; cemetery 1; salary of Rector $1800 per annum; arrears of salary none; number of free sittings, all, evening.

Money Receipts from all sources.—Pew rents $2694.40, offertory at Holy Communion $263.17, collections in Church $1053.82, subscriptions $250, donations $50, investments $167.50, other sources $1127. Total $5605.89.

Expenditures and Appropriations.—Current expenses (including salary of Rector) 3111.53, repairs and improvements $229.86, payment of debts $201.50, Episcopal and Convention Fund $75, support of Sunday Schools $58.17, for the Poor

$283.05, Missions, Foreign $24, Domestic $301, Diocesan $65, City Missions $123.44, for the Jews $20, Episcopal Hospital $115, Bibles, Prayer Books and Tracts $26.25, Christian and Theological Education $113, Disabled Clergymen $30.   Miscellaneous $716.55.   Total $5503.35.

St. Andrew's Church, Philadelphia. Admitted 1823. The Rev. Wilbur F. Paddock, D. D., Rector. Rev. Kinney Hall, Assistant. Thomas Robins and Frederick Brown, Wardens.

Baptisms, adults 9, infants 17, total 26; confirmed 24; communicants, added, new 24, by removal 15, died or removed 20, present number 833; marriages 9; burials 23; public services, on Sundays 104, on other days 84, total 188; children catechized monthly; Sunday Schools, officers and teachers 46, scholars 439; Bible Classes, teachers 3, members 157; Sewing Schools, teachers 12, scholars 138; Mother's Meeting, officers 3, members 124; Church 1; sittings 900; buildings, Chapel and sexton's house; cemetery 1; salary of Rector $3500 per annum; arrears of salary none.

Money Receipts from all sources.—Pew rents $6090; offertory at Holy Communion $578.92; collections in Church $5325.65; subscriptions $500; donations $6542.62; other sources $1193.44.   Total $20,230.63.

Expenditures and Appropriations.—Current expenses (including salary of Rector, $7847.31; Episcopal and Convention Fund $250; support of Sunday Schools $369.80; Parochial Missions $724.19; for the Poor $483.92; to Missions, Foreign $1012.52; Domestic $305.59; Diocesan $812.60; City Missions $582.27; for the Jews $95.12; Episcopal Hospital $450; Church Home for Children $250; Bibles, Prayer Books and Tracts $164.60; Christian or Theological Education $640.40; Disabled Clergymen $153.70; Church Endowment Fund $6317.62; Miscellaneous $212.05.   Total $20,-671.69.

Financial Condition.—Aggregate value of property of the Parish, real and personal $70,000; ground rent on Chapel $100; other indebtedness none.

All the Sunday Schools were decreased in number, and one

was obliged to be closed for the winter by reason of the prevailing sickness.

St. Matthew's Church, Francisville. Admitted 1825. The Rev. John B. Falkner, Rector. George M. Stroud and Joseph P. Mumford, Wardens.

Baptisms, adults, 15, infants 37, total 52; confirmed 42; communicants, added, new, 44, by removal 33, died or removed 35, present number about 400; marriages 6; burials 40; public services, on Sundays, morning and evening; on other days 64; children catechized 12 times; Sunday Schools, scholars about 500; Bible Classes, teachers 5, members 98. Other Parish Agencies—St. Matthew's Chapel, average attendance 60; Divine service every Sunday morning; St. Matthew's Young Men's Literary Association, 60 members. Church 1, sittings 640; Chapel (the statistics of which are included in this report) 1; sittings 250; school building 1; salary of Rector $3000 per annum; arrears of salary none.

Money Receipts from all sources.—Pew rents $4294.12; offertory at Holy Communion $278; collections in Church $591.13; subscriptions $868.07; others sources $817.77. Total $6849.09.

Expenditures and Appropriations.—Current expenses (including salary of Rector) $4310.89; repairs and improvements $415.57; Episcopal and Convention Fund $110; support of Sunday Schools $500; Parochial Missions $500; for the Poor $308; to Missions, Foreign $138.50; Domestic $225; Episcopal Hospital $66.86; Christian or Theological Education $201.55; Disabled Clergymen $42.72; sufferers by Chicago fire $280; Sunday School appropriations $250. Total $6849.09.

Financial Condition.—Encumbrances, mortgages on Church edifice $8000; on other buildings $2000.

Grace Church. Admitted 1827. The Rev. William Suddards, D. D., Rector. Rev. James S. Ellis, Assistant. Mr. William Gillespie, Rector's Warden and Mr. Isaac S. Williams, Accounting Warden.

Baptisms, adults 11, infants 35, total 46; confirmed 46; communicants, added, new 40, died or removed 26, present number 491 ; marriages 24; burials 36 ; public services, on Sundays 140, on other days about 100, total 240 ; children catechized monthly; Sunday Schools, officers and teachers 56, scholars 450 ; Bible Classes, teachers 3, members 80 ; other Parish Agencies, Pastoral Aid Society ; Church 1, sittings 1200; parsonage none ; cemetery none; salary of Rector $3500 per annum, arrears of salary none ; number of free sittings 336 ; extra Sunday services, free to all 36.

Money Receipts from all sources.—Pew rents $7604 ; offertory at Holy Communion $400; collections in Church $1513.36; subscriptions 953.50; investments $2000. Total, $12,470.86.

Expenditures and Appropriations.—Current expenses (including salary of Rector), $6814, repairs and improvements $650; Episcopal and Convention Fund $250 ; support of Sunday Schools $600 ; for the Poor $800 ; to Missions, Foreign $400 ; Domestic $300 ; Diocesan $100 ; City Missions $100 ; Episcopal Hospital $403.21 ; Bibles, Prayer Books and Tracts $120 ; Christian or Theological Education $275 ; Disabled Clergymen $114.36. Total, $10,926.36.

Financial Condition—Aggregate value of property of the Parish, real and personal $40,000. Encumbrances—Mortgages on Church edifices none ; ground rent on buildings or lands, none ; other indebtedness, none.

St. Mary's Church, West Philadelphia. Admitted 1827. Rev. T. C. Yarnall, D. D., Rector. George A. Wright and William Yarnall, Wardens.

Baptisms, adults 2, infants 9, total 11 ; confirmed 10 ; communicants, present number about 150 ; marriages 8 ; burials 9 ; public services, on Sundays 102, on other days 104, total 206 ; Sunday Schools, teachers 14 ; scholars 146.

Money Receipts from all sources, excepting contributions to the building fund for the new Church.—Pew rents $2262.42 ; collections in Church $500.50 ; offertory at Holy Communion $297.09 ; Sunday School offerings $192.08 ; other sources $450. Total $3702.09.

Expenditures and Appropriations.—Current expenses (including salary of Rector) $2712.84 ; Episcopal and Convention

Fund $50; support of Sunday School $400; Foreign Missions, including Sunday School contributions $167.20; Domestic $78.43; Episcopal Hospital $51.06; Christmas Fund $25.08; Chicago sufferers $148.93; Miscellaneous $375.44. Total $4009.

In March last we began to tear down the old Church edifice, preparatory to the erection of a new Church building, in which, we are now actively engaged. Subscriptions and contributions amounting to upwards of $25,000 have already been obtained for this work, which has been long and greatly needed. The Rector takes this opportunity of heartily thanking those who have generously helped him in this undertaking.

Church of the Epiphany. Admitted 1836. Rev. Richard Newton, D.D., Rector. Rev. Alex. Shiras, D. D., Assistant. Wm. G. Boulton and Samuel Ashhurst, M. D., Wardens.

Baptisms, adults 6, infants 58, total 64; confirmed 29; communicants, added 41, new 29, by removal 12, died or removed 8, present number 737; marriages 41; burials 19; public services, on Sundays 100, on other days 74, total 174; Sunday Schools, officers and teachers 75, scholars 952; Bible Classes, teachers 4, members 171; Church sittings 1500; Chapels (the statistics of which are included in this report) 1, sittings 250; salary of Rector $5000 per annum, arrears of salary none; number of free sittings 275.

Money Receipts from all sources.—Pew rents $10,228.05, offertory at Holy Communion $1756, collections in Church $7839.25, subscriptions $4959, donations $1969, other sources $2166.06. Total $30,027.

Expenditures and Appropriations.—Current expenses (including salary of Rector) $9332.86, repairs and improvements $472.25, Episcopal and Convention Fund $300, support of Sunday Schools $636.51, Parochial Missions $1690.86, for the Poor $3553.47, to Missions, Foreign $1177.79, Domestic $2055.17, Diocesan $625, City Missions $556, for the Jews $128.48, Episcopal Hospital $1677, Church building $500, Bibles, Prayer Books, Tracts $370, Book Societies $1548.58.

Christian or Theological Education $1578.04, Disabled Clergymen $900, Miscellaneous $2914.09. Total $30,027.

Financial Condition.—Aggregate value of property of the Parish, real and personal, $250,000.

Ascension Church, Philadelphia. Admitted A. D. 1837. Rev. Henry M. Stuart, Rector. Alfred Zantzinger and Thomas R. Maris, Wardens.

Baptisms, adults 4, infants 31, total 35; confirmed 17; communicants, added, new 17, by removal 15, died or removed 17, present number 225; burials 21; public services, on Sundays 107, on other days 55, total 162: children catechized 10 times; Sunday Schools, officers and teachers 19, scholars 160; Bible Classes, teachers 7, members 68. Other Parish agencies—Mothers' Meeting and Employment Society, officers 4, members 60; Parish Brotherhood, active members 25; Ladies' Missionary Society; Sunday School Missionary Society. Church 1, sittings 600; Sunday services, free to all, every evening.

Money Receipts from all sources.—Pew rents $813.75, offertory at Holy Communion $194.68, collections in Church $717.83, subscriptions $994.75, other sources $400.77. Total $3121.78.

Expenditures and Appropriations.—Current expenses (including salary of Rector) $2680.56, repairs and improvements $71.41, Episcopal and Convention Fund $30, support of Sunday Schools $51.05, for the Poor $207, to Missions, Foreign $84.40, Domestic $95.18, Diocesan $15, for the Jews $9, Episcopal Hospital $60.31, Disabled Clergymen $27.80, Chicago sufferers $77.47, Orphans' Homes $68. Total $3477.18.

Emmanuel Church, Philadelphia. Admitted 1837. Rev. William H. Munroe, Rector. Douglass McFadden and John Scanlin, Wardens.

Baptisms, adults 11, infants 83, total 94; confirmed 26; communicants, added, new 26, by removal 12, died or removed 16, present number 497; marriages 33; burials 65; public services, on Sundays 102, on other days 52, total 154; children catechized 10 times; Sunday Schools, officers and teach-

14

ers 40, scholars 626; Bible Classes, teachers 6, members 130; Church 1, sittings 800; salary of Rector $2000 per annum, arrears of salary, none; extra Sunday services free to all.

Money Receipts from all sources.—Pew rents $2400, offertory at Holy Communion $200.53, collections in Church $595.42, other sources $877.87. Total $4073.82.

Expenditures and Appropriations.—Current expenses (including salary of Rector) $2700, Episcopal and Convention Fund $60, support of Sunday Schools $187.87, Parochial Missions $150, for the Poor $203.53, to Missions, Foreign $50. Domestic $100, City Missions $55, for the Jews $8.88, Episcopal Hospital $22.76, Bibles, Prayer Books and Tracts $30, Book Societies $140, Christian and Theological Education $20, Disabled Clergymen $1889, Miscellaneous $326,86.

All Saints' Church, Philadelphia. Admitted 1838. Rev. Herman L. Duhring, Rector. William Stirling and William Ridings, Wardens.

Baptisms, adults 6, infants 59, total 65; confirmed 29; communicants, present number 380; marriages 16; burials 49; public services, on Sundays 120, on other days 50, total 170; children catechized 10 times; Sunday Schools, officers and teachers 40, scholars 500; Bible Classes, teachers 2, members 60. Other Parish agencies, Dorcas and Sewing Societies 2. Church 1, sittings 800; parsonage none; cemetery 1; salary of Rector $1900 per annum; arrears of salary, none.

Money Receipts from all sources.—Pew rents and collections $2819.37; offertory at Holy Communion $312.33, collections in Church $760.88, subscriptions $753.80, donations $185, interest from investments $186, other sources $830.50. Total $5847.88.

Expenditures and Appropriations.—Current expenses (including salary of Rector) $2779.51, repairs and improvements $412.28, Episcopal and Convention Fund $50, support of Sunday Schools $298.40, Parish Monthly $300, for the Poor $376.74, to Missions, Foreign $100, Domestic $200, Home Mission for Colored People $40, Diocesan $40, City Missions $37.73, Episcopal Hospital $200, Church parsonage $766,

Bibles, Prayer Books and Tracts $25, Christian or Theological Education $25, Disabled Clergymen $17.39, Miscellaneous $179.83. Total $5847.88.

St. Luke's Church, Philadelphia. Admitted 1840. Rev. Algernon Morton, Assistant Minister in charge. George L. Harrison, Warden.

Baptisms, adults 8, infants 44, total 52; confirmed 46; communicants, added 45, new 45, died or removed 16, present number 478; marriages 15, burials 30; public services, on Sundays 104, on other days 59, total 163; children catechized 6 times; Sunday Schools, officers and teachers 38, scholars 409; Bible Classes, Teachers 5, Members 149; Parish Schools, Teachers 2, Scholars 50. Other Parish agencies; Male Bible Class Association of St. Luke's Church 30; Colored School scholars 50, teachers 7. Church 1, sittings 1300; salary of Rector $5000 per annum; Assistant $1000.

Money Receipts from all sources. — Pew rents, one year $9415.70, offertory at Holy Communion and alms for Poor $1300, collections in Church $5137.93, donations $416. Total $16,269.63.

Expenditures and Appropriations.—Episcopal and Convention Fund $300, support of Parish Schools $320, Parochial Missions $200, to Missions, Foreign $820.09, Dorcas $431.75, Missionary Sewing Society $276, Indian Hope $444, Domestic, $852, private source $2000, Diocesan, $502.55, City Missions $478, for the Jews $58.28, Episcopal Hospital $1440,50. Christian or Theological Education $172.47, Disabled Clergymen $150, Miscellaneous $500, St. Luke's Home for Aged Females $773.76, from Foreign Missionary Boxes $180.08. Total $9,899.48.

Current expenses (including salary of Rector and Assistant), repairs and improvements, etc., about $9000.

Financial Condition.—Aggregate value of property of the Parish, real and personal, Church lot, building and furniture, cost about $90,000. A Home for Aged Lone Women is held in trust by the Vestry of St. Luke's Church. Cost of property and furniture about $16,000.

St. Philip's Church. Admitted 1841. Rev. James Pratt, D. D., Rector. John Agnew and George R. Kellogg, Wardens.

Baptisms, adult 1, infants 13, total 14; communicants, present number about 300; marriages 9; burials 16; public services, on Sundays 104, on other days 41, total 145; average attendance on Sundays 400; children catechized 12 times; Sunday Schools, officers and teachers 43, scholars 320; Bible Classes, teachers 2, members 38; Church 1, sittings 842; salary of Rector $2500 per annum.

Money Receipts from all sources.—Pew rents $4534, offertory at Holy Communion $400, collections in Church $562, donations $100. Total $5596.

Expenditures and Appropriations.—Current expenses (including salary of Rector) $4120, repairs and improvements $300, Episcopal and Convention Fund $150, support of Sunday Schools $450, for the Poor $400, to Missions, Foreign $300, Domestic $1400, City Missions $60, for the Jews $30.60, Episcopal Hospital $113.44, Christian or Theological Education $250, Miscellaneous, viz., Chicago sufferers $600. Total $8174.

Financial Condition.—Aggregate value of property of the Parish, real and personal, $50,000; Chapel building not used for Church purposes $4000. Encumbrance—Ground-rent on Chapel not used for our service $240.

The undersigned, after officiating for four months as temporary supply of St. Philips', became its Rector on the 1st of May. The above report embraces the official acts by his predecessor for *eight* months, and his own for the *four* remaining months of the year.

J. Pratt.

————

Advent Church. Admitted 1842. Rev. J. W. Claxton, Rector. Rev. F. W. Winslow, Assistant. Abel Reed and George Remsen, Wardens.

Baptisms, adults 18, infants 24, total 42; confirmed 36; communicants, added, new 39, by removal 12, died or removed 29, present number 370; marriages 16; burials 26; children catechized monthly; Sunday Schools, officers and teachers

21 ; scholars 402; Bible Classes, teachers 4; members 262 ; Parish Schools, teachers 16; scholars 134. Other Parish Agencies—Mothers' Meeting, members 100. Church 1, sittings 619; extra Sunday services, free to all, 1.

Money Receipts from all sources.—Pew rents $4050; offertory at Holy Communion $324.27 ; collections in Church $1703.03; subscriptions $1004.31 ; donations $1104.31 ; other sources $2235.83. Total $9417.44.

Expenditures and Appropriations.—Current Expenses (including salary of Rector) $4284.31 ; repairs and improvements $320.49 ; payment of debts $745.15 ; Episcopal and Convention Fund $125 ; support of Sunday Schools $342.02; of Parish Schools $85 ; Parochial Missions $1200 ; for the Poor $288.23 ; to Missions, Foreign $131 ; Domestic $267.80 ; Diocesan $140; City Missions $351.80 ; for the Jews 7.13 ; Episcopal Hospital $93.65 ; Bibles, Prayer Books and Tracts $47.25 ; Christian or Theological Education $82.61 ; Miscellaneous $900. Total $9417.44.

Financial Condition.—Aggregate value of the property of the Parish, real and personal, $40,000.

Church of the Evangelists, Philadelphia. Admitted 1842. Rev. Jacob Miller, Rector. Richard W. Sommers and Alexander C. Young, Wardens.

Baptisms, adults 5, infants 87, total 92; confirmed 25 ; communicants, added, new 23, by removal 7, died or removed 39, present number 380 ; marriages 12 ; burials 51 ; public services on Sunday 120, on other days 70, total 190; children catechized monthly; Sunday Schools, officers and teachers 40, scholars 520; Bible Classes, teachers 2; members 24. Other Parish Agencies—Union Association, Parish Missionary Society, Rector's Aid Society ; Church 1; sittings 1000; salary of Rector $1233.34 per annum.

Money Receipts from all sources.—Pew rents $2051.15; offertory at Holy Communion $149.15, collections in Church $539.12; donations $418.37; other sources $2091.73. Total $5249.52.

Expenditures and Appropriations.—Current expenses (in-

cluding salary of Rector) $3022.64; payment of debts
$2077.44; Episcopal and Convention Fund $30; for the Poor
(Parish Missionary Society) $37.25; to Missions, Foreign
$22.33, City Missions $67.13; Episcopal Hospital $12.16;
Disabled Clergymen $3.80; Chicago sufferers $74.17. Total
$5346.92.

Financial Condition.—Aggregate value of property of the
Parish, real and personal $35.000; ground-rent on buildings
or lands $440 per year; other indebtedness $3520.46.

This Parish is steadily increasing its means of usefulness.
The Sunday School is self-sustaining; and in addition to the
sum of $250.75 raised and expended in refitting the Lecture
Room, has contributed $26.30 towards the relief of destitute
children in Chicago.   The Rector returns thanks to his parishioners for the numerous favors received at their hands.

––––––

Emmanuel Church, Holmesburg. Admitted 1844. Rev. D. Caldwell Millett, D. D., Rector.
Presley Blakiston and Lewis Thompson, Wardens.

Baptisms, adults 2, infants 21, total 23; confirmed, no visitation; communicants, added, by removal 3, present number
128; marriages 2; burials 10; Parish Schools, teachers 12,
Scholars 120; parsonage 1; cemetery 1; Sunday services
free to all in evening.

Money Receipts from all sources—Offertory at Holy Communion, and other charitable objects $202.16.

Expenditures and Appropriations.—Expenses $184.87; re-
pairs and improvements $559.81; Episcopal and Convention
Fund $60; support of Sunday Schools $29.90; Parish Library
$24.16; to Missions, Domestic $74.20 Diocesan $25.62; City
Missions, $65; for the Jews, $5; Episcopal Hospital, $25;
Bibles, Prayer Books and Tracts, $16.12; Nashotah, $10;
Disabled Clergymen, $16.33; Society for increase of Ministry,
$26; Chicago Sufferers, $167.15; St. Angarius, $4; Festival,
$33.66; Bishop Morris, $50; Church Home, $25.   Total
$1603.98.

Six large boxes were sent to the sufferers in Michigan and
Wisconsin, also one large box of clothing and groceries, with

$20 in money to the Ponca Indian Mission. One barrel of clothing from the Ladies' Missionary Society for Rev. Mr. Hinman's Mission.

The Sunday School sent $25 to the Missions in Maine, (Bishop Neely). The Easter offerings of the Sunday School for books, was $19.22. The amount from the mite chest up to 1872, was $276.29.

St. James' Church, Kingsessing. Admitted 1844. Rev. Charles A. Maison, Rector. Robert Buist, Warden.

Baptisms, infants 27; confirmed 11; communicants, added, new 10, by removal 4, died or removed 12, present number 136; marriages 9; burials 14; public services, on Sundays 105, on other days 25, total 130; Sunday Schools, officers and and teachers 15, scholars 186; Parish schools, teacher 1, scholars 35; Church 1, sittings 500; school buildings 2; parsonage 1; cemetery 1; salary of Rector, $1500 per annum.

Money Receipts from all sources.—Pew rents $1268.30, offertory at Holy Communion $179.90, collections in Church $489.65, subscriptions $1239, donations $787.63, investments $972.73, other sources $121.92. Total $5059.13.

Expenditures and Appropriations.—Current expenses (including salary of Rector) $2636.44, repairs and improvements $1219.78; Episcopal and Convention Fund $60, support of Sunday Schools $203.04, of Parish schools $555, for the Poor $17.66, to Missions, Domestic $391, City Missions $28.85, for the Jews $9.05, Episcopal Hospital $42.33, Church Church Home $20.25, Bibles, Prayer Books and Tracts $3.30, Book Societies $11.09, Christian or Theological Education $117.42, Disabled Clergymen $5.31, Miscellaneous $20.45. Total $5340.97.

Financial Condition.—Aggregate value of property of the Parish, real and personal $50,000.

Occasional services have been held in the School house at Boon's Dam. Large improvements have been made at the Church, and others are in progress at the parsonage.

Gloria Dei Church, Philadelphia. Admitted 1836. Rev. Snyder B. Simes, Rector. John Redles and George M. Sandgran, Wardens.

Baptisms, adults 2, infants 42, total 48; confirmed 14; marriages 44; burials 27; Sunday Schools, officers and teachers 30, scholars 500; Bible Class, teacher 1, members 29; Church 1, sittings 470; School buildings 2; parsonage 1; cemetery 1; salary of Rector $1500 per annum and parsonage; arrears of salary none.

Money Receipts from all sources.—Pew rents $1541.22, offertory at Holy Communion $206.90, collections in Church $425.20, donations $1150.46, other sources $1558.94. Total $4882.72.

Expenditures and Appropriations.—Current expenses (including salary of Rector) $2612.76, payment of debts $1711.-67, Episcopal and Convention Fund $60, for the Poor $240.05, City Missions $55.70, Episcopal Hospital $25, Bibles, Prayer Books and Tracts $14, Book Societies $74.67. Total $4793.85.

Church of the Nativity. Admitted 1845. Rev. William Newton, Rector. Wm. B. Ridgely and W. Hobart Brown, Wardens.

Baptisms, adult 1, infants 7, total 8; funerals 12; marriages 9; public services, on Sundays 86, other days 33, total 119. The Rector was laid aside by severe illness for three months. Confirmed 18; communicants, added, new 18; by removal or letter 50, last reported 268, present number about 310. The communicants' list is yet imperfect; but, as far as a most patient examination of it has gone, the result, as at present shown, is as definite as the Rector has been able to make it. Sunday Schools, officers and teachers 36. Infant School 87, Bible Classes 77, Intermediate department 204, total 404; increase of School since last October 13 teachers and 130 scholars. Missionary collections for the last nine months $589.16. Other Parish operations are the Mothers' Meeting, the Girls' Sewing School, Cottage Lectures, and Rector's Bible Class. Church accommodation, edifice 1; parsonage none; property other than the Church building, and lot owned by the Church, none; amount of indebtedness none; salary of Rector $2500; arrears of salary none.

Collections and Contributions.—Offertory $260, Education Society $230, Episcopal Hospital $85.05, Aged and Infirm Clergy $46.42, Chicago $500, all other sources $4424.28. Total $5546.

The Rector would thankfully acknowledge the many proofs and tokens of growing interest and prosperity in the Parish, which meet him on every hand.

Church of the Redemption. Admitted 1846. Rev. Jno. Pleasonton Du Hamel, Rector. Alexander Crow, Accounting Warden. W. H. Eastwood, Rector's Warden.

Baptisms, adults 5, infants 67, total 72; confirmed 25 (two others prepared but prevented by sickness); communicants, added 33, new 27, by removal 6; lost, died* and removed 5, do. repelled 1, present number, as per register 231; marriages 39; burials 30; public services, on Sundays 104, on other days 84, total 188; children catechized, monthly in the Church; Sunday Schools, officers and teachers 22, scholars 282; Bible Classes 2, scholars 39. Other Parochial agencies—Parish Aid Society, Woman's Missionary Association, Girl's Sewing School, Mothers' Meeting, Young Men's Library Association; all of which are or have been, during the past winter, in successful operation in their respective spheres. Church 1, sittings 600; Sunday School and Lecture Room in basement of Church; Rectory 1; salary of Rector $1200 per annum, arrears of salary none.

Money Receipts from all sources.—Pew rents $1044, offertory at Holy Communion $138.85, collections in Church $373.78; other sources, from " Parish Aid" $38.15, for Parish work. Total $1624.78.

Expenditures and Appropriations.—Current expenses (including salary of Rector) $1576.38, repairs and improvements $1019.29, for Sunday School purposes $17.03, Episcopal and Convention Fund $20; Missions, City $23.49, to Jews $10.20, Foreign, congregation $17.28, Sunday School Mission Boxes $18.78, to Rev. Mr. Thomson, special towards the education

---

*The Rector feels bound to record his sense of thankfulness to Almighty God, that during the prevalence of the late epidemic he has not, from that cause, been called to chronicle the death of a single communicant.

of a Chinese girl $10, Woman's Missionary Association
$33.90; Domestic, Woman's Missionary Association $33.90;
Church Institutions, Episcopal Hospital $20, Church Home
for Children $27.44; Special, Chicago sufferers $70, Sunday
School offerings for all purposes $184.96.   Total $3082.65.

Church property, aggregate value $58,000.   Encumbrances
none.

Church of St. James' the Less, Falls of Schuylkill. Admitted 1846. Rev. Robert Ritchie, Rector.
Ellis Yarnall and Edward S. Buckley, Wardens.

Baptisms 22; confirmed 12; communicants, added 15; new
12; by removal 3; marriage 1; children catechized about
75 times; Sunday Schools, officers and teachers 10; scholars 150; Parish Schools, teacher 1; scholars 30; Holy
Communion administered about 87 times, publicly, besides
private celebrations.   Church 1, sittings 180; school buildings 2; parsonage 1; cemetery 1; salary of Rector $1500;
arrears of salary none; number of free sittings 180.

St. Mark's Church, Frankford, Philadelphia. Admitted 1846. Rev. D. S. Miller, D.D., Rector.
Rev. T. Tweedale, Assistant Minister. John Clayton, Esq., and Benjamin Rowland, Jr., Esq.,
Wardens.

Baptisms, adults 8; infants 93, total 101; confirmed 29;
marriages 21; communicants, added, new 33, by removal 10,
died or removed 136, present number 955; burials 64; public services, on Sundays 172, on other days 61, total 233; children catechized monthly; Sunday Schools, officers and
teachers 70, scholars 764, Bible Class scholars 565, Sunday
School total 1399; Parish School teachers 18, day scholars
180, night scholars 127, sewing scholars 140, school total
1864; Young Men's Club 70 members; Mothers' Meeting, 18
visitors, 300 members; Dispensary, 2 physicians, 2 attendants,
401 patients (in four months); Church 1; school building 1;
rectory 1; club house 1; salary of Rector $2000 per annum
and rectory; arrears of salary none; all weekly and Sunday
services entirely free to all.

Expenditures and Appropriations.—Current expenses (including salaries of Rector and Assistant Minister, repairs and

improvements) $5062.17, Episcopal and Convention Fund $100, support of Sunday and Parish Schools, Parish Libraries and Parochial Missions $2360.36; for the Poor $767.75, to Missions, Foreign $952.51, Domestic $608, Oregon $120, Indians $416.84, Home Missions for Colored People $240.35, Diocesan $432.22, City Missions $97.50, for the Jews $48.22, Episcopal Hospital $841.62, Bibles, Prayer Books and Tracts $90, Book Societies $265.08, Theological education $570.53, Disabled Clergymen $86.43, the Chicago fire $351.60, Orphans' Home $50, Mothers' Meeting Clothing Club $449.73, Sick Club $128.65, Young Men's Club $809.71, St. Mark's Dispensary (4 months) $303.73, Mothers' Aid Fund $128.50, Sewing School $41.59. No encumbrance of any kind. Total $15,323.09.

St. Stephen's, Bridesburg, and St. Paul's, Aramingo, make their own reports. I have this year cut off all I have lost by this colonizing, thus largely reducing my communicant list and other items. About 5800 visits were made this year. The diminution is due to the presence of infectious diseases and sickness, and absence among our workers. A successful Young Men's Club has been established, and a Dispensary opened and carried on since January 1st, with great benefit to the poor, to whom it is open without regard to creed.

Church of the Crucifixion. Admitted 1847. Rev. William H. Josephus, Minister in charge. Thomas R. Maris, Esq., and W. Beaumont Whitney, Esq., Wardens.

Baptisms, adults 2, infants 15, total 17; confirmed *; communicants, added, new 2, by removal 5, died or removed 4, present number 137; marriages 5; burials 7; public services, on Sundays 2, on other days 1, total 3; children catechized monthly; Sunday Schools, officers and teachers 447, scholars 431; other Parish Agencies, "Home for the Homeless," 708 Lombard street; Church 1; salary of Rector $780 per annum; number of free sittings, all; extra Sunday services, free to all, P.M. at "Home."

Money Receipts from all sources.—Offertory at Holy Communion $42.22; collections in Church $69.84; donations

----

* Candidates in preparation.

$1202.94; investments $68.70; other sources $182.43. Total $1566.13.

Expenditures and Appropriations.—Current expenses (including salary of Rector) $1249.07, repairs and improvements $202, Sunday Schools self-supporting, for the Poor $23.72, Domestic $6. Total $1480.79.

Financial Condition.—Encumbrances, ground-rent on Church building $2158.33, on other buildings $3000, other indebtedness none.

Church of the Messiah, Port Richmond. Admitted 1847. Rev. Rees. C. Evans, Rector. Henry Christian and William Rogers, Wardens.

Baptisms, adults 3, infants 37, total 40; communicants, added, by removal 1, died or removed 8, present number 52; marriages 2; burials 18; public services, on Sundays 114, on other days occasional; children catechized 52 times; Sunday Schools, officers and teachers 6, scholars 100; Church 1, sittings 500; parsonage 1; cemetery lot 1.

Money Receipts from all sources.—Pew rents $487, offertory at Holy Communion $31.55, collections in Church $99.01, donations to Church and Rectory $632.25, special collections $31.46, other sources $45.83. Total $1327.10.

Expenditures and Appropriations.—Current expenses (including salary of Rector) $699.05, repairs and improvements $539.39, Episcopal and Convention Fund $6, Episcopal Hospital $4, Disabled Clergymen $2.81, Chicago Sufferers $15.09, Home for Little Wanderers $6.18. Total $1272.52.

Financial Condition.—Aggregate value of property of the Parish, real and personal $15.000, ground-rent on buildings or lands $1200, other indebtedness none.

Church of the Atonement. Admitted 1847. Rev. Benjamin Watson, D. D., Rector. Towsend Whelen and William H. Hill, Wardens.

Baptism, adults 3, infants 33, total 36; confirmed 13; communicants, added, new 13, by removal 10, died or removed 10, present number 492; marriages 15; burials 23, public services on Sundays 100, on other days 84, total 184; Sunday Schools, officers and teachers 40, scholars 340, Bible Classes, teachers 8, members 60. Other Parish agencies—Mother's Meeting, Female Missionary, Sunday night Services for the Poor.

Church 1, sittings 1100, salary of Rector $3500 per annum, arrears of salary, none.

Money receipts from all sources.—Pew rents $7,000, offertory at Holy Communion $519.62, collections in Church $3663.59, Subscriptions $2700, Sunday School collections $350, other sources $200. Total $14,434.13.

Expenditures and Appropriations.—Current expenses (including salary of Rector) $7000; payment of debts $3000; Episcopal and Convention Fund $200; support of Sunday Schools $230.70; Parochial Missions $300; for the Poor $356.34; to Missions, Foreign $315.83; Domestic $202.96; Diocesan $100; City Missions $200; for the Jews $42; Episcopal Hospital $303.36; Christian or Theological Education $750; Disabled Clergymen $88.21; miscellaneous $1069.42; Chicago sufferers $279.85. Total $14,438.34.

St. Mark's Church, Philadelphia. Admitted 1848. Rev. Eugene Aug. Hoffmann, D. D., Rector. Rev. Francis D. Canfield, A. M., and Rev. John Coleman, Assistants. Richard R. Montgomery and W. A. M. Fuller, Wardens.

Baptisms, adults 15, infants 65, total 80; confirmed 36; communicants, added, new or by removal 83, died or removed 39, present number 673; marriages 18; burials 50; public services, on Sundays 208, on other days 628, total 832; average attendance on Sundays 900; children catechized 44 times; Sunday Schools, officers and teachers 17, scholars 214; Bible Classes, teachers 3, members 67; Parish Schools, teachers 2, Scholars 85. Other Parish Agencies—Night Schools 2, scholars 105; Industrial School 1, teachers 17, scholars 147; Working Women's Meeting, members 40; Working Men's Club and Institute, members 375. Church 1, sittings 900; School building 1; parsonage 1; salary of Rector $5000 per annum; arrears of salary none; number of free sittings 100; extra Sunday services, free to all 2.

Money Receipts from all sources.—Pew rents $13,210.53;

offertory at Holy Communion and collections in Church and subscriptions $35,015.34. Total $48,225.87.

Expenditures and Appropriations.—Current expenses (including salary of Rector) $14,000, repairs and improvements $5082.35, payment of debts $5000, Episcopal and Convention Fund $350, support of Sunday Schools $257.57, of Parish Schools $884, Parochial Missions $3342.18, for the Poor $1490.04, to Missions, Foreign $297.25, Domestic $6718.65, Home Mission for Colored People $476.25, Diocesan $448.25, City Missions $470.68, for the Jews 163.28, Episcopal Hospital $762.05, Bibles, Prayer Book and Tract Societies $368.55, Christian or Theological Education $123.26, Disabled Clergymen $332.04, Miscellaneous $7659.47. Total $48,225.87.

Church of the Mediator. Admitted 1848. Rev. Samuel E. Appleton, Rector. Rev. J. C. Hewlett, Assistant. Francis A. Lewis and Horace Everett, Wardens.

Baptisms, adults 5, infants 60, total 65; confirmed 14; communicants, added, new 22, by removal 19, died or removed 16, present number 405; marriages 23; burials 41; Sunday Schools, officers and teachers 32, scholars 390; Bible Classes, teachers 3, members 53; Church 1, sittings 600; School building 1; salary of Rector $2250 per annum; arrears of salary none.

Money Receipts from all sources.—Pew rents $3985, offertory at Holy Communion $368.06, collections in Church $1794.50, subscriptions $1053.43, donations $1261.03. Total $8462.02.

Expenditures and Appropriations.—Current expenses (including salary of Rector) $4060.09, repairs and improvements $448.60, Episcopal and Convention Fund $100, support of Sunday Schools $253.06, for the Poor $672.60, to Missions, Foreign, $399, Domestic $452.42, Diocesan $345.88, City Missions $359.32, Episcopal Hospital $84.60, Bibles, Prayer Books and Tracts $125.95, Christian or Theological Education $61, Disabled Clergymen $72.31, Miscellaneous $673.28, sufferers by Chicago fire $354. Total $8462.02.

Financial Condition.—Aggregate value of property of the

Parish, real and personal $25.000. No encumbrances or debts.

Five years have passed away since the organization of the Parish Missionary Societies, and it gives me pleasure to state that they are in a flourishing condition. During the past year, the sum of one thousand dollars was raised for Missions by the Societies, independent of Church collections.

St. Jude's Church. Admitted 1848. Rev. W. H. Graff, Rector. Charles R. Taylor and Jacob L. Smith, Wardens.

Baptisms, adults 3, infants 10, total 13; confirmed 8; communicants, added, new 47, died or removed 18, present number 135; marriages 4; burials 20; public services, on Sundays 103, on other days 114, total 217; average attendance on Sundays 250; children catechized about 40 times; Sunday Schools, officers and teachers 20, scholars 165. Other Parish Agencies—Brotherhood, Pastoral Aid Society, Young Ladies' Aid Society. Church 1, sittings 460; salary of Rector $1500 per annum; arrears of salary none; number of free sittings, all.

Money Receipts from all sources.—Church free to all, offertory at Holy Communion $171.95; collections in Church $855.06, subscriptions $1731.78, donations $1744.54, sale of investments $965. Total $5468.33.

Expenditures and Appropriations.—Current expenses (including salary of Rector) $3079.26, repairs and improvements $1294, Episcopal and Convention Fund $40, Sunday School work $238.49, Parish Library $34.45, for the Poor $460.12, to Missions, Foreign $18.87, City Missions $12.86, for the Jews $10.25, Episcopal Hospital $101.72, "Home and Abroad" $10, Disabled Clergymen $16.23, Miscellaneous, including work for Indians, &c., &c. $481.76. Total $5798.01.

Financial Condition.—Ground-rent on buildings or lands $5000, other indebtedness $1488.

Zion Church. Admitted 1849. Rev. C. W. Duane, Rector. Dell Noblit, Jr., and Thomas R. Alexander, Wardens.

Baptisms, adults 5, infants 18, total 23; confirmed 15; communicants, added, new 15, by removal 11, died or removed

28, present number 188; marriages 9; burials 14; public services, on Sundays 104, on other days 42, total 146; children catechized 9 times; Sunday Schools, officers and teachers 15, scholars 250; Bible Classes, teachers 3, members 50; Church 1, sittings 750; salary of Rector $1800 per annum; arrears of salary none.

Money Receipts from all sources.—Pew rents $2130.58, offertory at Holy Communion $237.28, collections in Church $187.17, subscriptions $4301.24, other sources $565.10. Total $7421.37.

Expenditures and Appropriations.—Current expenses (including salary of Rector) $3652.84, repairs and improvements $195.50, payment of debts $2958.10, Episcopal and Convention Fund $30, support of Sunday Schools $276.29, for the Poor 116.53, to Missions, Foreign $41.31, Domestic $83, Diocesan $42, for the Jews $5.12, Episcopal Hospital $70.45, Christian or Theological Education $25, Chicago sufferers $111.60. Total $7607.74.

Financial Condition.—Aggregate value of property of the Parish, real and personal $40,000. Encumbrances—mortgages on Church edifice $10,000, ground-rents on buildings or lands none, other indebtedness none.

St. Bartholomew's Church. Admitted 1849. Rev. James Saul, Rector. George W. Taylor and John C. Mitchell, Wardens.

Expenditures and appropriations.—To Missions, Foreign $8.40, Domestic $3.25, sufferers by fire at Chicago $50.

Referring to previous reports, I have only to observe that the suit for recovery of the Church property has not yet been decided by the court of last resort. The Church edifice is consequently out of possession of the Parish, so that public services cannot be held. And the prevalence of small-pox has caused the discontinuance of the School in the Hall on Saturdays. Under these circumstances, I accepted the Rectorship of Christ Church, Waterford, New Jersey, without dissolving my connection with this Diocese on changing my residence from Philadelphia.

The Parish of St. Bartholomew requires the sympathy and aid of the Clergy and Laity of its sister Parishes in this city.

St. David's Church, Manayunk. Admitted 1833. Rev. F. H. Bushnell, Rector. Orlando Crease and Edward Holt, Wardens.

Baptisms, adults 7, infants 51, total 58; confirmed 36; communicants, added, 18, died or removed 14, present number 242; marriages 9; burials 21; public services, on Sundays 104, on other days 45, total 149; children catechized 12 times; Sunday Schools, officers and teachers 33, scholars 500; Bible Classes, teachers 2, members 45. Other Parish Agencies—Mothers' Meeting, Bible teacher 1, members 71. Church 1, sittings 590; School building 1; parsonage 1; cemetery 1; salary of Rector $1300 per annum; arrears of salary none; number of free sittings 40; Sunday services, free to all, 1.

Money Receipts from all sources.—Pew rents $1639.34; offertory at Holy Communion $111.27, collections in Church $567, subscriptions $1047.15, donations $2441.02, other sources $811. Total $6616.78.

Expenditures and Appropriations.—Current expenses (including salary of Rector) $1786, repairs and improvements $647.25, Episcopal and Convention Fund $60, support of Sunday Schools $930.17, Parish Library $5, Parochial Missions $691, for the Poor $111.27, to Missions, Foreign $80, Domestic $343.46, Diocesan $125, City Missions $11.55, Episcopal Hospital $28, Church building $1250, Bibles, Prayer Books and Tracts $25, Christian or Theological Education $96, Disabled Clergymen $12.72, Miscellaneous $414.36. Total $6616.78.

Financial Condition.—Aggregate value of property of the Parish, real and personal $41,900.

There is included in the amounts under the head of "Donations" $1250, the value of a lot, situated in the lower part of Manayunk, given for the purpose of having erected thereon a School and Church building. $670, under the head "other sources," is money accumulated by the ladies of the congregation towards the erection of a Chapel or Sunday School building on this lot. Besides the sums mentioned in the

16

above report there has been subscribed for the enlargement of our present Sunday School building through a Mite Society $500, and by an ever generous member of the congregation $1000 more.

Church of the Resurrection. Admitted 1850. Rev. Thomas J. Davis, Rector.

Baptisms, adults 5, infants 4, total 9; confirmed 14; communicants, added, new 7, died or removed 3, present number 22; marriages 2; burials 5.

The re-erection of the Church edifice having been completed and ready for Divine worship, by reason of the absence of the Rt. Rev. Bishop Stevens, the Rt. Rev. Bishop Howe, of Central Pennsylvania, was invited to consecrate the Church and perform the Rite of Confirmation.

And, on the 8th March, 1872, the Church was solemnly consecrated and set apart for Divine worship, according to the provisions and authority of the Church in the United States of America.

By an amicable arrangement, at a meeting, the Vestry, March 22d, 1872, the Parish of St. George was united with the Church of the Resurrection. And thereupon, I resigned the Rectorship thereof, and was unanimously elected Rector Emeritus; likewise the Rev. Joseph R. Moore elected Rector. All of which was to take effect on Easter Monday, the 1st of April ensuing.

.   THOMAS J. DAVIS, *Rector Emeritus.*

Church of the Resurrection. Admitted 1850. Rev. Joseph R. Moore, Rector. Rev. Thomas J. Davis, Rector Emeritus.   John Zimmerling and Thomas Maddock, Jr., Wardens.

The Church having been closed since April 1st for necessary improvements, I have performed no official acts since the date of my taking charge of the Parish. The statistics of the Parish from May, 1871 to April 1st, 1872, will be reported by the Rev. Thomas J. Davis, who was Rector up to the latter date, when he became Rector Emeritus.

St. Andrew's Church, West Philadelphia.   Admitted 1852. Rev. Samuel E. Smith, Rector.
H. W. Siddall, M. D., and L. R. Massey, Wardens.

Baptisms, adults 5, infants 40, total 45 ; confirmed 16; communicants, added, new 11, by removal 19, died or removed 29, present number 121; marriages 10; burials 17; public services, on Sundays 106, on other days 82, total 188; children catechized 10 times; Sunday Schools, officers and teachers 24, scholars 195; Bible Classes, teachers 2, members 16; Church, 1 sittings 380; salary of Rector $1750 per annum; number of free sittings 35; Sunday evening services free to all.

Money Receipts from all sources.—Pew rents $1738.88; offertory at Holy Communion $119.06; collections in Church $715.88, subscriptions $382.75, other sources $121. Total $3077.37.

Expenditures and Appropriations.—Current expenses (including salary of Rector) $2216.76, repairs and improvements $148.15, payment of interest $450, Episcopal and Convention Fund $20, support of Sunday Schools $57.99, to Missions, Foreign $14, Domestic $20, Diocesan $26.14, City Missions $94, Episcopal Hospital $15, Disabled Clergymen $25, Miscellaneous, Chicago $90.20. Total $3177.24.

Financial Condition.—Aggregate value of property of the Parish, real and personal, $40,000; indebtedness $345.25.

It is gratifying to be able to report that the indebtedness on the Church edifice, mentioned in former report, has been entirely extinguished, and the building is now ready for Consecration.

Church of The Saviour, West Philadelphia. Admitted 1852. Rev. J. H. Eccleston, D.D., Rector. John D. Taylor and H. P. Rutter, Wardens.

Baptisms, adults 10, infants 29, total 39; confirmed 42; communicants, added, new 39, by removal 52, died or removed 6, present number 291; marriages 6; burials 19; public services, on Sundays 96, on other days 54, total 150; children catechized 10 times; Sunday Schools, officers and teachers 46, scholars 509; Bible Classes, teachers 2, members 32. Other Parish Agencies—Sewing School and Mothers' Meeting at Chapel. Church 1, sittings 500; Chapel (the statistics of which are included in this report) 1, sittings 250; salary of Rector $3000 per annum; all seats at Chapel free.

Money Receipts from all sources.—Pew rents $3646.14, offertory at Holy Communion $514.47, collections in Church $1514.80, subscriptions $1473.50, donations $155, other sources $1834.41. Total $9150.59.

Expenditures and Appropriations.—Current expenses (including salary of Rector) $4210.48, repairs and improvements $719.15, Episcopal and Convention Fund $150, support of Sunday Schools $261, Parochial Missions $1882, for the Poor $303.13, to Missions, Foreign $258.02, Domestic $242.40, Diocesan $20, City Missions $102.11, for the ·Jews $52.87, Episcopal Hospital $74.59, Church building $100. Christian or Theological Education $590.08, Disabled Clergymen $61.78, Miscellaneous $142.39. Total $9149.59.

Financial Condition.—Aggregate value of property of the Parish, real and personal, $4200. Ground rent on Chapel $2000.

The Chapel of the Holy Comforter has been entirely under the care of Mr. William H. Platt, acting under a license as Lay Reader.

Christ Church, Germantown. Admitted 1855. Rev. Theodore S. Rumney, D. D., Rector. Lewis D. Vail and Charles Spencer, Wardens.

Baptisms, adults 5, infants 21, total 26; confirmed*; communicants, added, new 35, by removal 12, died or removed 18, present number 304; marriages 6; burials 15; public services, on Sundays 106, on other days 115, total 221; children catechized, monthly in Church; Sunday Schools, officers and teachers 50, scholars 539; Bible Classes, teachers 9, members 95. Other Parish Agencies—Sewing School, Christ Church Mission, Mothers' Meeting, Parish Library, Ladies' Missionary Society. Church 1, sittings 700; School building 1; parsonage 1; salary of Rector $2500 per annum and Rectory; number of free sittings 176.

Money Receipts from all sources.—Pew rents $4467.14, offertory at Holy Communion (including Easter offering) $903.-85, collections in Church $5011.74, investments $1644, other sources $764.93. Total $12,793.66.

---

* A class of thirty persons ready for the Bishop, who is to visit the Parish on Whitsunday.

Expenditures and Appropriations.—Current expenses (including salary of Rector) $4938.54, Episcopal and Convention Fund $200, support of Sunday Schools $224.53, Seamen's Mission $50, Parochial Missions $262, for the Poor $400, to Missions, Foreign $895.78*, Domestic $1131.04, Diocesan $171, City Missions $546.88, for the Jews $71.09, Episcopal Hospital $265.50, Book Societies $48, Christian or Theological Education $238.95, Disabled Clergymen $50.75, Sunday School offerings to various objects $474.03, special for Indians $448.60, Miscellaneous $1674.09. Total $12,090.78.

Financial Condition.—Aggregate value of property of the Parish, real and personal, $80,000. Encumbrances, mortgages on Church edifice none, on other buildings $6067.00. Other indebtedness $128.91.

Over twenty boxes have been sent to the sufferers by fire in Michigan and Wisconsin; also to the Indians, valued at $800.

Trinity Church, Maylandville. Admitted 1853. Rev. J. H. Eccleston, D.D., Rector. Rev. C. T. Stout, Assistant. N. B. Browne and Robert Craven, Wardens.

Baptisms, infants 5, total 5; confirmed 1; communicants, present number 11; burials 3; public services, on Sundays 39, on other days 4, total 43; children catechized 8 times; Sunday Schools, officers and teachers 12, scholars 95. Other Parish Agencies—Mothers' Meeting and Men's Bible Class on Sunday evening. Church 1, sittings 150; salary of Assistant Rector $1000 per annum; number of free sittings all; extra Sunday services free to all.

Money Receipts from all sources.—Offertory at Holy Communion $9, collections in Church $15.23, subscriptions $1705, Total $1729.23.

Expenditures and Appropriations.—Current expenses (including salary of Assistant Rector) $694.97, repairs and improvements $715.78; no debt. Total $1410.75.

Trinity, Maylandville, has not for some time had the care of a regular Pastor, but since October last it has been under

---

* The above amount is exclusive of eleven hundred dollars, contributed by members of the congregation to this object.

the regular care of the Rev. C. T. Stout, who has had entire charge of it.

St. Clement's Church, Philadelphia. Admitted 1855. Rev. ——— ———, Rector. Rev. W. H. N. Stewart, LL D., Assistant Minister in charge. Walter H. Tilden, Rector's Warden, and M. Arnold, Jr., Accounting Warden.

Baptisms, adults 9, infants 38, total 47; confirmed 20; communicants, present number 275; marriages 8; burials 16; public services, on Sundays 168; children catechized 12 times; Sunday Schools, officers and teachers 20, scholars 150; Church 1, sittings 976; Parish buildings, number of free sittings 150; extra Sunday services, free to all, 104.

Money Receipts from all sources.—Pew rents $4412.50, offertory at Holy Communion $873.62, collections in Church $1166.88; donations $706.57, other sources $1204.67.

Expenditures and Appropriations.—Current expenses (including salary of the Clergy) $6623.06, repairs and improvements $790.80, Episcopal and Convention Fund $100, support of Sunday Schools $40, Parish Library $50, for the Poor $290.40, to Domestic Missions $518.10, Episcopal Hospital $20, Church Home $105, Female Tract Society $16, Christian or Theological Education $85.98, Miscellaneous $615.15

Financial Condition.—Aggregate value of property of the Parish, real and personal $115.000; Encumbrances, mortgage on Parish building $10,000, ground-rent issuing out of Church lot $23,333.33, yearly rent $1400; other indebtedness, "Organ bonds" $2200; floating debt $1650.

St. Paul's Church, Chestnut Hill. Admitted 1856. Rev. J. Andrew's Harris, Rector. M. Russell Thayer and Richard Norris, Wardens.

Baptisms, infants 20, total 20; confirmed, no visitation; communicants, added, new 2, by removal 8, died or removed 26, present number 131; marriages 7; burials 8; public services, on Sundays 147, on other days 90, total 237; children catechized 63 times; Sunday Schools, officers and teachers 6, scholars about 60; Parish Schools, teachers 2, scholars 52.

Of the communicants above reported, twenty-one (21) have not received the Holy Communion during the year.

Church 1, sittings 500; Chapels (the statistics of which are included in this report) 1 ; sittings 125 (free); School building 1 ; parsonage 1 ; cemetery none; arrears of salary none; number of free sittings in Church, besides those in Chapel 96.

Money Receipts from all sources.—Pew rents $3461.25, offertory at Holy Communion $529.37, collections in Church $2062.41, subscriptions $1021.60, donations $846.75, investments $37.40, other sources $627.36. Total $8586.14.

Expenditures and Appropriations.—Episcopal and Conven-Fund $125, support of Sunday Schools $133.49, of Parish Schools $688.47, Parish Library $10, Parochial Missions $47.97, for the Poor $285.13, to Missions, Foreign $261.75, Domestic $386.01, Home Mission for Colored People $20.75, Diocesan $29.46, for the Jews $14.33, Episcopal Hospital $172.50, Disabled Clergymen $37.75, Miscellaneous $6373.53. Total $8586.14.

Financial Condition.—Aggregate value of property of the Parish, real and personal, about $30,000; Encumbrances, mortgage on other buildings $5000.

The mortgage is on the parsonage. A Bible Class of about 40 members was held during part of the year, and was discontinued on account of the teacher's ill-health. The Rector endeavored to supply the deficiency by week-day lectures during the winter.

Church of the Holy Trinity, Philadelphia.   Admitted 1857.   Rev. Thomas A. Jaggar, Rector. Rev. William H. Neilson, Jr., and Rev. Joseph E. Miller, Assistant Ministers.   John Bohlen and Lemeul Coffin, Church Wardens.

Baptisms, adults 5, infants 21, total 26; confirmed 16; present number of communicants, about 750; marriages 5; burials 22; public services, on Sundays 110, on other days 46, total 156; average attendance on Sundays 1000; children catechized monthly; Sunday Schools, officers and teachers 64, scholars 692; Bible Classes, teachers 6, members 215; Sewing Schools, scholars 152; Night School, scholars 69; Church 1, sittings 1400; Chapel 1, sittings 400; School building 1 ; salary of Rector $5000 per annum, and Rectory; arrears of salary none; number of free sittings 150.

Money Receipts from all sources.—Pew rents $14,830.50, offertory at Holy Communion $1811.02, collections in Church and subscriptions $29,801.15. Total $46,442.67.

Expenditures and Appropriations.—Current expenses (including salary of Rector) $14,830.50, Episcopal and Convention Fund $350, support of Sunday Schools $835.69, Parochial Missions $7288.87, for the Poor $1811.02, Foreign Missions, $2377.52, Domestic Missions $979.77, Diocesan Missions $436.31, City Missions $1107.86, Indian Hope Mission $544, for the Jews $150, Episcopal Hospital $700, Bibles and Prayer Books $125, Theological Education $870.26, Disabled Clergymen $220, Chicago Relief Fund $1105.55, Miscellaneous $12,710.32. Total $46,442.67.

Financial Condition.—Aggregate value of property of the Parish, real and personal, $300,000; ground-rent on Church lot $37,500; principal, less Sinking Fund $7500.

Trinity Chapel, under charge of the Rev. William H. Neilson, Jr., Assistant Minister of the Church of the Holy Trinity.

Baptisms, adults 3, infants 30, total 33; confirmed 30; marriages 3; burials 22; communicants, about 150; Sunday Schools, teachers and officers 42, scholars 484; Bible Classes, teachers 3, scholars 117; Sewing School, scholars 200; Night School, scholars 211. Collections and contributions $2029.50.

Calvary Church (Monumental), Northern Liberties. Admitted 1857. Rev. Edw. A. Foggo, D.D. Rector. Rev. G. Woolsey Hodge, Assistant in charge.

Baptisms, adults 2, infants 37, total 39; confirmed 6; communicants, added, new 14, by removal 15, died or removed 9, present number 100; marriages 4; burials 12; public services, on Sundays 109, on other days 69, total 178; children catechized monthly; Sunday Schools, officers and teachers 12, scholars 122; Bible Class, teachers 2, members 25; Parish Schools, teachers 1, scholars 15. Other Parish Agencies— . Girls' Sewing School, teachers 8, scholars 60; Mothers' Meetings, lady in charge 1, members 42. Church 1, sittings 350; School buildings 1; sexton's house 1; Parsonage Fund $1640; two lots in Franklin Cemetery; salary of Minister in charge $600 per annum; number of free sittings all.

Money Receipts from all sources.—Balance for previous year $98.86, offertory at Holy Communion $104.25, other collections in Church $743.73, donations $267, investments $438.58, other sources $31.15, raised by the Sunday Schools $101.33. Total $1640.90.

Expenditures and Appropriations.—Current expenses (including salaries) $1376.45, Episcopal and Convention Fund $10, support of Sunday Schools $121.54, of Parish Schools $50, for the Poor $89.25, to Missions, Foreign $10, Domestic $54, for the Jews $6.78, Episcopal Hospital $24.10, Miscellaneous, Chicago sufferers $9.64. Total $1751.76.

Financial Condition.—No encumbrances.

Church of the Covenant. Admitted 1858. Rev. Charles E. Murray, Rector. J. A. Kirkpatrick and John P. Rhodes, Wardens.

Baptisms, infants 22, total 22; communicants, present number 400; marriages 14; burials 24; Sunday Schools, officers and teachers 31, scholars 240; Bible Classes, teachers 4, members 58, total teachers and scholars 293; Church 1, sittings 800; salary of Rector $2500 per annum; arrears of salary none.

Money Receipts from all sources.—Pew rents $4726.26, offertory at Holy Communion $306.08, collections in Church $2633.08, subscriptions $321.97, donations $311.70, other sources $849.80. Total $9148.89.

* Expenditures and Appropriations.—Current expenses (including salary of Rector) $5777.84, repairs and improvements $228.92, payment of debts $1056.07, Episcopal and Convention Fund $75, support of Sunday Schools $338.39, for the Poor $306.08, to Missions, Foreign $100, Domestic $332, City Missions $21.75, Episcopal Hospital $122.40, Christian or Theological Education $400, Miscellaneous $616.99. Total $9275.44.

17

St. John the Baptist Church, Germantown. Admitted 1858. Rev. William N. Diehl, Rector.

Baptisms, infants 6; communicants, added, new 11, removed 13, present number 70; marriages 8; burials 5; public services, on Sundays, 78, other days 26, total 104. The Rector was sick for several months, and unable to officiate. Children catechized frequently; Sunday Schools, officers and teachers 9, scholars 100; Parish School, teacher 1, scholars 30; Church 1, sittings 400; Chapel 1, sittings 200; Sunday and Infant School, seats for 250; Free Church; salary of Rector $600; arrears of salary $300.

Money Receipts.—Collections, communion alms, Sunday collections and Parish Guild $600, Sunday School for Missions $50, Episcopal and Convention Fund $25, Chicago $15.

Financial Condition.—Aggregate value of property $15,000; ground-rent on Church lot $139, other indebtedness none.

Calvary Church, Germantown. Admitted 1859. Rev. James DeW. Perry, Jr., Rector. Dr. Samuel K. Ashton and Jas. E. Caldwell, Wardens.

Baptisms, adults 3, infants 7, total 10; confirmed 13; communicants, added, new 13, by removal, 2, died or removed 5, present number 125; marriages 5; burials 9; public services, on Sundays 117, on other days 48, total 165; average attentendance on Sundays good; children catechized 20 times; Sunday Schools, officers and teachers 28, scholars 235; Bible Classes, teachers 6, members 30. Other Parish Agencies, Mothers' Meeting, Sewing Schools, Night Schools, &c. Church 1, sittings 450; School building 1; Parsonage 1; salary of Rector $2000 per annum; arrears of salary none; number of free sittings 50.

Money Receipts from all sources.—Pew rents $2561.64, offertory at Holy Communion $297.86, collections in Church $2108.03, subscriptions $2122.50, donations $674.75, other sources $81.28. Total $7846.06.

Expenditures and Appropriations.—Current expenses (including salary of Rector) $3479.16, repairs and improvements $1906.50, Episcopal and Convention Fund $125, support of Sunday Schools $229.18, Parish Library $23.50, Parochial Missions $352.40, for the Poor $297.86, to Missions, Foreign

$197.65, Domestic $561.97, Home Mission for Colored People
$65.44, Diocesan $122.53, City Missions $100, for the Jews
$30.30, Episcopal Hospital $201.75, Christian or Theological
Education $74.80, Disabled Clergymen $42.76, Miscellaneous
$299.01. Total $8109.81.

Financial Condition.—Aggregate value of property of the
Parish, real and personal $45,000. Encumbrances, mortgage
$3000 on Rectory, other indebtedness $1000.

A Sunday School has been organized, and Divine services
have been held in a building on Nicetown Lane. This work
has met encouragement and success. Efforts are making, and
contributions are solicited to erect a Chapel.

The Bishop's Church, Spring Garden. Admitted 1859. Rev. E. Owen Simpson, Rector. V.
F. Harrison and George H. Greenleaf, Wardens.

Baptisms, adult 1, infants 15, total 16; confirmed 33; communicants, added, new 35, by removal 3, died or removed 15,
present number 206; marriages 4; burials 18; public services, on Sundays 141, on other days 57, total 198; children
catechized 10 times; Sunday Schools, officers and teachers
37, scholars 350; Bible Classes, teachers 2, members 40;
Church 1, sittings 1000; salary of Rector $1800 per annum.

Money Receipts from all sources.—Pew rents $2265.37, of-
fertory at Holy Communion $193.43, collections in Church
$1239.54, donations $642.64, other sources $825.43, Sunday
School $473.90. Total $5640.31.

Expenditures and Appropriations.—Current Expenses (including salary of Rector) $3535.41, repairs and improvements
$439.53, Episcopal and Convention Fund $25, support of Sunday Schools $1058.29, for the Poor, $193.43, to Missions,
Foreign $29.68, Domestic $25, Episcopal Hospital $18.75,
Theological Education $200, Miscellaneous, Chicago Fund
$52.36, Surplices $32, Dorcas Society $26.25, Incidentals
$204.61. Total $5840.31.

The Church of St. Matthias. Admitted 1859. Rev. Richard N. Thomas, Rector. Henry S.
Godshall and Wm. H. Rhawn, Wardens.

Baptisms, adults 9, infants 18, total 27; confirmed 29; communicants, added, new 31, by removal 25, died or removed

10, present number 225; marriages 5; burials 14; public services, on Sundays 102, on other days 33, total 135; children catechized monthly; Sunday Schools, officers and teachers 31, scholars 350; Bible Classes, teachers 2, members 31. Other Parish Agencies—Ladies' Mite Society, Parish Association, Free Reading Room and Library, Young People's Association. Church now building; Chapel (the statistics of which are included in this report) 1, sittings 500; salary of Rector $2500 per annum; arrears of salary none.

Money Receipts from all sources.—Pew rents $4816.77, offertory at Holy Communion $225.88, collections in Church $1190.67, subscriptions $3150, donations $1088.40, investments $167.62, other sources $1200, Mite Society collections $357.67, Sunday School Offerings $410.72. Total $12,607.73. ·

Expenditures and Appropriations.—Current expenses (including salary of Rector) $4073.41, repairs, insurance and improvements $570.63, Episcopal and Convention Fund (1870 and 1871) $93, support of Sunday Schools $422.35, Parochial Missions $269.33, for the Poor $82.08, to Missions, Foreign $13.30, Domestic $41.38, for the Jews $18.52, Episcopal Hospital $61.82, Church Building $6874.99, Bibles, Prayer Books and Tracts $15.54, Christian or Theological Education $130, Disabled Clergymen $28, Miscellaneous $19.93, Chicago Relief Fund $409.17, also, 15 packages of Clothing, invested for Mite Society $1200.

Church of the Incarnation. Admitted 1860. Rev. Joseph D. Newlin, Rector. James M. Patton and John Rapson, Wardens.

Baptisms, adults 10, infants 45, total 55; confirmed 19; communicants, added, new 18, by removal 30, died or removed 48, present number 346; marriages 16; burials 27; public services, on Sundays, 104, on other days 92, total 196; children catechized monthly; Sunday Schools, officers and teachers 32, scholars 312; Bible Classes, teachers 2, members 49. Other Parish Agencies—Ladies' Missionary Society and Sewing Schools. Salary of Rector $2500 per annum; arrears of salary none.

Money Receipts from all sources.—Pew rents $6982, offertory at Holy Communion and collections in Church $3755.22, donations $470, other sources $2607.43. Total $13,814.65.

Expenditures and Appropriations.—Current Expenses (including salary of Rector) $6908, repairs and improvements $1037, payment of debts $4815, Episcopal and Convention Fund $60, support of Sunday Schools $191.75, for the Poor $229.22, to Missions, Foreign $65, Domestic $160.58, City Missions $69.30, for the Jews $28.15, Episcopal Hospital $65, Bibles, Prayer Books and Tracts $34.70, Miscellaneous $279.88. Total $13,943.58.

Financial Condition.—Aggregate value of property of the Parish, real and personal $130,000, ground-rent on buildings or lands $12,866.67, principal; other indebtedness $58,775, including loans.

___

Church of St. John the Evangelist. Admitted 1860. Rev. William F. B. Jackson, Rector. W. H. Myers and John Hackett, Wardens.

Baptisms, infants 29, total 29; communicants, by removal 8, died or removed 3, present number 150; marriages 3; burials 19; public services, on Sundays 104, on other days 50, total 154; average attendance on Sundays 300; children catechized 12 times; Sunday Schools, officers and teachers 30, scholars 426; Bible Classes, teachers 2, members 12; Church 1, sittings 610; salary of Rector $1500 per annum; arrears of salary none; free sittings 50.

Money Receipts from all sources.—Pew rents $654.73, offertory at Holy Communion $66.22, collections in Church $441.73, subscriptions $1345.75, donations $2224, other sources $6963.45. Total $11,695.88.

Expenditures and Appropriations.—Current expenses (including salary of Rector) $2367.31, repairs and improvements $50.40, payment of debts $1214.94, support of Sunday Schools $196, for the Poor (four months) $86.22, to Missions, Foreign $1150, City Missions, $20.50, Episcopal Hospital $7, Church building $7736.34, Disabled Clergymen $5.15, Miscellaneous $28. Total $11,703.36.

Financial Condition.—Aggregate value of property of the Parish, real and personal $47,000. Encumbrances, mortgages on Church edifice $6700, ground-rent on buildings or lands $400 per annum, other indebtedness $6154.

The present Rector entered upon his duties at the beginning of the New Year, in the new Church edifices, erected, under God, by the indefatigable labors of the previous Rector, and the noble band of working people in the Parish. The thanks of the Parish are due to the many generous friends in other Parishes, without whose assistance the work would have been well nigh hopeless. The number of communicants is considerably smaller than reported last year, owing to a probable mistake in the last reports.

St. Michael's Church, Germantown. Admitted 1860. Rev. John K. Murphy, Rector. S. Harvey Thomas and George E. Arnold, Wardens.

Baptisms, adults, 2, infants 27, total 29; confirmed 9; communicants, added, new 10, by removal 24, died or removed 15, present number 160; marriages 6; burials 16; public services, on Sundays 122, on other days 198, total 320; children catechized 12 times; Sunday Schools, officers and teachers 18, scholars 162; Church 1, sittings 320; School building 1; parsonage none; salary of Rector $2600 per annum; arrears of salary none; number of free sittings, all.

Money Receipts from all sources.—Pew rents none, collections in Church $3056.02, donations $800, other sources $1778.22. Total $5634.24.

Expenditures and Appropriations.—Current expenses (including salary of Rector) $3593.76, repairs and improvements $800, payment of debts $684.56, Episcopal and Convention Fund $50, support of Sunday Schools $147.96, for the Poor $146.56, Domestic Missions $44, Diocesan $25, Episcopal Hospital $49.80, Disabled Clergymen $25, Chicago Relief $67.60. Total $5566.64.

Financial Condition—Aggregate value of property of the Parish, real and personal $18,000. Encumbrances—Mortgages on Church edifice $2740.83, on other buildings $900; ground-rent on buildings or lands $1875.

This year we have taken two steps in advance. We have enclosed our Church and Rectory lot with a neat fence, at a cost of $800, raised by the exertions of an earnest member of the Parish; and we have reduced our Church debt about the same amount, the children of the Sunday School having collected over $500 for that object. Our next and greatest need is the possession of a parsonage. On the score of economy, as well as usefulness, the Parish cannot begin its erection too soon, even if it has to be heavily mortgaged from the start.

Church of St. Luke the Beloved Physician. Admitted 1861. Rev. H. A. Parker, Rector. Edward Evans and J. B. Willian, Wardens.

Baptisms, infants 4, total 4; communicants, added, by removal 3, died or removed 5, present number 33; burials 2; public services, on Sundays 103, on other days 70 or more; Church 1, sittings 250; Chapel sittings 125; parsonage 1; cemetery 1; salary of Rector $750, no arrears. Any seats not hired are free for the time being.

Money Receipts from all sources.—Pew rents $259.75, collections in Church $72.93, subscriptions $500, donations $50. Total $882.68.

Expenditures and Appropriations.—Current expenses (including salary of Rector) $910, Episcopal and Convention Fund $6. Money has been given to several charitable objects, and a present of new chandeliers for the Church has been received; also, a gift of repairs for the parsonage, and various books for the Parish and Sunday School libraries.

Sunday School teachers 9, scholars 60.

House of Prayer, Branchtown. Admitted 1861. Rev. A. T. McMurphey, Rector. Charles D. Barney and James Lowe, Wardens.

Baptisms, adults 2, infants 20, total 22; confirmed, no visitation; communicants, added, new 3, by removal 5, died or removed 4, present number 37; marriages 2; burials 4; public services, on Sundays 100, on other days 10, total 110; Sunday Schools, officers and teachers 15, scholars 155; Industrial Parish School, teachers 7, scholars 77; Church 1, sittings 140; salary of Rector $1000 per annum, arrears of salary $150.

Money Receipts from all sources.—Offertory at Holy Communion $39.45, collections in Church $170.68, Sunday School $162.06; subscriptions $3.25, by St. Paul's Church $5, total $8.25; donations $190.   Total $1337.87.

Expenditures and Appropriations.—Current expenses (including salary of Rector) $1200, repairs and improvements $25, Episcopal and Convention Fund $12, support of Sunday Schools $115, of Parish Schools $112, for the Poor $60, to Missions, Foreign $20, Domestic $20, Diocesan $20, City Missions $3, for the Jews $3, Episcopal Hospital $5, Sunday School building $250, Book Societies $15, Christian or Theological Education $10, Disabled Clergymen $3, sufferers of the Northwest $15, for Sunday School at the West $5.   Total $1896.

The growth of this Parish has been slow, but steady, and while its progress has not been all that could have been desired, yet it has been as great as could reasonably be expected under the circumstances.   With increased facilities, it is hoped that it will be more rapid, especially as there is a prospect of an increased population in the vicinity.   Twenty-two hundred dollars have been secured towards the erection of the Sunday School building, which it is hoped will be completed during the present year.   To those friends who have generously aided us by donations toward the support of the Rector, I would, on behalf of the Vestry, express our sincere thanks.

St. Alban's Church, Roxborough.   Admitted 1862.   Rev. Richardson Graham, Rector.   Jacob Castleberry and James L. Rahn, Wardens.

Baptisms, infants 11, total 11; communicants, present number unknown; marriage 1; burials 3; public services, on Sundays 104, on other days 8, total 112; Sunday Schools, officers and teachers 5, scholars 40; Church 1, sittings 250; School building 1; number of free sittings, all.

Money Receipts from all sources.—Offertory at Holy Communion $12.64, collections in Church $63, subscriptions $265, other sources $80.   Total $420.

Expenditures and Appropriations.—Current expenses (including salary of Rector) $433, repairs and improvements

$35, Episcopal and Convention Fund $6, support of Sunday Schools $33, City Missions $6.74; Miscellaneous, Chicago Fund $7. Total $520.74.

Financial Condition.—Aggregate value of property of the Parish, real and personal $6000. Encumbrances—mortgages on Church edifice none, on other buildings none; ground-rent on buildings or lands none; other indebtedness about $75.

St. Timothy's Church, Roxborough. Admitted 1862. Rev. Wm. Augustus White, Rector.
J. Vaughan Merrick and T. F. Cauffman, Wardens.

Baptisms, adult 1, infants 16, total 17; confirmed 8; communicants, added, new 8, by removal 16, died or removed 24, present number 84; marriages 7; burials 8; public services, on Sundays 142, on other days 57, total 199; average attendance on Sundays 200; children catechized 8 times; Sunday Schools, officers and teachers 14, scholars 92; Bible Classes, teachers 2, members 21; Church 1, sittings 250; School building 1; parsonage 1; cemetery 1; salary of Rector $1500 per annum; arrears of salary none; number of free sittings 62; extra Sunday services, free to all, 90.

Money Receipts from all sources.—Pew rents $1140.87, offertory at Holy Communion $132.73, collections in Church $1147.93, subscriptions $714.80, donations $6760, investments $119.36, other sources $837.10. Total $10,852.79.

Expenditures and Appropriations.—Current expenses (including salary of Rector) $2115.05, repairs and improvements $6814.43, payment of debts $1029.50, Episcopal and Convention Fund $25, support of Sunday Schools $113.57, for the Poor $132.73, Missions, Domestic $84.04, Diocesan $89.20, City Missions $66.06, Episcopal Hospital $218.98, Bibles, Prayer Books and Tracts $17.56, Christian or Theological Education $18.01, Disabled Clergymen $20, Miscellaneous $110.66. Total $10,852.79.

Financial Condition.—Aggregate value of property of the Parish, real and personal $25,000. Encumbrances—Mortgages on Church edifice none, on other buildings $2300; other indebtedness $906.17, less $170 U. S. Bonds.

18

The "improvements" alluded to in this report are of an unusually interesting and important character. A stone tower has been added at the eastern end of the north aisle. It is fourteen and a half feet square, and rises to the height of fifty-eight feet. The lower story opens into the Church, and contains a new organ of great power and excellent mechanical arrangements. The aisles and pews have been carpeted. A beautiful window has been put in place, in remembrance of a member of the Sunday School. The eastern wall, on each side of the chancel, has been decorated in a very satisfactory manner; happy in design and pleasing in color. This is the pious offering of a few young persons, through the proceeds of their own industry. Indeed, all the improvements are gifts to the Parish; the tower from one of the Wardens, and the organ from the family of a lately deceased parishioner, as a memorial to whom it has been erected.

The Women's Missionary Guild, organized February 20, 1872, after a few weeks of diligent labor sent out a valuable box to a Missionary in Missouri; and the Ladies' Sewing Society has, this year, reduced the debt on the Rectory $500. Ground-rent to the amount of $205 has also been paid off.

Grace Church, Mt. Airy, Germantown. Admitted 1862. Rev. Robert A. Edwards, Rector. Judge Stroud and C. M. Bayard, Wardens.

Baptisms, adult 1, infants 5, total 6; confirmed 8; communicants, died or removed 14, present number 82; burials 3; public services, on Sundays 104, on other days 30, total 134; Sunday Schools, officers and teachers 17, scholars 133; Church 1, sittings 240; cemetery lot.

Money Receipts from all sources.—Pew rents $1650, offertory at Holy Communion $138.06, collections in Church $384.66. Total $2172.72.

Expenditures and Appropriations.—Episcopal and Convention Fund $25, support of Sunday Schools $35, to Missions, Foreign $103.78, Domestic $545.75, Chicago and Northwest $147.10, Diocesan $38.25, City Missions $15, for the Indians $32.15, Episcopal Hospital $47.15, Church Home $30, Book

Societies $155.17, Christian or Theological Education $101.97, Disabled Clergymen $33.15; Miscellaneous, Seamen's Mission $20.25, Mission House $160.70. Total $1490.42.

The Free Church of St. John. Admitted 1864. Rev. Joseph A. Nock, Rector. Robert Whitechurch and John S. Lovell, Wardens.

Baptisms, adults 3, infants 22, total 25; confirmed 14; communicants, added, new 14, by removal 2, died or removed 13, present number 45; marriages 2; burials 34; public services on Sundays 118, on other days 40, total 158; average attendance on Sundays 80; children catechized 8 times; Sunday Schools, officers and teachers 15, scholars 200; Bible Classes, teacher 1, members 10. Other Parish Agencies—Ladies' Aid Society 1, Young Men's Guild 1; Night School, scholars 6; Church 1; arrears of salary none; number of free sittings, all free.

Money Receipts from all sources.—Collections in Church $447.89, other sources $386.50. Total $834.39.

Expenditures and Appropriations.—Current expenses, payment of debts $150, Episcopal and Convention Fund $6, support of Sunday Schools $101.50, for the Poor $75, Episcopal Hospital $2.47, Book Societies $10, Miscellaneous $23.25. Total $368.22.

Financial Condition.—Aggregate value of property of the Parish, real and personal, $15,000.

The present incumbent took charge on the 1st of July, under the auspices of the City Mission. The field is an extensive and almost entirely a Mission one; no little interest in the work, however, is manifested by the people, and it is hoped that in a few years this will come to be a flourishing self-sustaining Parish.

St. Thomas' Church. Admitted 1864. Rev. William J. Alston, Rector.

Baptisms, adults 3, infants 8, total 11; confirmed 7; communicants, added, 7; marriages 30; burials 19; public services, on Sundays 94, on other days 7, total 101; average attendance 120; children catechized 12 times; Sunday Schools, officers and teachers 8; Parish Schools, scholars 75; Church, sittings 500; parsonage 1; salary of Rector $600 per annum; arrears of salary none; number of free sittings 100.

Money Receipts from all sources.—Pew rents $700, offertory at Holy Communion $48, collections in Church $200, subscriptions $1000, donations $32.84. Total $1980.84.

Expenditures and Appropriations.—Current expenses (including salary of Rector) $1200, Episcopal and Convention Fund $6, Parish Library $5, for the Poor $48, for the Jews $5.50, Episcopal Hospital $10, Christian or Theological Education $100. About a thousand dollars in hand towards repairing and improving the old Church edifice.

St. James' Church, Hestonville. Admitted 1867. Rev. G. Livingston Bishop, officiating. John Halliwell and James M. Cadmus, Wardens.

Baptisms, infants 3, total 3; communicants, added, new 1, present number 45; burial 1; public services, on Sundays 104, on other days 2, total 106; average attendance on Sundays 60; Sunday Schools, officers and teachers, 14, scholars 90; Bible Class, teacher 1, members 7; Church 1, sittings 250; number of free sittings, all; extra Sunday services, free to all.

Money Receipts from all sources.—Collections in Church $157.25, subscriptions $644, donations $810.32. Total $1,-611.57.

Expenditures and Appropriations.—Current expenses (including salary of Rector) $750.88, payment of debts $810.32, Miscellaneous, Chicago sufferers $13. Total $1574.20.

Financial Condition.—Aggregate value of property of the Parish, real and personal $12,000. Other indebtedness $2000.

Church of the Holy Apostles. Admitted 1868. Rev. Charles D. Cooper, Rector. Lewis H. Redner and George C. Thomas, Wardens.

Baptisms, infants 61; confirmed, no appointment by the Bishop; communicants, present number 140; marriages 8; burials 30; public services, on Sundays 104, on other days 40, total 144; average attendance on Sundays 300; Sunday Schools, officers and teachers 40, scholars 475; Bible Classes, teachers 2, members 35 ; Church 1, sittings 1050; Chapel (the statistics of which are included in this report) 1, sittings 450. Salary of Rector $2000 per annum; arrears of salary none; number of free sittings, all.

Money Receipts from all sources.—Pew rents $1750, offertory at Holy Communion $120, collections in Church $670, subscriptions $3000. Total $5540.

Expenditures and Appropriations.—Current expenses (including salary of Rector) $3200, payment of debts $2220, Episcopal and Convention Fund $40, support of Sunday Schools $450, Parish Library and Free Reading Room $500, Episcopal Hospital $18.97, Disabled Clergymen $20. Total $6448.75.

Church of the Good Shepherd Admitted 1869. Rev. John A. Goodfellow, Rector. William A. Parke and Joseph M. Christian, Wardens.

Baptisms, adults 2, infants 10, total 12; communicants by removal 12, died or removed 10, present number 56; marriage 1; burials 8; public services, on Sundays twice, on other days, every Wednesday evening and on greater festivals; average attendance on Sundays 125; children catechized monthly; Sunday Schools, officers and teachers 18, scholars 213; Bible Class, teacher 1, members 7. Salary of Rector $1000 per annum.

Money Receipts from all sources.—Offertory at Holy Communion $44, collections in Hall $171.98, subscriptions $476.10, donations $300, investments $14.64, other sources $563.50. Total $1570.22.

Expenditures and Appropriations.—Current expenses (including salary of Rector) $789, Episcopal and Convention Fund $6, support of Sunday Schools $57.79, for the Poor $16, Domestic Missions $26, Episcopal Hospital $15, Disabled Clergymen $9, Miscellaneous $48.50. Total $967.29.

The services of this Parish are held at present in a Hall on the Southwest corner of Frankford Road and Adams Street, 19th Ward. But the Rector and Vestry have just begun to erect a temporary Chapel on their lot, at the corner of Cumberland and Collins Streets, worth $7000, which has been taken on ground-rent. The Chapel will be completed in 30 days, and will cost about $3500.

As the Parish was without a Rector the greater part of the past year, but little parochial work was done.

St. Stephen's Church, Bridesburg.   Admitted 1869.   Rev. Isaac Martin, Rector.   Newton A. Perkins and Isaac Wilson, Wardens.

Baptisms, adults 8, infants 46, total 54; communicants, added by removal 12, died or removed 7, present number 50; marriages 2; burials 8; public services, on Sundays 104, on other days 21, total 125; average attendance on Sundays 150; children catechized 12 times; Sunday Schools, officers and teachers 24, scholars 184; Bible Classes, teacher 1, members 20; other Parish Agencies, Mothers' Meeting and Sewing School; Church 1, sittings 250; School buildings, part of Church; salary of Rector $700 per annum; arrears of salary none; number of free sittings, all; extra Sunday services, free to all, one.

Money Receipts from all sources.—Offertory at Holy Communion $38, collections in Church $79, subscriptions $833.27, donations $100.   Total $1050.27.

Expenditures and Appropriations.—Current expenses (including salary of Rector) $826.57, Episcopal and Convention Fund $6, support of Sunday Schools $140.80, Parish Library $100, for the Poor $38, to Missions, Domestic $34, for the Jews $1.90, Episcopal Hospital $10.50, Bibles, Prayer Books and Tracts $5, Disabled Clergymen $6.50, Miscellaneous, Chicago sufferers and Church Home for Children $26.10. Total $1190.37.

Financial Condition.—Aggregate value of property of the Parish, real and personal $12,000.

Free Church of the Holy Innocents.   Admitted 1869.   Rev. D. Caldwell Millett, D. D., Rector.   Henry L. Foster and J. B. Peale, M D., Wardens.

Baptisms, adults 2, infants 9, total 11; confirmed, no visitation; communicants, added, new 4, present number 29; marriage 1; burial 1; Sunday Schools, officers and teachers 6, scholars 35; Sunday services, free to all.

Money Receipts from all sources.—Collections in Church $46.28.

Expenditures and Appropriations.—To Missions, Foreign $9.50, Episcopal Hospital $23.34, Disabled Clergymen $13.10. Total $92.22.

Lay service has been continued by Messrs. Foster and Chamberlain. The Holy Communion administered once a month, and on high festivals.

St. George's P. E. Church, Kenderton, Philada. Admitted 1870. Rev. Joseph R. Moore, Rector. Daniel Hertz and Elijah Wyatt, Wardens.

Baptisms, adult 1, infants 6, total 7; confirmed 9; communicants, added, new 18, by removal 6, died or removed 7, present number 42; marriages 4; burials 5; public services, on Sundays 110, on other days 44, total 154; children catechized weekly; Sunday Schools, officers and teachers 11, scholars 114; Night School, teachers 7, scholars 112; Church none, worship in hall; salary of Rector $1200 per annum.

Money Receipts from all sources.—Pew rents $450, offertory at Holy Communion $150.68, collections in Church $628.78, subscriptions $1035, donations $770, other sources $214.13. Total $3248.59.

Expenditures and Appropriations.—Current expenses (including salary of Rector) $1860, repairs and improvements $128.75, Episcopal and Convention Fund $10, support of Sunday Schools $159.96, Night Schools $54.42, to Missions, Foreign $50, Domestic $1.50, Episcopal Hospital $20.86, Church building $770, Christian or Theological Education $16.18, Disabled Clergymen $7, Miscellaneous (including $40.15 for sufferers by fire in Michigan) $169.49. Total $3248.59.

On Easter Monday, April 1st, St. George's P. E. Church, Kenderton, was united with that of the Church of the Resurrection, Rising Sun, on the following basis: The Rev. Thomas J. Davis, Rector of the Church of the Resurrection, resigned, and thereon was elected Rector Emeritus, with an annuity, together with the free use of the Rectory and the grounds attached, as long as he lives; and immediately thereafter the present Rector of St. George's P. E. Church, Kenderton, was elected Rector of the Parish; his congregation having paid, before the above arrangements were consummated, $823.50 of the debt against the Parish, besides assuming the mortgage of $3000 against the Rectory. Owing to the necessity of making improvements in the Church building, and providing proper accommodations for our Sunday School work, no service can be held in the Church, and we have therefore continued to worship in Tioga Hall.

Church of the Messiah. Admitted 1870. Rev. George Bringhurst, Rector. M. Mesier Reese and William Jordan, Wardens.

Baptisms, adults 9, infants 20, total 29; confirmed 42; communicants, added, new 42, by removal 13, died or removed 17, present number 137; marriages 26; burials 17; public services, on Sundays 116, on other days 40, total 156; children catechized 11 times; Sunday Schools, officers and teachers 22, scholars 225; Bible Classes, teachers 2, members 35.

St. George's Church. Admitted 1870. Rev. Charles A. Maison, Rector. Rev. J. H. B. Brooks, Assistant. Henry S. Henry and Hugh Whiteley, Wardens.

Baptisms, adults 18, infants 59, total 77; confirmed 42; communicants, added, new 34, by removal 19, died or removed 7, present number 79; marriages 4; burials 18; public services, on Sundays 103, on other days 34, total 137; average attendance on Sundays 250; children catechized 12 times; Sunday School, officers and teachers 25, scholars 275; Bible Classes, teachers 3, members 24. Other Parish Agencies, Ladies' Mite Society. Church 1, sittings 300.

Money Receipts from all sources.—Pew rents $842.74, offertory at Holy Communion $100.16, collections in Church $289.31, subscriptions $160, donations $203, other sources $1268.06. Total $2863.27.

Expenditures and Appropriations.—Current expenses (including salary of Assistant) $1109.84, Episcopal and Convention Fund $6, support of Sunday Schools $101.66, Chicago Relief $17.07, for the Poor $10, Church Home $10, Bell $400, Disabled Clergymen $4.50, Miscellaneous $1200.04. Total $2859.11.

Financial Condition.—Aggregate value of property of the Parish, real and personal, $15,000. Encumbrances, mortgage on Church edifice $6000.

St. Timothy's Church. Admitted 1871. Rev. J. L. Heysinger, Rector. Robert Briggs and Henry Plews, Wardens.

Baptisms, adults 2, infants 33, total 35; confirmed 12; communicants, present number 71; marriages 5; burials 8; public services, on Sundays 111, on other days 48, total 159; children catechized monthly; Sunday Schools, officers and teachers 15, scholars 200; Bible Classes, teacher 1, members 14; Church 1, sittings 480; school building 1; salary of Rector $1000 per annum; arrears of salary none; extra Sunday services, free to all, 8.

Money Receipts from all sources.—Pew rents $351.51, offertory at Holy Communion $61.71, collections in Church $768.75, subscriptions $419.11, donations $1347, other sources $325.96. Total $3274.04.

Expenditures and Appropriations.—Current expenses (including salary of Rector) $1371.63, repairs and improvements $233.20, payment of debts $1212.50, Episcopal and Convention Fund, no assessment, support of Sunday Schools $203.26, Chicago sufferers $59.60, for the Poor $61.71, to Missions, Foreign $18.70, Indian $10, City Missions $24.19, Episcopal Hospital $19.25, Bibles, Prayer Books and Tracts $20, Christian or Theological Education $23, Disabled Clergymen $17. Total $3274.04.

Financial Condition.—Aggregate value of property of the Parish, real and personal, $15,000. Encumbrances, mortgages on Church edifice none, on other buildings $2400. Ground-rent on buildings or lands none, other indebtedness none.

The Parish was organized in February, 1871, and the Rector took charge on the 11th of June following. Of the Baptisms reported, five were administered in April. The remaining items of the report are confined within the Conventional year. Owing to the heavy outlay required for refitting and improving the Church buildings, and for other necessary expenses, the Parish has not been able to do as much for general benevolence as would be otherwise desirable. Only by great energy and self-denial, both on the part of Rector and people, has the Parish been made self-sustaining during this first year of its history.

———

The Church of Our Merciful Saviour. Admitted 1872. Rev. E. Solliday Widdemer, Rector. A. L. Britton and William Trinkle, Wardens.

Baptisms, adults 6, infants 16, total 22; confirmed 17; communicants, died or removed 3, present number 71; marriages 4; burials 17; public services, on Sundays 156; on other days 50, total 256; average attendance on Sundays 200; Sunday Schools, officers and teachers 22, scholars 268; Bible Classes, teachers 4.

———

Church of the Redeemer, Seamen's Mission, Philadelphia. Founded 1847. Rev. Washington B. Erben, Rector. Joseph E. Hover and George W. Story, Wardens.

Baptisms, adults 8, infants 40, total 48; confirmed 7; communicants, present number about 50; marriages 12; burials 41; public services, on Sundays 116, on other days 42, total 158; children catechized 12 times; Sunday School officers and teachers 10, scholars 125; Church 1; sittings 300; parsonage 1; salary of Rector $1250 per annum; arrears of salary none; sittings all free.

Expenditures and Appropriations.—Current expenses (including salary of Rector) $1793.59, repairs and improvements $62.40, support of Sunday School $68, for relief of the Poor $189.50, to Missions, Diocesan $8.23, Domestic $5, Foreign $53, Home Mission for Colored People $5, Church Hospital $16.82, Bibles, Prayer Books, Tracts and Books for Seamen $99, Bishop White Prayer Book Society $5, Indian Missions $5, Philadelphia P. E. City Missions $15.66, Chicago sufferers $9.52, Missions to Maine $10.89. Total $2346.61.

Financial Condition.—Aggregate value of property of the Mission, Church building and ground $30,000, no encumbrance, Endowment Fund $6300, Building Fund about $1500. Total $37,800.

The Free Church of the Redeemer, for Seamen and their families, is maintained by the " Churchmen's Missionary Association for Seamen of the Port of Philadelphia," and the Association is dependent for support on voluntary contributions from individuals and Churches.

The Missionary and Parochial work in this field, which is on account of its specialty, of a very difficult and trying character, has been carried on during the past year without cessation and with encouraging results. The immediate neighborhood of the present Church is now chiefly devoted to heavy commercial traffic, and we shall soon be compelled to remove to a new and more eligible location. The Board of Managers are now engaged in an effort to raise funds to purchase a Church lot on South Front Street, on which a Church and Sunday School building will be erected with the proceeds of the present lot, when sold. The Bishop has given his approval and generous encouragement to this effort, and the Board are unanimous in favoring the project. About fifteen thousand dollars will be required, and subscriptions and pledges have already been received to the amount of over three thousand dollars.

To the Right Rev. William Bacon Stevens, D.D., Bishop in charge of the American Protestant Episcopal Church on the Continent of Europe.

The undersigned, Rector of the American Protestant Episcopal Church of Florence, Italy, begs leave to report that the congregation of this Church, for the past year has met for public worship in the restored old Chapel of the Piazza del Carmine, purchased for his use and rented to him by the proprietors.

The offertory and spontaneous subscriptions for this year (the fifth of the existence of the Church), have amounted to $1572, paying the expenses of the restoration and all the ordinary contingent ones, and leaving a balance of some hundred dollars for the Rector.

There have been no baptisms, marriages or burials. At a confirmation held in the British Episcopal Church in this city, three members of the congregation were confirmed by the Hon. and Rt. Rev. the Bishop of Gibraltar.

The average number of communicants from October to July, at each fortnightly celebration was thirty-six; the number on Easter Day, in spite of a heavy rain, was eighty-three.

All of which is respectfully submitted, by

PIERCE CONNELLY,

Presbyter of the Diocese of Penna.

Florence, Piazza del Carmine.

July 25th, 1872.

Report of the Rev. Robert J. Nevin, Rector of St. Paul's Church (formerly Grace), Rome, Italy. May 1st, 1872.

Services for the year ending May 1st, 1872: read service 130 times; preached 58 times; celebrated Holy Communion 24 times; baptized 3; married 1; confirmed 6; buried 6.

Collections.—Current support (including salary of Clergymen) $2740, Domestic and Foreign Missions and local Charities $432, Day Nursery for Infant Children $1050, Building Fund of new Church $7350. Total $11,572.

These figures are but approximate, as I am not able to refer to the full accounts to date. They show, however, a steady increase in our collections.

About $13,000 was secured toward the new Church by the Rector during his visit to the United States last summer.

This visit was made at the request of the Vestry, and was successful to the extent mentioned. The burning of Chicago made the latter part of the visit almost fruitless. The Rector returned to Rome in December, and remained on duty there until the middle of April, when it was again deemed advisable that he should return to America to solicit further help. He is happy to be able to report that during the past winter, an admirable building site has been bought for the new Church, on the Via Nazionale, at the corner of the Via Napoli. The Church will stand thus on the Main Street of the new city, in the immediate neighborhood of several very large Hotels, and in a quarter that is accessible, both to the new and older districts of the city.

The lot has cost, including the heavy registry fees, nearly $19,000. The greater part of this sum has already been given

in Rome, and the whole will be secured there.   The lot purchased has an area of something over 1600 square yards, and
gives room for Church, lecture-room, library, rectory, &c.

The design of the new Church, in Italian Gothic style, has
been prepared by Mr. G. E. Street, of London, and has been
already approved by the Building Commission of the Muni-
cipal Government of Rome.

The official sanction of the National Government of Italy
to our building in the locality named, has also been obtained,
through the special interest in the matter, of His Royal High-
ness, Prince Humbert, the hereditary Prince of Italy.

The Rector hopes to increase the subscriptions to the Building Fund during the present spring, to such an extent as will
justify the immediate prosecution of the work.   We have yet
within our hands the opportunity of building the first Protestant Church in Rome.   Forty-seven thousand dollars, however, are yet required for the completion of the work.   The
Rector desires to return to Rome in August, as it is almost
necessary that the work there should have his personal supervision.

On the 9th of the present month, the following named
gentlemen, *i. e.*—Hamilton Fish, John David Wolfe, Frederick
G. Foster, Henry Chauncey, John Welsh, George Kemp,
Robert J. Nevin, were created a body corporate by special
Act of the Legislature of the State of New York, under the
name and title of the Board of Trustees of St. Paul's American Protestant Episcopal Church, Rome, Italy, and empowered
to hold all real-estate and personal property necessary to said
congregation.   This Board is to perpetuate itself by election,
provided only, that no one shall be eligible to the office of
Trustee, who is not a Communicant member of the Protestant
Episcopal Church in the United States of America.   It is
proposed, on acceptance of this Act by the Vestry at Rome,
and subject to the approval of the Bishop in charge, and
Standing Committee of Foreign Churches, to vest the title of
the new Church in this Board.

The name St. Paul's Church has been assumed by the congregation at Rome, instead of the former title of "Grace Church," by unanimous Resolution of the Vestry, subject to the approval of the Bishop in charge. This approval was given by the Bishop then present in Rome.˙ The change was made because it was felt that the Church was about to assume in the City of Rome, an importance and permanence that she had never known before. The name "Grace Church" had never become popularly attached to it—it being known among the Roman people only as the "American Chapel." Further, it could not be conveniently rendered into Italian with its proper English signification, while, even if it could, it was felt that the name St. Paul, would carry with it more meaning, and was more appropriate in our peculiar relations in Rome.

In January, it was our privilege to receive an official visitation from the Rt. Rev. Wm. Bacon Stevens, the Bishop in charge, who confirmed four persons. The visit was of great benefit to the Parish, and was hailed especially as the first manifestation of the more definite Episcopal supervision which the Church provided for our foreign congregations at the last General Convention.

In March, the Rt. Rev. Dr. Harris, the Bishop of Gibraltar, officiated for one Sunday in our Chapel, and administered (at his regular Confirmation in the English Chapel) Confirmation to two of our candidates, who had not been sufficiently prepared to receive it at the time the Bishop in charge made his visitation.

The attendance of Americans at the Chapel during the past winter, has been unusually large, and it is already manifest, that the change of Government in Rome, will considerably increase both our resident and traveling American population.

This winter has been characterized in Rome by a very unusual awakening of interest in regard to the religious interests of the nation, and specially significant in this connection have been the following events :

1st. The establishment of an Old Catholic newspaper, entitled "L'Esperance di Roma."

2d. The discussion (officially authorized on the Roman part by the Pope himself) on the proposition that St. Peter had never been in Rome.

3d. The formation and public inauguration of an Italian Bible Society.

4th. A series of five public conferences on the Wounds of the Church, given by Pere Hyacinthe.

I do not propose to enter into any details in regard to these, but merely mention them as illustrations of a progress toward independence in matters of religion, which I hope may before many years eventuate in an organic and wholesome reform of the National Church of Italy.

Report of Rev. G. C. Bird.

I respectfully report that until October 1st, 1871, I continued in temporary charge of Memorial Church, Baltimore, Md.

Since that time, I have been rendering occasional services in Christ Church, West River, Md., and elsewhere, as I have been invited.

On the 15th of April, I accepted a call from the congregation and Vestry to the Rectorship of St. Martin's Church, Marcus Hook, Pa., and have just entered upon my duties in that Parish.

Report of the Rev. C. M. Butler, D.D., Professor of Ecclesiastical History in the Divinity School, West Philadelphia.

I have the honor to report that, with the exception of a week of sickness, and two weeks when I was providentially prevented from being at the institution, I have discharged the duties of my Professorship in the Divinity School; and have read prayers and preached about 20 times in various Churches.

Report of Rev. William V. Bowers.

By increasing age, with its infirmities, my annual ministerial work is diminishing and, doubtless, will soon be finished.

During the Conventional year ending May 1st, 1872, I have done as follows:

Preached 33 times; performed whole services 34 times, performed in part services 22 times; whole Communion services 8 times; assisted 5 times. Baptisms, adult 1, infant 1, total 2; burials, adults 2. These were in connection with Parishes. Addresses frequently; traveled in discharge of duty about 400 miles; remuneration $218; expense about $5.

I still have service twice a month at the Magdalen Asylum. For four months during the year this service was kindly performed for me by the Rev. J. G. Furey.

Last summer and autumn, I had in charge Christ Church, Waterford, New Jersey, for four months. What I did there is herein stated.

To the Rt. Rev. William Bacon Stevens, D.D , Bishop of Pennsylvania:

The Rev. F. L. Bush respectfully reports, that while spending the past year in Europe, for the benefit of his health, he has rendered occasional service in the American Chapels in Dresden, Florence and Rome, as well as in a number of English Chapels on the Continent.

Report of the Rev. Robert F. Chase.

I respectfully report that, in September last, I entered upon the duties of an Assistant of St. Peter's Church, Philadelphia, in charge of the Memorial Chapel; and that the statistics of my work are included in the report of St. Peter's Parish.

Report of the Rev. John A. Childs, D.D.

During the past year I have been engaged in my duties as usual, viz.: as the Secretary of the Bishop, Secretary of the Convention of the Diocese, Secretary of the Trustees and Overseers of the Divinity School, Secretary of the Hospital of the Protestant Episcopal Church in Philadelphia, Secretary of the Board of Missions; and have officiated nearly every Sunday in desk and pulpit.

Report of the Rev. R. Bethell Claxton, D.D.

My duties, as Professor in the Divinity School and in the Mission House, have been performed as usual.

During the Conventional year I have delivered 52 sermons

and lectures; have read prayer 85 times; have administered the Holy Communion 11 times; have baptized 2 infants; solemnized 1 marriage; and officiated at 3 funerals.

Report of the Rev. John Coleman, Philadelphia.

I respectfully report that, from September 1st, 1871, until May 1st, 1872, I was occupied in the duties of an Assistant Minister in St. Mark's Parish, Philadelphia. During this period of eight months, I performed the following acts: officiated in entire service 144 times; assisted in service 346 times; baptisms, adults 8, children 16, total 24; burials 6; assisted at Holy Communion 48 times; celebrated Holy Communion 21 times; sermons preached 28.

Report of the Rev. George Alexander Crooke, D.D., D.C.L., Philadelphia.

The Rev. Dr. Crooke reports that he has been engaged, during the last year, in the exercise of his ministry, whenever and wherever practicable. His various official acts are recorded in the reports of the Churches wherein he has officiated.

Report of the Rev. A. H. Cull.

Since the meeting of the Convention, last year, I have improved every opportunity that presented of doing duty in vacant Parishes, in the vicinity of the city of Philadelphia, in the Central Diocese of Pennsylvania, and also four or five services, or parts of services, in the Diocese of Pittsburgh. Immediately after New Year I made a trip to Canada, and visited many old and much valued friends, by whom I have been uniformly treated with great kindness. At the solicitation of the Rev. Mr. King, of Durham, who is still in Deacon's orders, I took part in the services, and delivered some five or six sermons or addresses; and administered the Holy Sacrament of the Lord's Supper three times, twice in public and once to a young man, I fear, on his death bed. I also made an address in the Church under the charge of the Rev. Mr. Roe, of Richmond. Both of these clergymen treated me

20

with special kindness, as did the good people committed to their charge.

I also preached twice, and gave Holy Communion once, at East St. Armand, by invitation from the Rector of the Church, the Rev. Mr. Davison.

I should have said that the services rendered in Durham were during the latter week in Lent.

Trinity Church, Falls of Schuylkill. Rev. J. P. Fugett, Rector. Thomas Grime and Thomas Dabbs, Wardens.

Baptisms, adult 1, infants 9, total 10; communicants, present number 25; burials 3; children catechized 25 times; Sunday School, teachers 10, pupils 80.

Collections and Contributions.—Parochial, alms for the Poor, Sunday School and Libraries, improvements and current expenses $2100; Extra Parochial, City Missions $16.70, collections for sufferers (Chicago fire) $63.75, total $80.45. Total of both $2180.45.

The foregoing statement has reference to the work of fourteen months, since March 5th, 1871, at which date the undersigned took charge of this new organization, which greatly *prospered* under his rectorship. The Rector resigned on the 4th instant.

Report of the Rev. Alexander Fullerton.

The Rev. Alexander Fullerton respectfully reports that he has officiated 148 times, preached 86 times, lectured 4 times, administered or assisted in administering the Holy Communion 23 times, baptized 4 adults and 22 children, and buried 12 persons, which acts are recorded in the registers of the several Parishes.

Report of Rev. John G. Furey, of the Philadelphia Protestant Episcopal City Mission, May 1, 1872.

The amount of work performed by me during the past year is nearly the same as in each of the preceding years since ·I have been acting in the capacity of a City Missionary. I am glad to be able to state that I find the same freedom and welcome as formerly in all the places to which I am in the habit of going, either regularly or occasionally. The numerous sermons and addresses demanded of me in my regular work in public institutions and elsewhere, require, of course, a great deal of time' for preparation, involving, as they do, much and careful study, in order to adapt my ministrations to the classes among whom these labors are performed. Most of my time during the afternoons and evenings is spent in visiting among the sick, needy, and distressed in every part of Philadelphia. The following summary will show the kind and degree of work done in a year:

Number of services, sermons, and addresses on all occasions about 300; special visits to sick, poor, distressed, etc., etc., 800; baptism of children and adults (the latter chiefly in sickness) 38; funerals attended 30; times in which I administered or assisted in administering the Holy Communion, 16; Bibles, Testaments, and Prayer Books given to individuals, 40; Charitable, Reformatory, Penal and other Institutions, in which I officiated, 12; Churches in the city and elsewhere, in which I officiated by request, 15; religious tracts distributed in every part of Philadelphia, 10,000.

Besides this enumeration of actual items of Missionary work, I made a large number of *personal* visits to individuals in the wards of the Insane Department, Blockley, those of the Pennsylvania Hospital, and in the cells of the County Prison, and elsewhere; giving in each case whatever the circumstances seemed to require or admit of instruction, consolation, and encouragement. I also made almost daily week-day visits to the office of the City Mission, 225 South Ninth street, to attend to calls for Missionary work, and to assist in carrying on the routine work of the same.

The past winter and spring were unusually severe on all those engaged in City Mission labors, owing to the vast amount of sickness of various kinds so long prevalent, and to the very great inclemency of the weather; both of which made the condition of the classes among whom our labors were needed an object of greater care and attention than usual. But amid the sickness, pestilence, and storm, our work went on, and now, under the care and favor of a kind Providence, I am enabled, for my part, to recount these results, which, it is humbly hoped and believed, were to the glory of God our Saviour, and to the good both of the bodies and souls of many who might otherwise have been in some degree neglected.

Report of the Rev. Daniel R. Goodwin.

During the past year, besides the discharge of my duties as Professor in the Divinity School in Philadelphia, my official acts have been as follows:

Preached 15 times; officiated in Divine service 20 times; administered the Holy Communion once, assisted in its administration 5 times; baptized 2 infants, and officiated at 2 funerals.

Report of Rev. S. Hazlehurst.

Since the last Convention, I have preached 36 times; officiated at 5 funerals; read service, and assisted at the Holy Communion 24 times. It affords me much pleasure to assist my brethren, whenever able.

Report of the Rev. G. Emlen Hare, D. D.

Throughout the current year, except in the vacations, or when prevented by extraordinary causes, I have preached, to Theological Students, 8 or 9 times per week.

G. EMLEN HARE,
Philadelphia Divinity School.

Report of the Rev. William H. Hare.

William H. Hare, Presbyter, begs leave to report that he has been engaged, during the past year, in the duties of his office, as Secretary and General Agent of the Foreign Committee of the Board of Missions.

Report of Thomas P. Hutchinson.

I would respectfully report, that since my resignation of St. James' Church, Hestonville, I have been engaged as Assistant to the Rector of St. Peter's, and as Itinerating Missionary. My official acts are embodied in the reports of the Rector of St. Peter's Church. I have also assisted Rev. Dr. Foggo, in Christ Church Parish.

Report of Rev. Isaac Martin, as Missionary to Seamen.

For the past year I have been engaged in visiting various ships, merchantmen and men-of-war, distributing among seamen the Word of God, the Prayer Book, and good reading tracts; have spent hours, conversing with inquiring seamen on the subject of duties to God and to themselves. It gives me great pleasure to witness an improved condition of morals, and to notice a greater thirst for true knowledge among them. It is due to the seamen to say that a thorough reformation is noticeable; but few of them drink ardent spirits to intoxication, and several are total abstainers from its use. Quite a number of officers and men are Christians, and honor their faith by a consistent, pious life. My summary of acts are as follows: ships visited 678; boarding-houses 118; Bibles given 42; Prayer Books 82; Sailors' Prayer Books 12; tracts distributed 3696; visits to Port Richmond 10; Receiving ship 20; Barracks Navy Yard 20; shipping agents 53; Fort Mifflin 2; baptisms 2.

Report of Rev. Arch. M. Morrison.

Since last report, the undersigned has not been engaged in any public, or recognized, ministerial work.

ARCH. M. MORRISON.

Report of Rev. Louis C. Newman.

With feelings of profound gratitude, I report, that although sickness has greatly hindered my work for the past eight months, God's special blessing has, nevertheless, attended my efforts among His anciently chosen people. Four children of Israel (3 adults and 1 infant) were baptized during the Conventional year. Details reported and published in Society's Report. Besides my regular Missionary work, I have also officiated about 185 times; preached 69 times; administered the Holy Communion 13 times; marriages 2; burials 3.

Report of W. S. Perkins, Bristol.

As my health would permit, I have been engaged, as formerly, in preaching and teaching, at the Orphans' Asylum of the Children of the Colored Soldiers of Pennsylvania, who were killed or died in the late war.

It was established some five years ago, by the State, in the buildings of old Bristol College, near this town.

Report of Rev. Alexander Shiras, D. D.

I would respectfully report that, as far as the condition of my voice allowed, I have been steadily employed during the Conventional year past, in the performance of ministerial duties. From the close of the last Convention until the first Sunday in July, I aided Bishop Lee in the services of St. Andrew's Church, Wilmington, Delaware. During July, I supplied the place of the absent Rector of St. John's Church, Norristown. For the remainder of the Summer, I was compelled to rest, except from occasional services. Since October 1st, I have been rendering, continuously, such assistance as lay within my power to the Rector of the Church of the Epiphany, Philadelphia, filling the intervals of Sunday and week-day services with educational engagements, on which I have mainly to rely for my support.

Report of Rev. W. H. N. Stewart, LL. D.

I beg to report that I have, during the last year, discharged the duties belonging to my Order, and offices as Assistant Minister and Priest in charge of St. Clement's Church, with such ability as God gave me. The numerical results are embodied in the report of St. Clement's Parish, and the other results are known to God, of whom I crave pardon for their imperfections.

Report of Rev. Enoch H. Supplee.

Besides the discharge of my scholastic duties, which have been greater this year than ever before, I have officiated in Divine service, since last Convention, as follows:

Preached 56 times; read service 71 times; administered

the Holy Communion 7 times; assisted in its administration 6 times; baptisms 3; funerals 4.

Most of these services were performed at St. Philip's, and the Church of the Good Shepherd, Philadelphia. The baptisms and funerals have been properly entered in Parish registers.

Report of Rev. Samuel Tweedale.

During the last Convention year, I have had two severe attacks of sickness, from which, by the blessings of our Heavenly Father, I have, in a great measure, recovered; I have received many acts of kindness from the Rector and the congregation, for which I am truly thankful. I have been enabled to assist at services on Sundays 88, on other days 40 times baptized 17 children; burials 44; visits made 498.

Report of the Rev. Henry Dana Ward.

I have to report, for the last and for the present Convention, that I have been exclusively engaged in the work of the ministry, with many opportunities of supplying vacancies, and of assisting brethren. While engaged in comparing the Gospel of the Kingdom, as held among our Protestant denominations, I was enabled to devote eight months to the same work among the Divines of Great Britain, ending this year in the publication of the "Faith of Abraham"—a work showing that the Jew's nationality, and Gentile's also, depart from the pattern, when they look for a city and for a possession of inheritance, to come in this world, whether in Judea or elsewhere. Laboring for Christ, crucified in the flesh, received up into heaven, and coming again in glory,

I am your brother in the faith.

Report of the Rev. Frank W. Winslow.

I have to report that, since October 22d, 1871, I have had charge of the 9 A.M. Free or Mission service, at the Church of the Advent; also, assisting the Rector in other ways. The attendance at this service, designed especially to accommodate

the large Bible Classes and Mothers' Meetings connected
with the Church, has been very regular and gratifying, and
demonstrates the feasibility of separate congregations, worshipping in the same city Church. The record of my official
acts, except of eight occasions, when I have supplied vacant
pulpits elsewhere, is included in the report of the Rector of
Advent Church.

Report of the Rev. Charles Woodward.

During the past Conventional year, besides discharging my
duties as Professor of Ancient and Modern Languages in this
Institution, and performing all the religious services required
of me as Chaplain of the same, I have, here and elsewhere,
preached 12 sermons, and delivered 58 short expository addresses; also, have regularly instructed a Bible Class of older
students; have solemnized 1 marriage; and assisted at 1
funeral.

Report of the Rev. Samuel Durborow.

I have been engaged, during the year, in attending to the
duties of my office, as Superintendent of the Philadelphia
Protestant Episcopal City Mission.

Baptisms, infants 19, adults 3, total 22; marriages 103;
burials 32. I have presented the cause of Missions in 48
Churches, and received for the work of the Mission $11,-
082.29.

Report of the Philadelphia Protestant Episcopal City Mission.　President, *ex officio*, the Bishop of the Diocese.　Superintendent, Rev. Samuel Durborow.

This Mission was organized May 1st, 1870. The following
general summary of results will exhibit the labors of the past
year. There are eight regularly established Mission Churches
and Halls. At two of these, viz.: The French Mission and
the Camac Street Mission, the services have resulted in making them almost self-supporting. At the other six, important
progress has been made.

Another feature of the Mission work is the constant visitation of the various public institutions. Eleven of these have been regularly attended, and the Word of Comfort carried to those who could not otherwise hear it.

House to house visitation, also, has been a very important part of the duties of the Missionaries; 8558 visits to the homes of the poor and sinful being paid during the past year. A fourth division of the work comes under the head of Charity. Over 400 families have been relieved, and heart-rending cases of destitution found out, and, as far as possible, attended to. This department of the Mission work is very valuable, and should be largely extended.

Total results of labor of all departments: special visits to the poor, sick and dying 8588; sermons and addresses 1287; funerals 172; baptisms 110; marriages 113; Holy Communion 60 times; cases sent to hospital 13. There are fully and regularly employed 6 Clerical and 6 Lay-Missionaries; and upwards of 100,000 tracts were distributed last year by those engaged in the work. The Treasurer's report shows an income of $11,164.26, including a small balance from last year, and an expenditure, on all accounts, of $10,840.94. Balance on hand May 1st, $323.32.

Thus, the work done is considerably greater than in the first year of the Mission's existence, and the promise is very hopeful for larger usefulness in the future.

Report of the Lincoln-Institution.

During the year 1871, the Lincoln Institution continued its useful work. It is now on a secure and firm basis.

In January last, there were 120 boys in the Institution, 84 of whom have been placed in stores and offices; these attend the night-school, which is under the control of the Board of Counsellors. This and also the day-school are in a flourishing condition, and receive attention of careful and competent teachers. Very many contributions have been made by various friends of the Institution, such as supplies of coal, &c. One gentleman has generously given $10,308, for the purpose of founding scholarships.

Eleven boys were confirmed during the past year, and the Counsellors, Managers, and all the other officers of the Institution are zealous in their efforts to secure the spiritual, as well as the temporal, welfare of those intrusted to their charge.

A charter has been obtained for an Institution called " The Educational Home for Boys," to be built upon a lot of ground on Forty-ninth Street, between Greenway Avenue and King-sessing Avenue, in West Philadelphia, generously presented by a gentleman and lady of this city, who feel a deep interest in the undertaking. This is intended to be a nursery for the smaller boys of the Lincoln Institution, and a home for orphans and destitute boys. Its charter provides that the officers of the Lincoln Institution shall always be ex officio members, thus legally binding them together.

GRAND SUMMARY OF DIOCESAN STATISTICS.

Baptisms.—Adults 568
          Infants 2,478
          Total. 3,046
Confirmed 1,547
Communicants 19,318
Public Services.—On Sundays 9,196
          On other days 5,436
Average attendance on Sundays. 64,217
Sunday Schools.—Teachers 2,503
          Scholars. 22,779
Bible Classes. 13
          Teachers. 168
          Members 4,421
Churches. 75
          Sittings 41,805
Sunday School Buildings. 31
Parsonages. 35
Cemeteries 26
Marriages 932
Burials 1,715
Chapels 15
          Sittings 3,185
Sewing Schools.—Teachers. 42
          Scholars. 995
Dorcas and Sewing Societies 3
District Visitors—Officers. 3
          Visitors 20
Parish Schools—Teachers 71
          Scholars 1,494
Mission Schools. 30
Mothers' Meeting.—Officers 8
          Members. 344
St. Matthew's Young Men's Literary Association.—Members. 60
Colored Schools.—Teachers. 1
          Scholars 50
Club House. 2
Dispensary.—Physicians 2
          Attendants 2
          Patients. 401
Night Schools.—Schools 2
          Teachers. 9
          Scholars 503
Industrial Schools.—Teachers. 17
          Scholars. 147
Working Women's Meeting.—Members. 40
Working Men's Meeting.—Members. 375
Children Catechized.—Times. 952
Candidates for Holy Orders.—Admitted 10
          Present number 21
Deacons ordained. 18
Presbyters. 11
Clergy dismissed. 20
  " received 11
Whole number of Clergy 176
Parishes admitted into union with the Convention 2
Whole number 113

MONEY RECEIPTS FROM ALL SOURCES.

Pew Rents	$196,904 00
Offertory at Holy Communion	22,514 38
Collections in Churches for Current Expenses	109,984 24
Other sources	62,875 89
Donations	44,456 85
Subscriptions	113,717 60
Investments	10,920 17
Collections for Coal	50 00
" Sunday School Library and Papers	1,625 00
" in Sunday Schools	2,069 67
Shannon Fund	100 00
Ground Rents	300 00
Sunday School Contributions	1,650 24
Episcopal Hospital	468 15
Church Home	80 56
Communion Alms	1,143 58
Five Per Cent. Parochial and Missionary Fund	585 40
Boyer Poor Fund	207 51
Domestic Missions	1,525 99
Convention Fund	281 00
Chicago Fund	1,282 00
Alms for Poor	26 53
Thanksgiving Day	38 68
Christmas Fund	11 60
Parish Aid	38 15
Mite Society	351 67
Foreign Missions	841 24
Disabled Clergymen	229 24
Alms for the Poor	610 00
Diocesan Missions	438 29
Evangelical Educational Society	2,639 00
Sunday School Offerings	2,729 92
Jewish Missions	112 75
Miscellaneous	116 50

Salaries of Rectors	$149,655
Arrears of salary	3,720

EXPENDITURES AND APPROPRIATIONS.

————:o:————

Current Expenses, including Salary of Rector	$245,285	00
Repairs and Improvements	86,802	00
Payment of Debts.—Interest	36,826	16
Episcopal Convention Fund.—Assessment	5,995	00
Support of Sunday Schools	15,178	74
Melodeon	125	00
For the Poor	18,183	02
Missions.—Parochial	19,622	34
Foreign	13,957	55
Domestic	29,027	57
Diocesan	6,159	14
Maine	10	89
Home Colored	1,442	23
City	6,391	46
For the Jews	1,521	37
Indian	2,605	23
Episcopal Hospital	17,301	54
Disabled Clergymen	5,573	45
Chicago and Northwestern Sufferers	8,215	24
Miscellaneous	46,424	24
Book Societies	2,515	39
Bibles, Prayer Books and Tracts	2,300	71
Church Building	36,499	62
Christian or Theological Education	8,735	87
Bible Society	22	25
A Parochial Sufferer	24	00
Parish Library and Reading Room	915	23
Families of Deceased Clergy	20	00
Church Home for Children	1,449	23
Bureau of Relief	41	16
Poor Children's Shoe Fund	50	00
Sunday School Offerings	1,436	51
Ladies' Missionary Aid Society	1,147	50
Dorcas	344	09
Offerings and Memorial Chapel	538	70
Bells	810	04
Church at Tioga	147	00
Church Endowment Fund	6,317	62
St. Luke's Home for Aged Females	773	76
St. Angarius	4	00
Mothers' Meeting Clothing Club	449	73
Sick Club	128	65
Young Men's Club	809	71
St. Mark's Dispensary, (4 months)	303	73
Mother's Aid Fund	128	50
Sewing School	41	59
Home for Little Wanderers	6	18
" Home and Abroad"	10	00
Female Tract Society	16	00
Mite Society, (15 Packages of Clothing)	1,200	00
Sunday School at the West	5	00
Bishop Morris, Oregon	75	00

FINANCIAL CONDITION.

Aggregate Value of the Property of the Parishes, Real and Personal	$2,460,000	00
Interest on Mortgages	4,632	47
Interest on Ground-Rents, &c	5,655	14
Other Indebtedness	93,546	12

FORM OF THE CERTIFICATE FOR LAY DEPUTIES TO CONVENTION.

It is hereby certified that at a meeting of the Vestry of   Church,   , in the County of
held on the   day of   18 , Mr.
was duly elected a lay deputy to the Convention of the Protestant Episcopal Church in the Diocese of Pennsylvania, to be held in   , on the   day of   next ; and that the said deputy is now, and has also been for not less than the six calendar months next before his election, a worshipper in the said   Church.

Dated this   of   , 18 .

} WARDEN.

} VESTRYMEN.

N. B.—If more than one deputy be chosen, a certificate in the above form may be given to each, or, which is better, the names of all may be included in one certificate, varying the language accordingly.

N. B.—According to Canon XI., "No other certificate or evidence of the appointment of any lay deputy or deputies to the Convention of this Diocese shall be allowed or received."

N. B.—*Resolved*, That the Churches of the Diocese be affectionately and earnestly requested to select their deputies to the Convention from such of their people as "come to the Holy Communion."—*Resolution of May 29, 1863.*

FORM OF PAROCHIAL REPORT.

————————————————————County.

—————————Church,　　Admitted—————————

The Rev.　　　　　　Rector.　　Rev.　　　　　　Assistant,
and　　　　　　　　　　　　　Wardens.

Baptisms—Adults,　　; Infants,　　; total,　　.

Confirmed,　　.

Communicants, added, new　　, by removal　　, died or removed　　,
present number　　.

Marriages　　.

Burials　　.

Public Services—On Sundays　　, on other days　　, total　　;
Average attendance on Sundays　　.

Children Catechized—Times　　.

Sunday Schools—Officers and Teachers　　, Scholars　　.

Bible Classes—Teachers　　, Members　　.

Parish Schools—Teachers　　, Scholars　　, other Parish agencies　　.

Church—Sittings　　; Chapels (the statistics of which are included in
this report), Sittings　　; School Buildings　　; Parsonage　　; Cemetery　　; Salary of Rector $　　 per annum; Arrears of salary　　;
Number of free sittings　　. Extra Sunday services, free to all　　.

MONEY RECEIPTS FROM ALL SOURCES.

Pew Rents, $　　; Offertory at Holy Communion, $　　; Collections in Church, $　　; Subscriptions, $　　; Donations, $　　.
Investments, $　　; Other Sources, $　　; Total, $　　.

EXPENDITURES AND APPROPRIATIONS.

Current Expenses (including Salary of Rector) $　　; Repairs and
Improvements, $　　; Payment of Debts, $　　, Episcopal and Con-
vention Fund, $　　· Support of Sunday Schools, $　　; of Parish
Schools, $　　; Parish Library, $　　; Parochial Missions, $　　;
For the Poor, $　　; To Missions, Foreign, $　　; Domestic, $　　;
Home Missions, for Colored People, $　　; Diocesan, $　　; City
Missions, $　　; For the Jews, $　　; Episcopal Hospital, $　　;
Church Building, $　　; Bibles, Prayer Books and Tracts, $　　;
Book Societies, $　　; Christian or Theological Education, $　　;
Disabled Clergymen, $　　; Miscellaneous, $　　; Total, $　　.

APPENDIX B.

THIRTEENTH ANNUAL REPORT OF THE BOARD OF MISSIONS OF THE DIOCESE OF PENNSYLVANIA.

In presenting their Thirteenth Annual Report, the Board of Missions of the Diocese of Pennsylvania cannot overlook the fact, that one period of our Diocesan history is past, and we begin a new year under entirely different circumstances.

The local boundaries of our field are extremely reduced; and the number of Parishes to whom we may appeal is (although not correspondingly) diminished. It is to be supposed that the Convention will deem it expedient to take some action, looking toward the gradual withdrawal of aid still extended to Central Pennsylvania.

MEMBERS OF THE BOARD:

At the time of the last Annual Report, the Board consisted of the following members, viz.:

The Rev. M. A. DeWolfe Howe, D.D.,	The Rev. E. A. Warriner,
" S. E. Appleton,	Mr. John Welsh,
" T. F. Davies,	" J. S. McCalla,
" W. P. Orrick,	" Edward L. Clark,
" Percy Browne,	" Frederick Fraley.

WHOSE TERM OF SERVICE EXPIRED JUNE, 1871.

The Rev. B. Watson, D.D.,	The Rev. R. C. Matlack,
" D. Washburn,	Mr. B. G. Godfrey,
" John Bolton,	" J. S. Biddle,
" J. K. Murphy,	" Lemuel Coffin,
" J. W. Claxton,	" Edward S. Buckley.

WHOSE TERM OF SERVICE EXPIRES JUNE, 1872.

The Rev. D. R. Goodwin, D.D.,	The Rev. A. Wadleigh,
" E. H. Foggo, D.D.,	Mr. Wm. Welsh,
" W. F. Paddock, D.D.,	" Abel Reed,
" J. A. Harris,	" James C. Booth,
" A. A. Marple,	" James S. Whitney.

22

The members whose term of service expired in June, 1871, were re-elected for the ensuing three years. At the meeting of the Standing Committee, in March, Rev. D. S. Miller, D.D., the Rev. J. B. Falkner, and Mr. George Hoffman, were elected members of the Board of Missions, in the places of the Rev. Dr. Howe, the Rev. P. Browne, removed, and Mr. Edward L. Clark, deceased. A minute has been placed upon our records, referring to the loss sustained by the decease of Mr. E. L. Clark.

MISSIONARIES AND STATIONS.

Missionaries appointed during the current year:

The following appointments were made during the year, viz.:

> The Rev. Chandler Hare, Tamaqua,
> " V. H. Berghaus, Lykens,
> " C. E. D. Griffith, Allentown,
> " W. W. Spear, St. Andrew's, West Vincent,
> " " " St. Mary's, Warwick,
> " " " St. Mark's, Honeybrook.

Missionaries resigned during the current year:

The following have resigned, viz.:

> Rev. J. L. Heysinger, New London and Oxford.
> " Thomas Burrows, Hulmeville and Attleboro'.
> " J. T. Carpenter, Minersville,
> " F. W. Bartlett, Allentown,
> " Wm. Moore, Northumberland.
> " J. H. Mac-El'Rey, Ashley.

Missionaries and Stations now aided by the Board:

Stations receiving aid from the Board in

CENTRAL PENNSYLVANIA:

Bedford,	Chambersburg,
Mahanoy City,	Minersville,
Hazleton,	Mansfield,
Green Ridge,	Allentown and Catasaqua,
Manheim,	Blossburg,
Troy,	Pleasant Mount,
New Milford and Great Bend,	Ashley,
Salem and Sterling,	Montoursville,

Northumberland.

IN PENNSYLVANIA:

Coatesville,	St. Andrew's, West Vincent,
New London and Oxford,	St. Mary's, Warwick,
Doylestown and Centreville,	St. Mark's, Honeybrook,
Hulmeville,	Gwynned,

Bucks County, Fallsington.

Missionaries now receiving aid from the Board:

Rev. Geo. P. Hopkins, Troy,
" J. A. Jerome, New Milford,
" R. H. Brown, Salem and Sterling,
" Chandler Hare, Tamaqua,
" Benjamin Hartley, Blossburg,
" W. G. Hawkins, Chambersburg,
" N. Barrows, Mansfield,
" H. C. Howard, Pleasant Mount,
" W. S. Heaton, Manheim,

Rev. J. W. Murphy, Mahanoy City,
" C. H. Van Dyne, Hazleton,
" Wm. Jarrett, Bedford,
" V. H. Berghaus, Lykens,
" C. E. Griffith, Allentown,
" J. MacAlpine Harding, Athens,
" Geo. J. Field, Coatesville,
" H. Baldy, Doylestown,

W. W. Spear, D. D.,   { St. Andrew's, West Vincent,
                        St. Mary's, Warwick,
                        St. Mark's, Honeybrook.

ABSTRACT OF TREASURER'S ACCOUNT.

During the year ending May 1st, 1872:

14 Churches out of Philadelphia contributed	$389.74
24 " in " "	4,204.87
Episcopal Hospital, Sunday School and Class	15.00
Individuals	1,415.00
Collection at Convention	85.80
Total Contributions	$6,110.41
Interest on U. S. Bonds	99.90
Total Receipts	$5,210.31

Of which were:

For general purposes	4,360.31	
" Missions of the Board	305.00	
" Missionaries of the Board and City Missions	1,200.00	
" Missions and objects not of the Board	345.00	
		$6,210.31
Balance in hand, May 1st, 1871		1,188.82
Proceeds of sale of U. S. Bonds		1,131.25
		$3,530.38

The expenditures have been:

For Missions of the Board and Secretary	$6,237.34
" " not of the Board	345.00
" City Missionaries	100.00
" Treasurer's Expenses	7.25
" Rent	150.00
" Printing	94.28
" Postage of Secretary	8.00
Total Payments	$6,941.87
Showing a Balance on hand, May 1st, 1872	$1,588.51

The following tables exhibit the financial condition of the Board for the last twelve years:

The total receipts for the year ending

May 1st, 1861			$5,740.18
"	1862		7,779.69
"	1863		5,336.55
"	1864		6,789.85
"	1865	including $200 reported to the Board,	8,026.44
"	1866		5,461.60
"	1867		8,206.07
"	1868	including $87.50 reported to the Board,	8,542.69
"	1869	" $30.00 " " "	8,821.04
"	1870		7,928.91
"	1871	including $121.97 reported to the Board	6,870.23
"	1872		6,210.31

The receipts from Churches were as follows:

Year ending	Churches out of Philadelphia.	Churches in Philadelphia.
May 1st, 1861	56—$ 946.92	27—$4,443.25
" 1862	83— 1,003.64	39— 5,525.83
" 1863	66— 1,208.71	33— 3,730.50
" 1864	55— 2,070.14	25— 4,339.70
" 1865	68— 2,087.11	37— 5,698.17
" 1866	40— 1,084.16	28— 4,233.58
" 1867	53— 1,292.34	37— 5,871.38
" 1868	43— 1,086.84	37— 6,499.39
" 1869	32— 1,047.17	29— 6,169.31
" 1870	33— 758.47	29— 5,703.93
" 1871	39— 829.60	26— 5,025.30
" 1872	14— 389.74	24— 4,204.87

It will be perceived, that our annual revenue reached its highest point in 1868, three years ago. Since then, it has steadily decreased. It was a thousand dollars less in 1870; another thousand dollars short in 1871. And during the present year, 1872, our receipts have fallen more than $600 behind those of 1871. This is by no means a gratifying or encouraging exhibit of financial affairs; but as it offers a true representation of noteworthy facts, the Board feels bound to present those facts distinctly, for due consideration by the Convention.

The Board does not, for a moment, admit or believe that the foregoing statements prove the present method of administering Diocesan Missions to be a failure. We see no reason, whatever, for pronouncing that the Convention of 1859 inaugurated an unwise or mistaken policy, when they committed the management of Missionary affairs to a Board of official appointment, recognized by the Convention and reporting to it.   On the contrary, we hold that the scheme has worked well in practical results; and has proved to be a decided improvement upon the prior plan of accomplishing similar ends.

For twelve years, the partisan element has been eliminated from the conduct of Diocesan Missions in Pennsylvania.   The records of this Board offer the plainest possible evidence that representatives of various schools of opinion in the Church can consult together in entire harmony, and carry forward important undertakings, with perfect concert of action.

We deem this a very valuable testimony.   For the harmony prevailing among us has not been the tranquility of stagnation.

The sessions of the Board have been well attended by its members; the proceedings have been characterized by lively interest; all propositions suggested, and all appointments considered, have elicited free comment and close scrutiny.   Yet party suggestions have never been introduced, and unanimous conclusions have been almôst invariably reached.

Moreover, as regards the prosecution of our work, it is worthy of remark, that no application for assistance, commending itself to the Board's approval, has ever been rejected; and our Missionaries have always been regularly paid. Those who have served in the Mission field can understand the importance of this point; and our Missionaries have constantly expressed their appreciation of its addition to their comfort.

Usually we have been enabled to add an annual gratuity to their stated salaries; the rule being to distribute, at the close of the fiscal year, all the money in hand, which it was prudent to spare from the near demands of the following year.   In making this extra allowance, the Board has, in the last two years, been greatly aided by anonymous contributions expressly designed for the "increase of salaries."

The following named Churches, formerly stations of the Board, have become self-supporting since the organization:

Grace—Allentown,	Eckley,
Bethlehem,	Marietta,
Altoona,	Downingtown,
Williamsport,	Pottstown,
Media,	Mauch Chunk
Montrose,	Scranton,
St. John's—Lancaster,	Lebanon,
Columbia,	St. Barnabas—Reading,
S. Wilkesbarre,	Sunbury,
Lewistown,	Franklin.
Conshohocken,	

The Parishes which have become self-supporting have generally large Churches, built in most cases since the stations were under the care of the Board. New Churches are built at the following present stations: Chambersburg, Coatesviile, Mansfield.

While, however, we feel assured that the past history of this Board illustrates, not failure, but success, we would ask whether the issues of any experiment can be declared final until the experiment itself has had a full, fair trial? Such trial, we may confidently claim, has not yet been granted to this Board.

When the present Missionary Qrganization of the Diocese was instituted, in 1859, the project received the votes of a large majority of the Convention; 74 Clergymen and 37 Parishes voting for its adoption.

Now, certainly, it might have been reasonably anticipated that our Churches would generally contribute, in proportion, for the vigorous administration of so important work; for the evangelization of needy souls, and the support of feeble Church enterprises in our own loved Diocese.

If some Rectors and Parishes, doubting the advantageous nature of an untried plan, had felt constrained to decline their aid at first, ought we not to suppose that they would subsequently grant their co-operation, unless they could point out manifest flaws in the practical working of the scheme? Especially, as by the terms of the resolutions under which this Board was created, and by the subsequent action by other societies, no general Missionary effort was, or has been since, expended in the Diocese, not emanating from the body holding its commission by virtue of Conventional institution, and the appointment of the Standing Committee. Yet what has been the case? Only about 90 Churches, in any one year since the Diocese of Pittsburg was set off, have given anything to our treasury; only 38 Parishes contributed during the current fiscal year. The Board of Diocesan Missions in Pennsylvania has been forgotten, thus far, in the distribution of their charities, by a large number of clerical and lay brethren, who were zealous in securing its original constitution. Forgotten with a systematic and unexceptional uniformity which it is difficult to understand.

.We are about to commence another year of labor. Our own proper range of territory is comparatively small; but, by a compact, of which the last Convention approved, we are bound to continue the salaries of all our appointed Missionaries in Central Pennsylvania until November, 1872. Still, while we shall eventually part from 17 of our old stations, we shall retain 10 in the boundaries of the Diocese of Pennsylvania; and we have ample opportunity of extending our work. Already the Board has ventured to sanction the adoption of certain places in Bucks County as points for itinerant oversight, and only waits to find a suitable person, who shall be at once entrusted with the charge. The whole support must come, during the first year at least, from the Board.

The Bishop also recommends that certain points in Chester County be immediately aided by the Board, on a largely advanced scale.

The Lincoln Institute, at Oxford, where there are several colored students, candidates for our Ministry, is included in the district named by Bishop Stevens.

We would like to increase the stipends of all Missionaries upon our roll, to make the salaries far better proportioned to the high cost of living which prevails.

Conscientious care is always exercised in the selection of our clerical laborers. They must be men who preach the

Gospel and do faithful work.   When they fail to fulfil either condition there is no hesitation in applying the remedy.

The Board has not yet fully digested its future plans of work, owing to the facts:

1. That the Central Pennsylvania Missions are to depend upon us until November next.

2. By reference to Journal of Convention of 1871, p. 53, it will be seen (Resolution 2d) that it was

Resolved, That the resolutions passed in 1858 [a mistake for 1859], establishing the Board of Missions, be suspended, so far as to remove the City of Philadelphia from the field of its labor.

It would seem necessary to await the action of this Convention, to ascertain its decision as to the permanence of this "suspension;" and, in fact, as to the general scope and character of the work henceforth to be assigned to the Board by the Convention.

We earnestly ask the Convention to give serious consideration to the subject of Diocesan Missions.   We urgently appeal for a fair share in the gifts of every Church in the Diocese.   Then the following year may indeed witness a due test applied, for the first time, to an exceedingly important department of our organized Church work.

PHILADA., MAY 7, 1872.

REV. J. W. CLAXTON,
  Chairman, &c.

DEAR SIR:—The following resolution was adopted by the Board of Missions of the Diocese of Pennsylvania, at a meeting held this day, viz.:

Resolved, That it be recommended to the Convention of this Diocese, to rescind its action by which the City of Philadelphia was withdrawn from its field of labor, in order that the Board may take entire charge of Missions in this Diocese.

Very truly, yours,

JNO. A. CHILDS,
Secretary.

TREASURER'S ACCOUNT.

BOARD OF MISSIONS

OF THE

DIOCESE OF PENNSYLVANIA.

DR.   *Board of Missions of the Diocese of Pennsylvania,*

1872.		
May 1.	Paid Rev. Benjamin Hartley..............................	$300 00
"	" do. (Special)....................	100 00
"	" George P. Hopkins..........................	300 00
"	" Rowland H. Brown..........................	300 00
"	" John T. Carpenter..........................	375 00
"	" do. (Special).....................	10 00
"	" John A. Jerome............................	250 00
"	" George G. Field...........................	250 00
"	" J. H. Hobart Millett.......................:	250 00
"	" F. Weston Bartlett..........................	212 50
"	" Thomas Burrows...........................	275 00
"	" do. (Special).....................	75 00
"	" W. George Hawkins.......................	350 00
"	" do. (Special).....................	70 00
"	" Napoleon Barrows.........................	300 00
"	" Horatio C. Howard..........................	250 00
"	" William S. Heaton..........................	300 00
"	" Joseph W. Murphy..........................	300 00
"	" Hurley Baldy...............................	150 00
"	" Charles H. Vandyne........................	250 00
"	" William Jarrett............................	275 00
"	" do. (Special......................	50 00
"	" Joseph H. MacEl'Rey.......................	187 50
"	" William Moore............................	100 00
"	" John L. Heysinger..........................	50 00
"	" John H. Babcock...........................	33 34
"	" Chandler Hare.............................	100 00
"	" V. Hummell Berghaus.......................	100 00
"	" W. W. Spear, D. D..........................	125 00
"	Supply for Bristol...............................	10 00
"	Services at Springville..........................	150 00
"	Rt. Rev. Bishop Stevens, for General Missionary Expenses...	139 00
"	Rev. John A. Childs, D. D., Secretary...............	250 00
"	" Robert Mackie.............................	50 00
"	" Rev. John G. Furey.........................	50 00
"	St. George's Church, Kenderton (Special)............	75 00
"	S. E. Convocation, do..............	20 00
"	for Treasurer's Book............................	6 25
"	Insurance on U. S. Bonds.........................	1 00
"	Rent..	150 00
"	Postage of Secretary............................	8 00
"	McCalla & Stavely, Printing......................	94 28
"	Church of Good Shepherd, Radnor (Special).........	250 00
	Total Payments.............................	$6941 87
	Amount carried forward........................	$6941 87

in account with James S. Biddle, Treasurer. CR.

By the following contributions from Parishes from May 1st, 1871, to May 1st, 1872:		
BERKS COUNTY.		
St. James' Church, Bristol, Sunday School.......	$125 00	
Trinity Church, Centreville....................	1 87	
St. Paul's Church, Doylestown................	11 00	
		$137 87
CHESTER COUNTY.		
St. Peter's Church, Great Valley..............	5 00	
St. Paul's Church, West Whiteland............	5 00	
		10 00
CUMBERLAND COUNTY.		
St. John's Church, Carlisle, special............		50 00
DELAWARE COUNTY.		
Christ Church, Media......................	13 92	
do. do. special................	10 00	
		23 92
LUZERNE COUNTY.		
St. Luke's Church, Scranton..................		20 00
MONTGOMERY COUNTY.		
St. James' Church, Perkiomen................	4 75	
Christ Church, Pottstown, special.............	20 00	
Church of Our Saviour, Jenkintown...........	59 00	
St. Paul's Sunday School, Upper Providence.....	10 20	
		93 95
PHILADELPHIA COUNTY.		
St. Peter's Church..........................	756 00	
St. James' Church..........................	382 59	
St. Andrew's Church........................	127 60	
do. do. special....................	20 00	
Church of the Ascension.....................	15 00	
Church of the Atonement....................	100 00	
St. Mark's Church..........................	473 25	
do. do. special................	75 00	
Church of the Mediator.....................	75 00	
Advent Church............................	100 00	
Zion Church.......	20 00	
do. do. Sunday School..................	22 00	
Trinity Church, Southwark..................	45 00	
St. Luke's Church, Germantown..............	82 17	
Trinity Church, Oxford......................	105 00	
All Saints' Church, Lower Dublin, special......	75 00	
Emmanuel Church, Holmesburg....	25 62	
St. Mark's Church, Frankford................	102 22	
do. do. special..........	300 00	
St. Andrew's Church, West Philadelphia........	26 14	
St. Paul's Church, Chestnut Hill..............	21 96	
Church of the Redeemer, Seamen's Mission.....	8 23	
St. Michael's Church, Germantown.............	26 50	
St. Timothy's Church, Roxborough.............	59 20	
Church of the Holy Trinity..................	436 31	
Amount carried forward....................		$3479 79

DR.   *Board of Missions of the Diocese of Pennsylvania*

1872.		
May 1.	Amount brought forward........................	$6941 87
	Balance, Cash in hand..............................	1588 51
		$8530 38

We have examined the foregoing account, compared it with the vouchers, and find it correct: the balance of $1588.51 being to the credit of the Treasurer in the Philadelphia National Bank. The Treasurer also exhibits a certificate of deposit of the Fidelity Insurance and Trust Co. for $1000, of U. S. 5-20 Bonds.

LEMUEL COFFIN, } *Auditing Committee.*
BENJ. G. GODFREY, }

PHILADELPHIA, May 29, 1872.

in account with James S. Biddle, Treasurer. CR.

Amount brought forward		$3479 79	$335 74
PHILADELPHIA,—Continued.			
St. Luke's Church		502 55	
Calvary Church, Germantown		122 53	
Grace Church, Philadelphia		100 00	
			$4204 87
WAYNE COUNTY.			
Grace Church, Honesdale		50 00	
St. Paul's Church, Pleasant Mount		4 00	
			54 00
Collection at Convention			85 80
Thomas Coleman, for Blossburg		100 00	
Rev. James Saul		100 00	
" F. W. Bartlett		15 00	
"Z.," for Missionaries of the Board and City Missions		1200 00	
Bishop Potter Bible Class, Episcopal Hospital		5 00	
Sunday School of Episcopal Hospital		10 00	
			1430 00
Interest on U. S. 5-20 Bonds			99 90
Total receipts			$6210 31
Add proceeds of sale of U. S. Bonds			1131 25
Add balance in hand May 1st, 1871			1188 82
			$8530 38
By balance in Philadelphia Bank			$1588 51

The above receipts were :
For general purposes...........$4360 31
" Missionaries of the Board and City Missions.......... 1200 00
Special for Missions of the Board.......... 305 00
 do.   do.   out of do.......... 345 00

Total..........$6210 31

JAMES S. BIDDLE, TREASURER,
1714 *Locust Street.*

Report of the Southeastern Convocation.

———o———

In accordance with the resolution passed at the last Convention (see Journal 1871, page 51), the Southeastern Convocation of the Diocese of Pennsylvania make the following report:

The Southeastern Convocation is the only such organization within the bounds of the present Diocese of Pennsylvania. According to lines indicated by the late Bishop, Alonzo Potter, it occupies the counties of Chester, Delaware and Montgomery; these three counties contain thirty Church organizations, and three Missionary stations. From these facts it is evident how large a Missionary field it presents.

In 1866, the Convocation resolved itself into a Missionary Association (to quote the language of the report), " with the view of the resuscitation of decayed parishes, the establishment of new stations, and the organization of parishes wherever practical and desirable within the Convocation boundaries." Accordingly, in February, 1866, Kennett Square was adopted as a Missionary Station, and the Rev. John Long appointed Missionary, at a salary of $1000 per annum.

In June, 1866, Convocation appropriated $200 per annum for two years, for the vacant Churches of St. Andrew's, St. Mary's and St. Mark's, in Chester Counties.

The Rev. Mr. Long, having resigned in the early part of 1867, the Rev. J. H. Mac-El'Rey, Deacon, was appointed his successor, who, with more or less of success, labored in this field in conjunction with that of St. John's, New London, until April 1, 1869, when the Rev. J. L. Heysinger succeeded him, taking charge of these points, and adding to them the Missionary Station of Oxford. He was assisted in these extended labors by Mr. (now Rev.) Arthur Brooks and Mr. C. E. Fessenden, divinity students. The Rev. Mr. Heysinger resigned as Missionary of the Convocation in July, 1871. Services were kept up at Kennett, by lay-reading, until the end of the year.

The centre of Missionary operations of the Convocation has lately been changed from Kennett to Parksburg, a growing town on the line of the Pennsylvania Railroad, where a good Church edifice has been procured, and the Rev. J. C. Carpenter elected Missionary, at a salary of $1200 per annum. He entered upon his duties April 1st, 1872.

Although the labors of these six years of Missionary effort have not been as successful in results, as was at first anticipated, yet they have been pursued with unremitting zeal, in faith that we were sowing the good seed of God's Word, and that in His good time He would cause it to spring up and bear fruit. Those acquainted with this field need not be told of the peculiar difficulties that present themselves everywhere within its limits, difficulties often much greater than those encountered in our new Western Dioceses, yet which we feel bound to grapple with; we have tried to carry on this work in patient faith, not looking for great results or immediate success, but endeavoring to spread the knowledge of Christ and Him crucified, among a people who, however blessed with this world's goods, have been and are now too generally ignorant of the True and Heavenly Riches.

DR.   *Rev. E. W. Appleton, Treasurer,*

1871.			
April 1,	Cash	Balance...	$ 1 28
" 3,	"	Holy Trinity, West Chester.......................	50 00
" 12,	"	Rev. F. E. Arnold...............................	10 00
" 24,	"	St. John's Church, Norristown....................	51 07
" 25,	"	St. Paul's, West Whiteland......................	10 00
" 25,	"	St. Peter's, Great Valley........................	10 00
May 9,	"	Christ Church, Media............................	40 00
" 11,	"	St. Paul's, West Whiteland, and St. Peter's, Great Valley	10 00
" 22,	"	St. Paul's, Cheltenham..........................	125 00
June 19,	"	Calvary Church, Rockdale........................	37 50
July 28,	"	Holy Trinity, West Chester......................	20 00
Sept. 26,	"	St. John's, Norristown..........................	35 00
" 26,	"	St. Paul's, Chester.............................	30 00
Oct. 30,	"	St. James', Perkiomen...........................	6 50
Nov. 3,	"	Holy Trinity, West Chester......................	50 00
Dec. 5,	"	Christ Church, Pottstown........................	20 00
" 13,	"	" " "	10 00
" 22,	"	Church of Our Saviour, Jenkintown...............	25 00
1872.			
Jan. 9,	Cash,	St. James' Church, Downingtown.................	25 00
" 9,	"	St. Timothy's, Roxborough.......................	30 00
" 15,	"	St. Paul's, Upper Providence....................	25 00
" 23,	"	Calvary Church, Rockdale........................	37 50
" 23,	"	St. Paul's, Chester.............................	40 00
" 23,	"	House of Prayer, Branchtown.....................	10 00
Mar. 4.	"	Holy Trinity, West Chester......................	30 00
			$738 85

in Account with S. E. Convocation.   CR.

1871.		
April 3,	Paid Rev. J. L. Heysinger..........................	$50 00
" 25,	" " "	30 00
June 7,	" " "	225 00
" 29,	" " "	25 00
July 19,	" Mr. C. E. Fessenden.........................	32 00
Sept. 29,	" " " "	32 00
Nov. 3,	" " " "	32 00
1872.		
Jan. 5,	Paid Mr. C. E. Fessenden.........................	56 00
" 9,	" Rev. S. Hazlehurst...........................	10 82
Feb. 22,	" Rev. J. H. MacEl'Rey........................	75 00
Mar. 30,	Balance..	171 03
		$738 85

24

APPENDIX C.

REPORT OF TREASURER OF CHRISTMAS FUND
FOR DISABLED CLERGYMEN.

Cr.   *R. P. McCullagh, Treasurer, in Acc't with Christmas Fund.*

1872.			
		Contributions received since May 1st, 1871 :	
BUCKS COUNTY,	Bristol,	St. James	$17 00
	Doylestown,	St. Paul..	15 10
CHESTER,	Coatesville,	Trinity	5 44
	Downingtown,	St. James	6 20
	Parkesburg,	Grace	1 50
	Pequea,	St. John..	15 35
	West Chester,	Holy Trinity.	23 90
DELAWARE,	Media,	Christ..	9 09
	Radnor,	Good Shepherd	6 66
	Rockdale,	Calvary.	22 50
MONTGOMERY,	Cheltenham,	St. Paul..	53 09
	Conshohocken,	Calvary.	5 70
	Jenkintown,	Our Saviour..	27 44
	Lower Merion,	Redeemer..	60 00
	Perkiomen,	St. James	3 55
	Pottstown,	Christ..	15 56
	Norristown,	St. John.	32 24
	Upper Providence,	St. Paul's Memorial . . .	18 91
	White Marsh,	St. Thomas	18 00
PHILADELPHIA,	Philadelphia,	Ascension.	27 80
	"	Atonement.	88 24
	"	Epiphany	250 00
	"	Good Shepherd	9 00
	"	Grace.	114 50
	"	Holy Apostles..	24 50
	"	Holy Trinity.	200 00
	"	Mediator	72 31
	"	Trinity Chapel.	6 67
	"	St. Andrew	143 70
	"	St. George.	4 50
	"	St. James.	241 65
	"	St. John the Evangelist .	5 15
	"	St. Luke	150 00
	"	St. Mark...	182 04
	"	St. Peter	225 50
	"	St. Stephen	232 25
	"	Mrs. Fallon	1 00
	Branchtown,	House of Prayer	3 00
	Bridesburg,	St. Stephen	6 53
	Chestnut Hill,	St. Paul	37 75
	Francisville,	St. Matthew.	42 72
	Frankford,	St. Mark.	86 43
	Germantown,	Calvary	42 76
	"	Christ	50 75
	"	" Special from a Parishioner.	50 00
	"	St. Michael	25 00
	"	St. Luke.	75 00
	"	" A Family Christmas Offering.	100 00
	Holmesburg,	Emmanuel	16 33
	Kenderton,	St. George.	7 00
	Kensington,	Emmanuel	19 00
	"	Ditto. 1870..	61 32
	"	Chapel, Epis. Hospital.. .	5 24
	Kingsessing,	St. James	5 31
	Lower Dublin,	All Saints	11 60
	Manayunk,	St. David	12 72
	Mount Airy,	Grace	33 35
	Moyamensing,	All Saints	17 39
	"	St. Timothy..	16 00
	Oxford,	Trinity.	186 00
	Port Richmond,	Messiah..	2 81
	Roxborough,	St. Timothy..	20 00
	Southwark,	Evangelist.	3 80
	"	Trinity	30 00
	Spring Garden,	Nativity	46 42
	"	Redemption	11 42
	"	St. Jude	16 23
	"	St. Matthias.	28 00
	Carried Forward		$3405 98

R. P. McCullagh, Treasurer, in Acc't with Christmas Fund.   Cr.

1872	Brought forward . . . . St. Andrew	$3405 98	
	PHILADELPHIA, West Philadelphia, St. Andrew	20 00	
	" St. Mary	25 08	
	" Saviour, 1870	44 22	
			$3495 28
1872 May 3.	To twelve (12) months' interest on $2650 U. S. six per cent. 5-20 Bonds $159 00		
	Premium on Gold, July 1, 1871, 13 per cent. $10 34		
	" " Jan. 6, 1872, 8⅝ " 7 06		
		$17 40	
			176 40
	To Interest on Balances in The Philadelphia Trust and Safe Deposit Company, for one year to date, at (4) per cent		121 00
	To Balance on hand at last Annual Report, May 3, 1871		2537 15
			$6329 83

Christmas Fund in Acc't with R. P. McCullagh, Treasurer.   DR.

1872.				
May 3.	By Appropriations paid to Beneficiaries during the year ending May 1, 1872, viz.:			
	Annual, to four Clergymen	$1375 00		
	" six widows of do	1500 00		
	" children of three do	650 00		
			$3525 00	
	Special, to two Clergymen	200 00		
	" five widows of do	500 00		
	" children of two do	200 00		
			900 00	
				4425 00
	Cash paid bills, &c., viz.:			
	Episcopal Register, publishing acknowledgments	11 10		
	Siddall Brothers, printing Receipts	4 00		
	Postage and Check Stamps, one year	6 90		
			22 00	
	Balance of cash on hand in the Philadelphia Trust and Safe Deposit Company to the credit of the Treasurer, on interest at four per cent		2882 83	
			$7329 83	
1872.				
May 3.	To Balance brought down		$2882 83	

E. E.

Philadelphia, May 3, 1872.

R. P. McCULLAGH,

Treasurer.

We have examined the foregoing Account, compared it with the vouchers, and found it correct, leaving a balance to the credit of the Treasurer, in the Philadelphia Trust and Safe Deposit Co., of Twenty-eight hundred and eighty-two dollars and eighty-three cents ($2882 83), together with the investment of twenty-six hundred and fifty (2650) dollars in United States Six Per Cent. Bonds of 1867.

THOMAS ROBINS,
THOS. H. MONTGOMERY, } *Committee.*

Philadelphia, May 7, 1872.

APPENDIX D.

ACCOUNT OF TREASURER OF CONVENTION AND EPISCOPAL FUNDS.

CR. *Convention Diocese Pa. in Acc't with B. G. Godfrey, Treasurer.*

Assessments. 1872.				Epis. F.	Con. F.
		To balances as per last Report		$2408 07	$919 42
		From Parishes:			
$12 50	Berks County,	Douglassville,	St. Gabriel.	7 50	5 00
22 00		Morgantown,	St. Thomas, '71--'71	13 50	8 50
6 00		Birdsboro',	St. Michael	3 50	2 50
8 00	Bradford,	Troy,	St. Paul.	4 50	3 50
13 50		Athens,	Trinity, 1870 and '71	7 50	6 00
50 00	Bucks	Bristol,	St. James	28 50	21 50
6 00		Hulmeville,	Grace.	3 50	2 50
6 00		Centreville,	Trinity.	3 50	2 50
20 00		Doylestown,	St. Paul	11 00	9 00
62 00	Carbon,	Mauch Chunk,	St. Mark	32 00	30 00
6 00		Summit,	St. Philip	3 50	2 50
16 00	Centre,	Philipsburg,	Trinity.	9 00	7 00
12 00	Chester,	Great Valley,	St. Peter. . . .	6 50	3 50
9 00		West Whiteland,	St. Paul	5 00	4 00
6 00		West Vincent,	St. Andrew. . . .	3 50	2 50
20 00		Phœnixville,	St. Peter. . . .	12 50	7 50
17 00		Pequea,	St. John, 1870 . . .	10 00	7 00
25 00		Coatesville,	Trinity, 1870 and '71	15 00	10 00
6 00	Columbia,	Centralia,	Holy Trinity. . . .	3 50	2 50
50 00	Cumberland,	Carlisle,	St. John.	28 00	22 00
6 00	Dauphin,	Harrisburg,	St. Paul	3 50	2 50
30 00	Delaware,	Radnor,	St. David	20 00	10 00
22 00		Concord,	St. John, '70 and '71	13 50	8 50
12 00		Rockdale,	Calvary.	7 00	5 00
50 00		Chester,	St. Paul, 1870 . .	32 00	18 00
20 00		Marcus Hook,	St. Martin, 1870 . .	13 00	7 00
30 00		Media,	Christ.	18 00	12 00
22 00	Lancaster,	Paradise,	All Saints, '70 and '71	13 00	9 00
5 00		Churchtown,	Bangor, 1870. . .	3 00	2 00
20 00		Columbia,	St. Paul	11 00	9 00
30 00	Lehigh,	Allentown,	Grace	20 00	10 00
6 00		"	Mediator.	3 50	2 50
75 00	Luzerne,	Wilkesbarre,	St. Stephen . . .	40 00	35 00
5 00		"	St. Clement, 1870. .	3 00	2 00
15 00		Eckley,	St. James, 1871. .	8 00	7 00
12 00		White Haven,	St. Paul	7 00	5 00
30 00		Scranton,	St. Luke, 1870. . .	19 00	11 00
6 00	Lycoming,	Montoursville,	Ch. of Our Saviour..	3 50	2 50
20 00		Muncy,	St. James . . .	13 00	7 00
5 00	Montour,	Exchange,	St. James, 1870. .	3 00	2 00
45 00	Montgomery,	White Marsh,	St. Thomas	30 00	15 00
75 00		Norristown,	St. John.. . . .	40 00	35 00
25 00		Pottstown,	Christ.	13 00	12 00
62 00		Lower Merion,	Redeemer.	40 00	22 00
55 00		Jenkintown,	Our Saviour, '70--'71	34 00	21 00
6 00		Conshocken,	Calvary... . . .	3 50	3 50
90 00		Cheltenham,	St. Paul.	50 00	40 00
37 00		Lower Merion,	St. John.. . . .	22 00	15 00
6 00		Upper Providence,	St. Paul	3 50	2 50
37 00	Northampton.	Bethlehem,	Nativity, 1870 . .	19 00	11 00
125 00	Philadelphia.	Philadelphia,	Christ.	75 00	50 00
210 00		"	St. Peter.		
75 00		"	St. Paul	45 00	30 00
200 00		"	St. James	125 00	75 00
325 00		"	St. Stephen	200 00	125 00
250 00		"	St. Andrew	140 00	110 00
300 00		"	. Epiphany	175 00	125 00
30 00		"	Ascension	19 00	11 00
300 00		"	St. Luke	155 00	145 00
200 00		"	Atonement.	125 00	75 00
350 00		"	St. Mark.	200 00	150 00
100 00		"	Mediator.	60 00	40 00
100 00		"	St. Clement	64 00	36 00
350 00		"	Holy Trinity. . . .	200 00	150 00
75 00		"	Covenant	40 00	35 00
$4222 00		Carried forward, ...		$4751 57	$2578 92

Convention Diocese Pa. in Acc't with B. G. Godfrey, Treas.   CR.

Assessments.			Epis. F.	Con. F.
$4222 00		Brought forward	$4751 57	$2578 92
5 00	PHILADELPHIA, Philadelphia,	St. Thomas, 1870..	3 00	2 00
50 00	Oxford,	Trinity	28 50	21 50
50 00	Lower Dublin,	All Saints... . . .	27 00	23 00
125 00	Northern Liberties,	Advent	70 00	55 00
12 00	"	Calvary Mon'tal . .	6 00	4 00
75 00	Southwark,	Trinity	39 00	36 00
30 00	"	Evangelists.	19 00	11 00
60 00	"	Gloria Dei	38 00	22 00
150 00	Spring Garden,	St. Philip	85 00	65 00
40 00	"	St. Jude.	25 00	15 00
50 00	"	St. Matthias . . .	30 00	20 00
60 00	"	Incarnation	35 00	25 00
60 00	Francisville,	St. Matthew.	35 00	25 00
50 00	West Philadelphia,	St. Mary.	30 00	20 00
20 00	"	St. Andrew.	11 00	9 00
150 00	"	Ch. of the Saviour .	80 00	70 00
60 00	Kensington,	Emmanuel	35 00	25 00
50 00	Moyamensing,	All Saints... . . .	27 00	23 00
150 00	Germantown,	St. Luke.	85 00	65 00
19 00	"	St. John Baptist, '68	12 00	7 00
6 00	"	1871	3 50	2 50
50 00	"	St. Michael	27 00	23 00
60 00	Holmesburg,	Emmanuel.	35 00	25 00
60 00	Kingsessing,	St. James	35 00	25 00
200 00	Germantown,	Christ.	125 00	75 00
30 00	North Penn,	St. James the Less .	17 00	13 00
100 00	Frankford,	St. Mark	60 00	40 00
6 00	Pt. Richmond,	Messiah	3 50	2 50
30 00	South Penn,	Zion	16 00	14 00
60 00	Manayunk,	St. David	38 00	22 00
125 00	Chestnut Hill,	St. Paul.	70 00	55 00
25 00	Roxborough,	St. Timothy. . . .	15 00	10 00
6 00	"	St. Alban.	3 50	2 50
6 00	Bustleton,	St. Luke.	3 50	2 50
12 00	Branchtown,	House of Prayer...	7 00	5 00
25 00	Mt. Airy,	Grace	15 00	10 00
6 00	Frankford Road,	St. John's Free. . .	3 50	2 50
40 00	"	Holy Apostles . . .	25 00	15 00
6 00	Bridesburg,	St. Stephen	3 50	2 50
6 00	"	Good Shepherd. . .	3 50	2 50
10 00	Kenderton,	St. George... . . .	6 00	4 00
12 00	"	Messiah.	7 00	5 00
6 00	"	St. George.	3 50	2 50
8 00	SCHUYLKILL, St. Clair,	Holy Apostles . .	4 50	3 50
12 00	Mahanoy,	Church of Faith . .	7 50	4 50
8 00	Ashland,	St. John	5 00	3 00
8 00	SUSQUEHANNA, New Milford,	St. Mark	4 50	3 50
6 00	Great Bend,	Grace	3 50	2 50
11 00	Springville,	St. Andrew . . . 1868	6 00	5 00
5 00	"	" . . . 1869	3 00	2 00
5 00	Dundaff,	St. James	3 00	2 00
6 00	TIOGA, Tioga,	St. Andrew	3 50	2 50
6 00	Blosburg,	St. Luke.	3 50	2 50
6 00	Mansfield,	St. James	3 55	2 00
50 00	WAYNE, Honesdale,	Grace.	30 00	20 00
6 00	Pleasant Mt.,	St. Paul	3 50	2 50
3 00	Sterling,	Zion 1870	2 00	1 00

$6515 00

FUND FOR THE SUPPORT OF THE EPISCOPATE—"Interest for the use of the Bishop for the time being of the P. E. Church in Pennsylvania, who shall have the City of Philadelphia within his Diocese," through Geo. W. Taylor, Esq., Treasurer of the Advancement Society Trustees:

Annual Interest on $8128.29 Penn'a 6 per cent. loan.	$487 70		
" " $100 Philad'a " " "	6 00		
		493 70	

Carried forward $6574 82 $3539 92

25

CR.   *Convention Diocese Pa. in Acc't with B. G. Godfrey, Treas.*

	Epis. F.	Con. F.
Brought forward............	$6574 82	$3539 92

RECEIPTS FROM THE INVESTMENTS FOR THE EPISCOPATE GENERAL FUND—The income of said Fund shall be exclusively appropriated for the use of the Bishop who shall have the City of Philadelphia in his Diocese. See Rev. Reg. vi.

			Epis. F.	Con. F.
Annual interest on $2400 Philadelphia City Loan . .	$144 00			
Less State Tax..................	7 20			
		136 80		
Annual interest on $25,350 Pennsylvania 6 per cent. loan..............		1521 00		
Annual interest on $1000 Pennsylvania 5 per cent. loan		50 00		
		1571 00		
Annual interest on $2000, 1881, U. S. 6 per cent. loan, in gold	120 00			
Do. $1000, 1865.	60 00			
Do. $1000, 10-40.	50 00			
		230 00		
Premium on gold.		26 58		
			1964 38	
ANDREW DOZ LEGACY—"In trust to, and for the only proper use, benefit, and behoof of the Bishop of the P. E. Church who shall have the Episcopalians of Philadelphia within his Diocese :				
Annual Interest on $2000 Pennsylvania 6 per cent. loan. .	120 00			
One year's ground-rent from Mrs. M. E. Stewart, Feb. 1..	144 00			
18 months' ground-rent from John Laurence ($36 in silver).	38 16			
			302 16	
KOHNE LEGACY—"For the Support of the Bishop of the P. E. Church who shall have the City of Philadelphia within his Diocese :"				
Annual Interest on $4600 Philadelphia 6 per cent. loan.	$276 00			
Less State Tax..	13 80			
		$262 20		
Annual Interest on $150 Pennsylvania 6 per cent. loan		9 00		
			271 20	
HUTCHINS LEGACY—To increase the Episcopate or Bishop's Fund of the Diocese of Pennsylvania, per G. W. Taylor, Treasurer, etc.:				
Annual Interest on $1888.35 Pennsylvania 6 per cent. loan			113 30	
PILMORE LEGACY—Towards the Support of the Episcopate in the Diocese of Pennsylvania, through G. W. Taylor, Esq., Treasurer :				
Annual Interest on $7983.36 Pennsylvania 6 per cent. loan			479 00	
Interest received from Philadelphia Safe Deposit Co., to date				198 43
			$9804 86	$3738 35

ASSESSMENTS FOR 1871, RECEIVED AFTER MAY 1ST, 1872.

1872.				
May 2,	St. Peter	Philadelphia..	$210 00	
	Nativity	Bethlehem	37 00	
3,	St. John	Lancaster	18 00	
	Grace	Philadelphia	250 00	
	Bishop's Church.	"	25 00	
	St. Thomas	"	6 00	
15,	Holy Trinity	West Chester	62 00	
	Calvary	Germantown, Philadelphia	125 00	
	Nativity	Philadelphia.	125 00	
	St. Martin	Marcus Hook	25 00	
	St. James	Downingtown	25 00	
18,	Christ	Danville.	40 00	
20,	St. Matthew, on account. . . .	Sunbury	3 00	
	St. John the Evangelist	Philadelphia	10 00	
	St. John	Pequea	21 00	
24,	St. Paul	Chester	62 00	
June 21,	St. Paul	Minersville.	10 00	
July 9,	St. John.	Philadelphia	20 00	
	St. James, 1870 and 1871	Hestonville, Philadelphia. . . .	15 00	
				$1089 00

Convention Diocese Pa. in Acc't with B. G. Godfrey, Treas.   DR.

1872.		Epis. F.	Con. F.
	Cash paid traveling expenses of the following named Clergymen in attendance on the Convention of May, 1871 :		
Rev.	A. P. Brush		$8 50
"	A. M. Abel, 1870		2 60
"	" " 1871		2 60
"	W. Paret		8 10
"	J. M. Martin		6 70
"	P. M. Peck		5 20
"	J. Hewitt		4 90
"	J. H. H. Millett		3 20
"	G. C. Drake		6 05
"	J. K. Karcher		20 70
"	N. Burrows		21 84
"	P. Russell		2 00
"	B. Hartley		20 00
"	Thomas Burrows		2 50
"	M. F. Keed		13 00
"	E. A. Warriner		16 02
"	M. McGlathery		3 80
"	C. Hare		7 80
"	J. C. Carpenter		3 15
"	J. P. Hammond		1 80
"	J. S. Reed		3 75
"	W. C. Leverett		6 00
"	R. J. Keeling		10 00
"	H. T. W. Allen		10 00
"	R. H. Brown		8 12
"	R H. Williamson		6 60
"	W. R. Stockton		1 00
"	H. Baldy		2 00
"	H. C. Howard		14 50
"	F. A. Irvine		12 00
"	W. S. Heaton		4 75
"	A. A. Marple		7 60
"	G. P. Hopkins		16 00
"	W. R. Gries		3 50
"	O. W. Landreth		15 00
"	J. Karcher		1 80
"	G. T. Burton		8 40
"	Wm. Moore		6 74
"	Geo. G. Field		1 50
"	P. R. Reese		3 60
"	H. R. Smith		2 10
"	D. Washburn		7 65
"	Jas. Walker		3 50
"	J. W. Murphy		3 50
"	W. G. Hawkins		9 70
"	F. W. Bartlett		3 30
"	Herbert M. Jarvis		13 78
May 19.	Paid Rt. Rev. Bishop Lee, by order of Convention	$200 00	
"	James Montgomery, for Services at the Convention		24 72
"	Rev. J. A. Childs, 1 year's salary as Secretary to Bishop . . .	500 00	
"	Rt. Rev. Bishop Stevens, 1 year's salary	6500 00	
"	" " traveling to date	201 00	
"	Philadelphia Safe Deposit, rent of Safe	16 00	
"	City and State Taxes on Episcopal Residence, 1872	412 48	
"	Water Rents on Episcopal Residence, 1872	15 00	
"	Rt. Rev. Bishop Howe, for carriage hire	13 00	
"	Rev. J. A. Childs, D.D., 6 months rent of Episcopal Rooms . .		125 00
"	McCalla & Stavely, Printing Journal of Convention of 1871 . .		2086 75
"	John Short, for Services, by order of the Standing Committee . .		18 50
"	Jas. Hogan, Stationery for Convention, 1871		13 42
"	Rev. John A. Childs, for Postage		55 00
"	Jos. Hover, Stationery for Convention		9 00
"	J. H. Nichols, for Postage, Telegram, etc., for Bishop		35 67
"	R. M'Cauley, for Binding 13 volumes		16 25
"	A. J. H. Nichols, for making Triennial Digest		50 00
"	" " Services, order Rev. Dr. Childs		25 00
	Carried forward	$7857 48	$2806 11

DR. *Convention Diocese Pa. in Acc't with B. G. Godfrey, Treasurer.*

1871.		Epis. F.	Con. F.
	Brought forward.	$7857 48	$2806 11
May 19.	Paid Miss Mary B. Reed, for written copy of Minutes of Convention of 1871.		25 00
"	Rt. Rev. Bishop Stevens, order Standing Committee.		22 75
"	Postage Stamps and Stationery for Treasurer.		21 00
"	Balance in Philadelphia Trust and Deposit Co. to credit of Episcopal Fund.	1847 38	
	Balance in Philadelphia National Bank to credit of Convention Fund		863 49
		$9704 86	$3738 35

The undersigned, appointed by the Standing Committee to audit the accounts of the Treasurer of the Convention, have examined the same, compared the vouchers with the various entries, and find them correct, leaving a balance in his hands of Two Thousand Seven Hundred and Ten Dollars and Eighty-seven Cents ($2710.87), of which sum $1847.38 are deposited in the Philadelphia Insurance, Trust and Safe Deposit Co., to the credit of the Episcopal Fund, and $863.49 in the Philadelphia National Bank, for the expenses of Convention.

They have also examined the Securities in which the funds of the Episcopate are invested, and find Certificates of Loans, namely, Twenty-seven Thousand Five Hundred ($27,500) Dollars of the Six per cent. Loan, and One Thousand ($1000) Dollars of the Five per cent. Loan (due July 1, 1870), all of the State of Pennsylvania; Seven Thousand ($7000) Dollars of Philadelphia City Six per cent. Loan (taxable); Two Thousand ($2000) Dollars United States Six per cent. Loan, due 1881; One Thousand ($1000) Dollars U. S. Six per cent. Loan, May, 1865-85; and One Thousand ($1000) Dollars Five per cent. Loan, Ten-forty; making a total of Thirty-nine Thousand Five Hundred Dollars. All of this sum composes the General Fund, with the exception of $4600 Philadelphia City Loan and $150 Pennsylvania Six per cent. Loan, which constitute the Kohne Legacy, and $2000 Pennsylvania Six per cent. Loan, which forms part of the Andrew Doz Trust.

RECAPITULATION.

GENERAL FUND :

Pennsylvania Six Per Cent. Loan.	$25,350	
" Five "	1,000	
Philadelphia Six Per Cent. Loan (taxable) . .	2,400	
United States Loan, 6 per cent, 1881	2,000	
" " " 1865-85. . . .	1,000	
" " 5 per cent., 10-40.	1,000	
		$32,750

KOHNE LEGACY :

Philadelphia Six Per Cent. Loan (taxable) . .	4,600	
Pennsylvania " "	150	
		4,750

ANDREW DOZ TRUST :

Pennsylvania Six Per Cent. Loan	2,000	
		$39,500

THOMAS ROBINS, } *Committee.*
WM. F. GRIFFITTS,

MAY 13, 1872.

APPENDIX D.

ACC'T OF B. G. GODFREY, TREAS. OF DIOCESE AS
TO FUNDS COLLECTED AND CONTRIBUTED
FOR SUFFERING PEOPLE OF CHICAGO.

Benjamin G. Godfrey, Treasurer, Diocese of Pennsylvania, in Acc't with Collections and Contributions, in response to the Pastoral Letter of Bishop Stevens, of October 10th, 1871, in behalf of the Suffering People of Chicago.

DR.

1871.			Special.	General.
October.	Cash, Church of the Evangelist and Sunday School . . . . Philadelphia			$74 17
"	St. John . . . . "	N. Liberties .		92 26
"	St. John the Evangelist . . . . . "			28 00
"	Emmanuel . . . . . "	Holmesburg .		167 15
"	Zion . . . . . . "			111 60
"	St. James the Less . . . . . . "			26 34
"	St. John the Baptist . . . . . . "	Germantown .		15 00
"	St. Michael . . . . . . "			67 60
"	Christ . . . . "			214 00
"	St. Luke . . . . . "			251 25
"	Calvary . . . . . "			239 27
"	Grace . . . . "	Mt. Airy . . .		105 10
"	St. Paul . . . . . "	Chestnut Hill.		431 25
"	Trinity Chapel . . . . . "			15 52
"	Church of the Nativity . . . . "			500 00
"	St. Luke . . . . . "			281 51
"	St. Timothy . . . . . "			59 66
"	Church of the Holy Apostles . . . "			78 30
"	St. Mark . . . . . "			474 91
"	Bible Class and Sunday School Episcopal Hospital . . . . . "			23 39
"	All Saints . . . . . "			102 00
"	French Congregation . . . . . "			25 00
"	Free Church of St. John . . . . "	Frankford Rd.		23 55
"	St. Peter (gold ring included) . . "			493 52
"	St. Mary . . . . . "	West Philad'a.		148 93
"	Church of the Mediator . . . . "			354 00
"	Gloria Dei (Swedes) . . . . "		$106 50	
"	Church of St. Matthias . . . . "			409 17
"	Episcopal Hospital (add.) . . . . "			1 50
"	St. Clement . . . . . "			120 34
"	St. Stephen . . . . . "			400 00
"	Ch. of the Redeemer (Seamen) . "			9 52
"	" " Redemption . . . . . "			70 00
"	" " Crucifixion . . . . . "			5 00
"	St. Philip . . . . . "			331 00
"	Bishop's Church . . . . . "			52 36
"	Church of the Advent . . . . . "			298 47
"	" " " Men's Bible Class . . . . "		6 75	6 75
"	St. Matthew . . . . . "			285 00
"	Church of the Saviour . . . . . "	West Philad'a.		142 39
"	St. Andrew . . . . . . "	" "		90 00
"	St. Stephen . . . . . "	Bridesburg . .		23 36
"	Trinity . . . . . . "	Southwark . . .	15 00	150 00
"	Christ . . . . "		471 44	
"	Church of the Incarnation . . . . "			170 00
"	Pupils of the Episcopal Academy, Rev. Mr. Robins . . . . . "			79 07
"	St. Alban . . . . . "	Roxborough .		7 00
"	St. Timothy . . . . "			110 66
"	Church of the Ascension, ... "			77 47
"	St. James . . . . . "			627 00
"	St. Paul . . . . "		100 00	54 56
"	" Sunday Schools . . . . "		20 00	
"	St. David . . . . . "	Manayunk . .		99 32
"	St. James . . . . . "	Kingsessing .		151 50
"	Atonement, ... "			283 85
"	St. Thomas . . . . . "			10 00
"	Church of the Covenant . . . . "			317 08
"	Grace . . . . . "			392 00
"	Epiphany . . . . . "		455 00	455 00
	Carried forward		$1174 69	$9632 65

B. G. Godfrey, Treas. in Acc't with Chicago Fund. DR.

1871.				Special.	General.
October.	Brought forward			$1174 69	$9632 65
	Cash, Calvary, "Monumental"	Philadelphia			9 64
"	Holy Trinity	"		200 00	925 55
"	Church of the Merciful Saviour	"			46 25
"	St. Mark (gold ring included)	"	Frankford	10 00	341 60
"	St. Andrew, add.	"			53 00
"	St. James	"	Hestonville		13 00
"	Emmanuel	"	Kensington	68 59	50 00
"	Church of the Messiah	"	Pt. Richmond		15 09
"	Misses M. and F. A. S.	"		5 00	
"	Mr. Chapman				5 00
"	St. Paul "Memorial"	Upper Providence			48 62
"	Christ	Reading			86 00
"	St. John	York			48 10
"	St. Paul	Columbia		22 71	31 37
"	Church of the Trinity	Coatesville			56 79
"	St. Peter	Hazleton			14 00
"	Free Church of St. John	Lancaster			30 00
"	Church of the Redeemer	Lower Merion			139 10
"	St. John	"			355 25
"	St. David	Radnor			52 96
"	St. Paul	Lock Haven			80 21
"	St. Martin	Marcus Hook			25 00
"	St. Michael	Birdsboro'			103 32
"	St. Luke, by Mrs. and Miss Henderson and Mrs. Dade	Bustleton			30 00
"	Trinity	Philadelphia, Oxford		125 00	180 62
"	Trinity Chapel	" Crescentville			22 97
"	Grace	Allentown			120 00
"	Christ	Pottstown			71 84
"	St. John	Carlisle			50 76
"	Holy Trinity	Centralia			5 00
"	Trinity	Pottsville			469 08
"	All Saints	Lower Dublin			112 68
"	St. John	Norristown		205 00	2 00
"	St. James	Muncy			31 25
"	St. Luke	Scranton			75 33
"	St. James	Eckley			127 70
"	St. Paul	Manheim			13 43
"	Hope	Mount Hope			2 14
"	Christ	Towanda			121 56
"	St. James	Downingtown			54 40
"	St. Paul	Philipsburg			35 38
"	Holy Trinity	West Chester			160 77
"	Good Shepherd	Scranton			42 11
"	St. James	Mansfield			10 25
"	St. Barnabas	Reading			30 00
"	Memorial Church of St. John	Ashland			80 00
"	St. Luke	Lebanon			36 00
"	St. Paul	Cheltenham			200 00
"	Church of the Nativity	Bethlehem			122 72
"	Grace	Great Bend			20 00
"	St. Mark	New Milford			20 00
"	St. Stephen	Wilkesbarre			200 00
"	St. John	Concord			12 25
"	St. Paul	Chester			132 00
"	Swedes	Bridgeport		47 20	50 00
"	St. Thomas	White Marsh			75 73
"	St. Peter	Phœnixville			14 00
"	Trinity	Shamokin			27 00
"	Trinity Sunday Schools	"			3 00
"	St. Paul	Doylestown			80 00
"	" Sunday Schools	"			15 55
"	Trinity	Centreville			19 75
"	" Sunday Schools	"			15 70
"	Christ	Danville			225 00
"	Christ	Williamsport		172 10	186 00
"	Trinity	"			102 00
"	Grace Church	Hulmeville		1 00	14 00
	Carried forward			$2031 29	$15,552 52

DR.   *B. G. Godfrey, Treas. in Acc't with Chicago Fund.*

1871		Special.	General.
	Brought forward	$2031 29	$15,552 52
October.	Cash, Grace Church Sunday School. . . Hulmeville	50	7 00
"	Mediator . . . . Allentown		2 10
"	Catasauqua Mission . . . . "		7 20
"	Drifton " . . . . Luzerne Co.		64 80
"	St. Luke . . . . Altona.		6 00
"	Grace . . . . Honesdale . . , ...		100 00
"	St. John . . . . Marrietta		32 82
"	Christ . . . . Media		50 00
"	St. James . . . . Lancaster		286 77
"	St. Paul . . . . Wellsboro'		35 00
"	St. Matthew . . . . Sunbury		50 00
"	St. James. . . . . Perkiomen		10 25
"	Calvary . . . . Conshohockon		56 06
"	St. Mark . . . . "	3165 40	
"	" Sunday Schools . . . . "		25 00
"	St. Philip . . . . Summit Hill..		9 80
"	St. Paul. . . . . White Haven.		15 05
"	St. Paul . . . . Bloomsburg		33 00
"	St. John . . . . Catawissa		4 50
"	Lehigh University, pr Dr. Coppee, South Bethlehem..		124 00
"	St. Mark. . . . . Northumberland.. . . .		2 50
"	Trinity . . . . Easton . . . . , ...		100 00
"	St. Luke . . . . Newtown.		17 76
"	St. Andrew . . . . Yardleyville		32 24
"	St. Paul . . . . Minersville		15 50
"	Trinity . . . . . - . . Athens	17 00	8 00
"	St. Paul . . . . Pleasant Mount . . .		4 00
"	Christ Chapel . . . . Edington, Bucks Co. . . .		9 70
"	Trinity Sunday School. . . . . Moorstown, N. J.	12 09	
"	St. James . . . . Bristol	100 00	
"	St. Luke . . . . Blosburg..		9 00
			5326 28
			$21,996 95

The undersigned Committee, appointed by the Standing Committee of the Diocese of Pennsylvania to examine the accounts of Benjamin G. Godfrey, Treasurer, have examined the above account, compared the vouchers with the various entries on page 5, and found the same correct, and that the entire amount, say Twenty-one Thousand Nine Hundred and Ninety-six Dollars and Ninety-five Cents have been forwarded as directed to the sufferers by the recent fires in Chicago and the Northwest.

THOMAS ROBINS,
WM. F. GRIFFITTS,   } *Committee.*

May 13th, 1872,

B. G. Godfrey, Treas. in Acc't with Relief Fund. CR.

1871.		North-west.	Chicago.
Oct. 19.	Cash Draft Rev. H. M. Thompson, D. D., order Rev. C. E. M'Ilvaine..		$205 00
"	" Rev. Clinton Locke, D. D., order Rev. Percy Brown .		331 00
"	" C. E. Cheney, order Rev. R. A. Edwards		105 10
"	" Clinton Locke, D D., order Dr. Foggo		70 00
"	" " " " Dr. Paret.		186 00
"	" Dr. Newton, order Church of Epiphany		455 00
"	" C. V. Kelly, D. D., order L. Coffin, Esq.		200 00
"	" Geo. C. Street, by direction of the Bishop, order of Rector of St. Paul's		100 00
Nov. 3.	" " Geo. C. Street, by direction of the Bishop, order Rector of Gloria Dei		106 50
"	" Geo. C. Street, by direction of the Bishop, order Rector of Christ Church		401 44
"	" Rt. Rev. Bishop Whitehouse, order Rector of St. James', Lancaster.		286 77
Dec. 5.	" Rev. Clinton Locke, D. D., order Rev. Leighton Coleman		1546 99
"	" " Clinton Locke, D. D., Chicago Relief Committee.		5000 00
"	" Wirt Dexter, Esq., Chairman Chicago Aid and Relief Committee		5000 00
"	" Rev. Clinton Locke, D D., Chicago Relief Committee.		679 87
"	" George M. Pullman, Esq., Treasurer Chicago Relief Committee.		679 87
Nov.	" Hon. H. B. Baldwin, Governor of Michigan, order Rev. Leighton Coleman	$821 71	
"	" Rt. Rev. Bishop Armitage, Wisconsin, order Rev. Leighton Coleman	821 70	
"	" Hon. H. B. Baldwin, Governor of Michigan, for Relief Committee	2500 00	
"	" Rt. Rev. Bishop Armitage, Wisconsin, for Relief Committee	2500 00	
		6643 41	
			$21,996 95

APPENDIX E.

Assessment of Churches for the Convention Fund, embracing the Support of the Episcopate, as well as the Expenses of the Diocesan and General Conventions, for the year 1872, payable on or before December 31, 1872, to Benjamin G. Godfrey, Treasurer, 245 Market Street.

COUNTY.	CHURCH.	PLACE.	RECTOR OR WARDEN.	AM'T.
Bucks..	St. James.	Bristol.	Rev. J. H. Drumm, D. D. .	$50 00
"	St. Andrew. . . .	Yardleyville . .	" W. S. Cochran	6 00
"	St. Luke.	Newtown. . . .	" " "	6 00
"	Grace	Hulmeville.. . .	" W. G. P. Brinckloe.. .	6 00
"	Trinity.	Centreville. . .	" H. Baldy.	6 00
"	St. Paul	Doylestown . .	" "	20 ob
Chester	St. Peter.. . . .	Great Valley .	John L. Philips, Warden .	12 00
"	St. John	New London..	Thos. M. Charlton, Warden.	6 00
"	St. Mary. . . .	Warwick . . .	Rev. W. W. Spear, D. D. .	6 00
"	St. John	Pequea.	" H. R. Smith	21 00
"	St. Paul	W. Whiteland .		9 00
"	St. Andrew. . . .	W. Vincent. . .	Rev. W. W. Spear, D.D .	6 00
"	St. Mark	Honeybrook . .	Rev. W. W. Spear, D. D. .	6 00
"	Holy Trinity . . .	West Chester. .	" John Bolton. . . .	75 00
"	St. Peter	Phœnixville . .	" W. R. Stockton. . . .	25 00
"	St. James	Downingtown. .	" R. F. Innes. . . .	25 00
"	St. James	W. Marlboro'. .		. . . .
"	Trinity.	Coatesville. . .	Rev. G. G. Field	15 00
"	Grace	Parkesburg. . .	" J. T. Carpenter	5 00
Delaware.	St. Paul	Chester. . . .	" H. Brown. . . .	62 00
"	St. Martin	Marcus Hook. .	" G. C. Bird	30 00
"	St. David. . . .	Radnor	" W. F. Halsey. . . .	30 00
"	St. John	Concord	" J. B. Clemson, D. D. .	12 00
"	Calvary	Rockdale. . . .	" William Ely	12 00
"	Christ.. . . .	Media	E. A. Price, Warden.. . .	30 00
"	Good Shepherd.. .	Radnor. . . .	Rev. H. Palethorp Hay, D.D	5 00
Montgomery.. .	St. James. . . .	Perkiomen.. .	" P. Russell	20 00
" .	St. Thomas. . . .	Whitemarsh . .	" P. W. Stryker	45 00
"	St. John.. . . .	Norristown. . .	John McKay, Warden . . .	75 00
"	Christ	Pottstown . .	Rev. B. McGann. . . .	25 00
"	Redeemer	Lower Merion .	" E. L. Lycett	62 00
"	Our Saviour	Jenkintown. . .	" R. Francis Colton. . .	50 00
"	Calvary	Conshohocken .	W. Cresson, Warden.. . .	6 00
"	St. Paul	Cheltenham. .	Rev. E. W. Appleton. . .	100 00
"	St. John	Lower Merion .	" C. L. Fischer. . . .	50 00
"	St. Paul	L. Providence .	" J. Rudderow	6 00
Philadelphia . . .	Christ	Philadelphia . .	" E. A. Foggo, D.D. . .	125 00
"	St. Peter. . . .	" . .	" T. F. Davies, D.D. .	250 00
"	St. Paul	" . .	" R. T. Roach, D.D. . .	75 00
"	Trinity.	Oxford.. . . .	" E. Y. Buchanan, D.D.	50 00
"	All Saints	Lower Dublin..	" F. W. Beasley, D.D...	60 00
"	St. James	Philadelphia . .	" H. J. Morton, D.D...	250 00
"	St. John	N. Liberties . .	" Charles Logan . . .	20 00
"	St. Luke. . . .	Germantown . .	" Albra Wadleigh. . . .	150 00
"	Trinity.	Southwark.. .	" J. Y. Burk	75 00
"	St. Stephen. . . .	Philadelphia . .	" Wm. Rudder, D.D. . .	325 00
"	St. Andrew. . . .	" . .	" W. F. Paddock, D.D..	250 00
"	St. Matthew	Francisville. . .	" J. Blake Falkner . . .	100 00
"	Grace..	Philadelphia. .	" W. Suddards, D.D.. .	250 00

$2905 00

Assessment of Churches for the Convention Fund, 1872.

COUNTY.	CHURCH.	PLACE.	RECTOR OR WARDEN.	AM'T.
Philadelphia	St. Mary	West Phila	Rev. T. C. Yarnall, D.D.	$50 00
"	St. David	Manayunk	" F. H. Bushnell	75 00
"	Epiphany	Philadelphia	" R. Newton, D.D	300 00
"	Ascension	"	" H. M. Stuart	30 00
"	Emmanuel	Kensington	" W. H. Monroe	100 00
"	All Saints	Moyamensing	" H. L. Duhring	75 00
"	St. Luke	Philadelphia	" C. G. Currie	300 00
"	St. Philip	Spring Garden	" James Pratt, D.D.	125 00
"	Advent	N. Liberties	" J. W. Claxton	125 00
"	Evangelists	Southwark	" Jacob Miller	30 00
"	Emmanuel	Holmesburg	" D. C. Millett, D.D.	60 00
"	St. James	Kingsessing	" C. A. Maison	60 00
"	Gloria Dei	Southwark	" S. B. Simes	60 00
"	Nativity	Spring Garden	" Wm. Newton	125 00
"	Redemption	Fairmount	" J. P. Du Hamel	12 00
"	St. James the Less	North Penn.	" Robert Ritchie	30 00
"	St. Mark	Frankford	" D. S. Miller, D.D.	125 00
"	Crucifixion	Moyamensing	" W. H. Josephus	
"	Messiah	Port Richmond	Henry Christian, Warden	6 00
"	Atonement	Philadelphia	Rev. B. Watson	200 00
"	St. Mark	"	" E. A. Hoffman, D.D.	350 00
"	Mediator	"	" S. E. Appleton	125 00
"	St. Jude	Spring Garden	" Wm. H. Graff	50 00
"	Zion	South Penn.	" C W. Duane	50 00
"	Resurrection	Rising Sun	" J. R. Moore	20 00
"	St. Andrew	West Phila	" S. E. Smith	20 00
"	The Saviour	"	" J. H. Eccleston, D.D.	150 00
"	Christ	Germantown	" T. S. Rumney, D.D.	200 00
"	Trinity	Maylandville	" J. H. Eccleston, D.D.	5 00
"	St. Clement	Philadelphia	M. Arnold, Jr., Warden.	100 00
"	St. Paul	Chestnut Hill.	Rev. J. A. Harris	125 00
"	Holy Trinity	Philadelphia	" T. A. Jaggar	350 00
"	Calvary Monumental	N. Liberties	" E. A. Foggo, D.D	12 00
"	Covenant	Philadelphia	" C. E. Murray	75 00
"	St. John the Baptist	Germantown	" W. N. Diehl	6 00
"	Calvary	"	" J. W. DePerry	125 00
"	Intercessor	Spring Garden	" Owen E. Simpson	25 00
"	St. Matthias	"	" R. N. Thomas	50 00
"	Incarnation		" J. D. Newlin	60 00
"	St. John Evangelist	Southwark	" W. F. B. Jackson	30 00
"	St. Michael	Germantown	" J. K. Murphy	60 00
"	St. Luke	Bustleton	" H. A. Parker	6 00
"	House of Prayer	Branchtown	" A. T. McMurphey	20 00
"	St. Timothy	Roxborough	" W. A. White	40 00
"	St. Alban	"	" A. A. Rickert	6 00
"	Grace	Mt. Airy	" R. H. Edwards	40 00
"	St. John	Frankford Road.	" J. A. Nock	6 00
"	St. Thomas	Philadelphia	Morris Brown, Warden	6 00
"	St. James	Hestonville	Rev. G. L. Bishop	8 00
"	Holy Apostles	Philadelphia	" C. D. Cooper	50 00
"	Good Shepherd	"	" J. W. Claxton	6 00
"	St. Stephen	Bridesburg	" I. Martin	6 00
"	Holy Innocents	Tacony	" D. C. Millett, D.D.	6 00
"	St. George	Kenderton	" J. R. Moore	5 00
"	St. Paul	Aramingo		
"	Messiah	Philadelphia	" George Bringhurst	20 00
"	St. George	"	" Charles A. Maison	6 00
"	St. Timothy	"	" J. L. Heysinger	10 00
"	St. Sauveur	"	" C. F. B. Miel	10 00
"	Merciful Saviour	"	" E. J. Widdemer	5 00
				$4127 00

ERRATUM.

The name of the Rev. George Alexander Crooke, D.D., D. C. L., Philadelphia, has been inadvertently omitted from the List of Clergy canonically and actually resident in the Diocese.

INDEX.

NOTICE.

The next Annual Convention of the Church in this Diocese, will be held in St. Andrew's Church, Philadelphia, on the second Tuesday in May, 1873, at 5 o'clock, P. M.

JOHN A. CHILDS, *Secretary,*
No. 708 Walnut Street, Philadelphia.

OFFICERS OF CHURCH INSTITUTIONS IN PHILADELPHIA.

Treasurer of Episcopal and Convention Fund,
BENJ. G. GODFREY, 245 Market Street.

Treasurer of Christmas Fund,
R. P. McCULLAGH, 421 Chestnut Street.

Treasurer of Board of Missions of Diocese of Pennsylvania,
JAMES S. BIDDLE, 1714 Locust Street.

Secretary of Hospital of the Protestant Episcopal Church, of Board of Missions of Diocese of Pennsylvania, and of the Trustees and Overseers of Divinity School,
Rev. JOHN A. CHILDS, D.D., 708 Walnut Street.

Treasurer of Hospital of Protestant Episcopal Church, and of City Missions,
WM. W. FRAZIER, Jr., 101 S. Front Street.

Secretary of Bishop White Prayer Book Society,
JAMES S. BIDDLE, 1714 Locust Street.

Treasurer of Corporation for Relief of Widows and Children of Deceased Clergymen,
J. SOMERS SMITH, 212 S. Fourth Street.

Registrar of the Diocese, and Head Master of the Academy of the Protestant Episcopal Church in Philadelphia,
Rev. J. W. ROBINS, 1821 DeLancey Place.

Treasurer of Clergy Daughters' Fund,
CHARLES W. CUSHMAN, 128 S. Delaware Avenue.

Treasurer of Evangelical Educational Society,
WM. C. HOUSTON, 1224 Chestnut Street.

General Agent of Evangelical Educational Society,
Rev. R. C. MATLACK, 1224 Chestnut Street.

Treasurer of Society for the Advancement of Christianity in Pennsylvania,
GEORGE W. TAYLOR, S. W. cor. Fifth and Market.

Corresponding Secretary of Society for Advancement of Christianity in Philadelphia,
Rev. E. A. FOGGO, D.D., 268 S. Ninth Street.

Treasurer of Society for the Promoting Christianity Among the Jews,
ZEBULON LOCKE, 1010 Market Street.